Minette Walters lives in Hampshire with her husband and two children. She has worked as a magazine editor but is now a full-time writer.

With her debut, *The Ice House*, she won the Crime Writers' Association John Creasey Award for the best first crime novel of 1992. Rapidly establishing a reputation as one of the most exciting crime novelists writing today, her second novel, *The Sculptress*, was acclaimed by critics as one of the most compelling and powerful novels of the year and won the Edgar Allan Poe Award for the best crime novel published in America in 1993.

In 1994 Minette Walters achieved a unique triple when *The Scold's Bridle* was awarded the CWA Gold Dagger for best crime novel of the year. Her following five novels, *The Dark Room*, *The Echo*, *The Shape of Snakes* and *Acid Row*, were also published to further critical acclaim throughout the world and her ninth novel, *Fox Evil*, won the 2003 CWA Gold Dagger for Fiction.

BBC TV has adapted all five novels with huge success, most recently *The Dark Room* starring Dervla Kirwan and James Wilby.

MINETTE WALTERS

The Echo
&
The Breaker

PAN BOOKS

The Echo first published 1997 by Macmillan.
First published in paperback 1998 by Pan Books.
The Breaker first published 1998 by Macmillan.
First published in paperback 1999 by Pan Books.

This omnibus first published 2007 by Pan Books
an imprint of Pan Macmillan Ltd
Pan Macmillan, 20 New Wharf Road, London N1 9RR
Basingstoke and Oxford
Associated companies throughout the world
www.panmacmillan.com

ISBN 978-0-330-45235-9

1 3 5 7 9 8 6 4 2

A CIP catalogue record for this book is available from
the British Library.

Printed and bound in Great Britain by
Mackays of Chatham plc, Chatham, Kent

The Echo

For Frank and Mary

The echo began in some indescribable way to undermine her hold on life . . . it had managed to murmur, 'Pathos, piety, courage – they exist, but are identical, and so is filth. Everything exists, nothing has value.'

E. M. FORSTER (1879–1970)

O Rose, thou art sick!
   The invisible worm
That flies in the night,
In the howling storm,

Has found out thy bed
   Of crimson joy:
And his dark secret love
Does thy life destroy.

WILLIAM BLAKE
(1757–1827)

Chapter One

IT WAS THE smell that Mrs Powell noticed first. Slightly sweet. Slightly unpleasant. She sniffed it on the air one warm June evening as she parked her car in her garage, but she assumed it came from her neighbours' dustbin on the other side of the low wall that divided the properties, and did nothing about it. The next morning the smell of decay eddied out from inside when she pulled open the garage doors, and curiosity led her to poke among the stack of boxes at the back after she had reversed her car on to the driveway. Certainly, she didn't expect to find a corpse. If she expected anything, it was that someone had abandoned their rubbish in there, and it shocked her badly to find a dead man huddled on sheets of flattened cardboard in the corner, his head slumped on his knees.

There was a flutter of media interest in the story, largely because of where the man was found – within the boundaries of an exclusive private estate bordering the Thames in London's old docklands – and because the pathologist gave cause of death as malnutrition. That a man should have died of starvation in one of the wealthiest parts of one of the wealthiest capitals of the

1

world as the twentieth century drew to a close was irresistible to most journalists, the more so when they learned from the police that he had passed away beside a huge chest freezer filled with food. The rat-pack arrived in force.

But they were to be disappointed. Mrs Powell was a reluctant interviewee and had already vanished from her house. Nor was there anyone to flesh out the dead man's life and make it worth writing about. He was one of the army of homeless who haunted the streets of London, an alcoholic without family or friends, whose fingerprints were recorded under the name of Billy Blake as a result of a handful of convictions for petty thieving. Among London's policemen he had a small reputation as a street preacher from his habit of shouting aggressively at passers-by about forthcoming doom and destruction whenever he was drunk, but as none of them had ever listened closely to his incoherent ramblings, nothing was added to their knowledge of the man through what he had preached. The only curious fact about him was that he had lied about his age when first arrested in 1991. The police had him on file as sixty-five; while the pathologist's estimate, as officially recorded at the inquest, was forty-five.

Mrs Powell's involvement in this bizarre tragedy was that she owned the garage in which Billy had died. However, he preyed upon her mind following her return two weeks later after the morbid press interest had died down and, because she could afford it, she put up the money for his cremation when the coroner finally released the body. She had no need to do it – as in other areas of social welfare, the trappings of death were covered by a state benefit – but she felt an obligation to her uninvited guest. She chose the second cheapest package offered, and presented herself at the crematorium on the due date at the due time. As she had expected, she and the vicar were the only people there, the undertaker's men having left after depositing the coffin on the rollers. It was a somewhat harrowing service, conducted to the accompaniment of taped music. Elvis Presley sang 'Amazing Grace' over the sound system at the beginning, the vicar and she struggled through the service and the responses together (while worrying independently if Billy Blake had even been a Christian), and a Welsh male voice choir gave a harmonious rendition of 'Abide with Me' as the coffin rolled through to the burners and the curtains closed discreetly behind it.

There was little more to be said or done and, after shaking hands and thanking each other for being there, Mrs Powell and the vicar went their separate ways. As part of the package, Billy Blake's ashes were placed in an urn in a small corner of the crematorium with a plaque giving his name and date of death. Sadly, neither piece of information was accurate, for the dead man had not been christened Billy Blake and the pathologist had miscalculated his temperature readings and underestimated the time of death by a few hours.

Whoever Billy Blake was, he died on Tuesday, 13 June 1995.

*

The two visitors who came to view Billy Blake's plaque a few days later went unnoticed. The older man jabbed a stubby finger at the words and made a derisory noise in his throat. 'See, what did I tell you? Died twelfth of June 1995. The frigging Monday. Okay? Happy now?'

'We ought to've brought some flowers,' said his young companion, looking at the profusion of wreaths that other mourners had left in last respects to the recently cremated.

'There'd be no point, son. Billy's dead and I've yet to meet a corpse 'oo appreciates floral arrangements.'

'Yeah, but—'

'But nothing,' said the old man firmly. 'I keep telling you, the bugger's gone.' He pushed the youngster forward. 'Satisfy yerself I'm right, and then we'll be off.' He glanced around with a look of distaste creasing his weathered face. 'I never did like these places. It ain't 'ealthy thinking too much on death. It comes soon enough as it is.'

Despite having her garage cleansed three times in six weeks by three different cleaning companies, Mrs Powell disposed of her chest freezer, shopped rather more frequently and started parking her car in the driveway. Her neighbour remarked on it to his wife, and said it was a pity there was no Mr Powell. No *man* would allow a perfectly serviceable garage to go to waste simply because a tramp had died in it.

(Extract from *Unsolved Mysteries of the Twentieth Century* by Roger Hyde, published by Macmillan, 1994)

missing persons

Precisely how many people leave home for good every year in Britain remains a mystery, but if we define 'missing' as 'whereabouts unknown', then the figure is believed to run into hundreds of thousands. Only a tiny percentage ever hit the headlines, and these are usually children who are abducted and subsequently murdered. Adults rarely attract attention. The most famous missing person of recent years is the Earl of Lucan, who vanished from his estranged wife's house on 7 November 1974, following the brutal murder of Sandra Rivett, his children's nanny, and the attempted murder of Lady Lucan. He was never seen again, nor was his body found, but there seems little mystery about why he chose to vanish. Less explicable were the disappearances of two other 'missing persons': Peter Fenton, OBE, a Foreign Office 'high flyer', and James Streeter, a merchant banker.

† † †

The Case of the Vanishing Diplomat – Peter Fenton, OBE

The disappearance of Peter Fenton during the evening of 3 July 1988, only hours before his wife's body was discovered in the bedroom of their Knightsbridge home, created a sensation in the British press. The house was less than a mile from where the terrible Lucan tragedy had been played out nearly fourteen years before, and the parallels between Peter Fenton and Lord 'Lucky' Lucan were startling. The two men had moved in similar social circles and both were known to have loyal friends who would help them; each man's car was later found abandoned on the south coast of England, leading to speculation that they had fled across the Channel to France; there was even a bizarre similarity in their appearance, both being tall, dark and conventionally handsome.

But comparisons with the Lucan case ended when the police revealed that, following detailed forensic examination of the house and body, they were satisfied that Verity Fenton had committed suicide. She had hanged herself from a rafter in the attic some time during the evening of 1 July while Peter Fenton was on a five-day visit to Washington. A reconstruction of the evidence suggested that, on his return from America during the afternoon of 3 July, he had found her suicide note on the hall table and then searched the house for her. There seems no doubt that it was he who cut her down and he who laid her out on the bed. Nor is there any doubt that he phoned his stepdaughter and asked her to come to the house that evening with her husband. He did not warn her of what she would find, nor did he mention that he wouldn't be there, but he told her he would leave the door on the latch. She described him as sounding 'very tired'.

Unlike Lord Lucan, who was formally committed for trial at the Central Criminal Court after the inquest into the death of Sandra Rivett, Peter Fenton was effectively absolved of blame for the death of his wife, Verity. A verdict of 'suicide while the balance of her mind was disturbed' was recorded, following evidence from her daughter that she had been unnaturally depressed while her husband was away. This was borne out by her suicide note which said simply: 'Forgive me. I can't bear it any more, darling. Please don't blame yourself. Your betrayals are nothing compared with mine.'

However, the question remained: why did Peter Fenton vanish? It seemed logical to many columnists that 'betrayals' referred to love affairs, and there was much speculation that he had run to the comforting arms of a mistress. But this did not explain why his car was found abandoned near a cross-Channel ferry port, nor why he continued in hiding after the inquest verdict had been published. Interest began to centre on his job in the Foreign Office and the two postings he had held in Washington (1981–3 and 1985–7), where he was thought to have had access to highly secret information about NATO.

Was it coincidence that Fenton had vanished only weeks after the arrest of Nathan Driberg* in America? Why had he made the five-day trip to Washington alone when it must have been clear to him that his wife was deeply depressed? Could it have been a desperate attempt to find out if Driberg was going to talk in order to then reassure Verity that he was safe? For why had she written of 'betrayals' before hanging herself unless she had known that her husband was a spy? Parallels were now drawn, not with Lord Lucan, but with Guy Burgess and Donald Maclean, the notorious Foreign Office spies of the 1930s and 1940s, who disappeared in 1951 after being warned by Kim Philby

---

* Nathan Driberg (b. 1941, Sacramento, California) joined the CIA from Harvard in 1962. Although a man of high intellect he failed to make progress within the CIA and is said to have become increasingly angry with the system. Some time during the early 1980s he conceived the idea of a syndicated spying ring whose aims would be purely profit-making and whose members would be known only to him. Information was supplied by syndicate members and sold on to a selected buyer. Purchasing countries are said to have included Russia, China, South Africa, Colombia and Iraq. The syndicate is believed to have contained other CIA agents, members of Congress, foreign diplomats, journalists and industrialists, but, as Driberg has consistently refused to name any other person, their identities remain a secret. The syndicate's activities were only discovered when one of its members, Harry Castilli, a CIA agent, began to adopt an overly lavish lifestyle. In return for immunity, he led investigators to Driberg and testified against him at his trial. Shortly after Driberg's arrest, a French diplomat and a prominent US Congressman both committed suicide. A UK diplomat, Peter Fenton, vanished.

that a counter-intelligence investigation by British and American agencies was closing in on them. Had Peter Fenton, like Donald Maclean, used his position of trust in our Washington Embassy to betray his country?

Sadly, we shall probably never know because, if Peter Fenton *was* a traitor, then he did it for the money and he is unlikely to resurface as Burgess and Maclean did in Moscow in 1956, claiming a long-standing allegiance to communism. With the sort of wealth that the Driberg syndicate is said to have made, he could have had millions stashed away in Switzerland with which to fund a new identity for himself. But, according to his step-daughter, Marilyn Burghley, it would be wrong to assume that he benefited from his treachery. 'You have to understand that Peter adored my mother. I never believed that "betrayals" meant he'd had affairs. Which means, I suppose, that I have to accept he was betraying his country, and that she knew about it. Perhaps he asked her to run away with him, and when she refused, he accused her of not loving him. I think they must have had a terrible row for her to kill herself like that. Whatever the truth, life without her would have been something he couldn't bear. My mother's death was a far worse punishment than anything the courts could have given him.'

An examination of Peter Fenton's earlier life and background sheds little further light on the mystery. Born on 5 March 1950, he was the adopted son of

Jean and Harold Fenton of Colchester, Essex. Jean always described him as her 'little miracle' because she was forty-two at the time of the adoption and had given up hope of a child. She and her husband were both teachers and lavished time and effort on their son. Their reward was a gifted child who won scholarships first to Winchester and then to Cambridge, where he read classics. However, he became gradually estranged from his parents during his teenage years, spending fewer vacations in Essex and preferring whenever possible to stay with friends in London. There is evidence that he resented his humble background and set out to rise above it. He showed little love for his adoptive parents.

In a letter to his brother in 1971, Harold Fenton wrote: 'Peter has broken Jean's heart and I shall never forgive him for it. When I tackled him about his gambling, he asked me if I'd rather he stole to buy his way out of our lives and our house. He's ashamed of us. Apparently, he intends joining the Foreign Office when he leaves Cambridge and he wanted to "warn" us that we will see very little of him once that happens. His career must come first. I asked him if he had any explanation for why God saw fit to bless us with so objectionable a child and he said: "I made you proud. What more did you want?" I would have struck him had Jean not been present.'

Peter Fenton joined the Foreign Office from Cambridge in 1972, and was spotted early by Sir

Angus Fraser, then ambassador in Paris. With Fraser's backing, Fenton seemed set for a glittering career. However, his marriage to Verity Standish in 1980 was seen by many as a mistake, and his meteoric rise looked like faltering. Verity, a widow with two teenage children, was thirteen years older than Fenton and, because of her age, was considered an unsuitable wife for a future ambassador. Interestingly, in view of what he had said to his father ten years earlier, Fenton chose to put his love for Verity before his career, and his decision would seem to have been vindicated when he won his first posting to Washington in September 1981.

There followed seven years of apparently blameless marriage and dedicated work. Fenton was awarded the OBE in 1983 for services to Her Majesty's Government during the Falklands War, and Verity proved a loyal wife and much-sought-after hostess for official functions. Her children, who spent their vacations with the couple in whichever part of the world they were, remember Fenton with affection. 'He was always very kind to us,' said Verity's son, Anthony Standish. 'He told me once that he always thought money and ambition were the only things that mattered in life until my mother showed him how to love. That's why I don't believe he was a traitor. The money wouldn't have attracted him. If you want my opinion, it was she who was having the affair. She was the sort of woman who needed constant demonstrations of love, probably because my real father was a womanizer and their marriage had been an unhappy one. Perhaps she felt neglected because Peter was working so hard at that time, and she slid into infidelity by default. If Peter found out about it and threatened to leave her, it would explain why she hanged herself.'

But, unfortunately, it explains nothing else. Why did Peter Fenton vanish? Is he alive or dead? Was he a spy, a philandering husband or a cuckold? Can we really believe that love for Verity transformed him from ambitious materialist to loving husband and stepfather? And, if he loved her as much as his stepchildren claim he did, what did he do before he left for Washington that sent his wife into such a spiral of despair that she killed herself? More intriguingly, in view of its anonymity and the absence of an envelope, was Verity's suicide note addressed to him or to someone else?

The truth may well lie in what Jean Fenton wrote in her diary on his fifth birthday: 'How Peter does love acting. Today he's playing the part of the perfect child. Tomorrow it will be the devil. I wish I knew which of these various Peters is the *real* one.'

The Case of the Absconding Merchant Banker – James Streeter

James Streeter was born on 24 July 1951, the elder son of Kenneth and Hilary Streeter of Cheadle Hulme in Cheshire. He was educated at Manchester Grammar School and Durham University, where he read modern languages. On graduation, he took a job in Paris with Le Fournet, a French merchant bank, where he remained for five years before moving to a sister bank in Brussels. While there, he met and married Janine Ferrer, but the marriage lasted less than three years and, following his divorce in 1983, he returned to Britain to take a job with Lowenstein's Merchant Bank in the City of London. In 1986 he married a promising young architect who was seven years his junior. Kenneth and Hilary Streeter describe the marriage as a stormy one. 'They had very little in common,' admits Hilary, 'which led to rows, but it's ridiculous to suggest that depression over his marital problems prompted James to become a thief. In any case, if the police are to be believed, he began embezzling a year before his marriage, so the facts don't even add up. It makes us so angry that our son's reputation can be destroyed like this simply because the police have taken everything at face value. It's his murderer who deserves to be reviled, not James.'

Taken at face value, James Streeter's disappearance is as self-explanatory as Lord Lucan's for, within days of deserting his desk at Lowenstein's Merchant Bank on Friday, 27 April 1990, and in his absence, he was charged with defrauding his employers of £10 million. The case against him appears a strong one. Only weeks before he vanished, certain irregularities were noticed by the bank's auditors and were drawn to the attention of the board. At issue was a £10 million discrepancy which seemed to stem from Streeter's department and, worse, to stretch back over a period of five years. In simple terms, the theft involved the creation of fraudulent accounts which were set up as conduits for large international transactions and then creamed of interest. Their operation relied on the bank's failure to introduce proper security functions into its computer system, with the result that the false accounts went unnoticed and the interest creamed over the years was substantial.

The board's decision, a mistaken one as events proved, was to authorize a clandestine in-house investigation in order to avoid panicking the bank's customers. It was badly handled, with its secrecy compromised from the start, and the outcome was a failure to identify the responsible employee, while at the same time alerting him/her to the existence of the investigation. When James Streeter chose to run on the night of 27 April, the conclusion drawn was that he had 'got away' with a fortune, particularly as his abrupt departure followed within hours of the board's reaching its belated decision to turn the investigation over to the police.

However, despite lengthy questioning of his wife and a prolonged investigation into his financial affairs, no trace of Streeter or the stolen money has ever been found. Sceptics argue that his escape route was in place for weeks, months or even years, and that the £10 million were transferred out of the country into a safe haven abroad. Supporters, most notably his parents and brother, argue that James was a scapegoat for someone else's criminal activity and that he was murdered to shield the real culprit from further investigation. In defence of their position, they quote a handwritten facsimile that was sent from James's office at 3.05 p.m. on Friday, 27 April 1990, to his brother's office in Edinburgh.

Dear John [it reads], Dad's pushing me to
book a room for the Ruby Wedding 'do'.
He's suggesting the Park Lane, but I
remember Mum saying that if they ever
celebrated a major anniversary she'd like to
go back to the hotel in Kent where they
had their reception. Am I imagining this?
And did she ever mention the name of the
hotel to you? Dad says it was somewhere
in Sevenoaks but, needless to say, can't
remember details. He claims his memory's
going but I suspect he was pissed as a rat
the whole day and <u>never</u> knew where he
was! I've tried the aunts and uncles, but
none of them can remember either. Failing
all else, I think we'll have to blow the

surprise and ask Mum. You know what
she's like. It'll offend her Puritan soul if we
spend a fortune on something she doesn't
really want, and then she won't enjoy
herself. I know it's still a long way off, but
the earlier we book the less likely we are to
be disappointed. I shall be home all
weekend, so give me a bell when you can.
I've told Dad I'll call back Sunday
lunchtime. Cheers. James.

'Whatever the police may argue,' says John
Streeter, 'my brother would not have written that
fax if he was planning to leave the country the
same evening. There were a hundred better ways of
allaying official suspicion about his alleged intentions. More likely he'd have referred to the visit that
I and my family were making to him in May. "See
you in two weeks" would have been far more telling
than "give me a bell when you can." And why
mention Dad? He couldn't afford to have two
members of his family worried about nonexistent
phone calls.'

The police take a more sceptical view. They cite
the climate of suspicion that already existed in
Lowenstein's and James's need to neutralize concern about his movements that weekend. Despite
the supposed secrecy of the bank's in-house investigation, most of the employees noticed that
security had been stepped up and that reports and
transactions were being closely monitored. Gossip

was rife and at least two people in Streeter's department are on record as saying they knew *before* he disappeared that some kind of fraud had been discovered and that suspicion centred on them. If, as the police believe, Streeter was biding his time until the investigation became serious enough to force him to run, then the fax to his brother was merely part of the smoke-screen he threw up to confuse the Lowenstein investigation. Almost every telephone call in the weeks preceding his disappearance contained invitations to business colleagues to meet on dates in April, May and June. His wife told police that around the beginning of April James became uncharacteristically sociable, encouraging her to organize dinner parties and weekend visits from friends, work colleagues and relations until well into July.

According to the police, he was working to a hidden agenda. They point to the fact that his secretary was instructed very early on in the 'clandestine' investigation to keep his desk diary up to date with social engagements, including private ones, and it is noticeable that April, May, June and July 1990 are significantly fuller than in the previous year. His brother admits this behaviour was unusual. 'Yes, we were surprised when they invited us to stay because James always said he found entertaining boring. The police argue that it was a successful attempt to lull the investigators into believing he had no idea the fraud had been discovered and would still be available for questioning through to

July. But it is equally logical to argue that, because he was as worried by the rumours as everyone else at Lowenstein's he acted out of character in trying to prove his commitment and dedication. Certainly, he wasn't the only employee to up his work schedule during that period and most of those diary dates refer to business meetings.'

His family go on to quote Streeter's computer illiteracy as further evidence of his innocence in this unsolved mystery. 'James simply didn't have the skill to work that fraud,' says John. 'His complete aversion to modern technology became something of a joke over the years. He could use a calculator and a fax machine but the idea of him being able to reprogram the bank's computer is laughable. When and where did he learn how to do it? He had no computer at home, and no one has ever come forward claiming to have taught him.'

But others have raised doubts about Streeter's alleged ignorance. There is evidence that he had an affair with a woman called Marianne Filbert, who was employed as a computer programmer by Softworks Limited. Softworks was invited to produce a report on Lowenstein's computer security in 1986, but they failed to complete the task and the report was never presented. James Streeter's detractors point to Marianne Filbert's access to that halfcompleted report as the key to the fraud, while his supporters dispute that he even knew Filbert. Alleged or otherwise, the affair was certainly over before the fraud was discovered because Filbert moved to America in August 1989. However, James Streeter's secretary has stated that on several occasions she found him using her word processor for personal correspondence, and colleagues testify to his easy understanding of the computer spread-sheet function. 'It took him no time at all to find an error I'd made,' claimed one member of his depart-ment. 'He said any fool could work the system if someone told him which buttons to press.'

Nevertheless, there remain several unanswered questions about James Streeter's disappearance which, in the opinion of this author, have never been adequately addressed. If we assume he *was* guilty of embezzling £10 million from Lowenstein's Merchant Bank, how did he know that the decision to involve the police was taken by the board on 27 April? The police allege that he had always planned to abscond if his fraud came to light and it was mere coincidence that his escape was scheduled for the day of the decisive board meeting. But, if that were true, why did he wait out the six weeks of the in-house investigation? Unless he had access to board documents, which the police admit is unlikely, then he could not have known the investi-gation was failing. And isn't it pushing the bounds of coincidence a little far that the last weekend in April, as recorded in James's office diary, was also the only weekend in April when his wife would be away, fulfilling a long-standing engagement with her mother, thus giving James – *or someone else* – two whole days to 'make good' his disappearance before his absence was reported?

The police argue that he chose that weekend to run because his movements could not be monitored, and that he would have gone whatever decision the board had reached, but this is to ignore the relationship that existed between James and his wife. According to Kenneth, one of the reasons the marriage was stormy was because the two people involved had more commitment to their careers than they had to each other. 'If James had said he had to fly to the Far East on Friday for a business meeting the following Monday, his wife wouldn't have turned a hair. That was what their lives were like. He didn't need to choose the one weekend she was away. Her absence only becomes important if someone else chose it.'

The police argument also ignores the fax James sent to his brother: 'I shall be home all weekend, so give me a bell when you can. I've told Dad I'll call back Sunday lunchtime.' The fact that John did telephone, but wasn't worried when there was no answer, may, as the police claim, have been entirely predictable, but it was a strange gamble for a guilty man to take. If we put that beside Kenneth Streeter's claim, tested and verified by a lie detector, that James promised to phone him on the Sunday with John's contribution to the Ruby Wedding debate, then the gamble becomes entirely unnecessary. Had John and Kenneth followed up the promised telephone calls, then James's absence might have been discovered earlier.

The Streeters' defence of their son relies heavily on a conspiracy theory – someone more highly placed than James and with access to privileged information manipulated decisions and events to avoid exposure – but without evidence to prove their case, their campaign to clear their son's name seems a hopeless one. Sadly, conspiracy theories work better in fiction than they do in real life, and on any objective reading of the evidence the conclusion must be that James Streeter *did* steal £10 million before running away and leaving his family to reap the bitter harvest of his betrayal.

Despite the Streeters' claims to the contrary, both James Streeter and Peter Fenton would appear to be genuine abscondees. They were mature men with settled backgrounds whose disappearances were bound to cause a stir within their communities and so provoke exhaustive investigations. However this is not true of the next two 'missing persons': Tracy Jevons, a troubled fifteen-year-old with a known history of prostitution; and Stephen Harding, a backward seventeen-year-old with a string of convictions for car theft . . .

Chapter Two

SIX MONTHS later, in the middle of a cold, wet December when flaming June and its sweltering heat were a distant memory, Mrs Powell was telephoned by a journalist from the *Street*, a self-styled politically left-of-centre magazine, who was compiling a feature on poverty and the homeless and wondered if she would agree to do an interview about Billy Blake. He gave his name as Michael Deacon.

'How did you get this number?' she asked suspiciously.

'It wasn't difficult. Your name and address were all over the newspapers six months ago and you're in the telephone book.'

'There's nothing I can tell you,' she said. 'The police knew more about him than I ever did.'

He was persistent. 'I won't take up much of your time, Mrs Powell. How about if I came round tomorrow evening? Say, eight o'clock.'

'What do you want to know about him?'

'Whatever you can tell me. I found his story very moving. No one seemed to be interested in him except you. The police told me you paid his funeral expenses. I wondered why.'

'I felt I owed him something.' There was a short silence. 'Are you the Michael Deacon who used to be with the *Independent*?'

'Yes.'

'I was sorry when you left. I like the way you write.'

'Thank you.' He sounded surprised, as if compliments were a rarity. 'In that case, surely I can persuade you to talk to me? You say you felt you owed Billy something.'

'Except I don't have the same liking for the *Street*, Mr Deacon. The only reason someone from that magazine would want to interview me about Billy would be to score cheap political points off the government, and I refuse to be exploited in that way.'

This time the silence was at Deacon's end while he reassessed his strategy. It would be helpful, he thought, if he could put an age and a face to the quiet, rather controlled voice of the woman he was talking to, more helpful if he genuinely believed this interview would produce anything of value. In his view the whole exercise was likely to be a waste of time and he was even less motivated than she was to go through with it. *However* . . .

'I don't make a habit of exploiting people, Mrs Powell, and I am interested in Billy Blake's story. Look, what have you got to lose by seeing me? You have my word that we'll abandon the whole thing if you don't like the way the interview's going.'

'All right,' she said, with abrupt decision. 'I'll expect you tomorrow at eight.' She rang off without saying goodbye.

*

23

The *Street* offices were a tired reminder that its namesake, Fleet Street, was once the glorious hub of the newspaper industry. The building still carried the masthead above its front door, but the letters were faded and cracked and few passers-by even noticed them. As with most of the broadsheets which had moved into cheaper, more efficient premises in the Docklands, the writing was on the wall for the *Street*, too. A new dynamic owner with ambitions to become a media tycoon waited in the shadows with plans to revamp the magazine by achieving lower costs, improved production and a twenty-first-century image through one galvanizing leap into pristine property in an outer London suburb. Meanwhile the magazine struggled on with outmoded work practices in elegant but impractical surroundings under an editor, Jim Pearce, who hankered after the good old days when the rich exploited the poor and everyone knew where he stood.

JP, still ignorant of what awaited them in the first few weeks of the new year (in his case enforced early retirement) but increasingly worried about the present owner's refusal to discuss anything that smacked of long-term strategy, sought out Deacon in his office the following afternoon. The only concessions to modernity were a word processor and an answering machine; otherwise the room looked as it had done for thirty years, with purple walls, an oak-panelled door covered in sheets of cheap white hardboard to smooth out unsightly bumps, and orange floral curtains at the window, all of which were the height of interior design in the heady, classless days of the 1960s.

'I want you to take a photographer with you when you interview Mrs Powell, Mike,' said Pearce in the belligerent tone that grew more ingrained as each worrying day passed. 'It's too good an opportunity to miss. I want tears and breast-beating from a Thatcherite who's seen the light.'

Deacon kept his eyes on his computer screen and continued typing. At six feet tall and weighing over thirteen stone, he wasn't easily bullied. In any case, he'd lied to Mrs Powell, and he didn't particularly want her to know it. 'No way,' he said bluntly. 'She did a runner the last time photographers turned up looking for pictures, and I'm not giving up precious time to go out and interview the silly cow only to have her slam the door in my face when she sees a camera lens.'

Pearce ignored this. 'I've told Lisa Smith to go with you. She knows how to behave, and if she keeps the camera out of sight till she's inside, the two of you should be able to talk Mrs Powell round.' He cast a critical eye over Deacon's crumpled jacket and five o'clock shadow. 'And, for Christ's sake, smarten yourself up, or you'll give the poor woman the screaming habdabs. I want a rich, well-fed Tory weeping over the iniquities of government housing policy, not someone scared out of her wits because she thinks a middle-aged mugger's come through her door.'

Deacon tilted his chair back and regarded his boss through half-closed lids. 'It won't make any difference what her blasted political affiliations are because I'm not including her unless she has something pertinent to say. She's your idea, JP, not mine. Homelessness is too big a social problem to be cheapened by one fat Tory weeping into her lace handkerchief.' He lit a cigarette and tossed the match angrily into an already overfull ashtray. 'I've sweated blood over this and I won't have it turned into a slanging match by the subs. I'm trying to offer some solutions here, not indulge in yah-boo politics.'

Pearce prowled across to the window and stared down on a wet, grey Fleet Street where cars crawled bumper to bumper in the driving rain and the odd window showed an ephemeral gaiety with lighted Christmas trees and sprayed-on snow. More than ever he had a sense of chapters ending. 'What sort of solutions?'

Deacon searched through a pile of papers on his desk and removed a typed sheet. 'The consensus sort. I've taken views from politicians, religious leaders and different social lobby groups to assess how the picture's changed in the last twenty years.' He consulted the page. 'There's across-the-board agreement that the figures on family breakdown, teenage drug and drink addiction and teenage pregnancies are alarming, and I'm using that agreement as a starting point.'

'Boring, Mike. Tell me something new.' He watched a progression of raised black umbrellas pass below the window, and he was reminded of all the funerals he'd attended over the years.

Deacon took in a lungful of smoke as he studied JP's back. 'Like what?'

'Tell me you've got a statement from a government minister saying all single mothers should be sterilized. Then maybe I'll let you off your interview with Mrs Powell. Have you?' His breath misted the glass.

'No,' said Deacon evenly. 'Oddly enough, I couldn't find a single mainstream politician who was that stupid.' He squared the papers on his desk. 'How about this for a quote? The poor are always with us and the only way to deal with them is to love them.'

Pearce turned round. 'Who said that?'

'Jesus Christ.'

'Is that supposed to be funny?'

Deacon gave an indifferent shrug. 'Not particularly. Thought-provoking, perhaps. In two thousand years no one's come up with a better solution. Certainly no politician anywhere at any time has managed to crack the problem. Like it or not, even communism has its share of paupers.'

'We're a political magazine, not an apologist for born-again Christianity,' said JP coldly. 'If mud-slinging offends you so much, then you should have kept your job on the *Independent*. Think about that the next time you tell me you don't want to get your hands dirty.'

Thoughtfully, Deacon blew a smoke ring into the air above his head. 'You can't afford to sack me,' he murmured. 'It's my byline that's keeping this rag afloat. You know as well as I do that until the tabloids raided my piece on the health service for scare stories about chaos in the A. and E. departments 99.99 per cent of the adult population of this country had no idea the *Street* was still being published. I'm a necessary evil as far as you're concerned.'

This was no exaggeration. In the ten months since Deacon had joined the staff, the circulation figures had begun to show a modest increase after fifteen years of steady decline. Even so, they were still only a third of what they had been in the late seventies and early eighties. It would require something more radical to revitalize the *Street* than the occasional publicity that one writer could generate, and in Deacon's view that meant a new editor with new ideas – a fact of which JP was very aware.

His smile held all the warmth of a rattlesnake's. 'If you'd written that story the way I told you to, *we* would have benefited from the scare stories and not the sodding tabloids. Why the hell did you have to be so coy about identifying the two children involved?'

'Because I gave my word to their parents. *And,*' said Deacon with heavy emphasis, 'I do not believe in using pictures of severely damaged children to sell copy.'

'They were used anyway.'

Yes, thought Deacon, and it still made him angry. He had taken great pains to keep the two families anonymous, but cheque-book journalism had seduced neighbours and friends into talking. 'Not because of anything I did,' he said.

'That's mealy-mouthed crap. You knew damn well it was only a matter of time before someone sold out.'

'I *should* have known,' corrected Deacon, squinting through the smoke from his cigarette. 'God knows I've spent enough time listening to your views on the subject. You'd sell your granny down the river for one more reader on the mailing-list.'

'You're an ungrateful bastard, Mike. Loyalty's a one-way street with you, isn't it? Do you remember coming here and begging me for a job when Malcolm Fletter bad-mouthed you round the industry? You'd been out of work for two months and it was doing your head in.' He levelled an accusing finger at the younger man. 'Who took you on? Who prised you out of that flat and gave you something to think about other than the self-induced misery of your personal life?'

'You did.'

'Right. So give me something in return. Smarten yourself up, and go chase pictures and quotes off a fat Tory. Put some spice into this article of yours.' He slammed the door as he left.

Deacon was half-inclined to pursue his irascible little boss and tell him that Malcolm Fletter had offered him his job back on the *Independent* less than two weeks previously; however, he was too soft-hearted to do it.

JP wasn't the only one who had a sense of chapters ending.

Lisa Smith whistled appreciatively when Deacon met her outside the offices at seven thirty. 'You look great. What's the occasion? Getting married again?'

He took her arm and steered her towards his car. 'Take my advice, Smith, and keep your mouth shut. I'm sure the last thing you want to do is rub salt in raw wounds. You're far too sweet and far too caring to do anything so crass.'

She was a beautiful, boisterous 24-year-old with a cloud of fuzzy dark hair and an attentive boyfriend. Deacon had lusted after her for months, but was too canny to let her know it. He feared rejection. More particularly he feared being told he was old enough to be her father. At forty-two, he was increasingly aware that he'd been abusing his body far too long and far too recklessly. What had once been lean, hard muscle had converted itself into alcoholic ripples that lurked beneath his waistband and escaped detection only because pleated chinos disguised what skin-tight jeans had formerly enhanced.

'But you're a different man when you take a little trouble, Deacon,' she said with apparent sincerity. 'The *enfant terrible* image was quite sweet in the sixties, but hardly something to cultivate into the nineties.'

He unlocked the doors and waited while she stowed her equipment on the back seat before folding her long legs into the front. 'How's Craig?' he asked, climbing in beside her.

She displayed a diamond hoop on her engagement finger. 'We're getting married.'

He fired the engine and drew out into the traffic. 'Why?'

'Because we want to.'

'That's no reason for doing anything. I want to screw twenty women a night but I value my sanity too much to do it.'

'It's not your sanity that would crack, Deacon, it's your self-esteem. You'd never find twenty women who were that desperate.'

He grinned. 'I wanted to marry both of my wives until I'd gone through with it and discovered they paid more attention to my bank statements than they did to my body.'

'Thanks.'

'What for?'

'The congratulations and the good wishes for my future.'

'I'm merely being practical.'

'No, you're not.' She bared her teeth at him. 'You're being bitter – as usual. Craig is very different from you, Mike. For a start, he likes women.'

'I *love* women.'

'Yes,' she agreed, 'that's your problem. You don't like them but you sure as hell love them as long as you think there's a chance of getting them into bed.' She lit a cigarette and opened her window. 'Has it never occurred to you that if you'd actually been friends with either of your wives you'd probably still be married?'

'Now you're sounding bitter,' he said, heading towards Blackfriars Bridge.

'I'm merely being practical,' she murmured. 'I don't want to end up as lonely as you.' She held the tip of her cigarette to the crack in the window and let the slipstream suck out the ash. 'So what's the MO for this evening? JP says he wants me to capture this woman's emotions while you ask her about some dead wino she found in her garage.'

'That's the plan.'

'What's she like?'

'I've no idea,' said Deacon. 'The nationals ran the story in June but, bar her name, which is Mrs Powell, and her address, which is expensive, there were no other details. She did a vanishing act before the rat-pack arrived and, by the time she came back, the story was dead. JP's

31

hoping for late fifties, immaculate grooming, strong right-wing political affiliations and a husband who's a stockbroker.'

Mrs Powell was certainly immaculately groomed but she was twenty years short of late fifties. She was also far too controlled ever to display the sorts of emotion that Lisa was hoping for. She greeted them with a brisk, professional courtesy before showing them into an impeccable sitting-room which smelt of rose-petal pot-pourri and had the clean, spare look of designer minimalism. She clearly liked space, and Deacon rather approved of the cream leather and chrome chairs and sofa that formed an island about a low glass coffee table in the middle of a russet-coloured carpet. Beyond them an expanse of window, framed by draped but undrawn curtains, looked across the Thames to the lights on the other side. There was very little else in the room: only a series of glass shelves above tinted glass cabinets which clearly contained a stereo system; and three canvases – one white, one grey and one black – which adorned the wall opposite the shelves.

He nodded towards them. 'What are they called?'

'The title's in French. *Gravure à la manière noire*. It means mezzotint in English. They're by Henri Benoit.'

'Interesting,' he said, glancing at her, although it wasn't clear if he was referring to the canvases or to the woman herself.

In fact he was thinking that her taste in interior design sat rather oddly with her choice of house. It was an uninteresting brick box on a new estate in the Isle of Dogs which would probably be billed in estate agents' jargon as 'an exclusive development of detached executive homes with views of the river'. He guessed the house to be about five years old, with three bedrooms and two reception rooms, and put its value at well outside an average price range. But why, he wondered, would an obviously wealthy woman with interesting taste choose something so characterless when, for the equivalent money, she could have had a spacious flat anywhere in the heart of London? Perhaps she liked detached houses, he thought rather cynically. Or views of the river. Or perhaps *Mr* Powell had chosen it.

'Do sit down,' she said gesturing towards the sofa. 'Can I get you something to drink?'

'Thank you,' said Lisa, who'd taken an instant dislike to her. 'Black coffee would be nice.' In the scheme of feminine competition, Mrs Powell oozed success. She appeared to have everything – even femininity – and Lisa looked around for something to criticize.

'Mr Deacon?'

'Do you have anything stronger?'

'Of course. Whisky, brandy, beer?'

'Red wine?' he suggested hopefully.

'I've a 1984 Rioja open. Would that do?'

'It would. Thank you very much.'

Mrs Powell disappeared down the corridor and they heard her filling the kettle in the kitchen.

'What's with black coffee, Smith,' murmured Deacon, 'when there's alcohol on offer?'

'I thought we were supposed to be behaving ourselves,'

she whispered. 'And, for Christ's sake, don't start smoking. There are no ashtrays. I've already looked. I don't want you putting her back up before she agrees to the photographs.'

He watched her critical appraisal of the room. 'What's the verdict?'

'JP was right about everything except her age and her husband. *She*'s the stockbroker. I'll bet the Mrs is a courtesy title to give her some status in a male-dominated world. There's no sign of a man living here. It's all too uncomfortable and it doesn't half stink of roses. She probably sprayed the room before we arrived.' She turned her mouth down. 'I hate women who do that. It's a kind of one-upmanship. They want to prove their house is cleaner than yours.'

He lifted an amused eyebrow. 'Are you jealous?'

'What's to be jealous of?' she hissed.

'Success,' he murmured, holding a finger to his lips as they heard Mrs Powell returning.

'If you want to smoke,' she said, passing a coffee cup to Lisa and a glass of red wine to Deacon, 'I'll find you an ashtray.' She put her own wine glass on the table near an armchair and looked at them both.

'No, thank you,' said Lisa, thinking of JP's instruction.

'Yes, please,' said Deacon, doubting he could stand the scent of rose petals for an hour. He wished Lisa hadn't mentioned them. Once noticed, the smell was cloying, and he was reminded of the second Mrs Deacon who had plundered his very mediocre fortune in order to dowse herself in Chanel No. 5. It had been the shorter of his two marriages, lasting a mere three years before

Clara had cleared off with a twenty-year-old toyboy and rather too much of her husband's capital. He took the china saucer Mrs Powell handed him, then placed a cigarette between his lips and lit it. The smell of burning tobacco immediately swamped the roses, and Deacon felt guilt and satisfaction in equal measures. He left the cigarette jutting from his mouth as he took a tape recorder and a notebook from his pocket and placed them on the table in front of him. 'Do you mind if I record what you say?'

'No.'

He set the tape in motion and reluctantly broached the subject of photographs. 'We'd like a small visual to accompany the piece, Mrs Powell, so have you any objections to Lisa photographing you?'

She stared at him as she sat down. 'Why would you want photographs of me if you're planning to write about Billy Blake, Mr Deacon?'

Why indeed? 'Because in the absence of pictures of Billy, which we've established don't exist,' he lied, transferring the cigarette to the ashtray, 'I'm afraid you're the next best thing. Is that a problem for you?'

'Yes,' she said flatly. 'I'm afraid it is. I've already told you I have no intention of being used by your magazine.'

'And, as I told you, Mrs Powell, I don't make a habit of using people.'

She had ice-blue eyes which reminded him of his mother's, and that was a shame, he thought, because in other respects she was quite attractive. 'Then surely you agree that it's absurd to illustrate an article on poverty and the homeless with a picture of a woman who lives in

35

an expensive house in an expensive part of London.' She paused for a moment, inviting him to speak. When he didn't she went on: 'In fact, there *are* pictures of Billy Blake. I have two which I'm prepared to lend you. One is a mugshot from when he was first arrested and the other was taken in the mortuary. Either would illustrate poverty better than a photograph of me.'

Deacon shrugged but didn't say anything.

'You said you were interested in Billy.'

She sounded put out, he thought, and that made him curious, for he'd been a journalist long enough to recognize that Mrs Powell was keener to tell her story than he was to hear it. *But why now, when she had refused to talk to the press at the time?* That question intrigued him. 'No pictures of you, no story, I'm afraid,' he said, reaching forward to switch off the tape. 'Editor's instructions. I'm sorry to have wasted your time, Mrs Powell.' He looked with regret at his untouched wine. 'And your Rioja.'

She watched him as he began to gather his bits and pieces together, clearly weighing something in her mind. 'All right,' she said abruptly, 'you can take your photographs. Billy's story needs to be told.'

'Why?' He shot the word at her as he depressed the record button a second time.

It was a question she had prepared for. The words came out so fluently that he was sure she'd rehearsed the answer in advance. 'Because we're in terrible trouble as a society if we assume that any man's life is so worthless that the manner of his death is the only interesting thing about him.'

'That's a fine sentiment,' he said mildly, 'but hardly very newsworthy. People die in obscurity all the time.'

'But why starve to death? Why here? Why does nobody know anything about him? Why had he told the police he was twenty years older than he actually was?' She searched his face intently. 'Aren't you at all curious about him?'

Of course! Curiosity wormed like a maggot in his brain, but he was far more interested in her than he was in the man who had died in her garage. *Why, for example, did she take Billy's death so personally that she was prepared to be exploited in order to have his story publicized?* 'Are you sure you didn't know him?' he suggested with apparent indifference.

Her surprise was genuine. 'No. Why would I need answers if I'd known him?'

He opened his notebook on his lap, and wrote: *Why does anyone need answers about a complete stranger six months after his death?* 'Which would you prefer,' he asked, 'that Lisa takes her photographs before we talk or while we're talking?'

'While.'

He waited as Lisa unzipped her bag and removed her camera. 'Do you have a Christian name, Mrs Powell?'

'Amanda.'

'Do you prefer Amanda Powell or Mrs Powell?'

'I don't mind.' She frowned into the camera lens.

'A smile would be better,' said Lisa. She snapped the shutter. Click. 'That's great.' Click. 'Could you look at the floor? Good.' Click. 'Keep your eyes cast down. That's really touching.' Click, click.

'Go on, Mr Deacon,' said the woman curtly. 'I'm sure you don't want me to be sick over my own carpet.'

He grinned. 'I prefer Deacon or Mike. How old are you?'

'Thirty-six.'

'What do you do for a job?'

She glanced at him as Lisa took another photograph. 'I'm an architect.'

'On your own or with a firm?'

'I'm with W. F. Meredith.' Click.

Not bad, he thought. Meredith was about as good as you could get. 'What are your political affiliations, Amanda?'

'None.'

'How about off the record?'

She gave a faint smile which Lisa caught. 'The same.'

'Do you vote?' She caught him watching her, and he looked away.

'Of course. Women fought long and hard to give me that right.'

'Are you going to tell me which party you usually vote for?'

'Whichever I think will do the least damage.'

'You seem to have little time for politicians. Is there a particular reason for that or is it just *fin-de-siècle* depression?'

The faint smile again as she reached for her wine glass. 'Personally, I'd hesitate to qualify a huge abstract concept like *fin-de-siècle* depression with "just", but for the purposes of your article it's as truthful as anything else.'

He wondered what it would be like to kiss her. 'Are you married at the moment, Amanda?'

'Yes.'

'What does your husband do?'

She raised the glass to her lips, momentarily forgetting the camera lens pointing at her, then lowered it with a frown as Lisa took another photograph. 'My husband wasn't here when I found the body,' she said, 'so what he does is irrelevant.'

Deacon caught the look of amused cynicism on Lisa's face. 'It's human interest,' he countered lightly. 'People will want to know what sort of man a successful architect is married to.'

Perhaps she realized that his curiosity was personal, or perhaps, as Lisa had guessed, there *was* no Mr Powell. In either case, she refused to expand on the matter. 'It was I who found the body,' she repeated, 'and you have my details already. Shall we continue?'

The pale eyes, so like his mother's, rested on Deacon's craggy face too long for comfort, and his mild fantasy about kissing her shifted from harmless fun to sadistic revenge. He could imagine what JP's reaction was going to be to the paucity of information that he'd managed to drag out of her so far. *Name, rank and number.* And he had little optimism that the photographs would be any better. Her features were so controlled that she might as well be a poker-faced prisoner of war backed against a wall. He wondered if fires had ever burned in her cool little face, or if her life had been entirely passionless. Predictably, the idea excited him.

'All right,' he agreed, 'let's talk about finding the body. You said you were shocked. Can you describe the experience for me? What sort of thoughts went through your mind when you saw him?'

'Disgust,' she said, careful to keep her voice neutral. 'He was behind a stack of empty boxes in the corner and he'd covered himself in an old blanket. The smell was really quite awful once I'd pulled it away from him. Also, his body fluids had seeped out all over the floor.' Her mouth tightened in sudden distaste and she blinked as the flash of the camera stung her eyes. 'Afterwards, when the police told me that he'd died of self-neglect and malnutrition, I kept wondering why he'd made no attempt to save himself. It wasn't just that I found him beside my chest freezer' – she gestured unhappily towards the window – 'everyone's so affluent on this estate that even the dustbins have perfectly edible food in them.'

'Any ideas?'

'Only that he was so weak by the time he found my garage that he hadn't the energy to do more than crawl into the corner and hide himself.'

'Why would he want to hide?'

She studied him for a moment. 'I don't know. But if he wasn't hiding, why didn't he try to attract my attention? The police think he must have entered the garage on the Saturday, because his only opportunity to get inside was when I went to the shops that afternoon and left the doors unlocked for half an hour.' In so far as she was capable of showing emotion, she did. Her hand flickered nervously towards her mouth before she

40

remembered the camera and dropped it abruptly. 'I found his body on the following Friday and the pathologist estimated he'd been dead five days. That means he was alive on the Sunday. I could have helped him if he'd called out and let me know he was there. So why didn't he?'

'Perhaps he was afraid.'

'Of what?'

'Being turned over to the police for trespass.'

She shook her head. 'Certainly not that. He had no fear of the police or of prison. I understand he was arrested quite regularly. Why should this time have been any different?'

Deacon made shorthand notes on his pad to remind himself of the nuances of expression that crossed her face as she talked about Billy. *Anxiety. Concern. Bewilderment even.* Curiouser and curiouser. *What was Billy Blake to her that he could inspire emotion where her husband couldn't?* 'Maybe he was just too weak to attract your attention. Presumably the pathologist can't say if he was conscious on the Sunday?'

'No,' she said slowly, 'but I can. There was a bag of ice-cubes in the freezer. Someone had opened it, and it certainly wasn't me, so I presume it must have been Billy. And one corner of the garage had been urinated in. If he was strong enough to move around the garage, then he was strong enough to bang on the connecting door between the garage and my hall. He must have known I was here that weekend because he could have heard me. The door's not thick enough to block out sound.'

'What did the police make of that?'

'Nothing,' she said. 'It made no difference to the pathologist's verdict. Billy still died of malnutrition whether through wilful self-neglect or involuntary self-neglect.'

He lit another cigarette and eyed her through the smoke. 'How much did the cremation cost you?'

'Does the amount matter?'

'It depends how cynical you believe the average reader to be. He might think you're being coy about the figure because you want everyone to assume you spent more.'

'Five hundred pounds.'

'Which is a great deal more than you would have given him alive?'

She nodded. Click. 'If I'd met him as a beggar in the street, I'd have thought I was being generous if I gave him five pounds.' Click. Click. She glanced with irritation at Lisa, looked as if she were about to say something, then thought better of it. Her face took on its closed expression again.

'You said yesterday that you felt you owed him something. What exactly?'

'Respect, I suppose.'

'Because you felt he hadn't been shown any in life?'

'Something like that,' she admitted. 'But it sounds ridiculously sentimental when it's put into words.'

He wrote for a moment. 'Do you have a religion?'

She turned away as another flash exploded in her eyes. 'Surely she's taken enough by now?'

Lisa kept the camera lens on her face. 'Just a couple more shots with the eyes cast down, Amanda.' Click.

'Yes, that's really nice, Amanda.' Click. 'More compassion maybe.' Click. 'Great, Amanda.' Click, click, click.

Deacon watched increasing irritation gather in the woman's eyes. 'All right, Smith. Let's call a halt, shall we?'

'How about a few more in the garage?' suggested the girl, reluctant to waste the end of the film. 'It won't take a minute.'

Mrs Powell stared into the blood-red depths of her glass before taking a sip. 'Be my guest,' she said without raising her head. 'The keys are on the table in the hall, and the light comes on automatically when the garage door is lifted. I don't use the connecting door any more.'

'I meant a few more of you,' said Lisa. 'I'll need you to come with me. If it's cold and damp out there, a few atmospheric shots could be really good. More in tune with a wino dying of starvation.'

The woman's stillness following this remark persuaded Lisa she hadn't been listening. She tried again. 'Five minutes, Amanda, that's all we'll need. You might like to stand near where you found him, look a bit upset, that sort of thing.'

The only sound in the room was the ticking of a clock on the mantelpiece, and it grew louder as Mrs Powell's silence lengthened. She seemed to Deacon to be waiting for something, and he held his breath and waited with her. It startled him to hear her speak. 'I'm sorry,' she said to the girl, 'but you and I are very different animals. I could no more pose weepy-eyed over where Billy died than I could wear your fuck-me clothes or your fuck-me make-up. You see, I'm neither so vulgar nor so desperate to be noticed.'

There were too many sibilants in the last sentence, and her careful diction abandoned her. With a slight shock, Deacon realized she was drunk.

Chapter Three

IT WAS dangerous to allow a silence to go on too long. The impact of her words did not diminish in a vacuum; instead they grew and gained in authority. Deacon was drawn to see Lisa through her eyes, and he was struck by how appropriate her description of the girl was. Compared with the snow queen in the chair opposite, Lisa's outlined pouting lips and bottom-hugging skirt were blatantly provocative, and he felt himself belittled to have lusted after her so long in silence when lust was what she was inviting. He saw himself as one of Pavlov's dogs, lured into salivating every time his greed was stimulated, and the idea offended him.

He took his keys from his pocket and suggested that Lisa use the car to drive herself back to the office with her equipment. 'I'll grab a taxi when I'm through,' he said. 'Leave the keys with Glen at the front desk and I'll pick them up from him.'

She nodded, glad of an excuse to leave, and immediately he regretted his perfidy. It wasn't a crime to display bright plumage; rather it was a celebration of youth. She left the camera out as she repacked the case, then with a curt nod in the older woman's direction let herself out of the sitting-room door.

They both heard the rattle of garage keys being lifted from the hall table. Amanda sighed. 'I was rude to her. I'm sorry. I find it hard to treat Billy's death quite as casually as you and she do.' She examined her glass for a moment, as if aware that she'd given herself away, then abandoned it on the coffee table.

'You certainly seem to take it very personally.'

'He died on my property.'

'That doesn't make you responsible for him.'

She looked at him rather blankly. 'Then who is responsible?'

The question was simplistic – it was what a child would ask. 'Billy himself,' said Deacon. 'He was old enough to make his own choices in life.'

She shook her head then leaned forward, searching his face earnestly. 'You said yesterday that you were moved by Billy's story, so could we talk about his life instead of his death? I know I said there was nothing I could tell you, but that wasn't strictly accurate. I know at least as much as the police do.'

'I'm listening.'

'According to the pathologist, he was forty-five years old, six feet tall and although his hair was completely white when he died, it would have been dark. He was first arrested four years ago for stealing some bread and ham from a high-street supermarket, and he gave his name as Billy Blake and his age as sixty-one, which, if the pathologist is right, was twenty years older than his actual age.' She spoke quickly and fluently, as if she had spent a

46

long time preparing the facts for just such a presentation. 'He said he'd been living rough for ten years, but refused to give any other information. He wouldn't say where he came from and he wouldn't say if he had a family. The police checked Missing Persons in London and the South-East, but nobody of his description had been reported missing in the previous ten years. His fingerprints, such as they were, weren't in the police files and he had nothing on him that could establish his identity. In the absence of any other information, the police recorded the details he gave them and for the next four years he lived and subsequently died as Billy Blake. He spent a total of six months in prison for stealing food or alcohol, with each sentence amounting to a one- or two-month stretch, and he preferred to doss down as near to the Thames as possible when he was out. His favourite pitch was a derelict warehouse about a mile from here. I've talked to some of the other old men who use it, but none of them admitted to knowing anything about Billy's history.'

Deacon was impressed by the extent of her interest and effort. 'What did you mean by "his fingerprints, such as they were"?'

'The police said he'd burnt his hands in a fire at some time and left them to heal on their own. Both were so badly scarred that his fingers were like claws. They think he may have mutilated himself deliberately to avoid some previous crime catching up with him.'

'Shit!' he said unguardedly.

She stood up and walked over to the glass cabinet on the far wall. 'As I said earlier, there *are* photographs of him.' She took an envelope from a shelf inside and came back with it, slipping the contents into her hand. 'I persuaded the police to give me two of them. This is the best they had out of the batch the pathologist took. It's not very pleasant and they say it's doubtful anyone would recognize him from it.' She handed it across. 'His face is very shrunken from lack of food, and because his forehead and jaw were so pronounced, it's likely that he was much fuller faced when he was healthy.'

Deacon examined the picture. She was right. It wasn't very pleasant. He was reminded of the corpses piled high inside Bergen-Belsen when the Allies liberated it. The face was almost fleshless, so tightly was the skin drawn across the bones. She handed him the other photograph. 'That's the one that was taken four years ago when he was first arrested. But it's not much better. He was skeletal even then, although it gives a slightly clearer idea of what he might have looked like.'

Could this really be the face of a 41-year-old? Deacon wondered. Old age had scored itself into deep lines round the mouth, and the eyes that looked into the camera were faded and yellow. Only the hair had any vitality where it sprang up from the high forehead, although its whiteness was startling against the sallowness of the complexion. 'Could the pathologist have been wrong about his age?' he asked.

'Apparently not. I understand he took a second opinion when the police didn't believe him. It did occur to me,' she went on, 'that someone with the right computer software might be able to build on the images, but I don't know anyone who specializes in that area. If

48

your magazine could do it, it would make a far better visual accompaniment to your article than the picture of me.'

'Why haven't the police done that?'

'He didn't commit a crime before he died, so they're not interested. I believe they put his description on to a missing persons computer file but it didn't match with anyone, so they've written him off.'

'Can I borrow these? We'll have some negatives made and then I can let you have them back.' He tucked the photographs between the pages of his notebook when she nodded agreement. 'Did the police ever come up with any other explanation for why he chose your garage, apart from the door being open on the day he went into it?'

She sat down again and folded her hands in her lap. Deacon was surprised to see how whitely her knuckles shone. 'They thought he might have followed me home from work, although they never produced a valid reason for why he might have wanted to do that. If he'd singled me out as someone worth following, then he'd have asked me for help. Would you agree with that?' She was appealing to him on an intellectual level, but Deacon was more inclined to respond to the tic of anxiety that fluttered at the corner of her mouth. He hadn't noticed it before. He was beginning to understand that her composure was a surface thing and that something far more turbulent was at work underneath.

'Yes,' he said. 'There's no sense in following you without a reason. So? Could there have been another reason?'

'Like what?'

'Perhaps he thought he recognized you.'

'As whom?'

'I don't know.'

'Wouldn't he have been even more likely to speak to me if he thought he knew me?' She darted the question at him so quickly that he guessed it was one she had asked herself many times.

Deacon scratched his jaw. 'Maybe he was too far gone by then to do anything other than collapse and die. Where exactly is your office?'

'Two hundred yards from the derelict warehouse where Billy used to doss. The whole area's up for redevelopment. W. F. Meredith rent office space in a warehouse which was refurbished three years ago during the first phase. The police felt the proximity of the buildings was too much of a coincidence, but I'm not sure I agree with them. Two hundred yards is a long way in a city like London.' She looked unhappy and he guessed she found this argument less convincing than she claimed.

He lifted the pages of his notebook to study the skull's-head photograph again. 'Was this house a Meredith construction?' he asked without looking up. 'Did you get a discount on it because you're part of the firm?'

She didn't answer immediately. 'I don't think that's any of your business,' she said then.

He gave a low laugh. 'Probably not, but a place like this costs a fortune, and you haven't exactly stinted on the furnishings. You're not short of a bob or two if you can afford all this and shell out five hundred pounds on an unknown man's cremation. I'm curious, Amanda. You're either a very successful architect or you have another source of income.'

'As I said, Mr Deacon, it's none of your business.' Briefly the drink slurred her words again. 'Shall we go back to Billy?'

He shrugged. 'Presumably you'd have noticed anyone like this watching you?' he asked her, tapping the celluloid face.

She straightened slowly, a troubled expression on her face. 'No, I don't think I would.'

'How could you have missed him?'

'By avoiding eye-contact,' she admitted reluctantly. 'It's the only way to escape being pestered. Even if I do give money to someone, I very rarely look at them. I certainly couldn't give a detailed description of them afterwards.'

Deacon reflected on the homeless youngsters he'd interviewed already for his article, and realized he'd have trouble describing any particular individual. It depressed him to admit it, but she was right. Through sheer embarrassment, one never looked too long on the destitute. 'All right,' he said, 'let's say it was pure coincidence that Billy chose your garage to die in. Then someone must have seen him. If he was walking along the road looking for a place to hide, particularly on an estate like this, he couldn't have gone unnoticed. Did any of your neighbours come forward as witnesses?'

'No one's mentioned it.'

'Did the police ask?'

'I don't know. It was all over in three or four hours. As soon as the doctor arrived and pronounced him dead, that was effectively it. The doctor said he'd died of natural causes, and the PC who answered my 999 call claimed they'd all known it was only a matter of time before Billy Blake turned up as a bundle of rags somewhere. His words were: "The silly old sod has been committing slow suicide for years. People can't live the way he did and expect to survive."'

'Did you ask him what he meant by that?'

'He said the only time Billy ate properly was when he was in prison. Otherwise he survived on a diet of alcohol.'

'Poor bastard,' said Deacon, eyeing her glass. 'I suppose life under anaesthetic was more bearable than life without.'

If she understood the personal import of his remark, she didn't show it. 'Yes,' was all she said.

'You suggested Billy Blake wasn't his real name, but one he adopted four years ago when he was first arrested. So where did he get the money to buy the alcohol? He'd need to register to get welfare payments.'

She shook her head again. 'I asked the old men in the warehouse about that, and they said he survived on charity rather than government hand-outs. He used to draw pavement pictures down on the embankment near the river cruisers, and he earned enough from the tourists to pay for his drink. It was only in the winter when the sightseers dried up that he resorted to stealing and, if you look at his prison record, you'll find that all his stretches were done during the winter months.'

'It sounds as though he had his life pretty well organized.'

'I agree.'

'What sort of things did he draw? Do you know?'

'He did the same picture each time. From the way the men describe it, he drew the nativity scene. He also used to preach to the passers-by about the damnation to come for all sinners.'

'Was he mentally ill?'

'It sounds like it.'

'Did he use the same pitch each time?'

'No. I gather he was moved on fairly regularly by the police.'

'But he only drew the one picture?'

'I believe so.'

'Was it any good?'

'The old men said it was. They described him as a real artist.' Unexpectedly she laughed, and mischief brightened her eyes. 'But they were drunk when I spoke to them, so I'm not sure how valid their artistic judgement is.'

The mischief vanished as quickly as it came, but once again Deacon fell prey to his fantasies. He persuaded himself that she was ignorant of real desire and that it needed an experienced man to release her passion . . . 'What else have you managed to find out?'

'Nothing. I'm afraid that's it.'

He reached forward to switch off his tape recorder. 'You said Billy's story needs to be told,' he reminded her, 'but everything you know about him will fit into two or three sentences. And if I'm honest, I'd say he doesn't justify even that much space.' He reflected for a moment, collating the information in his head. 'He was an alcoholic and a petty criminal who lied about his age and used an alias. He was running away from someone or something, probably a wife and an unhappy marriage, and he descended into destitution because he was either inadequate or mentally ill. He had some ability as an artist and he died in your garage because you live near the river and the door happened to be open.' He watched his abandoned cigarette expire in a long curl of ash in the saucer. 'Have I missed anything?'

'Yes.' The movement at the side of her mouth became suddenly more pronounced. 'You haven't explained why he was starving himself to death or why he burnt his hands to claws.'

He made a gesture of apology. 'That's what chronic alcoholics with severe depression do, Amanda. They drink instead of eating, which is why the pathologist included self-neglect as a cause of death, and they mutilate themselves as a way of externalizing their anguish about a life that holds no hope for them. I think your Billy was clinically ill and, because he drank to make himself feel better, he ended up dead in your garage.'

He could see from the resigned expression on her face that he hadn't told her anything she hadn't already worked out for herself, and his curiosity about her increased. Why this *idée fixe* about Billy Blake's life? There was something much deeper driving her, he thought, than simple compassion or high-minded sentiment about a man's value to society.

'I couldn't get anyone even remotely interested in trying to find out who he might have been,' she murmured, bending her head to the bowl of pot-pourri and sifting the petals idly between her fingers. 'The police were polite but bored. I've written to my MP and to the Home Office, asking for some attempts to be made to trace his family, and had replies saying it's not their responsibility. The only people who were at all sympathetic were the Salvation Army. They have his description on their files now and have promised to contact me if anyone tries to trace him, but they're not optimistic about it.' She looked very unhappy. 'I simply don't know what else to do. After six months I've reached a dead end.'

He watched her for several moments, fascinated by the play of expressions that crossed her face. He guessed that her look of unhappiness probably translated as deep despair for someone more demonstrative. 'If it's that important, why don't you hire a private detective?' he suggested.

'Have you any idea how much they charge?'

'You've explored the possibility then?'

She nodded. 'And I could never justify the expense. I was told it could take weeks, even months, and there's no guarantee of success at the end of it.'

'But we've already established that you're a rich woman, so who would you be justifying the expense to?'

A flicker of emotion – *embarrassment?* – crossed her face. 'Myself,' she said.

'Not your husband.'

'No.'

'Are you saying he wouldn't mind if you spent a fortune trying to trace a dead stranger's family?' The elusive Mr Powell intrigued him.

She didn't say anything.

'You've already recognized Billy's worth by paying for his funeral. Why isn't that enough for you?'

'Because it's life that matters, not death.'

'That's not a good enough reason, or not for the kind of obsession you've developed.'

She laughed again, and the sound startled Deacon. It was pitched far too high, but he couldn't decide if it was drink – *or fear?* – that had introduced the note of hysteria. She made a visible effort to bring herself under control. 'You know about obsession, do you, Mr Deacon?'

'I know there's something else to this story that you haven't told me. You seem to be going to extraordinary lengths to try and identify Billy Blake and trace his family. Almost,' he said thoughtfully, 'as if you felt under an obligation. I think you did speak to him, and I think he asked you to do something. Am I right?'

She stared through him with the same expression of disappointment that his mother had shown the last time he saw her. He had wished so often that he'd tried for a reconciliation then that he reached out now, in a strange, confused transposition, to do for a stranger what he hadn't done for Penelope. He put a sympathetic hand on Amanda's arm but her skin was cold and unresponsive to his touch, and if she noticed the gesture at all, she didn't show it.

Instead she leaned her head against the back of her chair to stare at the ceiling, and Deacon had a sense of doors closing and opportunities lost. 'Could you retrieve my garage keys when you return to your office?' she asked politely. 'Unless your friend is still out there, she's taken them with her.'

'What did he say to you, Amanda?'

She glanced at him for a moment but there was only boredom in her eyes. He was no longer of any interest to her. 'I've wasted your time and mine, Mr Deacon. I hope you find a taxi without too much trouble. It's usually easier if you turn left out of the entrance to the estate and walk up to the main road.'

He wished he was better at reading a woman's character. He was sure she was lying to him, but women had lied to him for years and he had never known when they were doing it.

There was a note with the two sets of keys at the front desk. *What a cow! Hope she didn't eat you alive after I left. I put her stupid keys in my pocket and forgot about them. Here they are with your car keys. Thought you should return them rather than me! If you're interested, I left the film with Barry. He said he'll develop it tonight. See you tomorrow. Love, Lisa.*

Deacon decided he was in no hurry, and wandered up to the third floor where Barry Grover doubled as film processor and archives' librarian. He was a somewhat pathetic character in his early thirties, very much a loner, short, pot-bellied and bug-eyed behind magnifying lenses, who pored over the picture cuttings in his library with the avidity of a collector and haunted the offices till all hours in preference to going home. The female staff avoided him whenever possible, and invented malicious gossip behind his back. Over the years they had described him variously, and always with conviction, as a paedophile, a Peeping Tom and a flasher, because it was the only way they could account for his infatuation with pictures. Deacon, who found him as unsympathetic as the women did, nevertheless felt sorry for him. Barry's was a peculiarly barren life.

'Still here?' he said with false bonhomie as he shouldered open the door and caught the man bent over a newspaper cutting on his desk.

'As you say, Mike.'

He propped a buttock on the edge of the desk. 'Lisa told me you were developing her film. I thought I'd drop in to see how it turned out.'

'I'll get the contact sheets for you.' Barry scuttled hurriedly out of the room like a fleshy white cockroach, and Deacon, watching him critically, decided it was the way he moved that set people's teeth on edge. There was something very effeminate about the rapid little steps he took, and he wondered, not for the first time, if Barry's problem had more to do with unresolved homosexuality than the heterosexual perversions of which the women accused him.

He lit a cigarette and turned the cutting that Barry had been reading towards himself.

The Guardian 6th May, 1990

Banker's Wife Released

Amanda Streeter, 31, was released without charge yesterday following two days of police questioning. 'We are satisfied,' said a police spokesman, 'that Mrs Streeter was not implicated in the theft of £10 million from Lowenstein's Merchant Bank, nor has any knowledge of her husband's whereabouts.' He confirmed that James Streeter, 38, is believed to have left the country some time during the night of 27 April. 'His description has been circulated around the world and we expect him to be found within days. As soon as we are notified of where he is, extradition procedures will begin.'

Amanda Streeter's solicitor issued the following statement to the press. 'Mrs Streeter has been deeply shocked by the events of the last eight days and has given the police as much assistance as she can in their search for her husband. Now that she has been ruled out of the investigation, she asks to be left in peace. There is nothing she can add to the information that is already in the public domain.'

The allegations against James Streeter are that, over a period of five years, he used his position at Lowenstein's to falsify accounts and steal over £10 million. The alleged irregularities came to light some six weeks ago but the details were kept in-house to avoid panicking the bank's customers. When it became clear that the bank's own investigation was going nowhere, the board decided to call in the police. Within hours of the decision being taken, James Streeter disappeared. Charges are being brought against him in his absence.

'I recognized her face.'

Deacon hadn't heard Barry return and was startled by the sudden, breathy voice in the silence. He watched the man's fat finger push the cutting to one side and point to a grainy photograph underneath.

'That's her with her husband before he ran. Lisa called her Mrs Powell, but it's the same woman. You probably remember the case. He was never caught.'

Deacon stared down at the photograph of Amanda Powell-Streeter, aged thirty-one. She was wearing glasses, her hair was shorter and darker and her face was in three-quarters profile. He wouldn't have recognized her, yet, knowing who it was, he saw the similarities. He looked thoughtfully at the husband for a moment or two, searching for a resemblance with Billy Blake, but nothing in life was ever that easy. 'How do you do it?' he asked Barry.

'It's what I'm paid for.'

'That doesn't explain how you do it.'

The other man smiled to himself. 'Some people say it's a gift, Mike.' He placed the contact sheets on the desk. 'Lisa's done a lousy job with these. There are only five or six that are good enough to pass muster. She needs to do them again.'

Deacon held the sheets to the light and examined them closely. They were uniformly bad, either out of focus or so poorly lit that Amanda Powell's face looked like granite. There were six perfect shots of an empty garage at the end of the sequence. He stubbed his cigarette out in an ashtray on Barry's desk which was placed beside a prominent notice saying: *In the interests of my health please don't smoke*. 'How the hell did she manage to produce crap like this?' he asked crossly.

Fastidiously, Barry emptied the ashtray into his waste-

60

paper basket. 'Obviously there's something wrong with her camera. I'll call it in for service tomorrow. It's a shame. She's usually very reliable.'

Considering how bad Lisa's photographs were, it was even more extraordinary that Barry had been able to make the connection. Deacon fished his notebook from his coat pocket and isolated the two photographs of Billy Blake. 'I suppose you don't recognize him?'

The little man took the prints and placed them side by side on his desk. He examined them for a long time. 'Maybe,' he said at last.

'What do you mean, maybe? Either you do or you don't.'

Barry looked put out. 'You don't know anything about it, Mike. Supposing I played a bar of Mozart to you, you might be able to identify it as Mozart, but you'd never be able to say which of his works it came from.'

'What's that got to do with identifying a photograph?'

'You wouldn't understand. It's very complicated. I shall have to work on it.'

Deacon felt suitably put in his place. And not for the first time that night. But thoughts of Barry were less likely to haunt him than thoughts of a woman who reminded him of his mother. 'How about making some good negatives for me? The chances are he looked nothing like this when he was fit and healthy, but we might be able to do something on the computer to flesh the face out a bit. That would give you a better base to start from, wouldn't it?'

'Possibly. Where did the prints come from?'

'Mrs Powell. He died in her garage under the name of Billy Blake, but she doesn't think that was his real name.' He gave Barry a quick summary of what Amanda had told him. 'She has a bee in her bonnet about trying to identify him and trace his family.'

'Why?'

Deacon touched the newspaper cuttings. 'I don't know. Perhaps it has something to do with what happened to her husband.'

'I can make the negatives easily enough. When do you want them?'

'First thing tomorrow?'

'I'll do them for you now.'

'Thanks.' Deacon glanced at his watch as he stood up and saw with surprise that it was after ten o'clock. 'Change of plan,' he said abruptly, reaching Barry's coat from a hook behind the door. 'I'm taking you for a drink instead. Christ, man, this bloody magazine doesn't own you. Why the hell don't you tell us all to get stuffed occasionally?'

Barry Grover allowed himself to be drawn along the pavement by Deacon's insistent hand on his shoulder, but he was a reluctant volunteer. He had been on the receiving end of such spontaneous invitations before. He knew the routine, knew he had only been invited because Deacon's irregular conscience had struck, knew he would be forgotten and ignored within five minutes of entering the pub. Deacon's drinking cronies would be lining the bar and Barry would be left to stand at the side, unwilling to intrude where he wasn't wanted, unwilling to draw attention to himself by leaving.

Yet, as usual, he was prey to a terrible ambivalence as the pub drew closer, because he both feared and yearned to go drinking with Deacon. He feared inevitable rejection, yearned to be accepted as Deacon's friend, for Deacon had shown him more casual companionship since he'd arrived at the *Street* than Barry had known in years. He told himself that to be accepted just once would suffice. It was such a small ambition for a man to hold, after all. To feel part of a social group for a single night, to tell a joke and raise a laugh, to be able to say the next morning: 'I went for a drink with a mate.'

He stopped abruptly outside the pub and started to polish his glasses furiously on a large white handkerchief. 'After all, Mike, I think I'd better get home. I hadn't realized how late it was and, if I'm to do those negatives for you, I can't afford to oversleep.'

'You've time for a pint,' said Deacon cheerfully. 'Where's home? I'll drop you off afterwards if it's on my way.'

'Camden.'

'It's a deal then. I'm in Islington.' He clapped a friendly arm across Barry's shoulders and escorted him through the doors of the Lame Beggar.

But the fat little man's forebodings were well founded. Within minutes, Deacon had been subsumed into a raucous pre-Christmas drinking throng, while Barry was left to blink his embarrassment and his loneliness in feigned insouciance by the wall. It was when he realized that Deacon was too drunk to drive him home, or even to remember the offer, that a terrible sense of injustice began to grow in him. Confused feelings of hero-worship turned angrily to bitter resentment. Hell could freeze over, as far as he was concerned, before Deacon would ever learn from him who Billy Blake really was.

11.00 p.m. – Cape Town, South Africa

It was a warm summer night in the Western Cape. A well-dressed woman sat alone in the glass-fronted restaurant of the Victoria and Alfred Hotel, toying with a cup of black coffee. She was a regular customer, although little was known about her other than that her name was Mrs Metcalfe. She always ate and drank sparingly, and it was a mystery to the waiters why she came at all. She seemed to take little pleasure in her solitary meal, and preferred to turn her back as far as possible on her fellow diners. She chose instead to gaze out over the harbour where, had it been daylight, she would have seen the seals that play among the moored ships. The night held fewer diversions and, as usual, her expression was bored.

At eleven o'clock, her driver presented himself at reception and, after settling her bill, she left. Her waiter pocketed his customary handsome tip and wondered, not for the first time, what brought her here every Wednesday evening to spend three hours doing something she found so uncomfortable.

Had she been remotely friendly, he might have asked her, but she was a typical tight-lipped, skinny white woman and their relationship was a professional one.

Chapter Four

IF DEACON was surprised that Barry Grover left the pub without saying anything, he didn't dwell on it. He had walked out on too many drinking sessions himself to regard it as anything unusual. In any case he was relieved to be shot of the responsibility of driving the man home. He wasn't as drunk as Barry had believed, but he was certainly over the limit and chose to abandon his car at the office and take a taxi. He was renting an attic flat, and he slouched dejectedly in his seat as Islington drew closer. He and Barry had something in common, he thought, assuming Barry's long hours at work meant he shared Deacon's aversion to going home. The parallel intrigued him suddenly. What were Barry's reasons, he wondered? Did he, like Deacon, fear the emptiness of a flat that contained nothing of a personal nature because there was nothing from his past that he wanted to remember?

He sank deeper into maudlin gloom, indulging himself in drink-inspired self-loathing. He was to blame for everything. His father's death. His failed marriages. His family's bitterness and their ultimate rejection of him. (*God, how he wished he could get that damn woman's eyes out of his mind. Memories of his mother had been haunting him all evening.*) No children. No friends because they'd all taken his first wife's side. He must have been out of his mind to betray one wife, only to find the second wasn't worth the price he'd paid for her.

From time to time, the cab driver flicked him a sympathetic glance in the rear-view mirror. He recognized the melancholy of a man who drank to drown his sorrows. London was full of them in the run-up to Christmas.

Deacon woke with a sense of purpose, which was unusual for him. He put it down to the fact that his subconscious mind had been replaying the tape of his interview with Amanda Powell, further whetting his curiosity about her. Why should mention of Billy Blake, a stranger, produce an emotional reaction when mention of her husband, James Streeter, produced none? Not even anger.

He pondered the question in the solitary isolation of his kitchen while he stirred his coffee and looked with disfavour at the blank white walls and blank white units that surrounded him. Predictably, his thoughts turned inwards. Did either of *his* wives show emotion when *his* name was mentioned? Or was he just a forgotten episode in their lives?

He could die like Billy Blake, he thought, slumped in a corner of this wretched flat, and when he was found, days later, it would almost certainly be by a stranger. Who would come looking, after all? JP? Lisa? His drinking pals?

Jesus wept! Was his life really as empty – and worthless? – as Billy Blake's . . .?

He arrived at the office early, consulted the phone book and an *A to Z* of London, left a message at the front desk to say he would be back later, then retrieved his car and headed east along the river towards what had once been the thriving port of London. As in so many other ports around the world, the shipping fleets and working docks had long since given way to pleasure vessels, expensive housing and marinas.

He made his way down the western shores of the Isle of Dogs and located the refurbished warehouse where W. F. Meredith, architects, had their offices, then drove on towards a filthy, boarded-up building that bore no resemblance to its neighbours except in its rectangular lines and gabled roof. Not that it required much imagination on his part to picture what this sad relic of Victorian London could become. He had lived in the capital long enough to witness the transformation of the old docklands buildings into things of beauty, and he had only to look at the converted warehouses around him to remind himself of what was achievable.

He parked his car, took a torch and a bottle of Bell's whisky from the dashboard pocket and made his way through a gap in the fence to the front of the building. He tested the boarding on the doors and windows before making his way round to the back. Five or six metres of exposed scrubland separated the rear wall from the river, and he pulled his coat more tightly about him as a bitterly cold wind whipped across the surface of the Thames and flayed the skin of his face. How anyone could expose themselves to such conditions was beyond him, yet a small group of men, apparently impervious to the morning cold and damp, sat huddled about a brazier of burning wood in an open doorway in the warehouse wall. They regarded him with suspicion as he approached.

'Hi,' he said, squatting down in a gap in the circle with the bottle between his feet, 'my name's Michael Deacon.' He took out his cigarette packet and offered it around. 'I'm a reporter.'

One of the men, much younger than the rest, gave a short laugh and mimicked Deacon's educated diction. 'Hi. My name's R. S. Hole. I'm a bum.' He took a cigarette. 'Ta. I'll save it for drinkies before dinner if you've no objections.'

'None at all, Mr Hole. Seems a shame to wait for dinner, though.'

The lad had a thin, washed-out face beneath a crudely shaven head. 'The name's Terry. What are you after, you bastard?'

He really was very young, thought Deacon, but there was street wisdom in the aggressive tilt of his jaw and a terrible cynicism in the narrowed eyes. With a slight shock, it occurred to him that Terry thought he was a middle-class homosexual in search of a rent-boy. 'Information,' he said matter-of-factly. 'About a man called Billy Blake who used to doss here when he wasn't in prison.'

'Who says we knew him?'

'The woman who paid for his funeral. She tells me she came here and got answers to some of her questions.'

'*Aye*-mander,' said one of the others. 'I remember 'er.

68

Saw 'er on the corner not so long ago and she gave me a fiver.'

Terry cut him off with an impatient hand. 'What does a reporter want with Billy? He's been dead six months.'

'I don't know yet,' said Deacon honestly. 'Maybe I just want to prove that Billy's life had value.' He clamped his hands over the bottle. 'Whichever one of you can tell me something useful gets the whisky.'

The older men watched the bottle; Terry watched Deacon's face. 'And what exactly does useful mean?' he asked with heavy irony. 'I know he couldn't give a shit about anything. Is that useful?'

'I could have guessed that, Terry, from the way he died. Useful means anything I don't know already, or anything that will lead me towards someone who might have information on him. Let's start with his real name. Who was he before he became Billy Blake?'

They shook their heads.

''E did pavement pictures,' said one old man. ''Ad a pitch down near the cruisers.'

'I know about that. Amanda tells me he always drew the same nativity scene. Does anyone know why?'

More shakes of heads. They were like something out of a *Star Wars* film, thought Deacon irrelevantly. Wizened little monkey-men, swathed in overcoats that were too big for them, but with bright, beady eyes that spoke of a cunning he would never possess.

'It were just a picture of a family that everyone would recognize,' said Terry. 'He weren't stupid, and he needed money. He wrote "Blessed are the poor" underneath, then lay beside it. He looked so fucking ill most of the time that people felt guilty when they saw the painting and read the message. He did pretty well out of it and he were only aggressive when he'd had a skinful and started preaching at the punters. But that just frightened them off, and he'd come home skint those days and have to sober up.'

The faces around him split into grins of reminiscence.

''E was a good artist when 'e was sober,' said the old man who'd spoken before. 'Bloody awful when 'e was drunk.' He cackled to himself, his leathery skin creasing inside the frame of a matted balaclava. 'Drew 'eaven when 'e was sober and 'ell when 'e was pissed.'

'You mean he did two different pictures?'

''E did 'undreds, s'long as 'e could get the paper.' The old head jerked towards the office blocks. 'Used to take piles of old letters out of the bins of an evening, draw his pictures all night on the backs, then abandon 'em in the morning.'

'What happened to them?'

'We burned 'em the next day.'

'Did Billy mind?'

'Nah,' said another. 'He needed to keep warm like the rest of us. Matter of fact, it used to make him laugh.' He screwed his finger into his forehead. 'He was mad as a sodding hatter. Always screaming about hell-fire and being cleansed by the devil's flames. Stuck his hand in the middle of a mound of blazing paper once and kept it there for ages before we dragged him off.'

'Why did he do that?'

A shrug of indifference rippled round the group like a

muted Mexican wave. There was no logic to the actions of a madman seemed to be their common thinking.

'He were always doing it,' said Terry. 'Sometimes it were both hands, more often just the right. It really used to bug me. There were days when he couldn't move his fingers at all because the blisters were so bad, but he'd still draw his sodding pictures. He'd stick the crayon between two fingers and move his whole hand to do the drawing. He said he needed to feel the pain of creation.'

'Young Terry reckoned 'e was schizo,' declared the leathery-faced ancient in the balaclava. 'Told 'im 'e should get medication, but Billy weren't interested. 'E said 'e didn't suffer from anyfing mental and 'e weren't going near no doctors. Death was the only cure for what ailed 'im.'

'Did he ever try to kill himself?'

Terry gave another short laugh and gestured around him. 'What d'you call this? Living or dying?'

Deacon acknowledged the point with a nod. 'I meant did he make specific attempts on his life?'

'No,' said the boy flatly. 'He said he hadn't suffered enough and needed to die slowly.' He drew his coat about his spare frame as another blast of wind whistled across the water and drew sparks from the blazing wood. 'Listen, mate, the poor bastard had galloping schizophrenia, just like Walt here.' He nudged the muffled shape beside him who sat, much as Billy must have done when Amanda Powell found him, with head slumped on knees. 'Walt gets medication, but half the time he forgets to take it. By rights he should be in hospital but there

71

ain't no hospitals any more. He stayed with his old mum for a while when the doctors said he was okay to live on the out, but he scared the poor old biddy out of her wits and she barred the door on him.' He turned to look into the warehouse. 'There's twenty more like him inside. It's us sane ones who're looking after them, and it's a bloody joke, if you ask me.'

Deacon agreed with him. What was society coming to when it was the down-and-outs who offered care in the community to the mentally ill? 'Did Billy ever mention being in a hospital?'

Terry shook his head. 'He never talked much about the past.'

'Okay. How about prison? Do you know which one he did his time in?'

Terry nodded towards the leathery-faced old man. 'Tom and him did a month in Brixton once.'

'Where did they keep him?' Deacon asked Tom. 'On the hospital wing or in a cell?'

'Cell, same as me.'

'Was he given any medication?'

'Not that I remember.'

'So he wasn't diagnosed schizophrenic in prison?'

Tom shook his head. 'The screws ain't got the time or the inclination to worry about a wino doing four weeks in the nick. It'd take 'im that long to dry out so, if 'e screams 'is 'ead off on a regular basis, they just put it down to DTs or anything else they fancy.'

'Did he act as crazy inside as he did on the out?'

Tom made a rocking motion with his hand. 'Bit up and down, got depressed every so often, but otherwise 'e

72

was okay. Went to chapel like a good'un and be'aved 'isself. Reckon it was the drink made 'im mad. 'E was only ever off his 'ead when 'e'd 'ad a skinful. Sane as you an' me when 'e was sober.'

Deacon offered his cigarettes round a second time, then raised his coat flap against the wind to light one for himself. 'And none of you knows where he came from, or who he might have been, or why he called himself Billy Blake?'

'What makes you think it wasn't his real name?' asked Terry. This time he chose to smoke his cigarette, pulling a brand from the fire to light it.

Deacon shrugged. 'I'm guessing.' He drew heavily on his cigarette in order to keep the tip alight. 'How did he speak? Did he have an accent?'

'Not so's you'd notice. I asked him once if he was an actor because he sounded pretty classy when he was raving. But he said no.'

'What did he do when he was raving?'

'Shouted anything that came into his head. Some of it rhymed, but I don't know if he was making it up himself or if he was quoting someone else. I remember some of it – and one bit more or less because he said it over and over again. It was bloody weird stuff, all about his mother groaning, his father weeping and demons leaping out of clouds.'

'Can you quote it?'

Terry looked at the others for inspiration. 'Not really,' he said when he didn't find any. 'He always began with "My mother groaned, my father wept" but I forget what came after.'

Deacon cupped his cigarette in his hands and dredged deep into his memory. '"My mother groaned, my father wept,"' he murmured, '"Into the dangerous world I leapt;/Helpless, naked, piping loud,/Like a fiend hid in a cloud."'

'Yeah,' said the young man with surprised respect. 'How the hell did you know that?'

'It's a poem entitled "Infant Sorrow" by a man called William Blake. I wrote a thesis on him years ago. He was an eighteenth-century poet and artist who was considered off the wall by his contemporaries because he claimed to see visions.' Deacon gave a faint smile. 'William wrote some wonderful poetry, but lived and died in virtual poverty because no one recognized his genius until after he was dead. I suspect your friend knew William and his work rather well.'

'Yeah,' said Terry with quick intelligence. 'William Blake, Billy Blake. What else did this guy write?'

'"Tyger! Tyger! burning bright/In the forests of the night" . . .' Deacon paused, inviting the lad to finish it.

'"What immortal hand or eye/Could frame *thy* fearful symmetry?"' said the youngster in triumph. 'Yeah, Billy were always spouting that one. I told him it didn't rhyme properly, and he said you had to stress "thy", which was where the rhyme was.'

Deacon nodded. Had Billy Blake been a teacher? he wondered. 'There's a line in the next verse that goes: "What the hand dare seize the fire?" Was he thinking of that, do you suppose, when he tried to burn his own hand?'

'I dunno. It depends what it means.'

'The tiger represents power, energy and cruelty. The poem describes this beautiful but uncontrollable creature being forged in flames and then goes on to question why his creator was brave enough to manufacture anything so dangerous.' Deacon could see he'd lost the others but there was keen interest still in Terry's face. 'It's the creator's hand that dared "seize the fire", so perhaps Billy thought he'd started something that he couldn't control.'

'Maybe.' A far-away look came into the young man's eyes as he stared across the river. 'Is the creator God?'

'*A* god. Blake doesn't specify which one.'

'Billy reckoned there were loads of gods. Gods of war. Gods of love. Gods of rivers. Gods of every-bloody-thing. He used to swear at them all the time. "It's your fault, you buggers," he used to shout, "so let me alone and let me die." I said he should just stop believing that the gods were there, then he wouldn't have to hate them. Makes sense, doesn't it?' The pinched face turned back towards the brazier.

'What did he think was the gods' fault?'

'It's not what he *thought*,' said Terry with careful emphasis, 'it's what he *knew*.' He reached out and gripped the air with his fingers. 'He strangled someone because the gods wrote it into his fate. That's why he stuck his hand in the fire. He called it the "offending instrument" and said "such sacrifices were necessary if the gods' anger was to be directed somewhere else." Poor bastard. He didn't know his arse from his elbow most of the time.'

*

On Terry's instructions, Deacon gave the bottle of Bell's whisky into the care of the old man in the balaclava before following Terry into the warehouse to see where Billy had slept. 'It's a waste of time,' the lad grumbled. 'He's been dead six months. What are you expecting to find?'

'Anything.'

'Listen, there've been a hundred dossers in his space since he kicked it. You won't find nothing.' But despite this he led Deacon into the gloom. 'You nuts or what?' he said in amusement as Deacon lit a small pool of light at their feet with his torch. 'That's not going to help you see a damn thing. Just wait, okay. Your eyes'll soon adjust. There's enough light comes through the door.'

A grey lunar landscape slowly developed in front of Deacon, a wasteland of twisted metal, piled bricks and abandoned warehouse wreckage. It was the aftermath of war where nothing recognizable existed any more, and only the acrid smell of urine suggested human presence. 'How long have you been here?' he asked Terry, as he began to pick out sleeping bodies among the rubble.

'Two years on and off.'

'Why here? Why not a squat or a hostel?'

The young man shrugged. 'I've done them. This ain't so bad.' He led the way past a pile of bricks and gestured to a makeshift structure, made out of polythene and old blankets. He pulled one of the blankets aside and reached in to light a battery-operated hurricane lamp. 'Take a look,' he invited. 'This is my pitch.'

Deacon experienced a strange sort of envy. It was a cobbled-together tent in the middle of a urine-smelling bomb site, but it had personality in a way his flat did not. There were posters of semi-nude women pinned to the polythene walls, a mattress on the floor with a handmade patchwork quilt, ornaments on a metal filing cabinet, a wicker chair with a dressing-gown on it, and a jam-jar of plastic red roses on a small painted table. He went in and sat on the chair, carefully folding the dressing-gown on to his lap. 'This is good. You've done it up well.'

'*I* like it. Got most of this stuff off the council tip. It's fucking amazing what people chuck out.' Terry squeezed in beside him and lay on the bed. He looked younger in repose than he did in tense concentration against the wind. 'It's freer than a hostel and not so cramped as a squat. People can get on your nerves in a squat.'

'Don't you have any family?'

'Nah. Been in and out of homes since I was six. One bloke told me once that my mother went to prison which is why I ended up in care, but I've never tried to find her. She's a loser, so it'd be a waste of time looking. I get by.'

Deacon made a point of examining the young face in order to remember it afterwards. But there was nothing memorable about the lad. He was like a hundred shaven-headed boys of the same age, uniformly colourless, uniformly unattractive. He wondered why Terry hadn't mentioned a father, but guessed the father was anonymous and therefore irrelevant. He thought of all the women he himself had slept with over the years. Had one of them fallen pregnant by him and given birth to a Terry whom she subsequently abandoned?

'Still, it can't be much fun living rough like this.'

'Yeah, well, I'm not the first to do it, and I sure as hell won't be the last. Like I said, I get by. Whatever man has done, man can do.'

The expression seemed an unlikely one for a youngster like Terry to use. 'Is that something Billy used to say?'

The lad gave an indifferent shrug. 'Maybe. He were always fucking preaching at me.' His voice took on a more refined tone. '"You cannot have rights without responsibility, Terry. Man's greatest sin is pride because he dethrones God at his peril. Be prepared – the Day of Judgement is closer than you think."' He reverted to his own, rougher accent. 'I'm telling you, it did your head in to listen to him. He were a right nutter most of the time, but he meant well and I reckon I learnt a thing or two off of him.'

'Like what?'

Terry grinned. 'Like, fools ask questions that wise men cannot answer.'

Deacon smiled. 'How old are you?'

'Eighteen.'

Somehow Deacon doubted that. For all Terry's readiness of speech and mind, which allowed him to dominate the derelict old men he was living with, the fluff on his chin was still downy and he was growing too fast for his thin frame to keep pace. His great bony hands hung out of his sleeves like paddles, and it would be a while yet before maturity bulked his chest and shoulders. It made Deacon all the more curious about the preacher – *and teacher?* – who had befriended him.

'How long did you know Billy?' he asked.

'A couple of years.'

Since he'd been in the warehouse then. 'Was his doss as good as this?'

Terry shook his head. 'He wanted to suffer. I told you, he was a real head-case. I found him prancing around in the fucking nude this time last year. You wouldn't believe how cold it was. He was blue from head to toe. I said, what the fuck are you doing, you fucking idiot, and he said he was mortifying the flesh – ' he paused, unsure if he'd used the right word – 'or something like that. He never built himself a place, just used to roll in an old blanket and doss down by the fire. He didn't have nothing, you see, didn't want nothing, didn't see the point in making himself comfortable. He knew the gods would get him in the end, and he reckoned he'd make it as easy for the rotten bastards as he could.'

'Because he was a murderer?'

'Maybe.'

'Did he say if it was a man or a woman that he killed?'

Terry linked his hands behind his head. 'I don't remember.'

'Why did he tell you and not the others?'

'How do you know he didn't tell them?'

'I was watching their faces.'

'They're so drunk most of the time they don't remember nothing.' Terry closed his eyes. 'It might come back for a tenner.'

Deacon's snort of laughter fanned the corner of one of the posters. 'I wasn't born yesterday, sunshine.' He took a card from his wallet and flipped it on to Terry's chest. 'Give me a ring any time you can come up with something I can verify, but don't ring me with crap. And the information had better be good if you want money for it.' He stood up and looked down on the youthful face. 'How old are you really, Terry?' Sixteen was his guess.

'Old enough to recognize a tight-fisted bastard when I meet one.'

On his return to the office, Deacon found a note from Barry Grover on his desk with the original prints of Billy Blake in a transparent plastic envelope. *I cannot trace this man in my files*, he'd written, *but I've passed the negatives and fresh prints to Paul Garrety. He is seeing what he can do with them on the computer. B. G.*

Paul Garrety, the art editor, shook his head when Deacon sought him out and asked him how he was getting on with the Billy Blake pictures. JP had been persuaded to invest heavily in computer equipment for the art department on the promise that technology could do for *Street* style and design, and therefore improved sales, what an army of graphics artists had previously failed to do. But he was too attached to the old look of the magazine to give Paul free rein with the equipment, and Garrety, like Deacon, spent most of his working day at loggerheads with his boss.

'You need an expert, Mike,' he said now. 'I can give you a hundred different versions of him, but it'll take someone with a knowledge of physiognomy to tell you which is the most accurate.' He pointed to his computer screen. 'Watch this. You can have a fuller face, which is just fattening up the whole thing. You can have fuller cheeks, which is puffing up the lower half. You can have double chins, you can have fleshy eyes, you can have thicker hair. The permutations are endless, and every one looks different.'

Deacon watched the alternatives appear on the screen. 'I see what you mean.'

'It's a science. Your best bet is to find yourself a pathologist or an Identikit artist who specializes in faces. We could choose any one of these variations but the chances are it'll look nothing like your dead guy.'

'Any hope of JP running the original alongside my copy?'

Garrety laughed. 'None at all, and for once I'd agree with him. It'd put the punters right off their breakfast. Be fair. Who wants to eat cornflakes looking at a shrivelled old wino who died of starvation?'

'He was only forty-five,' said Deacon mildly. 'Three years older than I am, and ten years younger than you. It's not so funny when you think of it in those terms, is it?'

Michael Deacon's feature on poverty and homelessness appeared in that week's *Street* without any mention of Amanda Powell or Billy Blake. Indeed, the final draft was precisely as he had envisaged at the outset. A thoughtful analysis of changing social trends which concentrated on causes and long-term solutions. JP doubted it would appeal to their readers ('It's bloody boring, Mike. Where's the human interest, for God's sake?'), but, without a decent photograph of either Billy or Mrs Powell, there seemed little point in going with the uninspired statements that Mrs Powell had made on the subject of homelessness in general. JP repeated his threats about the non-renewal of Deacon's contract if he didn't recognize that political mud-slinging was the magazine's stock in trade, and Deacon answered sarcastically that if the sales figures were anything to go by, the *Street* readership enjoyed having its intelligence insulted about as much as the rest of the electorate did.

Amanda Powell, who had received her garage keys and the two photographs of Billy through the post with an anonymous *Street* compliments slip, was disappointed, but not surprised, to find herself and Billy excluded from Deacon's article. But she read it with interest, particularly the paragraph describing a derelict warehouse and its community of mentally disturbed residents who were being cared for by a handful of old men and a young boy.

There was a look of relief in her eyes as she laid the magazine aside.

Chapter Five

A LITTLE research during a quiet afternoon produced the names and addresses of James Streeter's parents and brother, plus some imaginative – *and deliberately libellous?* – press releases from the Friends of James Streeter Campaign which was based at the brother's address in Edinburgh. The last one was dated August 1991.

Despite twelve months of determined lobbying, not a single newspaper has followed up the claims of the Friends of James Streeter Campaign that James was murdered on the night of Friday, 27 April 1990, in order to protect a member of Lowenstein's board and save the bank from the catastrophic collapse that would inevitably result from loss of confidence in its management.

In the interests of justice, the following facts must be investigated:
- James Streeter did not have the knowledge to work the fraud of which he is accused. It is alleged that he gained his computer skills while abroad in France and Belgium.

The FoJSC has collected witness evidence from his previous employers and his first wife that he did not. (See enclosures.)

- James Streeter had no access either to the progress of Lowenstein's in-house investigation or to board decisions, therefore he could not have known the 'ideal' date to leave the country. The FoJSC has witness statements to this effect from his secretary and members of his department. (See enclosures.)

- James Streeter made reference to friends and colleagues in the six months before his disappearance about the incompetence of Nigel de Vriess, his line manager, who was a member of the Lowenstein board in 1990 and who has since left the bank. The FoJSC has three sworn statements which testify that James said in January 1990 that Mr de Vriess was 'at best incompetent and at worst criminally motivated'. (See enclosures.)

- Much reliance has been placed on the damaging allegations made by Amanda Streeter against her husband in a written statement to police. They were: (1) That James was having an affair with a woman who worked for a computer software company – name, Marianne Filbert, whereabouts unknown. (2) That he once remarked, 'Any fool could work the system if someone told him which buttons to press.' (3) That he was obsessed with wealth.

- The FoJSC refutes all three allegations. (1) and (3) depend entirely on the word of Amanda Streeter. (2) refers to a statement made by one of James's colleagues who has since admitted that he wasn't sure even in 1990 if it was James who made the remark.

Further:

- The FoJSC has obtained proof that it was Amanda herself who was having the affair and that her lover was Nigel de Vriess. We have photocopies of bills and eye-witness statements which refer to two secret meetings the couple had in 1986 and 1989 at the George Hotel, Bath. The first occurred only weeks before her marriage to James, the second three years after it. (See enclosures.)

We accuse Amanda Streeter and Nigel de Vriess.

- James Streeter's murder has gone unpunished. Unless the press shakes off its apathy and acts now, the guilty will continue to profit from an innocent man's death. The FoJSC urges, indeed demands, a proper enquiry into the activities of Nigel de Vriess and his lover, Amanda Streeter. Please fax or phone on the above numbers for assistance and/or further information. John and Kenneth Streeter are available for interview at any time.

Two evenings later, and because he had nothing better to do, Deacon dialled John Streeter's number in Edinburgh. A woman answered.

'Hello,' she said in a soft Scottish accent.

Deacon introduced himself as a London-based journalist who was interested in talking to a spokesman from the Friends of James Streeter Campaign.

'Oh, lord!'

He waited a moment. 'Is this a problem for you?'

'No, it's just – well, to be honest, it's over a year since – look, just hang on a moment, will you?' A hand went over the receiver. 'JOHN! JO-OHN!' The hand was removed. 'It's my husband you need to talk to.'

'Fine.'

'I'm sorry I didn't catch your name.'

'Michael Deacon.'

'He'll be here in a minute.' The hand again, and this time her voice was muffled. 'For God's sake, hurry. It's a journalist and he wants to talk about James. His name's Michael Deacon. No, you must. You promised your father you wouldn't give up.' She came back, louder. 'Here's my husband.'

'Hello,' said a man's much deeper voice. 'I'm John Streeter. How can I help you?'

Deacon flicked the trigger on his biro and pulled forward his notepad. 'Does the fact that it's three and a half years since you sent out your last press release mean you've now accepted your brother's guilt?' he said bluntly.

'Are you with a national newspaper, Mr Deacon?'

'No.'

'Then you're freelance?'

'As far as these questions are concerned, yes.'

'Have you any idea how many freelancers I've spoken to over the years?' He paused, but Deacon didn't rise to the bait. 'Approximately thirty,' he went on, 'and the number of column inches I've had out of them is nil because no editor would take the story. I'm afraid I'd be wasting both our time if I answered your questions.'

Deacon tucked the telephone more firmly under his chin and drew a spiral on his pad. 'Thirty is nothing, Mr Streeter. I've known campaigns like yours approach hundreds of journalists before they get anywhere. That apart, most of what you allege in your press releases is actionable. Frankly, you're lucky to have avoided a libel suit this far.'

'Which proves something in itself, don't you think? If what we're claiming is defamatory, why does no one challenge us?'

'Because your targets aren't that stupid. Why give your campaign the adrenalin of publicity when it's dying a death of its own accord? It would be a different matter if you managed to persuade an editor to go against his better judgement. Are you saying nothing has ever been published in defence of your brother?'

'Only a grudging piece in a compilation of unsolved mysteries that came out last year. I spent two days talking to Roger Hyde, the author, only to have him write a bland summary which ended with his own half-baked conclusion that James was guilty.' He sounded angry and frustrated. 'I'm growing rather tired of beating my head against a brick wall.'

'Then perhaps you're less persuaded of your brother's innocence than you were five years ago?'

There was a smothered obscenity. 'That's all you lot ever want, isn't it? Confirmation of James's guilt.'

'Except I'm giving you an opportunity to defend him which you don't seem very keen to take.'

John Streeter ignored this. 'My brother came from an honest, hard-working background, just as I did. Have you any idea what it's done to my parents to have their son labelled a thief? They're decent, respectable people and they can't understand why journalists like you won't listen to them.' He drew another angry breath. 'You're not interested in facts, only in trying to further destroy a man's reputation.'

'Aren't you playing the same game?' Deacon murmured unemphatically. 'Unless I've misread your releases, your defence of James rests entirely on blackening Nigel de Vriess and Amanda Streeter.'

'With reason. There's no proof of her assertion that James was having an affair, but we've found evidence of hers with de Vriess. He stripped the bank of ten million and she aided and abetted him in pushing the blame on to her husband.'

'That's some accusation. Can you prove it?'

'Not without access to their bank and investment accounts, but you only need to look at their respective addresses to realize there was an injection of cash from somewhere. Amanda bought herself a £600,000 house on the Thames within months of James's disappearance and de Vriess bought himself a mansion in Hampshire shortly afterwards.'

'Do they still see each other?'

'We don't think so. De Vriess has had at least five lovers in the last three years, while Amanda's kept herself to herself and remained celibate.'

'Why do you think that is?'

Streeter's voice hardened. 'Probably for the same reason she's never sought a divorce. She wants to give the impression that James is alive somewhere.'

Deacon consulted some photocopies of the press releases. 'Okay, let's talk about James's alleged affair with – ' he isolated a paragraph – 'Marianne Filbert. If there's no proof of its existence why did the police accept Amanda's word on it? Who is Marianne Filbert? Where is she? What does she say about it?'

'I'll answer those questions in order. The police accepted Amanda's word because it suited them. They needed a computer expert in the frame, and Marianne fitted the bill. She was part of a research-and-development team working for Softworks Limited in the mid-eighties. Softworks was commissioned to prepare a report for Lowenstein's Bank in '86, although no one knows if Marianne Filbert was involved with that. She went to America in '89.' He paused briefly. 'She was employed for six months by a computer software company in Virginia before moving on to Australia.'

'And?' prompted Deacon, when he didn't continue.

'There's no trace of her after that. If she went to Australia, which now seems doubtful, she was using another name.'

'When did she leave the Virginian company?'

'April 1990,' said the other reluctantly.

Deacon felt sorry for him. John Streeter wasn't a fool, and blind faith clearly made him uncomfortable. 'So the police see a connection between your brother's disappearance and hers? He told her when to run, in other words.'

'Except they haven't established that James and Marianne even knew each other.' Streeter's furious indrawn breath was audible down the wire. 'We believe it was de Vriess and Amanda who gave her the green light to disappear.'

'A three-way conspiracy then?'

'Why not? It's just as plausible as the police theory. Look, it was Amanda who gave them Marianne Filbert's name and Amanda who told them she'd gone to America. Without that evidence, there'd have been no computer link and no way that James could have worked the fraud. The entire police case rests on James having access to expert knowledge, but Amanda's testimony about his alleged affair with Marianne has never been independently substantiated.'

'I find that hard to believe, Mr Streeter. According to the newspapers, Amanda spent two days answering police questions, which means she was high on their list of suspects. It also means she must have had something more convincing than just a name to give them. What was it?'

'It wasn't proof of anything,' said John Streeter stubbornly.

Deacon lit a cigarette while he waited.

'Are you still there?' demanded Streeter.

'Yes.'

'She couldn't prove a relationship between them. She couldn't even prove they knew each other.'

'I'm listening.'

'She gave the police a series of photographs, most of which were pictures of James's car parked outside the block of flats in Kensington where Marianne Filbert lived before she went to the States. There were three blurred shots of a couple kissing who, she claimed, were Marianne and James but frankly could have been anybody, and there was a back view of a man, wearing a coat

similar to James's, entering the front door of the building. As I say, it proves nothing.'

'Who took the photographs?'

'A private detective hired by Amanda.'

The same one she consulted about Billy Blake? 'Were
they dated?'

'Yes.'

'From when to when?'

'January to August '89.'

'You say most of the pictures were of James's car. Was
he in it when they were taken?'

'Someone was, but the quality of the photographs
isn't good enough to say whether or not it was James.'

'Perhaps it was Nigel de Vriess,' murmured Deacon
with an irony that was lost on the other man. He was
beginning to think that John Streeter's obsession to
prove his brother innocent was even greater than Amanda's to establish Billy Blake's true identity. Did the seeds
of paranoia find fertile ground in the aftermath of
betrayal?

'We certainly believe the man to have been de Vriess,'
said Streeter.

'So they were deliberately setting your brother up as a
fall-guy?'

'Yes.'

'That's one hell of a conspiracy theory, my friend.'
This time Deacon ladled the sarcasm into his voice.
'You're saying these people worked out a year in advance
of the event how they were going to murder a completely
innocent man, irrespective of anything that might happen

in the intervening period. And you feel happy with that scenario?' Ash dropped from the cigarette in his mouth, powdering the lapel of his jacket. 'Is your sister-in-law a monster, Mr Streeter? She would need to be, I think, to share a house indefinitely with a man whose murder she'd already planned. So? Who are we talking about here? Medusa?'

Silence.

'And what sort of idiot would rely on a status quo existing indefinitely? James was a free agent. He could have walked out on his wife or his job at any time, and where would the conspiracy have been then?' He paused, inviting the other to speak, but went on when he didn't: 'The obvious explanation is the one the police have accepted. James was having an affair with Marianne Filbert and Amanda put a stop to it by having him followed and photographs taken. She then brought pressure to bear which resulted in Marianne banishing herself, or being banished, to the States.'

'How could she tell the police where to find Marianne?'

'Because she's not stupid. Part of the deal for rescuing the marriage would be proof that Marianne was out of harm's way. And the only proof worth having would be something verifiable, like an address or a legal contract with a company's name on it.'

'Have you spoken to her?'

'Who?'

'Amanda.'

'No,' lied Deacon. 'You're my first contact on this,

Mr Streeter. I came across your press releases and they interested me enough to make this call. Tell me,' he went on with the easy fluency of practised deceit, 'what set you looking for a connection between Amanda and de Vriess in the first place?'

'She met James through de Vriess at some official function. De Vriess was married then, but it was an open secret that he was planning to leave his wife for Amanda. He used to parade her whenever his wife was away. It seemed logical, once we realized de Vriess was behind the fraud, that Amanda was involved too, so we set out to find evidence that the affair was an on-going one.'

'Except your evidence seems to be as flawed as your logic.' He pulled the relevant photocopies towards him. 'You have a hotel bill, signed by de Vriess and dated 1986, plus a description of a woman who *might* have been Amanda Streeter. Your 1989 witness account is even vaguer.' He moved the top copy aside and ran his pen down the one underneath. 'A waiter claims to have taken champagne to a couple in Room 306 who, he says, were the same two people, but there's no signed bill to back it up. You can't even prove the man was de Vriess, let alone that the woman was Amanda.'

'He paid cash the second time.'

'What name was on the bill?'

'Mr Smith.'

Deacon stubbed out his cigarette. 'And you're surprised that no one's prepared to publish? None of your allegations is sustainable.'

'We've limited funds and limited influence. We need

a reporter on a national newspaper to wield a bit of clout. We've been told there's more in the hotel files if we're prepared to pay for it.'

'It'll be an expensive ride with nothing at the end of it.'

'I'd back my brother's honesty any day against his wife's.'

'Then you're deluding yourself,' said Deacon bluntly. 'His *dis*honesty isn't in doubt. He was cheating on his wife and she was able to prove it, and you've allowed your anger over that to cloud your judgement. Your starting point should have been recognition that James played a part in his own destruction.'

'I knew this would be a waste of time,' said the other angrily.

'You keep firing at the wrong targets, Mr Streeter. That's where you've been wasting your time.'

The line went dead.

Deacon's enquiries of the Isle of Dogs police about Billy Blake had produced little of value, despite his suggestion that Billy might have been a murderer. This elicited the surprising response that the police had investigated just that possibility at the time of Billy's first arrest.

'I went through his file for the coroner,' said the uniformed constable who had overseen the removal of Billy's corpse. 'He was first arrested in 1991 for a series of food thefts from supermarkets. He was starving even then, and there was a bit of debate over whether to charge him or get him into supervised care. In the end a decision was made to have him remanded for psychiatric reports because he'd burnt off his fingerprints. Some bright spark decided he'd done it on purpose to beat a murder charge, and people started getting twitched about whether he constituted a danger to society.'

'And?'

The PC shrugged. 'He was interviewed in Brixton, and was given the all-clear. The psychiatrist's view was that he was more of a danger to himself than to anyone else.'

'What was his explanation for the burnt fingerprints?'

'As far as I remember, he called it a morbid interest in mortification. He described Billy as a penitent.'

'What does that mean?'

Another shrug. 'Maybe you should ask the psychiatrist.'

Deacon took out his notebook. 'Do you know his name?'

'I can find out.' He came back in ten minutes and handed Deacon a piece of paper with a name and address on it. 'Is there anything else?' he asked, keen to get on with something more pressing than a dead wino.

Reluctantly, Deacon stood up. 'The information I had was fairly specific.' He tucked the notebook back into his pocket. 'I was told that Billy Blake said he'd strangled someone.'

The PC showed mild interest until Deacon admitted that his informant had no details beyond what Billy had screamed one drunken night when the snakes of alcohol were writhing and squeezing in his brain. 'Would that someone be a man or a woman, sir?'

'I don't know.'

'Can you give me a name?'

'No.'

'Where did this murder happen?'

'I don't know.'

'When?'

'I don't know.'

'Then I'm sorry, sir, but I don't think we can be of any assistance.'

Deacon had visited Westminster Pier where the cruisers docked, but had looked in vain for someone to question about a pavement artist who had once earned charity there. He was impressed by how hostile the river seemed in winter, how stealthily its water lapped the hibernating pleasure cruisers, how black and secretive its depths. He remembered what Amanda Powell had said: '... *he preferred to doss down as near to the Thames as possible.*' But why? What was the bond that tied Billy to this great sinew at the heart of London? He leaned forward and stared into the water.

An elderly woman paused in her progress along the walkway. 'Premature death is never a solution, young man. It raises far more questions than it answers. Have you taken into account that there may be something waiting for you on the other side, and that you may not be prepared yet to face it?'

He turned, unsure whether to be offended or touched. 'It's all right, ma'am. I'm not planning to kill myself.'

'Not today perhaps,' she said, 'but you've thought about it.' She had a tiny white poodle on a lead which wagged its stumpy tail at Deacon. 'I can always tell the ones who've thought about it. They're looking for answers that don't exist because God has not chosen to reveal them yet.'

He squatted down to scratch the little creature's ears. 'I was thinking about a friend of mine who killed himself six months ago. I was wondering why he didn't drown himself in the river. It would have been a less painful way to die than the one he chose.'

'But would you be thinking about him if he hadn't died painfully?'

Deacon straightened. 'Probably not.'

'Then perhaps that's why he chose the method he did.'

He took out his wallet and removed the first photograph of Billy. 'You might have seen him. He was a pavement artist here in the summers. He used to draw pictures of the nativity with "Blessed are the poor" written underneath. Do you recognize him?'

She studied the thin face for several seconds. 'Yes, I think I do,' she said slowly. 'I certainly remember a pavement artist who drew pictures of the Holy Family, and I think this was the man.'

'Did you speak to him?'

'No.' She returned the photograph. 'There was nothing I could say to him.'

'You spoke to me,' Deacon reminded her.

'Because I thought you'd listen.'

97

'And you didn't think he would?'

'I *knew* he wouldn't. Your friend wanted to suffer.'

On the off-chance that Billy had been a teacher, and in the absence of a national register, which he had established did not exist, Deacon wined and dined a contact at NUT headquarters, told him what he knew and asked him to search the union backlist for any English teachers whose subscriptions had lapsed in the last ten years without good reason.

'You're pulling my leg, I hope,' said his acquaintance with some amusement. 'Have you any idea how many teachers there are in this country and what the turnover is? At the last count there were upwards of four hundred thousand full-time equivalents in the maintained sector alone, and that's excluding the universities.' He pushed his plate to one side. 'And what does "without good reason" mean anyway? Depression? That's very common. Physical disability inflicted by fifteen-year-old thugs? More common than anyone wants to admit. At the moment, I'd guess there are more inactive teachers than active ones. Who wants the hell of the classroom if there's something more civilized on offer? You're asking me to search for the needle in the proverbial haystack. You have also, and rather conveniently, forgotten the Data Protection Act, which means I couldn't give you the information even if I could find it.'

'The man's been dead six months,' said Deacon, 'so you won't be betraying any confidences, and his subscription was probably stopped at least four years before that.

You'll be looking at lapsed membership between say, 1984 and 1990.' He smiled suddenly. 'All right, it was a long shot, but it was worth a try.'

'I can give you several more apt descriptions than long shot. Try damp squib, non-starter or absolute no-no. You don't know his name, where he came from or even if he was a member of the NUT. He might have belonged to one of the other teachers' unions. Or to no union at all.'

'I realize that.'

'Matter of fact, you don't even know if he was a teacher. You're guessing he might have been because he could recite poems by William Blake.' The man smiled amiably. 'Do me a favour, Deacon, go boil your head in cooking oil. I'm an overworked, underpaid union official, not a ruddy clairvoyant.'

Deacon laughed. 'Okay. Point taken. It was a bad idea.'

'What's so important about him, anyway? You didn't really explain that.'

'Maybe nothing.'

'Then why the pressure to find out who he was?'

'I'm curious about what drives an educated man to self-destruct.'

'Oh, I see,' said the other sympathetically. 'It's a personal thing then.'

THE STREET, FLEET STREET, LONDON EC4

Dr Henry Irvine,
St Peter's Hospital,
London SW10

10th December 1995

Dear Dr Irvine,
Your name has been given to me in connection
with a prisoner you interviewed at Brixton Prison
in 1991. His name was Billy Blake and you may
have read about his death by starvation in a
garage in London's docklands in June of this year.
I have become interested in his story, which seems
a tragic one, and I wonder if you have any
information that might help me establish who he
was and where he came from.

I believe he chose the alias William Blake
because there were echoes of the poet's life in his
own. Like William, Billy was obsessed with God
(and/or gods), and while he preached their
importance to anyone who would listen, his
message was too arcane to be understood; both
men were artists and visionaries, and both died in
poverty and destitution. It might interest you to
know that I wrote my MA thesis on William Blake,
so I find these echoes particularly interesting.

From the little information I have been able to
gather so far, Billy was clearly a tortured

individual who may or may not have been schizophrenic. In addition one of my informants (not very reliable) says that Billy confessed to strangling a man or woman in the past. Is there anything you can tell me that would confirm or refute that statement?

Whilst I fully accept that your interview(s) with Billy were of a confidential nature, I do believe his death demands investigation, and anything you can tell me will be greatly appreciated. I have no desire to compromise your professional reputation and will only use what you send me to further my research into Billy's story.

You may already know my work but, in case you do not, I enclose some examples. I hope they will give you the confidence to trust me.

Yours sincerely,

Michael Deacon

Michael Deacon

Dr Henry Irvine MB, FRCP,
St Peter's Hospital,
London

17th December 1995

Dear Michael Deacon,

Thank you for your letter of 10th December. My report on Billy Blake has been in the public domain since 1991 so I cannot see that it's a breach of confidence to give you the information you want. Also, I agree that his death demands investigation. I was upset when my access to him was denied after I advised that Billy's self-mutilation was more likely the result of private trauma than criminal offence, because I firmly believe that further sessions would have allowed me to help him. While I offered him free treatment when he left prison, I could not force him to accept it and, inevitably, I lost touch with him. Your letter is the only follow-up on his case that I have ever had.

To put my role into perspective, the police were not satisfied that Billy Blake's first crime was the theft of bread and ham from a supermarket. They recognized that he was using an alias, and they were suspicious of his mutilated hands which defied fingerprint analysis. However, despite lengthy questioning, they failed to 'break' him and fell back on the charge of shoplifting to which he had already admitted. I was asked to write a psychological report prior to sentencing because of the bizarre nature of the man. In simple terms my brief was to discover if Billy was a danger to the community, the argument being that he would not have scarred his fingers so badly unless he was afraid of a previous, violent crime being brought home to him.

Despite having only three meetings with him, Billy made an extraordinary impact on me. He was desperately thin with a shock of white hair and, though clearly suffering acute alcohol-withdrawal symptoms, he was always in command of himself. He had a powerful presence and considerable charm, and the best description I can give of him is 'fanatic' or 'saint'. These may seem strange epithets in the London of the nineties, but his commitment to the salvation of others while suffering torment himself makes any other description invalid once the more obvious mental disorders were ruled out. He was rather a fine man.

I enclose the concluding paragraphs of the psychiatric report and a transcript of part of a conversation I had with him, which may interest you. I confess to having missed the William Blake association, but Billy's conversation was certainly of a visionary nature. If I can be of any further assistance please don't hesitate to contact me.

With best wishes,

Henry Irvine

Henry Irvine

P.S. Re: the transcript – it was, of course, the answers Billy declined to give that tell us most about him.

Psychiatric Report
Subject: Billy Blake * */5387
Interviewer: Dr Henry Irvine

- page 3 -

In conclusion:
Billy has a fully developed understanding of moral and
ethical codes, but refers to them as 'ritual devices for
the subjugation of individual to tribal will', from which I
infer that his own morality is in conflict with social and
legal definitions of right and wrong. He exhibits
extraordinary self-control and gives no insight into his
background or history. Billy Blake is almost certainly
an alias, although questions about specific crimes
elicit no reaction from him. He has a high IQ and it is
difficult to assess his reasons for refusing to talk about
his past. He has a morbid interest in hell and
mortification, but poses more of a threat to himself
than to the community. I can find no evidence of a
dangerous mental disorder. He seems to have a clear
rationale for his choice of lifestyle – I would describe it
as a penitent's life – and I consider it far more likely
that some private trauma, unrelated to any crime,
motivates him.

He presents himself as a passive individual
although I have noticed signs of agitation whenever
he is pressed about where he was and what he was
doing before he first came to police attention. I agree

that there may be a crime in his past – he is quite single-minded enough to mutilate himself to achieve a purpose – but I think it unlikely. He quickly developed a strong resistance to my questions on the matter, and it is doubtful that further sessions will persuade him to be more forthcoming. It is my considered opinion, however, that he would benefit from therapy as I believe his 'exile' from society, involving as it does an almost fanatical desire to suffer through starvation and deprivation, will result in his unnecessary and premature death.

Henry Irvine

Henry Irvine

Transcript of taped interview with Billy Blake –
12.7.91 (part only)

IRVINE: Are you saying that your personal code of
ethics is of a higher order than the religious
codes?

BLAKE: I'm saying it's different.

IRVINE: In what way?

BLAKE: Absolute values have no place in my
morality.

IRVINE: Can you explain that?

BLAKE: Different circumstances demand different
codes of ethics. For example, it isn't always sinful
to steal. Were I a mother with hungry children, I
would think it a greater sin to let them starve.

IRVINE: That's too easy an example, Billy. Most
people would agree with you. What about
murder?

BLAKE: The same. I believe there are times and
occasions when murder, premeditated or not, is
appropriate. (Pause) But I don't think it's possible
to live with the consequences of such a crime.
The taboo against killing a member of our own
species is very strong, and taboos are difficult to
rationalize.

IRVINE: Are you speaking from personal
experience?

BLAKE: (Gave no answer)

IRVINE: You seem to have inflicted severe
punishment on yourself, particularly by burning
your hands. As I'm sure you already know, the

police suspect a deliberate attempt to obscure
your fingerprints.

BLAKE: Only because they can conceive of no
other reason why a man should want to express
himself upon the only thing that truly belongs to
him – namely his body.

IRVINE: Self-mutilation is normally an indication
of a disordered mind.

BLAKE: Would you say the same if I had disfigured
myself with tattoos? The skin is a canvas for
individual creativity. I see the same beauty in my
hands as a woman sees when she paints her face
in a mirror. (Pause) We assume we control our
minds when we don't. They're so easily
manipulated. Make a man destitute and you make
him envious. Make him wealthy and you make
him proud. Saints and sinners are the only free-
thinkers in a governed society.

IRVINE: Which are you?

BLAKE: Neither. I'm incapable of free thought. My
mind is bound.

IRVINE: By what?

BLAKE: By the same thing as yours, doctor. By
intellect. You're too sensible to act against your
own interests, therefore your life lacks
spontaneity. You will die in the chains you've
made for yourself.

IRVINE: You were arrested for stealing. Wasn't
that acting against your own interests?

BLAKE: I was hungry.

IRVINE: You think it's sensible to be in prison?

BLAKE: It's cold outside.

IRVINE: Tell me about these chains I've made for myself.

BLAKE: They're in your mind. You conform to the patterns of behaviour that others have prescribed for you. You will never do what you want because the tribe's will is stronger than yours.

IRVINE: Yet you said your mind is as constrained as mine, and you're no conformist, Billy. If you were, you wouldn't be in prison.

BLAKE: Prisoners are the most diligent of conformists, otherwise places like this would be in perpetual riot and rebellion.

IRVINE: That's not what I meant. You appear to be an educated man, yet you live as a derelict. Is the loneliness of the streets preferable to the more conventional existence of home and family?

BLAKE: (Long pause) I need to understand the concept before I can answer the question. How do you define home and family, doctor?

IRVINE: Home is the bricks and mortar that keeps your family – wife and children – safe. It's a place most of us love because it contains the people we love.

BLAKE: Then I left no such place when I took to the streets.

IRVINE: What *did* you leave?

BLAKE: Nothing. I carry everything with me.

IRVINE: Meaning memories?

BLAKE: I'm only interested in the present. It's how

we live our present that predicts our past and our future.

IRVINE: In other words, joy in the present gives rise to joyful memories and an optimistic view of the future?

BLAKE: Yes. If that is what you want.

IRVINE: Isn't it what *you* want?

BLAKE: Joy is another concept that is incomprehensible to me. A destitute man takes pleasure in a butt-end in the gutter, while a wealthy man is disgusted by the self-same object. I am content to be at peace.

IRVINE: Does drinking help you achieve peace?

BLAKE: It's a quick road to oblivion, and I would describe oblivion as being at peace.

IRVINE: Don't you like your memories?

BLAKE: (Gave no answer)

IRVINE: Can you recall a bad memory for me?

BLAKE: I've found men dead of cold in the gutter, and I've watched men die violently because anger drives others to the point of insanity. The human mind is so fragile that any powerful emotion can overturn its precepts.

IRVINE: I'm more interested in memories from before you took to the streets.

BLAKE: (Gave no answer)

IRVINE: Do you think it's possible to recover from the kind of insanity you've just described?

BLAKE: Are you talking about rehabilitation or salvation?

IRVINE: Either. Do you believe in salvation?

BLAKE: I believe in hell. Not the burning hell and torment of the Inquisition but the frozen hell of eternal despair where love is absent. It's difficult to conceive how salvation can enter such a place unless God exists. Only divine intervention can save a soul condemned for ever to exist in the loneliness of the bottomless pit.

IRVINE: Do you believe in God?

BLAKE: I believe that each of us has the potential for divinity. If salvation is possible, then it can only happen in the here and now. You and I will be judged by the efforts we make to keep another's soul from eternal despair.

IRVINE: Is saving that other soul a passport to heaven?

BLAKE: (Gave no answer)

IRVINE: Can we earn salvation for ourselves?

BLAKE: Not if we fail others.

IRVINE: Who will judge us?

BLAKE: We judge ourselves. Our future, be it now or in the hereafter, is defined by our present.

IRVINE: Have you failed someone, Billy?

BLAKE: (Gave no answer)

IRVINE: I may be wrong but you seem to have judged and condemned yourself already. Why is that, when you believe in salvation for others?

BLAKE: I'm still searching for truth.

IRVINE: It's a very bleak philosophy, Billy. Is there no room for happiness in your life?

BLAKE: I get drunk whenever I can.

IRVINE: Does that make you happy?

BLAKE: Of course, but then I define happiness as intellectual absence. Your definition is probably different.

IRVINE: Do you want to talk about what you did that makes stupefied oblivion your only way of coping with your memories?

BLAKE: I suffer in the present, doctor, not the past.

IRVINE: Do you enjoy suffering?

BLAKE: Yes, if it inspires compassion. There's no way out of hell except through God's mercy.

IRVINE: Why enter hell at all? Can you not redeem yourself now?

BLAKE: My own redemption doesn't interest me. (Billy refused to say anything further on the subject and we talked for several minutes on general subjects until the session ended.)

Chapter Six

THERE WERE two Christmas cards on Deacon's desk one morning. The first was from his sister, Emma. *Hugh keeps seeing your byline in the* Street *so we're assuming this will find you*, she had written. *We are none of us getting any younger, so isn't it time we called a truce? At least ring me if you won't ring Ma. Surely it's not that difficult to say sorry and start again.* The other was from his first wife, Julia. *I bumped into Emma the other day and she said you're working for the* Street. *Apparently your mother's been very ill this last year but Emma has promised she won't tell you because Penelope doesn't want you coming back out of guilt or pity. As I've made no such promise, I thought you should know. However, unless you've changed radically in the last five years, you'll probably tear this up and do nothing about it. You were always more stubborn than Penelope.*

As Julia had predicted he tore up her card, but stood Emma's on his desk.

Despite spending long hours on Paul Garrety's computer in an attempt to make a match between Billy Blake's image and James Streeter's, Deacon got nowhere. Paul pointed out that it would always be a waste of time unless he could find a better picture of James. 'You're not comparing like with like,' he explained. 'Billy's shots are full-face and the one of James is three-quarters. You need to go back to his wife and see what she's got in the way of old snapshots.'

'It's a waste of time, full stop,' said Deacon in disgust, tilting back his chair and staring at the faces. 'They're two different men.'

'Which is what I've been telling you for the last three days. Why can't you accept it?'

'Because I don't believe in coincidences. It makes sense if Billy was James and none at all if he wasn't.' He ticked the points off on his fingers. 'James had a reason to seek out his wife – a stranger didn't. Amanda paid for his funeral out of guilt, but her guilt is only logical if she was burying her husband – illogical if she was burying a stranger. She's obsessed with finding out who Billy was, but why, if he was completely unknown to her?' He rapped out a tattoo on his desk. 'I think she's telling the truth when she says she didn't know he was there. I also think she's telling the truth when she says she didn't recognize him. But I'm convinced she rapidly came to the conclusion *afterwards* that the man who died in her garage was James.'

Paul was doubtful. 'Why didn't she tell the police?'

'Out of fear that they'd think she locked him in the garage on purpose.'

'Then why get you interested? Why not let the story die?

Deacon shrugged. 'I can think of two reasons. The first, simple curiosity. She wants to know what happened to James after he walked out of her life. The second, freedom. Until he's declared officially dead, she'll always be tied to him.'

'She could divorce him tomorrow on the grounds of desertion.'

'But as far as everyone else was concerned he'd still be alive, which means people like me would always be turning up on her doorstep asking questions.'

Paul shook his head. 'That's a crap argument, Mike. Now if you'd said she wanted him declared dead for mercenary reasons, I'd probably go along with you. Let's say he spoke to her before he died and told her how to lay her hands on his fortune. As his widow she'd inherit the lot. Think on that, my friend.'

'My theory only works if she *didn't* speak to him,' declared Deacon mildly. 'We're into a whole new ball game if she *did*. In any case, it looks to me as if she got her hands on the fortune a long time ago.'

'You've never been in the ball game, chum. That guy – ' he tapped the photograph of Billy Blake – 'is not James Streeter.'

'Then who was he and what the hell was he doing in her garage?'

'Get Barry on to it. He's your best bet.'

'I've tried already. He doesn't know. Whoever Billy was he's not in Barry's files.'

Paul Garrety looked surprised. 'Did he tell you that?' Deacon nodded. 'Then how come he strings me along for weeks before he'll admit defeat?'

'Perhaps you've upset him,' said Deacon with unconscious irony.

With time on his hands the weekend before Christmas, Deacon telephoned Kenneth Streeter, mentioned his conversation with John and asked if he could drive out to Bromley and have a chat with James's parents. Kenneth was friendlier and more amenable than his younger son, and made an appointment for the Sunday afternoon.

They lived in a tired-looking terraced house in an unfashionable road, and Deacon was struck by the contrast between this and Amanda's house. *Where had her money come from?* He rang the doorbell and smiled pleasantly at the elderly man who opened the door. 'Michael Deacon,' he said, offering his hand.

Kenneth ignored the hand but gestured him inside. 'You'd better come in,' he said ungraciously, 'but only because I don't want our neighbours listening to what I have to say.' He closed the door but kept Deacon pinned behind it in the dark hallway. 'I don't take kindly to being tricked, Mr Deacon. You gave me to understand that John would approve of my talking to you, but I spoke to him this morning and discovered that the opposite is true. I will not allow the press to drive a wedge between me and my remaining son, so I'm afraid this has been a wasted trip for you.' He reached for the door handle again. 'Good day to you.'

'Your son misunderstood me, Mr Streeter. He assumed that because I said James played a part in his own destruction I was referring to the theft of the £10 million when in fact I was referring to his wife's rejection of him.' He moved forward as the door met his back. 'In simple terms, if you want your wife to stand by you when the chips are down, you don't lose her trust by having affairs.'

'She's the one who was having the affair. She never gave de Vriess up,' said the other bitterly.

'Are you sure about that? The evidence is very flimsy.' He hurried on when the pressure on his back relaxed slightly. 'I suggested to John that he's been firing at the wrong targets, which is not the same as saying that James was guilty of theft. Let's say he was murdered, as you and John believe, how will you get at the truth if you keep denying that James had an affair with Marianne Filbert? If the evidence was strong enough to convince the police, then it ought to be strong enough to convince you.'

A tear glittered in the other man's eye. 'If we give in on that point, we have nothing left except our knowledge of James. And what use is a father's word about his son's honesty? Who would believe me?'

'No one that matters,' said Deacon brutally. 'You'll have to prove it.'

'In this country it's guilt that must be proved, not innocence,' said the old man obstinately. 'I fought for that right fifty years ago and it's outrageous that James has been condemned without any proper hearing of the evidence.'

'I agree with you, Mr Streeter, but to date his defence has been poorly focused. You can't fight a campaign based on a lie. If nothing else, you've alienated the one person who's best placed to help you.'

'Meaning Amanda?'

Deacon nodded.

'We believe she was party to his murder.'

'But you've no proof that he was murdered.'

'He never contacted us. That's proof enough.'

Deacon took the mugshot of Billy Blake from his breast pocket. 'Does this man remind you of James at all?'

Bewilderment furrowed Kenneth's brow. 'How could he? He's too old.'

'He was in his mid-forties when this photograph was taken six months ago.'

Streeter pulled the door wide to examine the picture in daylight. 'This isn't my son,' he said. 'What on earth made you think it was?'

'He was a down-and-out, using an alias, and he died in your daughter-in-law's garage. He didn't speak to her or reveal that he was there, but she paid for his funeral and she's been trying to find out who he was ever since. The only obvious explanation for her interest is that she's afraid he may have been James.'

There was a long silence while Streeter stared at Billy Blake's face. 'It can't be,' he said at last, but there was less certainty in his tone. 'How could he have aged so much in five years? And why would he live as a down-and-out when he was always welcome here?'

'He would have been arrested if he came here. You couldn't have kept him hidden from your neighbours.'

'Are you trying to tell me that this *is* James?'

'Not necessarily,' said Deacon. 'I'm saying that for your daughter-in-law to think it might have been, she had to believe he was still alive when this man turned up dead in her garage in June. And that means she can't have been a party to James's alleged murder five years ago.'

'Then what happened to him?' asked the older man in despair. 'He wasn't a thief, Mr Deacon. He was brought up to earn money honestly, and it simply wouldn't have occurred to him to take short cuts. You see, he wanted the status that wealth brings, just as much as he wanted wealth itself, so theft and the danger of imprisonment would never have attracted him.' He gave another bewildered frown. 'At the time he disappeared, he and Amanda had just sunk all their capital into an old school on the Thames at Teddington, which they were planning to develop into luxury flats, and James was as excited about it as she was. They stood to make a handsome profit if the project went through. But why would he be excited by half a million if he was already sitting on ten?'

Because it represented a legitimate way to start laundering the rest, thought Deacon cynically. 'What happened to the project?'

'It was completed in '92 by a construction firm called Lowndes, but we can't find out if Amanda saw it through herself or whether Lowndes bought the property from her. We've written several letters of enquiry, but we've never had an answer. Either way, we'd like to know how she put together enough money to buy her present house in '91. If she sold the school first, she couldn't have raised more than the four hundred thousand she and James put towards the purchase of it. But it was probably a great deal less after nine months' interest on bank loans, and certainly not enough to buy into an expensive estate on the Thames. If she didn't sell the school but saw the project through, then she'd have had no capital at all in '91.' He smiled unhappily. 'You see now why we're so suspicious of her.'

'Perhaps she and James had other investments which they never told you about.'

But Kenneth wouldn't accept that. Four hundred thousand was already more spare capital than most young couples could lay their hands on, he pointed out, and it was honestly earned. James had cashed in his stocks and shares to support the project. Deacon acknowledged the point with a smile while his mind pursued its own line of thought. That would explain why Amanda hadn't wanted a divorce. If the investments were jointly owned, she had access to everything as long as she didn't dissolve the partnership before he could be legally presumed dead seven years after his disappearance. And if there were other investments in James's name – *dishonestly earned?* – then she still had another two years to wait before she could inherit as his widow.

How much simpler if he'd died in her garage six months ago . . .

'Do you have a photograph of James that you could lend me, Mr Streeter? Preferably a full-face one. I can let you have it back by Tuesday.'

. . . and how frustrating if she couldn't prove it . . .

'The police must have searched James's bank accounts

at the time he disappeared,' he said, taking the snapshot Kenneth Streeter produced for him. 'Did they find anything that shouldn't have been there?'

'Of course not. There was nothing to find.'

'Have you told them your suspicions about Amanda's new-found wealth?'

A look of weariness crossed the older man's face. 'So regularly that I've had an official caution for wasting police time. It's harder than you think to prove a man's innocence, Mr Deacon.'

He phoned an old colleague, now retired, who had spent most of his working life on the financial desks of different newspapers, and arranged to meet him that evening in a pub in Camden Town. 'I'm supposed to be off the bloody booze,' Alan Parker had growled down the wire, 'so I can't invite you here. There's not a drop worth drinking in the house.'

'Coffee won't kill me,' said Deacon.

'It's killing *me*. I'll see you in the Three Pigeons at eight o'clock. Make mine a double Bell's if you get there first.'

Deacon hadn't seen Alan for a couple of years and he was shocked by the sight of his old friend. He was desperately thin and his skin had the yellow tinge of jaundice. 'Should I be doing this?' Deacon asked him as he paid for their whiskies.

'You'd better not tell me I look like death, Mike.'

He did, but Deacon just smiled and pushed the Bell's

towards him. 'How's Maggie?' he asked, referring to Alan's wife.

'She'd have my guts for garters if she knew where I was and what I was doing.' He raised the glass and sampled a mouthful. 'I can't get it through to the silly old woman that I'm a far better judge of what's good for me than the blasted quacks.'

'So what's the problem? Why have they ordered you off the booze?'

Alan chuckled. 'It's the newest form of tyranny, Mike. No one's allowed to die any more, so you're expected to live out your last months in misery. I mustn't smoke, drink or eat anything remotely tasty in case it kills me. Apparently, dying of boredom is politically correct while succumbing to anything that gives you pleasure isn't.'

'Well, don't peg out here, for God's sake, or Maggie will have *my* guts for garters. Where does she think you are, as a matter of interest? Church?'

'She knows exactly where I am, but she's a tyrant with a soft centre. I'll be hauled over the coals for this when I get back, but in her heart of hearts she'll be glad I was happy for half an hour. So? What did you want to talk to me about?'

'A man called Nigel de Vriess. The only information I have on him is that he lives in a mansion in Hampshire which he bought in '91, and was on the board of Lowenstein's Merchant Bank, which he's since left. Do you know him? I'm interested in where he got the money to buy the mansion.'

'That's easy enough. He didn't buy it because he already owned it. If I remember right, his wife took the marital home in Hampstead and he took Halcombe House, although I can't recall now if it was his first divorce or his second. Probably the second because it was a clean-break settlement. It was the first marriage that produced the kids.'

'I was told he bought it.'

'He did, when he made his first million. But that was twenty-odd years ago. He came something of a cropper in the eighties when he invested in a transatlantic airline that went bust during the cartel war, but he managed to hang on to the properties. The only reason he joined Lowenstein's was to buy a period of stability while the market recovered. In return for a damn good salary, he expanded their operations in the Far East and gave them footholds round the Pacific rim. He did well for them, too. They owe their place on the map to de Vriess.'

'What about this guy James Streeter, who ripped them off for ten million?'

'What about him? Ten million's chicken feed these days. It took eight *hundred* million to bring down Baring's Bank.' Alan swallowed another mouthful of whisky. 'The mistake Lowenstein's made was to force the guy to run and bring the whole thing into the open. They recouped their ten million within forty-eight hours' trading on the foreign-exchange markets but the bad publicity set them back six months in terms of credibility.'

Deacon took out his cigarette packet and proffered it to Alan with a lift of his eyebrows. 'I won't tell Maggie if you don't.'

'You're a good lad, Mike.' He placed a cigarette reverently between his lips. 'The only reason I stopped was because the silly old cow kept crying. Would you believe that? I'm dying in misery so she won't be miserable watching me die. And she always said I was the most selfish man alive.'

Deacon found a laugh from somewhere – though God only knew where. 'She's right,' he said. 'I'll never forget that time you invited me out to dinner, then made me pay because you claimed you'd left your wallet at home.'

'I had.'

'Bullshit. I could see the bulge it was making in your jacket.'

'You were very young and green in those days, Mike.'

'Yes, and you took advantage of it, you old sod.'

'You've been a good friend.'

'What do you mean, *been* a good friend? I still am. Who bought the whisky?' He saw a cloud pass over Alan's face and changed the subject abruptly. 'What's de Vriess doing now?'

'He bought a computer software company called Softworks, renamed it de Vriess Softworks or DVS, sacked half the staff and turned the damn thing round in two years by producing a cheaper version of Windows for the home computer market. He's an arrogant SOB, but he has a knack for making money. He started with a paper round at thirteen and he's never looked back.'

'You said he came a cropper in the eighties,' Deacon reminded him.

'A temporary blip, Mike, hence the job with Lowenstein's. Now he's back to where he was before the crash.

Shares have recovered, and he's found a nice little earner in DVS.'

'There was a woman who used to work for Softworks called Marianne Filbert. Does that name mean anything to you?'

Alan shook his head. 'What's the connection with de Vriess?'

Briefly, Deacon explained John Streeter's theory about the conspiracy against James. 'I suspect his whole argument is based on wishful thinking, but it's interesting that de Vriess bought the company where James Streeter found his computer expert.'

'It's highly predictable if you know de Vriess. I imagine Softworks was put under a microscope to see if the bank's money had found its way into their books, and in the process de Vriess spotted an opportunity. He's as sharp as a bloody ferret.'

'You sound as if you admire him.'

'I do. The guy has balls. Mind, I don't like him much – few people do – but he doesn't lose sleep over trifles like that. Women love him, which is all he cares about. He's a randy little toad.' He gave another chuckle. 'Rich men often are. Unlike the rest of us, they can afford to pay for their mistakes.'

'You always were a cynical bastard,' said Deacon affectionately.

'I'm dying of liver cancer, Mike, but at least my cynicism remains healthy.'

'How long have you got?'

'Six months.'

'Are you worried about it?'

124

'Terrified, old son, but I cling to Heinrich Heine's dying words: "God will forgive me. It's his job."'

Barry Grover held the snapshot of James Streeter under the lamplight and examined it carefully. 'It's a better angle,' he said grudgingly. 'You'll have more chance of making comparisons with this than with the other one.'

Deacon perched casually on the edge of the desk, looming over Barry in a way the little man hated, and planted a cigarette in the corner of his mouth. 'You're the expert,' he said. 'Is that Billy or not?'

'I'd rather you didn't smoke in here,' muttered Barry, poking fussily at his *In the interests of my health please don't smoke* notice. 'I have asthma and it's not good for me.'

'Why didn't you say so before?'

'I assumed you could read.' He shoved a folder against Deacon's hip in an attempt to dislodge him from the desk, but Deacon just grinned at him.

'The smell of cigarette smoke is preferable any day to the smell of your feet. When did you last buy yourself a new pair of shoes?'

'It's none of your business.'

'The only colour you ever wear is black and, believe me, if I've noticed that, then the whole damn building's noticed it. I'm beginning to think you only have one pair, which probably explains your asthma.'

'You're a very rude man.'

Deacon's grin broadened. 'I suppose you were out on the razzle last night? Hence the lousy mood.'

'Yes,' lied the little man bitterly. 'I went for a drink with some friends.'

'Well, if it's a hangover, I've got some codeine in my office, and if it's not, then buck up, for Christ's sake, and give me an opinion on this picture. Does it look like Billy to you?'

'No.'

'They're pretty alike.'

'The mouths are different.'

'Ten million buys a lot of plastic surgery.'

Barry took off his glasses and rubbed his eyes. 'If you want to identify someone, you don't just compare a couple of photographs and dismiss anything that doesn't fit as plastic surgery. It really is a little more scientific than that, Mike.'

'I'm listening.'

'Lots of people look like each other, particularly in photographs, so you have to examine what you know about them as well. It's quite pointless finding similarities in faces if one belongs to a man in America and the other to a man in France.'

'But that's the whole point. James went missing in 1990 and Billy didn't surface at a police station until '91 with his fingers like claws because he'd been burning off his prints. It's certainly possible that they're one and the same.'

'But highly improbable.' Barry looked at the photograph again. 'What happened to the rest of the money?'

'I don't follow.'

'How could he become a penniless derelict within

months of having his face altered by plastic surgery? What happened to the rest of the money?'

'I'm still working on that.' Deacon interpreted Barry's expression correctly as one of scathing disbelief, although as usual it looked rather silly on the owlish face. 'Okay, okay. I agree it's improbable.' He stood up. 'I promised to send that snapshot back today. Do you have time to make a negative for me?'

'I'm busy at the moment.' Barry shuffled pieces of paper around his desk as if to prove the point.

Deacon nodded. 'No problem. I'll find out how Lisa's placed. She can probably do it for me.'

After he'd gone, Barry drew his own full-face photograph of James Streeter from his top drawer. If Deacon had seen this version, he thought, there'd have been no stopping him. The likeness to Billy Blake was extraordinary.

Purely out of curiosity, Deacon phoned Lowndes Building and Development Corporation and asked to speak to someone about a block of flats they had converted on the Thames at Teddington in 1992. He was given the address of the flats, but was told there was no one available to discuss the mechanics of the conversion. 'To be honest,' said a flustered secretary, 'I think it may have been Mr Merton who saw it through, but he was sacked two years ago.'

'Why?'

'I'm not sure. Someone said he was on cocaine.'

'Any idea how I can contact him?'

'He emigrated somewhere, but I don't think we have his address.'

Deacon pencilled Mr Merton in as someone to follow up after Christmas, alongside Nigel de Vriess.

It was the twenty-first of December. Deacon was crawling in a slow-moving traffic jam and his mood grew blacker as the compulsory office party drew nearer. God, how he loathed Christmas! It was the ultimate proof that his life was empty.

He had spent the afternoon interviewing a prostitute who, under the guise of 'researcher', claimed to have had regular access to the Houses of Parliament for paid sex romps with MPs. *Good God almighty! And this was news?* He despised the British thirst for sleaze, which said more about the repressed sexuality of the average Briton than it ever did about the men and women whose peccadilloes were splashed across the newspapers. In any case, he was sure the woman was lying (if not about the paid sex sessions, then certainly about the regular access) because she hadn't known enough about the internal layout of the buildings. He was equally sure that JP, who was of the 'never let the facts get in the way of a good story' school of journalism, would have him chasing the sordid little allegations for weeks in the hopes there was some truth in them. Ah, Jesus! Was this all there was?

He put his depression down to Seasonal Adjusted Disorder – SADness – because he couldn't face the alternative of inherited insanity. Every damn thing that had ever gone wrong in his life had happened in bloody

December. It couldn't be coincidence. His father had died in December, both his wives had abandoned him in December, he'd been sacked from the *Independent* in December. And why? Because he couldn't steer clear of the booze at Christmas and had punched his editor during a disagreement over copy. (If he wasn't careful, he was going to punch JP over the very same issue.) In the summer he was objective enough to recognize that he was caught in a vicious circle – things went wrong at Christmas because he was drunk, and he got drunk because things went wrong – but objectivity was always in rare supply when he most needed it.

He abandoned a congested Whitehall to drive up past the Palace. The bitter east wind of the past few days had turned to sleet, but beyond the metronome clicking of his windscreen wipers was a London geared for festivity. Signs of it were everywhere, in the brilliantly lit Norwegian spruce that annually supplanted Nelson's domination of Trafalgar Square, in the coloured lights that decorated shops and offices, in the crowds that thronged the pavements. He viewed them all with a baleful eye and thought about what lay ahead of him when the office shut for Christmas.

Days of waiting for the bloody place to reopen.

An empty flat.

A desert.

JP decided the prostitute's story had 'legs' and told him to rake as much muck as he could.

*

129

If there was any gaiety about the office party, then it was
happening in another room. Feeling like a trespasser at
some interminable wake, Deacon made a half-hearted
pass at Lisa and was slapped down for his pains.

'Act your age,' she said crossly. 'You're old enough to
be my father.'

With a certain grim satisfaction, he set out to get very
drunk indeed.

Chapter Seven

IT WAS NEARLY midnight. Amanda Powell would have ignored the ringing of her doorbell if whoever was doing it had had the courtesy to remove his finger from the buzzer, but after thirty seconds she went into the hall and peered through the spyhole. When she saw who it was, she glanced thoughtfully towards her stairs as if weighing the pros and cons of retreating up them, then opened the door twelve inches. 'What do you want, Mr Deacon?'

He shifted his hand from the bell to the door and leaned on it, pushing it wide, before lurching past her to collapse on a delicate wicker chair in the hall. He waved an arm towards the street. 'I was passing.' He made an effort to sound sober. 'Seemed polite to say hello. It occurred to me you might be lonely, what with Mr Streeter being away.'

She looked at him for a moment, then closed the door. 'That's an extremely valuable antique you're sitting on,' she said evenly. 'I think it would be better if you came into the drawing-room. The chairs in there aren't quite so fragile. I'll call for a taxi.'

He rolled his eyes at her, making himself ridiculous.

'You're a beautiful woman, Mrs Streeter. Did James ever tell you that?'

'Over and over again. It saved him having to think of anything more original to say.' She put a hand under his elbow and tried to lift him.

'It's really bad, what he did,' said Deacon, oblivious to the sarcasm. 'You probably wonder what you did to deserve him.' Whisky gusted on his breath.

'Yes,' she said, drawing her head away, 'I do.'

Tears bloomed in his eyes. 'He didn't love you very much, did he?' He put his hand over hers where it lay on his arm and stroked it clumsily. 'Poor Amanda. I know what it's like, you see. It's very lonely when no one loves you.'

With an abrupt movement, she curled the fingers of her other hand and dug her sharp nails in under his chin. 'Are you going to get up before you break my chair, Mr Deacon, or am I going to draw blood?'

'It's only money.'

'Hard-earned money.'

'That's not what John and Kenneth say.' He leered at her. 'They say it's stolen money and that you and Nigel murdered poor old James to get it.'

She kept up the pressure under his chin, forcing him to look at her. 'And what do you say, Mr Deacon?'

'*I* say you'd never have thought Billy was James if James was already dead.'

Her face became suddenly impassive. 'You're a clever man.'

'I worked it out. There are five million women in London, but Billy chose you.' He wagged a finger at her.

'Now why did he do that, Amanda, if he didn't know you? That's what I'd like to know.'

Without warning, she got going with her nails again, and he focused rather unsuccessfully on the frosty blue eyes.

'You're so like my mother. She's beautiful too.' He struggled upright under the painful prodding of her fingers. 'Not when she's angry, though. She's horrible when she's angry.'

'So am I.' Amanda drew him through the sitting-room door, then pushed him unceremoniously on to the sofa. 'How did you get here?'

'I walked.' He curled up on the sofa and laid his head on the arm.

'Why didn't you go home?'

'I wanted to come here.'

'Well, you can't stay. I'll call a cab.' She reached for the telephone. 'Where do you live?'

'I don't live anywhere,' he said into the cream leather. 'I exist.'

'You can't exist in my house.'

But he could and he did because he was already unconscious, and nothing on earth was going to wake him.

He opened his eyes on grey morning light and stared about him. He was so cold that he thought he was dying, but lethargy meant he did nothing about it. There was pleasure in passivity, none at all in action. A clock on a glass shelf gave the time as seven thirty. He recognized

133

the room as somewhere he knew but couldn't remember whose it was or why he was there. He thought he could hear voices – *in his head?* – but the cold numbed his curiosity, and he slept again.

He dreamt he was drowning in a ferocious sea.

'Wake up! WAKE UP, YOU BASTARD!'

A hand slapped his cheek and he opened his eyes. He was lying on the floor, curled like a foetus, and his nose was filled with the putrid smell of decay. Bile rose in his throat. 'Devourer of thy parent,' he muttered. 'Now thy unutterable torment renews.'

'I thought you were dead,' said Amanda.

For a moment, before memory returned, Deacon wondered who she was. 'I'm wet,' he said, touching the saturated neck of his shirt.

'I threw water over you.' He saw the empty jug in her hand. 'I've been rocking you and pushing you for ten minutes and you didn't stir.' She looked very pale. 'I thought you were dead,' she said again.

'Dead men aren't frightening,' he said in an odd tone of voice, 'they're just messy.' He struggled into a sitting position and buried his face in his hands. 'What time is it?'

'Nine o'clock.'

His stomach heaved. 'I need a lavatory.'

'Turn right and it's at the end of the hall.' She stood aside to let him pass. 'If you're going to be sick, could you make sure you wipe the bowl round afterwards with the brush? I tend to draw the line at cleaning up after uninvited guests.'

As Deacon weaved along the corridor, he sought for explanations. *Dear God, what the hell was he doing here?*

She had opened the windows and sprayed the room with air freshener by the time he returned. He looked slightly more presentable, having dried his face and straightened his clothes, but he had the shakes and his skin was the queasy grey of nausea. 'There's nothing I can say to you,' he managed from the doorway, 'except sorry.'

'What for?' She was sitting in the chair she'd sat in before and Deacon was dazzled by how vibrant and colourful she was. Her hair and skin seemed to glow, and her dress fell in bright yellow folds about her calves, tumbling like a lemon pool on to the autumn leaves of the russet carpet.

Too much colour. It hurt his eyes, and he pressed on his lids with his fingertips. 'I've embarrassed you.'

'You may have embarrassed yourself but you certainly haven't embarrassed me.'

So cool, he thought. *Or so cruel?* He longed for kindness. 'That's all right then,' he said weakly. 'I'll say goodbye.'

'You might as well drink your coffee before you go.'

He longed for escape as well. The room smelled of roses again and he couldn't bring himself to intrude his rancid breath and rancid sweat into the scented air. *What had he said to her last night?* 'To be honest, I'd rather leave now.'

'I expect you would,' she said with emphasis, 'but at least show me the courtesy of drinking the coffee I made for you. It will be the politest thing you've done since you entered my house.'

He came into the room but didn't sit down. 'I'm sorry.' He reached for the cup.

'Please' – she gestured towards the sofa – 'make yourself comfortable. Or perhaps you'd prefer to have another go at breaking the antique chair in the hall?'

Had he been violent? He gave a tentative smile. 'I'm sorry.'

'I wish you wouldn't keep saying that.'

'What else can I say? I don't know what I'm doing here or why I came.'

'And you think *I* do?'

He shook his head gently in order not to incite the nausea that was churning in his stomach. 'This must seem very odd to you,' he murmured lamely.

'Good *lord*, no,' she said with leaden irony. 'What on *earth* gives you that idea? It's quite the norm for me these days to find middle-aged drunks slumped in heaps on my floors. Billy chose the garage, you chose the drawing-room. Same difference, except that you had the decency not to die on me.' Her eyes narrowed, but whether in anger or puzzlement he couldn't tell. 'Is there something about me and my house that encourages this sort of behaviour, Mr Deacon? And will you sit *down*, for Christ's sake?' she snapped in sudden impatience. 'It's very uncomfortable having you towering over me like this.'

He lowered himself on to the arm of the sofa and tried to reknit the fabric of his tattered memory, but the effort was too much for him and his lips spread in a ghastly smile. 'I think I'm going to be sick again.'

She took a towel from behind her back and passed it over. 'I find it's better to try and hang on, but you know where to go if you can't.' She waited in silence for several seconds while he brought his nausea under control. 'Why did you say you'd devoured your parents and that your unutterable torment was renewing? It seems an odd comment to make.'

He looked at her blankly as he wiped the sweat from his forehead. 'I don't know.' He read irritation on her face. 'I don't KNOW!' he said, with a surge of anger. 'I was confused. I didn't know where I was. Okay? Is that *allowed* in this house? Or does everyone have to be in control of himself at all bloody times?' He bent his head and pressed the towel over his eyes. 'I'm sorry,' he said after a moment. 'I didn't mean to be rude. The truth is, I'm struggling a bit here. I can't remember anything about last night.'

'You arrived about twelve.'

'Was I on my own?'

'Yes.'

'Why did you let me in?'

'Because you wouldn't take your finger off the door-bell.'

Sweet Jesus! What had he been thinking of? 'What else did I say?'

'That I reminded you of your mother.'

He lowered the towel to his lap and set about folding it carefully. 'Is that the reason I gave for being here?'

'No.'

'What reason did I give?'

'You didn't.' He looked at her with so much relief in his strained, sweaty face that she smiled briefly. 'Instead you called me Mrs Streeter, talked about my husband, my brother-in-law and my father-in-law, and implied that this house and its contents came from the proceeds of theft.'

Hell! 'Did I frighten you?'

'No,' she said evenly, 'I'm long past being frightened by anything.'

He wondered why. Life itself frightened him. 'Someone at the magazine recognized your face from when you were questioned at the time of James's disappearance,' he said by way of explanation. 'I was interested enough to follow it up.'

The tic above her lip started working again, but she didn't say anything.

'John Streeter seemed an obvious person to talk to, so I telephoned him and heard his side of the story. He has – er – reservations about you.'

'I wouldn't describe calling your sister-in-law a whore, a murderer and a thief as "having reservations", but perhaps you're more worried about being sued than he is.'

Deacon put the towel to his mouth again. He was in no condition for this conversation, he thought. He felt like something half-alive on a dissecting bench, waiting for the scalpel to slice through its gut. 'You'd win huge damages if you took him to court,' he told her. 'He has no evidence for his accusations.'

'Of course not. None of them is true.'

He drained his coffee cup and put it on the table.

' "Devourer of thy parent, now thy unutterable torment renews" is a line from William Blake,' he said suddenly, as if he had been thinking about that and nothing else. 'It's in one of his visionary poems about social revolution and political upheaval. The search for liberty means the destruction of established authority – in other words, the parent – and the push for freedom means every generation suffers the same torment.' He stood up and looked towards the window and its view of the river. 'William Blake – Billy Blake. Your uninvited guest was a fan of a poet who's been dead for nearly two hundred years. Why is this house so cold?' he asked abruptly, drawing his coat about him.

'It isn't. You've got a hangover. That's why you're shivering.'

He stared down at her where she sat like a radiant sun in her expensive designer dress in her expensive scented environment. But the radiance was skin deep, he thought. Underneath the immaculate façade of her and her house, he sensed despair. 'I smelt death when I woke up,' he said. 'Is that what you're trying to mask with the pot-pourri and the air spray?'

She looked very surprised. 'I don't know what you're talking about.'

'Perhaps I imagined it.'

She gave a ghost of a smile. 'Then I hope your imagination returns to normal when the alcohol's out of your system. Goodbye, Mr Deacon.'

He walked to the door. 'Goodbye, Mrs Streeter.'

*

Outside the estate he found a small grassed area with a bench seat overlooking the Thames. He huddled into his coat and let the wind suck the poisonous alcohol out of his system. The tide was out, and on the mud bank in front of him four men were sorting through the debris that had been washed up overnight. They were of indeterminate age, muffled like him in heavy overcoats, with nothing to show who they were or what their backgrounds were, and whatever assumptions he made about them would probably be as wrong as their assumptions about him. Deacon was struck again, as he had been when he met Terry, by how unremarkable most faces were, for he realized that he would not recognize these men in a different setting. Ultimately the various arrangements of eyes, nose, ears and mouth had more in common than they had apart, and it was only adornment and expression that gave them individuality. Change those, he thought, and anonymity was guaranteed.

'So what's your verdict, Michael?' asked a quiet voice beside him. 'Are any of us worth saving or are we all damned?'

Deacon turned to the frail old man with silver hair who had slipped quietly on to the bench beside him and was studying the industry on the shore with as much concentration as he was. He frowned, trying to recall the face from his past. It was someone he'd interviewed, he thought; but he talked to so many people and he rarely remembered their names afterwards.

'Lawrence Greenhill,' prompted the old man. 'You did an interview with me ten years ago for an article on euthanasia called "Freedom to Die". I was a practising solicitor and I'd written a letter to *The Times* pointing out the practical and ethical dangers of legalized suicide both to the individual and to his family. You didn't agree with me, and described me unflatteringly as "a righteous judge who claims the moral high ground for himself". I've never forgotten those words.'

Deacon's heart sank. *He didn't deserve this, not when he'd been through one guilt trip already this morning.* 'I remember,' he said. *Rather too well in fact.* The old bugger had been so complacent about biblical authority for his opinion that Deacon had come close to throttling him. But then Greenhill hadn't known how touchy he was on the whole damn subject. *Suicide in any form is wrong, Michael . . . we damn ourselves if we usurp God's authority in our lives . . .*

'Well, I'm sorry,' he went on abruptly, 'but I still don't agree with you. My philosophy doesn't recognize damnation.' He stubbed out his cigarette, while wondering if he even believed what he was saying. *Damnation had been real enough to Billy Blake.* 'Nor does it recognize *sal*vation because the whole concept worries me. Are we being saved *from* something or *for* something? If it's the former, then our right to live by our own code of ethics is under threat from moral totalitarianism, and if it's the latter, then we must blindly follow negative logic that something better awaits us when we die.' He glanced pointedly at his watch. 'Now you'll have to excuse me, I'm afraid.'

The old man gave a quiet laugh. 'You give up too easily, my friend. Is your philosophy so fragile that it can't defend itself in debate?'

'Far from it,' said Deacon, 'but I have better things to do than stand in judgement on other people's lives.'

'Unlike me?'

'Yes.'

His companion smiled. 'Except I try never to judge anyone.' He paused for a moment. 'Do you know those words by John Donne? "Any man's death diminishes me because I am involved in mankind."'

Deacon finished the quote: '"Therefore never send to know for whom the bell tolls; it tolls for thee."'

'So tell me, is it wrong to ask a man to go on living, even though he's in pain, when his life is more precious to me than his death?'

Deacon experienced a strange sort of dislocation. Words hammered in his brain. *Devourer of thy parent . . . now thy unutterable torment renews . . . Is any man's life so worthless that the manner of his death is the only interesting thing about him . . .* He stared rather blankly at Lawrence. 'Why are you here? I remember going to Knightsbridge to interview you.'

'I moved seven years ago after my wife died.'

'I see.' He rubbed his face vigorously to clear his head. 'Well, look, I'm sorry but I have to go now.' He stood up. 'It's been good talking to you, Lawrence. Enjoy your Christmas.'

A twinkle glittered in the old man's eyes. 'What's to enjoy? I'm Jewish. Do you think I like being reminded that most of the civilized world condemns my people for what they did two thousand years ago?'

'Aren't you confusing Christmas with Easter?'

Lawrence raised his eyes to heaven. 'I talk about two

thousand years of isolation and he quibbles over a few months.'

Deacon lingered, seduced by the twinkle and the outrageous racial blackmail. 'Enjoy Hanukka then, or are you going to tell me that that's impossible, too, because there's no one to enjoy it with?'

'What else can a childless widower expect?' He saw hesitation in the younger man's face, and patted the seat. 'Sit down again and give me the pleasure of a few minutes' companionship. We're old friends, Michael, and it's so rare for me to spend time with an intelligent man. Would it relieve your mind if I said I've always been a better lawyer than I've been a Jew, so your soul is in no danger?'

Deacon persuaded himself that he only sat down out of curiosity but the truth was he had no weapons against Lawrence's frailty. Death was in the old man's face just as clearly as it had been in Alan Parker's, and Deacon's sensitivity to death was always more acute as Christmas drew nearer.

'In fact, I was thinking how alike we all are and how easy it would be to drop out of our boring lives and start again,' said Deacon, nodding towards the men on the shore. 'Would you recognize them, for example, if the next time you saw them was in the Dorchester?'

'Their friends would know them.'

'Not if they came across them in a different environment. Recognition is about relating a series of known facts. Change those facts and recognition becomes harder.'

'Is a new identity what you want, Michael?'

He scraped the stubble on his chin. 'It certainly has its attractions. Did you never think about dropping out and wiping the slate clean?'

'Of course. We all have mid-life crises. If we didn't, we wouldn't be normal.'

Deacon laughed. 'To be honest, Lawrence, I'd rather you'd said I was different. The last thing a red-blooded male with unrealized ambitions wants to hear is that he's *normal*. I've done damn-all with my life and it's driving me round the bend.'

'I tend to give Christmas a wide berth,' said Deacon, lighting a fresh cigarette. 'I'd rather be at work than pretending I'm enjoying myself.'

'What does giving it a wide berth usually involve?'

Deacon shrugged. 'Ignoring it, I suppose. Keeping my head down till it's all over and sanity's restored. I don't have any children. It might be different if I had children.'

'Yes, we suffer when we have no one to love.'

'I thought it was the other way round,' he said, watching one of the men tug at a piece of wood in the mud's embrace. *No woman had ever held on to him so tenaciously as the mud held the wood.* 'We suffer when no one loves *us*.'

'Perhaps you're right.'

'I know I'm right. I've had two wives and I fucked my brains out trying to express my love for both of them. It was a waste of time.'

Lawrence smiled. 'My *dear* fellow,' he murmured. 'So much fucking for so little result. How terribly exhausting for you.'

Deacon grinned. 'It clearly served some purpose if it amuses you.'

'It reminds me of the woman who gave her husband a DIY kit when he told her he wanted a good screw.'

'Is there a moral to this story?'

'Five or six at least, depending on whether it was a genuine misunderstanding or whether the wife was teaching her husband a lesson.'

'Meaning she thought he was taking her for granted? Well, I never took either of the Mrs Deacons for granted, or not until it was obvious the marriages were on the skids. It was they who took me' – he drew morosely on his cigarette – 'for every damn penny they could. I had to sell two bloody good houses to give them each a half of my capital, lost most of my possessions in the process and now I'm shacked up in a miserable rented flat in Islington. Is there anything in your morality tale to account for that?'

Lawrence chuckled. 'I don't know. I'm a little confused now about who was screwing whom. What was the purpose of these marriages, Michael?'

'What do you mean, what was the purpose? I loved them, or at least I thought I did.'

'I love my cats but I don't intend to marry any of them.'

'What *is* the purpose of marriage then?'

'Isn't that the question you need to answer before you try again?'

'Do me a favour,' said Deacon. 'I don't intend to have my balls chopped off a third time.'

'You sound as if you're sulking, Michael.'

'Clara – she was my second wife – kept accusing me of going through the male menopause. She said I was only interested in sex.'

'Naturally. Wanting babies isn't a female prerogative. I still want babies, and I'm eighty-three years old. Why did God give me sperm if it wasn't to make babies? Look at Abraham. He was geriatric when he had Isaac.'

Deacon's rugged face broke into a smile. 'Now you're sulking, Lawrence.'

'No, Michael, I'm complaining. But old men are allowed to complain because it doesn't matter how positive their mental attitude, they still have to persuade a woman under forty to have sex with them. And that's not as easy as it sounds. I know because I've tried.'

'I can't pretend it was anything other than lust. Clara was – is – beautiful.'

'Who am I to argue? I had to have my tomcat neutered six months ago because the neighbours kept complaining about his insatiable appetite for their pretty little queens.'

'I wasn't that bad, Lawrence.'

'Neither was my tom, Michael. He was only doing what God programmed him to do, and the fact that he preferred the pretty ones merely demonstrated his good taste.'

'I don't think I ever told Clara I wanted children. I mentioned it to Julia a couple of times, but she always said there was plenty of time.'

'There was, until you deserted her for Clara.'

'I thought you were trying to persuade me to feel less guilty about that. Didn't I do it out of desperation to keep the Deacon line going?'

'There's no excuse for inefficiency, Michael. If children are what you want, then you must find a woman who wants them too. Surely the moral of the DIY story is that people have different priorities in life.'

'So where do I go from here?' asked Deacon with wry amusement. 'Singles bars? Dating agencies? Or maybe I should try an ad in *Private Eye*?'

'I think it was Chairman Mao who said, "Every journey begins with the first step." Why do you want to make that first step so difficult?'

'I don't understand.'

'You need a little practice before you throw yourself in at the deep end again. You've forgotten how simple love is. Relearn that lesson first.'

'How do I do that?'

'As I said, I love my cats but I don't plan to marry them.'

'Are you telling me to get a pet?'

'I'm not telling you anything, Michael. You're intelligent enough to work this one out for yourself.' Lawrence took a card from his inside pocket. 'This is my phone number. You can call me at any time. I'm almost always there.'

'You might live to regret it. How do you know I won't take you up on it and drive you mad with endless phone calls?'

The old eyes twinkled with what looked to Deacon like genuine affection. 'I hope you will. It's such a rarity for me to feel useful these days.'

'You're the most dreadful old fraud I've ever met.'

'Why do you say that?'

'"It's such a rarity for me to feel useful these days,"' he quoted. 'I bet you say that to all the waifs and strays you pick up. As a matter of interest, does everyone get emotionally blackmailed or am I peculiarly privileged?'

The old man chortled happily. 'Only those who inspire me with hope. You can only feed the hungry, Michael.'

It was a startling trigger to Deacon's memory. Images of skeletal Billy Blake floated to the surface of his mind. He felt for his wallet and took out a print of the dead man's mugshot. 'Did you ever talk to him? He was a derelict who lived in a warehouse squat about a mile from here and died of starvation six months ago on that estate behind us. He called himself Billy Blake but I don't think it was his real name. I need to find out who he was.'

Lawrence studied the photograph for several seconds then shook his head regretfully. 'I'm afraid not. I'm sure I'd remember if I had. It's not a face you can easily forget, is it?'

'No.'

'I remember the story. It caused quite a stir here for a day or two. Why is he important to you?'

'The woman whose garage he died in asked me to find out who he was,' said Deacon.

'Mrs Powell.'

'Yes.'

'I've seen her once or twice. She drives a black BMW.'

'That's the one.'

'Do you like her, Michael?'

Deacon thought about it. 'I haven't decided yet. She's a complicated woman.' He shrugged. 'It's a long story.'

'Then save it for your phone call.'

'It may never happen, Lawrence. My wives would tell you I score very low on reliability.'

'One little call, Michael. Is that so much to ask?'

'But it's not one little call, is it?' he growled. 'You're after people's souls, and don't think for one moment I don't know it.'

Lawrence glanced at the back of the photograph. 'May I keep this? I know quite a number of the homeless community and one of them might recognize him.'

'Sure.' Deacon stood up. 'But it doesn't mean I'll phone you, so don't raise your hopes. I'm going to be very embarrassed about this tomorrow.' He shook the old man's hand. 'Shalom, Lawrence, and thanks. Go home before you freeze to death.'

'I will. Shalom, my friend.'

He watched the younger man walk away across the grass, then smiled to himself as he took out his address book and made a careful note of Deacon's name, followed by the address and telephone number of the *Street* which Barry Grover had thoughtfully stamped on the back of the photograph. Not that he expected to need

them. Lawrence's faith in God's mysterious ways was
absolute, and he knew it was only a question of time
before Michael phoned him.

The old man turned his face upstream and listened to
the wind and the waves rebuking each other.

Chapter Eight

THE FIGHT THAT broke out inside the warehouse was a bloody affair, started by one of the more aggressive schizophrenics who decided the man next to him wanted to kill him. He pulled a flick-knife from his pocket and plunged it into his neighbour's stomach. The man's screams acted on the other inmates like a strident alarm, bringing some to his rescue and driving the rest to stampede in fear. Terry Dalton and old Tom snatched up pieces of lead piping and waded in to try to break up the affray but, like a fighting dog, the aggressor ignored the rain of blows that descended on his back and concentrated his energy on his victim. It ended, as so many of these fights ended, only when the man's stamina ran out and he retired, bruised and battered, to nurse his wounds.

Tom knelt beside the pathetic, curled figure of the man who'd been stabbed. 'It's poor old Walter,' he said. 'That bastard Denning's done for 'im good an' proper. If 'e ain't dead now, 'e soon will be.'

Terry, who was shaking from head to toe in the aftermath of heightened adrenalin, flung his piece of pipe to the ground and stripped his coat from his thin body. 'Put this over Walt and keep him warm. I'm calling an ambulance,' he said. 'And get yourselves ready for when the Old Bill gets here. This time I'm having Denning put away good and proper. He's too fucking dangerous.'

'You can cut that kind of talk, son,' said Tom, laying the coat over the body. 'There's no one gonna thank you for dropping the law on us like a ton of bricks. We'll shift Walt out and let the coppers think it 'appened in the street. The poor bastard's leaking like a stuck pig, so there'll be enough blood on the pavement to persuade 'em it were a gang of louts what did for 'im.'

'No!' snapped Terry. 'If you shift him, you'll kill him quicker.' He clenched his fists. 'We have rights, Tom, same as everyone else. Walt's right is to be given his chance, and our right is to get shot of a psycho.'

'There ain't no rights in 'ell, son,' said Tom dismissively, 'never mind Billy filled your 'ead with claptrap about 'uman dignity. You bring the bizzies in 'ere and it won't be just Denning for the 'igh jump. You think about what's in your pockets before you go calling in the filth.' He touched a gnarled hand to the wounded man's face. 'Walt's had it anyway, so it won't make no difference where 'e dies. We'll get shot of Denning ourselves, send 'im back on the streets where 'e'll likely die of cold before too long. 'E's tired 'isself out with this, so 'e won't be no trouble.'

He spoke with the authority of a man who expected to be obeyed, for, despite Deacon's impression that Terry's quick mind allowed him to dominate the group, it was Tom who governed the warehouse, and there was no place in Tom's philosophy for sentiment. He'd seen too many derelicts die to care much about this one.

'NO!' roared the youngster, making for the doorway. 'You move Walt, and you'll answer to me. We're not fucking savages, so we don't fucking behave like them. YOU HEAR ME?' He pushed his way furiously through the crowd around the door.

The phone rang in Deacon's flat as he emerged from a shower. 'I need to speak to Michael Deacon,' said an urgent voice.

'Speaking,' he said, rubbing his hair dry with a towel.

'Do you remember that warehouse you came to a couple of weeks back?'

'Yes.' He recognized his caller. 'Are you Terry?'

'Yeah. Listen, are you still after information on Billy Blake?'

'I am.'

'Then get yourself down to the warehouse in the next half-hour and bring a camera with you. Can you do that?'

'Why the hurry?'

'Because the cops are on the way, and there's stuff in there that belonged to Billy. I reckon half an hour tops before the barricades go up. You coming?'

'I'll be there.'

Terry Dalton, muffled inside an old donkey-jacket and with a black bobble hat pulled down over his shaven head, was leaning against the corner of the building, watching for Deacon's arrival. As Deacon drew into the kerb in front of an empty police car, Terry pushed himself off the wall and went to meet him.

'There's been a stabbing,' he said in a rush, as the older man got out, 'and it was me called the coppers. I reckoned it wouldn't do no harm to have a journalist in on the act. Tom reckons they're going to use this as an excuse to evict us and maybe charge us with other offences, but we've got rights, and I want them protected. In return, I'll give you everything I've got on Billy. Is it a deal?' He looked down the road as another police car rounded the corner. 'Move yourself. We ain't got much time. Did you bring a camera?'

Confused by this babble of information, Deacon allowed himself to be drawn into the lee of the building. 'It's in my pocket.'

Terry gestured along the way. 'There's a way in through one of the windows which the Old Bill don't know about. If I get you inside, they'll think you were there all the time.'

'What about the policemen already in there?'

'There's just the two of them, and they didn't get here till after the medics. They won't have a clue who was inside and who wasn't. It's too bloody dark, and they were more interested in keeping Walt alive. They didn't start asking questions till five minutes ago when the ambulance left.' He eased aside a piece of boarding. 'Okay, remember this. It were Walter what got stabbed and a psycho called Denning what did it. It's something you'd know if you'd been here a while.'

Deacon put a hand on the boy's shoulder to restrain him as he prepared to climb through the window. 'Hang on a minute. I'm not a lawyer. What are these rights you're expecting me to protect? And how am I supposed to do it?'

Terry rounded on him. 'Take pictures or something. Jesus, I don't know. Use your imagination.' His expression changed to bitterness when Deacon gave a doubtful shake of his head. 'Look, you bastard, you said you wanted to prove that Billy's life had value. Well, start by proving that Walt, Tom, me and every other damn sod in here have value. I know it's a fucking shit-hole, but we've got squatters' rights over it and it's where we live. It was me as rung the police, not the police as had to come looking, so they've no call to treat us like scum.' His pale eyes narrowed in sudden desperation. 'Billy always said that press freedom was the people's strongest weapon. Are you telling me he was wrong?'

'Okay, you lot, out,' said a harassed police constable, pushing resistant bodies. 'Let's have you in the light where we can see you.' He caught at an arm and swung the man to face the doorway. 'Out! Out!'

The flash of Deacon's camera startled him, and he turned, open-mouthed, to be caught in a second flash. A sudden silence descended on the warehouse as the light popped several times in quick succession.

'They'll be mounted in a series across the front page,' said Deacon, swinging the camera towards another policeman whose foot was nudging a sleeping man, 'with a caption like "Police use concentration-camp tactics on the homeless".' He pointed the lens at the first policeman again, zooming in for a close-up. 'How about a repeat of the "*'Raus! 'Raus! 'Raus!*"? That should stir a few worrying memories among the great and the good.'

'Who the hell are you?'

'Who the hell are you, *sir*?' said Deacon, lowering the camera to offer a card. 'Michael Deacon, and I'm a journalist. May I have your name, please, and the names of the other officers present?' He took out his notebook.

A plain-clothes policeman intervened. 'I'm Detective Sergeant Harrison, sir. Perhaps I can be of assistance.' He was a pleasant-looking individual in his thirties, solidly built and with thinning blond hair, which lifted in the breeze from the warehouse doorway. His eyes creased in an amiable smile.

'You could begin by explaining what's going on here?'

'Certainly, sir. We are asking these gentlemen to clear the site of an attempted murder. As the only free area is outside, we have requested them to vacate the building.'

Deacon raised the camera again, pointed the lens the length of the warehouse and took a photograph of its vast interior. 'Are you sure about that, sergeant? There seems to be acres of free space in here. As a matter of interest, when did the police adopt this policy?'

'What policy's that, sir?'

'Forcing people to leave their homes when a crime's been committed inside. Isn't the normal procedure to invite them to sit in another part of the house, usually the kitchen, where they can have a cup of tea to calm their nerves?'

'Look, sir, this is hardly run-of-the-mill, as you can see for yourself. It's a serious crime we're investigating. There are no lights. Half these guys are comatose on drink or drugs. The only way we can find out what's been going on is to move everyone out and introduce some order.'

'Really?' Deacon continued to take pictures. 'I thought the more usual first step was to invite witnesses to come forward and make a statement.'

Briefly, the sergeant's guard slipped and Deacon's camera caught his look of contempt. 'These guys don't even know what co-operation means. However' – he raised his voice – 'a man was stabbed in here in the last hour. Would anyone who saw the incident or has information about it please step forward?' He waited a second or two, then smiled good-humouredly at Deacon. 'Satisfied, sir? Now perhaps you'll let us get on.'

'*I* saw it,' said Terry, sliding out from behind Deacon's back. His eyes searched the darkness for Tom. 'And I weren't the only one, though you'd think I was for all the guts the rest of them are showing.'

Silence greeted this remark.

'Jesus, you're pathetic,' he went on scathingly. 'No wonder the Old Bill treat you like dirt. That's all you know, isn't it? How to lie down in the gutter while anyone who wants to walks all over you.' He spat on the floor. 'That's what I think of men who'd rather let a psycho loose on the streets than stand up and be counted once in their fucking lives.'

'Okay, okay,' said a disgruntled voice from the middle of the crowd. 'Leave off, son, for Christ's sake.' Tom shouldered his way to the front and glared malignantly at Terry. 'Anyone'd think you were the Archbishop of flaming Canterbury the way you're carrying on.' He nodded at the sergeant. 'I saw it too. 'Ow's tricks, Mr 'Arrison?'

The demeanour of the detective sergeant changed. He gave a broad grin. 'Good God! Tom Beale! I thought you were dead. Your old lady did, too.'

Tom's face creased into lines of disgust. 'I might as well be for all she cares. She told me to bugger off the last time you got me sent down, and I never saw 'er or 'eard from 'er again.'

'Bull! She was on my back for months after you were released, pressuring me to find you. Why the hell didn't you go home like you were supposed to?'

'There weren't no point,' said Tom morosely. 'She made it clear she didn't want me. In any case the silly cow went and died on me. I thought I'd pay 'er a visit a couple of years ago, and there were a load of strangers in the 'ouse. I were that upset, you wouldn't believe.'

'That doesn't mean she's dead, for God's sake. The council moved her into a flat six months after you scarpered.'

Tom looked pleased. 'Is that right? You reckon she wants to see me?'

'I'd put money on it.' The DS laughed. 'How about we get you home for Christmas? God only knows why, but you're probably the present your old lady's been waiting for.' He turned his watch face towards the light. 'Better than that, if we can get this mess sorted out PDQ,

158

we'll have you home in time for supper. What do you say?'

'You're on, Mr 'Arrison.'

'Okay, let's start with names and descriptions of everyone involved.'

'There were only the one.' Tom nodded towards the sleeping man and the policeman standing over him. 'That's the bastard you want. Name of Denning. 'E's out for the count at the moment because 'e wears 'isself out with 'is rages, but you want to be careful 'ow you tackle 'im. Like Terry says, 'e's a psycho and 'e's still got the knife on 'im.' He cackled again and produced a cigar from one of his pockets. 'We don't want no accidents, not when we're all getting along so well. I tell you what, Mr 'Arrison, I've never been so pleased to see the Old Bill in my life. 'Ere, 'ave a cigar on me.'

Because he was a professional, Deacon caught the presentation on film and made a few pounds out of the picture by selling it to a photographic agency. It appeared after Christmas in one of the tabloids with the caption **'Havana nice cigar'** and a sentimental version of Tom's reunion with his wife, together with Sergeant Harrison's part in the little drama. It was a parody of the truth, glossed up by a staff reporter to stimulate a New Year feel-good factor, for the facts were that Tom preferred the company of men, his wife preferred her cat and Sergeant Harrison was furious when he discovered the cigar was part of a consignment stolen from a hijacked lorry.

The whole episode left a sour taste in Deacon's

mouth. It offended him that police even-handedness should turn on the warmth that one sergeant felt for one destitute man. This wasn't reality. Reality was Terry's shit-hole of a warehouse where dereliction ruled and the manner of a man's death was the most interesting thing about him.

Terry caught up with him as he was unlocking his car door. 'They're saying I have to go down the nick and make a statement.'

'Is that a problem?'

'Yeah. I don't want to go.'

Deacon glanced beyond Terry to the policeman who had followed him. 'You can't have it both ways, you know. If you want your rights respected, then you have to show willing in return.'

'I'll go if you come with me.'

'There'd be no point. Lawyers are the only people allowed in interview rooms.' He searched the lad's anxious face. 'Why the change of heart? You were all fired up to make a statement twenty minutes ago.'

'Yeah, but not down the nick on my own.'

'Tom'll be there.'

A terrible disillusionment curled the boy's lip. 'He doesn't give a toss about me or Walt. He's only interested in licking the sergeant's arse and getting home to his missus. He'll drop me in the shit, quick as winking, if it suits him.'

'What does he know that the rest of us don't?'

'That I'm only fourteen, and that my name's not

Terry Dalton. I ran away from care at twelve and I ain't going back.'

Jesus wept. 'Why not? What was so bad about it?'

'The bastard in charge was a sodding shirt-lifter, that's what.' Terry clenched his fists. 'I swore I'd kill him if I ever got the chance, and if they send me back, that's what I'm gonna do. You'd better believe that.' He spoke with intense aggression. 'Billy believed it. It's why he watched out for me. He said he didn't want another murder on his conscience.'

Deacon relocked the car door. 'Why do I get the feeling my fate is inextricably linked with Billy Blake's?'

'I don't get you.'

'Does death by starvation sound familiar?' He cuffed the boy lightly across the back of the head. 'There's no food in my flat,' he grumbled, 'and I was planning to do all my shopping this afternoon. It'll be bedlam tomorrow.' He steered Terry towards the policeman. 'Don't panic,' he said more gently as he felt him tense, 'I won't abandon you. Unlike Tom, I have no desire to see either of my wives again.'

'Is that you, Lawrence? It's Michael – Michael Deacon . . . Yes, as a matter of fact, I do have a problem. I need a respectable lawyer to tell a couple of little white lies for me . . . Only to the police.' He held his mobile telephone away from his ear. 'Look, you're the one who told me to get a pet, so I reckon you owe me some support here . . . No, it's not a dangerous dog and it hasn't bitten anyone. It's a harmless little stray . . . I can't prove ownership, so they look like impounding him over Christmas . . . Yes, I agree. It's a shame . . . That's it. All I need is a sponsor . . . You will? Good man. It's the police station on the Isle of Dogs. I'll reimburse the taxi fare when you get here.'

Terry was hunched in the passenger seat of Deacon's car in an East End back street. 'You should've told him the truth. He'll blow a fuse when he gets here and finds I'm a bloke. There's no way he's going to tell lies for someone he doesn't know.' He put his fingers on the door handle. 'I reckon I should take off now while the going's good.'

'Don't even think about it,' said Deacon evenly. 'I promised Sergeant Harrison you'd be at the nick by five o'clock, and you're going to be there.' He offered the boy a cigarette and took one himself. 'Look, no one's forcing you to make this statement. You're volunteering it, so you won't be put through the third degree unless Tom decides to drop you in it. Even then, you'll be treated with kid gloves because children aren't allowed to be interviewed without an adult present. I guarantee it won't even come to that, but if it does, Lawrence will get you out.'

'Yeah, but—'

'Trust me. If Lawrence says your name's Terry Dalton and you're aged eighteen, then the police will believe him. He's very convincing. He looks like a cross between the Pope and Albert Einstein.'

'He's a fucking lawyer. If you tell him the truth, he'll have to pass it on to the Old Bill. That's what lawyers do.'

'No, they don't,' said Deacon with more conviction than he felt. 'They represent their clients' interests. But, in any case, I won't tell Lawrence anything unless I have to.'

Terry was grinning broadly as he left the interview room. 'You coming?' he asked Deacon and Lawrence as he passed them in the waiting-room on his way out.

They caught up with him in the street. 'Well?' demanded Deacon.

'No problem. It never crossed their minds I wasn't who I said I was.' He started to laugh.

'What's so funny?'

'They warned me off you and Lawrence because they reckoned you were a couple of chutney ferrets after my arse. Otherwise, why'd you be hanging around when all I was doing was making a statement?'

'God almighty,' snarled Deacon. 'What did you say?'

'I said they needn't worry because I don't do that kind of stuff.'

'Oh, great! So our reputations go down the pan while you come out smelling of roses.'

'That's about the size of it,' said Terry, retreating behind Lawrence for safety.

Lawrence chuckled joyfully. 'To be honest, I'm flattered anyone thinks I still have the energy to do anything so active.' He tucked his hand into Terry's arm and drew him along the pavement towards a pub on the corner. 'What was the term you used? Chutney ferret? Of course, I'm a very old man, and not at all in touch with modern

163

idiom, but I do think gay is preferable.' He paused in front of the pub door, waiting for Terry to open it for him. 'Thank you,' he said, gripping the boy's hand to steady himself as he carefully mounted the step at the entrance.

Terry threw an anguished glance over his shoulder at Deacon which clearly said, *This old guy's got his hand in mine, and I think he's a fucking woofter*, but Deacon only bared his teeth in a savage smile. 'Serves you right,' he mouthed, following them inside.

Barry Grover looked up rather guiltily as the security guard opened the cuttings library door and stepped inside. 'All right, son, let's have you out of here,' said Glen Hopkins firmly. 'The office is closed and you are supposed to be on holiday.'

He was a blunt-spoken retired chief petty officer, and after much deliberation, and having listened to the vicious gossip about Barry that came from the women, he had decided to take the little man in hand. He knew exactly what his problem was, and it was nothing that practical advice and straight speaking couldn't put right. He had come across Barry's type in the Navy, although admittedly they were usually younger.

Barry covered what he was doing. 'I'm working on something important,' he said priggishly.

'No, you're not. We both know what you're up to, and it's not work.'

Barry took off his glasses and stared blindly across the

room. 'I'm afraid I don't know what you're talking about.'

'Oh, yes, you do, and it isn't healthy, son.' Glen moved heavily across the floor. 'Listen to me, a man of your age should be out having fun, not shutting himself away in the dark looking at snapshots. Now, I've a few cards here with some addresses and telephone numbers on them, and my best advice to you is to choose the one you like and give her a ring. She'll cost a bob or two and you'll need a condom, but she'll get you up and running, if you follow my drift. There's no shame in having a helping hand at the start.' He placed some prostitutes' cards on the desk, and gave Barry a fatherly pat on the shoulder. 'You'll find the real thing's a damn sight more fun than a boxful of pictures.'

Barry blushed a fiery red. 'You don't understand, Mr Hopkins. I'm working on a project for Mike Deacon.' He uncovered the pictures of Billy Blake and James Streeter. 'It's a big story.'

'Which explains why Mike's at the other desk helping you, I suppose,' said Glen ironically, 'instead of out on the tiles as per usual. Come on, son, no story's so important that it can't wait till after Christmas. You can say it's none of my business, but I'm a good judge of what a man's problems are and you're not going to solve yours by staying here.'

Barry shrank away from him. 'It's not what you think,' he mumbled.

'You're lonely, lad, and you don't know how to cure it. Your mum's the nosy type – don't forget it's me who answers the phone if she rings of an evening – and if you'll forgive the plain speaking, you'd have done better to get out from under her apronstrings a long time ago. All you need is a little confidence to get started, and there's no law that says you shouldn't pay for it.' His lugubrious face broke into a smile. 'Now, hop it, and give yourself the sort of Christmas present you'll never forget.'

Thoroughly humiliated, Barry had no option but to pick up the cards and leave, but the shame of the experience brought tears to his eyes and he blinked forlornly on the pavement as the front door was locked behind him. He was so afraid that Glen would quiz him on how he'd got on that he finally made his way to a phone box and called the first number in the pile that the man had selected for him. Had he known that, in the simplistic belief that sex cured all ills, Glen habitually passed prostitutes' cards to any male colleague whom he deemed to be going through a bad patch, Barry might have thought twice about what he was doing. As it was, he assumed his virginity would become common gossip if he didn't fulfil Glen's ambitions for him, and it was more in dread of being the butt of office jokes than in anticipation of pleasure that he agreed to pay £100 for Fatima, the Turkish Delight.

Chapter Nine

'NOW,' SAID LAWRENCE, when they were settled at a table with drinks in front of them, 'perhaps Terry would like to tell me why I'm here.'

Terry ducked the question by burying his nose in his pint of beer.

'It's quite simple—' began Deacon.

'Then I should like Terry to explain it,' said the old man with surprising firmness. 'I'm a lover of simplicity, Michael, but so far you've only confused me. I am very doubtful that Terry is who he says he is, which means you and I could be in the invidious position of accessories after the fact to a crime he committed previously.'

A resigned expression settled on Terry's face. 'I knew this were a bad idea,' he told Deacon morosely. 'For a kick-off, I don't understand a bleeding word he says. It's like listening to Billy. He were always using words the rest of us had never heard of. I told him once to speak fucking English, and he laughed so much you'd of thought I'd just told the best joke in the world.' His pale eyes fixed on Lawrence. 'People get hung up on names,' he said fiercely, 'but what's so important about a fucking name? If it comes to that, what's so important about a

167

person's age? It's the age you act that matters, not the age you are. Okay, maybe my name isn't Terry and maybe I'm not eighteen, but I like 'em both because they give me respect. One day, I'm gonna *be* somebody, and people like you will want to know me whatever I'm calling myself. It's me that's important' – he tapped his chest above his heart – 'not my name.'

Deacon passed Terry a cigarette. 'There's no crime involved, Lawrence,' he said matter-of-factly.

'How do you know?'

'What did I tell you?' demanded Terry aggressively. 'Fucking lawyers. Now he's calling me a liar.'

Deacon made a dampening motion with his hand. 'Terry ran away from care two years ago at the age of twelve, and he doesn't want to be sent back because the man in charge is a paedophile. To avoid that happening he's added four years to his age and has been living under an alias in a squat. It's as simple as that.'

Lawrence clicked his tongue impatiently, unintimidated by Terry's seething anger beside him. 'You call it simple that a child has been living in dreadful circumstances without education or loving parental control during two of the most important years of his life? Perhaps I should remind you, Michael, that it's only five hours since you were telling me you wanted to be a father.' He raised a thin, transparent hand towards Terry. 'This young man is no harmless stray who can be left to his own devices now that you've prevented the police from exercising their responsibility towards him. He's in need of the care and protection that a civilized society—'

'There were Billy,' broke in Terry fiercely. 'He were caring.'

Lawrence looked at him for a moment, then took the photograph Deacon had given him from his wallet. 'Is this Billy?'

Terry glanced at the haggard face then looked away. 'Yeah.'

'It must have grieved you to lose him.'

'Not so's you'd notice.' He lowered his head. 'He weren't that bloody brilliant. Half the time he were off his head, so it were *me* looking after *him*.'

'But you did love him?'

The boy's hands clenched into fists again. 'If you're saying me and Billy were sodding poofs, I'll belt you one.'

'My dear boy,' murmured the old man gently, 'such a thing never crossed my mind. I dread to think what kind of world you inhabit where men are frightened to express their fondness for each other because of what others might think. There are a thousand ways to love a person, and only one of them is sexual. I think you loved Billy as a father and, from the way you describe him, he loved you as a son. Is that so shameful that you have to deny it?'

Terry didn't say anything and a silence developed. Deacon broke it eventually because it was becoming uncomfortable.

'Look, I don't know about anyone else,' he said, 'but I had a terrible night last night, and I wouldn't mind calling it a day. My personal view is that Terry's a streetwise kid with a hell of a lot going for him – he's certainly got more nous than I had at his age. There's a spare bed in my flat, I look like spending a miserable Christmas on my own, and I'd welcome some company. What do you say, Terry? My place or the warehouse for the next few days? You and I can enjoy ourselves while Lawrence does the worrying about the future.'

'I thought you said there was no food,' he muttered ungraciously.

'There isn't. We'll grab a takeaway tonight and go looking for turkey tomorrow.'

'Except you don't really want me. It's only because Lawrence reckons you'd make a lousy father that you thought of it.'

'Right. But I *have* thought of it, so what's the answer?' He looked at the bowed head. 'Listen, you miserable little sod, I haven't done badly by you so far today. Okay, I don't know the first damn thing about parenting but a small thank you for the efforts I have made wouldn't go amiss.'

Terry grinned suddenly and raised his head. 'Thanks, Dad. You've done good. How about we make it an Indian takeaway?'

There was a gleam of triumph in the lad's pale eyes which came and went too swiftly for Deacon to notice. But Lawrence saw it. Being older and wiser, he had been looking for it.

Lawrence refused Deacon's offer of a lift home but took the Islington address in case he was contacted by the police. He advised Terry to use his few days' grace to consider whether a return to the warehouse was in his best interests, warned him that his true age and identity would undoubtedly be discovered if and when he was required to give evidence against Denning in court, and suggested he think about regularizing his position voluntarily before he was forced into it. He then asked Terry to call him a taxi from the phone at the bar and, while the boy was out of earshot, he cautioned Deacon against naivety. 'Retain a healthy scepticism, Michael. Remember the kind of life Terry's been leading and how little you actually know about him.'

Deacon smiled slightly. 'I was afraid you were going to tell me to clutch him to my heart with expressions of love. Healthy scepticism I can cope with. It's what I know best.'

'Oh, I don't think you're quite so hardened as you think you are, my dear fellow. You've accepted everything he's told you without blinking an eyelid.'

'You think he's lying?'

Lawrence shrugged. 'We've had a conversation filled with references to homosexuality, and that troubles me. You'll be very vulnerable to a charge of attempted rape if you take him back to your flat. And that will leave you no option but to pay whatever he demands from you.'

Deacon frowned. 'Come on, Lawrence, he's completely paranoid on the whole subject. He'd never let me near enough to touch him, so how could he accuse me of rape?'

'*Attempted* rape, dear chap, and do please recognize

how effective his paranoia is. He's lulled you into thinking it's safe to take him home, which I'm bound to say is not something I would feel confident doing.'

'Then why were you pushing me into it?'

Lawrence sighed. 'I wasn't, Michael. I was hoping to persuade you both that Terry should be returned to care.' He was watching the boy as he spoke. The barman was trying to give him a telephone directory, which he seemed reluctant to take. 'Tell me, what will your reaction be when he screams and tears his clothes, and threatens to run to one of your neighbours with stories of imprisonment and sexual assault?'

'Why would he want to do that?'

'I would imagine because he's done it before and knows it works. You really mustn't go into this with your eyes closed, my dear chap.'

'Great,' said Deacon, lowering his head wearily into his hands. 'So what the hell am I supposed to do now? Tell the little bastard to get stuffed?'

Lawrence chuckled. 'Dear, dear, dear! What a fellow you are for losing heart. The least generous but probably most sensible course would be to hand him back to the police and let the social workers deal with him, but that would be very unkind when you've just offered him Christmas in your flat. Forewarned is, after all, forearmed. I think you must honour your invitation to the poor lad but keep one step ahead of him all the time.'

'I wish you'd make up your mind,' growled Deacon. 'Half a minute ago the *poor lad* was planning to con me out of thousands.'

'Why should the two be mutually exclusive? He's an

unloved, ill-educated, half-formed adolescent who, through living rough, will have learned some sophisticated tricks to keep him in clothes, food, drink and drugs. The truth may be that you're exactly the person he needs to bring him back into the fold.'

'He'll run rings around me,' said Deacon gloomily.

'Surely not,' murmured Lawrence, looking towards the bar where Terry had finally asked the barman to locate a minicab firm for him in the directory. 'At least you have the advantage of literacy.'

Barry experienced only humiliation at the hands of Fatima, who spoke very poor English. The light in her bed-sitting room was dim, and he looked in fastidious alarm at the tumbled bed, which still seemed to bear the imprint of a previous client. There was a strong Turkish atmosphere in the frowsty room which owed more to Fatima herself than to the array of joss sticks burning on a dressing-table.

She was a well-covered woman, somewhere in her middle years, with a routine that was well established and made no allowance for time-wasting. She recognized rapidly that she was dealing with a virgin and looked repeatedly at her clock while Barry stumbled through an inarticulate introduction of himself as he tried to work out how to extricate himself from this dreadful situation without offending her.

'One hunra,' she broke in impatiently, stroking her palm. 'And take zee trowse off. Who care you call Barree? *I* call you sweeties. What you like? Doggy-doggy? Oil?'

She pursed her full lips into a ripe rosebud. 'You nice clean boy. For a hunra and fifty Fatima do sucky-sucky. You like sucky-sucky? Sounds good, eh, sweeties?'

Terrified that she wouldn't let him go without some sort of payment, Barry fumbled his wallet out of his coat pocket and allowed her to remove five twenties. It was a mistake. Once the money had changed hands, and when Barry didn't immediately start shedding his clothes, she set about doing it for him. She was a strong woman and clearly expected to fulfil her side of the contract.

'Come on, sweeties. No need to be shy. Fatima, she know all the tricks. There, you see, no problem. You beeg boy.' With deft hands she plucked a condom from a nearby drawer, applied it with consummate artistry and proceeded to practise her Turkish delights at speed.

Barry was no match for her skill and matters reached a conclusion in seconds.

'There you are, sweeties,' she said, 'all done, all enjoyed. You really *beeg* boy. You come back any time as long as you have a hunra. Fatima always willing. Next time less talk, more fun, okay? You pay for good sex, and Fatima give good sex. Maybe you like doggy-doggy and fondle Fatima's nice round arse. Now put zee trowse back on and say bye-bye.'

She had the door open before he was properly dressed and, because he didn't know what else to do with it, he put the condom in his pocket. She called after him as he walked away: 'You come back soon, Barree,' and his heart swelled with loathing for her and all her sex.

*

'What was the old guy saying to you while I was on the phone?' demanded Terry suspiciously as he and Deacon made their way back to the car.

'Nothing much. He's concerned about your future and how best to handle it.'

'Yeah, well, if he does the dirty on me and goes to the police, he'd better watch his back.'

'He gave you his word he wouldn't. Don't you believe him?'

Terry kicked at the kerb. 'I guess so. But he's a bit fucking heavy on the hand-patting and calling everyone dear. D'you reckon he's bent?'

'No. Would it make a difference if he were?'

'Bloody right it would. I don't hold with poofs.'

Deacon inserted his key in the car door, but paused before turning it to look across the roof at his would-be passenger. 'Then why do you keep talking about them?' he asked. 'You're like an alcoholic who can't keep off the subject of booze because he's dying for his next drink.'

'I'm not a bloody poof,' said Terry indignantly.

'Then prove it by keeping off the subject.'

'Okay. Can we stop at the warehouse?'

Deacon eyed him thoughtfully. 'Why?'

'There's things I need. Extra clothes and such.'

'Why can't you come as you are?'

'Because I'm not a fucking tramp.'

After ten minutes of drumming his fingers on the steering wheel and with no sign of Terry's re-emergence from the dark building, Deacon wondered if he should go after him. He could hear Lawrence's voice in his ear: '*You think this is good parenting, Michael? You let a fourteen-year-old boy go into a den of thieves, and you call that responsible?*'

He postponed one difficult decision by making another. He picked up his mobile telephone and dialled his sister's number. 'Emma?' he said when a woman's voice answered at the other end.

'No, it's Antonia.'

'You sound like your mother.'

'Who is this, please?'

'Your Uncle Michael.'

'God!' said the voice at the other end in some awe. 'Listen, hang on, okay? I'll get Mum.' The phone clattered on to a table and he heard her shouting for her mother. 'Quick, quick! It's Michael.'

His sister's breathless voice came down the line. 'Hello, hello! Michael?'

'Calm down and get your breath back,' he said in some amusement. 'I'm still here.'

'I ran. Where are you?'

'In a car outside a warehouse in the East End.'

'What are you doing there?'

'Nothing of any interest.' He could see the conversation being hijacked by irrelevancies, for, like him, Emma was adept at postponing anything difficult. 'Look, I got your card. I also got one from Julia. I gather Ma's not well.'

There was a short silence. 'Julia shouldn't have told you,' she said rather bitterly. 'I hoped you'd rung because you wanted to end this silly feud, not because you feel guilty about Ma.'

'I don't feel guilty.'

'Out of pity then.'

Did he feel pity either? His strongest emotion was still anger. '*Do not bring that whore into my house,*' his mother had said when he told her he'd married Clara. '*How dare you sully your father's name by giving it to a cheap tart? Was killing him not enough for you, Michael?*' That had been five years ago and he hadn't spoken to her since. 'I'm still angry, Emma, so maybe I'm phoning you out of filial duty. I'm not going to apologize to her – or you for that matter – but I am sorry she's ill. What do you want me to do about it? I'm quite happy to see her as long as she's prepared to keep a rein on her tongue, but I'll walk out the minute she starts having a go. That's the only deal you or she will get, so do I come or not?'

'You haven't changed one little bit, have you?' Her voice was angry. 'Your mother's virtually blind and may have to have her leg amputated as a result of diabetes, and you talk about deals. Some filial duty, Michael. She was in hospital for most of September, and now Hugh and I are paying through the nose for private nursing care at the farm because she won't come and live with us. *That*'s filial duty, making sure your mother's being looked after properly even if it means hardships for yourself.'

Deacon looked towards the warehouse with a frown in his dark eyes. 'What happened to her investments? She had a perfectly good income five years ago, so why isn't she paying for the nursing care herself?'

Emma didn't answer.

'Are you still there?'

'Yes.'

'Why isn't she paying herself?'

'She offered to put the girls through school and used her capital to buy their fees in advance,' said Emma reluctantly. 'She left herself enough to live on but not enough to pay for extras. We didn't *ask*,' she went on defensively. 'It was her idea, but none of us knew she was going to be struck down like this. And it's not as if there was any point keeping anything for you. As far as the rest of us were aware, you were never going to speak to us again.'

'That's right,' he agreed coolly. 'I'm only speaking to you now because Julia was so damn sure I wouldn't.'

Emma sighed. 'Is that the only reason you phoned?'

'Yes.'

'I don't believe you. Why can't you just say sorry and let bygones be bygones?'

'Because I've nothing to be sorry for. It's not my fault Pa died, whatever you and Ma like to think.'

'That's not what she was angry about. She was angry about the way you treated Julia.'

'It was none of her business.'

'Julia was her daughter-in-law. She was very fond of her. So was I.'

'You weren't married to her.'

'That's cheap, Michael.'

'Yes, well, I can't accuse you of that, can I? Not when you and Hugh have scooped the pot,' said Deacon

178

sarcastically. 'I've never taken a cent from Ma and don't intend to start now, so if she wants to see me, it'll have to be on my terms because I don't owe her a damn thing, never mind how many bloody legs she's about to lose.'

'I can't believe you said that,' snapped his sister. 'Aren't you at all upset that she's ill?'

If he was, he wasn't going to admit it. 'My terms, Emma, or not at all. Have you a pen? Okay, this is my telephone number at home.' He gave it to her. 'I presume you'll be at the farm for Christmas, so I suggest you talk this over with Ma and ring me with your verdict. And don't forget I promised to deck Hugh the next time I saw him, so take that into account before you reach a decision.'

'You can't hit Hugh,' she said indignantly. 'He's fifty-three.'

Deacon bared his teeth at the receiver. 'Good, then one punch should do it easily.'

There was another silence. 'Actually, he's been want-ing to apologize for ages,' she said weakly. 'He didn't really mean what he said. It just sort of came out in the heat of the moment. He regretted it afterwards.'

'Poor old Hugh. It's going to be doubly painful then when I break his nose.'

Terry appeared from the warehouse with two filthy suitcases which he parked on the back seat. He offered the explanation that as the warehouse was full of fucking thieves, he was safeguarding his possessions by bringing them with him. Deacon thought it looked more like wholesale removal to what promised to be luxury living.

'Doesn't the endless "fucking" get a little boring after a while?' he murmured as he drew away from the kerb.

They ate their takeaway perched on the bonnet of Deacon's car. They were in danger of freezing to death in the night air, but he preferred that to having his upholstery splattered with red tandoori chicken dye. Terry wanted to know why they hadn't eaten in the restaurant.

'I didn't think we'd ever get served,' said Deacon rather grimly, 'not after you called them wogs.'

Terry grinned. 'What d'you call them then?'

'People.'

They sat in silence for a while, gazing down the street ahead of them. Fortunately it was well-nigh deserted, so they attracted little curiosity. Deacon wondered who would have been the more embarrassed, himself or Terry, had some acquaintance passed by and seen them.

'So what are we going to do next?' asked Terry, cramming a last onion bhaji into his mouth. 'Go down the pub? Visit a club maybe? Get stoned?'

Deacon, who had been looking forward to putting his feet up in front of the fire and dozing through whatever film was on the television, groaned quietly to himself. *Pubbing, clubbing or getting stoned?* He felt old and decrepit beside the hyperactivity of movement – fidgeting, scratching, position-changing – that had been going on beside him for over an hour now. This, in turn, meant that his mind toiled with the threats of fleas, lice and bedbugs, and the problem of how to get Terry into a bath and every stitch of his clothing into the washing-machine without having his motives misconstrued.

One thing was certain. He had no intention of giving house room to Terry's wildlife.

The row between Emma and Hugh Tremayne had reached stentorian levels and, as usual, Hugh had resorted to the whisky bottle. 'Have you any idea what it's like to be the only man in a houseful of domineering women?' he demanded. 'Don't you think I've been tempted to do what Michael did and walk out? Nag, nag, nag. That's the only thing you and your mother have any talent for, isn't it?'

'I'm not the one who called Michael a sack of worthless shit,' said Emma furiously. 'That was your wonderful idea, although what made you think you could order him out of his own house I can't imagine. The only reason you're in our family is because you married me.'

'You're right,' he said abruptly, replenishing his glass. 'And what the hell am I still doing here? I sometimes think the only member of your family I've ever really liked was your brother. He's certainly the least critical.'

'Don't be so childish,' she snapped.

He stared at her moodily over the rim of his glass. 'I never liked Julia – she was a frigid bitch – and I certainly didn't blame Michael for taking up with Clara. Yet I let myself get dragged into defending you and your mother when I should have told Michael to go ahead and smash the house up with you and Penelope in it. As far as I'm concerned, he was well within his rights. You'd been screaming at him like a couple of fishwives for well over an hour before he lost his temper, and you had the damn nerve to accuse his *wife* of being common as muck.' He shook his head and moved towards the door. 'I'm not interested any more. If you want Michael's help, then you'd better persuade your mother to treat him with a little respect.'

Emma was close to tears. 'If I try, she won't talk to him at all. It's Julia's fault. If she hadn't told him Ma was ill, he'd probably have rung anyway.'

'You're running out of people to blame.'

'Yes, but what are we going to do?' she wailed. 'She's got to sell the farm.'

'It's your blasted family,' he growled, 'so you sort it out. You know damn well I never wanted your mother's money. It was obvious she'd use it as a stick to beat us with.' He slammed the door behind him. 'And I'm not going to the farm for Christmas,' he yelled from the hall. 'I've done it for sixteen bloody years, and it's been sixteen years of undiluted misery.'

'This is how we're going to play it,' said Deacon, pausing outside the door to his flat after carrying a suitcase up three flights of stairs. 'You're going to remove everything washable from these cases out here on the landing. We will then put it all into black dustbin bags which I will empty into the washing-machine while you're having your bath. You will leave what you're wearing outside the bathroom door, and when you're locked inside, I will take your clothes away and replace them with some of my own. Are we agreed?'

In the half-light of the landing, Terry looked a great deal older than fourteen. 'You sound like you're scared of me,' he remarked curiously. 'What did that old bugger Lawrence really say?'

'He told me how unhygienic you were likely to be.'

'Oh, right.' Terry looked amused. 'You sure he didn't tell you about the rape scam?'

'That, too,' said Deacon.

'It always works, you know. I met a guy once who scored five hundred off of it. Some old geezer took him in out of the goodness of his heart, and the next thing he knew this kid was screaming rape all over the place.' He smiled in a friendly way. 'I'll bet Lawrence tore strips off you for inviting me back here – he's sharp as a tack, that one – but he's wrong if he thinks I'd turn on you. Billy taught me this saying: never bite the hand that feeds you. So you've got nothing to worry about, okay? You're safe with me.'

Deacon opened the front door and reached inside for the light switch. 'That's good news, Terry. It lets us both off the hook.'

'Oh, yeah? You had something planned just in case, did you?'

'It's called revenge.'

Terry's smile broadened into a grin. 'You can't take revenge on an under-age kid. The cops'd crucify you.'

Deacon smiled back, but rather unpleasantly. 'What makes you think you'd still be a kid when it's done or that I'm the one who'd do it? Here's another saying Billy should have taught you: revenge is a dish best eaten cold.' His voice dropped abruptly to sound like sifted gravel. 'You'll have a second or two to remember it when a psycho like Denning does to you what was done to Walter this afternoon. And, if you're lucky, you'll *live* to regret it.'

'Yeah, well it's not going to happen, is it?' muttered Terry, somewhat alarmed by Deacon's tone. 'Like I said, you're safe with me.'

Terry was deeply critical of Deacon's flat. He didn't like the way the front door opened into the sitting-room – 'Jesus, it means you've got to be well tidy all the time'; nor the narrow corridor that led off it to the bathroom and the two bedrooms – 'It'd be bigger without these stupid walls all over the place'; only the kitchen passed muster because it was attached to the sitting-room – 'I guess that's pretty handy for TV dinners.' Once all his underlying odours had been effectively soaked away, he prowled around it in a pair of overwide jeans and a jumper, shaking his head over the blandness of it all. He reeked strongly of Jazz aftershave ('Nicked from a chemist,' he said proudly), which Deacon had to admit introduced an exotic quality into the atmosphere that hadn't been there before.

The final verdict was damning. 'You're not a boring bloke, Mike, so how come you live in such a boring place?'

'What's boring about it?' Deacon was using a long-handled wooden spoon to poke Terry's patchwork quilt with infinite care into the washing-machine. He kept his eyes peeled for anything that looked like hopping, although as his only plan was to try to whack the offending parasites with the head of the spoon, it was fortunate they never emerged.

Terry waved an arm in a wide, encompassing circle. 'The only room that's even half-way reasonable's your bedroom, and that's only because there's a stereo and a load of books in there. You ought to have more bits and pieces at your age. I reckon I've got more fucking stuff – sorry – and I ain't been knocking around half as long as you.'

Deacon produced his cigarettes and handed one to the boy. 'Then don't get married. This is what two divorces can do to you.'

'Billy always said women were dangerous.'

'Was he married?'

'Probably. He never talked about it though.' He pulled open the kitchen cupboard doors. 'Is there anything to drink in this place?'

'There's some beer in the fridge and some wine in a rack by the far wall.'

'Can I have a beer?'

Deacon took two cans from the fridge and tossed one across. 'There are glasses in the cupboard to your right.'

Terry preferred to drink from the can. He said it was more American.

'Do you know much about America?' Deacon asked him.

'Only what Billy told me.'

185

Deacon pulled out a kitchen chair and straddled it. 'What did Billy say about it?'

'He didn't rate it much. Reckoned it'd been corrupted by money. He liked Europe better. He were always talking about commies. Said they took after Jesus.'

The phone rang, but as neither of them answered it, the tape went into action. *'Michael, it's Hugh,'* said his brother-in-law's tipsy voice over the amplifier. *'I'll be in the Red Lion in Deanery Street tomorrow at lunchtime. I'm not going to apologize now because it's only fair you break my nose first. I'll apologize afterwards. Hope that's okay.'*

Terry frowned. 'What was that about?'

'Revenge,' said Deacon. 'I told you, it's a dish best eaten cold.'

Chapter Ten

THREE MILES AWAY in Fleet Street, Barry Grover skulked in the shadows waiting for Glen Hopkins's shift to finish. Only when the replacement, Reg Linden, had been *in situ* for fifteen minutes did he scuttle across the road and let himself in. Reg, who as nightwatchman had very little contact with *Street* employees, had long since ceased to question Barry's nocturnal visits to the offices, even looked forward to them for the company they offered. He took as much interest in Barry's researches as Barry did himself, and his view – untarnished by female gossip – was that the little man's problem was a tendency to insomnia. In that peculiarly uncomplicated way reserved to men who don't seek to know too much about each other, he and Barry were friends.

He smiled affably. 'Still trying to identify your dead wino?' he asked.

Barry nodded. Had Reg been a little more perceptive, he might have wondered at the little man's agitation, he might even have questioned why Barry's fly was undone, but fate had ruled him an unobservant man.

'This might help,' he said, producing a paperback from under the desk. 'You want chapter five – missing persons. No pictures, I'm afraid, but some useful information on James Streeter. Mrs Linden came across it in a bookshop and thought you might like it. She's always been interested in your projects.' He waved Barry's thanks aside, and promised to bring him a cup of tea when he made one for himself.

Deacon emptied another bag of washing into the machine. 'You said there was stuff in the warehouse that belonged to Billy,' he reminded Terry. 'Was that a ploy to get me down there or was it true?'

'True, but you'll have to pay if you want to see it.'

'Where is it?'

Terry jerked his head towards the sitting-room, where the suitcases stood in a corner. 'In there.'

'What's to stop me going through the cases myself?'

'One of these.' The lad clenched his right hand into a fist. 'I'll lay you flat, and if you hit me back, I'll have proof of assault.' He smiled engagingly. 'Sexual or the other kind, depending on my mood.'

'How much do you want?'

'My mate got five hundred off of his old geezer.'

'Bog off, Terry. Billy can go hang for all I care. I'm bored with him.'

'Like hell you are. He's bugging you, same as he bugs me. Four hundred.'

'Twenty.'

'One hundred.'

'Fifty, and it'd better be good' – Deacon clenched his own hand into a fist – 'or *you*'ll be on the receiving end of one of these. And to hell with the consequences, frankly.'

'It's a deal. Give us the fifty.' Terry uncurled his palm. 'Cash only, or all bets are off.'

Deacon nodded towards the kitchen cabinets. 'Third cupboard along, biscuit tin on the second shelf, take five tens and leave the rest.' He watched the boy locate the tin, remove the wad of notes inside it and peel off £50.

'Jesus, but you're a weird bastard, Mike,' he said resuming his seat. 'There must be another two hundred in there. What's to stop me nicking it, now you've shown me where it is?'

'Nothing,' said Deacon, 'except it's mine, and you haven't earned it. Not yet, anyway.'

'What'd I have to do to earn it?'

'Learn to read.' He saw the cynical look in Terry's eyes. 'I'll teach you.'

'Sure you will, for two miserable days. And when I still can't read at the end of it, you'll get mad and I'll've wasted my time for nothing.'

'Why didn't Billy teach you?'

'He tried once or twice,' said the boy dismissively, 'but he couldn't see well enough to teach anything 'cept what was in his head. It were another of his punishments. He poked a pin into his eye one time, which meant he couldn't read very long without getting a headache.' He took another cigarette. 'I told you, he were a right nutter. He were only happy when he were hurting himself.'

*

189

They were the most meagre of possessions: a battered postcard, some crayons, a silver dollar, and two flimsy letters which were in danger of falling apart from having been read so often. 'Is this all there was?' asked Deacon.

'I told you before. He didn't want nothing and he didn't have nothing. A bit like you if you think about it.'

Deacon spread the items across the table. 'Why weren't these on him when he died?'

Terry shrugged. 'Because he told me to burn them a few days before he buggered off that last time. I hung on to them in case he changed his mind.'

'Did he say why he wanted them burned?'

'Not so's you'd notice. It was while he was in one of his mad fits. He kept yelling that everything was dust, then told me to chuck this lot on the fire.'

'Dust to dust and ashes to ashes,' murmured Deacon, picking up the postcard and turning it over. It was blank on one side and showed a reproduction of Leonardo da Vinci's cartoon of *The Virgin and Child with St Anne* on the other. It was worn at the edges and there were crease marks across the glossy surface of the picture, but it required more than that to diminish the power of da Vinci's drawing. 'Why did he have this?'

'He used to copy it on to the pavement. That's the family he drew.' Terry touched the figure of the infant John the Baptist to the right of the picture. 'He left this baby out' – his finger moved to the face of St Anne – 'turned this woman into a man and drew the other woman and the baby that's on her knee the way they are. Then he'd colour it in. It were bloody good, too. You could see what was what in Billy's picture whereas this one's a bit of a mess, don't you reckon?'

Deacon gave a snort of laughter. 'It's one of the world's great masterpieces, Terry.'

'It ain't as good as Billy's. I mean, look at the legs. They're all mixed up, so Billy sorted them. He gave the bloke brown legs and the woman blue legs.'

With a muffled guffaw, Deacon lowered his forehead to the table. He reached surreptitiously for a handker-chief from his pocket and blew his nose loudly before sitting up again. 'Remind me to show you the original one day,' he said a little unsteadily. 'It's in the National Gallery in Trafalgar Square and I'm not as convinced as you that the legs need – er – sorting.' He took a pull at his beer can. 'Tell me how Billy managed to do these paintings if he couldn't see properly.'

'He could see to draw – I mean, he were drawing every night on bits of paper – and, anyway, he made his pavement pictures really big. It were only reading that gave him a headache.'

'What about the writing that you said he put at the bottom of the picture?'

'He did it big like the painting, otherwise people wouldn't have noticed it.'

'How do you know what it said if you can't read?'

'Billy learned it to me so I could write it myself.' He pulled Deacon's notebook and pencil towards him and carefully formed the words across the page.

Blessed are the poor

'If you can do that,' said Deacon matter-of-factly, 'you can learn to read in two days.' He took up one of the letters and spread it carefully on the table in front of him.

Cadogan Square
April 4th

Darling,
Thank you for your beautiful letter, but how I wish you could enjoy the here and now and forget the future. Of course I am flattered that you want the world to know you love me, but isn't what we have more perfect because it is a secret? You say your glass shall not persuade you you are old, so long as youth and I are of one date, but, my darling, Shakespeare never named his love because he knew how cruel the world could be. Do you want me pilloried as a calculating bitch who set out to seduce any man who could offer her security? For that is what will happen if you insist on acknowledging me publicly. I adore you with all my heart but my heart will break if you ever stop loving me because of what people say. Please, please, let's leave things the way they are. Your loving V.

Deacon unfolded the second letter and placed it beside the first. It was written in the same hand.

Paris
Friday

Darling,
Don't think me mad but I am so afraid of dying. I

*have nightmares sometimes where I float in black space
beyond the reach of anyone's love. Is that what hell is,
do you think? For ever to know that love exists while for
ever condemned to exist without it? If so, it will be my
punishment for the happiness I've had with you. I can't
help thinking it's wrong for one person to love another
so much that she can't bear to be apart from him.
Please, please, don't stay away any longer than is
necessary. Life isn't life without you. V.*

'Did Billy read these to you, Terry?'

The boy shook his head.

'They're love letters. Rather beautiful love letters, in
fact. Do you want to hear them?' He took Terry's shrug
for assent and read the words aloud. He waited for a
reaction when he'd finished, but didn't get one. 'Did
you ever hear him talking about someone whose name
began with a "v"?' he asked then. 'It sounds as if she was
a lot younger than he was.'

The boy didn't answer immediately. 'Whoever she is,
I bet she's dead,' he said. 'Billy told me once that hell
was being left alone for ever and not being able to do
nothing about it, and then he started to cry. He said it
always made him cry to think of someone being that
lonely, but I guess he was really crying for this lady.
That's sad, isn't it?'

'Yes,' said Deacon slowly, 'but I wonder why he
thought she was in hell.' He read through the letters
again but found nothing to account for Billy's certainty
about V's fate.

'He reckoned *he*'d go to hell. He kind of looked

forward to it in a funny sort of way. He said he deserved all the punishment the gods could throw at him.'

'Because he was a murderer?'

'I guess so. He went on and on about life being a holy gift. It used to drive Tom up the wall. He'd say' – he fell into a fair imitation of Tom's cockney accent – '"If it's so effing 'oly, what the fuck are we doing living in this soddin' 'ell of a cess-pit?" And Billy'd say' – Terry now adopted a classier tone – '"You are here by choice because your gift included free will. Decide now whether you seek to bring the gods' anger upon your heads. If the answer's no, then choose a wiser course."'

Deacon chuckled. 'Is that what he actually said?'

'Sure. I used to say it for him sometimes when he was too pissed to say it himself.' He returned to his mimicking of Billy's voice. '"You are here by choice because your gift included free will." Blah-blah-blah. He were a bit of a pillock really, couldn't see when he was annoying people. Or if he did, he didn't care. Then he'd get rat-arsed and start yelling, and that was worse because we couldn't understand what he was on about.'

Deacon fetched another two beer cans from the fridge, and chucked the empties into the bin. 'Do you remember him saying anything about repentance?' he asked, propping himself against the kitchen worktop.

'Is that the same as repent?'

'Yes.'

'He used to shout that a lot. "Repent! Repent! Repent! The hour is later than you think!" He did it that time he took all his clothes off in the middle of the fucking winter. "Repent! Repent! Repent!" he kept screaming.'

194

'Do you know what repentance is?'

'Yeah. Saying sorry.'

Deacon nodded. 'Then why didn't Billy follow his own advice and say sorry for this murder? He'd have been looking to heaven then instead of hell.' *Except that he'd told the psychiatrist his own redemption didn't interest him* . . .

Terry pondered this for some time. 'I get what you're saying,' he declared finally, 'but, see, I never thought about it before. The trouble with Billy was he was well noisy most of the time, and it did your head in to listen to him. And he only spoke about the murder once, when he were really worked up about something.' His eyes screwed in concentrated reflection. 'In any case, he stuck his hand in the fire straight afterwards and wouldn't take it out till we all pulled him off of it, so I guess no one thought to ask why he didn't repent himself.' He shrugged. 'I expect it's quite simple. I expect it was his fault his lady went to hell, so he felt he ought to go there too. Poor bitch.'

Deacon remembered his suspicions the first time he heard this story, when it was obvious to him that Terry was relating an incident that the other men at the warehouse knew nothing about. They had recalled the hand in the fire, but not the revelations of murder. 'Or maybe there was nothing to repent,' he suggested. 'Another way to go to hell is to destroy the gods' gift of life by killing *yourself*. For centuries, suicides were buried in wasteland to demonstrate that they had put themselves beyond the reach of God's mercy. Isn't that the path Billy was taking?'

'You asked me that one already, and I already told you, Billy never tried to kill himself.'

'He starved himself to death.'

'Nah. He just forgot to eat. That's different, that is. He were too drunk most of the time to know what he was doing.'

Deacon thought back. 'You said he strangled someone because the gods had written it in his fate. Were those the actual words he used?'

'I can't remember.'

'Try.'

'It were that or something like it.'

Deacon looked sceptical. 'You also said he burned his hand as a sacrifice to direct the gods' anger somewhere else. But why would he do that if he wanted to go to hell?'

'Jesus!' said Terry in disgust. 'How should I know? The guy was a nutter.'

'Except your definition of a nutter isn't the same as mine,' said Deacon impatiently. 'Didn't it occur to you that Billy was ranting and raving all the time because he was with a bunch of bozos who couldn't follow a single damn word he was saying? I'm not surprised he was driven to drink.'

'It wasn't our fault,' said the boy sullenly. 'We did our best for the miserable sod, and it wasn't easy keeping our cool when he were having a go at us.'

'All right, try this question. You said he was worked up about something just before he told you he was a murderer, so what was he worked up about?'

Terry didn't answer.

'Was it something personal between you and him?' said Deacon with sudden intuition. 'Is that why the others didn't know about it?' He waited for a moment. 'What happened? Did you have a fight? Perhaps he tried to strangle you and then thrust his hand in the fire out of remorse?'

'No, it were the other way round,' said the boy unhappily. 'It were me tried to strangle *him*. He only burned his bloody hand so I'd remember how close I came to murder.'

The awful irony of Barry's situation came home to him forcibly in the semi-darkness of the cuttings library when he realized he was no longer content to look at photographs of beautiful men and fantasize harmlessly about what they could do for him.

His hands trembled slightly as he separated out the photographs of Amanda Powell.

He knew everything about her, including where she lived and that she lived alone.

As far as Terry could remember, it had happened two weeks after his fourteenth birthday, during the last weekend in February. The weather had been bitter for several days, and tempers in the warehouse were frayed. It was always worse when it was cold, he explained, because if they didn't go daily to one of the soup kitchens for hot food, survival became impossible. More often than not, the older ones and the madder ones refused to emerge from whatever cocoon they had made for themselves, so Terry and Tom took it upon themselves to bully them into moving. But, as Terry said, it was a quick way to make enemies, and Billy was more easily riled than most.

'One of the reasons Tom didn't want me calling the coppers this afternoon was because of what's stashed away in that warehouse.' He produced a small wad of silver foil from his pocket and placed it on the table. 'I do puff' – he nodded to the wad – 'and maybe some E if I go to a rave. But that's kids' stuff compared to what some of them are on. There's bodies all over the shop most days, stoned on anything from jellies to H, and half the bastards don't even live there but come in off the streets for a fix because they reckon it's safer. And then there's the nicked stuff – booze and fags and the like – that people have hidden in the rubble. You have to be bloody careful not to go stumbling on someone's stash or you get a knife in the ribs the way Walter did. It can get pretty bad sometimes. This last week there's been two beatings and the stabbing. It gets to you after a while.'

'Is that why you called the police today?'

'Yeah, and because of Billy. I've been thinking about him a lot recently.' He returned to his story. 'Anyway, it were no different last February – worse, if anything, because it were colder than now, so there were more bodies than usual. If they slept on the streets, they froze where they lay, so Tom and the others let them doss inside.'

'Why didn't they go to the government-run hostels?

Surely a bed there has to be better than a floor in a warehouse?'

'Why'd you think?' said Terry scathingly. 'We're talking druggies and psychos who don't even trust their own fucking shadows.' He fingered the silver-foil wad. 'Tom was doing really well out of it. He'd let any sodding bastard in as long as he got something in exchange. He even took a guy's coat once because it was the only thing he had, and the poor bloke froze to death during the night. So Tom had him carried into the street – like he was going to do with Walter – in case the cops came in. And that's what made Billy flip his lid. He went ballistic and said it all had to stop.'

'What did he do?' prompted Deacon when the boy didn't go on.

'The worst thing he could've done. He started breaking people's bottles, and searching the rubble for stashes, and yelling that we had to get rid of the evil before it swallowed us up. So I jumped the silly bugger and tied him up in my doss before one of the psychos could kill him, and that's when he started on me.' Terry reached for another cigarette and lit it with a hand that shook slightly. 'Even you'd've said he was a nutter if you'd seen him that day. He was off his sodding rocker – shaking, screaming—' The boy pulled a wry face. 'See, once he got going he couldn't stop. He'd go on and on till he got so tired he'd give up. But he wouldn't give up this time. He kept spitting at me, and saying that I was the worst kind of scum, and when I didn't take no notice of that he started yelling out that I was a rent-boy and that anyone who wanted a bit of my arse should just come in the tent and take it.' He drew heavily on his cigarette. 'I wanted to kill him, so I put my hands round his neck and squeezed.'

'What stopped you?'

'Nothing. I went on squeezing till I thought he was dead.' He fell into a long silence which Deacon let drift. 'Then I got scared and didn't know what to do, so I untied him and pushed him about a bit to see if he really was dead, and the bugger opened his eyes and smiled at me. And that's when he told me about this bloke he'd killed, and how anger made people do things that could ruin their lives. Then he said he wanted to show the gods that it was his fault and not mine, so he went outside and stuck his hand in the fire.'

Deacon wished there had been a woman there to hear Terry's story, one who would have wrapped him in her arms and petted him, and told him there was nothing to worry about, for that most obvious course of action was denied to him. He could only look away from the tears that brightened the boy's eyes and talk prosaically about the mechanics of how to dry Terry's wet clothes overnight without the benefit of a tumble-drier.

Reg brought up Barry's tea and placed the mug on the desk beside the book his wife had bought. It was lying face down and he pointed to a quote on the back of it. '*Immensely readable*. Charles Lamb, THE STREET.'

'The wife is always happier with a recommendation,' he said, 'but, as I pointed out, it's surprisingly short for Mr Lamb. If he likes a book, he tends to go overboard.

Could "immensely readable" be the only words of praise in the review, I wonder? An example, perhaps, of a publisher's creative *dis*counting?'

One of the reasons why Reg enjoyed Barry's company so much was that Barry allowed him to practise his ponderous wit, and Barry chuckled dutifully as he picked up the paperback and turned to the imprint page. 'First published by Macmillan in 1994, so the review will have come out last year. I'll find it for you,' he offered. 'Consider it a small thank you for the book and the tea.'

'It could be interesting,' said Reg prophetically.

... Another mixed bag of a book is Roger Hyde's **Unsolved Mysteries of the Twentieth Century** (published by Macmillan at £15.99). Immensely readable, it nevertheless disappoints because, as the title suggests, it raises too many unanswered questions and ignores the fact that other writers have already shed light on some of these 'unsolved' mysteries. There are the infamous Digby murders of 1933, when Gilbert and Fanny Digby and their three young children were found dead in their beds of arsenic poisoning one April morning with nothing to suggest who murdered them or why. Hyde describes the background to the case in meticulous detail – Gilbert and Fanny's histories, the names of all those known to have visited the house in the days preceding the murders, the crime scene itself – but he fails to mention M. G. Dunner's book **Sweet Fanny Digby** (Gollancz, 1963) which contained evidence that Fanny Digby, who had a history of depression, had been seen to soak flypaper in an enamel bowl the day before she and her family were found dead. There is the case of the diplomat Peter Fenton, who walked out of his house in July 1988 after his wife Verity committed suicide. Again, Hyde describes the background to these events in detail, referring to the Driberg syndicate and Fenton's access to NATO secrets, but he makes no mention of Anne Cattrell's Sunday Times feature '**The truth about Verity Fenton**' (17 June 1990) which revealed the appalling brutality suffered by Verity at the hands of Geoffrey Standish, her first husband, before his convenient death in a hit-and-run accident in 1971. If, as Anne Cattrell claims, this was no accident, and if Verity did indeed meet Fenton six years earlier than either of them ever admitted, then the solution to her suicide and his disappearance lies in Geoffrey Standish's coffin and not in Nathan Driberg's prison cell . . .

Out of interest, Barry searched the microfiche files for the *Sunday Times* of 17 June 1990. He held his breath as Anne Cattrell's feature appeared with a full-face photograph of Peter Fenton, OBE.

He was as sure as he could be that he was looking at Billy Blake.

The truth about Verity Fenton
by Anne Cattrell

There have been few more effective smoke-screens than that thrown up by Peter Fenton when he vanished from his house on 3 July 1988, leaving his wife's dead body on the marital bed. It began as a sensational Lucan-style murder hunt until Verity Fenton was found to have committed suicide. There followed a rampage through Peter's history, looking for mistresses and/or treachery, when it was discovered that he had access to NATO secrets. Interest centred on his sudden trip to Washington, and easy links were drawn with the anonymous members of the Driberg syndicate.

And where did Verity Fenton's suicide feature in all this? Barely at all is the answer because minds were focused on Peter's inexplicable disappearance and not on the reasons why a 'neurotic' woman should want to kill herself. The coroner's verdict was 'suicide while the balance of her mind was disturbed', relying largely on her daughter's evidence that she had been 'unnaturally depressed' while Peter was in Washington. Yet no real explanation for her depression was sought, as the assumption seems to have been that Peter's disappearance meant that her reference in her suicide note to his betrayals was true, and these were shocking enough to drive a woman to suicide.

Two years on from these bizarre events of July 1988, it is worth reassessing what is known about Peter and Verity Fenton. Perhaps the first thing to strike anyone researching this story is the complete lack of evidence to show that Peter Fenton was a traitor. He certainly had access to confidential NATO information during 1985–7, but sources within the organization admit that three different investigations have failed to trace any leakage of information to him or to his desk.

By contrast, there is a

wealth of evidence about his 'sudden' trip to Washington at the end of June, which was painted as a 'fishing' expedition to find out if Driberg was about to name his associates. The details of the trip were made available at the time by his immediate superior at the Foreign Office but they were ignored in the scramble to prove Fenton a traitor. The facts are that he was briefed on 6 June to attend high-level discussions in Washington from 29 June to 2 July. It is difficult now to understand how three weeks' notification came to be interpreted as 'sudden' or why, if he *were* part of the Driberg syndicate, he should have waited until eight weeks after Driberg's arrest to go 'fishing'.

The Fenton tragedy takes on a very different perspective if suggestions that Peter was a traitor are dismissed. The question that must then be asked is: what were the betrayals that Verity talked about in her suicide note? She wrote: '*Forgive me, I can't bear it any more, darling. Please don't blame yourself. Your betrayals are nothing compared with mine.*'

But why have Verity's own betrayals been so consistently under-examined? The simple answer is that, as the wife of a diplomat, she was always less interesting than her husband. What or who could a 'neurotic' woman possibly have betrayed that could compete with treachery in the Foreign Office? Yet it was imperative, even in 1988, that her betrayals be examined because she claimed they were worse than her husband's, and *he* was branded a spy.

Born Verity Parnell in London on 28 September 1937, she was brought up alone by her mother after her father, Colonel Parnell, died in 1940 during the evacuation from Dunkirk. She and her mother are believed to have spent the war years in Suffolk but returned to London in 1945. Verity was enrolled at a preparatory school before transferring to the Mary Bartholomew School for Girls in Barnes in May 1950. Although considered bright enough to go on to university, she chose instead to marry Geoffrey Standish, a handsome, 32-year-old stockbroker who was fourteen years her senior, in August 1955. The marriage caused an estrangement between herself and her mother, and it is not clear whether she saw Mrs Parnell again before the woman's death some time in the late fifties. Verity gave birth to a daughter, Marilyn, in 1960 and a son, Anthony, in 1966.

The marriage was a disaster. Geoffrey was described, even by close friends, as 'unpredictable'. He was a gambler, a womanizer and a drunk, and it soon became clear to those who knew him that he was taking out his frustrations on his young wife. There was a history of 'accidents', days of indisposition, a reluctance to do anything that might upset Geoffrey, an obsessive protectiveness towards her children. It is not surprising then that, according to one of her neighbours, Verity described her husband's death in March 1971 as a 'blessed relief'.

Like so much in this story the details surrounding Geoffrey's death are obscure. The only verifiable facts are these: he had arranged to spend the weekend alone with friends in Huntingdon; he phoned them at 5.00 p.m. on the Friday night to say he wouldn't be with them until the following day; at 6.30 a.m. on the Saturday, a police patrol recorded his car abandoned with an empty petrol tank beside the A11 near Newmarket; at 10.30 a.m. his bruised and battered body was found sprawled in a ditch some two miles up the road; his injuries were consistent with having been run over by a car.

On the face of it, it was a straightforward case of hit-and-run while Geoffrey was walking through the dark in search of petrol, but because of the last-minute alterations in his plans, the police attempted to establish why he was in the vicinity of Newmarket. They had no success with that line of enquiry, but in the course of their investigation they unearthed the unpalatable details of the man's character and life-style. Although they were never able to prove it, it is clear from the reports that the Cambridgeshire police believed he was murdered.

Verity herself had a cast-iron alibi. She was admitted to St Thomas's Hospital on the Wednesday before Geoffrey's death with a broken collar-bone, fractured ribs and a perforated lung, and was not discharged until the Sunday. Her children were being cared for by a neighbour, so there is some doubt about Geoffrey's whereabouts on the Friday. Certainly he did not go to work that day, and this led to police speculation that someone, whose sympathies lay with Verity, removed him from his house during the Thursday night and cold-bloodedly planned his murder over the Friday.

Unfortunately, from the police point of view, no such sympathizer could be traced, and the file was closed through lack of evidence. The coroner recorded a verdict of 'man-slaughter by person or persons unknown', and Geoffrey Standish's prema-ture death remains unpunished to this day.

Now, however, with our knowledge of the events of 3 July 1988 it is logical to look back from the suicide of a desperate woman and the disappearance of her second husband to Geoffrey's death in 1971, and ask whether the person whose sympathies lay with Verity was a young and impressionable Cambridge undergraduate called Peter Fenton. Newmarket is less than 20 miles from Cambridge, and Peter was known to make frequent visits to the family of a friend from his Winchester College days who lived ten doors away from Geoffrey and Verity Standish in Cadogan Square. There is no evidence to rebut Peter's and Verity's own claims that their first meeting was at a party at Peter's friend's house in 1978, but it would be curious if their paths hadn't crossed earlier. Certainly, the friend, Harry Grisham, remembers the Standishes being regular guests at his parents' dinner parties.

But, assuming Peter's

involvement, what could have happened seventeen years after Geoffrey's murder to drive Verity into killing herself and Peter into vanishing? Did one of them betray the other inadvertently? Had Verity been ignorant of what Peter had done, and learned by accident that she'd married her first husband's murderer? We may never know, but it is a strange coincidence that two days before Peter left for Washington the following advertisement appeared in the personal column of *The Times*:

'**Geoffrey Standish**. Will anyone knowing anything about the murder of Geoffrey Standish on the A11 near Newmarket 10.3.71 please write to Box 431.'

Chapter Eleven

TERRY WAS PUT out to discover that his clothes were still wet when he finally stumbled out of his bedroom in an old T-shirt and shorts of Deacon's, rubbing his shaven head and yawning sleep away. 'I can't go out in your God-awful stuff, Mike. I mean, I've got a reputation to consider. Know what I'm saying? You'll have to go shopping on your own while I wait for this lot to dry.'

'Okay.' Deacon consulted his watch. 'I'd better get moving then or I'll miss the chance to break Hugh's nose.'

'You really going to do that?'

'Sure. I was also planning to buy you some new gear for a Christmas present, but if you're not there to try it on—' He shrugged. 'I'll get you some reading books instead.'

Terry was back, fully dressed, in under three minutes. 'Where did you put my coat?'

'I chucked it in the bin downstairs while you were having your bath.'

'What you want to do that for?'

'It had Walter's blood all over it.' He took a Barbour from a hook on the wall. 'You can borrow this till we buy you a new one.'

'I can't wear that,' said Terry in disgust, refusing to take it. 'Jesus, Mike, I'll look like one of those poncy gits who drive around in Range Rovers. Supposing we meet someone I know?'

'Frankly,' growled Deacon, 'I'm more concerned about meeting someone *I* know. I haven't worked out yet how to explain why a foul-mouthed, shaven-headed thug is (A) staying in my flat and (B) wearing my clothes.'

Terry put on the Barbour with bad grace. 'Considering how much of my puff you smoked last night, you ought to be in a better mood.'

Barry lay in bed and listened to his mother's heavy tread on the stairs. He held his breath while she held hers on the other side of his door. 'I know you're awake,' she said in the strangulated voice that seemed to start somewhere in her fat stomach and squeeze up out of her blubbery mouth. The door handle rattled. 'Why have you locked the door?' The voice dropped to a menacing whisper. 'If you're playing with yourself again, Barry, I'll find out.'

He didn't answer, only stared at the door while his fingers gripped and squeezed her imaginary neck. He fantasized about how easy it would be to kill her and hide her body somewhere out of sight – in the front parlour, perhaps, where it could sit for months on end with no visitors to disturb it. Why should someone so unlovely and unloved be allowed to live? And who would miss her?

Not her son . . .

Barry fumbled for his glasses and brought his world back into focus. He noticed with alarm that his hands were trembling again.

'Why haven't you ever been arrested?' asked Deacon as Terry selected a pair of Levis, saying they'd be 'a doddle to nick'. (He made a habit of locating security cameras and staying blind-side of them, Deacon noticed.)

'What makes you think I ain't?'

'You'd have been sent back into care.'

The boy shook his head. 'Not unless I told them the truth about myself, which I ain't never done. Sure, I've been arrested, but I was always with old Billy when it happened so he took the rap. He reckoned I'd have trouble with poofs if I went into an adult prison, or be sent back to the shirt-lifter if I gave my right name, so it were him what did the time and not me.' His gaze shifted restlessly about the shop. 'How about a jacket then? They're on the far side.' He set off purposefully.

Deacon followed behind. Were all adolescents so ruthlessly self-centred? He had an unpleasant picture of this terrible child latching on to protectors like a leech in order to suck them dry, and he realized that Lawrence's advice about keeping one step ahead was about as useful as pissing in the wind. Any half-way decent man with a sense of moral duty was putty in Terry's hands, he thought.

'I like this one,' said Terry, taking a donkey-jacket off

a coat hanger and thrusting his arms into the sleeves. 'What d'you think?'

'It's about ten times too big for you.'

'I'm still growing.'

'I'm damned if I'll be seen walking around with a mobile barrage balloon.'

'You ain't got the first idea of fashion, have you? Everyone wears things big these days.' He tried the next size down. 'Tight stuff's what guys like you pranced around in in the seventies, along with flares and beads and long hair and that. Billy said it was good to be young then, but I reckon you must've looked like a load of poofs.'

Deacon lifted his lip in a snarl. 'Well, you've got nothing to worry about then,' he said. 'You look like a paid-up member of the National Front.'

Terry looked pleased with himself. 'I ain't got a problem with that.'

Barry stood in the doorway and watched the back of his mother's head as she was slumped on a chair in front of the television, her feet propped on a stool. Sparse, bristly hair poked out of her pink scalp and cavernous snores roared from her mouth. The untidy room smelt of her farts, and a sense of injustice overwhelmed him. It was a cruel fate that had taken his father and left him to the mercies of a . . .

his fingers flexed involuntarily.

. . . *PIG!*

*

211

Terry found a shop that was selling Christmas decorations and posters. He selected a reproduction of Picasso's *Woman in a Chemise* and insisted Deacon buy it.

'Why that one?' Deacon asked him.

'She's beautiful.'

It was certainly a beautiful painting, but whether or not the woman herself was beautiful depended on taste. It marked the transition between Picasso's blue and rose periods, so the subject had the cold, emaciated melancholy of the earlier period enlivened by the pink and ochre hues of the later. 'Personally, I prefer a little more flesh,' said Deacon, 'but I'm happy to have her on my wall.'

'Billy drew her more than anyone else,' said Terry surprisingly.

'On the pavements?'

'No, on the bits of paper we used to burn afterwards. He copied her off of a postcard to begin with but he got so good at it that he could do her out of his head in the end.' He traced his finger along the clear lines of the woman's profile and torso. 'See, she's real simple to draw. Like Billy said, there's no mess in this picture.'

'Unlike the Leonardo?'

'Yeah.'

It was true, thought Deacon. Picasso's woman was glorious in her simplicity – and so much more delicate than da Vinci's plumper Madonna. 'Maybe you should become an artist, Terry. You seem to have an eye for a good painting.'

'I've been up Green Park once or twice to look at the stuff on the railings, but that's crap. Billy always said he'd take me to a proper gallery but he never got around to it. They probably wouldn't've let us in anyway, not with Billy roaring drunk most of the time.' He was flicking through the poster rack. 'What d'you reckon to this? You reckon this painter saw hell the same way Billy's lady did? Like being alone and afraid in a place that doesn't make sense to you?'

He had pulled out Edvard Munch's *The Scream* with its powerful, twisted imagery of a man screaming in terror before the elemental forces of nature. 'You really do have an eye,' said Deacon in admiration. 'Did Billy draw this one as well?'

'No, he wouldn't have liked it. There's too much red in it. He hated red because it reminded him of blood.'

'Well, I'm not having that on my wall or I'll think about hell every time I look at it.' *And blood*, he thought. He wished he and Billy had less in common.

They settled on reproductions of the Picasso (for its simplicity), Manet's *Luncheon in the Studio* (for its harmonious symmetry – 'That one works real good,' said Terry), Hieronymus Bosch's *The Garden of Earthly Delights* (for its colour and interest – 'It's well brilliant,' said Terry) and finally Turner's *The Fighting Téméraire* (for its perfection in every respect – 'Shit!' said Terry. 'That's one beautiful picture').

'What happened to Billy's postcard of the Picasso?' asked Deacon as he was paying.

'Tom burned it.'

'Why?'

'Because he was well out of order. He and Billy were drunk as lords and they'd been having a row about women. Tom said Billy was too ugly ever to've had one, and Billy said he couldn't be as ugly as Tom's missus or Tom wouldn't've walked out on her. Everyone laughed and Tom was gutted.'

'What did that have to do with the postcard?'

'Nothing much, except Billy really loved it. He kissed it sometimes when he was drunk. Tom was that riled at having his missus insulted, he went for something he knew'd send Billy mad. It worked, too. Billy damn near throttled Tom for burning it, then he burst into tears and said truth was dead anyway, so nothing mattered any more. And that were the end of it.'

It was six years since Deacon had last visited the Red Lion. It had been his local when he and Julia had lived in Fulham and Hugh had been in the habit of meeting him there a couple of times a month on his way home to Putney. The outside had changed very little over the years and Deacon half-expected to find the same landlord and the same regulars inside when he pushed open the doors. But it was a room full of strangers where the only recognizable face was Hugh's. He was sitting at a table in the far corner, and he raised a tentative hand in greeting when he saw Deacon.

'Hello, Michael,' he said, standing up as they approached. 'I wasn't sure if you'd come.'

'Wouldn't have missed it for the world. It might be the only chance I ever get to flatten you.' He beckoned Terry forward. 'Meet Terry Dalton. He's staying with me for Christmas. Terry, meet Hugh Tremayne, my brother-in-law.'

Terry gave his amiable grin and stuck out a bony hand. 'Hi. How ya doing?'

Hugh looked surprised but shook the offered hand. 'Very well, thank you. Are we – er – related?'

Terry appraised his round face and overweight figure. 'I don't reckon so, not unless you were putting it about a bit in Birmingham fifteen years ago. Nah,' he said. 'I think my dad was probably a bit taller and thinner. No offence meant, of course.'

Deacon gave a snort of laughter. 'I think Hugh was wondering if you were related to my second wife, Terry.'

'Oh, right. Why didn't he say that then?'

Deacon turned to the wall and banged his head against it for several seconds. Finally he took a deep breath, mopped his eyes with his handkerchief and faced the room again. 'It's a touchy subject,' he explained. 'My family didn't like Clara very much.'

'What was wrong with her?'

'Nothing,' said Hugh firmly, afraid that Deacon was going to embarrass him and Terry with references to tarts and sluts. 'What are you both having? Lager?' He escaped to the bar while they divested themselves of their coats and sat down.

'You can't hit *him*,' said Terry. 'Okay, he's a pillock, but he's about six inches shorter than you and ten years older. What did he do, anyway?'

Deacon propped his feet on a chair and laced his hands behind his head. 'He insulted me in my mother's house and then ordered me out of it.' He smiled slightly. 'I swore I'd deck him the next time I saw him, and this is the next time.'

'Well, I wouldn't do it if I were you. It don't make you any bigger, you know. I felt well gutted after what I did to Billy.' He nodded his thanks as Hugh returned with their drinks.

There was a painful silence while Hugh sought for something to say and Deacon grinned at the ceiling, thoroughly enjoying his brother-in-law's discomfort.

Terry offered Hugh a cigarette, which he refused. 'Maybe if you apologized, he'd forget the beating,' he suggested, lighting his own cigarette. 'Billy always said it were harder to hit someone you'd had a natter with. That's why guys who do violence tell people to keep their mouths shut. They're scared shitless of losing their bottle.'

'Who's Billy?'

'An old geezer I used to know. He reckoned talking was better than fighting, then he'd get rat-arsed and start attacking people. Mind, he were a bit of a nutter, so you couldn't really blame him. His advice was good, though.'

'Stop meddling, Terry,' said Deacon mildly. 'I want some answers before we get anywhere near an apology.' He lowered his feet from the chair and leaned across the table. 'What's going on, Hugh? Why am I so popular suddenly?'

Hugh took a mouthful of lager while he weighed up his answer. 'Your mother isn't well,' he said carefully.

'So Emma told me.'

'And she's keen to bury the hatchet with you.'

'Really?' He reached for the cigarette packet. 'Would that explain the daily phone messages at my office?'

Hugh looked surprised. 'Has she?'

'No, of course she hasn't. I haven't heard a word from her in five years, not since she accused me of killing my father. Which is odd, don't you think, if she wants to bury the hatchet?' He bent his head to the match.

'You know your mother as well as I do.' Hugh sighed. 'In sixteen years I've never heard her admit to being wrong about anything, and I can't see her starting now. I'm afraid you're expected to make the first move.'

Deacon's eyes narrowed suspiciously. 'This isn't what Ma wants, is it? It's what Emma wants. Is she feeling guilty about stripping Ma of her capital? Is that what this is about?'

Hugh toyed unhappily with his beer glass. 'Frankly, I've had about as much of your family squabbles as I can take, Michael. It's like living in the middle of a war zone being married to a Deacon.'

Deacon gave a low chuckle. 'Be grateful you weren't around when my father was alive then. It was worse.' He tapped his cigarette against the ashtray. 'You might as well spit it out. I'm not going anywhere near Ma unless I know why Emma wants me to.'

Again, Hugh appeared to weigh his answer. 'Oh, to hell with it!' he said abruptly. 'Your father did make a new will. Emma found it, or should I say the pieces, when she was sorting through your mother's things while she was in hospital. She asked us to pay her bills and keep everything ticking over while she was off games. I suppose she'd forgotten that the will was still sitting

217

there, although why she didn't burn it or throw it away—'
He gave a hollow laugh. 'We stuck it back together
again. His first two bequests were made out of duty. He
left the cottage in Cornwall to Penelope plus enough
investments to provide her with an income of ten thousand a year, and he left Emma a lump sum of twenty
thousand. The third bequest was made out of love. He
left you the farmhouse and the residue of the estate
because, and I quote, "Michael is the only member of
my family who cares whether I live or die." He made it
two weeks before he shot himself, and we assume it was
your mother who tore it up as she's the only one who
benefited under the old will.'

Deacon smoked thoughtfully for a moment or two.
'Did he appoint David and Harriet Price as executors?'

'Yes.'

'Well, at least that vindicates poor old David.' He
thought back to the furious row his mother had had with
their then next-door neighbours when David Price had
dared to suggest that Francis Deacon had talked about
making a new will with him as executor. '*Show it to me,*'
she had said, '*tell me what's in it.*' And David had had to
admit that he had never seen it, only agreed in principle
to act as executor should Francis revoke his previous will.
'Who drew it up?'

'We think your father did it himself. It's in his
handwriting.'

'Is it legal?'

'A solicitor friend of ours says it's properly worded
and properly witnessed. The witnesses were two of the
librarians in Bedford general library. Our friend's only

caveat was whether your father was in sound mind when he made it, bearing in mind he shot himself two weeks later.' He shrugged. 'But, according to Emma, he had been right as rain for months prior to his suicide and only became really depressed the day before he pulled the trigger.'

Deacon glanced at Terry who was wide-eyed with curiosity. 'It's a long story,' he said, 'which you don't want to hear.'

'You can shorten it, can't you? I mean, you know all about me. Seems only fair I should know a bit about you.'

It was on the tip of Deacon's tongue to say he didn't even know what Terry's real name was, but he decided against it. 'My father was a manic depressive. He was supposed to take drugs to control the condition, but he wasn't very reliable and the rest of us suffered.' He saw that Terry didn't understand. 'Manic depression is typified by mood swings. You can be high as a kite in a manic phase – it's a bit like being stoned – and suicidal in a depressed phase.' He drew on his cigarette then ground the butt out under his heel. 'On Christmas Day 1976, while depressed, my father put his shotgun in his mouth at four o'clock in the morning and blew his head away.' He smiled slightly. 'It was very quick, very loud and very messy, and it's why I try to forget that Christmas even exists.'

Terry was impressed. 'Shit!' he said.

'It's also why Emma and Michael are so difficult to live with,' said Hugh drily. 'They're both scared to death they've inherited manic depressive psychosis, which is why they resist feeling happy about anything and view mild *un*happiness as the onset of clinical depression.'

'It's in the genes then, is it? Billy were big on genes. He always said you couldn't escape what your parents programmed into you.'

'No, it's not in the genes,' said Hugh crossly. 'There's evidence suggesting hereditary predisposition but innumerable other factors would have to come into play to precipitate the same psychosis in Emma and Michael as occurred in Francis.'

Deacon laughed. 'That means I'm not a nutter yet,' he told Terry. 'Hugh's a civil servant, so he likes to be precise in his definitions.'

Terry frowned. 'Yeah, but why'd your mother accuse you of killing your dad if he topped himself?'

Deacon drank his lager in silence.

'Because she's a bitch,' said Hugh flatly.

Deacon stirred himself. 'She said it because it's true. He told me at eleven o'clock on Christmas Eve that he wanted to die, and I gave him the go-ahead to do it. Five hours later he was dead. My mother thinks I should have persuaded him out of it.'

'Why didn't you?'

'Because he asked me not to.'

'Yeah, but—' The boy's puzzled eyes searched Deacon's face. 'Didn't you mind if he died? I was well gutted every time Billy tried to hurt himself. I mean, you feel responsible like.'

Deacon held his gaze for a moment then looked down at his glass. 'It's a good expression – gutted. It's exactly how I felt when I heard the shot. And, yes, of course I

220

minded, but I'd stopped him before, and this time he said he was going to do it anyway and would rather do it with my blessing than without. So I gave him my blessing.' He shook his head. 'I hoped he wouldn't go through with it, but I wanted him to know I wouldn't condemn him if he did.'

'Yeah, but—' said Terry again. He was more disturbed by the story than Deacon would have expected, and he wondered if there were resonances in it of his friendship with Billy. Had Terry lied about Billy not trying to kill himself? he wondered. Or perhaps, like Deacon, he had lost interest and had aided and abetted a suicide through apathy?

'But what?' he asked.

'Why didn't you say something to your mum, give her a chance like to stop him?'

Deacon looked at his watch. 'How about we leave that question till later?' he suggested. 'We've still got food to buy and I haven't settled what I'm going to do to Hugh's nose yet.' He lit another cigarette and studied his brother-in-law through the smoke for a second or two. 'Why didn't Emma throw the pieces of this will away when she found them?' He smiled rather cynically at Hugh's expression. 'Let me guess. She didn't realize he'd only left her twenty thousand until she'd stuck it back together again, by which time you and your girls had seen it too.'

'She was curious. She'd have brought it home anyway. But, yes, she hoped – we both hoped – that he'd left her enough to wipe out the debt we owe your mother. As things stand, Penelope's used money that's rightfully yours, so we're actually in debt to you. And I swear to you, Michael, it's not money we even asked for. Your mother went on and on and on about how she wanted to do something for the only grandchildren she was going to have, then I mentioned one day that we were worried about Antonia's poor grades, and that was it. Penelope set up an educational trust and Antonia and Jessica were in private boarding school within a couple of months.'

Deacon took that with a pinch of salt. Knowing Hugh and Emma, there would have been endless little hints until Penelope paid up. 'Are they doing well?'

'Yes. Ant's doing A levels and Jesse's doing GCSEs.' He rubbed a worried hand across his bald head. 'That trust was set up to pay the equivalent of twelve years' schooling – five years for Ant because she was two years older when it started, and seven for Jesse – and they've already had nearly ten between them. We're talking a lot of money, Michael. You've probably no idea how expensive private boarding education is.'

'Let me guess. Upwards of a hundred and fifty thousand so far?' He lifted an amused eyebrow. 'You obviously didn't read my piece on selective education. I researched the whole subject in depth, including cost. Has it been money well spent?'

Hugh shrugged unhappily, forced to consider his daughters' merits. 'They're very bright,' he said, but Deacon had the impression he would've liked to have said they were nice. 'We need to sort this out, Michael. Frankly, it's a nightmare. As I see it, the situation is this.

Your mother deliberately tore up your father's will and stole her children's inheritance, for which she will be prosecuted if the whole thing's made public. She has materially altered your father's estate by selling the cottage in Cornwall and by setting up a trust fund for the girls. Against that, had you inherited what Francis left you, presumably Julia would have taken half its value in her divorce settlement and Clara would have taken half of what was left in hers, leaving you with a quarter share of what you inherited. For all I know, they may still be entitled to do that.' He raised his hands in a gesture of despair. 'So where do we go from here? What do we do?'

'You've left out your resentment at paying through the nose for Ma's private nursing care,' murmured Deacon. 'Doesn't that play a part in this complicated equation?'

'Yes,' Hugh admitted honestly. 'We accepted the trust money in good faith, believing it to be a gift, but the quid pro quo seems to be that Emma and I must fork out indefinitely for a live-in nurse, which we can't afford. Your mother claims she's dying, which means the expenditure won't go on for very much longer, but her doctors say she's good for another ten years.' He pressed finger and thumb to the bridge of his nose. 'I've tried to explain to her that if we could afford that level of private nursing care, we wouldn't have had to use her money to pay the girls' school fees, but she won't listen to reason. She refuses to sell her house, refuses to come and live with us. She just makes sure the weekly bill is sent to our address.' His voice hardened. 'And it's driving me mad. If I thought I could get away with it, I'd have put a pillow over her face months ago and done us all a favour.'

Deacon studied him curiously. 'What do you expect me to achieve by talking to her? If she won't listen to you, she certainly won't listen to me.'

Hugh sighed. 'The obvious way out of the mess is for her to sell the farm, invest the capital and move into a nursing home somewhere. But Emma thinks she's more likely to accept that suggestion if it comes from you.'

'Particularly if I hold Pa's will over her head?'

Hugh nodded.

'It might work.' Deacon reached for his coat and stood up. 'Assuming I was remotely interested in helping you and Emma out of your hole. But I have a real problem understanding why you think you're entitled to so much of Pa's wealth. Here's an alternative suggestion. Sell your own house and pay Ma back what you owe her.' His smile was not a friendly one. 'At least it means you'll be able to look her in the eye the next time you call her a bitch.'

Chapter Twelve

DEACON SELECTED A frozen turkey and chucked it into the supermarket trolley. He had been like a bear with a sore head since they'd left the pub, and Terry had been careful not to antagonize him further since remarking in the car that it wasn't surprising Deacon's old man had shot himself if all the women in his family were such cows.

'What would you know about it?' Deacon had asked in an icy voice. 'Did Billy make life so difficult for you that no one wanted to know you? Would it have mattered anyway? You can't get much lower than the gutter in all conscience.'

They hadn't spoken for half an hour, but now Deacon leaned on the trolley bar and turned to the youngster. 'I'm sorry, Terry. I was out of order. It doesn't matter how angry I was, it was no excuse for rudeness.'

'It were true, though. You can't get no lower than the gutter, and it ain't rude to tell the truth.'

Deacon smiled. 'There's a lot lower than the gutter. There's the sewer and there's hell, and you're a long way from both.' He straightened. 'You're not in the gutter either, not while you're under my roof, so choose your favourite foods and we'll eat like kings.'

After five minutes he returned to something that had been nagging at him. 'Did Billy ever tell you how old he was?'

'Nope. All I know is he was old enough to be my grandfather.'

Deacon shook his head. 'According to the pathologist, he was somewhere in his mid-forties. Not much older than me, in fact.'

Terry was genuinely astonished. He stood open-mouthed with a packet of cornflakes in his hand. 'You've gotta be joking. Shit! He looked well ancient. I reckoned he was the same age as Tom, near enough, and Tom's sixty-eight.'

'But he said it was good to be young in the seventies.' He knocked the cornflakes out of the boy's hand into the trolley. 'And the seventies were only twenty years ago.'

'Yeah, but I wasn't born then, was I?'

'What's that got to do with anything?'

'It means it was a long time ago.'

'Why did Billy say truth was dead?' asked Deacon as they drove home after packing the boot with food. 'What's that got to do with a postcard?' He recalled a line from Billy's interview with Dr Irvine. '*I am still searching for truth.*'

'How the hell should I know?'

Deacon held on to his patience with difficulty. 'You

lived with the man for two years on and off but, as far as I can see, you never questioned a single damn thing he said. Where was your curiosity? You ask *me* enough bloody questions.'

'Yeah, but you answer them,' said Terry, smoothing the front of his donkey-jacket with satisfaction. 'Billy got really angry if I said "why" too many times, so I gave up asking. It wasn't worth the aggro.'

'Presumably he said it in the present tense?'

'What?'

'"Truth *is* dead so nothing matters any more."'

'Yeah, I already told you that.'

'Another word for truth is verity,' mused Deacon gnawing at it like a dog with a bone. 'Verity is a girl's name.' He glanced sideways. 'Do you think V stood for Verity? In other words when he said, "Truth is dead," did he mean "Verity is dead"? *I am still searching for Verity?* 'And don't say, "How the hell should I know?" because I might be inclined to stop the car and ram the turkey down your throat.'

'I'm not a fucking mind reader,' said Terry plaintively. 'If Billy said, "Truth is dead," I reckon he meant, "Truth is dead."'

'Yes, but *why?*' growled Deacon. 'Which truth was he talking about? Absolute truth, relative truth, plain truth, gospel truth? Or was he talking about one particular truth – say, the murder – where the truth had never been uncovered?'

'How the—' Hastily Terry bit his tongue. 'He didn't say.'

'Then I'm going with V for Verity,' said Deacon

decisively. He drew up at some traffic lights. 'I'll go further. I'm betting she looked like the woman in Picasso's painting. Do you think that's a possibility? You said he loved the postcard and kissed it when he was drunk. Doesn't that imply she reminded him of someone?'

'Don't see why,' said Terry matter-of-factly. 'I mean, one of the guys has a picture of Madonna. He's always slobbering over her, but in his wildest dreams he never had a bird like that. I reckon it's the only way he can get a hard-on.'

Deacon let out the clutch. 'There's a difference between a photograph of a living woman who enjoys exploiting male fantasies and a portrait painted nearly a hundred years ago.'

'There probably wasn't at the time,' said Terry, after giving the matter some serious thought. 'I bet Picasso had a hard-on when he was painting his bird, and I bet he hoped other blokes'd get one, too, when they looked at her. I mean, you have to admit she's got nice tits.'

1.00 p.m. – Cape Town, South Africa

'Who *is* that woman?' asked an elderly matron of her daughter, nodding towards the solitary figure at a window table. 'I've seen her here before. She's always on her own, and she always looks as if she'd rather be somewhere else.'

Her daughter followed her gaze. 'Gerry was introduced to her once. I think her name's Felicity Metcalfe.

228

Her husband owns a diamond mine or something. She's absolutely rolling in it, anyway.' She looked with some dissatisfaction on her small solitaire engagement ring.

'I've never seen her with a man.'

The younger woman shrugged. 'Maybe she's divorced. With a face like that, she's almost bound to be.' She smiled unkindly. 'You could cut diamonds with it.'

Her mother subjected the lonely figure to a close scrutiny. 'She is very thin,' she agreed, 'and rather sad too, I think.' She returned to her food. 'It's true what they say, darling – money doesn't buy happiness.'

'Neither does poverty,' said her daughter rather bitterly.

While Terry decorated the flat that afternoon, Deacon sat at the kitchen table and made a stab at drawing conclusions from what little information he had. He threw out questions from time to time. Why did Billy choose to doss in the warehouse? *For the same reason as the rest of us, I guess.* Did he have a thing about rivers? *He never said.* Did he mention the name of a town where he might have lived? *No.* Did he mention a university or a profession or the name of a company he might have worked for? *I don't know any universities, so I wouldn't know, would I?*

'WELL, YOU BLOODY WELL SHOULD!' roared Deacon, losing his temper. 'I have never met anyone who knows as little about what matters as you do.'

Terry poked his head round the kitchen door with a broad grin splitting his face in two. 'You'd be dead in a week if you had to live the way I do.'

'Who says?'

'Me. Any guy who reckons the names of universities are more important than knowing how to graft for food ain't got a chance when the chips are down. What matters is staying alive, and you can't eat fucking universities. D'you want to see what I've done in here? It looks well brilliant.'

He was right. After two years, Deacon's flat had a homely feel about it.

Deacon simplified his notes down to names, ages, places and connecting ideas, and grouped them together logically on a page of A4 paper, putting Billy in the centre. He propped the sheet against the wine bottle. 'You're the artist. See if you can spot patterns. I'll help you with anything you can't manage.' He crossed his arms and watched the boy scrutinize the page, reading words out loud every time Terry pointed a questioning finger.

The Thames (any river?)

Terry Dalton (14)

Tom Beale (68)   Cadogan Square   Paris

The warehouse   HELL   (V) - Verity? - (45+)

SUICIDE   Billy Blake (45)   IDENTITY

MURDER

James Streeter (44)

Amanda Powell (36)

MONEY

W.F. Meredith   Nigel de Vriess (?)
(architects)

Teddington flats   Lowenstein's Bank

Thamesbank Estate   Marianne Filbert (?)

'What's this hang-up with rivers?' Terry asked.

'Amanda said Billy liked to doss down as near the Thames as possible.'

'Who told her that?'

Deacon checked through a transcript he'd made of his recorded conversation with her. 'The police presumably.'

'First I've heard of it. He really hated the river. He moaned about the damp getting into his bones, and said the water reminded him of blood.'

'Why on earth should it remind him of blood?'

'I dunno. It was something to do with the river being the cord between the mother and the baby but I can't remember its name.'

'The umbilical cord.'

'That's it. He said London's full of shit and she sends her shit along the river to infect the innocent places further down.'

'You said he had a thing about genes. Was he drawing an analogy?'

'If you speak English,' said Terry scathingly, 'then I might be able to give you an answer.'

Deacon smiled. 'Do you think he was talking about his own mother? Was he saying that his mother had passed on bad genes to him through the umbilical cord?'

'He only ever mentioned London.'

'Or maybe he meant all parents pass on bad genes?'

'He only ever mentioned London,' repeated Terry stubbornly.

'I heard you the first time. It was a rhetorical question.'

'Jesus! You're so like him. Lahdy-bloody-dah, and

never mind no one knew what the fuck he was talking about.' He pointed to the 45+ beside the name Verity. 'I thought you reckoned V was younger than Billy,' he said, 'so how come you've made her the same age?'

'I've added a plus sign,' said Deacon, 'which means I'm now convinced she was older than he was.' He pulled forward V's letters. 'I was thinking about it last night. There are two ways of reading "your glass shall not persuade you you are old, so long as youth and I are of one date". Either she took the quote verbatim from her correspondent's letter or she reinterpreted it for the purposes of hers. When I first read it, I assumed it was an interpretation because she didn't put it into quotation marks, and in Shakespeare's sonnet it reads: "my glass shall not persuade me I am old", et cetera, et cetera. Now I'm more inclined to think it was a direct quote and her correspondent was talking about *her* age and *her* glass.' He shook his head at Terry's obvious incomprehension. 'Forget it, sunshine. Just accept that the letter makes more sense if V was older than her correspondent. Youth is eternally optimistic, and age is wary, and V seems to be a damn sight warier of revealing their affair than whoever she was writing to.'

'Which was Billy?'

'Probably.'

'But not definitely?'

'Right. He could have found the letters anywhere.'

Terry whistled appreciatively. 'This is well interesting. I'm beginning to wish I'd asked the old bugger a few more questions.'

'Join the club,' murmured Deacon sarcastically.

Terry demanded an explanation of the lower half of the page. Who were de Vriess, Filbert and Streeter? Why were W. F. Meredith, Teddington flats and Thamesbank Estate included? Deacon gave him a summary of the Streeter connection with Amanda Powell.

'Thamesbank Estate is where Amanda lives and Billy died,' he finished. 'Teddington is where she and James were planning a development of flats and W. F. Meredith is the firm she works for. Its offices are in a converted warehouse about two hundred yards from yours.'

'So, are you saying Billy was this Streeter guy?'

'Not unless he had some pretty radical plastic surgery.'

'But you reckon there's a connection?'

'There has to be. The odds against one woman being associated with two men who both dropped out of their lives are so high they're not worth considering. There are a thousand garages between the warehouse and Amanda's estate, so Billy *must* have had a reason for going all the way to hers.' He ran a thoughtful hand around his jawline. 'I can think of three possible explanations. First, some of the letters he liberated from the bins were hers and he found out her address and who she was by reading them. Second, he saw her coming out of the Meredith building, recognized her as someone he'd known in the past and followed her home. Third, somebody *else* recognized her and followed her, then handed that information on to Billy.'

Terry frowned. 'The second one can't be right. I mean, if he recognized Amanda, then she'd've recognized him. And she wouldn't've come round asking about him if she already knew who he was, would she?'

'It depends how much he'd changed. Don't forget, you thought he was twenty years older than he actually was. It may have gone something like this. Out of the blue, Amanda finds a dead wino in her garage who's known to the police as Billy Blake, aged sixty-five. She's sorry but not unduly concerned until she learns that his name was assumed, his age was forty-five, he was dossing near her offices and there was a good chance he had chosen her garage deliberately, at which point she pays for his cremation and goes to great lengths to find out something about him. What does that suggest to you?'

'That she thought Billy was her old man.'

Deacon nodded. 'But she must have realized she was wrong the minute she got hold of the police photographs. So why is she still obsessed with Billy?'

'Maybe you should ask her?'

'I have.' He threw the boy a withering look. 'It's not a question she wants to answer.'

Terry shrugged. 'Maybe she can't. Maybe she's as puzzled by it all as you and me. I mean, she told us she didn't know he was there till he were dead, so he can't have spoken to her. And, see, you've not explained why he went there. If he *did* recognize her, why should that make him want to die in her garage? And if he *didn't* recognize her – well, why'd he want to die in a stranger's garage? Do you get what I'm saying?'

'Yes, but you're assuming she told you the truth. Supposing she was lying about not speaking to him?' Deacon stretched his hands towards the ceiling, easing the muscles of his shoulders. He watched the boy for a moment out of the corner of his eye. 'He must have been in a pretty bad way to die as quickly as he did, so why did you let him go off on his own like that?'

'You can't blame me. Billy never listened to anything I said. In any case, he was okay the last time I saw him.'

'He can't have been, not if he was dead of starvation a few days later.'

'You've got that wrong. None of us'd seen him for about three, four weeks before he pegged it.' The memory seemed to worry him, as if he knew that it was his own apathy that had killed Billy. *Just as Deacon's apathy had killed his father*. 'He buggered off in May some time, and the next we knew was when Tom read in a newspaper that he'd turned up dead in this woman's garage.'

Deacon digested this surprising piece of information in silence for a moment or two. For some reason he had always assumed that Billy had gone directly from the warehouse to the garage. 'Do you know where he went?'

'At the time we thought he was probably banged up in one of the London nicks, but thinking about it after' – he hesitated – 'well, like Tom said, no nick would have let him starve himself, so I guess he was holed up in a place where he just stopped eating.'

'Had he done that before?'

'Sure. Loads of times when he was depressed or he'd had enough of the likes of Denning. But it was never for more than a few days and he always came back. Then I'd get him down to a soup kitchen and feed him up again. I used to look after him pretty damn well, you know, and I was gutted about the way he died. There weren't no need for it.'

'Do you know where he might have gone?'

Terry shook his head. 'Tom reckoned he went out of town, seeing as no one saw hide nor hair of him.'

'Do you know why?'

Another shake of his head.

'What was he doing before he left?'

'Got rat-arsed, same as always.'

'Anything else?'

'Like what?'

'I don't know,' said Deacon, 'but something must have persuaded him to up stumps and vanish for four weeks.' He cupped his hands and beckoned with his fingers. 'Talk to me. Was he begging that day? Did he speak to anyone? Did he see someone he recognized? Did he do anything unusual? Did he say anything before he left? What time did he go? Morning? Evening? *Think*, Terry.'

'The only thing I remember that were different,' said Terry, after obliging Deacon with several seconds of eye-screwing concentration, 'was that he got pretty excited about a newspaper he found in a bin. He used to flick through them, looking at headlines, but this time he read one of the pages and gave himself a headache. He were in a bloody awful mood for the rest of the day, then he passed out on a bottle of Smirnoff. He were gone by the next morning and we never saw him again.'

Chapter Thirteen

AS NEAR AS TERRY could remember, Billy had left some time during the week beginning the fifteenth of May. Having prised this piece of information out of him, Deacon bundled him into the car and drove to the *Street* offices. Terry grumbled the entire way, complaining that pubs and clubs were supposed to be the order of the evening, not looking through newspapers ... Deacon's trouble was he was so old he'd forgotten how to enjoy himself ... The fact that he hated Christmas didn't mean everyone else had to be miserable with him ...

'ENOUGH!' roared his long-suffering host as they approached Holborn. 'This won't take long, so for Christ's sake, shut it! We can go to a pub afterwards.'

'All right, but only if you tell me about your mother.'

'Does the word "silence" make up part of your vocabulary, Terry?'

''Course it does, but you promised to answer my question about not giving her a chance to stop your dad killing himself.'

'It's simple enough,' said Deacon. 'She hadn't spoken

to him for two years, and I couldn't see her starting that night.'

'Didn't they live in the same house?'

'Yes. One at each end. She looked after him, did his washing, cooked his meals, made his bed. She just never spoke to him.'

'That sucks,' said Terry indignantly.

'She could have divorced him and left him to fend for himself,' Deacon pointed out mildly, 'or even had him institutionalized if she'd tried hard enough. That sort of thing was easier twenty years ago.' Briefly, he glanced at the boy's profile. 'He was impossible to live with, Terry – charming to people one day, abusive the next. If he didn't get his own way, he became violent, particularly if he'd been drinking. He couldn't hold down a job, loathed responsibility, but complained endlessly about everyone else's mistakes. Poor old Ma put up with it for twenty-three years before she retreated into silence.' He turned down Farringdon Street. 'She should have done it sooner. The atmosphere improved once the rows stopped.'

'How come he had all this money to leave if he didn't work?'

'He inherited it from his father who happened to own a piece of land that the government needed for the M1. My grandfather made a small fortune out of it and willed it to his only child, along with a rather beautiful farmhouse which has a six-lane motorway at the bottom of its garden.'

'Jesus! And that's what your mother's nicked off of you?'

239

Deacon turned into Fleet Street. 'If she has, she earned it. She sent me and Emma away to boarding school at eight years old so that we wouldn't have to spend too much time under the same roof with Pa.' He drove down the alleyway beside the offices and parked in the empty car park at the back. 'The one reason he and I were still speaking at the end was because I had less to do with him than either Ma or Emma. I avoided the place like the plague, and only ever went home for Christmas. Otherwise I stayed with school and university friends.' He switched off the engine. 'Emma was far more supportive, which is why Pa left her only twenty thousand. He grew to hate her because she took Ma's side.' He turned to the youngster with a faint smile, visible in the backwash of the headlamps. 'You see, none of it's the way you thought it was, Terry. Pa made that second will out of spite, and the chances are he was the one who tore it up anyway. Hugh knows that as well as I do, but Hugh's in a mess and he's looking for a way out.'

'Are all families like yours?'

'No.'

'Well, I don't get it. You sound as though you quite like your mother, so why aren't you speaking to her?'

Deacon switched off the headlights and plunged them into darkness. 'Do you want the twenty-page answer or the three-word answer?'

'Three-word.'

'I'm punishing her.'

*

'What's up with everyone tonight?' asked Glen Hopkins as Deacon signed in. 'I've had Barry Grover here for the last two hours.' He studied Terry with interest. 'I'm beginning to think I'm the only person whose home holds any charms for him.'

Terry smiled engagingly and leaned his elbows on the desk. 'Dad here' – he jerked a thumb at Deacon – 'wanted me to see where he worked. You see, he's pretty choked about the fact Mum's been on the game since he kicked her out, and he wants to show me there are better ways of earning a living.'

Deacon seized his arm and spun him round towards the stairs. 'Don't believe a word of it, Glen. If this git carried even one of my genes, I'd throw myself off the nearest bridge.'

'Mum warned me you'd get violent,' whined Terry. 'She said you always hit first and asked questions later.'

'Shut up, you cretin!'

Terry laughed, and Glen Hopkins watched the two of them vanish up the stairs with a look of intense curiosity on his usually lugubrious face. For the first time that he could remember, Deacon had looked positively cheerful, and Glen began to imagine similarities of bone structure between the man and the boy that didn't exist.

Barry Grover was equally curious about Terry, but he had spent a lifetime masking his true feelings and merely stared at the two from behind his pebble glasses as they barged noisily through the door into the cuttings' library.

He made a strange sight, isolated as he was at a desk in the middle of the darkened room with a pool of lamplight reflecting off his lenses. Indeed his resemblance to some large, shiny-eyed beetle was more pronounced than usual and, with an abrupt movement, Deacon snapped on the overhead lights to dispel the uncomfortable image.

'Hi, Barry,' he said in the artificially hearty tone he always used towards the man, 'meet a friend of mine, Terry Dalton. Terry, meet the eyes of the *Street*, Barry Grover. If you're even remotely interested in photography and photographic art, then this is the guy you should talk to. He knows everything there is to know about it.'

Terry nodded in his friendly fashion.

'Mike's exaggerating,' said Barry dismissively, fearing he was about to be made to look a fool. He had already suffered the humiliation of Glen's knowing looks and poorly disguised curiosity when he arrived. Now he turned his back on the newcomers and pushed the photographs of Amanda Powell under a sheaf of newspaper clippings.

Terry, who was largely insensitive to undercurrents of emotion unless they had a basis in paranoid schizophrenia or drug addiction, wandered over to where Barry was sitting while Deacon got to work on the microfiche monitor in search of newspaper files from May 1995. This was not an environment Terry knew, so it didn't occur to him to question why this fat, bug-eyed little man with his pernickety gestures should be closeted alone in the semi-darkness of a large room. If he and

Deacon were there, then presumably it was quite natural for Barry Grover to be there, too.

He perched on the side of the desk. 'Mike told me you were the best in the business as we were coming up the stairs,' he confided. 'Says you've been trying to work out who Billy Blake was.'

Barry drew away a little. He found the youngster's casual invasion of his work space intimidating, and suspected Deacon of putting him up to it. 'That's right,' he said stiffly.

'Billy and me were friends, so if there's anything I can do to help, just say the word.'

'Yes, well, I usually find I work better on my own.' He made sweeping gestures with his hands, as if to clear the desk of obstruction, and in the process uncovered an underexposed print of Billy's mugshot in which the eyes, the nostrils and the line between the lips were the only clearly defined features.

Terry picked it up and examined it closely. 'That's clever,' he said with frank admiration in his voice. 'No fuss means you can see what you're looking for.' He picked up another similarly underexposed print and laid the two side by side. They were very alike, with only minor variations in the spatial relationships between the features. 'That's amazing.' Terry touched the second photograph. 'So who's this geezer?'

Barry took off his glasses and polished them on his handkerchief. It was an indication of mental torment. He couldn't bear to have his painstaking efforts pawed by this shaven-headed thug. 'He's a lorry driver called

243

Graham Drew,' he snapped, moving the photographs out of Terry's reach.

'How did you know he looked like Billy?'

'I have his photograph on file.'

'Jesus! You really *are* something else. You mean, you can remember all the pictures you've got?'

'It would be irresponsible to rely on memory,' Barry said severely. 'Naturally, I have a system.'

'How does that work?'

It didn't occur to Barry that the youngster's interest might be genuine. He assumed, because he had come with Deacon, that he was more sophisticated than he was and interpreted his persistent questioning as a form of teasing. 'It's complicated. You wouldn't understand.'

'Yeah, but I'm a fast learner. Mike reckons my IQ's probably above average.' Terry hooked a spare chair forward with his foot and dropped into it beside his new guru. 'I'm not promising anything but I reckon I'd be more use helping you than helping him.' He jerked his head towards Deacon. 'Words aren't my thing – know what I'm saying? – but I'm good with pictures. So, what's your system?'

Barry's hands trembled slightly as he replaced his glasses. 'On the assumption that Billy Blake was an alias, I'm working through photographs of men who have avoided police capture in the last ten years. One is looking,' he finished pedantically, 'for people who felt it necessary to change their identities.'

'That's well brilliant, that is. Mike said you were a genius.'

Barry pulled forward a folder from the back of the

desk. 'Unfortunately, there are rather a lot of them, and in some cases the only record I have is a photofit picture.'

'Why're the Old Bill after this Drew bloke?'

'He drove a cattle truck containing his wife, two children, thirty sheep and £2 million of gold bullion on to a cross-Channel ferry, and vanished somewhere in France.'

'Shit!'

Barry tittered in spite of himself. 'That's what I thought. The sheep were found wandering around a French farmer's field, but the Drews, the gold and the cattle truck were never seen again.' Nervously, he opened the folder to reveal prints and newspaper clippings. 'We could go through these together,' he invited, 'and sort them into those that are worth a second look and those that aren't. They represent the hundred or so men sought by the police in 1988.'

'Sure,' agreed the boy cheerfully. 'Then what do you say to coming out for a drink with me and Mike afterwards? Are you game or what?'

Deacon spun his chair round an hour later. 'Oi! You two! Shift your arses! Come and read this.' He cocked both forefingers at them in triumph. 'If this isn't what made Billy go walkabout, I'll eat my hat. It's the only damn thing in the news during the first half of May that makes a connection with what we've got already.'

Nigel offers small consolation

Following her divorce from restaurateur Tim Grayson, 58, Fiona Grayson is believed to have returned to her first husband, entrepreneur Nigel de Vriess, 48. According to her friend, Lady Kay Kinslade, Fiona is a frequent visitor to Halcombe House, Nigel's home near Andover. 'They have a lot in common, including two grown-up children,' said Lady Kay. She drew a discreet veil over the bitter divorce ten years ago when Nigel abandoned Fiona for a brief affair with Amanda Streeter, whose husband, James, later vanished with £10 million from the merchant bank that also employed Nigel de Vriess. 'Time heals everything,' said Lady Kay. She denied that Fiona is having money problems.

Nigel, who once described himself as 'the man most likely to succeed', has had a chequered career. He made his first million by the age of 30, but after disastrous losses in a failed trans-atlantic airline venture, he joined the board of Lowenstein's Merchant Bank in 1985. He left in 1991 'by mutual consent' after entering the computer software business through the purchase of Softworks, a small, underfunded company with hidden potential. He renamed it DVS, recruited a new workforce with new ideas, and turned it round in four years to become a major player in the lucrative home computer market.

Less successful in love, Nigel has been married twice and his name has been linked with some of Britain's most beautiful women. But Fiona clearly remembers him more fondly than most. One of his ex-lovers, actress Kirstin Olsen, described him memorably as: 'undersized, tight-fisted and performs better on top'. Kirstin Olsen's new romance is Arnold Schwarzenegger look-alike Bo Madesen, voted 'the sexiest hunk in the world' by readers of *Hello!* magazine.

Deacon read it aloud for Terry's benefit and chuckled when the boy laughed. 'It probably serves him right, but I feel sorry for the poor bastard. He obviously didn't compensate Ms Olsen adequately for the effort she put into her orgasms.'

'Hell has no fury like a woman scorned,' quoted Barry ponderously.

'I know that one,' said Terry. 'Billy taught it me.' He fell into his imitation of Billy's voice and declaimed theatrically: '"*Heav'n* has no rage like love to hatred turned, nor *Hell* a fury like a woman scorn'd.' However*, Terry, that doesn't mean *fury* as in anger, it means *Fury* with a capital eff, as in the winged monsters sent by the gods to create *hell* on earth for sinners."' He beamed at the two men and returned to his own mode of speech. 'Billy reckoned they came after him every time he got pissed. It was one of his punishments, to have Furies claw at him whenever he was off his head.'

'He had a passion for hurting himself,' Deacon explained to Barry. 'He'd thrust his hands into a fire to cleanse them whenever they offended him.'

'The Furies sound more like DTs,' said Barry.

'Yeah, well, it was him used to claw himself, but he always said he was fighting off the Furies when he was doing it.' Terry pointed a finger at the monitor screen. 'So are you reckoning Billy went looking for this Nigel geezer? Why'd he want to do that?'

Deacon shrugged. 'We'll have to ask Nigel.'

'I expect this is too simplistic,' said Barry slowly, 'but could Billy just have wanted Amanda Streeter's address?

If he didn't know she was calling herself Amanda Powell, how else would he find her?'

'That's gotta be right,' said Terry admiringly. 'And that means Billy must've known James, seeing as how Amanda didn't know Billy. Know what I'm saying? So all you've gotta do now is find out the names of blokes that James knew and you'll have Billy sussed.'

Deacon shook his head in mock despair. 'We could work out who he was in five minutes if we knew how to access the information you already have in your head.' He arched an amused eyebrow. 'The man was clearly educated, he was a preacher, he was a fan of William Blake, quoted Congreve, knew his art, his classics, had views on European politics, believed in a code of ethics. Above all, he seems to have been a theologian with a particular interest in the Olympian gods and their cruel and arbitrary meddling in people's lives. So? What kind of man has those characteristics?'

Barry removed his glasses and set to work on them again. His self-loathing had become a physical pain in the pit of his stomach, and he was afraid of what he might do this time if Deacon abandoned him. He knew the other man well enough to know that if he divulged Billy's identity now, what little interest Deacon had in him would vanish. Deacon would set off with Terry in hot pursuit of Fenton, leaving Barry to the terrible confusion that had reigned in his soul for twenty-four hours. He thought of what awaited him at home, and in despair he clung to the hope that his hidden knowledge offered him. Deacon didn't need to know who Billy was

– *not yet anyway* – but he did need to know that Barry would deliver eventually.

'My father was fond of misquoting Dr Johnson,' he murmured nervously, as if fearing he was about to make a fool of himself. '"If patriotism is the last refuge of the scoundrel," he used to say, "then theism is the last refuge of the weak." I could be wrong, of course, but—' He hesitated, glanced at Terry and fell silent.

'Go on,' Deacon encouraged him.

'It's not fair to speak ill of the dead, Mike, particularly in front of their friends.'

'Billy was a murderer,' said Deacon evenly, 'and it was Terry who told me about it. I doubt he could have shown a greater weakness than that, could he?'

Barry replaced his glasses and peered at them both with a look of immense satisfaction. 'I thought it must be something like that. You see, his character was flawed. He ran away. He was a drunk. He killed himself. These are not the attributes of a strong man. Strong men face their problems and resolve them.'

'He might have been ill. Terry describes him as a nutter.'

'You told me he'd been living as Billy Blake for a minimum of four years.'

'So?'

'How could a mentally ill man maintain a false identity for four years? He would forget the rationale behind it every time he hit rock-bottom.'

It was a good point, Deacon admitted. *And yet . . .* 'Doesn't the same logic apply to a drunk?'

Barry turned to Terry. 'What did he say when he'd been drinking?'

'Not much. He usually passed out. I reckon that's why he did it.'

I define happiness as intellectual absence . . .

'You told me he used to rant and rave when he was drunk,' Deacon reminded him sharply. 'Now you're saying he passed out. Which was it?'

The boy's expression was pained. 'I'm doing my best here, okay? He ranted when he was half-cut and passed out when he was paralytic. But half-cut doesn't mean he didn't know what he was saying. That's when he got going on poetry and the day sex machine crap—'

'The what?' demanded Deacon.

'Day – sex – machine,' repeated Terry with slow emphasis.

'What's that supposed to mean?'

'How the hell should I know?'

Deacon frowned while his mind tried to make sense of the sounds. '*Deus ex machina?*' he queried.

'That's it.'

'What else did he say?'

'A load of bull usually.'

'Can you remember his exact words and how he said them?'

Terry was becoming bored. 'He said hundreds of things. Can't we go and have a drink? I'll remember better once I've had a pint. Barry wants one, too, don't you, mate?'

'Well—' The little man cleared his throat. 'I'd need to put things away first.'

Deacon looked at his watch. 'And I need to make a photocopy of this piece on de Vriess. How about giving us ten minutes' worth of Billy in a rant, Terry, while Barry and I finish off? Then we'll go pubbing and forget about it for the rest of the evening.'

'Is that a promise?'

'That's a promise.'

Terry's performance was a *tour de force* which Deacon captured on a tape cassette. The youngster had an extraordinary talent for sustaining a different voice from his own but whether it sounded anything like Billy was impossible to tell. He assured Deacon it was a perfect imitation until Deacon replayed the first thirty seconds and Terry collapsed in heaps of laughter because he sounded like an 'upper-class twit'. The content of the speech was largely irrelevant, in so far as it was a repetition of Billy's belief in gods and retribution together with the few snippets of poetry that Terry had already recalled for Deacon. Also, and disappointingly, Terry left out any reference to *deus ex machina* because, as he said afterwards, he'd never really understood what Billy was talking about, so it made it more difficult to remember the words he'd used.

Deacon, who had been thoroughly entertained by the entire proceedings, gave him a friendly punch on the arm and told him not to worry about it. However, Barry, to whom most of it was new, had listened with grave attention, and rewound the tape to isolate a small passage which followed a listing of gods.

'. . . *and the most terrible of all is Pan, the god of desire. Close your ears before his magical playing drives you insane and the angel comes with the key to the bottomless pit and casts you down for ever. You will wait in vain for the one who descends in clouds to raise you up. Only Pan is real* . . .'

'Couldn't "the one who descends in clouds to raise you up" be Billy's *deus ex machina*?' he suggested. 'Think of pantomimes and the good fairy emerging from dry-ice vapour to wave her wand and effect a happy ending.'

'And if it is?' Deacon prompted him.

'Well' – Barry marshalled his thoughts – 'Pan was a Roman god, but if I remember correctly "the angel with the key to the bottomless pit" comes from the Book of Revelation, which is of Judaeo-Christian inspiration. So Billy seems to have believed that it was the *pagan* gods who ensnared men into sin, but the *Judaeo-Christian* God who exacted punishment. Which must have left him very confused about where salvation lay. Should he placate the pagan gods, as he seems to have done with this business of burning his hand, or the Christian God through his preaching?'

'Where does "the one descending in clouds" fit in?'

'I think that's his symbolic view of salvation. He talks about waiting "in vain", so he obviously doesn't believe in it – or not for himself anyway – but if it does happen, it will be in the form of a *deus ex machina*, a sudden amazing apparition who reaches into the bottomless pit to raise him up.'

'Poor bastard,' said Deacon with feeling. 'I wonder what sort of murder it was that made him think he was beyond the pale of salvation?' He shivered suddenly and noticed that Terry was rubbing his hands in an effort to keep warm. 'Come on, it's damn cold in here. Let's go and get that drink.'

Barry watched Terry play the fruit machines with money supplied by Deacon. 'He's a nice lad,' he said.

Deacon lit a cigarette and followed his gaze. 'He's been living on the streets since he was twelve years old. It sounds as if he has Billy to thank for the fact that he's as straight as he is.'

'What will you do with him when Christmas is over?'

'I don't know. He needs educating but I can't see him agreeing to going back into care. It's a bit of a poser really, one of those bridges you only cross when you come to it.' He turned back to Barry. 'Was he helpful on the photographs?'

'A little quick to discard the improbables, but it doesn't seem to register with him that Billy was much younger than he looked. I had to rescue one or two.' He took an envelope from his pocket which contained various prints. He spread them across the table. 'What do you think of these?'

Deacon isolated a high-quality photocopy of a young fair-haired man staring directly into the camera. 'I recognize this one. Who is he?'

Barry tittered happily. 'That's James Streeter, taken twenty-odd years ago when he graduated from Durham University. He was brought up in Manchester so, out of interest, I applied to the local newspapers and one of them produced that. It's extraordinary, isn't it?'

'He's a dead ringer for Billy.'

'Only because he was thinner and appears to have had his hair bleached.'

Deacon took out his print of Billy and laid it beside the young James Streeter. 'Have you compared these two on the computer?'

'Yes, but they're not the same man, Mike. It's a closer match because we're looking at a similar relationship between camera angle and subject, but the differences are still obvious. Most notably the ears.' He picked up the cigarette packet and placed it across the bottom half of Billy's face with the upper edge touching the bottom of an ear lobe. 'It *is* all about angle, of course, but Billy's lobes are larger than James's and their bottom edge is roughly in line with his mouth.' He moved the packet to the other photograph and placed it in the same position. 'James has hardly any lobe at all and the bottom edge is in line with his nostrils. If you synchronize the eyes, nose and mouth on the computer, the ears immediately part company, and if you tilt the angles to synchronize the ear lobes then the rest parts company.'

'You're pretty good at this, aren't you?'

Pleased colour tinged Barry's plump cheeks. 'It's something I enjoy doing.' He nudged the other prints, artfully isolating a profile shot of Peter Fenton. 'Do you recognize anyone else?'

Deacon shook his head. He took a last look at James Streeter, then pushed the photographs aside. 'It's a wild-goose chase,' he said dispiritedly. 'I'm beginning to think Billy's a side issue anyway.'

'In what way?'

'It depends what Amanda Powell's agenda was when she told me about him. She must have known I'd find out about James, so whose story am I supposed to be investigating? Billy's or James's?' He drew thoughtfully on his cigarette. 'And where does Nigel de Vriess fit in? Why would he give Amanda's address to a complete stranger?'

'Perhaps he doesn't like her,' said Barry, tacitly disclosing his own prejudices.

'He did once. He left his wife for her. In any case, however much you dislike someone, you don't give their address to any old nutter who turns up.' He eyed Barry curiously. 'Do you?'

'No.' Barry looked uncomfortably at the photograph of Peter Fenton. 'I suppose it's possible they knew each other from before.'

Deacon followed his gaze. 'Nigel and Billy?'

'Yes.'

He looked sceptical. 'Wouldn't he have told Amanda who he was? Why talk to me if Nigel could have given her his name?'

'Maybe they're no longer in contact.'

Deacon shook his head. 'I wouldn't bet on that. She's not the type a man could forget very easily. And de Vriess likes women.'

'Do you like her, Mike?'

'You're the second person to ask me that' – he held the other's gaze for a moment – 'and I don't know the answer. She's out of the ordinary, but I don't know whether that makes her likeable or ruddy peculiar.' He grinned. 'She's damn fanciable. I'll say that for her.'

Barry forced himself to smile.

Chapter Fourteen

TERRY HAD TURNED on the overhead light in Deacon's bedroom and was prodding the slumbering man's shoulder aggressively. Deacon opened one eye and looked with extreme disfavour on his protégé. 'Stop – doing – that,' he said slowly and clearly. 'I am not a well man.' He rolled over and prepared to go back to sleep again.

'Yeah, right, but you've got to get up.'

'Why?'

'Lawrence is on the phone.'

Deacon struggled to a sitting position and groaned as his hangover hit him behind the eyes. 'What does he want?'

'Don't ask me.'

'Why didn't you leave the machine to take a message?' growled Deacon, glancing at his clock and seeing that it was six fifteen in the morning. 'That's what it's for.'

'I did, the first four times, but he just kept ringing back. How come you didn't hear it? Are you deaf or what?'

With muttered imprecations, Deacon stumbled through to the sitting-room and picked up the receiver.

'What's so important that you have to wake me at the crack of dawn on Christmas Eve, Lawrence?'

The old man sounded worried. 'I've just been listening to the radio, Michael. I sleep so little these days. I'm guessing that either you or I or both of us can expect a visit from the police shortly. I know Terry's there because he answered the telephone, but can you vouch for his movements last night?'

Deacon rubbed his eyes vigorously. 'What's this about?'

'Another incident at what I assume is Terry's warehouse. Look, find a news bulletin on your radio and listen to it. I may be completely wrong, but it sounds to me as if the police are looking for your lad. Call me back as soon as you can. You may need me.' He rang off.

It was the top story, with details breaking as the newscaster was on air. Following an attempted murder and the arrest of a suspect on Friday afternoon, further trouble had erupted among the homeless community in a docklands warehouse in the early hours of Christmas Eve when several men had been doused with petrol and their clothes set alight. The police were looking for a youth, five feet eleven inches tall, shaven-headed and wearing a dark coat, who was seen running from the warehouse following the incident. Although they had not released his name, the police were looking for a known suspect who was believed to hold a grudge against the warehouse community following the attempted murder on Friday.

For all Terry's surface bravura, he was only fourteen years old. He stared at the radio in tearful panic. 'Someone's grassed me up,' he stormed. 'What am I gonna fucking do? The Old Bill'll crucify me.'

'Don't be an idiot,' said Deacon sharply. 'You've been here all night.'

'How would you know, you bastard?' demanded Terry angrily, his fear sparking further aggression. 'I could have gone and come back without you knowing anything about it. Shit, you didn't even hear your phone ringing.'

Deacon pointed at the sofa. 'Sit down while I phone Lawrence back.'

'No chance. I'm out of here.' He bunched his hands into fists. 'I ain't gonna let the fucking pigs anywhere near me.'

'SIT DOWN,' roared Deacon, 'BEFORE I GET **REALLY** ANGRY!' Afraid that Terry would bolt if he left the room to search out Lawrence's number, he switched to the loudspeaker, pressed 1471 to give him a voiced number recall of the last person who had phoned him, then pressed 3 to dial that person back. 'Hi, Lawrence, it's Michael and Terry on the amplifier. We can both hear you and both talk to you. We think you're right. We think the guys at the warehouse have grassed Terry, and we think the police will come knocking. So what do we do?'

'Can you vouch for his movements?'

'Yes and no. We got back here about two o'clock in the morning, courtesy of a taxi. I abandoned my car in Fleet Street because I was over the limit. We were with a chap called Barry Grover until about one fifteen a.m. We were pissed as rats. The last thing I remember is telling

Terry to stop giggling like a schoolgirl and go to bed. I crashed out immediately and the next thing I knew was Terry giving me grief because you were on the phone. I can't swear he was here between two and when he woke me' – he squinted at his watch – 'which means four and a quarter hours are unaccounted for. It's a hypothetical possibility that he went out, but a practical no-no. He could hardly stand when I pushed him into his bedroom, and I am one hundred per cent certain that he's been there ever since.'

'Can you hear me, Terry?'

'Yeah.'

'Did you leave Michael's flat after you got back to it at two o'clock this morning?'

'No, I fucking didn't,' said the boy sullenly. 'And I've got a fucking headache, so I'm not answering fucking questions about what I didn't fucking do.'

Lawrence's dry laughter floated into the room. 'Then I'm sure we're worrying unnecessarily – perhaps there are two shaven-headed youths known to the police after Friday – but I do urge you to purify the flat. Our friends in the police force tend to react unfavourably to anything that requires chemical identification. Let me know if you run into trouble, won't you?'

'Why can't he speak English occasionally?' asked Terry ungraciously as Deacon put the phone down. 'What was he saying? That I'm guilty of something?'

'Yes. Possessing a class-C drug. How much cannabis have you got left?'

'Hardly any.'

'None' – Deacon banged the table – 'as of now. It's

going straight down the bog.' He fixed the boy with a gaze that would have pinned butterflies to a board. 'Do it, Terry.'

'Okay, okay, but it cost me a fortune, you know.'

'Not half as much as it's going to cost me if it's found here.'

Terry's natural ebullience resurfaced. 'You're more scared than I am,' he said with a knowing leer. 'Ain't you never wanted to live a little? See how much bottle you've got when the cops've got you pinned to the canvas?'

Deacon chuckled as he made for his bedroom. 'I tell you what, Terry, I'm more interested to see how much bottle you've got. You're the one they'll be using for target practice, so I wouldn't give them too much to aim at if I were you.'

They were fully dressed and eating breakfast when the police arrived half an hour later in the shape of two detective sergeants, one of whom was DS Harrison. When Deacon answered the door and agreed that he did know where Terry Dalton was – sitting at his kitchen table, as it happened – Harrison expressed surprise that they were up so early on a Sunday morning.

'It's Christmas Eve,' said Deacon, taking them through the flat. 'We're visiting my mother in Bedfordshire, so we wanted to make an early start.' He resumed his place and tucked into his cereals again. 'What can we do for you, sergeant? I thought Terry gave you a statement on Friday.'

Harrison glanced at the boy, who was happily engaged

on his third bowl of cornflakes. 'He did. We've come about a different matter. Can you tell us where you were at three o'clock this morning, Mr Dalton?'

'Here,' said Terry.

'Can you prove that?'

'Sure. I were with Mike. Why d'you want to know anyway?'

'There's been another incident at the warehouse. Five comatose men were saturated with petrol, then set alight. They're all in hospital and two of them are critical. We wondered if you knew anything about it.'

'Not fucking likely,' said Terry indignantly. 'I ain't been near the place since Friday night. Ask Mike.'

Harrison turned back to Deacon. 'Is that right, sir?'

'Yes. I invited Terry to spend Christmas with me after he made his statement to you. We stopped off at the warehouse on our way home on Friday to pick up a few of his things, and he's been in my company ever since.' He frowned. 'When you say you wonder if Terry might know something, are you suggesting he was involved?'

'We're not suggesting anything at this stage, sir, just making enquiries.'

'I see.'

There was a short silence while Deacon and Terry continued with their breakfast.

'When you said you were with this gentleman last night,' Harrison asked Terry, 'what did you mean exactly?'

'What d'you think I meant?'

'Let me put it another way, sir. If you and Mr Deacon shared a bed last night, then it's doubtful you could have left the bed without him noticing. Is that what you meant when you said you were with him?' The sergeant's expression was neutral but there was a look of amusement on his colleague's face.

A stillness settled on the boy which Deacon interpreted as anger, but when Terry raised his head there was cunning in his eyes. 'I reckon it's down to Mike to answer that,' he said off-handedly. 'This ain't my pad. He's the one calls the shots around here.'

Deacon located the youngster's naked toe under the table and ground his metal-tipped shoe heel into the unprotected flesh. 'Sorry,' he murmured as Terry yelped, 'did I hurt you? My foot slipped, sweetheart.' He pursed his lips into a rosebud and prepared to blow a kiss in Terry's direction.

'Bog off, Mike!' He glared from Deacon to the two policemen. ''Course we didn't share a sodding bed. I'm no pillow biter, and he's no sausage jockey. Got it? He were in his bed and I were in mine, but that don't mean I buggered off in the middle of the night to go torching the guys at the warehouse. We didn't get back here till round two, and I was out like a light the minute I hit the sack.'

'We've only your word on that.'

'Ask Mike. He's the one pushed me through the door of my room. Ask Barry, if it comes to that. We said goodnight to him at past one, and he'll tell you I was too rat-arsed to go looking for the warehouse in the middle of the night. And while you're about it, ask the taxi driver who gave us a ride. He only brought us back because it was on his way home and Mike paid up front and over the odds in case him and me puked all over the sodding seats. Which we didn't.' He drew breath. 'Shit! Why'd I want to set fire to anyone anyway? The old geezers there are looking after my mattress.'

'Who's Barry?'

'Barry Grover,' said Deacon. 'He works for the *Street* magazine and lives in Camden somewhere. We were with him from eight thirty to one fifteen.'

'Was it a black cab or a minicab?'

'Black cab. The driver was about fifty-five, grey-haired, skinny and wearing a green jumper. He picked us up on the corner of Fleet Street and Farringdon Street.'

'You were lucky,' said Harrison drily. 'Black cabs are usually pretty thin on the ground at Christmas time.'

Deacon just nodded. He didn't think it necessary to mention that he'd climbed on the taxi's bonnet at the traffic lights and refused to budge until the driver agreed to a fifty-quid fee. It was a rip-off but preferable to passing out in the gutter.

'Do you mind if we look around your flat, sir?' Harrison asked next.

Deacon eyed him curiously. 'Why would you want to do that?'

'To satisfy ourselves that your beds were slept in last night.'

'You should make them get a search warrant,' Terry said.

'What on earth for?' asked Deacon.

'The Old Bill aren't allowed to go poking round people's private things just when they fancy it.'

'Well, I've no objection at all to them looking at my

room, but if you've got a problem—' He broke off with a shrug.

''Course I ain't got a problem,' said Terry crossly.

'Then what are you bellyaching about?' Deacon stood up. 'This way, gentlemen.'

The two sergeants accepted a cup of coffee and relaxed enough to join Deacon and Terry in a smoke. 'Terry fits the description of a youth seen running from the scene after the incident,' Harrison told them.

'So do a million others,' said Deacon.

'How would you know, sir?'

'We heard the description on the radio.'

'I thought you might have done. May I ask who alerted you?'

'My solicitor, Lawrence Greenhill,' said Deacon. 'He heard the bulletin and warned us to expect a visit from you.'

'So you were lying when you said you were visiting your mother?'

'No. We'll be leaving as soon as you've gone, but I will admit we were woken rather earlier than I'd intended. If you hang around, my alarm will go off in approximately' – he consulted his watch – 'thirty minutes.'

'When do you expect to be back?'

'This evening.'

'And you're happy for us to check your story with Barry Grover and the taxi driver?'

'Be our guests,' said Deacon. 'You can do more.

Check that we were in the Lame Beggar until ten thirty, and then at Carlo's in Farringdon Street until one in the morning when we were finally thrown out.'

'Your mother's address please, sir.'

'I don't want to see your mother,' said Terry morosely, hunched in the corner of the passenger seat as they set off for the M1 after collecting Deacon's car from the *Street* car park following yet another taxi ride, 'and she won't want to see me.'

'She probably won't want to see me either,' murmured Deacon, calculating that he'd shelled out a fortune in incidental expenses since Terry had moved in. He was coming to the conclusion that teenagers cost more than wives. Terry's appetite alone – he'd eaten enough breakfast to sink a battleship – would beggar most people.

'Then why are we going?'

'Because it seemed like a good idea when I first thought of it.'

'Yeah, but that was just an excuse for the Old Bill.'

'It's good for the soul to do something you don't want to do.'

'Billy used to say that.'

'Billy was a wise man.'

'No, he weren't. He were a bloody pillock. I've been thinking about it, and d'you know what I reckon? I reckon he never starved himself to death at all but let someone else do it for him. And if that ain't stupid, I don't know what is.'

Deacon glanced at him. 'How could someone else do it for him?'

'By keeping him permanently pissed so he didn't think to eat. See, food were only important to him when he was sober – like when he were in the nick – otherwise he'd forget that it's eating that keeps you alive.'

'Are you saying someone kept him supplied with booze for four weeks so that he'd drink himself to death?'

'Yeah, I mean, it's the only thing that makes sense, isn't it? How else could he've stayed rat-arsed long enough to starve? He couldn't't've bought the sodding stuff because he didn't have no money, and if he'd been sober, he'd've come back to the warehouse. Like I said, he used to bugger off from time to time, but he always came back when the booze ran out and he started to get hungry again.'

DS Harrison had rung the bell of the Grovers' terraced house in Camden several times before it opened a crack and Barry's sweaty face peered through it. 'Mr Grover?' he asked.

He nodded.

'DS Harrison, sir, Isle of Dogs police station. May I come in?'

'Why?'

'I'd like to ask you a few questions about Michael Deacon and Terry Dalton.'

'What have they done?'

'I'd rather discuss this inside, sir.'

'I'm not dressed.'

'It'll only take a minute.'

There was a pause before the security chain rattled and Barry opened the door wide. 'My mother's asleep,' he whispered. 'You'd better come in here.' He opened the door of the front parlour, then closed it quietly behind them.

Harrison sniffed the cold, musty air and looked about him. He was in a time capsule from a forgotten era. Drab velvet curtains hung beside the windows with pale stripes where the sun had bleached their colour, and ancient wallpaper showed a tide mark of rising damp from the ground outside. Photographs of a man in First World War uniform crowded the mantelpiece, and a portrait of a young woman in Edwardian dress smiled sweetly above it. The furniture had the dark and heavy imprint of the Victorian age, and the atmosphere was heavy with the weight of years, as if the door of the room had been closed on a day in the distant past and never reopened.

He rested a hand on the back of a mildewed chair, feeling its dirt and its dampness soil his palm, and he thought unquiet thoughts about what sort of people chose to inhabit so oppressive an environment.

'You mustn't touch anything,' whispered Barry. 'She'll go mad if she thinks you've touched something. It's her grandparents' room.' He pointed to the photographs and the painting. 'That's them. They brought her up when her own mother ran away and abandoned her.'

He smelt of sickness and stale drink, and presented a pathetic picture in a worn towelling dressing-gown that barely met across his fat stomach and striped pyjamas. The sergeant was torn between sympathy towards a fellow traveller – Harrison had been on too many jags himself not to know the pain of the morning after – and a strange flesh-crawling antipathy. He put it down to the bizarreness of the room and the man's unpleasant smell, but his sense of revulsion remained with him long after the interview was over.

'Michael Deacon says you'll confirm that you were with him and a youth called Terry Dalton from eight thirty last night until approximately one fifteen this morning. Are you able to do that?'

Barry nodded carefully. 'Yes.'

'Can you tell me what they were doing when you last saw them?'

'Mike stopped a taxi by climbing on the bonnet, then he and Terry got into it. There was a bit of a row because the driver didn't want to carry drunks, and Mike said it was obligatory as long as the customer could pay. I think he gave the driver the money in advance, and then they left.' He pressed a queasy hand to his stomach. 'What's happened? Were they in an accident or something?'

'No, nothing like that, sir. There was some trouble last night at the squat Terry Dalton's been living in, and we wanted to assure ourselves that he wasn't involved in it. How would you describe his condition when you saw him off in the taxi?'

Barry wouldn't meet his eye. 'Mike more or less had to drag him into the cab and I think he was lying on the floor when it left.'

'And how did you get home, sir?'

The question clearly alarmed Barry. 'Me?' He hesitated. 'I took a taxi, too.'

'From Farringdon Street?'

'No, Fleet Street.' He took off his glasses and started to polish them on his dressing-gown hem.

'A black cab or a minicab?'

'I phoned for a minicab from the *Street* offices. Reg Linden let me use the phone in reception.'

'And did you have to pay in advance as well?'

'Yes.'

'Well, thank you for your help, sir. I'll see myself out.'

'No, I'll see you out,' said Barry with an odd little giggle. 'We don't want you turning the wrong way, sergeant. It wouldn't do at all if you woke my mother.'

Deacon drove through the farmhouse gates and parked in the lee of the red-brick wall that bordered the drive-way. The drone of motorway traffic was muted behind the baffle and the house slumbered in the winter sunshine that had emerged from the clouds as they travelled north. He peered up at the façade to see if their arrival had been noticed but there was no sign of movement in any of the windows that looked their way. There was a car he didn't recognize outside the kitchen door (which he rightly attributed to the live-in nurse), but otherwise the place looked exactly the same as when he had stormed out of it five years before, vowing never to return.

'Come on then,' said Terry when Deacon didn't move. 'Are we going in or what?'

'Or what probably.'

'Jesus, you can't be that nervous. You've got me, ain't you? I won't let the old dragon bite you.'

Deacon smiled. 'All right. Let's go.' He opened his car door. 'Just don't take offence if she's rude to you, Terry. Or not immediately anyway. Hold your tongue till we're back in the car. Is that a deal?'

'What if she's rude to you?'

'The same thing applies. The last time I came here I was so angry I damn nearly wrecked the place, and I never want to be that angry again.' He stared towards the kitchen door, recalling the episode. 'Anger's a killer, Terry. It destroys everything it touches, including the one it's feeding on.'

'Looks like we've caught our arsonists,' said Harrison's partner as he re-entered the station an hour later. 'Three subhumans by the names of Grebe, Daniels and Sharpe. They were picked up thirty minutes ago still reeking of petrol. Daniels made the mistake of boasting to his girlfriend about how he and his mates had done the local community a service by getting rid of undesirables, and she rang us. According to her, Daniels heard about the trouble at the warehouse on Friday and decided to go in and torch it last night. He says all homeless people are scum, and he's buggered if their kind should be allowed to infect the streets of the East End. Charming, eh?'

'And I've just wasted six hours chasing after Terry Dalton,' said Harrison sourly, 'ending up with the weirdest bloody bloke you've ever seen in Camden.' He shuddered theatrically. 'You know who he reminded me of? Richard Attenborough playing Christie in the film *10*

Rillington Place. If it comes to that, the house reminded me of a flaming film set.'

'Who's Christie?'

'A nasty little pervert who killed women so that he could have sex with their corpses. Don't you know anything?'

'Oh, *that* Christie,' said his partner solemnly.

The live-in nurse was an attractive Irish woman with soft grey hair and a buxom figure. She opened the kitchen door to Deacon's tap and invited them in with a warm smile of welcome. 'I recognize you from your photographs,' she told Deacon, wiping floury hands on her apron. 'You're Michael.' She shook his hand. 'I'm Siobhan O'Brady.'

'How do you do, Siobhan.' He turned to Terry who was skulking in his shadow. 'This is my friend Terry Dalton.'

'I'm pleased to meet you, Terry.' She put an arm around the boy's shoulder and drew him inside before shutting the door. 'Will you take a cup of tea after your journey?'

Deacon thanked her, but Terry seemed to find her mothering instincts overpowering and was bent on extricating himself from her embrace as soon as he decently could. 'I need a piss,' he said firmly.

'Through the door to your right, then first left,' said Deacon, hiding a smile, 'and mind your head as you go. There isn't a doorway in this house higher than six feet.'

Siobhan busied herself with the kettle. 'Is your mother expecting you, Michael? Because she hasn't said a word to me if she is. She's a little forgetful these days, so it may have slipped her mind, but there's nothing to worry about. I can find a little extra to feed you and the lad.' She chuckled happily. 'How did we manage before the deep-freeze? That's what I'm always asking myself. I remember my own mother pickling eggs to tide us over the lean periods, and nasty-looking things they were too. There were fourteen of us and it was a struggle to make any of us eat them.'

She paused to spoon tea into the pot and Deacon seized the opportunity to answer her first question. She was a garrulous woman, he thought, and wondered how his mother, who was the opposite, put up with her. 'No,' he said, 'she's not expecting me. And please don't worry about lunch. She may refuse to speak to me, in which case Terry and I will leave immediately.'

'We'll keep our fingers crossed then that she does no such thing. It would be a shame to come so far for so little.'

He smiled. 'Why do I get the feeling that you *were* expecting me?'

'Your sister mentioned the possibility. She said if you came at all, it would be unannounced. I think she was afraid I'd ring the police first and ask questions later.' She poured boiling water on to the tea-leaves and took some mugs from a cupboard. 'You'll be wanting to know how your mother is. Well, she's not as fit as she was – who is at her age? – but, despite what she's claiming, she's nowhere near death's door. She has impaired vision, which means she can't read, and she has difficulty walking because one of her legs is packing up. She needs constant supervision because her increasing immobility has caused her to take shortcuts on her diet, which, of course, means she could pass out with hypoglycaemia at any moment.'

She poured a cup of tea and passed it to him with a jug of milk and the sugar bowl. 'The obvious place for her is some sort of nursing home where she can retain her independence *and* be given round-the-clock care, but your mother is very resistant to the idea. We have all tried to explain to her that she could live for another ten years, but she has a bee in her bonnet about being gone in a couple of months and is determined to die here.' She fixed him with a knowing eye. 'I can see from your expression that you're wondering what business this is of mine – why is the nurse siding with Emma and Hugh? you're thinking, when they're only after getting shot of their debts – but, my dear, the truth is I can't bear to see a patient of mine so unhappy. She sits day after day in her sitting-room, with no one to visit her and no one to care, and her only companion is a talkative, middle-aged Irish woman with whom she has nothing in common. It breaks my heart to watch her struggling to be civil to me in case I up my stumps and leave. Almost anything would be preferable to that. Would you not agree, Michael?'

'I would, yes.'

'Then you'll try to persuade her to be sensible?'

He smiled apologetically and shook his head. 'No. If her mind's all right, then she's capable of making her own decisions. I'm damned if I'll interfere. I wouldn't begin to know what's sensible and what's not. I can't even make rational judgements for myself, let alone for someone else. Sorry.'

Siobhan seemed less troubled by this answer than he expected. 'Shall we find out if your mother will see you, Michael? Either she will or she won't, and there's little sense in putting it off.'

Cynically (and accurately) he guessed that Siobhan's complacency was based on her knowledge that Penelope Deacon would do the exact opposite of anything her son suggested.

Chapter Fifteen

AMANDA POWELL'S elderly neighbour looked up from where she was preparing lunch and was alarmed to see a man fiddling with the lock on Mrs Powell's garage. She knew the house was empty because Amanda had told her earlier that morning that she was spending the Christmas holiday with her mother in Kent. Shortly afterwards, she had driven away. The woman hurried through to the sitting-room to alert her husband, but by the time they returned to the kitchen window the man had gone.

Her husband sallied forth – somewhat reluctantly, it must be said – to discover where the would-be intruder had gone. He tried the garage door, but it was firmly locked. The same was true of the front door. He glanced up and down the quiet road, then with a shrug rejoined his wife.

'Are you sure you didn't imagine it, darling?'

'Of course I didn't imagine it,' she said crossly. 'I'm not senile. He'll have nipped across the gardens at the back and be trying somebody else's house by now. There'll be quite a few of them empty this weekend. You must ring the police.'

'They'll want a description.'

She paused in her peeling and stared out of the window, picturing the scene. 'He was about six feet tall, thin, and he had on a dark coat.'

Muttering that it seemed unkind to trouble the police on Christmas Eve, and anyway every house had an alarm system, her husband nevertheless made the call. But as he put down the telephone after receiving an assurance that a patrol car would be sent to check the house, it occurred to him that he had seen a man fitting that description once before.

When he had stood outside Mrs Powell's garage and watched the police lay a dead tramp on a stretcher . . .

He decided not to mention that to his wife.

'I don't know why we're bothering,' she said as he went back into the kitchen. 'It's not as though she ever does anything for us.'

'No,' he agreed, peering through the window. 'But then she doesn't like people very much, does she?'

There was a surreal quality to the scene that met Deacon's eyes as he and Siobhan approached the open sitting-room door. Far from being marooned in a chair as Siobhan had described, his mother was upright, leaning on Terry's arm, and peering at a painting on the wall. 'Of course, I can't really see it now,' she was saying, 'but if I remember correctly, it's a George Chambers Junior. Can you make out the signature in the bottom left-hand corner?'

Terry made a pretence of reading the artist's scrawl. 'You've got an amazing memory, Mrs D. George

Chambers Junior it is. Did he always paint the sea then?'

'Oh, I'm sure he must have done other things, but he and his father were famous marine artists of the last century. I bought that years ago for £20 in a down-at-heel gallery in south London somewhere, and I had it valued at Sotheby's a week later for hundreds. Goodness only knows what it's worth now.' She urged him to move on. 'Do you see a portrait of me in the alcove? A big, bold one with lots of rich colour. Read the signature on that,' she said triumphantly. 'He's a wonderful artist and it was such a thrill to be painted by him.'

Terry stared in agony at the canvas.

'John Bratby,' said Deacon from the doorway.

Terry flashed him a relieved smile. 'Yeah, well done, Mike. It's a John Bratby all right. Mind you, Mrs D., considering how beautiful you are, do you really reckon he's done you proud? It's bold, like you said, but it ain't pretty. D'you know what I'm saying?'

'Yes, I do, but my character isn't pretty, Terry, and I think John captured that perfectly. Can we turn round?'

'Sure.' He assisted her to face her son.

'Come in, Michael,' said Penelope. 'To what do I owe this unexpected pleasure?'

He smiled uncomfortably. 'Why do you always ask the hardest questions first, Ma?'

'Terry seemed to find it easy enough. When I asked him who he was and what he was doing here, he said you and he had a visit from the – er – Old Bill this morning and it seemed like a good idea to get out of London for a while. Was he lying to me?'

'No.'

'Good. I'd rather you came because you're on the run from the police than because you've been talking to Emma. I won't have any more browbeating, Michael.' She nudged Terry in the ribs. 'Take me back to my chair, please, young man, and then go and sort out some drinks for us in the kitchen. There's gin, sherry and wine but if you'd rather have beer, I expect there's some in the cellar. Siobhan will help you find it.' She resumed her seat. 'Sit down where I can see you, Michael. Did you shave before you left?'

He took a chair, facing the window. 'Afraid not. I didn't have time before the police came, and forgot about it afterwards.' He rubbed his jaw thoughtfully. 'The eyesight's not that bad then?'

She ignored the remark. 'Who is Terry and why is he with you?'

'He's a lad I interviewed for a story on homelessness, and when I discovered he had nowhere to go for Christmas, I suggested he stayed with me for a few days.'

'How old is he?'

'That has nothing to do with why the police came this morning, Ma.'

'I don't remember saying it did. How old, Michael?'

'Fourteen.'

'Dear God! Why aren't his parents looking after him?'

Deacon gave a hollow laugh. 'He'd have to find them first.' He was shocked by how much his mother had changed. She was an older, smaller, thinner shadow of herself, and the piercing blue gaze had dimmed to grey. He had been prepared for a wounded dragon who could still breathe fire, but not for one whose fires had gone out. 'Don't waste your sympathy on him, Ma. Even if he knew where his parents were, he wouldn't go back to them. He's far too independent.'

'Like you then?'

'Not really. I was never as self-sufficient at his age. He has social skills that I still don't possess. I could no more have walked into this room at fourteen and struck up a conversation with a complete stranger than fly over the moon. What did he say to you, as a matter of interest?'

A faint smile hovered round her lips. 'I called out when I heard him tiptoeing along the corridor. I said: "Whoever that is, will they please come in here?" And when he came in he said: "Have you got ears in the back of your head or what?" Then he took great trouble to assure me he wasn't a burglar but that, if he were, there were some "well brilliant" pictures that might take his fancy. I gather this house resembles a palace while your flat is as boring as a men's public lavatory. What are you going to do with him when Christmas is over?'

'I don't know. I haven't thought about it yet.'

'You should, Michael. You have a nasty habit of taking on a responsibility lightly and then discarding it when it bores you. I blame myself. I should have forced you to face up to unpleasantness instead of encouraging you to avoid it.'

He looked at her. 'Is that what you did?'

'You know it is.'

'No, I don't. What I know is that I watched you martyr yourself for no good reason, and I made up my mind that nothing on earth would induce me to go down the same route. Julia and I loathed each other, never mind what she said afterwards. Believe me, she was as glad of the divorce as I was. Okay, I was the one who had the affair, but you try sleeping with a woman who doesn't want sex, doesn't want babies and makes it abundantly clear that she only got married in the first place because Mrs Deacon was a preferable title to Miss Fitt.' He stood up and walked restlessly to the window. 'Haven't you ever wondered why she never remarried, and why she continues to call herself Julia Deacon?' Briefly he glanced back at her. 'Because getting out from under her parents was all she was interested in, and I was the sap who helped her do it.'

'And what was Clara's reason for getting married? How long did that one last, Michael? Three years?'

'At least she gave me a bit of warmth after eight frigid years with Julia.'

Penelope Deacon shook her head. 'So why didn't she produce any children?' she asked. 'Perhaps, after all, it's you who don't want them, Michael?'

'You're wrong. She didn't want to lose her blasted figure.' He pressed his forehead to the glass. 'You've no idea how much I envy Emma. I'd give my right arm to have her daughters.'

'No, you wouldn't,' said Penelope with a dry laugh. 'They're perfectly revolting. I can only tolerate them for a couple of minutes before their simpering starts to annoy me. I did hope you'd give me a grandson. Boys aren't so affected as girls.'

*

DS Harrison raised his hand in greeting to two uniformed policemen who were getting out of their car as he exited the station. 'I'm off,' he said. 'Five days' hard-earned leave, and I'm planning to enjoy every damn minute.'

'You jammy bastard,' said the driver enviously, opening the rear door of the car and grabbing the occupant by the arm. 'Come on, sunshine. Let's be having you.'

Barry Grover emerged blinking into the sunlight.

Harrison paused. 'I know this guy,' he said slowly. 'What's the story?'

'Acting suspiciously in a woman's garden. More accurately, wanking his little heart out over a photograph of the occupant. What name do you know him by?'

'Barry Grover.'

'How about giving us ten minutes then, sarge? He's claiming to be a Kevin Powell of Claremont Cottage, Easeby, Kent. Says he's related to the Mrs Amanda Powell who owns the house. We thought it pretty unlikely, seeing what he was doing to her photograph but, according to her neighbours, she does have relations in Kent. She drove down there this morning to stay with her mother.'

Harrison looked at Barry in disgust. 'His name's Barry Grover,' he repeated, 'and he lives with his mother in Camden. Jesus Christ! I hope to God wanking's the least of his crimes or we'll be digging out bodies from under his floorboards.'

*

281

'My son and I have never seen eye to eye,' Penelope Deacon told Terry, 'so much so that I can't think of a single decision he's made in life that I've agreed with.'

'You were thrilled when I said I was marrying Julia,' murmured Deacon from his position by the window.

'Hardly thrilled, Michael. I was pleased that you'd finally decided to settle down, but I remember saying that Julia would not have been my first choice. I always preferred Valerie Crewe.'

'You would,' he said. 'She agreed with everything you said.'

'Which shows how intelligent she was.'

'Terrified, more like. She used to quake every time she came into the house.' He dropped a wink in Terry's direction. 'Ma viewed every girl I brought home as potential marriage material, and she used to put them through the mill to find out if they were suitable. Who were their parents? Which school did they go to? Was there a history of insanity in their family?'

'If there had been, it would have been pointless your marrying them,' declared Penelope tartly. 'Both sets of genes would have been so tainted, your children wouldn't have stood a chance.'

'We'll never know, will we?' said Deacon equally tartly. 'Every time you brought up the so-called insanity on our side, the girls did a runner. It probably explains why Julia and Clara baulked at having children.'

Terry grinned. 'That can't be right, Mike. I mean, okay, I've only lived with you for a couple of days but it don't take that long to see you're not a nutter.'

'Who asked you to interfere?'

Terry was sitting on the floor, stroking an ancient, moth-eaten cat that had been around so long no one knew how old it was. It purred with raucous pleasure at Terry's ministrations, which Penelope said was unusual because senility had made it irritable with strangers.

'Yeah, but you need your heads knocking together,' said the boy. 'I mean, you should listen to yourselves. Argue, argue, argue. Don't you never get tired of it? There might be some sense if it were going somewhere, but it isn't, is it? Me, I think Mrs D. probably said a load of things she shouldn't've done about you killing your dad, but you've got to admit she weren't far off in what she said about your wives. I mean, they can't have been much cop – either of them – or you'd still be married to them. Know what I'm saying?'

The contents of Barry's pockets and the envelope he'd been carrying were spread out in front of him on the table of an interview room, and sergeants Harrison and Forbes stared at them in perplexity. There were the prostitutes' cards and a stiffened condom that told them, without benefit of forensic analysis, what it had been used for. There were a dozen head shots of different men, some fully exposed, some underexposed, a paperback entitled *Unsolved Mysteries of the Twentieth Century*, and a folded newspaper clipping. There was the sodden photograph of Amanda Powell, now discreetly wrapped in cellophane to preserve the evidence of Barry's shame, a leather wallet containing money and credit cards, and a dog-eared snap of Barry cradling a toddler in his arms.

The tape had been running for fifteen minutes, and Barry hadn't said a word. Tears of humiliation ran from his eyes, and his flaccid cheeks wobbled pathetically.

'Come on, Barry, for God's sake talk to us,' said Harrison. 'What were you doing at Mrs Powell's house? Why her?' He poked at the photographs. 'Who are all these men? Do you wank on them as well? Who's this child you're holding? Maybe you've got a thing about kids? Are we going to find pictures of children all over your walls when we go searching your mother's house? Is that what you're so worried about?'

With a sigh, Barry slid off his chair in a dead faint.

The police doctor accompanied Harrison into the corridor. 'He's certainly not dying,' he said, 'but he's scared out of his wits. That's why he fainted. He says he's thirty-four but I suggest you take twenty years off that to get an approximation of his emotional age. My best advice is to ask a parent or a friend to sit with him while you ask him questions, otherwise he'll probably collapse again. Work on the basis that you're dealing with a juvenile, and you might get somewhere.'

'His mother's not answering the phone and, judging by the shrine she's made to her grandparents in the front room of their house, she's barking mad anyway.'

'Which would explain his delayed development.'

'What about a solicitor?'

The doctor shrugged. 'My professional opinion, for what it's worth, is that a solicitor will terrify him even more. Find a friend – he must have some – otherwise you'll end up with a false confession. He's the type, Greg, believe me, so don't expect me to stand up in court and say anything different.'

The telephone rang in the kitchen. A few seconds later Siobhan popped her head round the sitting-room door. 'It's for you, Michael. A Sergeant Harrison would like a few words.'

Deacon and Terry exchanged glances. 'Did he say why?'

'No, but he made a point of stressing that it has nothing to do with Terry.'

With a shrug in the boy's direction, Deacon followed the woman out.

'Michael seems to be developing quite a relationship with the police,' Penelope remarked drily. 'Is this a recent thing?'

'If you're asking is it my fault, then I guess it is, sort of. The Old Bill wouldn't even know his name if it weren't for me. But you don't need to worry about *him* getting into trouble, Mrs D. He's a good bloke. He don't even drink and drive.' He watched her out of the corner of his eye. 'He's been well kind to me, bought me clothes and such, taught me stuff I didn't know. A hundred other guys wouldn't've given me the time of day.'

She didn't say anything and Terry ploughed on doggedly.

'So I reckon it wouldn't do no harm to show him you're pleased to see him. I remember this old geezer I used to know – he were a bit of a preacher – telling me a story about a rich bloke who took half his dad's loot, spent it all on women and gambling and ended up on the streets. He was really poor and really miserable until he remembered how nice his old dad had always been to him before he left home. Then he thought, why am I bumming crusts off strangers when Dad'll give them to me with no questions asked? So he took himself home, and his dad was that pleased to see him he burst into tears because he thought the silly bastard had died years ago.'

Penelope smiled slightly. 'You've just related the parable of the prodigal son.'

'D'you get the point, though, Mrs D? Never mind what sort of mess the bloke made of his life, his dad was over the moon to see him.'

'But for how long?' she asked. 'The son hadn't changed, so do you think his father would still be pleased to have him around when he started making a mess of his life again?'

Terry thought about it. 'I don't see why not. Okay, maybe they'd have the odd spat now and then, and maybe they couldn't live in the same house, but the dad wouldn't never be so unhappy as when he thought his son was dead.'

She smiled again. 'Well, I'm not going to burst into tears of joy, Terry. First, I'm far too crabby to do anything so sentimental and, secondly, poor Michael would be appalled. He can't cope with weepy women, which is why both his wives walked off with so much of his money despite the fact neither of them had children.

Certainly Julia knew how to turn on the waterworks when it mattered, and I've no doubt Clara was equally adept. In any case, I think you'll find he already knows I'm pleased to see him, otherwise he wouldn't be talking as freely as he is.'

'If you say so,' said Terry doubtfully. 'I mean, you seem like two straight-up types to me and, let's be honest, if I were looking for a mum – which I *ain't*,' he pointed out carefully, 'I'd as soon have you as the nurse out there who can't keep her paws off of me. Plus, she don't half talk a lot. Yabber, yabber, yabber. I reckon I heard her entire life history while I was looking for the gin.' He laid a gentle hand on the cat's head and drew forth another rumbling purr. 'What's a pickled egg anyway? It sounded right horrible.'

Penelope was laughing as Deacon came back into the room and he was surprised to see how young she looked. He remembered a Jamaican friend telling him once that laughter was the music of the soul. Was it also the fountain of youth? Would Penelope live longer if she learned to laugh again?

'We have to go back to London,' he told Terry. 'I'm a bit hazy on details, but Harrison says Barry's been arrested for acting suspiciously in Amanda Powell's garden. Barry won't say a word, and they want to know if I can shed any light on some photographs he has in his possession.' He frowned. 'Did he say anything to you about going to see her?'

Terry shook his head. 'No, but if he don't want to talk, that's his business. Don't see why we have to go stirring things up just because the Old Bill says jump.'

'Except there's something very odd going on and I want to know what it is. According to Harrison, they had to call in a doctor because Barry collapsed in a dead faint the minute they started asking him questions.' He turned to his mother. 'I'm sorry about this, Ma, but I do need to go. It's a story I've been working on for weeks. It's how I met Terry.'

'Ah, well,' she said with a sigh of resignation. 'It's probably for the best. Emma and her family are due some time this afternoon, and I've no doubt there'll be a terrible row if you're still here when they arrive. You know what you and she are like.'

Nobly, her son bit his tongue. More often than not it was Penelope's stirring that had set her children at each other's throats. 'I'm a reformed character,' he said. 'I stopped arguing with my nearest and dearest five years ago.' He stooped to peck her on the cheek. 'Look after yourself.'

She caught his hand and held on to it. 'If I sell this house and move into a nursing home,' she said, 'there'll be nothing for you when I die, particularly if I live as long as the doctors say I'm going to.'

He smiled. 'You mean, the threats of disinheritance if I married Clara were hogwash?'

'She was a gold digger,' said Penelope bitterly. 'I hoped they'd put her off.'

'They might have done if I'd ever repeated them to her.' He gave her hand a quick squeeze. 'Is this the only thing that's stopping you from moving?'

She didn't answer directly. 'It worries me that Emma will have had so much and you will have had so little.

Your father always intended you to have the house, and I made that clear to Emma when I set up the trust. Now she's pressing me to sell the wretched place, and put aside a similar amount for you as she's already had, and use the balance to pay for a nursing home.'

'Then do it,' said Deacon. 'It sounds fair to me.'

'Your father wanted you to have the house,' repeated Penelope stubbornly, withdrawing her hand from his in irritation. 'It's been owned by Deacons for two centuries.'

He looked down on her fluffy white hair and had a sudden urge to bury his nose in it as he had done as a child. He suspected he had just heard the nearest thing she would ever make to an apology for tearing up his father's will. 'Then don't sell it,' he said.

'That's hardly helpful.'

'Sorry,' he said with an indifferent shrug, 'but it's no skin off my nose if you bankrupt your daughter and spend the rest of your life with a series of nurses so that I can flog the place the minute you're gone. Let's face it, I've never shared your passion for living on the motorway, so I'd use the money to buy myself somewhere decent in London.' He dropped another sly wink at Terry. 'If anything's pissed me off about my divorces it's ending up in a miserable rented flat after losing two perfectly good houses.'

'Which is a very good reason *not* to let you have this one,' said Penelope, rising obligingly to the bait. 'Easy come, easy go. That's your philosophy, Michael.'

'Then take that into the equation when you decide what to do. If you want another two centuries of

Deacons living here, Ma, then you'd better leave the house to the Wimbledon branch of the family. I seem to remember they gave birth to a son about ten years ago.' He glanced at his watch. 'We really must go, I'm afraid. I promised the sergeant we'd be there in under two hours.'

She smiled a little bitterly. 'As I said, easy come, easy go.' She held out a hand to Terry who had stood up. 'Goodbye, young man. I've enjoyed meeting you.'

'Yeah, me too. I hope things work out for you, Mrs D.'

'Thank you.' She raised her eyes to look at him and he was startled by how blue they suddenly became in the sunlight shafting through the window. 'What a pity your mother is lost to you, Terry. She'd be proud of the man her son is becoming.'

'Do you think she's right?' Terry asked after several minutes of subdued thought in the car. 'Do you think my mum would be proud of me?'

'Yes.'

'It don't make no difference, though, does it? She's probably dead of an overdose by now, or banged up in a nick somewhere.'

Deacon stayed silent.

'She'll've forgotten all about me anyway. I mean, she wouldn't've got rid of me if I mattered to her.' He looked despondently out of the window. 'Don't you reckon?'

Yes, thought Deacon, but he said: 'Not necessarily,'

as he drove up the slip road on to the motorway. 'If you were put into care because she went to prison, that doesn't mean you didn't matter to her. It only means she wasn't in a position to look after you.'

'Why didn't she come searching after she got out then? I were there for nigh on six years, and she can't have been banged up that long, not unless she killed someone.'

'Perhaps she thought you were better off without her.'

'I could go looking for her, I suppose.'

'Is that what you'd like to do.'

'I think about it sometimes, then I get frightened she and me'll hate each other. I just wish I could remember her. I don't want some old tart with a drug problem whose frigging door's always open to any man as wants a shag.'

'What *do* you want?'

Terry grinned. 'A rich bitch with a fast Porsche, and no one to leave it to.'

Deacon laughed. 'Join the queue,' he said, moving into the fast lane and putting his foot down, 'but I don't want mine for a mother.'

Amanda Powell opened the door of Claremont Cottage and frowned enquiringly at the Kent policeman on the doorstep. The frown deepened as she listened to what he said. 'I don't know anyone called Barry Grover and I've no idea why he had a photograph of me. Did he succeed in breaking into my garage?'

'No. According to the information we've been given,

he was arrested in your garden but there were no signs of forced entry to any of the buildings.'

'Are the London police expecting me to go back and answer questions about this?'

'Not unless you want to. We were merely requested to pass on the information.'

She looked worried. 'All I told my neighbours was that I was spending a few days with my mother in Kent, so who gave you this address?'

The policeman consulted a piece of paper. 'Apparently Grover gave his name as Kevin Powell of Claremont Cottage, Easeby, when he was first arrested. We were asked to check the address and we discovered that a Mrs Glenda Powell lives here. It seemed likely she is your mother.' He frowned in his turn. 'He does seem to have a lot of information on you. Are you sure you don't know who he is?'

'Quite sure.' She pondered for a moment. 'Why might I know him? What does he do?'

He checked the paper again. 'He works for a magazine called the *Street*.' He heard her indrawn breath and looked up. 'Does that mean something to you?'

'No. I've heard of it, that's all.'

He wrote on a page of his notebook and tore it out. 'The investigating officer in London is DS Harrison and you can reach him on the top number. I'm PC Colin Dutton and my number's the bottom one. There's probably nothing to worry about, Mrs Powell. Grover's in custody, so he certainly won't be bothering you for a while, but if you're worried at all, then phone Sergeant Harrison or myself. Happy Christmas to you.'

She watched him walk past her BMW to the gate, and smiled brightly when he turned for a last look at her. 'Happy Christmas, constable,' she said.

'What's wrong?' called her mother on a note of anxiety from the sitting-room.

'Nothing,' said Amanda calmly, taking the brooch from her lapel and driving the pin under her thumbnail. 'Everything's fine.'

Deacon shook his head when Harrison finished. 'I really don't know much about Barry,' he said. 'I don't think anyone does. He never talks about his home life.' He looked in distaste at the besmirched photograph of Amanda Powell which had been cast like an island into the middle of the table. 'As far as I know, his only connection with Mrs Powell was when he developed some film after an interview I did with her. One of our photographers took some shots' – he jerked his chin at the table – 'and that was the best of them.'

'Why did you interview her?'

'I was writing a piece on the homeless and she was in the news in June when a man called Billy Blake died of starvation in her garage. We thought she might have general views on the subject, but she didn't.'

Light dawned in Harrison's eyes. 'I knew her name was familiar but I couldn't place it. I remember that incident. So why is Barry still interested in her?'

Deacon lit a cigarette. 'I don't know, unless it's something to do with the fact that he's been trying to help me identify Billy Blake.' He took one of his own prints of the dead man from his inside pocket and handed it across. 'That's him when he was arrested four years ago. We think Billy Blake was an assumed name and that he may have committed a crime in the past. He used to doss in the warehouse with Terry Dalton and Tom Beale.'

Harrison lifted an envelope from the floor and emptied its contents on to the table. 'So these headshots are your possible suspects?' He isolated the underexposed print of Billy's mugshot. 'And this is the dead guy?'

Deacon nodded.

Harrison unfolded a photocopy and flattened it on the table. 'This one's pretty close.'

Although Deacon was looking at it upside down, he knew Billy's face like the back of his hand and the shock of recognition was enormous.

Shi-it!

It was an enlarged copy of the picture of Peter Fenton that had accompanied Anne Cattrell's piece.

The little bastard had been holding out on him!

'It's close,' he agreed, 'but you need a computer to be sure.' *He'd fucking KILL Barry if the police got the story before he did!* 'Do you remember James Streeter?' Harrison nodded. 'We're more interested in him.' Disingenuously, he turned the graduation picture of James to face Harrison, and lined it up beside Billy's mugshot. 'That's probably why Barry's so interested in Amanda Powell. She was Amanda Streeter before James stole £10 million and left her to face the music alone.'

The sergeant's smile would have done credit to a cat. 'It's the same bloke.'

'Looks like it, doesn't it?'

'So what are you saying? James came back with his tail between his legs, and she starved him to death in her garage?'

'Could be.'

Harrison pondered for a moment. 'It still doesn't explain why Barry was in her garden wanking on her photograph.' He fingered idly through the prostitutes' cards. 'Guys with this kind of thing in their pockets worry me. And why does he carry a picture of himself with a kid? Who was the child and what happened to it?'

Deacon ran his thumbnail down the side of his jaw. 'You say he hasn't opened his mouth since he got here?'

'Not a dicky bird.'

'Then let me talk to him. He trusts me. I'll persuade him to give you what you want.'

'Even if it means he gets charged?'

'Even if it means he gets charged,' agreed Deacon rather savagely. 'I don't like perverts any more than you do, and I certainly don't want to work with one.'

Chapter Sixteen

BARRY'S SPECTACLES had been removed, giving him a naked look. He sat on the cell bed, head hanging forward, shoulders slumped in defeat. Deacon was told later that there was a fear he might break the lenses and try to cut his wrists – he was deemed a suicide risk – which also explained his lack of belt and shoelaces. He peered blindly towards the cell door when it opened, more like a sad-faced clown than a cockroach, and his plump little body shook with dread.

'Visitor for you,' said the custody sergeant, ushering Deacon in and leaving the door open. 'Ten minutes.'

Deacon watched the policeman walk away, then lowered himself on to the bed next to Barry. He expected to feel his usual antipathy but found himself pitying the man instead. It wasn't hard to imagine the sort of nightmare Barry was going through. There was precious little dignity to be found in a police cell at the best of times, none at all when your first experience of it was after committing a lewd act in public.

'It's Mike Deacon,' he said, wondering how much Barry could see without his glasses. 'Sergeant Harrison phoned me, told me you were in need of a friend.' He fished out his cigarettes. 'Are you going to let me smoke?' He watched the other's eyes fill with tears and punched him lightly on the shoulder. 'Is that a yes?'

Barry nodded.

'Good man.' He bent his head to the lighter. 'We haven't much time, so you're going to have to talk to me if you want my help. Let's start with the easy stuff first. You had a photograph of a man holding a child. The sergeant thinks the man's you, but I think it might be your father holding you as a toddler. Who's right?'

'You,' whispered Barry.

'You could be his double.'

'Yes.'

'Okay, next question. Why do you carry prostitutes' cards in your pocket? Is that how you spend your time when you're not working?'

Barry shook his head.

'Then why were they in your pocket?' He paused for an answer, but went on when he didn't get one. 'Talk to me,' he said kindly. 'You're not the first man in the world to be caught wanking, Barry, and you certainly won't be the last, but the police are putting the worst interpretation on it because they think you spend your time sniffing round toms.'

'Glen Hopkins gave them to me on Friday,' whispered Barry.

'Why?'

'He said there was no shame in paying for it.' Distress flowed in waves from the quivering body. 'But I *was* ashamed. I didn't like it.' He started to weep.

'I'm not surprised,' Deacon said matter-of-factly. 'I

297

suppose she had one eye on the clock and the other on your wallet. We've all been there, Barry.' He smiled slightly. 'Even the Nigel de Vriesses of this world have to pay for it. The only difference is they call their toms lovers and their shame becomes public property.' He sat forward with his hands between his knees, matching Barry's own body language. 'Look, does it make you feel any better if I tell you Glen tosses those cards about like bloody confetti? He gave me some a couple of months back when he decided my bad temper was due to lack of sex. I told him to ram them up his arse, where they belonged.' He glanced sideways. 'He caught you on a bad day, and you got ripped off. My best advice is to put it down to experience, and tell Glen to get stuffed the next time he tries it on.'

'He said it was – unhealthy – ' it clearly hurt him to say the word – 'looking at photographs. He said the real thing was more fun. But—' His voice tailed off.

'It wasn't?' suggested Deacon, offering him a hand-kerchief to dry his tears.

'No.'

Deacon reflected on his first sexual encounter at the age of sixteen, when he had fumbled his way through the act of intercourse without caring too much about satisfying the girl because his own arousal was so intense that every thought in his head was concentrated on not ejaculating before he got inside. To this day, he couldn't think of his and Mary Higgins's loss of virginity without embarrassment. She had claimed it was the worst experience of her life and never spoke to him again.

'You're not unusual,' he said sympathetically. 'Most

men find their first time pretty humbling. So what happened this morning? Why did you go to Amanda's house?'

The story was muddled but Deacon made what he could of it. After Barry's humiliation at the hands of the prostitute his anger, which should have been directed against Fatima – or even Glen – became fixated on Amanda instead. (There was a strange logic to it. He had been studying pictures of her when Glen had accused him of unhealthy practices, and in his mind's eye she had assumed the proportions of a Jezebel.)

Had he known less about her, it wouldn't have mattered, but his interest in Billy Blake and James Streeter had led him to build up a file of press cuttings on her. The reasons why he should have wanted to go out to her house and confront her were obscure, but they seemed to lie in his total confusion about whether he had hated or enjoyed the sex act. He wouldn't have gone at all had Deacon and Terry not filled him with Dutch courage on Saturday night. Tight as a tick, he had waved them off in a taxi, then called one for himself and told the driver to take him to the Thamesbank Estate.

He wasn't very sure now what his intentions were – certainly he hadn't expected to find her lights on – but at two o'clock in the morning he had stood in her garden and watched through her open curtains as she made love to a man on her sitting-room carpet. (Deacon asked him if he recognized the man, but Barry said no. Interestingly, he described him in detail but he barely mentioned Amanda.)

'It was exciting,' he said simply.

Yes, thought Deacon, it would have been. 'But illegal,' he said. 'I'm not sure if you can be charged with voyeurism, but you can certainly be charged with trespass and indecent behaviour. Why did you go back this morning anyway? It was broad daylight, so you were bound to be spotted.'

The simple explanation was that Barry had put the envelope of photographs on the ground the night before (to leave his hands free, Deacon guessed) and forgotten them. The more complex explanation seemed to concern his extraordinarily ambivalent attitude to living with his mother ('I don't want to go back,' he kept saying), his barely remembered love of his father and a half-understood desire to rekindle his excitement of a few hours earlier. But the house was clearly empty, and the only excitement left to him was to desecrate Amanda's photograph. 'I'm so ashamed,' he said. 'I don't know why I did it. It just – happened.'

'Well, if you want my opinion, it's a good thing the police caught you,' said Deacon bluntly, squeezing the burning tip out of his cigarette. 'Maybe it'll persuade you to wise up to the facts of life. You've got more going for you than to end up as some grubby little man who can only get a hard-on outside a window. Admittedly I'm no psychiatrist, but I'd say there are a couple of areas you need to sort out pretty damn quick. One, get out from under your mother and, two, come to terms with your sexuality. There's no sense in directing your anger against women if your preference is for men, Barry.'

Helplessly, Barry shook his head. 'What would my mother say?'

'A hell of a lot, I should imagine, if you're silly enough to tell her.' Deacon clapped him on the back. 'You're a grown man, Barry. It's time you acted like one.' He smiled. 'What were you planning to do, as a matter of interest? Wait till she was dead before you could be the person you wanted to be?'

'Yes.'

'Bad plan. That person would have died long before she did.' He stood up. 'Are you going to let me tell the sergeant what you've told me? Depending on what he says, you may want a solicitor with you when he questions you. And you'd better be prepared for the fact that Glen Hopkins will be asked to confirm that he gave you those cards on Friday. Are you ready for all that?'

'Will they let me go if I tell the truth?'

'I don't know.'

'Where will I go if they do? I can't go home.' His eyes welled again. 'I'd rather stay here than go home.'

God almighty! Just don't say it, Deacon. 'You can use my sofa while we sort something out.' *We-ell . . . It was Christmas . . .*

And . . .

. . . Barry knew who Billy Blake was . . .

Harrison was sceptical. 'You're being naive. I know the type. It's the classic profile of a sex criminal. A repressed loner with an unhealthy appetite for spying on people. Lives with his mother but doesn't like her. Can't make adult relationships. First offence is exposing himself in public. We'll be banging him up for rape and/or child molestation next.'

'On that basis you'll be locking me up as well,' said Deacon with a friendly smile. 'I'm a loner. I disliked my mother so much that I didn't speak to her for five years. I can't make successful adult relationships – as evidenced by my two divorces – and the worst offence I ever committed, judging by the thrashing I received, was when I bought a pornographic magazine at the age of twelve and attempted to smuggle it into my house with the intention of admiring my erections in front of a mirror.'

The sergeant chuckled. 'It's a serious point, though. You were twelve, Barry's thirty-four. You were going to practise in your bedroom, he was practising in somebody else's garden. At twelve, the damage you can do to someone else is hopefully limited by your size. At thirty-four, you're likely to be very dangerous indeed, particularly if you're thwarted.'

'But you can't charge him with what he *might* do. At worst, you've got him for trespass and indecency, and that's not going to keep him off the streets for long. Look,' he said persuasively leaning forward, 'you can't label a man a pervert for one aberrant episode. It wouldn't have happened if Glen Hopkins had kept his stupid ideas to himself, or if Barry had had more sense than to try something he wouldn't enjoy. The poor guy's hopelessly confused. He loved his father, who died when he was ten, he's terrorized by his mother and he'd just paid a hundred quid to lose his virginity to a woman who treated him like a lump of meat. On top of all that, Terry and I got him drunk – for the first time in his life as far as I can make out – and he found himself watching live sex inadvertently.' He gave a low laugh. 'Then you turned up on his doorstep this morning and scared him out of his wits because he thought Amanda must have seen him. He only went back for his photographs, for God's sake, and had a quiet wank in her absence because he was still aroused. Is this *really* the profile of a classic sex criminal?'

Harrison tapped his pen against his teeth. 'He was trying to break into Mrs Powell's garage. Where does that fit in?'

Deacon frowned. 'You haven't mentioned that before.'

'It's how we caught him. Her neighbours reported a possible intruder, and we sent out a patrol car.' He pushed a piece of paper across the table. 'It's all there in black and white.'

Deacon read the incident report. 'This man's described as six feet tall, thin and wearing a dark coat. Barry's about six inches shorter, fat and the only coat I've ever seen him in is a blue anorak. It's in his cell at the moment.'

The sergeant shrugged. 'I wouldn't rely on that description. The neighbours are in their eighties.'

Deacon studied him with amusement. 'God help you if my mother heard you say that. Surely you can see there were two different men? You've nicked the easy one –

the wally. My best advice, if you want a result, is to look for the tall guy.'

'If he exists,' said Harrison cynically.

Terry was bored to distraction by the time Barry and Deacon emerged from the inner recesses of the police station. 'You've been two hours,' he said crossly, pointing to the clock in the waiting area. 'What did Barry do then? It must have been something pretty bad if it took this long to sort.'

Deacon shook his head. 'He was watching Amanda's house, and got nicked in mistake for a man who tried to break into her garage half an hour earlier. It's taken all this time to establish that he doesn't answer the description of a tall, skinny bloke in a dark coat.'

'No kidding! You want to get Lawrence on to it. He'd soon sort these bastards out. That's harassment, that is, banging up a bloke for no reason. You all right, Barry? You don't look too good.'

Deacon shoved him through the front door into the freezing evening air before the desk sergeant could set him straight. 'Barry's coming home with us,' he murmured in Terry's ear. 'His family kicked up rough because we sent Harrison round there this morning, so I've said he can sleep on the sofa for a day or two. Do you have a problem with that?'

'Why would I?' asked the boy suspiciously.

'It'll be crowded with three of us.'

'Do me a favour,' he said scornfully. 'The warehouse was *crowded*.' He looked expectantly at Barry, who had followed them out. 'I hope you can cook, mate, because Mike's sodding useless. He can't even boil an egg without burning it.'

Barry looked nervous. 'Only self-taught, I'm afraid.'

'Yeah, well, me and Mike ain't been taught at all, so you get the job.' He jerked his head impatiently towards the car. 'Let's get going then, shall we? I'm starving. You realize we ain't had nothing to eat since seven o'clock this morning?'

While Terry escorted Barry into the kitchen and kept him captive there until he cooked something edible, Deacon took the telephone into his bedroom and made a call to Lawrence. 'I'm sorry to keep bothering you,' he said, 'but I need some advice and I don't know who else to ask.'

'I'm honoured,' said Lawrence.

'You haven't heard what the problem is yet.' As briefly as he could he related the details of Barry's arrest. 'I persuaded them he deserved a second chance, so they gave him one hell of a bollocking and released him. As long as nothing else comes to light, he's in the clear.'

'So what's the problem?'

'I said he could stay here with me and Terry.'

'Dear, dear. A latent homosexual who performs acts of gross indecency living cheek by jowl with a disturbed adolescent who will probably have no compunction at all about leading him on in order to blackmail him. You certainly have an appetite for trouble, Michael.'

Deacon sighed. 'I knew I could rely on you to be

objective. So what do I do? Barry's under strict instructions not to tell Terry why he was arrested, but Terry's no fool and he'll have worked it out for himself by tomorrow.'

Lawrence's happy laugh rippled down the wire. 'Start praying?'

'Ha! Ha! How about this? Come to Christmas lunch tomorrow and help me keep the peace. Being a lonely old Jew without family who rarely feels useful, you can't possibly be doing anything. Can you?'

'Even if I were, my dear chap, I couldn't resist so charming an invitation.'

DS Harrison was shrugging on his coat when a colleague popped his head round the door to say there was a Mrs Powell to see him. 'Tell her I've gone,' he growled. 'Dammit, I've already lost six hours' leave because of her blasted trespassers.'

'Too late,' said the colleague with a jerk of his head. 'Stewart told her you're here and she's waiting down the corridor.'

'Damn!' He followed the other man out.

'Detective Sergeant Harrison,' he introduced himself to the woman. 'How can I help you, Mrs Powell?' She was quite a looker, he thought, a great deal more attractive in the flesh than in her photograph, and he wasn't surprised that watching her make love on her carpet had set Barry's hormones racing.

She gave an uncertain smile. 'I'm frightened to go home,' she said simply. 'I live alone' – she gestured unhappily towards a window – 'and it's dark. This man you caught in my garden? He is locked up, isn't he?'

Harrison shook his head. 'We've released him pending further enquiries. But our understanding was that you wouldn't be home until after Christmas, and we asked Kent police to inform you of our decision together with our reasons for doing it. There's obviously been a breakdown in communications.' He wiped a hand over his face in irritation. 'I don't think you've anything to fear, Mrs Powell. In our opinion, the man acted out of character after getting drunk and won't be troubling you again. He's currently staying with a friend of his, Michael Deacon, whom I think you know, and we don't antici-pate any further trouble.'

Her eyes opened wide in alarm. 'But Michael Deacon forced his way into my house only four days ago when *he* was drunk.' She shivered suddenly. 'I don't understand. Why did no one talk to me about any of this? I've never heard of this man Barry Grover, but if he's a friend of Mr Deacon's—' She caught at Harrison's sleeve. 'I *know* someone's been watching me,' she said urgently. 'I've seen him at least twice. He's a short man with glasses and he wears a blue anorak. He was standing outside my house about ten days ago when I turned into my drive, and he walked away when he saw me. Is that the man you arrested?'

Harrison frowned uncomfortably. 'It certainly sounds like him but he claims he didn't go near your house until Saturday night.'

'He's lying,' she said flatly. 'I saw him again about a week ago. It was very dark but I'm sure it was the same person. He was standing under a tree at the entrance to the estate and his glasses caught my headlamps as I drove in.'

'Why didn't you call the police?'

She pressed trembling fingers to her forehead as if she had a headache. 'You can't report every man who looks at you,' she said. 'It only becomes frightening when they start to behave oddly. According to the policeman who came to tell me about the arrest, he was exposing himself over a photograph of me.' Her voice rose slightly. 'If that's true, why aren't you prosecuting him? He's not going to stop now, not if he's been allowed to get away with it. By letting him go, you've given him the right to terrorize me.'

Harrison turned back to his office and opened the door for her. 'I'll need a statement from you, with details of when and where you saw him previously. And you'd better include this incident with Michael Deacon.' He checked his watch surreptitiously and stifled a sigh. His wife would not forgive him for this.

Terry took his silver-foil wad out of his pocket. 'Who wants a spliff?' he asked.

'I told you to get rid of that,' said Deacon.

'I did. Up my arse till the heat was off.' He glanced at Barry. 'Barry wants one, don't you, mate? Matter of fact, he deserves one after that meal,' he told Deacon. 'Bloody brilliant, it was. Knocks spots off anything you've managed to produce.' He set to work splitting the tobacco out of Deacon's Benson and Hedges. 'So what were you doing round Aye-mander's place, Barry? I don't buy that cobblers you and Mike gave me earlier. Even the fuzz don't take six hours to tell the difference between a short, fat bloke and a tall, skinny one.' He paused momentarily to fix his pale – and intimidating – gaze on the man opposite. 'You looked shit-scared when you came out.'

Barry's small bubble of confidence over the success of his cooking shrank away. His fear of being thrown out of the flat if this adolescent boy found out what he'd done was greater than his fear of the police. 'I – er—'

'He had every reason to be scared,' said Deacon coldly, levelling a finger at Barry's face. 'He's worked out who Billy is – he's even carrying a picture of him in his pocket – and he knew I'd rip his head off if the police got that information before I did.' His voice hardened. 'Jesus, you're such an arsehole, Barry. I still can't believe you'd jeopardize all the work we've put into this sodding story just for the sake of seeing what that silly bitch looks like in real life.'

'Leave off,' said Terry, peeling cigarette papers from a Rizla packet. 'How could he know the Old Bill was going to turn up? Come on then, Barry, who was he? Anyone I've heard of?'

Barry held Deacon's gaze for a moment, and there was a look of gratitude in his over-damp eyes. 'I wouldn't think so,' he said then. 'He went missing when you were seven years old.' He took off his glasses and started to polish them. 'You saw the photograph?' he asked Deacon. 'And you're sure it's Billy?'

'Yes.'

'But I showed another version of him to you yesterday, Mike, and you didn't even give him a second glance.'

Deacon took a carving knife out of the table drawer and balanced it in the palm of his hand. 'I wasn't joking when I said I'd rip your head off,' he murmured. 'Are you going to tell me who he is before Terry and I start wiping you off the floor?'

The WPC put her arms around a weeping Amanda and looked accusingly at the sergeant. 'Be fair, sarge, you swallowed that scumbag's story hook, line and sinker. He said he watched her making love on her carpet and you believed him, but he was bound to say that or something similar. For your average pervert, a woman semi-clothed or naked in her own house is justification for anything. "It wasn't my fault, guv, it was the woman's fault. She didn't pull her curtains. She knew I was out there and she wanted to excite me." It sucks, for Christ's sake.' She sounded very angry. 'I'm sick to death of men trying to excuse themselves by smearing women. In any case, it doesn't make a blind bit of difference whether Amanda was having sex or not that night. It's still no reason for inadequate little men to jerk off afterwards over their photographs.'

Wearily, Harrison held up his hands. 'I agree. All right? I agree.' He closed his eyes. 'I was merely trying to establish some facts, and I am sorry if Amanda took offence at anything I said.' When a man was wedged

between a rock and a hard place, the only way out was
to exploit a weakness.

Deacon read what Barry had on Peter Fenton, finishing
with Anne Cattrell's piece, then propped his chin on his
hands and stared in frustration at the cover of *Unsolved
Mysteries of the Twentieth Century*. 'It's all here – a
hundred reasons for a man to abscond and live the rest
of his life in torment – but no damn reason at all for
choosing Amanda Powell's garage to die in.' His own
collection of notes was lying on the table beside him and
he picked out the cutting on Nigel de Vriess. 'Why
should this get him excited? Where's the connection
between the Streeter story and the Fenton story?'

'Maybe there isn't one,' said Barry. 'You're only
guessing that's what Billy read before he left the warehouse because you want to establish a pattern, but I keep
asking myself why Mrs Powell told you Billy's story if she
had anything to fear from what you might find out.' He
placed Billy's mugshot beside the photograph of the
young James Streeter. 'Superficially, there's a pattern
here, but it takes a computer to show you there isn't.'
He smiled apologetically. 'Perhaps it's a case of truth
being stranger than fiction, Mike.'

Terry, dreamily engaged on smoking the joint that the
other two had rejected in favour of another bottle of
wine, spoke through the blue haze that surrounded him.
'That's the biggest load of crap I've ever heard. You're
talking through your arse, mate.'

'What's your theory?'

'Well, look at it this way. What happens to the average wife whose husband dumps her in the shit and vanishes with all the loot? She don't bloody come up smelling of roses, that's for sure.'

'This one does,' said Deacon thoughtfully. 'Reeks of the damn things, as a matter of fact.'

'There you are then,' said Terry owlishly, not too clear what Deacon was talking about.

'So what?'

'Means she's scored, doesn't it? Means she ain't no pushover.' He sought to express himself. 'Means she don't reckon men too high. Ah, shit!' he said, looking at their bewildered faces. 'Don't you understand nothing?'

'We might if you spoke in words of more than two syllables,' said Deacon drily. 'Man has not spent centuries developing sophisticated language to have it reduced to grunts, glottal stops and endless double negatives that convey absolutely nothing. Work out what you want to say and try again.'

'Jesus, you're a poncy git sometimes,' said Terry scathingly, but he made an effort to collect his thoughts. 'Okay, try this. Even when he were drunk, Billy had reasons for what he did. They may not have been *good* reasons, but they were reasons. Do you understand that?'

The two men nodded.

'Right, next point. Amanda's done pretty well for herself, never mind her husband's a criminal and dropped her in it. That makes her a clever bloody bitch. Do you understand that?'

Two more nods.

'So put those two together, and what do you get? You get Billy going to Amanda's house for a reason, and Amanda using her brains afterwards.'

Deacon ground his teeth. 'Is that it?'

Terry sucked the cannabis deep into his lungs. 'My money's on Amanda. If she's cleverer than you and Billy put together, she's going to win, isn't she?'

'Win what?'

'How the hell should I know? You're the one who's playing the game with her, not me. I'm just along for the ride.'

313

Chapter Seventeen

WHEN THE DOORBELL rang unexpectedly the three men showed varying degrees of alarm. None of them doubted it was the police. Terry bolted for the lavatory and belatedly flushed his guilt into the sewers; Deacon flung open the kitchen window and sought frantically for an air freshener; but Barry, showing more composure than either of them, turned the gas up under the dirty frying pan, crushed garlic into the sizzling fat and started chopping onions. 'I've been expecting them,' he said in resignation. 'I'll not forgive myself if they arrest you, too, Mike. None of this is your fault.'

Harrison grew tetchy when it seemed clear that Deacon intended to keep him indefinitely on the front step of the flats. 'If you carry on like this,' he warned him, 'I'll be back in half an hour with an arrest warrant for the whole damn lot of you. Come on, let me in. I need to talk to Barry again, and you're just making me suspicious with these delaying tactics. What the hell's going on up there? Is Barry shafting that little boyfriend of yours?'

Deacon let him pass. 'Maybe it's time you retired,' he

said dispassionately. 'Even I wouldn't stoop so low as to make a remark like that, and I'm a journalist.'

Harrison surveyed him with weary amusement. 'You're an amateur, Mr Deacon. A raw recruit could get past you.'

The smell in the flat was revolting, a mixture of burnt fat, garlic, onions and, overall, the exotic reek of Jazz aftershave which Terry had sprinkled liberally over Deacon's sofa. The kitchen door was shut and Terry and Barry were sitting, none too relaxed, watching the television in the corner.

The sergeant stood on the threshold for a moment, then took out his cigarettes and offered one to Deacon. 'Interesting atmosphere,' he said mildly.

Deacon agreed. He accepted a cigarette with some relief. 'DS Harrison has a few more questions for Barry,' he announced to the room in general. 'So maybe Terry and I should make ourselves scarce for ten minutes.'

Harrison closed the door of the flat. 'I'd rather you stayed, Mr Deacon. I have some questions for you, too.'

'Not Terry, though.' Deacon took five pounds from his pocket and jerked his head at the boy. 'There's a pub on the corner. We'll join you there when we've finished.'

Terry shook his head. 'No way. What'll I do if you never turn up?'

'Why wouldn't we?'

Terry flicked a suspicious glance at the sergeant. 'He ain't come round to pass the time of day, Mike. My guess is he's going to arrest Barry again over that Powell woman. Am I right, Mr Harrison?'

The sergeant shrugged noncommittally. 'I want some

answers to a few more questions, that's all. As far as I'm concerned, you're not involved, so you can go or you can stay. I'm easy either way.'

'But I'm not,' said Deacon firmly, reaching the spare key off a shelf by the door. 'Come on, lad, hop it. If we don't join you in half an hour, you can let yourself back in.'

'No,' said the boy stubbornly. 'I'm staying. Billy were a mate, same as you and Barry are, and you don't walk out on mates when they need you.'

'Let's get on with it,' said Harrison impatiently, lowering himself into a chair and leaning forward to stare at Barry. 'Mrs Powell tells a different story from you, my friend. According to her, you've been stalking her for a couple of weeks, and you're terrifying her out of her wits. She's seen you on at least two occasions, described you down to what colour shoes you wear and denies absolutely that anyone was with her last night or that she was making love on her sitting-room carpet at two o'clock in the morning. She wants you locked up because, until you are, she's too frightened to stay in her house.' He switched his gaze to Deacon. 'She has also described in meticulous detail how your friend here forced his way in on Thursday night and refused to leave. She says he was drunk, violent and abusive, and refused to explain at any point why he was there. So? What the hell's going on with you two and this woman?'

There was a short silence.

'She's very beautiful,' Deacon said slowly, 'and I *was* very drunk, but she's relying on the fact that I told her the next morning I couldn't remember anything.' He strolled across to the television and switched it off before leaning his back against the wall beside it. 'It was true at the time, but not after a decent breakfast and several cups of coffee. She can almost get away with saying I forced my way in, because I leaned on her door when she opened it and it would have been difficult for her to shut me out at that point. But I wasn't violent and I wasn't abusive and there was nothing to stop her calling the police if she was afraid of me. We had a brief conversation before I passed out on her sofa, and the next morning she made me drink a cup of coffee before she let me go. I said sorry so many times that it started to get on her nerves, and when I asked her if I'd frightened her, she said she was long past being frightened by anything.' He smiled slightly. 'She can accuse me of lousy timing and lousy technique' – his eyes narrowed – 'but she can't accuse me of anything else. I hardly ever become aggressive under the influence of alcohol, sergeant. Merely embarrassing.'

'That's true,' said Terry. 'He told me and Barry he wanted babies when he got drunk last night. He were weeping all over the bloody shop.'

Deacon looked at him with disfavour. 'I was not weeping.'

'Near enough,' said Terry with a wicked smile.

Harrison ignored this exchange and turned to Barry. 'You swore you hadn't been near Mrs Powell's house before last night.'

Barry flushed guiltily. 'I hadn't.'

'I don't believe you.'

The little man shook with nerves. 'I hadn't,' he repeated.

'She described you in detail, told me where you were standing when she saw you. How could she do that if she didn't see you?'

'I don't know,' said Barry helplessly.

'Did she say when she saw him?' asked Deacon.

'She's not sure of the exact dates, but the first occasion was about ten days ago, and the second two or three days later.' He took a notebook from his pocket and flipped over the pages. 'She described him as a short man with glasses, wearing a blue anorak, grey slacks and light-coloured shoes which were probably suede. She said he was standing outside her house when she approached it in her car, but walked away when she turned into her drive. Do you still deny that it was you, Barry?'

'Yes.' He looked in desperation towards Deacon. 'It can't have been me, Mike. I never went there before.'

Deacon frowned. 'It sounds like you,' he pointed out, wondering if he had been wrong and Harrison right. 'It's one hell of an accurate description.'

'Jesus, it's a good thing I didn't go for that drink,' said Terry scornfully. 'You two'd be lost without me.' He turned aggressively on Barry. 'What was it I said to you in the kitchen? Sad people wear anoraks, but *really* sad people wear suede shoes. And what did you say to me? It's a pity you didn't meet me on Thursday because that's when you bought the shoes. I told you that bitch was clever. She's got one of those coppers to give her a description of you and fed it back to Mr Harrison here.

If you paid for those shoes with a credit card, mate, you're in the clear, ain't you? There's no way you could've been wearing them ten days ago.'

Barry's sad face brightened. 'I did,' he said. 'I've even got the receipt. It's in my room at home.'

'And how many other pairs of suede shoes do you own?' asked Harrison, unimpressed by Terry's reasoning.

'None,' said Barry with rising excitement. 'I bought these as a Christmas present to myself because all my shoes are black. Mike knows that. He's the one who told me black shoes were boring.'

'Yes,' said Deacon thoughtfully, 'I did.' He bent to flick ash into the ashtray on the coffee table, using the pause for some rapid thinking. 'Give me a description of the man she was with last night, Barry,' he said, 'the one she's denying was there.'

'I've already told you,' said Barry uncomfortably.

'Tell me again.'

'Fair, good-looking . . .' he petered out in an embarrassed silence, unwilling to revisit his shameful voyeuristic excitement. The thrill of the experience had long since vanished for him.

'The description Barry gave me this afternoon,' Deacon told Harrison, 'was tall, slim, blond, tanned and with a tattoo or birthmark on his right shoulder blade. He didn't recognize him, and I don't recognize the description, but let's say I can prove to you that such a man exists and that Amanda Powell is well acquainted with him?'

Harrison wasn't against the proposition. He still smarted from the drubbing he had received when he dared to question her denial. *But* . . . 'What difference would it make?'

'It might persuade you to ask her why she's lying about him being there.'

'I repeat, what difference does it make? There's no law against her having a man in her house, and Barry could have seen him on one of the other occasions she says he was there. In itself, the man's existence proves nothing.'

'But, just for the moment, assume Barry's telling the truth. Accept that he hadn't been to Mrs Powell's house before and that he did see a man there last night. Aren't you curious about why she's lying? I know I am.'

Harrison held his gaze for a moment. 'Mrs Powell is very' – he sought for a word – 'convincing.' He looked as if he were about to say something else, then thought better of it.

'Too convincing?' Deacon suggested.

'I didn't say that.'

Deacon stubbed out his cigarette, then moved to the telephone and consulted the address book beside it. He dialled a number. 'Hello, Maggie, it's Mike Deacon here. Yes, I know it's late, but I really do need to talk to Alan rather urgently.' He waited, then smiled into the receiver. 'Yes, you old buzzard, it's me again. How are you feeling?' He laughed. 'She let you have a Bell's? Things are looking up then. A small favour over the phone, that's all. I'm going to switch over to the loudspeaker because there are three other people in the room, and they're all interested in what I hope you're about to say.

320

I want you to describe Nigel de Vriess for me.' He pressed the loudspeaker button and replaced the handset.

'What he looks like, you mean?' barked Alan Parker's gravelly voice.

'Yes. You might just confirm that you've never given me a description of him before.'

'Only if you tell me what this is all about. I may be on my last legs, but I'm still a journalist. What's the oily toad been up to?'

'I'm not sure yet. You'll be the first to know after me.'

'And pigs might fly.' Alan chuckled. 'All right, I've never given you his description before. To the best of my recollection he's about my height – which is five eleven – and has blond hair which he dyes to cover the grey. He's always impeccably dressed in dark suits, probably from Harrods. Wears a white carnation in his button-hole. Good-looking, suave. Think of Roger Moore as James Bond and you won't go far wrong. Anything else you want to know?'

'We were given a description of a man I believe to be him.' Deacon's grin reflected itself in his voice. 'But he was bollock-naked at the time, so how he dresses doesn't help us much. He was described as having an all-over body tan and a tattoo or a birthmark on his right shoulder blade. Can you verify either of those facts?'

'Hah! I can't speak for the tan, but he certainly has a birthmark on his shoulder blade. Legend has it, put about by him, of course, that it's shaped like the devil's number – 666 – which is why he was a millionaire by the age of thirty, the devil looking after his own and all that twaddle. But one of his floozies described it as looking more like a dog's pizzle. Never seen it myself, so can't say either way.' His voice took on a wheedling tone. 'Come on, Mike. What *is* all this? I'll have your hide if DVS is on the skids, and you've kept it to yourself. I've got shares in the bloody thing.'

'To the best of my knowledge, this has nothing to do with his business, Alan.' With renewed promises to keep his old friend posted, Deacon cut the line and lifted an eyebrow in Harrison's direction. 'Amanda's in-laws have been claiming for five years that she and Nigel de Vriess conspired to defraud Lowenstein's Bank of £10 million, then made a scapegoat of her husband by murdering him. No one, including the police, has ever taken the claims seriously because there was no evidence that Nigel and Amanda had anything to do with each other after she married James.'

Harrison digested this in silence for a moment. 'There still isn't,' he pointed out. 'Everything your friend said is presumably in the public domain. What was to stop you or Barry looking it up and then using it to compromise Mrs Powell?'

'Nothing at all,' said Deacon evenly, lighting another cigarette. 'In fact, that's exactly what I was planning to do after Christmas. The first opportunity I had, I intended to make an appointment to interview de Vriess. You'll have to take my word for it that the only research I've done on him so far was to treat Alan Parker to a drink last Sunday and ask him how de Vriess funded the purchase of his mansion in Hampshire, which is the area that's been exercising the brains – and curiosity – of the Streeter family.'

'And I never even knew of him before last night,' put in Barry tentatively.

Deacon retrieved his notes from the kitchen, and shut the door hurriedly on the heavy fetid air that seeped out of it like sump oil. He handed the *Mail* Diary piece to Harrison and explained briefly why he'd been looking for it, or something like it. 'We're after anything that might connect Billy Blake to Amanda Powell,' he finished.

'Have you found a connection?'

Deacon's expression was neutral. 'We're still working on it. As I told you this afternoon, the most likely explanation is that Billy was her husband. But we can't prove it.'

There was a long pause while Harrison considered the implications of what Deacon had told him.

'If Billy was James, then her in-laws are wrong,' he pointed out. 'She and de Vriess couldn't have murdered him five years ago if he was still alive in June.'

Deacon grinned. 'Even we amateurs worked that one out, so I'm beginning to think it's the crux of the whole thing. It's so blindingly obvious, after all.'

He resumed his position against the wall and told Harrison at length how he believed Amanda had seized upon the fortuitous death of a strange man in her garage, who bore an odd resemblance to her husband, to clear herself of lingering suspicions of murder and at the same time formalize her position as a widow. 'My only role, as

I see it, was to be the objective observer who generated official interest,' he finished. 'But she must be very worried now if she thinks Barry saw her and Nigel together. She can't afford doubts being raised about her relationship with him.'

Harrison clearly found the arguments convincing and asked if he could borrow the photographs of Billy's mugshot and the young James Streeter. 'How would you expect her to react when I show her these?' he queried, tucking them into his coat pocket.

But Deacon shook his head. 'I've no idea,' he said honestly, remembering how her nails had dug into his chin when he had made the suggestion himself.

'Why didn't you tell Mr Harrison about Billy being this Fenton geezer?' asked Terry after the DS had gone.

'Do you know what a scoop is?'

'Sure.'

'That's why I didn't tell him.'

'Yeah, but you just gave him a load of bull instead. I mean, Amanda ain't stupid, is she? She can't never have thought it'd be that easy to have James declared dead. The Old Bill'd need loads more proof than a couple of snapshots.'

Deacon grinned. 'She called me a clever man when *I* put the theory to her.'

'Do you fancy her?'

'What on earth makes you think that?'

'Why else'd you want to pass out on her sofa?'

Deacon rubbed his jaw. 'She has the same blue eyes as my mother,' he said reflectively. 'I felt homesick.'

Harrison dropped in at the station before going on to Amanda's house. He made a few enquiries of his colleagues, then put through a call to PC Dutton in Kent. Had Mrs Powell been informed of Barry Grover's release? Yes. And how much information had Dutton given her about him? A full description was the answer, and details of when he had been outside her house. Was this wrong? There had been nothing on the faxed information requesting confidentiality, and Mrs Powell had pointed out quite reasonably that she needed to know who to look for in case he troubled her again.

Harrison had worked himself into a fine fury by the time he reached the Thamesbank Estate.

The WPC who was minding Amanda pending Harrison's return from re-interviewing Barry answered the door. 'Where is she?' demanded the sergeant, pushing past her.

'In the sitting-room.'

'Right. I want a witness to this. You'll make notes of everything she says, and if you bat one eyelid at what *I* say, you'll damn well wish you hadn't. Have you got that?' He shouldered open the door to the sitting-room and sat himself squarely on the sofa facing Amanda. 'You've been lying to me, Mrs Powell.'

She drew away from him.

'There *was* a man in this house last night.'

She leaned forward to sift the rose-petal pot-pourri, scattering the scent through her slender fingers. 'You're quite wrong, sergeant. I was on my own.'

Harrison ignored this. 'We've tentatively identified your' – he chose the next word carefully – '*companion* as Nigel de Vriess. Will he also deny being here?'

Something shifted at the back of her eyes, and he felt his vestigial hackles rise in response. She reminded him suddenly of a bad-tempered Siamese cat his grandmother had once owned. As long as it was left alone, it was beautiful; touched, it clawed and spat. When it tore deep tramlines in her face one day, his grandmother had it put down. 'Beauty is as beauty does,' she had remarked without regret.

'I would imagine so,' Amanda remarked.

'When did you last see him?'

'I've no idea. It's so long ago I couldn't possibly say.'

'Before or after your husband went missing?'

'Before.' She shrugged. 'Long before.'

'So if I ask his partner where Nigel was last night, she'll probably say he was at home with her?'

The tip of her pink tongue played across her lips, moistening them. 'I wouldn't know.'

'I *will* be asking her, Mrs Powell, and I'm sure she'll ask me why I'm asking.'

She shrugged again. 'I have no interest in either of them.'

'Then why were you so determined to discredit Barry Grover earlier?'

She didn't answer.

Harrison dipped a hand into his pocket. 'Tell me

about Billy Blake,' he invited. 'Did you recognize him when you found him in your garage?'

She took the change of tack with only the mildest of frowns. 'Billy Blake?' she echoed. 'Of course I didn't recognize him. Why would I? He was a stranger.'

He produced the borrowed photographs, and aligned them carefully on the coffee table. 'The same man?' he suggested.

Her shock was so extreme that he couldn't doubt it was genuine. Whatever else she might be guilty of, he thought, it had clearly never crossed her mind that Billy Blake might be mistaken for her missing husband.

But then Deacon had omitted to mention that she'd heard that very same theory on Thursday night.

Deacon replaced the telephone receiver with a gleam of amusement in his dark eyes. 'Harrison's pissed off with being sent on wild-goose chases,' he remarked. 'Apparently Mrs Powell looked poleaxed when he showed her the photos.'

'I'm not surprised,' said Terry. 'Like Barry said, if you forget the difference in age, it takes a computer to tell them apart. Maybe she's shitting bricks right this minute because she's suddenly clicked that it might've been James after all.'

'No,' said Deacon slowly, 'she didn't blink an eyelid when I suggested it to her. She's always known it wasn't him, so why throw a wobbly for Harrison?' He looked at his watch. 'I'm going out,' he said abruptly. 'You two can watch a late movie till I get back.'

'Where are you going?' demanded Terry.

'Never you mind.'

'You're planning a Peeping Tom act like old Barry, ain't you? You're going to sneak into her garden and drool while she gets rogered by Nigel.'

Deacon stared down at him. 'You've got a grubby little mind, Terry. Unless Sergeant Harrison's blind as a bat, Nigel de Vriess is long gone.' He levelled a finger at the boy. 'I won't be more than a couple of hours, so behave yourself. I'll skin you alive if you try anything on while I'm out of this flat.'

Terry flicked a thoughtful glance in Barry's direction. 'You can trust *me*, Mike.'

The traffic was thin at that time of night, and it took only half an hour to drop down through the City and head east along the river to the Isle of Dogs. He kept a wary eye on his rear-view mirror, regretting his decision to open the second bottle of wine. Lights blazed in Amanda's house and he toyed with the idea of acting out Terry's fantasy by sneaking round the back and peeping through her sitting-room windows. The idea was more attractive than he liked to admit, but he abandoned it for fear of the consequences. Instead he fulfilled one of Billy's prophecies. *'You will never do what you want because the tribe's will is stronger than yours.'*

He rang the doorbell and listened to the sound of her footsteps in the hall. There was a brief silence while she put her eye to the spy-glass. 'I'm not going to open this door, Mr Deacon,' she said from the other side, 'so I suggest you leave before I call the police.'

'I doubt they'll come,' he said, stooping to smile amiably into the pinhole. 'They're bored with the both of us. At the moment they can't decide which of us is telling more lies, although you seem to have the edge. Sergeant Harrison's deeply put out by your refusal to admit that Nigel de Vriess was in this house last night.'

'He wasn't.'

'Barry saw him.'

'Your friend's sick.'

He leaned his shoulder against the door and took out a cigarette. 'A little confused, perhaps, like me. I had no idea I'd frightened you so much on Thursday night, Amanda, not when you were so charming to me the next morning.' He paused, waiting for an answer. 'Sergeant Harrison's surprised you didn't call the police when I passed out on the sofa. It's what most women would have done when faced with a violent and abusive intruder.'

'What do you want, Mr Deacon?'

'A chat. Preferably inside where it's warmer. I've found out who Billy was.'

There was a long silence before the chain rattled and she opened the door. The light in the hall was very bright and he was taken aback by her appearance. She seemed unwell. Her face was drawn and colourless, and she looked nothing like the radiant woman in the yellow dress who had dazzled him three days ago.

He frowned. 'Are you all right?'

'Yes.' She was staring at him rather oddly, as if she expected to see a reaction in his eyes, and relaxed visibly when he showed none. She stepped back. 'You'd better come in.'

He looked around the hall and noticed a suitcase at the bottom of the stairs. 'Going somewhere?'

'No. I've just come back from my mother's.'

'What's wrong?'

'Nothing.'

He followed her into the sitting-room and noticed immediately that the scent of roses was absent. Instead, the window was open and the rotten smell of the exposed river banks seemed to be drifting in on the night air. 'The tide must be out,' he said. 'You should have kept one of the flats in Teddington, Amanda. There's no tide above the locks.'

What little colour remained in her face leached out of it. 'What are you talking about?'

'The smell. It's not very pleasant. You should shut your window.' He lowered himself on to the sofa and lit his cigarette, watching her as she sprayed the room with air freshener before fluttering the pot-pourri between her fingers to disperse its scent.

'Is that better?' she asked him.

'Can't you tell?'

'Not really. I'm so used to it.' She took the chair opposite. 'Are you going to tell me who Billy was?'

The tic was working furiously at the corner of her mouth, and he wondered why she was so agitated and why she looked so deathly pale. Whatever he may have told Harrison, it would take more than Barry's chance

330

sighting of her with Nigel de Vriess to give credence to the Streeters' theory of conspiracy to murder. She had impressed him as a woman of cool composure, and he was puzzled by her lack of it now. The paradox was that he found her infinitely less attractive in despair – so much so that he wondered why he had ever lusted after her – but a great deal more likeable. Vulnerability was a quality he recognized and understood.

'His name was Peter Fenton. You probably remember the story. He was a diplomat – believed to have been a spy – who vanished from his house in 1988 and was never seen again. Not as Peter Fenton, anyway.'

She didn't say anything.

'You don't seem very impressed.'

She pressed her hands to her lips for a moment, and he realized that her silence owed more to the fact that she couldn't speak than that she didn't want to. 'Why did he come here?' she managed at last.

'I don't know. I hoped *you* would tell *me*. Did you or James know him?'

She shook her head.

'Are you sure? Do you know everyone James knew?'

'Yes.'

Deacon took the *Mail* Diary piece on de Vriess from his pocket and handed it to her. 'Billy read that three weeks before he ended up dead in your garage. Let's say he went to Halcombe House with the intention of getting Amanda Streeter's address out of Nigel because he didn't know you were calling yourself Amanda Powell or that you lived and worked within a mile or so of where he was dossing.' He thought for a moment and, in the absence of an ashtray, tapped ash into his palm. 'The fact that he arrived here meant Nigel must have told him how to find you, which makes your lover a bit of a bastard, Amanda. First, for giving out your address to any old drunken bum who asks for it, and secondly for not telling you to expect a visitor. He didn't, did he?'

She licked her lips. 'How do you know Billy read this?'

Deacon lied. 'One of the men at the warehouse told me. So what's it all about? Why should Peter Fenton be so intent on finding Amanda Streeter? And why would Nigel help him? Did *they* know each other?'

She rubbed her temples with trembling fingers. 'I don't know.'

'Okay, try this. What might Peter have known about you that sent him chasing after you when he read your name in the newspaper? Maybe he had something on you *and* Nigel, and Nigel wriggled out by persuading him it was you he needed to talk to?'

She withdrew into her chair and closed her eyes. 'Billy never spoke to me. I didn't know he was here until he was dead. I don't know who he was or why he came to my house. Most of all, I don't know why—' She fell silent.

'Go on.'

'I feel ill.'

Deacon glanced towards the window. 'Tell me about Nigel,' he prompted. 'Why would he give your address to Peter without telling you he'd done it?'

'I don't know.' She gave a troubled shake of her head.

'Why do you think he knew him as Peter Fenton? It was Billy Blake who died in my garage.'

'Okay. Why give your address to Billy?'

'I don't know,' she said again. 'What sort of man was he?' Her eyes opened wide, and Deacon feared she was about to vomit.

'If you mean Billy, he was a fine man.' He took a handkerchief from his pocket. 'I find it's easier to hold on,' he said with a faint smile, 'but you know where the lavatory is if you need it.' He waited till her gagging ceased. 'A psychiatrist who had three sessions with him described him as half-saint, half-fanatic. I've read a transcript of part of their interview. Billy believed in the salvation of souls and the mortification of the flesh, but he felt himself to be personally damned.' He studied her for a moment. 'From my own experience of him, through the medium of Terry Dalton – a youngster he befriended and cared for – I'd say Billy was a man of honour and integrity despite being a drunk and a thief.'

'Why should any of that make him want to come here?'

Deacon got up and went to the window to toss his dog-end into the garden. The air that blew in was sweet and clean and smelt faintly of the sea. He turned back to the cloying atmosphere of her spare, minimalist sur-roundings and he began to understand why her car was always parked in her driveway, why she drenched the room in rose-scented spray and, ultimately, why six months after Billy's death she had been so desperate to find out who her uninvited guest had been. He had had an inkling of it once before, but hadn't believed it. He held the back of his hand to his nose, and he saw recognition in her eyes because he was reacting the way she had expected when he first entered the house. 'What did you do to him, Amanda?'

'Nothing. If I'd known he was there, I'd have helped him as I helped you.'

She had put on a hell of a performance for Harrison in the last few hours, but was she acting now? Deacon didn't think so, but then he was no judge. 'Why did you lie to Harrison about me and Barry?' he asked, opening all the windows to let in the freezing air. Anything was better than the sweet, sickly smell of death.

She shook her head, unable to cope with the sudden switch of direction.

'Are the Streeters right? Did you and Nigel work the fraud and then murder James?'

She lowered the handkerchief. 'James worked the fraud. Everyone knows that except his family. They were so proud of the success he made of his life that they forgot what he was really like. He loathed them, never went near them in case their penny-pinching poverty rubbed off on him.' She sounded very bitter. 'He was always on the make, always after insider knowledge of stocks that might double in value overnight. I've never been less surprised about anything than when the police told me he'd embezzled £10 million.'

'Where did he get the knowledge to bypass the computer system? Did Marianne Filbert help him?'

Amanda shrugged. 'She must have done. Who else was there?'

'Nigel de Vriess?' he suggested. 'It's too much of a coincidence that he bought out Softworks after James and Marianne disappeared.'

She rested her head against the back of her chair. 'If Nigel was involved,' she said wearily, 'then he covered his tracks extremely well. He was investigated along with everyone else, but all the evidence pointed to James. I'm sorry the Streeters can't see that but it is the truth.'

'If you dislike James so much, why are you still married to him?'

'I didn't want any more publicity. And why get divorced if you don't want to marry again?' Unexpectedly she smiled. 'There's a simple explanation for everything, Mr Deacon, even this house. Lowndes, the company that developed the Teddington flats, also built this estate. I negotiated a straightforward exchange. I gave them full title to the Teddington property in return for full title to this house. And they did rather better out of the deal than I did. Converting the school was easy because I'd already done the drawings and obtained planning permission, and the flats were sold even before they were finished. Lowndes had far more trouble shifting these houses because they'd overpriced them, and the housing market was in the doldrums in 1991. You may not believe it, but I did them a favour by taking this one off their hands.' Her voice took on its bitter note again. 'If the bank hadn't threatened to pull the rug out from under me because of the uncertainty over James, I'd have made a great deal more by seeing the development through than by accepting this house in lieu.'

Were explanations ever that simple? Why hadn't she

fought harder to see her project through? She was no pushover, in all conscience. *And once she'd cleared herself of involvement in the fraud . . .* 'You told me Billy liked to doss down as near the river as possible,' he said, 'but the same is true of you. Teddington's on the river. This house is on the river. Your office is on the river. Could the river be the connection between you?'

She raised the handkerchief to her mouth. There was still no colour in her face except the blue of her eyes, which followed every movement he made. 'If I knew the answer to that—' She paused. 'I thought – well, I hope it's enough just to identify him. If I can put the right name on his plaque—' She fell silent.

'He'll rest in peace?'

She nodded. 'It's not always like this, you know.' She gestured unhappily towards the window. 'It's been worse since you came to the house.'

'Has he ever spoken to you?'

'No.'

'I think I heard him,' Deacon said matter-of-factly. 'Either that or I was dreaming. "Devourer of thy parent, now thy unutterable torment renews,"' he explained. 'I heard that.'

'Why would Billy say that?'

'I don't know. He was obsessed with religion. I think he may have murdered somebody and that's why he believed he was damned. Both he and his wife seemed to see hell as their inevitable destiny.' *'My own redemption doesn't interest me . . .' Whose then? Verity's? Amanda's?* He eyed her curiously. 'He preached repentance to others but seemed to see his own salvation in terms of a divine hand reaching down into the bottomless pit to pull him out. He said there's no way out of hell except through God's mercy.'

Her fingers tightened round the handkerchief, compressing it into a tight ball. 'What does that have to do with me?'

Or me, thought Deacon. *Why do I get the feeling that my fate is inextricably linked with Billy's ...? He said London was full of shit ... I've watched men die violently ... The water reminded him of blood ... She sends her shit along the river to infect the innocent places further down ...*

'I need to talk to Nigel de Vriess,' he said abruptly. 'If he gave Billy your address, then Billy may have explained why he wanted it' – he paused to reflect – 'although it doesn't explain why Nigel didn't warn you to expect him.' He smiled slightly. 'I would have said he didn't like you, Amanda, if Barry hadn't witnessed what you and he were up to last night.'

She shrugged indifferently. 'Your friend's quite capable of coming up with sick fantasies about what he saw through my window. What he did to my photograph was disgusting. Even you must recognize he's an unreliable witness.'

Deacon drew his coat about him. It was very cold although Amanda seemed unaffected by it. 'I don't. He's totally reliable when it comes to anything visual. Is the Streeters' conspiracy theory right? Is that why it's so important to keep denying that Nigel was here?'

'You've already asked me that, and I've already given you my answer.'

'Do you have de Vriess's telephone number?'

'Of course not. I haven't seen him in five years.'

He gave a low laugh. 'Then for your sake, I hope he's as good a liar as you are. You're too elegant to end up with egg on your face.' He raised a hand in farewell. 'Happy Christmas, Amanda.'

'Happy Christmas, Mr Deacon.' She held out his handkerchief.

'You keep it,' he said. 'Something tells me you'll be needing it more than I do.'

Terry Dalton (14)
Lived with Billy from 1993   Cadogan Square   Paris
                                     Geoffrey Standish's house?   Embassy? Peter Fenton

Tom Beale (68)   m. (1956)   m. (1980)
Lived with Billy from – ?
                                     Verity
                                     (1937–1988)

                                     Anthony & Marilyn

The warehouse
(How long derelict?)   HELL

SUICIDE   Peter Fenton/Billy Blake (45)   IDENTITY
                     (Winchester, Cambridge, Foreign Office)
                                     (1950–1995)
                              (Vanished 3 July 1988)
                 Geoffrey Standish died 10.3.71 – 20 mls from Cambridge

The Thames   MURDER   Nigel de Vriess (48)
                                                (Softworks/DVS/left
                                                Lowenstein's – 1990)

                                                Amanda Streeter-Powell (36)
                                                m. (1986)
                                                James Streeter (44)
                                                (Vanished 27 April 1990)

                              MONEY

W.F. Meredith (architects)   Lowenstein's Bank
Teddington flats (c. 1900)
Thamesbank Estate   Marianne Filbert
(Amanda moved 1991)   (Left UK for USA – 1989)
(From where?)   (Vanished April 1990)

                     Where was Billy in April 1990?

Chapter Eighteen

'I RECKON YOU and Mike take me for a mug,' said Terry, opening another can of lager and sprawling on the sofa again. 'I don't swallow this bullshit about you wanting to know what Amanda looked like. I've seen the way you watch Mike, and I've seen the way he watches you, and my guess is you're panting for him to do some uphill gardening, and he don't fancy the idea.'

Barry wouldn't look at him. 'I don't understand what you're talking about,' he said.

'Sure you do. You're a faggot, Barry. So what were you after when you went round Amanda's? And what did the Old Bill nick you for?' He put a cigarette between his lips and rolled it from side to side with the tip of his tongue. 'Know what I think? I think you got well worked up having a drink with me and Mike, and then went out to do some damage to the competition. I bet it really sticks in your gullet that he fancies Amanda more than he fancies you. Am I right or am I right?'

Barry reached forward to switch up the volume on the television. 'I don't want to talk to you,' he said.

'Stands to reason. You might hear something you don't want to hear, like Mike ain't so unavailable as he's making out.' His lips thinned to a cruel line as he lit his cigarette. 'He's pretty fucking keen on me, that's for sure.'

Barry didn't say anything.

'How about you then? You keen on me, too, are you? You were getting mighty close last night when we were going through them photos.' He propped himself on one elbow and drank noisy mouthfuls of lager.

'You shouldn't be talking like this.'

'Why not?' said the boy with a sneer. 'It makes you excited, doesn't it?'

Barry doubted anything would excite him again. Fear was the only emotion he understood now. He should have trusted his first impression that Terry was a shaven-headed thug, then he could have saved himself this terrible disappointment. He took off his glasses and stared blindly at the screen. 'If I were a different kind of man – a braver one,' he said after a moment, 'I'd stand up to you. Not for me, but for Mike. It doesn't matter what you say about me, I've had people talk about me behind my back all my life, but Mike deserves better. The sad thing is, he thinks you're a decent lad.' He squeezed the bridge of his nose between his fingers as if trying to hold back tears. 'But he couldn't be more wrong, could he?'

'Yeah, well, it ain't your place to lecture me about decency, being as how you most likely got arrested for *in*decency.'

'Did you abuse Billy's friendship the way you're abusing Mike's?'

'If I knew what it meant, I might be able to tell you.'

'Yes, I forgot. You're ignorant as well as despicable.'

Terry grinned. 'You want to be careful what you say to me, Barry. I ain't scared of no queer.' He blew a stream of smoke disdainfully in Barry's direction.

'Don't do that,' said the fat little man in a stifled voice. 'I suffer from asthma.'

'Jesus wept. If you weren't such a girl, you'd've hit me. Ain't you got no bottle at all?'

He was quite unprepared for the speed with which Barry launched himself at his throat, and equally unprepared for the little man's deceptive weight and strength. As his lungs started to struggle under the combined constriction of his throat and Barry's solid knee in the centre of his chest, he realized he'd tried the rape scam on the wrong person. He looked despairingly into Barry's unseeing eyes and saw only madness.

'Where's Terry?' asked Deacon as he let himself back into the flat.

'In his room.'

'Asleep?'

'Probably. He's been in there half an hour. Can I get you something, Mike? Coffee? A drink?'

Deacon looked around the room, noticed Terry's abandoned cigarettes on the floor and the stain on the carpet where his lager had fallen over. 'What's been going on?'

Barry followed his gaze. 'I'm sorry about that. He knocked the can over accidentally. He's tired, Mike. Don't forget he's only fourteen.'

'Did he try something on?'

'I'd rather you asked him.'

'Okay. How about a coffee? I'll check on him while you're making it.' He watched the other man go into the kitchen then went down the side corridor and tapped lightly on the spare bedroom door.

'If that's you, you murdering bastard,' said Terry's suspicious voice from the other side, 'you can bog off. I ain't coming out till Mike gets back.'

'It is Mike.'

'Jesus,' said the boy, pulling the door wide, 'am I pleased to see you. Barry's round the fucking twist. He tried to kill me.' He pointed to his throat. 'Look at that. Fucking finger prints.'

'Nasty,' said Deacon, looking at the red marks on the boy's neck. 'Why did he do it?'

'Because he's a nutter, that's why.' Terry poked his head nervously round the door jamb. 'By rights I should have the law on him. He's well dangerous, he is.'

'What's stopping you?' Deacon's eyes narrowed. 'You weren't so backward when Denning went mad.'

'That were different.'

'Meaning Denning didn't have a reason to attack Walt but Barry had a damn good reason for attacking you? You're a fool, Terry. I warned you to behave while I was out. Frankly, if you're not prepared to treat Barry with respect, you'd better leave now.'

'How do you know it weren't him started it?'

'It's the law of the jungle. Rabbits never attack weasels unless they're cornered. Plus, you're still alive, which you wouldn't be if Barry was a nutter.' He started to walk away. 'You've got two choices, sunshine,' he said over his shoulder. 'Apologize or go.'

'I ain't apologizing to no pervert. It's him tried to kill *me*.'

Deacon turned round. 'You didn't learn a damn thing from Billy, did you?' he said wearily. 'He put his hand in the fire for you to teach you the dangers of uncontrollable anger, be it yours or anyone else's, but you were too stupid to understand the message. I think I'm wasting my time with you, just as he did. You'd better start packing.'

It was a subdued Terry who joined them in the kitchen ten minutes later. There was a revealing redness about his eyes, and his walk was less cocky than usual. Deacon, who was reworking his chart, glanced up briefly, expression neutral, then returned to what he was doing. Terry thrust his bony hand at Barry. 'Sorry, mate,' he said. 'I were well out of order. No hard feelings, eh?'

Barry, who had been sitting in an uncomfortable silence while Deacon ignored him, took the hand in surprise. 'I think – ' he looked at the marks on Terry's neck – 'well, it's I who should apologize.'

'Nah. Mike's right. It were me pushed you into it. You're braver than you think. You said you'd stand up, and you did. It were my fault.'

Barry looked as if he was about to agree with him until he caught Deacon's gaze on him and changed his mind. The only thing Deacon had said to him since he'd returned to the kitchen was: 'I don't care what he said to you, Barry, but if you ever lift a hand against a child again, I'll take you apart at the seams.'

Now Deacon pointed to an empty chair as he pushed the chart to one side. 'Sit down,' he invited, listening to the distant sound of bells ringing out for midnight mass. 'Perhaps we should have gone to church,' he said, nodding towards the window. 'We always used to go to midnight mass when I was a child and it's the only time I can remember us functioning as a normal family.'

Terry, accepting this for what it was – a truce – perked up again. 'Did you go the night your dad shot himself?'

Deacon smiled slightly at Barry's horrified expression but the horror was for Terry's insensitivity, he thought, and not his father's messy death. 'No. If we had, he wouldn't have done it. We stopped going to church when he and Ma stopped talking.'

'Billy said the family that prays together stays together.'

Deacon didn't reply because he didn't want to disillusion the boy. He often thought it was the accruing disappointment of the thousand prayers that went unanswered that had led his family to disintegrate. *Please God, let Pa be nice to my friends . . . Please God, let Pa be ill so that he won't come to sports day . . . Please God, let Pa die . . .*

'My father was an atheist,' said Barry apologetically, as if he, too, didn't want to disillusion the boy.

'What happened to him?' asked Terry.

'He died of a heart attack when I was ten.' Barry sighed. 'It was very sad. My mother changed afterwards. She used to be such a happy person, but now, well, the

345

trouble is I look so like my father – she resents that, I think.'

The conversation lapsed and they listened in silence to the pealing bells. Deacon regretted stirring memories, however good the cause. In twenty years he had not rid himself of the terrible sight of his father's blood-spattered study and the shapeless huddle that had once been Francis. Suicide, he thought, was the least forgivable of deaths because there was no time to prepare for the shock of bereavement. Whatever grief he had felt had been subsumed in disgust as he had wiped his father's blood and brains off walls, paintings, shelves and books.

It led him to think of that other suicide. 'I wonder why Verity hanged herself,' he murmured.

'I don't reckon she did,' said Terry. 'I reckon it were Billy killed her.' He gripped the air as he had done beside the brazier the first time Deacon had met him. 'That'd be more than enough to send him off his rocker.'

Deacon shook his head. 'That's the first thing the police would have looked at. The evidence of suicide must have been very convincing to persuade them otherwise.'

'Surely Anne Cattrell's right,' said Barry. 'If Verity found out by accident that she'd married her husband's murderer, wouldn't that be reason enough to kill herself?'

'I don't see why. She hated Geoffrey.' Deacon tapped his pencil against his teeth. 'According to Roger Hyde's book, her son thought she was having an affair.' He ringed Verity's name and drew a line down to James Streeter. 'How about that? Think how alike James and

Peter were. She'd have been attracted to James on looks alone. It's one explanation for Billy's interest in Amanda's address.'

'Meaning he was after revenge?' queried Terry doubtfully. 'I don't see that, Mike. First off, he'd be taking revenge on the wrong person and, second off, the dish wouldn't just be cold, it'd be fucking freezing.'

Deacon chuckled. He would never tell the boy how much he admired the guts he'd just shown in that handshake with Barry, but it didn't mean the admiration wasn't there. *Shades of his relationship with his mother? In the end, perhaps love was stronger for being disguised. Clara had never ceased declaring her love right up until the day she left him.* 'All right, hot shot, give me a better idea.'

'I ain't got one. I just reckon it's all to do with fate. See, Amanda could've talked to any journalist, but she picked the one who'd get hung up on it enough to keep going. You said yourself you and Billy are linked by fate.'

'She didn't pick me,' said Deacon. 'I picked her or, more accurately, my editor picked her and sent me off against my will to interview her. Depending on what she was expecting to achieve, she was either lucky or unlucky that events in Billy's life have faint echoes in mine.'

But Terry was not to be dissuaded. 'And then there's me. I weren't never going to phone you about Billy, but then I had to because of Walt. And if Mr Harrison hadn't recognized Tom, I wouldn't have been worried about him dropping me in it, and if you hadn't met old Lawrence and persuaded him to come and hold our hands, then he wouldn't've stuck his nose in about good parenting' – he paused for breath – 'and I wouldn't be here now. Plus, Barry wouldn't've got pissed and taken himself off to gawp at Amanda and none of us would know that Nigel was still shafting her. That's fate, that is,' he finished triumphantly. 'Ain't that right, Barry?'

Barry ducked his head to take off his glasses. He was so tired after the emotional buffeting of the last twenty-four hours that he was finding it increasingly difficult to follow the conversation. 'I suppose it depends on whether you think, as my father did, that everything happens accidentally,' he said slowly. 'He believed there was no purpose to life beyond the furtherance of the species, and that you could either suffer your pointless existence or enjoy it. But to enjoy it you had to plan ahead in order to minimize the threat of unpleasant accidents.' He smiled ruefully. 'Then he died of a heart attack.'

'Do you agree with him?' asked Deacon curiously.

'Oh, no, I agree with Terry. I think fate plays a part in our destinies.' He replaced his spectacles and sheltered nervously behind them like an inexperienced knight preparing for battle. 'I can't help feeling that it doesn't really matter why Verity hanged herself, or not as far as Amanda Powell is concerned anyway.' He put a fat finger on Deacon's chart where it said: *Where was Billy in April 1990?* 'This is Billy Blake's fate, not Peter Fenton's. Peter Fenton died in 1988.'

Far away, the bells fell silent as Christmas Day began.

*

Such strange dreams inhabited Deacon's mind that night. He put them down to the fact that he opted for the sofa in order to have Barry and Terry securely shut in bedrooms with himself as a physical barrier between them. But he sometimes thought afterwards that it was too easy to say it was a bad night, coupled with subconscious fears of homosexual rape scams and memories of his father, that led him to dream about James Streeter covered in blood.

He started out of sleep in a threshing frenzy at four o'clock in the morning with his mind full of the knowledge that *he* was James and that he had woken seconds before the final crushing blow that was going to kill him. His face was awash with sweat – *blood?* – and his heartbeat hammered in the silence of the night. *And when the heart began to beat, what dread hand and what dread feet* . . . Was this a dream? *My mother groaned, my father wept, into the dangerous world I leapt* . . . Who am I? *Devourer of thy parent, now thy unutterable torment renews* . . .

It soon became clear that the old adage 'Too many cooks spoil the broth' was a true one. Barry began patiently enough but, faced with Deacon's and Terry's natural incompetence in the kitchen, he progressed rapidly through irritation to outright tyranny. 'My mother would have your head for this,' he remarked acidly, pushing Deacon away from a bowl of saturated stuffing and transferring it to the sink.

'How am I supposed to get it right if I don't have a measuring jug?' asked Deacon sulkily.

'You use your intelligence and add the water a little more slowly,' said Barry, pressing the soggy mess into a sieve and squeezing out the excess liquid. 'It may come as a surprise to you, Mike, but you're not supposed to *pour* the stuffing into the turkey, you're supposed to *stuff* it in. That's why it's called stuffing. If you poured it in, it would be called pouring.'

'All right, all right, I get the message. I'm not a complete idiot.'

'I told you he couldn't cook,' said Terry self-righteously.

Barry turned his indignation on the boy and lifted a tiny sprout from the meagre pile on the draining board. 'What's this?' he demanded.

'A sprout.'

'Correction. It *was* a sprout. Now it's a pea. When I said take off the outer leaves, I meant one layer, not two centimetres' worth. We're supposed to be eating these, not swallowing them with a glass of water.'

'You need a drink,' said Deacon's shaven-headed incubus prosaically. 'You aren't half ratty when you're sober.'

'A drink?' Barry squeaked, stamping his little feet. 'It's nine o'clock in the morning and we haven't even got the turkey in yet.' He pointed a dramatic finger at the kitchen door. 'Out of here, both of you,' he ordered, 'or you can forget lunch.'

Deacon shook his head. 'We can't do that. I've invited Lawrence Greenhill over. He'll be very disappointed if there's nothing to eat.' He watched fury rise like a red tide in Barry's face and flapped his hands placatingly as he backed towards the kitchen door. 'Don't panic. He's a great guy. You'll like him. I'm sure he won't mind waiting if the meal isn't ready on the dot of one o'clock. Look, here's an idea,' he said, as if he was the one who had thought of it, 'why don't Terry and I make ourselves scarce so that you can get on with things? We'll be back at midday to lay the table.'

'That's good,' said Terry, raising two thumbs in salute. 'Cheers, Barry. Just make sure you do loads of roast potatoes. They're my favourite, they are.'

Deacon caught him by the collar and hoicked him through the door before their chef vanished in a puff of spontaneously combusted smoke.

'Where are we going?' asked Terry as they climbed into the car. 'We've got three hours to kill.'

'Let's muddy some waters first.' Deacon reached for his mobile and dialled Directory Enquiries. 'Yes, the number of N. de Vriess, please, Halcombe House, near Andover. Thank you.' He took a pen from his inner pocket and wrote the number on his shirt cuff before switching off the telephone.

'What are you going to do?'

'Phone him and ask him what he was doing at Amanda Powell's house on Saturday night.'

'Supposing his wife answers?'

'The conversation will be even more interesting.'

'You're cruel, you are. It's Christmas Day.'

Deacon chuckled. 'I shouldn't think anyone will answer. It'll be his secretary's number. Guys like de

Vriess don't make their private numbers public.' He squinted at his cuff as he punched the digits. 'In any case, I'll hang up if Fiona answers,' he promised, putting the phone to his ear. 'Hello?' He sounded surprised. 'Am I speaking to Nigel de Vriess? . . . Is he there? . . . He's away? Yes, it is important. I've been trying to contact him on a business matter since Friday . . . My name's Michael Deacon . . . No, I'm phoning from a mobile . . .' A long pause. 'Would it be possible to speak to his wife? . . . Can you give me a number where I can find Nigel? . . . Then perhaps you can give me an idea of when he'll be back? . . . My home number? Yes, I should be there from midday onwards. Thank you.' He gave his telephone number at the flat, then disconnected and frowned thoughtfully at Terry. 'Nigel's gone away for a few days and his wife is too unwell to speak to anyone.'

'Jesus, what a bastard! I betcha he's ditched the poor cow for Amanda.'

Deacon drummed his fingers on the steering wheel. 'Except I'd put every cent I've got on that being a policeman who answered the phone, and you don't call in the police just because your notorious husband is shagging another woman.'

'What makes you think he was Old Bill?'

'Because he was too damn efficient. He cut me off after I gave my name in order to see if it meant anything to whoever was in the room with him.'

'Could've been a butler. You're likely to have a butler if you live in a mansion.'

Deacon fired the engine. 'Butlers speak first,' he said, 'but there was silence on that line till I asked for Nigel de Vriess.' He drew out into the road. 'You don't think he's done a bunk, do you?'

'Like James?'

'Yes.'

'Why'd he want to do that?'

'Because Amanda warned him that Barry saw him in her house and he's decided to run.'

'Then why hasn't she gone, too?'

Deacon recalled the suitcase that he'd seen in her hall. 'Maybe she has,' he said rather grimly. 'That's what we're going to find out.'

They drove into the Thamesbank Estate and parked across the road from Amanda's house. It had a deserted look about it. The curtains were open but, despite the greyness of the morning, there were no lights inside and the car was gone from in front of her garage.

'She could be at church,' said Terry without conviction.

'You stay here,' Deacon said. 'I'm going to have a look through her sitting-room windows.'

'Yeah, well, just don't forget what happened to Barry when he did that,' said the boy morosely. 'If the neighbours see you, we'll be carted off to the flaming nick to answer more bloody questions, and I ain't going without my lunch two days in a row.'

'I won't be long.' True to his word, he was back in five minutes. 'No sign of her,' he said, easing in behind the wheel and fishing out his cigarettes. 'So what the hell do I do about it?'

'Nothing,' said Terry firmly. 'Let the Old Bill work it out for themselves. I mean, you're gonna look a right plonker if you go steaming in with stories about Nigel and Amanda scarpering when all that's happened is they've holed up in a hotel somewhere to hump each other. You've got a real thing about her, except I can't decide whether you fancy her something rotten or think she's a hard-nosed bitch. On balance, I reckon you fancy her because you sure as hell don't like the fact she's still fucking Nigel.' He cast a mischievous glance at Deacon's profile. 'You look like you're sucking lemons every time the subject comes up.'

Deacon ignored this. 'All these houses are identical and hers is the tenth. Why did Billy choose hers?'

'Because the garage door was open.'

'Number eight's open now.'

'So what? It weren't open when Billy came here.'

Deacon looked at him. 'How do you know?'

There was a momentary pause before Terry answered. 'I'm guessing. Look, are you planning to sit here all day or what? Barry ain't gonna like it one little bit if Lawrence turns up and we ain't back.'

Despite Terry's protests, Deacon dropped in at the police station to request Sergeant Harrison's home telephone number. Sir was joking, of course. Did he think private numbers were given out to any Tom, Dick or Harry who asked for them? Had he forgotten that it was Christmas Day and that policemen, like ordinary mortals, welcomed the peace and quiet of the precious little time they spent

with their families? Deacon persisted, and finally compromised on the officer's promise to phone Harrison 'at a
reasonable time' to relay the message that Michael
Deacon needed to talk to him on a matter of urgency
regarding Amanda Streeter and Nigel de Vriess.

'It's ten thirty,' said Deacon, tapping his watch. 'Why
isn't this a reasonable time?'

'*Some* people go to church on Our Lord's birthday,'
was the sharp response.

'But most people don't,' murmured Deacon.

'More's the pity. A God-fearing society has fewer
criminals.'

'And so many whited sepulchres that you can't believe
a word anybody says.'

'Do you want me to make this phone call, sir?'

'Yes, please,' said Deacon meekly.

When they were within a mile of the flat, Deacon drew
the car into a kerb and killed the engine. 'You've been
lying to me,' he said pleasantly. 'Now I'd like the truth.'

Terry was deeply offended. 'I ain't lied to you.'

'I'll hand you back to social services if you don't start
talking pretty damn quick.'

'That's blackmail, that is.'

'Exactly.'

'I thought you liked me.'

'I do.'

'Well, then.'

'Well, then, what?' asked Deacon patiently.

'I want to stay with you.'

355

'I can't live with a liar.'

'Yeah, but if I told the truth, would you let me stay?'

It was a strange little echo of what Barry had said yesterday . . . 'Will they let me go if I tell the truth?' . . . But what was truth? . . . Verity? . . .

'You mean, heads you win, tails I lose.'

'I don't get you.'

'Presumably you've spent the last three days trying to weasel your way in by not telling me the truth.' Deacon toyed with the idea of revisiting Terry's behaviour of last night, but thought better of it. He knew from his own experience that post-mortems were bitter affairs which achieved little beyond continuing warfare.

'I reckoned you needed time to get to know me. It took Billy a couple of months before he realized I was the next best thing to sliced bread. Anyway, you can't kick me out. Not yet. I ain't learnt to read, and I want to earn that money you promised to pay me.'

'You've already cost me a fortune.'

'Yeah, but you're rich. Your ma's house alone has gotta be worth a bob or two, so you can easily afford another mouth to feed.'

'I told her to sell it.'

'She won't, though. She's well gutted about tearing up your dad's will and giving your fortune away to your sister. When the time comes – which is the few months she's given herself – she'll fade away. She's made up her mind to it, and there ain't nothing you can do to stop it unless you make it worth her while to stick around a bit longer.'

'And how do I do that?'

A sort of ancient wisdom glimmered in the boy's pale eyes. 'Billy said it's curiosity that keeps people alive, being as how we all want to know what happens next. And them that kill themselves or lie down and die before they need to reckon there's nothing left to be curious about.' He spoke seriously. 'You and your ma ain't got nothing to talk about except the stuff that made you angry enough to walk out on her, so you've got to give her something else to think about. Like me. She'd be well excited if you told her you was gonna keep me. She'd be on the phone all the time, sticking her nose into our business.'

'That's enough to put me off the idea for good.'

'Except if you don't give her a reason to talk to you, then another five years'll go by. And you don't want that any more than she does.'

'Are you sure you're only fourteen?' Deacon asked suspiciously. 'You talk like a forty-year-old sometimes.'

Terry looked injured. 'I'm mature. Anyway, I'm nearer fifteen than fourteen.'

'Social services won't allow you to stay with me,' said Deacon handing him a cigarette. 'If I expressed even mild interest in taking care of you, they'd label me a paedophile. It's dangerous these days for men to like anyone under the age of sixteen.' He held a match to the tip. 'Also, I'm irresponsible. I shouldn't let you smoke these damn things for a start.'

'Give over. I didn't get none of this grief from Billy. He just took me on board like I was his long-lost kid. I ain't asking you to adopt me, and chances are I'll be off out of it in a couple of months. Look, I just want to stay or a while longer, learn to read, meet Mrs D. again. It's a free country, and if you ain't doing nothing wrong, 'cept giving a homeless bloke a bed, why should the bastards at social services interfere?'

'Because that's what they're paid for,' said Deacon cynically, staring through the windscreen. 'How much is it going to cost me to keep a six-foot-tall teenager in food, clothes, beer and cigarettes for weeks on end?'

'I'll go begging. That'll help out.'

'No way. I'm not having a beggar in my flat or an illiterate with an impoverished vocabulary. You need educating.' *Don't say it, Deacon* ... 'You're going to bankrupt me, probably land me in prison, and at the end of it all you'll bugger off leaving me to wonder what the hell came over me.'

'I ain't like that. I stood by Billy, didn't I? And he weren't half as easy to like as you are.'

Deacon glanced at him. 'If you put one foot out of line and drop me in it with social services or the police, I'll come after you with an axe the minute I'm out of prison. Is that a deal?' He held out his hand, palm up.

Terry gripped it excitedly. 'It's a deal. Now can I phone Mrs D. and wish her happy Christmas?' He reached for the mobile. 'What's her number?'

Deacon gave it to him. 'You really like her, don't you?' he said curiously.

'She's an older version of you,' said Terry matter-of-factly, 'and I ain't never met two people who treated me straight off with respect. Even old Hugh was okay, so maybe you're none of you as bad as you like to make out. Have you ever thought of that?'

Chapter Nineteen

WHAT TERRY HAD withheld was that he *had* seen Billy again before he died, just once, at the warehouse. It was early in the morning and the boy had been sitting on the scrubland at the back, staring out over the river. There had been a dawn mist over the water, which the warming sun had begun to burn off. He described himself as feeling 'fucking depressed'.

'Life weren't the same when old Billy weren't around. Okay, he were a pain in the butt most of the time, but I'd kind of got used to him. Know what I mean? Lawrence got it about right. It were like having a dad about the place – nah, more like a granddad. Anyway, I turned round at one point and the bastard was sitting next to me. It gave me a shock because I hadn't heard him coming. Matter of fact, I don't know how I didn't have a heart attack.' He paused to reflect. 'To be honest, I thought he were a ghost,' he went on. 'He looked about as bad as I'd ever seen him – with white skin, and lips that looked as if there was no blood in them.' He shuddered at the memory. 'So I asked him what he'd been doing and he said, "Toning."'

Deacon waited. 'Did he say anything else?' he asked when Terry didn't go on.

'Yeah, it didn't make much sense though. He said, "untoned sin's the invisible worm."'

Pensively, Deacon stroked his jaw. 'I should think he said "*a*toning" and "un*a*toned". The atonement of sins is the same as repentance.' He brooded for a while, searching through his memory for word associations. 'Blake wrote a poem called "The Sick Rose",' he said at last. 'It's about a beautiful rose that's dying inside because an invisible worm is eating away at its heart.' He stared out at the windscreen. 'You can interpret its symbolism any way you like, but Billy presumably interpreted the worm as unexpiated sin.' He paused again. 'He can't have been talking about his own atonement because he was torturing himself for his sins,' he said slowly, 'which leaves only Amanda. Do you understand all that?'

'Sure, I'm not totally dumb, you know, and you said she reeked of roses. In any case, it was her place he made me take him to.'

'How do you mean "*made*"?'

'He just set off. All I could do was follow. He didn't say a word the whole way, then just walked in her garage and shut the door behind him.'

Deacon regarded him curiously. 'Did you know it was her house?'

'No. It was just a house.'

'How did Billy know the garage door would be open?'

Terry shrugged. 'Luck?' he suggested. 'None of the others were.'

'Did he say anything before he went into it?'

'Only goodbye.'

Deacon shook his head in bewilderment at the boy's apparent acceptance of Billy's bizarre behaviour. 'Didn't you ask him what he was doing? Why he wanted to go there? What it was all about?'

''Course I did, but he didn't answer. And he looked that ill, I thought he'd peg out on me at any moment, so I weren't keen to make matters worse by pestering. You couldn't never stop Billy doing what he wanted to do.'

'But weren't you worried when he didn't come back to the warehouse? Why didn't you go and fetch him?'

The injured look reappeared on Terry's face. 'I did, sort of. I went and hung around the entrance to the estate the next day, but there weren't no sign of him, and I was too scared to go in there two days in a row in case the cops came down on me like a ton of bricks for casing the joint. Anyway, I was afraid of getting Billy in shit if he were holed up somewhere cosy. So me and Tom talked it over, and we'd got to the point of thinking we'd go round and suss the place out when Tom read in a newspaper that Billy'd snuffed it in Amanda's garage.' He shrugged. 'And that were the end of it.'

'Can you remember which day you took Billy there?'

Terry looked uncomfortable. 'Yeah, but Tom reckons I was stoned on cannabis most of that week and got everything muddled. It ain't true, but it's the only thing that makes sense. Me and him went all the way to the cemetery after Amanda told us she'd done the honours for Billy, just to make sure she weren't lying about it, and it was there in black and white. Billy Blake, died June twelfth, 1995.'

Deacon flicked through his diary. 'The twelfth was a Monday, and the pathologist estimated he'd been dead five days when the body was found on the following Friday. So which day did you see him?'

'The Tuesday. And it was the Wednesday I hung about outside the estate, the Thursday me and Tom talked it over and the Friday we reckoned we'd go round to take a butcher's. It were about eight o'clock at night, we was on our way, Tom lifts an *Evening Standard* from a bin, and there's this steaming great headline saying: "Homeless man starves to death." So he reads it and goes: "Jesus, you're an arsehole, Terry, the bastard's been dead for days and you've suckered me into looking for a corpse."'

Deacon was silent for so long that Terry eventually spoke again.

'Yeah, well, maybe Tom was right. Maybe it was the Tuesday before, and I was so stoned I let a whole week go by before I did anything.'

'According to the police he went into the garage on Saturday, the tenth.'

'It weren't a Saturday when I saw him,' said the boy decidedly. 'Saturdays are good tourist days, so I'd've been out begging.'

Deacon felt for the key in the ignition. 'How long after Billy died did Amanda come asking questions?'

'A few weeks. She'd paid for his cremation by then because she told us about it.'

The engine fired and Deacon put it into gear. 'Why didn't you tell her Billy was still alive on the Tuesday?'

Terry stared despondently out of the window. 'For the same reason I didn't tell you. I don't reckon he was, see. Matter of fact, I don't like to think about it too much. I mean, *d'you* believe in ghosts?'

Deacon recalled the smell of death that had been in Amanda's house and wondered uneasily about the nature of Billy's *deus ex machina.*

. . . I believe in hell . . .

. . . I have nightmares sometimes where I float in black space beyond the reach of anyone's love . . .

. . . Only divine intervention can save a soul condemned for ever to exist in the loneliness of the bottomless pit . . .

. . . Please, please, don't stay away longer than is necessary . . .

DS Harrison slept badly. At the back of his mind all night was the disturbing knowledge that he had missed something. He was temporarily distracted by the mayhem of Christmas morning, as his excited children opened their presents and his wife set to work on the lunch preparations, but shortly after eleven o'clock a call came through from the station relaying Deacon's message.

'He refused to explain what this matter of urgency was,' said the desk sergeant, 'and, to be honest, I didn't take it too seriously. But this name, Nigel de Vriess, has now come up in another connection. Hampshire and

Kent are alerting forces across the South to watch out for him. Apparently, his Rolls-Royce was reported abandoned last night in a field outside Dover. What do you want me to do about it? Pass this Deacon's number on to the DCI?'

'No, I'm coming in. Tell the DCI I'm on my way.'

'Amanda must've done something pretty bad to get Billy worked up like that,' said Terry suddenly. 'I mean, he didn't rate stealing and drugs too high, but he didn't lose his rag overly much at the guys who did them. Do you get what I'm saying? It were murder that made him go ape-shit and stick his hands in the fire and talk about sacrifices. Like the time Tom took the geezer's coat off of him and the geezer froze to death in the night. That's when Billy spent the night in the nude to take the blame on himself. He damn near died for it. It were only because Tom got really upset about what he'd done that we were able to get Billy back in his clothes again. So do you reckon she killed Billy by letting him starve to death?'

'No,' said Deacon, whose thoughts had been following similar lines. 'Barry's right. She wouldn't have told me Billy's story if she was afraid of what I'd find out. In any case, I can't see Billy caring too much about his own death.'

. . . My own redemption doesn't interest me . . .

'Whose then?'

. . . I'm still searching for truth . . . There's no way out of hell except through God's mercy . . . I'm still searching

*for truth ... Why enter hell at all? ... I'm searching for
Verity...*

'Verity's?' suggested Deacon.

Terry shook his head. 'Verity murdered herself.'

*... You and I will be judged by the efforts we make to
keep another's soul from eternal despair ... Do you enjoy
suffering? Yes, if it inspires compassion. There's no way out
of hell except through God's mercy ... I'm searching for
Verity...*

'James's?'

'Yeah.' Terry nodded. 'I reckon the bitch murdered
her old man, and Billy watched her do it. He mentioned
once that he dossed west of London before he came to
the warehouse. But I didn't pay no mind. It weren't
important then. It makes sense now, though, doesn't it?'

'Yes,' said Deacon slowly, thinking of the river above
Teddington, where the water level remained constant
because the lock gates held back the tides.

Harrison telephoned through to a Chief Superintendent
Fortune in Hampshire. 'I have a possible sighting of de
Vriess on Saturday night,' he told him. 'He was with a
woman called Amanda Powell, previously known as
Amanda Streeter. She's the wife of James Streeter, who
absconded in 1990 with £10 million. According to my
information, she and de Vriess have been intimately
acquainted since the mid-eighties.'

'Who's your informant?'

'A journalist called Michael Deacon. He's been investigating the Streeter disappearance.'

There was a momentary silence. 'He phoned de Vriess's house this morning claiming to be a business colleague. We're sending someone up to question him. What's he like?'

'I think he's protecting his story. Look, I suggest your officer talks it through with me here first. The situation's fairly complicated, and it'll probably help to have me there when you question Deacon. He's not the only one involved.' Briefly he recounted Barry Grover's part in the proceedings. 'He hasn't positively identified the man as Nigel de Vriess,' he warned, 'but he described him as having a birthmark on his shoulder, and that's mentioned as a distinguishing characteristic in your bulletin.'

'Where can we find Grover?'

'He's staying with Deacon.'

'What about Amanda Powell? You say she was in her house last night. Is she still there?'

'We're not sure. We've had a car in position across the road for about thirty minutes, but there's been no movement inside. We've also suggested that Kent police stake out her mother's house in Easeby. She was there most of yesterday and only returned to London in the late evening.'

'How far is Easeby from Dover?'

'Twenty miles.'

'Right. There'll be two of us coming up.' He reeled off a number. 'I'll keep that line open for you. The traffic shouldn't be too bad, so expect us between one and one thirty.'

*

Barry was in fine good humour when Deacon and Terry returned. Left to his own devices and with a clear goal in view, he had brought order to the proceedings and appetizing smells drifted from the oven. He beamed at them happily as they came through the door, and Deacon was struck by how different he seemed from the unhappy man who haunted the *Street* offices.

'You're a genius,' he said honestly, accepting a glass of chilled white wine.

'It's not so difficult, Mike. I remembered reading once about cooking turkeys in very hot ovens, and that's what I've chosen to do. It's important to keep the flesh moist, so I've stuffed bacon and mushrooms under the skin.'

He used the same slightly overbearing tone as when talking about his talent with pictures, and Deacon felt sorry for him because he realized that Barry's self-esteem was so fragile that he could blossom only when he could prove to himself that he was better than his peers. On balance, he preferred Barry bossy to Barry in tears, so he kept to himself that Lawrence was Jewish and that bacon might prove difficult.

'And I've made extra roast potatoes for Terry.'

'Wicked,' said the boy admiringly.

'And if you'll pardon the liberty, Mike, I used your telephone to call my mother. It occurred to me she might be worried about what had happened to me.'

'And was she?'

Barry's pleasure was unmistakable. 'Yes,' he said. 'She's been worried out of her mind. It surprised me a little. She never shows any concern when I stay late at the office.'

Deacon wanted to warn him – *Be objective . . . Mother love is jealous . . . As loneliness becomes a memory for you, it becomes a reality for her . . . She's using you* – but he suspected that much of Barry's renewed confidence stemmed from his conversation with his mother, and he held his tongue.

Terry, untrammelled by tact or sensitivity, jumped in with both feet. 'Jesus, she's a two-faced bitch, isn't she? Doesn't lift a finger for you when you're in bother and then goes lovey-dovey on you when your mates help you out. I bet she's hopping-mad Mike's offered you a bed. I hope you told her to bog off,' he finished severely.

'She's not that bad,' murmured Barry loyally.

'I don't suppose mine is either,' said Terry, 'but you wouldn't know it from the way she's treated me. I like Mike's mum the best. She's a bit of an old dragon but at least she's straight.' He took himself off to the bathroom.

Deacon watched the little man toy unhappily with the laid cutlery on the table. 'Everything's black and white with him,' he said. 'He takes people at face value and assumes that what he sees is what he gets.'

And all too often it worked, he thought. Terry's conversation with his mother on the telephone had been a revelation. (*'Hi, Mrs D. Happy Christmas. Guess what? I'm going to stay with Mike for a while. I knew you'd be pleased. Yeah, of course we'll come and see you. How about next weekend? Sure thing. We'll have a New Year's Eve party.'* And his mother to him afterwards: *'For once in your life, Michael, you've made a decision I agree with, but I shall be very angry if you're making promises that you can't keep. That child deserves better than to be tossed aside when something more attractive comes along.*')

'Do you think he's right about my mother?' asked Barry. It was years since she had spoken to him with such warmth, and he longed for Deacon to hand him a straw of comfort.

But Deacon could only think of the little man's ambivalence in the police station when he had expressed fear and hatred of the woman in one breath, then wept for her in the next. Indeed, Harrison had been so concerned by Barry's peculiarity on the subject that he had sent a patrol car to check that Mrs Grover was still alive.

'I don't know,' he said honestly, clapping a friendly hand on Barry's shoulder, 'but natural law determines that offspring must make their own way in life, so I'd keep your mother dangling if I were you. Apart from anything else, if she's this keen to see you after one night away, she'll be eating out of your hand if you make her wait a week.'

'I've nowhere else to go.'

'You can stay here till we sort something out.'

Barry turned away towards the oven, releasing himself from Deacon's comforting hold. 'You make it sound so simple,' he said rather wretchedly, opening the door and peering at the turkey.

'It is,' said Deacon cheerfully. 'Goddammit, if I can put up with Terry, I'm sure I can put up with you.'

But Barry didn't want to be 'put up with'; he wanted to be loved.

*

369

'Frankly, we thought it more likely we were dealing with a kidnap,' said Superintendent Fortune. 'Neither de Vriess's wife nor his business colleagues report money problems, there's no history of depression and, while he has a fairly murky reputation with the ladies, the general view is that he hasn't strayed since his ex-wife returned to him in May. You can't put much reliance on her word, of course – her husband was hardly likely to keep her up to date with his affairs – but she's adamant that he's had no contact with Amanda Powell in the last seven months.'

'Until Saturday,' said Harrison. 'Mind you, his wife's probably right about the seven-month abstinence. It's not that long if he was trying to make a go of it with his wife.'

'So why break out on Saturday?'

Harrison shook his head. 'I don't know, unless Michael Deacon triggered some kind of panic when he pushed his way in there on Thursday night.'

'It's the time scale that worries me,' said Harrison's DCI. 'According to Kent, the Rolls-Royce was first spotted in the field at lunchtime yesterday, but the farmer did nothing about it because he thought it was a courting couple. He only reported it after he saw it still there as it was getting dark and checked to find the doors unlocked and the car empty. But Mrs Powell wasn't informed of the full extent of Barry Grover's Peeping Tom act until approximately five o'clock, therefore the two incidents can't be connected. Put simply, Nigel vanished from his car several hours *before* there was any evidence that he needed to.'

'Assuming the two of them conspired to murder her husband in 1990?'

'Precisely. And there's no evidence that they did.' Fortune pondered for a moment. 'To be honest, gentlemen, I'm not sure where we go from here. Before DS Harrison's phone call I had a man who'd been missing for two days and an abandoned Rolls-Royce in a Kent field. Now I have him in the company of a former mistress thirty-six hours ago and the only motive for him to do a bunk or for her to get rid of him – which is always a possibility, I suppose – is ruled out because the car was abandoned too soon. I can't possibly justify using precious resources on a wild-goose chase. On the pooled evidence, we can't even point to a crime having been committed.'

'There's still Michael Deacon,' said Harrison.

'Yes,' said his DCI. 'There's also Amanda Powell's house. I think our resources will stretch to lawful entry in order to lay official concerns to rest *vis-à-vis* Mr de Vriess's welfare, bearing in mind that was the last place he was seen alive.'

Lawrence arrived with presents and had to be assisted up three flights of stairs when he collapsed in a breathless heap on the doorstep. 'Dear, dear, dear,' he said, gripping Deacon's hand tightly as he lowered himself on to the sofa, 'I'm not the man I used to be. I couldn't have managed on my own.'

'That's what I told Mike,' said Terry, omitting his own refusal to be the supporting arm 'in case the old poofter tries a grope on the way up'. 'Can we open these now?' he demanded eagerly, tapping the presents. 'We ain't got nothing for you, though.'

The old man beamed at him. 'You're giving me lunch. What more could I ask? Won't you introduce me to Barry first? I've been so looking forward to meeting him.'

'Yeah, right.' He grabbed the little man's arm and dragged him forward. 'This is my mate, Barry, and this is my other mate, Lawrence. Stands to reason you two're going to like each other because you're both mates of me and Mike.'

Lawrence, accepting this naive statement at face value, took Barry's hand in both of his and shook it joyfully. 'This is such a pleasure for me. Mike tells me you're an expert on photography. I do envy you, my dear fellow. An artist's eye is a precious gift.'

Deacon turned away with a smile as the ready flush of pleasure coloured Barry's face. Lawrence's secret, he thought, was that he was incapable of sounding insincere, but whether his feelings were really as genuine as they appeared it was impossible to say. 'Whisky, Lawrence?' he asked heading for the kitchen.

'Thank you.' Lawrence patted the seat beside him. 'Sit next to me, Barry, while Terry tells me who made such a wonderful job of the festive decorations.'

'That was me,' said Terry. 'They're good, ain't they? You should've seen this place when I first got here. It was well unfriendly. No colour, nothing. Do you know what I'm saying?'

'It lacked atmosphere?' suggested the old man.

'That's the word.'

Lawrence looked towards the mantelpiece, where Terry had arranged the *objets d'art* from his doss in the warehouse. There was a small plaster replica of Big Ben, a conch shell and a brilliantly coloured garden gnome squatting on a toadstool. He doubted they represented Deacon's taste in ornaments, so attributed them correctly to Terry. 'I congratulate you. You've certainly made it very friendly now. I particularly like the gnome,' he said with a mischievous glance at Deacon, who was returning with the whisky.

'I'm glad you said that,' murmured Deacon, putting the glass on a table at Lawrence's knee and retrieving his own. 'I've been racking my brains for something to give you, and we wouldn't miss the gnome, would we, Terry?'

'Mike hates it,' confided the boy, reaching it down, 'probably because I nicked it out of somebody's garden. Here, it's yours, Lawrence. Happy Christmas, mate.'

Deacon gave his evil grin. 'I tell you what, if there's a mantelpiece in your sitting-room, then that's the place for it. As Terry says, you can't go wrong with spots of bright colour about the place.' He raised his glass to their guest.

Lawrence placed it on the table. 'I'm overwhelmed by so much generosity,' he said. 'First a party, then a present. I feel I don't deserve either. My gifts to you are so humble by comparison.'

Deacon's lip curled. He had a nasty feeling the old buzzard was about to shame them.

'Can we open them now?' asked Terry.

'Of course. Yours is the largest one, Barry's is the one wrapped in red paper and Michael's is in green paper.'

Terry handed Deacon and Barry theirs and ripped open his own. 'Shit!' he said in amazement. 'What d'you reckon to this, Mike?' He held up a worn leather bomber jacket with a sheepskin collar and the Royal Air Force insignia sewn onto the breast pocket. 'These cost a packet down Covent Garden.'

Deacon frowned as the boy thrust his arm into a sleeve, then glanced towards the old man with a questioning look in his eyes which said: *Are you sure?* Lawrence nodded. 'You'd never find that in Covent Garden,' Deacon said then. '*That*'s the real thing. What did you fly?' he asked. 'Spitfires?'

Lawrence nodded again. 'But it's a long time ago, and the jacket has been looking for a home for many years.' He watched Barry finger his package on his lap. 'Aren't you going to open yours, Barry?'

'I wasn't expecting anything,' said the little man shyly.

'Then it's a double surprise. Please. I can't bear the suspense of not knowing if you like it.'

Barry carefully slit the Sellotape, as was his character, and unfolded the paper neatly to reveal a Brownie box-camera wrapped in layers of tissue-paper. 'But this is pre-war,' he said in amazement, turning it over with immense care. 'I can't possibly accept this.'

Lawrence raised his thin hands in protest. 'But you must. Anyone who can tell the age of a camera just by looking at it should certainly possess it.' He turned to Deacon. 'Now it's your turn, Michael.'

'I'm as embarrassed as Barry.'

'But I'm *delighted* with my gnome.' His eyes twinkled mischievously. 'And I shall do exactly as you suggest and put it on the mantelpiece in my drawing-room. It will look very well beside my collection of Meissen porcelain.'

Deacon bit off a snort of laughter and pulled the wrapping from his present. He didn't know whether to be relieved or dismayed, for while the gift had no material value, its sentimental value was clearly enormous. He turned the pages of a closely written diary, spanning many years of Lawrence's life. 'I'm honoured,' he said simply, 'but I'd rather you left it to me in your will as something to remember you by.'

'Then there'd be no pleasure in it for me. I want you to read it while I'm alive, Michael, so that I shall have someone to reminisce with from time to time. As far as you are concerned, I have been entirely selfish in my choice of a present.'

Deacon shook his head. 'You've already hijacked my soul, you old bastard. What more do you want?'

Lawrence reached out a frail hand. 'A son to say Kaddish for *my* soul.'

The smell of decay that poured out like a tide of sewage when the police burst open the door of Amanda Powell's house drove the team of policemen staggering backwards. So thick and putrid was the stench that it stung eyes and nostrils and loosened the contents of stomachs. The very fabric of the house seemed to ooze with the liquid of corruption.

Superintendent Fortune clapped a handkerchief to his mouth and rounded angrily on Harrison. 'What the hell kind of fool do you take me for? There's no way you could have missed this if you were here last night.'

Harrison dropped to his haunches and attempted to keep his guts from turning inside out. 'There was a WPC here as well,' he muttered. 'I asked her to stay with Mrs Powell while I spoke to Deacon. Believe me, she didn't notice it either.'

'It's clearing, sir,' said Fortune's Hampshire colleague, approaching the doorway warily. 'There must be a draught blowing it through.' Gingerly, he poked his head into the hall. 'It looks like the connecting door to the garage is open.'

There was no immediate response from the remaining policemen. To a man they dreaded what they knew they were going to see, for Nature has not endowed its works of beauty with the smell of death. At the very least they expected rivers of blood around a scene of brutal carnage.

However, when they finally found the courage to enter the house and look into the garage, there was a single naked corpse, intact and uncorrupted, propped against a stack of unopened bags of cement in the corner, gazing wide-eyed in their direction. And while no one put the thought into words, they all wondered how something so cold and pure could reek so vilely of corruption.

Chapter Twenty

'I'M BEGINNING TO wish I'd never met you,' said DS Harrison, stepping wearily across Deacon's threshold and introducing his companion. 'Chief Superintendent Fortune of Hampshire police.'

'I left a message for you to phone.'

'Events overtook me,' said Harrison laconically.

Deacon took in their sombre expressions and belatedly removed the paper hat from his head and tucked it into his pocket. The all-too-simple pleasures of getting gently smashed while eating Barry's turkey dinner and reading dire jokes out of crackers palled rather rapidly in the face of official sobriety. 'Is something wrong?'

The superintendent, a lean, somewhat intimidating individual with eyes that had been trained to see more than they gave away, gestured him forward. 'After you, Mr Deacon. If you please.'

With a shrug, he led the way upstairs and introduced them to his guests. 'If you're from Hampshire,' he said to Fortune, resuming his seat, 'then this must be to do with Nigel de Vriess.'

'How much do you know about him?' asked the superintendent.

'Very little.'

'Then why did you phone his house this morning?'

Deacon glanced at Terry, wondering if the boy could be relied on to keep his mouth shut. *Trust me* was the response in his disarmingly innocent expression. 'It occurred to me that the man Mrs Powell's neighbours saw tampering with her garage door yesterday might have been Nigel, so I thought I'd check to see if he ever went home.' He stroked his nose. 'Apparently he didn't.'

'Later you left a message at the station, saying you wanted to contact me on a matter of urgency regarding Amanda and Nigel,' said Harrison. 'What was that about?'

Deacon consulted his watch. 'It's after three. It won't be urgent any more.' He read impatience in Harrison's face and, with an amused smile, outlined his theory that Amanda and Nigel had done a bunk once they knew Barry had seen them together. 'Terry and I drove to the docklands this morning and checked her house,' he explained. 'It seemed empty and her car had gone. I thought it worth passing on that information if I could, but your desk sergeant was reluctant to bother you.'

'We're talking quite an epidemic here,' said Harrison. 'First James absconds, then Amanda and Nigel. Is this a serious theory you're proposing, Mr Deacon?'

Terry grinned. 'I told you you'd look a plonker.'

Deacon offered the two policemen a drink, which they refused. 'I'm sorry to have wasted your time,' he said refilling the glasses of the others. 'Put it down to the fact that I've had missing persons on the brain for weeks.'

'Meaning James Streeter.'

'Among others.'

Lawrence stirred. 'I doubt you'd be here, gentlemen, if you knew where Amanda and Nigel were, so are we to be given an explanation or left in the dark? I should add that I think it's a little unfair to pour scorn on Michael's theory if you have none of your own.'

The two policemen exchanged glances. 'After all, I think I will have that drink,' said the superintendent unexpectedly. 'It's been a bugger of a twenty-four hours.'

Harrison looked relieved, although whether because he needed a drink or because his colleague had shown a weakness, Deacon couldn't tell. 'I wouldn't say no either.'

They chose beer and, as Terry poured it for them, Fortune gave a brief account of the events that had brought him to London to consult with DS Harrison. 'A short while ago we took the decision to enter Amanda Powell's house.' He paused to drink from the glass Terry handed him. 'We found Nigel de Vriess dead in the corner of her garage,' he went on bluntly. 'He was naked and appears to have died from a blow to the back of his head. It's a rough estimate, but we're looking at death occurring approximately thirty-six hours ago, presumably during the hours following Mr Grover's sighting of him in the sitting-room.'

There was a long silence.

Deacon wondered what the reaction would be if he admitted that he had visited Amanda's house the night before. He suspected that theories on the inexorability of fate would go down like a lead balloon with London's and Hampshire's finest, particularly as Harrison already had his doubts about his and Barry's involvement with the damn woman. He thought of her pallor, and the way her eyes had watched his every movement. Was she afraid he would stumble across the corpse? How close had he come to it, for God's sake? *And how the hell could she have been so calm and collected when the body of her dead lover was secreted in her house and on her conscience?*

He rolled the stem of his wine glass between his finger and thumb, turning it in a slow circle on the table cloth. 'If she had a dead body on the premises, then I'm surprised she complained to you about Barry,' he said to Harrison. 'She's either very cool or very stupid.'

'Cool,' said Harrison, recalling his own impressions of a woman who had calmly allowed the police into her house with a dead man in the garage. 'I'm guessing she wanted to find out how much he'd told us before deciding what to do next. Presumably the original idea was to abandon his car in Dover before disposing of the body somewhere else, but she did a bunk when she realized she couldn't discredit Barry's evidence.' He paused. 'It still gives us a logistical problem. Who drove the Rolls-Royce to Kent if its owner was lying dead in a London garage?'

No one answered.

'If Amanda took it there,' he continued, 'how did she get back in time for her neighbours to speak to her at nine o'clock and then watch her drive away to spend Christmas with her mother? She certainly couldn't have done it afterwards because she was in her mother's house at midday when Kent police informed her of Barry's arrest. Which makes the timeframe too narrow to switch cars, drive the Rolls to Dover and return for the BMW.'

'She could have left home at three o'clock in the morning and caught an early train to London from Dover,' Deacon pointed out. 'That would have got her back by nine o'clock, wouldn't it?'

The sergeant shook his head. 'The first train on a Sunday doesn't reach Waterloo until after nine o'clock.'

'She could have hitched a lift.'

'In the early hours of Christmas Eve? In the dark? Right to her doorstep in time to be bright-eyed and bushy-tailed for her neighbours?'

Lawrence was watching him closely. 'What's your theory, sergeant?'

'We think there was someone else involved, sir. Admittedly this is pure speculation, but let's say de Vriess was struck on the back of the head *while* he was making love to Amanda, which is the only sensible explanation for his nudity. Let's say then that it was the accomplice who collected de Vriess's Rolls-Royce from wherever he had left it – it certainly wasn't parked outside her house or her neighbours would have noticed it – and drove the Rolls to Dover. I think you'd agree that's a more likely sequence of events, given what we have.'

Lawrence smiled. 'I'm a lawyer, my dear fellow. You can't expect me to agree any such thing. An equally likely sequence of events is that de Vriess was so aroused by Amanda that he forgot to lock his car and it was subsequently hijacked by joy-riders. Meanwhile, following their satisfactory session on the sitting-room floor, he took a shower, slipped on the tiles and killed himself accidentally. Amanda, appalled at what had happened, hid the body in the garage and has now fled to think things over. Have you any evidence to disprove my version of events?'

Both policemen looked at Barry. 'Perhaps Mr Grover can help us,' suggested Superintendent Fortune. 'How long did you watch what was going on in that sitting-room, sir?'

Barry looked at his hands. 'Not long.'

'You left before they finished?'

He nodded.

'Are you sure about that, sir? Most men in your situation would have waited till the end. You were unobserved. You stumbled on it by accident. You said yourself it was exciting. So much so' – he glanced briefly at the other three, as if wondering how graphic he could be – 'that you went back a few hours later for a second helping. Why leave before you had to?'

Barry licked his lips. 'I thought she'd seen me. She made him get up suddenly and pull the curtains.'

Fortune showed him a photograph of Nigel de Vriess. 'Was this the man?'

'Yes.'

'Why did you think Amanda had seen you?'

'Because he only got up after she looked at the window.'

'Was there anyone else in the room?'

Barry shook his head.

'Did you look in any of the other windows?'

'No. I was scared of being caught. I went straight back to the main road and took a taxi home.'

'You can't have been that scared,' Harrison said bluntly. 'You were there again in under eight hours.'

'He left his folder of photographs behind,' said Deacon reasonably. 'That's why he went back.' He looked thoughtfully across at Barry. 'She drives a black BMW which she always parks in her driveway. Was it there that night?'

Barry shook his head again.

'Then it was premeditated murder and she didn't need an accomplice,' he said matter-of-factly. 'She made two trips to Dover. The first on Saturday in her own car, which she left down there, returning to London by train, and the second early on Sunday morning in the Roller, returning in her BMW.' He fingered a cigarette from the packet on the table, wondering if she'd made the same round trip nearly six years before. 'The interesting question is what was she planning to do with Nigel's body?' He held the lighter to the tip of his cigarette. 'She must have been very sure of her hiding place or she wouldn't have gone to the trouble of leaving his car near a ferry port.'

The superintendent was watching him closely. 'The only problem with that scenario, sir, is that her neighbours recollect her car being outside her house all Saturday.'

Deacon shrugged. 'If Barry says it wasn't there, then it wasn't there.'

'Sounds to me like they're trying to frame him for the murder,' said Terry aggressively. 'I mean, he's a sitting duck if they reckon she had some patsy helping her.' He nudged Lawrence in the ribs. 'You shouldn't let them question him like this. They ain't given him a caution or nothing.'

'Oh, I think you do our police friends an injustice, Terry. They know as well as you and I that Barry would not have told them he'd seen a man in Amanda's house if he were guilty of murdering him.' He frowned slightly. 'It's quite a problem, isn't it? Assuming Nigel was murdered, then one must accept that Amanda was party to the murder. Yet, she's such a lovely young woman.'

'Do you know her, sir?'

'I've seen her once or twice. She and I are distant neighbours and, as Michael will tell you, I like to sit on the riverbank and watch the world go by.'

'Go on, sir,' said Fortune when Lawrence came to a halt.

'Forgive me. I was wondering how far human depravity can sink without its showing. You see, if Michael is right, then Mrs Powell must have encouraged Nigel to make love to her in order to facilitate his murder, and that would make her very depraved indeed.' He smiled a little wistfully. 'By and large, I prefer to think well of people.'

The superintendent smiled politely, hiding his impatience over an old man's ramblings. 'In my experience there's no relationship between how a person looks and how they behave.'

'Normally I would agree with you.' He took the photograph of Nigel de Vriess from Barry and examined it with interest. 'It's a cruel face, don't you think? But then he was a very arrogant man, and arrogance is a dangerous quality. I can say quite truthfully that Nigel de Vriess was one of the nastier by-products of a civilized society.'

'Did you know him, sir?'

'In a manner of speaking. One of my younger partners handled his affairs for several years.' He tapped the photograph. 'The occasion when he refused to act for de Vriess again was when he was instructed to buy off a young woman who had been beaten to within an inch of her life during sexual intercourse. De Vriess put a value of £10,000 on her physical and mental well-being, but my colleague was so shocked by the damage done to her that he severed our firm's connection with him. He described de Vriess as a psychopath, and nothing I have ever read or heard about him leads me to think any differently. Society should never allow a man like this to accrue wealth. When money is in the wrong hands then justice, the bedrock on which our democracy rests, can always be corrupted.'

Deacon's expression was thoughtful as he looked at his elderly friend.

'I'm not sure I understand the point you're making, sir,' said Fortune.

Lawrence looked surprised. 'I'm so sorry. I assumed it was obvious. You see, I can believe in de Vriess's depravity far more readily than I can believe in Mrs Powell's.'

'But it's de Vriess who is dead, sir, and not his ladyfriend.'

Barry cleared his throat nervously. 'She didn't look at all happy,' he confessed. 'He was pulling her round the room by her hair at one point, and then he made her

385

bend over a little table so that he could – well—' He faltered to a halt. 'I think he might have been raping her,' he added in a whisper.

Five pairs of eyes swivelled in his direction.

'Why the hell didn't you tell us this yesterday?' demanded Harrison.

Barry looked terrified.

'You didn't ask him,' Deacon pointed out. But, by God, it explained much of Barry's confused behaviour over the last twenty-four hours. No wonder he had been able to describe the dominant male with such accuracy . . .

Daily Express

27.12.95

Stop Press: Police took the unusual step this afternoon of releasing the name and photograph of a woman they want to interview in connection with the disappearance of missing entrepreneur Nigel de Vriess, whose Rolls-Royce was found abandoned in Dover. She is Amanda Powell of Thamesbank Estate, London E14, formerly known as Amanda Streeter. She is thought to be in hiding somewhere in the UK.

Daily Express

30.12.95

Stop Press: Following a sighting by a member of the public, police have charged Amanda Streeter-Powell with the murder of her one-time lover, Nigel de Vriess. She was discovered last night in a cottage in Sway in the New Forest which is only 40 miles from de Vriess's home in Andover. Neighbours say she was a regular weekend visitor there. Neighbours in London E14 and colleagues at work describe themselves as 'dumbfounded' by her arrest. 'She's a nice woman,' said one. 'I can't believe she's a murderess.'

Telephone message

From: DS Greg Harrison   Date: 3.01.96
To: Michael Deacon (Room 104)   Dictated to: Mary Petty

Greg Harrison is fed up with your calls. He says he
spends more time talking to you than he does to his
wife, and he loves her!

Amanda Powell has been charged with murder and
is on remand at Holloway, and, no, he can't take you to
see her because you'll probably be called as a witness
at her trial, along with Barry. In any case it would be a
waste of time your talking to her because she has
nothing to add to what she told the police almost six
years ago about James's disappearance. She spent the
weekend of 27th/28th/29th April 1990 with her mother
in Kent, and her mother confirms this. Her alibi satisfied
the investigating officers then and continues to satisfy
them. Without more evidence, there is no justification
for wasting taxpayers' money by trawling the Thames
at Teddington.

With regard to de Vriess's murder, and for Christ's
sake don't quote Greg as this is all *sub judice* and he
could get the sack for talking out of turn (Greg asked
me to underline that), Amanda agrees with Fiona Grayson. There had been no contact between her and Nigel
for months. Amanda claims she had a chance meeting
with Nigel in Knightsbridge on Saturday morning (they

were both Christmas shopping, apparently), he became very excited about seeing her again and twelve hours later forced his way into her house in order to rape her. Barry's evidence supports this. When Nigel finally released her, she lashed out at his face and he fell backwards on to the brass doorstop. The forensic evidence (bruise on his cheek/traces of blood on the doorstop) supports this. We are still looking for witnesses who may have seen her BMW in Dover during the Saturday, but have found none to date. The neighbours continue to support her statement that it was parked in her driveway (although they're a little less sure than previously, as they are very used to it being left there).

The reason Amanda didn't dial 999 was because she panicked. She says she realized immediately that she needed to put as much distance between her and Nigel's Rolls-Royce as possible, so drove it to Dover, a town she knows well because her mother lives only 20 miles away. She agrees it's ridiculous that she thought getting rid of the car was more important than getting rid of the body, but she was confused and frightened following the rape. She hitched a lift out of Dover with a French lorry driver, arriving home by 8.30 a.m.

At the moment none of this can be disproved, but Greg is working on it.

Communicate by fax in future. Hard-working policemen can't afford to spend hours on the telephone.

Chapter Twenty-One

DEACON PUT THROUGH another call to Edinburgh. 'It's Michael Deacon,' he told John Streeter when the man came on the line. 'I presume you've read that your sister-in-law's been charged with the murder of Nigel de Vriess?'

'Yes.'

'Have you any idea why she did it, Mr Streeter?'

'Not really. I spoke to her the Friday before Christmas, suggesting a truce. She was surprisingly amenable.'

'What kind of truce?'

There was a short silence. 'The kind you suggested,' he said then. 'I told her we now believed she'd been telling the truth and asked her to use her influence with de Vriess to let us search through the DVS personnel files for anything that might lead us to Marianne Filbert. She agreed and asked me to contact her again in the new year with a view to proceeding.'

'Did she seem worried by the suggestion?'

'She was puzzled by it. She asked me why we believed her now when we hadn't before, and I said you'd become interested in James's story and had persuaded us to work with her rather than against her.'

'What was her answer to that?'

'As far as I remember, she said it was a pity we hadn't attracted your interest five years ago before quite so much water had gone under the bridge.'

'Did you ask her what she meant by that?'

'No. I assumed she was saying there'd have been a lot less anguish for everyone if the truth had come out at the time of James's disappearance.'

'Anything else?'

'No. We wished each other a happy Christmas and said goodbye.' Streeter paused again. 'Do you know if the police have questioned her about James?'

'Yes, but her story hasn't changed. She still denies knowing anything about what happened to him.'

There was a sigh. 'You'll keep us posted, I hope.'

'Of course. Goodbye, Mr Streeter.'

With cast-iron guarantees that her part in the story would never be written, Deacon persuaded Lawrence to talk to his partner about the woman who had been offered £10,000 by de Vriess to keep her mouth shut. 'All I want to know,' he told the old man, 'is whether she reported the incident to the police, and if she didn't, why not?'

Lawrence frowned. 'I imagine because the money was an inducement to stay silent.'

'How can it have been if he had time to go to his solicitor? Most women dial 999 the minute their attacker walks out of the door. They don't give him time to get legal advice. That ten thousand sounds more like severance pay than inducement.'

Lawrence phoned through the answer a couple of days later. 'You were right, Michael. It was in the nature of a pay-off, and she did not report the incident to the police. There had been a history of abuse against the poor woman, which ended in the injuries my colleague witnessed. In fact he urged her to prosecute' – he chuckled happily – 'somewhat unethically, it must be said, because he was still acting for de Vriess at the time, but she was too frightened to do it.'

'Of de Vriess?'

'Yes and no. She refused to give any details but my colleague believes de Vriess was blackmailing her. She was a stockbroker and his best guess is that she used insider knowledge to buy shares, and de Vriess found out about it.'

'Why stop? Why pay her?'

'De Vriess claimed it was a one-off incident when he'd acted out of character because he was drunk. The woman said it was the culmination of a series of such incidents. My colleague believed her and promptly severed our firm's connection with a man he considered to be extremely dangerous. His view is that de Vriess realized he'd gone too far – he broke her arm and her jaw – and decided to release her with a lump sum. His instructions were to offer the woman £10,000 on the clear under-standing that there would be no further contact between the two parties.'

'Did she ever get paid?'

Another chuckle. 'Oh, yes. My colleague screwed £25,000 out of de Vriess before refusing any further business from him.'

'You realize this would help Amanda's case considerably? It proves Nigel had a taste for rape.'

'Oh, I don't think so. It wouldn't suit her book at all to have it demonstrated that Nigel blackmailed women in order to make them party to their own rape. As I understand it, her defence is that this had never happened before, that Nigel forced his way into her house in a state of high arousal and that his death was an accident when she lashed out after managing to get free of him.'

'She's lying.'

'I'm sure she is, my friend, but she's fighting for her life, poor creature.'

'Will she get off?'

'Undoubtedly. Barry's witness evidence alone will persuade a jury to acquit.'

'She wouldn't have been arrested but for him,' said Deacon, 'and now she's looking to him to save her. As Terry would say, that's well ironic.'

Lawrence tittered. 'How's his reading coming along?'

'Faster than I expected,' said Deacon drily. 'He's discovered the joys of looking up dirty words in the dictionary, and he's sending me round the bend by reading the definitions out loud.'

'And how's Barry?'

There was a long pause. 'Barry's decided to be honest about his feelings,' said Deacon even more drily, 'and, unless he puts a sock in it pretty rapidly, I'm planning to do the job for him by ripping his balls off and stuffing them in his mouth. I'm a tolerant man, as you know, but I draw the line at being the object of someone else's fantasies.'

393

FACSIMILE TRANSMISSION   DATED: 4.01.96

THE STREET, FLEET STREET, LONDON EC4

From: Michael Deacon
To: DS Greg Harrison

**Nota bene: <u>You're not the only person I've been
telephoning!</u>**

1. John Streeter called Amanda the week before
   Christmas (on my advice), asking for a truce
   and saying that the Friends of James Streeter
   were planning to approach Nigel de Vriess in
   the new year with a view to searching through
   the Softworks/DVS personnel files to try and
   get an angle on Marianne Filbert.
2. Wise up! It's about as likely that Amanda met
   Nigel by chance in Knightsbridge on the
   Saturday before Christmas as you or I winning
   the lottery. The odds against it are phenomenal.
   For Christ's sake, the world and his wife would
   have been there looking for last-minute
   presents. She made an arrangement with him to
   come to her house for some Christmas jollies.
   See below.
3. Who owns the cottage in Sway? Amanda or
   Nigel? If Nigel, then his wife knew nothing
   about it, and her evidence that there was no
   contact between Nigel and Amanda doesn't
   hold water. I'm betting Amanda was required to
   get herself down there whenever Nigel said

'jump'. (He <u>knew</u> she'd murdered James, and was using her as his personal punchbag whenever he felt like sex. Lawrence has told you what a bastard Nigel was, and Barry says he was <u>raping</u> her – what more proof do you need that Nigel had a hold over her?)

4. How did she know where Nigel had left his Rolls if it wasn't outside her house? Did he pause in mid-rape to tell her where he'd parked it?

5. If her car <u>was</u> parked in her driveway, why didn't she reverse into her garage, load Nigel into the boot and dump him somewhere before getting rid of the Rolls? The fact that she didn't is the best proof you've got that the BMW wasn't there.

6. How does she explain the sacks of cement in her garage when we have photographic evidence that the garage was empty at the beginning of December?

7. Why have rumpy-pumpy in London when they could have gone to Sway, considering she was going there anyway and it was only 40 miles from Halcombe House? Because the disappearing act would have been harder to work from Sway, that's why! It <u>had</u> to be London for easy access to Dover; and it <u>had</u> to be somewhere he wasn't known. So she phoned him and persuaded him to come to <u>London</u> for a change!

This was premeditated murder, which would have worked if Barry hadn't thrown a spanner in the works. While Kent & Hampshire police were running around like headless chickens looking for a kidnapped/absconded entrepreneur she would have been spending a quiet Christmas with her mother (who gives solid alibis!). The only risk was leaving the body in her garage over the holiday, but she didn't have time to dispose of the Rolls and Nigel all in one night, so she probably thought it was a risk worth taking. It was never going to be as easy as disposing of James. If she'd tipped Nigel over her garden wall he'd be sitting on a mudbank when the tide went out, and someone would want to know what was in the concrete overcoat. You really must trawl the river beside the Teddington flats. I guarantee you'll find a bag of bones weighted down with hardened cement, and you can use John Streeter for DNA comparison. I've met Amanda's mother, by the way, and the alibi's lousy. The poor old thing's been arthritic for years and knocks herself out every night with sleeping pills. Amanda could have murdered half of England and Mrs Powell Snr wouldn't have known a damn thing about it.

Best Wishes

Mike

From: Greg Harrison
To: Michael Deacon

1. Hearsay evidence. Amanda denies John Streeter said any such thing. Her version is that he verbally abused her as he has done every Christmas since James vanished.
2. We can't prove she didn't meet him in Knightsbridge.
3. The cottage in Sway belongs to a Mrs Agnes Broadbent. The lessee for the past five years has been Amanda Powell.
4. She told Nigel she didn't want to see him and said she would call a taxi. He said: 'Don't bother, I'm going. The Rolls is parked in Harbour Lane.' Then he attacked her. A witness remembers seeing a Rolls-Royce in Harbour Lane that night.
5. She thought about lifting Nigel into the boot of her car but he was too heavy for her. She only just managed to drag him into the garage.
6. She is planning to have the patio relaid in the garden. Some of the stones have worked loose.
7. Sway doesn't enter the equation. De Vriess's only intention was to rape her, so he forced his way into her house to do just that. His death was an accident. (You understand I don't necessarily believe this, but am merely quoting her.)

Have you any idea how much it *costs* to trawl rivers? We've no more reason to search the Thames at

Teddington than any other stretch of water. We need evidence that a body is there. You seem to have it in for Amanda. Why is that?'

Yours

Greg.

PS. You're placing a lot of trust in Barry and Lawrence. Their evidence of Nigel's 'brutality' towards women is very slight. Are you looking for trouble with his family?

FACSIMILE TRANSMISSION   DATED: 15.01.96

···

THE STREET, FLEET STREET, LONDON EC4

···

From: Michael Deacon
To: DS Greg Harrison

Lawrence and Barry have no reason to lie, unlike
Nigel's family. And far from 'having it in' for
Amanda, I'm trying to help her so, as Terry would
say, I'm 'well gutted' about the assistance I gave
you in finding her. I should have protected her
story as assiduously as I'm protecting Billy's, then
I'd have been able to interview her. Why the hell
didn't you charge her with manslaughter, on the
grounds of provocation, and agree to bail instead
of having her banged up in the nick? That way I
could have effected a chance meeting. I guarantee
I'd have got more out of her than your lot ever
will.

In passing, are <u>you</u> to blame for my being
designated a potential witness? Get real! What did
I ever <u>see</u>? Okay, I was in her house on Christmas
Eve, but as far as I was concerned the poor bitch
was trying to cope with the smell that you lot have
seen fit to put down to Nigel. Listen, even I, a
humble journalist, know that bodies don't go off
that badly after 36 hours in the middle of a cold
winter. <u>That</u> was Billy Blake who has been her
constant companion since June in a so far vain
attempt to force her into an admission of murder.
Okay, I know it sounds crazy, but 'there are more

things in heaven and earth than are dreamt of in
your philosophy', my friend!

Do yourselves a favour, trawl the river by the
flats at Teddington and find James. That's her real
crime: losing her temper and striking out at a two-
timing bastard who was about to skedaddle off to
his mistress with £10 million in a numbered Swiss
bank account. Not that I blame her, particularly.
The more I learn about James, the less I like him,
and she's certainly paid her dues by being Nigel
de Vriess's plaything for the past six years.

As to that garbage you sent me last week:

John Streeter's wife heard his side of the phone
call, so there's independent proof of what he said;
search Nigel's bank accounts for the rent payments
on Sway; Amanda will have told Nigel to park in
Harbour Lane; if Amanda managed to get Nigel
atop the sacks of cement, she could get him into
her boot (she's an architect, therefore must know
something about the mechanics of lifting); no one
relays patio stones in the middle of winter – frost
cracks cement. Go with your gut instincts. Ask
yourself why Nigel raped Amanda. BECAUSE
SHE WOULDN'T REPORT HIM. Why not?
BECAUSE THE BASTARD HAD A HOLD OVER
HER?

*I'm guessing that the James scenario went something
like this:*
- James Streeter was a thief and a liar. He began a
  mini-fraud in 1985 to fund his stockmarket
  dreams. When he met Marianne Filbert in '88,
  he learned how to cream millions and the fraud
  became more sophisticated.

- In the meantime he'd married Amanda, whom he met through Nigel de Vriess. I can only explain this marriage in terms of escape for her as she must have discovered by then what Nigel was really like. It's harder to say what James's motives were. A bit of social-climbing perhaps (i.e. if Amanda was good enough for the boss, then she was worth having). His father describes him as 'status-conscious'.
- The marriage was a stormy one and James was soon casting around for someone more amenable. Meanwhile, he encouraged Amanda to pursue the Teddington flats project, possibly to legitimize some of his 'dirty' money. (The title deeds were registered in her name only – for tax purposes? – which was why she had no trouble exchanging the property for the house in Thamesbank.)
- As soon as the fraud came to light, Nigel, from his position on the Lowenstein board, guessed that James was responsible. He may even have sussed him through the Marianne Filbert/ Softworks/DVS connection – the bank's inhouse investigation will have unearthed the abandoned Softworks security report. Either way, there's a good chance he took a cut in return for tipping James off about when to run.
- I think he also tipped off Amanda out of spite because she certainly learned that James was about to vanish and leave her to face the music alone.
- She killed James in anger, then sheltered behind the fact that all the evidence pointed to him

absconding. Her problem was that Nigel knew what she'd done and held the knowledge over her. I'm guessing he *did* tip Amanda off and *did* take a cut off James and Marianne. When Marianne contacted him to say that James had failed to arrive, he realized that James had never left the UK. After that he put two and two together, worked out that Amanda had disposed of James in the river, weighted down with bags of cement from the building site, and threatened to go to the police. (The MO was so effective, she was going to repeat it with Nigel.)

- The evidence for all of this lies in Nigel's treatment of Amanda, as witnessed by Barry. How could a man like de Vriess afford to do what he did <u>unless</u> he knew she wouldn't go to the police? Dammit, he had <u>everything</u> to lose if she screamed rape the minute he left the house.

Best wishes,

Mike

Mike

402

Amanda Powell
HM Prison
1X Parkhurst Road
Holloway
London N7 ONU

15th January 1996

Dear Amanda,

I have no idea if Billy's views on hell and
damnation have any validity. He described
purgatory as 'a place of eternal despair where love
is absent'. However, he saw it not as an eternity of
ignorance but as an eternity of terrifying
awareness. The condemned soul knows that love
exists, but is condemned for ever to exist without
it. I believe he was so appalled by this vision that,
as Billy Blake, he set out to save sinners from the
dangers of unredeemed sin.

For others, he thrust his hands into the fire or
subjected himself to intense cold. For you, he died.
That is not to say you should carry his death on
your conscience because death was what he
wanted. Without it, he had no hope of rescuing his
much loved wife, Verity, from the loneliness of the
bottomless pit to where, as a suicide, she would
have been banished. He believed there was no

salvation from that terrible place except through divine compassion, and he hoped that if he led a life of extreme penitence before dying voluntarily of self-neglect, he could achieve the miracle of plucking Verity from hell through God's merciful intervention.

You can argue that his mind was completely unhinged by shock, grief, alcohol abuse and persistent malnutrition. Certainly, some of his friends believe he was an undiagnosed schizophrenic. But I agree with the sentiments you expressed the first time I met you. 'We're in terrible trouble as a society if we assume that any man's life is so worthless that the manner of his death is the only interesting thing about him.' Billy's worth was in the efforts he made to save you, because the only reason he sought you out was to persuade you to pay in this life for the murder of James, rather than postpone your suffering into eternity.

The irony is that you were prepared to give an unmourned derelict the dignity in death that you have denied to James, and perhaps that was Billy's intention all along. It's what brought me to see you, after all. Billy must have known that walking to Andover in the middle of a hot summer to learn your address from Nigel de Vriess (although Nigel was abroad at the time, and it was Fiona who told him how to find you) would destroy what little reserves of energy he had. This meant that his death in your garage would be the inevitable consequence of his actions. As you said yourself, he could have attracted your attention, or eaten food from your freezer, but he did neither, just quenched his thirst on ice-cubes and quietly died. He wasn't interested in judging you, you see – he was a murderer himself – he was only interested in reminding you of that other man who had gone unburied and unmourned.

I enclose a summary of what I think happened, which I have sent to DS Greg Harrison. I have omitted Billy's part in the proceedings because he never reported it at the time and because I doubt the police will accept a dead man's witness. But I am confident he was watching in the shadows when you killed James. Neighbours in Teddington remember a squatter in the old school, and Tom Beale from the warehouse tells me Billy mentioned 'dossing upriver from Richmond' before he moved to the Isle of Dogs.

You may ask why he didn't come looking for you sooner. The simple answer is he only knew you as Amanda Streeter, the woman who bought the school where he was squatting, and when you reverted to your maiden name and moved house he lost sight of you until he read your name in connection with Nigel de Vriess. But the real answer is that he wasn't ready. An elderly woman talked to me once about suicide. She said: 'Have you taken into account that there may be something waiting for you on the other side, and that you may not be prepared yet to face it?' Billy understood better than anyone, I think, that he needed to be prepared, and his preparation came through suffering. He always said he hadn't suffered enough.

I don't intend to do any more than I have done already – which is to leave justice to the authorities – except to tell the Streeters that their son <u>was</u> murdered. None of us is all bad, Amanda, and we each deserve to be mourned. Billy's salvation I leave to you. My own view is that it makes no difference if he was mad or sane. He believed that saving another soul from hell would earn God's compassion.

You asked me to prove that Billy's life had value, but I'm sure you realize now that you're the only person who can do that. It is in your hands whether, through your own redemption, you also redeem him and Verity.

With best wishes,

Michael Deacon

Michael Deacon

PS. Please don't think there is any animosity behind this letter. I have always liked you.

THE ECHO

From: DS Greg Harrison
To: Michael Deacon

Amanda Powell has come clean about James. We start trawling tomorrow at 08.30 am. See you at Teddington!

Yours

Greg.

Greg

Chapter Twenty-Two

As Deacon rounded the corner of the converted school building, he was reminded of the first time he had visited the docklands warehouse. This was another bleak landscape, enlivened by people in shapeless, dark overcoats. A group of men stood in a huddle a few feet from the riverbank, staring out across grey water, coat collars raised against the biting wind. They were younger and more uniform in their dress, but the cold pinched their faces no less fiercely than it had pinched the faces of the warehouse derelicts. Beyond them, police divers in wetsuits bobbed beside a dinghy which was holding station against the current some yards out from where a twenty-foot stretch of lawn sloped down towards the river, ending at a wooden walkway that formed a towpath along the front of the property. The lawn was planted with shrubs and flowerbeds, curving in to give a framed perspective across the water, and Deacon wondered if this had been Amanda's vision when she drew up the plans for the conversion.

He noticed her suddenly, dressed in black, standing slightly apart with a prison officer and staring as intently at the river as the policemen were. She turned to look in

Deacon's direction as he approached across the grass, a faint smile of recognition lifting the corners of her mouth. She raised a hand in greeting, then let it drop, afraid perhaps that she'd put herself beyond the pale of human sympathy. He raised his own hand in acknowledgement.

DS Harrison peeled off from the group to steer him away from contact with Amanda. He glanced at the camera in Deacon's hand and shook his head. 'No photographs this time, old son,' he said.

'Just one?' murmured Deacon, nodding towards the woman. 'For my personal collection and not for publication. She looks great in black.'

'She would,' said the sergeant. 'She kills her lovers after copulation.'

'Is that a yes or a no?'

He shrugged. 'It's a "be it on your own head". She's trouble, Mike.'

Deacon grinned. 'You're a red-blooded male, for Christ's sake. Haven't you ever wanted to live a little? Don't you think the quid pro quo for the male black widow getting eaten is the best fucking sex he's ever had in his life?'

'It'll be the *only* sex he ever has,' said Harrison sourly. 'In any case she'll be an ugly old woman by the time she's served two life sentences.'

A wetsuited diver lifted a glistening, seal-like head above the surface of the river, and made a thumbs-down gesture to the watchers on the shore. The scene was both colourless and beautiful. Grey sky over grey water, with the black silhouette of the dinghy against a white winter sun. Before Harrison could stop him, Deacon raised his camera and recorded the moment for posterity. 'Nothing in life is ugly,' he said, swivelling the lens towards Amanda and using the zoom to bring her close, 'unless you choose to see it that way.'

'Wait till we pull James out. You'll think differently then.' He offered Deacon a cigarette. 'You were right about de Vriess tipping her off,' he said, cupping his hands around a match, 'except that at the time she didn't know where the information had come from. He sent her a photocopy of the original brief for the bank's in-house investigation, with James mentioned as a suspect. It arrived on the morning of Friday, the twenty-seventh of April, and she spent the day in a panic.' He broke off to light his own cigarette. 'She was due at her mother's that evening but she rang James at his office and asked him to meet her here at the school at six o'clock, ostensibly to discuss one or two problems that had arisen over the conversion plans. She says her only intention was to find out the truth, but it turned into a fight when James started boasting about how clever he'd been. They were inside the school, and she pushed him down a flight of stairs. She thinks he must have broken his neck on the way down.'

He paused as a second diver surfaced. 'According to her, the body's wedged under the boardwalk. That was the obligatory first phase of the construction. Rebuilding the dilapidated towpath in return for the right to convert the school. Supports were driven in to carry the pathway, and she put James in behind them.'

'At six o'clock on an April evening?' said Deacon in disbelief. 'It would have been broad daylight.'

'She didn't do it then.' Harrison drew heavily on his cigarette, sheltering it from the wind with his coat lapel. 'She left James dead at the bottom of the stairs and drove to Kent in a state of shock, expecting the police to be waiting for her when she got there. When they weren't, she began to calm down and realized she'd either have to confess to the murder or get rid of the body. She came back at two o'clock in the morning while her mother was asleep and disposed of it then.'

Deacon was watching Amanda while Harrison spoke. 'How? She's no Arnold Schwarzenegger, and she must have been working in the dark.'

'She's a resourceful woman,' said Harrison, 'and she brought a torch with her from her mother's house. As far as I can make out, she rolled him on to an old door and used the lever principle and a pile of breeze blocks to raise the door high enough to slide him into a wheelbarrow. The plan was to tip him off the boardwalk into the river and hope that when his body washed up further down, his death would be put down to a tragic accident. But she was tired, couldn't control the barrow properly and the whole thing tipped over this side of the walkway.' He gestured towards the shrubs on the left-hand side. 'Five years ago there was a two-yard gap where the bank had eroded, so rather than go through the whole palaver with the door and the breeze blocks again, she launched the body head-first through the gap, assuming it would be sucked out into the main stream.'

'But it wasn't?' asked Deacon when he didn't go on.

Harrison shrugged. 'He never surfaced, so she thinks he must have got snagged on one of the supports, and was then buried under the ballast and cement that the builders tipped in to fill the gaps along the board-walk.'

'Wouldn't they have seen the body?'

'She says she came back on the Monday morning to check, and there was no sign of it. After that, she thought it was just a matter of time before one of us knocked on her door and told her that, far from absconding, James had been dead for weeks.'

'But it never happened?'

'No. She's a jammy bitch.'

'If he's under a ton of ballast, what are the divers expecting to find?'

'Anything to indicate she's telling the truth. They're looking for metallic objects, his Rolex watch, belt buckle, shoe studs, buttons, even his fly. If they find them, we start digging out the ballast looking for the poor sod's skeleton.'

Deacon glanced across at Amanda again. 'Why wouldn't she be telling the truth?'

'No one understands why she's suddenly decided to come clean. She has every chance of walking away from the de Vriess murder because Barry's evidence of rape means she can plead self-defence. We're still working on proof of premeditation but we're having very little suc-cess. There's no record of any phone calls, no trace of her car in Dover, and if Nigel ever visited Sway, then no one saw him there.' He jerked his chin towards the river.

'So why give us this for free? What does she expect to achieve by it?'

'A clear conscience?' suggested Deacon.

Harrison dropped his butt to the grass and ground it out with his toe. 'You're a romantic, Mike. This is the end of the twentieth century, and people don't have consciences any more. They have clever solicitors instead. Do you seriously think Amanda would have told us about James if she hadn't been charged with Nigel's murder?' He shook his head. 'The pressure's been building up on her to account for James's disappearance, and she can't afford two separate trials for two separate murders. She might be found innocent once, but never twice, and the last thing she wants is for us to unearth James *after* she's beaten the de Vriess verdict. I'm betting there won't be enough of him left to show how he died, and she wants an assurance before she goes to court that there'll be no more charges pending. What price conscience then, eh?'

Deacon didn't answer immediately, and they stood in silence watching the police industry in the river. 'How did she find out it was Nigel who sent her the photocopy about the fraud?' he asked then.

'He rang to offer his sympathy after James disappeared, and mentioned it then. He said he wanted to warn her that James might be arrested but couldn't do it officially because of his position on the board. She denies your theory about him having a hold over her,' he went on. 'She says Nigel knew nothing about James's death, and claims their relationship had always been amicable until he forced his way into her house and raped her.'

413

Deacon gave a low laugh which was whipped away by the wind. 'She can't say anything else, not if she wants to plead self-defence.'

Harrison eyed him curiously. 'Why are you so keen to prove it wasn't?'

'I'm not any more.'

'I don't follow.'

Deacon trod his own butt into the ground. 'I'm only interested in her admission that she killed James. As far as Nigel's concerned, I'd say he got what he deserved whether he raped her once or a hundred times.'

'But you're damn sure it was the latter.'

'Yes.' He thrust his hands into his pockets to keep them warm. 'I think he owned her body and soul because he knew she'd murdered her husband. I've spoken to Lawrence's partner and he describes de Vriess as an animal. He says Nigel wouldn't have hesitated to abuse a woman he had a hold over.' He lifted an amused eyebrow. 'Look, there had to be some reason for the bastard's murder. *You* may believe she killed two men in accidental self-defence, but I don't. I think she's probably been planning how to get rid of Nigel for the last five years, but when John Streeter phoned to announce a change of tactics it was the push she needed. It's one thing to be the butt of libellous press releases that no sensible editor has ever touched with a barge pole, quite another to sit idly by while people you fear form alliances on the advice of a journalist.'

Harrison pulled a wry face. 'Where's the evidence? Justice isn't served by idle speculation.'

'It is in this case,' countered Deacon amiably. 'Justice

was served the minute she admitted to killing James, and you can thank Billy Blake for that. He's the one who persuaded her to talk.'

'You're not going to tell me she killed him as well?'

'No. Billy died of self-neglect.'

'What's your theory on why Nigel gave Billy her address?'

'He didn't. Nigel was abroad the last two weeks in May.' He thought back to the bitter woman who had spilled her heart out to him a few days before. 'It was Fiona who told Billy how to find Amanda.'

God knows, I hate her . . . She's ruined my life . . . Nigel and I were divorced because of her, and now she's killed him . . . Yes, I did tell that old tramp where she lived . . . He was completely mad . . . He said he was an instrument of God . . . And then he asked for her address . . . Did it worry me that I was sending a madman after her? . . . Not in the least. It amused me . . . Oh, I've always known where she was and what she was calling herself . . . I'd have been mad not to . . .

There was sudden activity in the water as a diver surfaced and gestured excitedly to the watchers on the bank. Harrison moved forward with a group of policemen, leaving Deacon to cross the twenty-yard gap that separated him from Amanda Powell. She was watching him, not the river, and he felt the pull of her attraction just as he had the first time he met her.

He often wondered why he didn't go to her.

Instead, he retraced his steps up the slope without a backward glance.

THE STREET, FLEET STREET, LONDON EC4

Lawrence Greenhill
23 Wharf Way
LONDON E14

22nd January 1996

Dear Lawrence,
What can you tell me about the following? I came
across it last night in your diary.

*London – 19th December 1949: A new client, Mrs P., a
war widow, came to me today, seeking advice about her
13-yr-old daughter's pregnancy. Should she seek to
prosecute the man in question or keep quiet for the sake
of her child? At 7+ months the pregnancy is too
advanced for abortion – dear God, the poor soul thought
it was puppy fat and my heart bleeds for her. She
welcomed GS into her home as a friend. He is 27, only
five years younger than she is, and she was flattered by
his attentions. Her confusion is the greater because she
clearly entertained hopes of marriage herself and is
devastated to find that he was more interested in
seducing her daughter, V. I have advised silence and
adoption, and given her the address of a convent in
Colchester where her daughter can retreat before her
condition becomes noticeable to friends and teachers.
The nuns will find suitable parents when the time*

416

*comes. But I am at war with myself tonight. What sort
of world are we living in where innocent children,
orphaned by war, become the prey of monsters? Surely
such a man should be prosecuted, even if at the expense
of his wretched victim's reputation?*

Terry says it's fate. Is it? Or is this your God at
work? I should have put you at the centre of my
chart, and not Billy Blake, for it was you who held
the key to both stories. Billy was 'still searching for
truth' while you have always known it.

Yours ever,

Michael Deacon

P.S. I've taken your advice and sent Barry home
to his mother after he got drunk for the third night
on the trot. It's Terry's fault. He teases the poor
little sod unmercifully. That being said, I can't
take any more protestations of love!

Wednesday, 7 February 1996 – 9.00 p.m. –
Cape Town, South Africa

The young waiter shrugged expressively, and jerked his head towards the figure at the window table. 'She's been crying ever since she got here,' he said. 'I don't know what to do. She won't order, and she won't go.'

The older man approached the table. 'Are you all right, Mrs Metcalfe? Is there anything I can do for you?'

She raised drowned eyes to his face, then rose unsteadily to her feet. 'No,' she said. 'I'm fine.'

As she walked away, he looked down at the English newspaper that she'd taken from the hotel rack when she'd arrived. But he was none the wiser for the banner headline.

DNA proves bones in river were
James Streeter

A Parable of Our Time
by Michael Deacon

THE tragic story of Verity Fenton's suicide and Peter Fenton's subsequent disappearance is well known. Unknown until recently is what happened to Peter, because the truth was buried in a suicide's grave.

'BILLY BLAKE – died 12 June 1995 of starvation.' So says the plaque at a London crematorium which commemorates the death of a homeless man. It should read: 'PETER FENTON OBE. Born 5 March 1950 – died 13 June 1995 of mortification.'

It's hard to conceive how a man like Peter Fenton, so prominent in the twin environments of Knightsbridge and the Foreign Office, could walk out of his house and vanish into thin air unless one understands why he did it. At the time, it was assumed he had run away, so the search was concentrated abroad. What never occurred to anyone was that he had chosen the life of a penitent by embracing poverty in the gutters of London.

Is it any wonder he vanished so successfully when none of us looks too long on the destitute in case eye-contact proves dangerous or embarrassing?

But transformations take time, and Peter, a handsome, darkhaired 38-year-old, should have been recognizable for weeks until poor hygiene and diet reduced him to the skeletal figure of Billy Blake, well-known to the police as a 60-year-old human derelict and street preacher. How could he have changed so radically and in so short a time? The answer, I think, is that the shock of Verity's suicide destroyed him. He was already aged beyond recognition when he entered the anonymous world of the vagrant.

It would be true to say that Peter Fenton died on 3 July 1988 when he walked out of the family home in Cadogan Square. Certainly, he had no interest in being that man again. Peter Fenton was a professional diplomat, an assured and confident man with an enviable intellect and no obvious vices. By contrast, Billy Blake was a tortured individual, who delighted in self-inflicted pain and preached damnation to anyone who would listen. He was an unrepentant alcoholic, thief and beggar, but he strove, often at terrible cost to himself, to protect others from the evil that he had done himself. The irony was that Billy, destitute, was a good man and Peter Fenton, advantaged, was not.

Peter was a murderer who went on to seduce and marry the wife of his victim, Geoffrey Standish. There can be no doubt that he knew exactly who Verity was when he first made love to her, for even if Geoffrey Standish was a stranger when Peter killed him, he will have learned about the man from newspaper reports afterwards. We can speculate that this knowledge added to the thrill of Verity Standish's seduction or we can take a kinder view and say that Peter simply fell in love at first sight with a frail and vulnerable woman whose suffering at the hands of her brutal first husband had left its indelible imprint.

She was a tiny, fine-drawn woman with huge doe eyes, and Peter was by no means the first man to offer her protection. He was, however, the youngest, and Verity, after years of abuse by Geoffrey, who was fourteen years her senior, saw safety in a relationship with a younger man. Nevertheless, she wasn't keen to publicize her love for a toyboy. There is evidence that she didn't want to legitimize the affair because she was afraid of what people might say. But, while she may have married Peter against her better judgement, her fears about the inappropriateness of the match were quickly laid to rest. Their marriage has been described by friends as 'an idyll', 'the greatest love since Abelard and Eloise', 'sweet to watch', 'so intense that it was close to idolatry', 'it's hard to say who adored the other more'.

How tragic then that, obsessed with love of Peter,

she began to ignore the two children she'd had with Geoffrey. It's easy to understand why. At the time of her marriage, her daughter Marilyn, 20, was at university and her son Anthony, 14, was at boarding school. She was no longer so important to them, and her role as Peter's wife took her overseas.

'They always paid for us to fly out in the holidays if we wanted to go,' says Marilyn, 'but it was no fun playing gooseberry for weeks on end. It was harder for Anthony because he was younger. Not that he ever blamed Peter. It was Mother he resented because she never made a secret of how much she'd hated our father. In the end, when Anthony became depressed after his girlfriend walked out on him, his resentment boiled over and he put that advertisement in *The Times*. He knew Mother would read it, and he wanted to jolt her out of her complacency. We'd both heard the rumours that she'd had Father killed, and Anthony wanted to remind her of them. You see, he was only five in 1971, and he never believed that Geoffrey was as bad as everyone said.'

Anthony Standish was 22 years old in 1988. He was an unhappy young man, whose depression over a failed love affair became confused with a long-standing resentment of his mother's coolness towards him. His bitterness found expression in the following advertisement:

'**Geoffrey Standish**. Will anyone knowing anything about the murder of Geoffrey Standish on the A11 near Newmarket 10.3.71 please write to Box 431.'

Anne Cattrell first put forward the theory that Peter had murdered Geoffrey in her article 'The Truth about Verity Fenton' (*Sunday Times*, 17 June 1990). She argued that Peter and Verity may have met much earlier than they ever admitted, and that Peter was Verity's avenging arm. There's no evidence of that, but there is a wealth of evidence to show that Geoffrey and Peter had something else in common in 1971. Which was gambling.

As Billy Blake, Peter confessed to killing a man, and it's reasonable to assume that that man was Geoffrey Standish. Billy's penance was too long and too tortured for his victim to have been unconnected with Verity's suicide. But as Billy Blake, he also preached against the dangers of sudden and uncontrollable anger which leads men to commit acts of violence that they later regret. This would suggest that Geoffrey's murder was the result of a similar anger, making it an unplanned act and not a premeditated one.

We can only speculate twenty-five years after the event, but university friends of Peter talk about his 'illicit Friday-night card games at a private house somewhere in Cambridge' which allowed him to pursue his goals of 'money' and 'the good life'. It is certainly possible that Geoffrey, who was on his way to Huntingdon on Friday, 9 March 1971, learned of such a card game and gained entry to it after phoning his hosts to say he would be delayed. It is also possible that a fight broke out over money and ended, tragically, in death.

There must have been other people present who witnessed what happened. Indeed Peter may not have been alone in the killing, which would explain why it was so successfully disguised as a road traffic accident. More likely, perhaps, is that Geoffrey attacked first – his aggressiveness is well documented – which would have exonerated the other participants, at least in their own minds, of murderous intent. Whatever the truth, the decision was made to protect everyone involved by dumping the body as far as possible from the illegal gambling house and make the death look like a hit-and-run accident.

While there is no evidence to support this theory above any other (except perhaps Peter's abrupt decision to give up gambling 'some time in '71', according to friends) it makes it easier to understand how Verity could have married Peter in ignorance of his crime. For, as Anne Cattrell argued elsewhere in her article, did Verity kill herself because she learned by accident that she'd married her first husband's murderer?

The answer is that it was not an accident. Peter told her himself, during a bitter confrontation between Verity and Anthony after the advertisement appeared in *The Times*. 'I accused her of killing my father and when she burst into tears Peter got very angry and said *he'd* done it. I know it sounds ridiculous,' Anthony says now, 'but I didn't believe him. I thought he was just trying to diffuse the row. It's what he always did. Every time she and I fell out over anything, Peter would take the blame on to himself. It used to make me so angry. My mother was very childish in many ways. She seemed unable to take responsibility for anything.

'I've lived with the guilt of that row for eight years. I wish I'd waited until Peter had come back from the States instead of attacking her the day before he left. It's one of those terrible truisms, that you only realize how much you love a person when you've lost them. I was hurting very badly after my girlfriend left me, but it's no excuse for what I did. I never really believed that my mother had killed my father, but when she hanged herself I assumed she must have done and that Peter had rejected her as a result. I always hoped he'd come back one day, which is why I've never spoken about this before.'

But if Verity didn't hang herself out of guilt, then why? Was it in sudden revulsion against the man she adored? In panic because she was afraid her husband's crime would catch up with him now that Anthony knew the truth? Either explanation could be true but neither satisfies. For all her frailty, Verity was stronger than that. She had put up with years of abuse from Geoffrey, and it seems unlikely that revulsion or panic would drive her to suicide.

My own view is that something infinitely more terrible pushed Verity over the edge. It was a secret she had kept for forty years, and I learned of it by chance from a lawyer whom Verity's mother, Mrs Isobel Parnell, consulted in 1949 about Geoffrey Standish's seduction of her 13-year-old daughter.

'It was a terrible story,' said Lawrence Greenhill. 'Isobel had hoped to marry Geoffrey herself, and she hated Verity for causing her so much pain. The baby, a boy, was put up for adoption, and Verity was sent away to boarding school. The tragedy was that no one considered Verity's pain. At one stroke Isobel had deprived her of child, lover and mother, and one can only wonder what loneliness the poor girl must have suffered. With the benefit of hindsight, it's obvious she would seek to pay Isobel back by marrying the man who had ruined their lives. How could a disturbed adolescent possibly distinguish between love and lust when the woman who loved her rejected her and the man who seduced her continued to pursue her?'

But there are no neat solutions to this story. Peter was not Verity's long-lost son, nor could she ever have believed he was. It is the Registrar General's job to check for just such anomalies before granting marriage licences, and no questions were raised at the time of Peter's and Verity's wedding.

In her rational mind, Verity must have known there was nothing improper about their relationship, despite the intensity of her love for Peter. But in her irrational mind, alone in the awful silence of their empty house after Peter had gone to America, did she start to brood on the unnatural love she had for the murderer of her first husband and did she begin to question the legality of the adoption papers?

Her suicide note speaks of betrayals, and it's tempting to assume she was thinking of her mother and her adopted son when she wrote it. But perhaps a more likely explanation is that she finally recognized she had betrayed everyone, *even Peter*, through her inability to express love naturally. For it's unlikely Peter would have been forced to betray himself to Anthony had Verity loved him less and Anthony more.

As Lawrence Greenhill suggests, Verity Fenton's

real tragedy was her confusion of love with desire. She couldn't adequately express her love for Anthony because desire for a son is illegal, so she chose to consume her surrogate son, Peter, with all the passion in her nature. But, as she dwelt on the consequences of his admission of murder, alone and isolated in Cadogan Square, did it begin to dawn on her that her worship of the man who'd killed the father of *all* her children was a betrayal too far?

And did she decide to kill herself because she realized it made no difference, and that she would want this man to possess her as long as she lived – be he father-slayer *or* son?

(Extracts taken from *Oedipus* by Michael Deacon, to be published by Macmillan, 8 November 1996)

Epilogue

THE FLAT WAS empty when Deacon returned to it, for which he was grateful. He was in no mood for Terry's cannabis-inspired inanity, having had his third row in as many days with the new editor of the *Street*.

Who could have believed he would ever regret JP's departure?

'Different times, different customs, Mike,' JP had said as he left. 'Anodyne's the word I'd use for the new management. You won't be chasing prostitutes any more, just sound bites from trained politicians.'

'I can live with that,' Deacon replied.

'Don't be too sure,' JP had warned prophetically. 'You may not have shared my ideas on what made a good story, but you were always free to write it in any way you chose.' He picked up Deacon's copy on Peter Fenton, which was lying on the desk, and isolated the final two pages which discussed why Billy Blake had died in Amanda Powell's garage. 'I can guarantee you won't get these last seven hundred words into print. I know you want to go public on why and how the poor bastard died, but there's no way the new lot will risk being sued, and particularly not by a prisoner on remand. It's too

426

damned contentious. It almost certainly infringes the *sub judice* rules and it's bound to damage Amanda's right to a fair trial for the murder of de Vriess. And that's not to mention the trouble you'll have from the DV's family when you accuse him of being a multiple rapist.'

'Would you have risked it?'

'Of course. I'd argue that the matter isn't *sub judice* yet because Amanda hasn't been charged with James's murder.' His expression grew cynical. 'And won't be, unless the boffins can come up with a cause of death. Is it true she's withdrawn her confession?'

Deacon nodded.

'Even more reason to publish and be damned then, and if and when we raised enough steam to force a prosecution, I'd make hay out of the fact that our efforts resulted in her being convicted of *both* murders instead of walking away scot-free as she looks like doing at the moment.'

'And if the magazine got taken to the cleaners for libel?'

'We'd have served a kind of justice, on both her *and* that bastard de Vriess.' JP chuckled. 'It's why they've kicked me out, of course. It's all about profit these days, and social consciences like mine come expensive.'

Deacon pressed the 'messages' button on his answer phone. 'Barry's been arrested again,' said Greg Harrison's unemotional voice. 'Drunk and disorderly right on our doorstep this time. His mother's adamant she won't have him back, so he wants to give your address in case he's bound over. You're going to have to sort this, Mike. He says he only gets drunk because he's in love with you.' There was a short pause. *For laughter?* Deacon wondered sourly. 'Look, call me back when you can.'

Lawrence's voice next. 'I'm so sorry, my dear fellow. I see your article has had its teeth drawn. How very disappointing for you. I know how much you wanted to demonstrate that Billy's life had a purpose. Is it any consolation to think of him as Terry's mentor? In the end, surely, that is where Billy's true value lay.'

As the messages came to an end, the emptiness of the flat began to make itself felt. Picasso's *Woman in a Chemise* had gone, along with the television and the stereo that Terry had moved from the bedroom into the sitting-room. Big Ben and the conch shell no longer stood on the mantelpiece, and Turner's *Fighting Téméraire* was just a memory on a blank wall. Deacon went into the kitchen and inspected the biscuit jar. It contained a folded piece of paper.

Cheers, mate. I reckon I've earned what I've taken by learning to read and write. Anyway, it's a lot less than the five hundred quid I could have had off you at the beginning. Give my love to Lawrence and Mrs D. They're good people. You, too. I'll look you up some time. Your friend, Terry.

P.S. Tell that editor to get stuffed and concentrate on book-writing. Do your own thing, mate. I mean, like Billy always said: any man who dies in chains probably deserves to.

The Breaker

For Marigold and Anthony

Acknowledgements

With particular thanks to
Sally and John Priestley of *XII Bar Blues*
and Encombe House Estate.

Admiralty chart of Chapman's Pool © British Crown
Copyright/MOD. Reproduced with the
permission of the Controller of Her Britannic
Majesty's Stationery Office.

Chapman's Pool   Emmetts Hill   Quarry Valley   St Alban's Head

Eastern Perspective

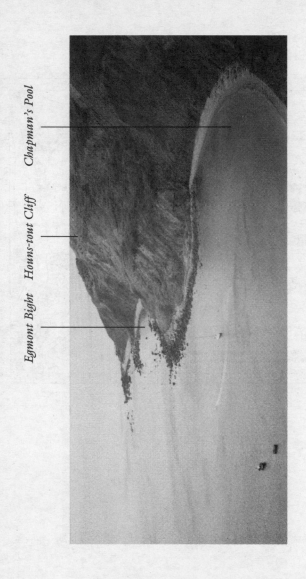

Egmont Bight *Houns-tout Cliff* *Chapman's Pool*

Western Perspective

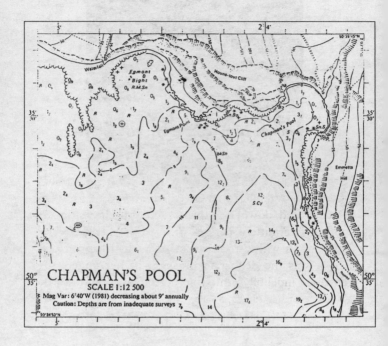

CHAPMAN'S POOL
SCALE 1:12 500
Mag Var: 6°40′W (1981) decreasing about 9′ annually
Caution: Depths are from inadequate surveys

Sunday, 10 August 1997 – 1.45 a.m.

SHE DRIFTED with the waves, falling off their rolling backs and waking to renewed agony every time salt water seared down her throat and into her stomach. During intermittent periods of lucidity when she revisited, always with astonishment, what had happened to her, it was the deliberate breaking of her fingers that remained indelibly printed on her memory, and not the brutality of her rape.

Sunday, 10 August 1997 – 5.00 a.m.

THE CHILD sat cross-legged on the floor like a minia-ture statue of Buddha, the grey dawn light leeching her flesh of colour. He had no feelings for her, not even common humanity, but he couldn't bring himself to touch her. She watched him as solemnly as he watched her, and he was enthralled by her immobility. He could break her neck as easily as a chicken's, but he fancied he saw an ancient wisdom in her concentrated gaze, and the idea frightened him. Did she know what he'd done?

Prologue

Extract from: *The Mind of a Rapist* by Helen Barry

THE most widely held view is that rape is an exercise in male domination, a pathological assertion of power, usually performed out of anger against the entire sex or frustration with a specific individual. By forcing a woman to accept penetration, the man is demonstrating not only his superior strength but his right to sow his seed wherever and whenever he chooses. This has elevated the rapist to a creature of legendary proportions – demoniacal, dangerous, predatory – and the fact that few rapists merit such labels is secondary to the fear the legend inspires.

In a high percentage of cases (including domestic, date and gang rape) the rapist is an inadequate individual who seeks to bolster poor self-image by attacking someone he perceives to be weaker than himself. He is a man of low intelligence, few social skills, and with a profound sense of his own inferiority in his dealings with the rest of society. A deep-seated fear of women is more common to the rapist than a feeling of superiority, and this may well lie in early failure to make successful relationships.

Pornography becomes a means to an end for such a person because masturbation is as necessary to him as the regular fix is to a heroin addict. Without orgasm the sex-fixator experiences nothing. However, his obsessive nature, coupled with his lack of achievement, will make him an unattractive mate to the sort of woman his inferiority complex demands, namely a woman who attracts successful men. If he has a relationship at all, his partner will be someone who has been used and abused by other men which only exacerbates his feelings of inadequacy and inferiority.

It could be argued that the rapist, a man of limited intelligence, limited sensation and limited ability to function, is more to be pitied than feared, because his danger lies in the easy ascendancy society has given him over the so-called weaker sex. Every time judges and newspapers demonize and mythologize the rapist as a dangerous predator, they merely reinforce the idea that the penis is a symbol of power . . .

Chapter One

THE WOMAN LAY on her back on the pebble foreshore at the foot of Houns-tout Cliff, staring at the cloudless sky above, her pale blonde hair drying into a frizz of tight curls in the hot sun. A smear of sand across her abdomen gave the impression of wispy clothing, but the brown circles of her nipples and the hair sprouting at her crotch told anyone who cared to look that she was naked. One arm curved languidly around her head while the other rested palm-up on the shingle, the fingers curling in the tiny wavelets that bubbled over them as the tide rose; her legs, opened shamelessly in relaxation, seemed to invite the sun's warmth to penetrate directly into her body.

Above her loomed the grim shale escarpment of Houns-tout Cliff, irregularly striped with the hardy vegetation that clung to its ledges. So often shrouded in mist and rain during the autumn and winter, it looked benign in the brilliant summer sunlight. A mile away to the west on the Dorset Coast Path that hugged the clifftops to Weymouth, a party of hikers approached at a leisurely pace, pausing every now and then to watch cormorants and shags plummet into the sea like tiny guided missiles.

To the east, on the path to Swanage, a single male walker passed the Norman chapel on St Alban's Head on his way to the rock-girt crucible of Chapman's Pool whose clear blue waters made an attractive anchorage when the wind was light and offshore. Because of the steep hills that surround it, pedestrian visitors to its beaches were rare, but at lunchtime on a fine weekend upwards of ten boats rode at anchor there, bobbing in staggered formation as the gentle swells passed under each in turn.

A single boat, a thirty-two-foot Princess, had already nosed in through the entrance channel, and the rattle of its anchor chain over its idling engines carried clearly on the air. Not far behind, the bow of a Fairline Squadron carved through the race off St Alban's Head, giving the yachts that wallowed lazily in the light winds a wide berth in its progress towards the bay. It was a quarter past ten on one of the hottest Sundays of the year, but out of sight around Egmont Point the naked sunbather appeared oblivious to both the shimmering heat and the increasing likelihood of company.

The Spender brothers, Paul and Daniel, had spotted the nudist as they rounded the Point with their fishing rods, and they were now perched precariously on an unstable ledge some hundred feet above her and to her right. They took it in turns to look at her through their father's expensive binoculars which they had smuggled out of the rented holiday cottage in a bundle of T-shirts, rods and tackle. It was the middle weekend of their two weeks' holiday, and as far as the elder brother was concerned, fishing had only ever been a pretext. This remote part of the Isle of Purbeck held little attraction for an awakening adolescent, having few inhabitants, fewer distractions and no sandy beaches. His intention had always been to spy on bikini-clad women draped over the expensive motor cruisers in Chapman's Pool.

'Mum said we weren't to climb the cliffs because they're dangerous,' whispered Danny, the virtuous ten-year-old, less interested than his brother in the sight of bare flesh.

'Shut up.'

'She'd kill us if she knew we were looking at a nudie.'

'You're just scared because you've never seen one before.'

'Neither've you,' muttered the younger boy indignantly. 'Anyway, she's a dirty person. I bet loads of people can see her.'

Paul, the elder by two years, treated this remark with the scorn it deserved – they hadn't passed a soul on their way round Chapman's Pool. Instead, he concentrated on the wonderfully accessible body below. He couldn't see much of the woman's face because she was lying with her feet pointing towards them, but the magnification of the lenses was so powerful that he could see every other detail of her. He was too ignorant of the naked female form to question the bruises that blotched her skin, but he knew afterwards that he wouldn't have questioned them anyway, even if he'd known what they meant. He had fantasized about something like this happening – discovering a quiescent, unmoving woman who allowed him to explore her at his leisure, if only through binoculars. He found the soft flow of her breasts unbearably erotic and dwelt at length on her nipples, wondering what it would be like to touch them and what would happen if he did. Lovingly he traversed the length of her midriff, pausing on the dimple of her belly button, before returning to what interested him most, her opened legs and what lay between them. He crawled forward on his elbows, writhing his body beneath him.

'What are you doing?' demanded Danny suspiciously, crawling up beside him. 'Are you being dirty?'

''Course not.' He gave the boy a savage thump on the arm. 'That's all you ever think about, isn't it? Being dirty. You'd better watch it, penis-brain, or I'll tell Dad on you.'

In the inevitable fight that followed – a grunting, red-faced brawl of hooked arms and kicking feet – the Zeiss binoculars slipped from the elder brother's grasp and clattered down the slope, dislodging an avalanche of shale in the process. The boys, united in terror of what their father was going to say, abandoned the fight to wriggle back from the brink and stare in dismay after the binoculars.

'It's your fault if they're broken,' hissed the ten-year-old. 'You're the one who dropped them.'

But for once his brother didn't rise to the bait. He was more interested in the body's continued immobility. With an awful sense of foreboding it dawned on him that he'd been masturbating over a dead woman.

Chapter Two

THE CLEAR WATERS of Chapman's Pool heaved in an undulating roll to break in rippling foam around the pebble shore of the bay. By now three boats were anchored there, two flying the red ensign – *Lady Rose*, the Princess, and *Gregory's Girl*, the Fairline Squadron; the third, *Mirage*, a French Beneteau, flew the tricolour. Only *Gregory's Girl* showed any sign of real activity with a man and a woman struggling to release a dinghy whose winching wires had become jammed in the ratchet mechanism of the davits. On *Lady Rose*, a scantily clad couple lounged on the flying bridge, bodies glistening with oil, eyes closed against the sun, while on *Mirage*, a teenage girl held a video camera to her eye and panned idly up the steep grassy slope of West Hill, searching for anything worth filming.

No one noticed the Spender brothers' mad dash around the bay, although the French girl did zoom in on the lone male walker as he descended the hillside towards them. Seeing only with the tunnel vision of the camera, she was oblivious to anything but the handsome young man in her sight, and her smitten heart gave a tiny leap of excitement at the thought of another chance encounter with the beautiful Englishman. She had met him two days before at the Berthon Marina in Lymington when, with a gleaming smile, he'd told her the computer code for the lavatories, and she couldn't believe her good luck that he was here . . . today . . . in this shit-hole of boring isolation which her parents described as one of England's gems.

To her starved imagination he looked like a longer-haired version of Jean-Claude Van Damme in his sleeveless T-shirt and bottom-hugging shorts – tanned, muscled, sleek dark hair swept back from his face, smiling brown eyes, grittily stubbled jaw – and in the narrative tale of her own life, romanticized, embellished, unbelievably innocent, she pictured herself swooning in his strong arms and capturing his heart. Through the intimacy of magnification she watched his muscles ripple as he lowered his rucksack to the ground, only for the lens to fill abruptly with the frantic movements of the Spender brothers. With an audible groan, she switched off the camera and stared in disbelief at the prancing children who, from a distance, appeared to be showing enthusiastic delight.

Surely he was too young to be anybody's father?
But . . . A Gallic shrug . . .
Who knew with the English?

Behind the questing mongrel which zigzagged energetically in pursuit of a scent, the horse picked its way carefully down the track that led from Hill Bottom to the Pool. Tarmac showed in places where the track had once been a road, and one or two sketchy foundations among the overgrown vegetation beside it spoke of buildings long abandoned and demolished. Maggie Jenner had lived in this area most of her life but had never known why the handful of inhabitants in this corner of the Isle of Purbeck had gone away and left their dwellings to the ravages of time. Someone had told her once that 'chapman' was an archaic word for merchant or pedlar but what anyone could have traded in this remote place she couldn't imagine. Perhaps, more simply, a pedlar had drowned in the bay and bequeathed his death to posterity. Every time she took this path she reminded herself to find out, but every time she made her way home again she forgot.

The cultivated gardens that had once bloomed here had left a lingering legacy of roses, hollyhocks and hydrangeas amid the weeds and grasses, and she thought how pleasant it would be to have a house in this colourful wilderness, facing south-west towards the channel with only her dog and her horses for company. Because of the threat of the ever-sliding cliffs, access to Chapman's Pool was denied to motorized traffic by padlocked gates at Hill Bottom and Kingston, and the attraction of so much stillness was a powerful one. But then isolation and its attendant solitude was becoming something of an obsession with her, and occasionally it worried her.

Even as the thought was in her head, she heard the sound of an approaching vehicle, grinding in first gear over the bumps and hollows behind her, and gave a surprised whistle to bring Bertie to heel behind Sir

Jasper. She turned in the saddle, assuming it was a tractor, and frowned at the approaching police Range Rover. It slowed as it drew level with her and she recognized Nick Ingram at the wheel before, with a brief smile of acknowledgement, he drove on and left her to follow in his dusty wake.

The emergency services had rushed into action following a nine-nine-nine call to the police from a mobile telephone. It was timed at 10.43 a.m. The caller gave his name as Steven Harding and explained that he had come across two boys who claimed a body was lying on the beach at Egmont Bight. The details were confused because the boys omitted to mention that the woman was naked, and their obvious distress and garbled speech led Harding to give the impression that 'the lady on the beach' was their mother and had fallen from the cliff while using a pair of binoculars. As a result the police and coastguards acted on the presumption that she was still alive.

Because of the difficulty of retrieving a badly injured person from the foreshore, the coastguards dispatched a Search and Rescue helicopter from Portland to winch her off. Meanwhile, PC Nick Ingram, diverted from a burglary investigation, approached via the track that skirted the inappropriately named West Hill on the eastern side of Chapman's Pool. He had had to use bolt cutters to slice through the chain on the gate at Hill Bottom and, as he abandoned his Range Rover on the hard standing beside the fishermen's boatsheds, he was hoping fervently that rubber-neckers wouldn't grab the opportunity to follow him. He was in no mood to marshal petulant sightseers.

The only access from the boatsheds to the beach where the woman lay was by the same route the boys had taken – on foot around the bay, followed by a scramble over the rocks at Egmont Point. To a man in uniform, it was a hot and sweaty business, and Nick Ingram, who stood over six feet four inches and weighed upwards of sixteen stone, was drenched by the time he reached the body. He bent forward, hands on knees, to recover his breath, listening to the deafening sound of the approaching SAR helicopter and feeling its wind on his damp shirt. He thought it a hideous intrusion into what was obviously a place of death. Despite the heat of the sun, the woman's skin was cold to the touch and her widely staring eyes had begun to film. He was struck by how tiny she seemed, lying alone at the bottom of the cliff, and how sad her miniature hand looked waving in the spume.

Her nudity surprised him, the more so when it required only the briefest of glances about the beach to reveal a complete absence of towels, clothes, footwear or possessions. He noticed bruising on her arms, neck and chest, but it was more consistent with being tumbled over rocks on an incoming tide, he thought, than with a dive off a clifftop. He stooped again over the body, looking for anything that would indicate how it had got there, then retreated rapidly as the descending stretcher spiralled dangerously close to his head.

The noise of the helicopter and the amplified voice of

15

the winch-operator calling instructions to the man below had attracted sightseers. The party of hikers gathered on the clifftop to watch the excitement while the yachtsmen in Chapman's Pool motored out of the bay in their dinghies to do the same. A spirit of revelry was abroad because everyone assumed the rescue wouldn't have happened unless the woman was still alive, and a small cheer went up as the stretcher rose in the air. Most thought she'd fallen from the cliff; a few thought she might have floated out of Chapman's Pool on a lilo and got into difficulties. No one guessed she'd been murdered.

Except, perhaps, Nick Ingram who transferred the tiny, stiffening body to the stretcher and felt a dreadful anger burn inside him because Death had stolen a pretty woman's dignity. As always, the victory belonged to the thief and not to the victim.

As requested by the nine-nine-nine operator, Steven Harding shepherded the boys down the hill to the police car which was parked beside the boatsheds where they waited with varying degrees of patience until its occupant returned. The brothers, who had sunk into an exhausted silence after their mad dash round Chapman's Pool, wanted to be gone, but they were intimidated by their companion, a twenty-four-year-old actor, who took his responsibilities *in loco parentis* seriously.

He kept a watchful eye on his uncommunicative charges (too shocked to speak, he thought) while trying to cheer them up with a running commentary of what he could see of the rescue. He peppered his conversation with expressions like: '*You're a couple of heroes . . .*' '*Your mum's going to be really proud of you . . .*' '*She's a lucky lady to have two such sensible sons . . .*' But it wasn't until the helicopter flew towards Poole and he turned to them with a smile of encouragement, saying: 'There you are, you can stop worrying now. Mum's in safe hands,' that they realized his mistake. It hadn't occurred to either of them that what appeared to be general remarks about their own mother applied specifically to the 'lady on the beach'.

'She's not our mum,' said Paul, dully.

'Our mum's going to be *really* angry,' supplied Danny in his piping treble, emboldened by his brother's willingness to abandon the prolonged silence. 'She said if we were late for lunch she'd make us eat bread and water for a week.' (He was an inventive child.) 'She's going to be even angrier when I tell her it's because Paul wanted to look at a nudie.'

'Shut up,' said his brother.

'*And* he made me climb the cliff so he could get a better look. Dad's going to kill him for ruining the binoculars.'

'Shut *up*.'

'Yeah, well, it's all your fault. You shouldn't have dropped them. *Penis*-brain!' Danny added snidely, in the safe knowledge that their companion would protect him.

Harding watched tears of humiliation gather in the older boy's eyes. It didn't take much reading of the references to 'nudie', 'better look', 'binoculars' and 'penis-brain' to come up with a close approximation of the facts. 'I hope she was worth it,' he said matter-of-factly. 'The first naked woman I ever saw was so old and ugly, it was three years before I wanted to look at another one. She lived in the house next to us and she was as fat and wrinkled as an elephant.'

'What was the next one like?' asked Danny with the sequential logic of a ten-year-old.

Harding exchanged a glance with the elder brother. 'She had nice tits,' he told Paul with a wink.

'So did this one,' said Danny obligingly.

'Except she was dead,' said his brother.

'She probably wasn't, you know. It's not always easy to tell when someone's dead.'

'She was,' said Paul despondently. 'Me and Danny went down to get the binoculars back.' He unravelled his bundled T-shirt to reveal the badly scratched casing of a pair of Zeiss binoculars. 'I – well, I checked to make sure. I think she drowned and got left there by the tide.' He fell into an unhappy silence again.

'He was going to give her the kiss of life,' said Danny, 'but her eyes were nasty, so he didn't.'

Harding cast another glance in the older brother's direction, this time sympathetic. 'The police will need to identify her,' he said matter-of-factly, 'so they'll probably ask you to describe her.' He ruffled Danny's hair. 'It might be better not to mention nasty eyes or nice tits when you do it.'

Danny pulled away. 'I won't.'

The man nodded. 'Good boy.' He took the binoculars from Paul and examined the lenses carefully before

18

pointing them at the Beneteau in Chapman's Pool. 'Did you recognize her?' he asked.

'No,' said Paul uncomfortably.

'Was she an old lady?'

'No.'

'Pretty?'

Paul wriggled his shoulders. 'I guess so.'

'Not fat then?'

'No. She was very little, and she had blonde hair.'

Harding brought the yacht into sharp focus. 'They're built like tanks, these things,' he murmured, traversing the sights across the bay. 'Okay, the bodywork's a bit scratched but there's nothing wrong with the lenses. Your dad won't be that angry.'

Maggie Jenner would never have become involved if Bertie had responded to her whistle, but like all dogs he was deaf when he wanted to be. She had dismounted when the noise of the helicopter alarmed the horse and natural curiosity had led her to walk him on down the hill while the rescue was under way. The three of them rounded the boatsheds together and Bertie, overexcited by all the confusion, made a beeline for Paul Spender's crotch, shoving his nose against the boy's shorts and breathing in with hearty enthusiasm.

Maggie whistled, and was ignored. 'Bertie!' she called. 'Come here, boy!'

The dog was a huge, fearsome-looking brute, the result of a night on the tiles by an Irish wolfhound bitch, and saliva drooled in great white gobbets from his jaws.

19

With a flick of his hairy head, he splattered spittle across Paul's shorts and the terrified child froze in alarm.

'BERTIE!'

'It's all right,' said Harding, grabbing the dog by the collar and pulling him off, 'he's only being friendly.' He rubbed the dog's head. 'Aren't you, boy?'

Unconvinced, the brothers retreated rapidly to the other side of the police car.

'They've had a tough morning,' explained Harding, clicking his tongue encouragingly and walking Bertie back to his mistress. 'Will he stay put if I let him go?'

'Not in this mood,' she said, pulling a lead from her back trouser pocket and clipping one end into the collar before attaching the other end to the nearest stirrup. 'My brother's two boys adore him and he doesn't understand that the rest of the world doesn't view him in quite the same way.' She smiled. 'You must have dogs yourself, either that or you're very brave. Most people run a mile.'

'I grew up on a farm,' he said, stroking Sir Jasper's nose and studying her with frank admiration.

She was a good ten years older than he was, tall and slim with shoulder-length dark hair and deep brown eyes that narrowed suspiciously under his assessing gaze. She knew exactly what type she was dealing with when he looked pointedly at her left hand for the wedding ring that wasn't there. 'Well, thanks for your help,' she said rather brusquely. 'I can manage on my own now.'

He stood back immediately. 'Good luck then,' he said. 'It was nice meeting you.'

She was all too aware that her distrust of men had

now reached pathological proportions, and wondered guiltily if she'd jumped to the wrong conclusion. 'I hope your boys weren't too frightened,' she said rather more warmly.

He gave an easy laugh. 'They're not mine,' he told her. 'I'm just looking after them till the police get back. They found a dead woman on the beach so they're pretty shook up, poor kids. You'd be doing them a favour if you persuaded them Bertie's just an overgrown hearthrug. I'm not convinced that adding canophobia to necrophobia all in one morning is good psychology.'

She looked undecidedly towards the police car. The boys did look frightened, she thought, and she didn't particularly want the responsibility of inspiring a lifelong fear of dogs in them.

'Why don't we invite them over,' he suggested, sensing her hesitation, 'and let them pat him while he's under control? It'll only take a minute or two.'

'All right,' she agreed half-heartedly, 'if you think it would help.' But it was against her better judgement. She had the feeling that once again she was being drawn into something she wouldn't be able to control.

It was after midday by the time PC Ingram returned to his car to find Maggie Jenner, Steven Harding and the Spender brothers waiting beside it. Sir Jasper and Bertie stood at a distance, secure in the shade of a tree, and the aesthete in Nick Ingram could only admire the way the woman displayed herself. Sometimes he thought she had no idea how attractive she was; other times, like now, when she placed herself side by side with natural, equine and human beauty, demanding comparison, he suspected the pose was deliberate. He mopped his forehead with a large white handkerchief, wondering irritably who the Chippendale was and how both he and Maggie managed to look so cool in the intolerable heat of that Sunday morning. They were looking at him and laughing, and he assumed, in the eternal way of human nature, they were laughing at him.

'Good morning, Miss Jenner,' he said with exaggerated politeness.

She gave a small nod in return. 'Nick.'

He turned enquiringly to Harding. 'Can I help you, sir?'

'I don't think so,' said the young man with an engaging smile. 'I think we're supposed to be helping you.'

Ingram was Dorsetshire born and bred and had no time for wankers in dinky shorts, sporting artificial tans. 'In what way?' There was a hint of sarcasm in his voice that made Maggie Jenner frown at him.

'I was asked to bring these boys to the police car when I made the emergency call. They're the ones who found the dead woman.' He clapped his hands across their shoulders. 'They're a couple of heroes. Maggie and I have just been telling them they deserve medals.'

The 'Maggie' wasn't lost on Ingram although he questioned her enthusiasm for being on Christian-name terms with such an obvious poser. She had better taste, he thought. Ponderously, he shifted his attention to Paul and Danny Spender. The message he had received couldn't have been clearer. Two boys had reported seeing their mother fall from a cliff while using a pair of binoculars. He knew as soon as he saw the body – not enough bruises – that it couldn't have fallen, and looking at the boys now – too relaxed – he doubted the rest of the information. 'Did you know the woman?' he asked them.

They shook their heads.

He unlocked his car door and retrieved a notebook and pencil from the passenger seat. 'What makes you think she was dead, sir?' he asked Harding.

'The boys told me.'

'Is that right?' He examined the young man curiously then deliberately licked the point of his pencil because he knew it would annoy Maggie. 'May I have your name and address, please, plus the name of your employer if you have one?'

'Steven Harding. I'm an actor.' He gave an address in London. 'I live there during the week, but if you have trouble getting hold of me you can always go through my agent, Graham Barlow of the Barlow Agency.' He gave another London address. 'Graham keeps my diary,' he said.

Bully for Graham, thought Ingram sourly, struggling to suppress rampant prejudices against pretty boys . . . Chippendales . . . Londoners . . . actors . . . Harding's address was Highbury, and Ingram would put money on the little poser claiming to be an Arsenal fan, not because he'd ever been to a match but because he'd read *Fever Pitch*, or seen the movie. 'And what brings an actor to our neck of the woods, Mr Harding?'

Harding explained that he was in Poole for a weekend break and had planned to walk to Lulworth Cove and back that day. He patted the mobile telephone that was attached via a clip to his waistband, and said it was a good thing he *had* otherwise the boys would have had to hoof it to Worth Matravers for help.

'You travel light,' said Ingram, glancing at the phone. 'Aren't you worried about dehydrating? It's a long walk to Lulworth.'

The young man shrugged. 'I've changed my mind. I'm going back after this. I hadn't realized how far it was.'

Ingram asked the boys for their names and addresses together with a brief description of what had happened. They told him they'd seen the woman on the beach when they rounded Egmont Point at ten o'clock. 'And then what?' he asked. 'You checked to see if she was dead and went for help?'

They nodded.

'You didn't hurry yourselves, did you?'

'They ran like the clappers,' said Harding, leaping to their defence. 'I saw them.'

'As I recall, sir, your emergency call was timed at 10.43, and it doesn't take nearly three-quarters of an hour for two healthy lads to run round Chapman's Pool.' He stared Harding down. 'And while we're on the subject of misleading information, perhaps you'd care to explain why I received a message saying two boys had seen their mother fall from a clifftop after using a pair of binoculars?'

Maggie made a move as if she was about to say

something in support of the boys, but Ingram's intimidating glance in her direction changed her mind.

'Okay, well, it was a misunderstanding,' said Harding, flicking his thick dark hair out of his eyes with a toss of his head. 'These two guys' – he put a friendly arm across Paul's shoulders – 'came charging up the hill shouting and yelling about a woman on the beach beyond the Point and some binoculars falling, and I rather stupidly put two and two together and made five. The truth is, we were all a bit het-up. *They* were worried about the binoculars and *I* thought they were talking about their mother.' He took the Zeisses from Paul's hands and gave them to Ingram. 'These belong to their father. The boys dropped them by accident when they saw the woman. They're very concerned about how their dad's going to react when he sees the damage, but Maggie and I have persuaded them he won't be angry, not when he hears what a good job they've done.'

'Do you know the boys' father, sir?' asked Ingram, examining the binoculars.

'No, of course not. I've only just met them.'

'Then you've only their word that these belong to him?'

'Well, yes, I suppose so.' Harding looked uncertainly at Paul and saw the return of panic in the boy's eyes. 'Oh, come on,' he said abruptly. 'Where else could they have got them?'

'Off the beach. You said you saw the woman when you rounded Egmont Point,' he reminded Paul and Danny.

They nodded in petrified unison.

'Then why do these binoculars look as if they've fallen down a cliff? Did you find them beside the woman and decide to take them?'

The boys, growing red in the face with anxiety about their peeping Tom act, looked guilty. Neither answered.

'Look, lighten up,' said Harding unwarily. 'It was a bit of fun, that's all. The woman was nude so they climbed up for a better look. They didn't realize she was dead until they dropped the binoculars and went down to get them.'

'You saw all this, did you, sir?'

'No,' he admitted. 'I've already told you I was coming from St Alban's Head.'

Ingram turned to his right to look at the distant promontory topped by its tiny Norman chapel, dedicated to St Alban. 'You get a very good view of Egmont Bight from up there,' he said idly, 'particularly on a fine day like this.'

'Only through binoculars,' said Harding.

Ingram smiled as he looked the young man up and down. 'True,' he agreed. 'So where did you and the boys run into each other?'

Harding gestured towards the coastal path. 'They started shouting at me when they were halfway up Emmetts Hill, so I went down to meet them.'

'You seem to know the area well.'

'I do.'

'How come, when you live in London?'

'I spend a lot of time here. London can be pretty hellish in the summer.'

Ingram glanced up the steep hillside. 'This is called

West Hill,' he remarked. 'Emmetts Hill is the next one along.'

Harding gave an amiable shrug. 'Okay, so I don't know it *that* well, but normally I come in by boat,' he said, 'and there's no mention of West Hill on the Admiralty charts. This whole escarpment is referred to as Emmetts Hill. The boys and I ran into each other approximately there.' He pointed towards a spot on the green hillside above them.

Out of the corner of his eye, Ingram noticed Paul Spender's frown of disagreement but he didn't remark on it.

'Where's your boat now, Mr Harding?'

'Poole. I sailed her in late last night but as the wind's almost non-existent and I fancied some exercise' – he favoured Nick Ingram with a boyish smile – 'I took to my legs.'

'What's the name of your boat, Mr Harding?'

'*Crazy Daze*. It's a play on words. Daze is spelt D-A-Z-E, not D-A-Y-S.'

The tall policeman's smile was anything but boyish. 'Where's she normally berthed?'

'Lymington.'

'Did you come from Lymington yesterday?'

'Yes.'

'Alone?'

There was a tiny hesitation. 'Yes.'

Ingram held his gaze for a moment. 'Are you sailing back tonight?'

'That's the plan, although I'll probably have to motor if the wind doesn't improve.'

The constable nodded in apparent satisfaction. 'Well, thank you very much, Mr Harding. I don't think I need detain you any longer. I'll get these boys home and check on the binoculars.'

Harding felt Paul and Danny sidle in behind him for protection. 'You will point out what a good job they've done, won't you?' he urged. 'I mean, but for these two, that poor little woman could have floated out on the next tide and you'd never have known she was there. They deserve a medal, not aggro from their father.'

'You're very well informed, sir.'

'Trust me. I know this coast. There's a continuous south-south-easterly stream running towards St Alban's Head, and if she'd been sucked into that the chances of her resurfacing would have been nil. It's got one hell of a back eddy on it. My guess is she'd have been pounded to pieces on the bottom.'

Ingram smiled. 'I meant you were well informed about the woman, Mr Harding. Anyone would think you'd seen her yourself.'

Chapter Three

'WHY WERE YOU so hard on him?' asked Maggie critically as the policeman shut the boys into the back of his Range Rover and stood with eyes narrowed against the sun watching Harding walk away up the hill. Ingram was so tall and so solidly built that he cast her literally and figuratively into the shade, and he would get under her skin less, she often thought, if just once in a while he recognized that fact. She only felt comfortable in his presence when she was looking down on him from the back of a horse, but those occasions were too rare for her self-esteem to benefit from them. When he didn't answer her, she glanced impatiently towards the brothers on the back seat. 'You were pretty rough on the children, too. I bet they'll think twice before helping the police again.'

Harding disappeared from sight around a bend, and Ingram turned to her with a lazy smile. 'How was I hard on him, Miss Jenner?'

'Oh, come on! You all but accused him of lying.'

'He *was* lying.'

'What about?'

'I'm not sure yet. I'll know when I've made a few enquiries.'

'Is this a male thing?' she asked in a voice made silky by long-pent-up grudges. He had been her community policeman for five years, and she had much to feel resentful for. At times of deep depression, she blamed him for everything. Other times, she was honest enough to admit that he had only been doing his job.

'Probably.' He could smell the stables on her clothes, a musty scent of hay dust and horse manure that he half-liked and half-loathed.

'Then wouldn't it have been simpler just to whip out your willy and challenge him to a knob-measuring contest?' she asked sarcastically.

'I'd have lost.'

'That's for sure,' she agreed.

His smile widened. 'You noticed then?'

'I could hardly avoid it. He wasn't wearing those shorts to disguise anything. Perhaps it was his wallet. There was precious little room for it anywhere else.'

'No,' he agreed. 'Didn't you find that interesting?'

She looked at him suspiciously, wondering if he was making fun of her. 'In what way?'

'Only an idiot sets out from Poole for Lulworth with no money and no fluid.'

'Maybe he was planning to beg water off passers-by or telephone a friend to come and rescue him. Why is it important? All he did was play the good Samaritan to those kids.'

'I think he was lying about what he was doing here. Did he give a different explanation before I got back?'

She thought about it. 'We talked about dogs and

horses. He was telling the boys about the farm he grew up on in Cornwall.'

He reached for the handle on the driver's door. 'Then perhaps I'm just suspicious of people who carry mobile telephones,' he said.

'Everyone has them these days, including me.'

He ran an amused eye over her slender figure in its tight cotton shirt and stretch jeans. 'But you don't bring yours on country rambles whereas that young man does. Apparently he leaves everything behind except his phone.'

'You should be grateful,' she said tartly. 'But for him, you'd never have got to the woman so quickly.'

'I agree,' he said without rancour. 'Mr Harding was in the right place at the right time with the right equipment to report a body on a beach and it would be churlish to ask why.' He opened the door and squeezed his huge frame in behind the wheel. 'Good day, Miss Jenner,' he said politely. 'My regards to your mother.' He pulled the door to and fired the engine.

The Spender brothers were in two minds who to thank for their untroubled return home. The actor because his pleas for tolerance worked? Or the policeman because he was a decent bloke after all? He had said very little on the drive back to their rented cottage other than to warn them that the cliffs were dangerous and that it was foolish to climb them, however tempting the reason. To their parents he gave a brief, expurgated account of what had happened, ending with the suggestion that, as the boys' fishing had been interrupted by the events of the morning, he would be happy to take them out on his boat one evening. 'It's not a motor cruiser,' he warned them, 'just a small fishing boat, but the sea bass run at this time of year and if we're lucky we might catch one or two.' He didn't put his arms round their shoulders or call them heroes, but he did give them something to look forward to.

Next on Ingram's agenda was an isolated farmhouse where the elderly occupants had reported the theft of three valuable paintings during the night. He had been on his way there when he was diverted to Chapman's Pool and, while he guessed he was wasting his time, community policing was what he was paid for.

'Oh God, Nick, I'm so sorry,' said the couple's harassed daughter-in-law who, herself, was on the wrong side of seventy. 'Believe me, they did *know* the paintings were being auctioned. Peter's been talking them through it for the last twelve months but they're so forgetful, he has to start again from scratch every time. He has power of attorney, so it's all quite legal, but, honestly, I nearly *died* when Winnie said she'd called you. And on a *Sunday*, too. I come over every morning to make sure they're all right but *sometimes . . .* ' She rolled her eyes to heaven, expressing without the need for words exactly what she thought of her ninety-five-year-old parents-in-law.

'It's what I'm here for, Jane,' he said, giving her shoulder an encouraging pat.

'No it's not. You should be out catching criminals,' she said, echoing the words of people across the nation who saw the police only as thief-takers. She heaved a huge sigh. 'The trouble is their outgoings are way in excess of their income and they're incapable of grasping the fact. The home help *alone* costs over ten thousand pounds a year. Peter's having to sell off the family silver to make ends meet. The silly old things seem to think they're living in the 1920s when a housemaid cost five bob a week. It drives me mad, it really does. They ought to be in a home, but Peter's too soft-hearted to put them there. *Not* that they could afford it. I mean *we* can't afford it, so how could they? It would be different if Celia Jenner hadn't persuaded us to gamble everything on that beastly husband of Maggie's but . . .' She broke off on a shrug of despair. 'I get so angry sometimes I could scream, and the only thing that stops me is that I'm afraid the scream would go on for ever.'

'Nothing lasts for ever,' he said.

'I know,' she said mutinously, 'but once in a while I think about giving eternity a hand. It's such a pity you can't buy arsenic any more. It was so easy in the old days.'

'Tell me about it.'

She laughed. 'You know what I mean.'

'Should I order a post-mortem when Peter's parents finally pop their clogs?'

'Chance'd be a fine thing. At this rate I'll be dead long before they are.'

The tall policeman smiled and made his farewells. He didn't want to hear about death. *He could still feel the touch of the woman's flesh on his hands . . .* He needed a shower, he thought, as he made his way back to his car.

The blonde toddler marched steadfastly along a pavement in the Lilliput area of Poole, planting one chubby leg in front of the other. It was 10.30 on Sunday morning so people were scarce, and no one took the trouble to find out why she was alone. When a handful of witnesses came forward later to admit to the police that they'd seen her, the excuses varied. *'She seemed to know where she was going.' 'There was a woman about twenty yards behind her and I thought she was the child's mother.' 'I assumed someone else would stop.' 'I was in a hurry.' 'I'm a bloke. I'd have been strung up for giving a lift to a little girl.'*

In the end it was an elderly couple, Mr and Mrs Green, who had the sense, the time and the courage to interfere. They were on their way back from church and, as they did every week, they made a nostalgic detour through Lilliput to look at the art deco buildings that had somehow survived the post-war craze for mass demolition of anything out of the ordinary in favour of constructing reinforced concrete blocks and red-brick boxes. Lilliput sprawled along the eastern curve of Poole Bay and, amid the architectural dross that could be found anywhere, were elegant villas in manicured gardens and art deco houses with windows like portholes. The Greens adored it. It reminded them of their youth.

They were passing the turning to Salterns Marina when Mrs Green noticed the little girl. 'Look at that,' she said disapprovingly. 'What sort of mother would let a child of that age get so far ahead of her? It only takes a stumble and she'd be under a car.'

Mr Green slowed. 'Where's the mother?' he asked.

His wife twisted in her seat. 'Do you know, I'm not sure. I thought it was that woman behind her, but she's looking in a shop window.'

Mr Green was a retired sergeant major. 'We should do something,' he said firmly, drawing to a halt and putting the car into reverse. He shook his fist at a motorist who hooted ferociously after missing his back bumper by the skin of his teeth. 'Bloody Sunday drivers,' he said, 'they shouldn't be allowed on the road.'

'Quite right, dear,' said Mrs Green, opening her door.

She scooped the poor little mite into her arms and sat her comfortably on her knee while her eighty-year-old husband drove to Poole police station. It was a tortuous journey because his preferred speed was twenty miles an hour and this caused mayhem in the one-way system round the Civic Centre roundabout.

The child seemed completely at ease in the car, smiling happily out of the window, but once inside the police station, it proved impossible to prise her away from her rescuer. She locked her arms about the elderly woman's neck, hiding her face against her shoulder and clung to kindness as tenaciously as a barnacle clings to a rock. Upon learning that no one had reported a toddler missing, Mr and Mrs Green sat themselves down with commendable patience and prepared for a long wait.

'I can't understand why her mother hasn't noticed she's gone,' said Mrs Green. 'I never allowed my own children out of sight for a minute.'

'Maybe she's at work,' said the woman police constable who had been detailed to make the enquiries.

'Well, she shouldn't be,' said Mr Green reprovingly. 'A child of this age needs her mother with her.' He pulled a knowing expression in WPC Griffiths's direction which resolved itself into a series of peculiar facial jerks. 'You should get a doctor to examine her. Know what I'm saying? Odd people about these days. Men who should know better. Get my meaning?' He spelled it out. 'P-A-E-do-*fills*. S-E-X criminals. Know what I'm saying?'

'Yes, sir, I know exactly what you're saying, and don't worry' – the WPC tapped her pen on the paper in front of her – 'the doctor's at the top of my list. But if you don't mind we'll take it gently. We've had a lot of dealings with this kind of thing and we've found the best method is not to rush at it.' She turned to the woman with an encouraging smile. 'Has she told you her name?'

Mrs Green shook her head. 'She hasn't said a word, dear. To be honest, I'm not sure she can.'

'How old do you think she is?'

'Eighteen months, two at the most.' She lifted the edge of the child's cotton dress to reveal a pair of disposable trainer pants. 'She's still in nappies, poor little thing.'

The WPC thought two years old was an under-estimation, and added a year for the purposes of the paperwork. Women like Mrs Green had reared their children on terry towelling and, because of the washing involved, had had them potty-trained early. The idea that a three-year-old might still be in nappies was incomprehensible to them.

Not that it made any difference as far as this little girl was concerned. Whether she was eighteen months old, two years old or three, she clearly wasn't talking.

With nothing else to occupy her that Sunday afternoon, the French girl from the Beneteau, who had been an interested observer of Harding's conversations with the Spender brothers, Maggie Jenner and PC Ingram through the video camera's zoom lens, rowed herself into shore and walked up the steep slope of West Hill to try to work out for herself what the mystery had been about. It wasn't hard to guess that the two boys had found the person who had been winched off the beach by helicopter, nor that the handsome Englishman had reported it to the police for them, but she was curious about why he had re-emerged on the hillside half an hour after the police car's departure to retrieve the rucksack he'd abandoned there. She had watched him take out some binoculars and scan the bay and the cliffs before making his way down to the foreshore beyond the boatsheds. She had filmed him for several minutes, staring out to sea, but she was no wiser, having reached his vantage point above Chapman's Pool, than she'd been before and, thoroughly bored, she abandoned the puzzle.

It would be another five days before her father came across the tape and humiliated her in front of the English police . . .

At six o'clock that evening the Fairline Squadron weighed anchor and motored gently out of Chapman's Pool in the direction of St Alban's Head. Two languid girls sat on either side of their father on the flying bridge, while his latest companion sat, alone and excluded, on the seat behind them. Once clear of the shallow waters at the mouth of the bay, the boat roared to full power and made off at twenty-five knots on the return journey to Poole, carving a V-shaped wake out of the flat sea behind it.

Heat and alcohol had made them all soporific, particularly the father who had overexerted himself in his efforts to please his daughters, and after setting the autopilot he appointed the elder one lookout before closing his eyes. He could feel the daggers of his girlfriend's fury carving away at his back and, with a stifled sigh, wished he'd had the sense to leave her behind. She was the latest in a string of what his daughters called his 'bimbos' and, as usual, they had set out to trample on the fragile shoots of his new relationship. Life, he thought resentfully, was bloody . . .

'Watch out, Dad!' his daughter screamed in sudden alarm. 'We're heading straight for a rock.'

The man's heart thudded against his chest as he

wrenched the wheel violently, slewing the boat to star-board, and what his daughter had thought was a rock slid past on the port side to dance in the boisterous wake. 'I'm too old for all of this,' he said shakily, steering his three hundred thousand-pound boat back on to course and mentally checking the current state of his insurance. 'What the hell was it? It can't have been a rock. There are no rocks out here.'

The two youngsters, eyes watering, squinted into the burning sun to make out the black, bobbing shape behind them. 'It looks like one of those big oil drums,' said the elder.

'Jesus wept,' growled her father. 'Whoever let that wash overboard deserves to be shot. It could have ripped us open if we'd hit it.'

His girlfriend, still twisted round, thought it looked more like an upturned dinghy but was reluctant to voice an opinion for fear of attracting any more of his beastly daughters' derision. She'd had a bucketful already that day, and heartily wished she had never agreed to come out with them.

'I bumped into Nick Ingram this morning,' said Maggie as she made a pot of tea in her mother's kitchen at Broxton House.

It had been a beautiful room once, lined with old oak dressers, each one piled with copper pans and ornate crockery, and with an eight-foot-long, seventeenth-century refectory table down its middle. Now it was merely drab. Everything worth selling had been sold. Cheap white wall and floor units had replaced the wooden dressers and a moulded plastic excrescence from the garden stood where the monks' table had reigned resplendent. It wouldn't be so bad, Maggie often thought, if the room was cleaned occasionally, but her mother's arthritis and her own terminal exhaustion from trying to make money out of horses meant that cleanliness had long since gone the way of godliness. If God was in his heaven, and all was right with the world, then he had a peculiar blind spot when it came to Broxton House. Maggie would have cut her losses and moved away long ago if only her mother had agreed to do the same. Guilt enslaved her. Now she lived in a flat over the stables on the other side of the garden, and made only intermittent visits to the house. Its awful emptiness was too obvious a reminder that her mother's poverty was her fault.

'I took Jasper down to Chapman's Pool. A woman drowned in Egmont Bight and Nick had to guide the helicopter in to pick up the body.'

'A tourist, I suppose?'

'Presumably,' said Maggie, handing her a cup. 'Nick would have said if it was someone local.'

'Typical!' snorted Celia crossly. 'So Dorset will foot the bill for the helicopter because some inept creature from another county never learnt to swim properly. I've a good mind to withhold my taxes.'

'You usually do,' said Maggie, thinking of the final reminders that littered the desk in the drawing room.

Her mother ignored the remark. 'How was Nick?'

'Hot,' said her daughter, remembering how red-faced

he had been when he returned to the car, 'and not in the best of moods.' She stared into her tea, screwing up the courage to address the thorny issue of money, or more accurately lack of money, coming into the riding and livery business she ran from the Broxton House stableyard. 'We need to talk about the stables,' she said abruptly.

Celia refused to be drawn. 'You wouldn't have been in a good mood either if you'd just seen a drowned body.' Her tone became conversational as a prelude to a series of anecdotes. 'I remember seeing one floating down the Ganges when I was staying with my parents in India. It was the summer holidays. I think I was about fifteen at the time. It was a horrible thing, gave me nightmares for weeks. My mother said . . .'

Maggie stopped listening and fixed instead on a long black hair growing out of her mother's chin which needed plucking. It bristled aggressively as she spoke, like one of Bertie's whiskers, but they'd never had the kind of relationship that meant Maggie could tell her about it. Celia, at sixty-three, was still a good-looking woman with the same dark brown hair as her daughter, touched up from time to time with Harmony colour rinses, but the worry of their straitened circumstances had taken a heavy toll in the deep lines around her mouth and eyes.

When she finally drew breath, Maggie reverted immediately to the subject of the stables. 'I've been totting up last month's receipts,' she said, 'and we're about two hundred quid short. Did you let Mary Spencer-Graham off paying again?'

Celia's mouth thinned. 'If I did it's my affair.'

'No it's not, Ma,' said Maggie with a sigh. 'We can't afford to be charitable. If Mary doesn't pay then we can't look after her horse. It's as simple as that. I wouldn't mind so much if we weren't already charging her the absolute minimum but the fees barely cover Moondust's fodder. You really must be a bit tougher with her.'

'How can I? She's almost as badly off as we are, and it's our fault.'

Maggie shook her head. 'That's not true. She lost ten thousand pounds, peanuts compared with what we lost, but she knows she only has to turn on the waterworks for half a second and you fall for it every time.' She gestured impatiently towards the hall and the drawing room beyond. 'We can't pay the bills if we don't collect the money, which means we either decide to hand everything over now to Matthew and go and live in a council flat or you go to him, cap in hand, and beg for some kind of allowance.' She gave a helpless shrug at the thought of her brother. 'If I believed there was any point in my trying, I would, but we both know he'd slam the door in my face.'

Celia gave a mirthless laugh. 'What makes you think it would be any different if I tried? That wife of his can't stand me. She'd never agree to keeping her mother-in-law and sister-in-law in what she chooses to call the lap of luxury when her real pleasure in life would be to see us destitute.'

'I know,' said Maggie guiltily, 'and it serves us right. We should never have been rude about her wedding dress.'

'It was difficult not to be,' said Celia tartly. 'The vicar nearly had a heart attack when he saw her.'

Her daughter's eyes filled with humour. 'It was the greenfly that did it. If there hadn't been a plague of the blasted things the year they got married, and if her wretched veil hadn't collected every single one in a twenty-mile radius while she walked from the church to the reception . . . What was it you called her? Something to do with camouflage.'

'I didn't call her anything,' said Celia with dignity. 'I congratulated her for blending so well into her surroundings.'

Maggie laughed. 'That's right, I remember now. God, you were rude.'

'You found it funny at the time,' her mother pointed out, easing her bad hip on the chair. 'I'll talk to Mary,' she promised. 'I can probably bear the humiliation of dunning my friends rather better than I can bear the humiliation of begging off Matthew and Ava.'

Chapter Four

**Physical/psychological assessment of
unidentified toddler: 'Baby Smith'**

Physical: The child's general health is excellent. She
is well nourished and well cared for, and is not
suffering from any disease or ailment. Blood test
indicates minute traces of benzodiazepine (possibly
Mogadon) and stronger traces of paracetamol in her
system. There is no evidence of past or recent
abuse, sexual or physical, although there is some
evidence (see below) that she has suffered past,
continuing or recent psychological trauma. The
physical evidence suggests that she was separated
from her parent/guardian within 3–4 hours of being
found – most notably in terms of her overall
cleanliness and the fact that she hadn't soiled herself.
In addition she showed no signs of dehydration,
hypothermia, hunger or exhaustion which would have
been expected in a child who had been abandoned
for any length of time.

Psychological: The child's behaviour and social skills are typical of a two-year-old, however her size and weight suggest she is older. She presents evidence of mild autism although knowledge of her history is needed to confirm a diagnosis. She is uninterested in other people/children and reacts aggressively when approached by them. She is overly passive, preferring to sit and observe rather than explore her environment. She is unnaturally withdrawn and makes no attempt to communicate verbally, although will use sign language to achieve what she wants. Her hearing is unimpaired and she listens to everything that's said to her; however, she is selective about which instructions she chooses to obey. As a simple example, she is happy to point to a blue cube when asked, but refuses to pick it up.

While she is unable or unwilling to use words to communicate, she resorts very quickly to screams and tantrums when her wishes are thwarted or when she feels herself stressed. This is particularly evident when strangers enter the room, or when voices rise above a monotone. She invariably refuses any sort of physical contact on a first meeting but holds out her arms to be picked up on a second. This would indicate good recognition skills, yet she evinces a strong fear of men and screams in terror whenever they intrude into her space. In the absence of any indication of physical or sexual abuse, this fear may stem from: unfamiliarity with men as a result of being raised in a sheltered, all-female environment;

witnessing male aggression against another – e.g. mother or sibling.

Conclusions: In view of the child's backward development and apparent stress-related disorders, she should not be returned to her family/guardians without exhaustive enquiries being made about the nature of the household. It is also imperative that she be placed on the 'at risk' register to allow continuous monitoring of her future welfare. I am seriously concerned about the traces of benzodiazepine and paracetamol in her bloodstream. Benzodiazepine (strong hypnotic) is not recommended for children, and certainly not in conjunction with paracetamol. I suspect the child was sedated, but can think of no legitimate reason why this should have been necessary.

N.B. Without knowing more of the child's history, it is difficult to say whether her behaviour is due to: (1) autism; (2) psychiatric trauma; (3) taught dependence which, while leaving her ignorant of her own capabilities, has encouraged her to be consciously manipulative.

Dr Janet Murray

Chapter Five

IT HAD BEEN a long twenty-four hours and WPC Sandra Griffiths was yawning as her telephone started to ring again at noon on Monday. She had done several local radio and television interviews to publicize Lily's abandonment (named after Lilliput where she was found), but although the response to the programmes had been good, not one caller had been able to tell her who the child was. She blamed the weather. Too many people were out in the sunshine; too few watching their sets. She stifled the yawn as she picked up the receiver.

The man at the other end sounded worried. 'I'm sorry to bother you,' he told her, 'but I've just had my mother on the phone. She's incredibly het-up about some toddler wandering the streets who looks like my daughter. I've told her it can't possibly be Hannah, but' – he paused – 'well, the thing is we've both tried phoning my wife and neither of us can get an answer.'

Griffiths tucked the receiver under her chin and reached for a pen. This was the twenty-fifth father to phone since the toddler's photograph had been broadcast, and all were estranged from their wives and children.

She had no higher hopes of this one than she'd had of the previous twenty-four but she went through the motions willingly enough. 'If you'll answer one or two questions for me, sir, we can establish very quickly whether the little girl is Hannah. May I have your name and address?'

'William Sumner, Langton Cottage, Rope Walk, Lymington, Hampshire.'

'And do your wife and daughter still live with you, Mr Sumner?'

'Yes.'

Her interest sharpened immediately. 'When did you last see them?'

'Four days ago. I'm at a pharmaceutical conference in Liverpool. I spoke to Kate – that's my wife – on Friday night and everything was fine, but my mother's positive this toddler's Hannah. It doesn't make sense though. Mum says she was found in Poole yesterday, but how could Hannah be wandering around Poole on her own when we live in Lymington?'

Griffiths listened to the rising alarm in his voice. 'Are you phoning from Liverpool now?' she asked calmly.

'Yes. I'm staying in the Regal, room number two-two-three-five. What should I do? My mother's beside herself with worry. I need to reassure her that every-thing's all right.'

And yourself, too, she thought. 'Could you give me a description of Hannah?'

'She looks like her mother,' he said rather helplessly. 'Blonde, blue eyes. She doesn't talk very much. We've been worrying about it but the doctor says it's just shyness.'

'How old is she?'

'She'll be three next month.'

The policewoman winced in sympathy as she put the next question, guessing what his answer was going to be. 'Does Hannah have a pink cotton dress with smocking on it and a pair of red sandals, Mr Sumner?'

It took him a second or two to answer. 'I don't know about the sandals,' he said with difficulty, 'but my mother bought her a smocked dress about three months ago. I think it was pink – no, it *was* pink. Oh God' – his voice broke – 'where's Kate?'

She waited a moment. 'Did you drive to Liverpool, Mr Sumner?'

'Yes.'

'Do you know roughly how long it will take you to get home?'

'Five hours maybe.'

'And where does your mother live?'

'Chichester.'

'Then I think you'd better give me her name and address, sir. If the little girl *is* Hannah, then she can identify her for us. Meantime I'll ask Lymington police to check your house while I make enquiries about your wife here in Poole.'

'Mrs Angela Sumner, Flat Two, The Old Convent, Osborne Crescent, Chichester.' His breathing became laboured – *with tears?* – and Griffiths wished herself a million miles away. How she hated the fact that, nine times out of ten, she was the harbinger of bad news. 'But there's no way she can get to Poole. She's been in a wheelchair for the last three years and can't drive. If she could, she'd have gone to Lymington to check on Kate and Hannah herself. Can't I make the identification?'

'By all means, if that's what you prefer. The little girl's in the care of a foster family at the moment, and it won't harm her to stay there a few more hours.'

'My mother's convinced Hannah's been abused by some man. Is that what's happened? I'd rather know now than later.'

'Assuming the little girl is Hannah, then, no, there's no evidence of any sort of physical abuse. She's been thoroughly checked and the police doctor's satisfied that she hasn't been harmed in any way.' She glossed over Dr Murray's damning psychological assessment. If Lily were indeed Hannah Sumner, then that particular issue would have to be taken up later.

'What kind of enquiries can you make about my wife in Poole?' he asked in bewilderment, reverting to what she'd said previously. 'I told you, we live in Lymington.'

The hospital kind . . . 'Routine ones, Mr Sumner. It would help if you could give me her full name and a description of her. Also the type, colour and registration number of her car and the names of any friends she has in the area.'

'Kate Elizabeth Sumner. She's thirty-one, about five feet tall and blonde. The car's a blue Metro, registration F52 VXY, but I don't think she knows anyone in Poole.

Could she have been taken to hospital? Could something have gone wrong with the pregnancy?'

'It's one of the things I'll be checking, Mr Sumner.' She was flicking through the RTA reports on the computer while she was talking to him, but there was no mention of a blue Metro with that registration being involved in a road accident. 'Are your wife's parents living. Would they know where she is?'

'No. Her mother died five years ago and she never knew her father.'

'Brothers? Sisters?'

'She hasn't got anyone except me and Hannah.' His voice broke again. 'What am I going to do? I won't be able to cope if something's happened to her.'

'There's no reason to think anything's happened,' said Griffiths firmly, while believing the exact opposite. 'Do you have a mobile telephone in your car? If so I can keep you up to date as you drive down.'

'No.'

'Then I suggest you break your journey at the halfway mark to ring from a callbox. I should have news from Lymington police by then, and with luck I'll be able to set your mind at rest about Kate. And try not to worry, Mr Sumner,' she finished kindly. 'It's a long drive from Liverpool, and the important thing is to get yourself back in one piece.'

She put through a call to Lymington police, explaining the details of the case and asking for a check to be made of Sumner's address, then as a matter of routine dialled the Regal Hotel in Liverpool to enquire whether a Mr William Sumner had been registered in room two-two-three-five since Thursday. 'Yes, ma'am,' said the receptionist, 'but I can't put you through, I'm afraid. He left five minutes ago.'

Reluctantly, she started on the list of hospitals.

For various reasons, Nick Ingram had no ambitions to move away from his rural police station where life revolved around community policing and the hours were predictable. Major cases were handled thirty miles away at County HQ Winfrith, and this left him free to deal with the less glamorous side of policing which for 95 per cent of the population was the only side that mattered. People slept sounder in their beds knowing that PC Ingram had zero tolerance for lager louts, vandals and petty thieves.

Real trouble usually came from outside, and the unidentified woman on the beach looked like being a case in point, he thought, when a call came through from Winfrith at 12.45 p.m. on Monday, 11 August. The Coroner's Office at Poole had ordered a murder inquiry following the postmortem, and he was told to expect a DI and a DS from headquarters within the hour. A scene of crime team had already been dispatched to search the beach at Egmont Bight but Ingram was requested to stay where he was.

'I don't think they'll find anything,' he said helpfully. 'I had a bit of a scout round yesterday but it was fairly obvious the sea had washed her up.'

'I suggest you leave that to us,' said the unemotional voice at the other end.

Ingram gave a shrug at his end. 'What did she die of?'

'Drowning,' came the blunt response. 'She was thrown into the open sea after an attempt at manual strangulation which failed. The pathologist guestimates she swam half a mile to try and save herself before she gave up from exhaustion. She was fourteen weeks pregnant, and her killer held her down and raped her before pitching her over the side.'

Ingram was shocked. 'What sort of man would do that?'

'An unpleasant one. We'll see you in an hour.'

Griffiths drew a series of blanks with the name Kate Sumner – there was no record of her at any hospital in Dorset or Hampshire. It was only when she made a routine check through Winfrith to see if there was any information on the whereabouts of a small blonde woman, aged thirty-one, who appeared to have gone missing from Lymington within the last forty-eight hours that the scattered pieces of the jigsaw began to come together.

The two detectives arrived punctually for their meeting with PC Ingram. The sergeant, an arrogant, pushy type with ambitions to join the Met, who clearly believed that every conversation was an opportunity to impress, went down like a lead balloon with his rural colleague and Ingram was never able afterwards to remember his name. He talked in bullet points 'reference a major investigation' in which 'speed was the essence' before the murderer had a chance to get rid of evidence and/ or strike again. Local marinas, yacht clubs and harbours were being 'targeted' for information on the victim and/or her killer. Victim identification was the 'first priority'. They had a possible lead on a missing IC/1 female, but no one was counting chickens until her husband identified a photograph and/or the body. The second priority was to locate the boat she'd come off and give forensics a chance to strip it top-to-bottom in search of non-intimate samples that would connect it to the body. Give us a suspect, he suggested, and DNA testing would do the rest.

Ingram raised an eyebrow when the monologue came to an end but didn't say anything.

'Did you follow all that?' asked the sergeant impatiently.

'I think so, si-rr,' he said in a broad Dorsetshire burr, resisting the temptation to tug his forelock. 'If you find some of her hairs on a man's boat that'll mean he's the rapist.'

'Near enough.'

'That's amazing, sir-rr,' murmured Ingram.

'You don't sound convinced,' said DI Galbraith, watching his performance with amusement.

He shrugged and reverted to his normal accent. 'The only thing that non-intimate samples will prove is that she visited his boat at least once, and that's not proof of rape. The only useful DNA tests will have to be done on her.'

'Well, don't hold your breath,' the DI warned. 'Water doesn't leave trace evidence. The pathologist's taken swabs but he's not optimistic about getting a result. Either she was in the sea too long and anything useful was flushed away or her attacker was wearing a condom.' He was a pleasant-looking man with cropped, ginger hair and a smiling, freckled face that made him look younger than his forty-two years. It also belied a sharp intelligence that caught people unawares if they were foolish enough to stereotype him by his appearance.

'How long was long?' asked Ingram with genuine curiosity. 'Put it this way, how does the pathologist know she swam half a mile? It's a very precise estimate for an unpredictable stretch of water.'

'He based it on the condition of the body, prevailing winds and currents, and the fact that she must have been alive when she reached the shelter of Egmont Point,' said John Galbraith, opening his briefcase and extracting a sheet of paper. 'Victim died of drowning at or around high water which was at 1.52 a.m. British Summer Time on Sunday, 10 August,' he said, skip-reading the document. 'Several indicators, such as evidence of hypothermia, the fact that a keeled boat couldn't have sailed too close to the cliffs and the currents around St Alban's Head suggest she entered the sea' – he tapped the page with his finger – 'a *minimum* of half a mile west-south-west of where the body was found.'

'Okay, well assuming the minimum, that doesn't

mean she swam half a mile. There are some strong currents along this part of the coast, so the sea would have caused her eastward drift. In real terms she would only have swum a couple of hundred yards.'

'I presume that was taken into account.'

Ingram frowned. 'So why was she showing evidence of hypothermia? The winds have been light for the last week and the sea's been calm. In those conditions, an average swimmer could cover two hundred yards in fifteen to twenty minutes. Also, the sea temperature would have been several degrees higher than the night air, so she'd be more likely to develop hypothermia on the beach than she would in the water, especially if she was naked.'

'In which case she wouldn't have died from drowning.'

'No.'

'So what's the point you're making?' asked Galbraith.

Nick shook his head. 'I don't know except that I'm having trouble reconciling the body I saw with what the pathologist is saying. When the lifeboat crew at Swanage fished a corpse out of the sea last year, it was black with bruises and had swelled to twice its normal size.'

The DI consulted the paper again. 'Okay, well there's a time constraint. He says the time of death must have coincided with high water to leave it stranded on the beach as the tide receded. He also makes the argument that if she hadn't reached the shelter of Egmont Point before she drowned, the body would have been pulled under by back eddies and towed out round St Alban's Head. Put those two together and you have your answer, don't you? In simple terms she must have died within yards of the shore and her body was stranded shortly afterwards.'

'That's very sad,' said Ingram, thinking of the tiny hand waving in the spume.

'Yes,' agreed Galbraith who had seen the body in the mortuary and was as moved by the unnecessary death as Ingram was. He found the constable easy to like. But then he always preferred policemen who showed emotion. It was a sign of honesty.

'What evidence is there that she was raped if everything useful was flushed away?'

'Bruising to the inside of her thighs and back. Rope marks on her wrists. Bloodstream full of benzodiazepine . . . probably Rohypnol. Do you know what that is?'

'Mmm. The date-rape drug . . . I've read about it . . . haven't come across it, though.'

Galbraith handed him the report. 'It'll be better if you read it yourself. They're preliminary notes only, but Warner never commits anything to paper unless he's pretty damn sure he's right.'

It wasn't a long document and Ingram read it quickly. 'So you're looking for a boat with bloodstains?' he said, laying the pages on the desk in front of him when he'd finished.

'Also skin tissue if she was raped on a wooden deck.'

The tall policeman gave a doubtful shake of his head. 'I wouldn't be too optimistic,' he said. 'He'll hose down the deck and the topsides the minute he gets into a marina and what the sea hasn't already taken, fresh water will finish off.'

'We know,' said Galbraith, 'which is why we need to get a move on. Our only lead is this tentative identification which, if it's true, suggests the boat she was on might have come from Lymington.' He took out his notebook. 'A three-year-old kid was found abandoned near one of the marinas in Poole yesterday and the description of the missing mother matches our victim. Her name's Kate Sumner and she lives in Lymington. Her husband's been in Liverpool for the last four days but he's on his way back now to make the identification.'

Ingram picked up the incident report he'd typed that morning and squared it between his large hands. 'It's probably just coincidence,' he said thoughtfully, 'but the guy who made the emergency call keeps a boat in Lymington. He sailed it into Poole late on Saturday night.'

'What's his name?'

'Steven Harding. Claimed to be an actor from London.'

'You think he was lying?'

Ingram shrugged. 'Not about his name or his occupation, but I certainly think he was lying about what he was doing there. His story was that he'd left his boat in Poole because he fancied some exercise, but I've done a few calculations and by my reckoning there's no way he could have made it on foot in time to make the call at 10.43. If he was berthed in one of the marinas then he'd have to have taken the ferry to Studland but as the first crossing isn't until seven that means he had to cover sixteen-odd miles of coastal path in just over three hours. If you take into account that a good percentage is sandy beach and the rest is a roller-coaster ride of hills, I'd say it was an impossibility. We're talking an average of over five miles an hour and the only person I can think of who could sustain that sort of speed on that kind of terrain is a professional marathon runner.' He pushed the report across. 'It's all in there. Name, address, description, name of boat. Something else that's interesting is that he sails into Chapman's Pool regularly and knows everything there is to know about the back eddies. He's very well informed about the seas round here.'

'Is he the one who found the body?'

'No, that was two young lads. They're on holiday with their parents. I doubt there's any more they can tell you but I've included their names and the address of their rented cottage. A Miss Maggie Jenner of Broxton House talked to Harding for an hour or so after he made the call, but he doesn't appear to have told her much about himself except that he grew up on a farm in Cornwall.' He laid a hand the size of a dinner plate on the report. 'He was sporting an erection, if that's of any interest. Both Miss Jenner and I noticed it.'

'Jesus!'

Ingram smiled. 'Don't get too excited. Miss Jenner's a bit of a looker, so it may have been her that brought it on. She has that effect on men.' He lifted his hand. 'I've also included the names of the boats that were anchored in the bay when the body was found. One was registered in Poole, one in Southampton and the third was French, although it shouldn't be too hard to find. I watched it leave yesterday evening and it was heading for Weymouth so I guess they're on holiday and working their way along the coast.'

'Good work,' said Galbraith warmly. 'I'll be in touch.' He tapped the pathologist's report as he turned to go. 'I'll leave this with you. Maybe something will strike you that hasn't struck any of us.'

Steven Harding woke to the sound of a dying outboard motor, followed by someone banging his fist on the stern of *Crazy Daze*. It was at its permanent mooring, a buoy in Lymington river, and was well out of reach of casual visitors unless they had a dinghy of their own. The swell was sometimes unpleasant, particularly when the Lymington to Yarmouth ferry went past on its way to the Isle of Wight, but it was affordable, private and suitably remote from prying eyes.

'Hey, Steve! Get up, you bastard!'

He groaned as he recognized the voice, then rolled over in his bunk, pulling the pillow over his head. His brain was splitting from a piledriver of a hangover and the last person he wanted to see at crack of dawn on Monday morning was Tony Bridges. 'You're banned from coming aboard, arsehole,' he roared angrily, 'so bugger off and leave me alone!'

But *Crazy Daze* was sealed up as tight as a can of beans and he knew his friend couldn't have heard him. The boat tilted as Tony climbed aboard after securing his dinghy next to Harding's on the aft cleat.

'Open up!' he said, hammering on the companion-way hatch. 'I know you're in there. Have you any idea what time it is, you stupid sod? I've been trying to get you on your mobile for the last three hours.'

Harding squinted at his watch. Three ten, he read. He sat bolt upright and banged his already aching head on the planked ceiling. 'Fucking Ada!' he muttered, crawling off his bunk and stumbling into the saloon to pull the bolt on the hatch. 'I was supposed to be in London by midday,' he told Tony.

'So your agent keeps telling me. He's been calling me non-stop since 11.30.' Tony pulled back the main hatch and dropped down into the saloon, sniffing the ripe atmosphere with an expression of distaste. 'Ever heard of fresh air?' he asked, pushing past his friend to open the forward hatch in the cabin and create a through draft. He looked at the rumpled sheets and wondered what the hell Steve had been doing. 'You're a bloody fool,' he said unsympathetically.

'Go away. I'm sick.' Harding groaned again as he slumped on to the port settee in the saloon and dropped his forehead into his hands.

'I'm not surprised. It's like an oven in here.' Tony handed him a bottle of mineral water from the galley. 'Get some of this into you before you die of dehydration.' He stood over him until he'd downed half the bottle then lowered himself on to the facing settee. 'What's going on? I talked to Bob and he said you were supposed to be crashing at his place last night and catching the early train to town this morning.'

'I changed my mind.'

'So I gather.' Tony looked at the empty bottle of whisky on the table between them and the photographs scattered across its surface. 'What the hell's up with you?'

'Nothing.' He pushed the hair out of his eyes with a frown of irritation. 'How did you know I was here?'

Tony jerked his head towards the stern. 'I spotted your dinghy. Also I've tried everywhere else. Graham's after your blood in case you're interested. He's pissed off that you missed the audition. It was in the bag, according to him.'

'He's lying.'

'Your big chance, he said.'

'Fuck that!' said Harding dismissively. 'It was a bit part in a kids' TV series. Three days' filming with spoilt brats to make something I wouldn't be seen dead in. Only idiots work with children.'

Malice stirred briefly in Tony's eyes before he cloaked his anger behind a harmless smile. 'Is that a dig at me?' he asked mildly.

Harding shrugged. 'No one forced you to be a teacher, mate. It was your choice.' He rocked his flattened palm. 'Your funeral when the little bastards finally do your head in.'

Tony held his gaze for a moment then picked up one of the photographs. 'So how come you don't have a problem with this kind of crap?' he said, jabbing his finger at the image. 'Doesn't this count as working with kids?'

No answer.

'You're being exploited by experts – *mate* – but you can't see it. You might as well sell your arse in Piccadilly

Circus as let perverts drool over tacky porno pics of you in private.'

'Shut it,' growled Harding angrily, touching his fingertips to his eyelids to suppress the pain behind them. 'I've had enough of your bloody lectures.'

Tony ignored the note of warning. 'What do you expect if you keep behaving like an idiot?'

An unfriendly smile thinned the other man's lips. 'At least I'm up front about what I do' – his smile broadened – 'in every respect.' He stared Bridges down. 'Unlike you, eh? How's Bibi these days? Still falling asleep on the job?'

'Don't tempt me, Steve.'

'To do what?'

'Shop you.' He stared at the photograph in a confusion of disgust and jealousy. 'You're a fucking deviant. This kid's barely fifteen.'

'Nearly sixteen . . . as you damn well know.' Harding watched him tear the photograph to shreds. 'Why are you getting so het up about it?' he murmured dispassionately. 'It's only acting. You do it in a movie and they call it art. You do it for a mag and they call it pornography.'

'It's cheap filth.'

'Wrong. It's *exciting* cheap filth. Be honest. You'd swap places with me any day. Hell, the pay's three times what you get as a teacher.' He raised the bottle of mineral water to his mouth and tilted his head back, smiling cynically. 'I'll talk to Graham,' he said, wiping his wet lips with the back of his hand. 'You never know.

A little guy like you might go down a wow on the Internet. Paedophiles like 'em small.'

'You're sick.'

'No,' said Harding, dropping his head into his hands, energy spent. 'Just broke. It's inadequate bastards who jerk off over my pictures who're sick.'

Chapter Six

Forensic Pathology Report
UF/DP/5136/Interim: Ref: GFS/Dr J. C. Warner

- General description: Natural blonde – 30 yrs
  (approx) – height 5′ – weight: 6 st 12 lbs – blue
  eyes – blood group O – excellent health – excellent
  teeth (2 fillings; RL wisdom removed) – no surgical
  scars – mother of at least one child – 14 weeks
  pregnant (foetus male) – non-smoker – small
  traces of alcohol in blood – consumed last meal
  approx 3 hrs before drowning – contents of
  stomach (other than sea water): cheese, apple –
  pronounced indentation 3rd finger L-hand indicates
  recent presence of ring (wedding or otherwise).

- Cause of death: Drowning. The evidence
  prevailing conditions – wind, tide, rocky
  shoreline; **good condition of body** – had she
  entered the sea on or near the shoreline she was
  obviously determined enough to save herself, and

while there is some post-mortem bruising, there is
not enough to suggest that the corpse remained
long in the water after death – points to her coming
off a boat in the open sea, alive, and swimming for
some considerable time before exhaustion led to
drowning within shelter of land.

- Contributory factors in victim's death: 0.5 litres of
sea water in stomach – fingertip bruising either side
of voicebox, indicative of attempted manual
strangulation – residual benzodiazepine in
bloodstream and tissues (Rohypnol?) – bruising
and abrasions to back (pronounced on shoulder
blades and buttocks) and inside of thighs,
indicative of forced intercourse on a hard surface,
such as a deck or an uncarpeted floor – some
blood loss from abrasions in vagina (vaginal swabs
negative, either due to prolonged immersion in sea
water or assailant using a condom) – severe
fingertip bruising on upper arms, indicative of
manual restraint and/or manual lift (possibly
inflicted during ejection from boat) – incipient
hypothermia.

- Condition of body: Death had occurred within 14
hrs of being examined – most likely time of death:
at or around high water at 1.52 a.m. BST on
Sunday, 10 August (see below) – general condition
good, although hypothermal evidence, condition of
skin and vasoconstriction of the arterial vessels
(indicative of prolonged stress) suggests victim

spent considerable time in the sea before drowning
– extensive abrasions to both wrists, suggesting
she was bound with rope and made efforts to
release herself (impossible to say whether she
succeeded, or whether her killer released her prior
to drowning her) – two fingers on L-hand broken;
all fingers on R-hand broken (difficult at this stage
to say what caused this – it may have been done
deliberately or may have happened accidentally if
the woman tried to save herself by catching her
fingers on a railing?) – fingernails broken on both
hands – post-mortem bruising and grazing of back,
breasts, buttocks and knees indicate the body was
dragged to and fro across rocks/pebbles prior to
being stranded.

- Ambient conditions where found: Egmont Bight is a
shallow bay, inaccessible to boats other than keel-
less vessels such as ribs/dinghies (lowest recorded
depth = 0.5 m; variation between low and high
water = 1.00–2.00 m). Kimmeridge Ledges to the
west of Egmont Bight make sailing close to the
cliffs hazardous and sailors steer well clear of the
shoreline (particularly at night when that part of the
coast is unlit). Due to a back eddy, a continuous
SSE stream runs from Chapman's Pool towards St
Alban's Head, which suggests victim was inside the
shelter of Egmont Point before she died and was
stranded on the shoreline as the tide receded. Had
she drowned farther out, her body would have
been swept round the Head. SW winds and

currents mean she must have entered the water WSW of Egmont Bight and was towed along the coast in an easterly direction as she swam towards the shore. In view of the above factors,* we estimate the victim entered the sea a minimum of 0.5 miles WSW of where the body was found.

- Conclusions: The woman was raped and subjected to a manual strangulation attempt before being left to drown in the open sea. She may also have had her fingers broken prior to immersion with the possible aim of hampering her efforts to swim towards the shore. She was certainly alive when she entered the water, so the failure to report her fall overboard suggests her killer expected her to die. The removal of distinguishing features (wedding ring, clothing) suggests a premeditated intent to hinder an investigation should the body surface or be washed ashore.

***NB: In view of the fact that she came so close to saving herself, it is possible that she made the decision to jump while the boat was still in sight of land. However, both the failure to report her 'missing

---

* These estimates are calculated on what an average swimmer could achieve in the conditions.

These conclusions are predicated on the rape taking place on board a boat, most probably on deck.

Difficult at this stage to say to what extent the benzodiazepine would have affected her ability to operate. Further tests required.

overboard' and the evidence of premeditation leaves little room for doubt that her death was intended.

***Rohypnol** (manufactured by Roche) Much concern is being expressed about this drug. A soluble, intermediate-acting hypnotic compound – known on the street as the 'date-rape drug', or more colloquially as a 'roofie'. It has already been cited in several rape cases, two being 'gang-rape' cases. Very effective in the treatment of severe and disabling insomnia, it can induce sleep at unusual times. Used inappropriately – easily dissolved in alcohol – it can render a woman unconscious without her knowledge, thus making her vulnerable to sexual attack. Women report intermittent bouts of lucidity, coupled with an absolute inability to defend themselves. Its effects on rape victims have been well-documented in the US where the drug is now banned: temporary or permanent memory loss; inability to understand that a rape has taken place; feelings of 'spaced-out' disconnection from the event; subsequent and deep psychological trauma because of the ease with which the victim was violated against her will (often by more than one rapist). There are enormous difficulties in bringing prosecutions because it is impossible to detect Rohypnol in the bloodstream after seventy-two hours, and few victims regain their memories quickly enough to present themselves at police stations in time to produce positive semen swabs or benzodiazepine traces in the blood.

***NB: The UK police lag well behind their US counterparts in both understanding and prosecution of these types of cases.

J. C. Wonnt

Chapter Seven

SALTERNS MARINA LAY at the end of a small cul-de-sac off the Bournemouth to Poole coastal road, some two hundred yards from where the Greens had rescued the blonde toddler. Its approach from the sea in a pleasure craft was through the Swash Channel and then via the North Channel which allowed a passage between the shore and the numerous moored boats that flew like streamers from the buoys in the centre of the bay. It was a popular stopping-off place for foreign visitors or sailors setting out to cruise the south coast of England, and was often crowded in the summer months.

An enquiry at the marina office about traffic in and out over the previous two days, 9/10 August, produced the information that *Crazy Daze* had moored there for approximately eighteen hours on the Sunday. The boat had come in during the night and taken a vacant berth on 'A' pontoon, and the nightwatchman had recorded the arrival at 2.15 a.m. Subsequently, when the office opened at 8.00 a.m., a man calling himself Steven Harding had paid for a twenty-four-hour stay, saying he was going for a hike but planned to be back by late afternoon. The harbour master remembered him. 'Good-looking chap. Dark hair.'

'That's the one. How did he seem? Calm? Excited?'

'He was fine. I warned him we'd need the berth again by the evening and he said, no problem, because he'd be heading back to Lymington by late afternoon. As far as I recall he said he had an appointment in London on Monday – this morning in other words – and was planning to catch the last train up.'

'Did he have a child with him?'

'No.'

'How did he pay?'

'Credit card.'

'Did he have a wallet?'

'No. He had the card tucked into a pocket inside his shorts. Said it was all you needed these days to go travelling.'

'Was he carrying anything?'

'Not when he came into the office.'

No one had made a note of *Crazy Daze*'s departure, but the berth was empty again by 7.00 p.m. on Sunday evening when a yacht out of Portsmouth had been logged in. On this initial enquiry, there were no reports of an unaccompanied toddler leaving the marina, or a man taking a toddler away with him. However, several people pointed out that marinas were busy places – even at eight o'clock in the morning – and anyone could take anything off a boat if it was wrapped in something unexceptional like a sleeping bag and placed in a marina trolley to transport it away from the pontoons.

Within two hours of Lymington police being asked to check William Sumner's cottage in Rope Walk, another request came through from Winfrith to locate a boat by the name of *Crazy Daze* which was moored somewhere in the tiny Hampshire port's complex of marinas, river moorings and commercial fishing quarter. It took a single telephone call to the Lymington harbour master to establish its exact whereabouts.

'Sure I know Steve. He moors up to a buoy in the dog-leg, about five hundred yards beyond the yacht club. Thirty-foot sloop with a wooden deck and claret-coloured sails. Nice boat. Nice lad.'

'Is he on board?'

'Can't say. I don't even know if his boat's in. Is it important?'

'Could be.'

'Try phoning the yacht club. They can pick him out with binoculars if he's there. Failing that, come back to me and I'll send one of my lads up to check.'

William Sumner was reunited with his daughter in Poole police station at half-past six that evening after a tiring two hundred and fifty-mile drive from Liverpool, but if anyone expected the little girl to run to him with joyful smiles of recognition, they were to be disappointed. She chose to sit at a distance, playing with some toys on the floor, while making a cautious appraisal of the exhausted man who had slumped on a chair and buried his head in his hands. He apologized to WPC Griffiths. 'I'm afraid she's always like this,' he said. 'Kate's the only one she responds to.' He rubbed his red eyes. 'Have you found her yet?'

Griffiths moved protectively in front of the little girl, worried about how much she understood. She exchanged a glance with John Galbraith who had been waiting in the room with her. 'My colleague from Dorset Constabulary Headquarters, DI Galbraith, knows more about that than I do, Mr Sumner, so I think the best thing is that you talk it through with him while I take Hannah to the canteen.' She reached out an inviting hand to the toddler. 'Would you like an ice cream, sweetheart?' She was surprised by the child's reaction. With a trusting smile, Hannah scrambled to her feet and held up her arms. 'Well, that's a change from yesterday,' she said with a laugh, swinging her on to her hip. 'Yesterday, you wouldn't even look at me.' She cuddled the warm little body against her side and deliberately ignored the danger signals that shot like Cupid's arrows through her bloodstream, courtesy of her frustrated thirty-five-year-old hormones.

After they'd gone, Galbraith pulled forward a chair and sat facing Sumner. The man was older than he'd been expecting, with thinning dark hair and an angular, loose-limbed body that he seemed unable to keep still. When he wasn't plucking nervously at his lips, he was jiggling one heel in a constant rat-a-tat-tat against the floor, and it was with reluctance that Galbraith took some photographs from his breast pocket and held them loosely between his hands. When he spoke it was with deep and genuine sympathy. 'There's no easy way to tell you this, sir,' he said gently, 'but a young woman, matching your wife's description, was found dead yesterday morning. We can't be sure it's Kate until you've identified her but I think you need to prepare yourself for the fact that it might be.'

A look of terror distorted the man's face. 'It will be,' he said with absolute certainty. 'All the way back I've been thinking that something awful must have happened. Kate would never have left Hannah. She adored her.'

Reluctantly, Galbraith turned the first close-up and held it for the other man to see.

Sumner gave an immediate nod of recognition. 'Yes,' he said with a catch in his voice, 'that's Kate.'

'I'm so sorry, sir.'

Sumner took the photograph with trembling fingers and examined it closely. He spoke without emotion. 'What happened?'

Galbraith explained as briefly as possible where and how Kate Sumner had been found, deeming it unnecessary at this early stage to mention rape or murder.

'Did she drown?'

'Yes.'

Sumner shook his head in bewilderment. 'What was she doing there?'

'We don't know but we think she must have fallen from a boat.'

'Then why was Hannah in Poole?'

'We don't know,' said Galbraith again.

The man turned the photograph over and thrust it at Galbraith, as if by putting it out of sight he could deny its contents. 'It doesn't make sense,' he said harshly. 'Kate wouldn't have gone anywhere without Hannah, and she hated sailing. I used to have a Contessa 32 when we lived in Chichester but I could never persuade her to come out on it because she was terrified of turning turtle in the open sea and drowning.' He lowered his head into his hands again as the meaning of what he'd said came home to him.

Galbraith gave him a moment to compose himself. 'What did you do with it?'

'Sold it a couple of years ago and put the money towards buying Langton Cottage.' He lapsed into another silence which the policeman didn't interrupt. 'I don't understand any of this,' he burst out then in despair. 'I spoke to her on Friday night and she was fine. How could she possibly be dead forty-eight hours later?'

'It's always worse when death happens suddenly,' said the DI sympathetically. 'We don't have time to prepare for it.'

'Except I don't believe it. I mean, why didn't someone try to save her? You don't just abandon people when they fall overboard.' He looked shocked suddenly. 'Oh, God, did other people drown as well? You're not going to tell me she was on a boat that capsized, are you? That was her worst nightmare.'

'No, there's no evidence that anything like that happened.' Galbraith leaned forward to bridge the gap between them. They were on hardbacked chairs in an empty office on the first floor and he could have wished for friendlier surroundings for a conversation like this one. 'We think Kate was murdered, sir. The Home Office pathologist who performed the post-mortem believes she was raped before being deliberately thrown into the sea to die. I realize this must be a terrible shock to you, but you have my assurance that we're working round the clock to find her killer and if there's anything we can do to make the situation easier for you, we will of course do it.'

It was too much for Sumner to take in. He stared at the detective with a surprised smile carving ridges in his thin face. 'No,' he said, 'there's been a mistake. It can't have been Kate. She wouldn't have gone anywhere with a stranger.' He reached out a tentative hand for the photograph again, then burst into tears when Galbraith turned it over for him.

The wretched man was so tired that it was several minutes before he could stem his weeping but Galbraith kept quiet because he knew from past experience that sympathy more often exacerbated pain than ameliorated it. He sat quietly looking out of the window which faced towards the park and Poole Bay beyond, and only stirred when Sumner spoke again.

'I'm sorry,' he said, striking the tears from his cheeks. 'I keep thinking how frightened she must have been. She wasn't a very good swimmer which is why she didn't want to go sailing.'

Galbraith made a mental note of the fact. 'If it's any comfort, she did everything in her power to save herself. It was exhaustion that beat her, not the sea.'

'Did you know she was pregnant?' Tears gathered in his eyes again.

'Yes,' said Galbraith gently, 'and I'm sorry.'

'Was it a boy?'

'Yes.'

'We wanted a son.' He took a handkerchief from his pocket and held it to his eyes for several moments before getting up abruptly and walking to the window to stand with his back to Galbraith. 'How can I help you?' he said then in a voice stripped of feeling.

'You can tell me about her. We need as much background information as you can give us – the names of her friends, what she did during the day, where she shopped. The more we know the better.' He waited for a response which never came. 'Perhaps you'd rather leave it until tomorrow? I realize you must be very tired.'

'Actually, I think I'm going to be sick.' Sumner turned an ashen face towards him, then, with a small sigh, slid to the floor in a dead faint.

The Spender boys were easy company. They demanded little from their host other than the odd can of Coke, occasional conversation and help with threading their hooks with bait. Ingram's immaculate fifteen-foot day-boat, *Miss Creant*, sat prettily on the surface of a calm turquoise sea off Swanage, her white topsides turning pale pink in the slowly setting sun and a fine array of rods bristling along her rails like porcupine quills. The boys loved her.

'I'd rather have *Miss Creant* any day than a stupid cruiser,' said Paul after helping the mighty policeman launch her down the Swanage slip. He had allowed the boy to operate the winch at the back of his ancient Jeep while he himself had waded into the sea to float her off the trailer and make her fast to a ring on the slip wall. Paul's eyes had gleamed with excitement because boating was suddenly more accessible than he'd realized. 'Do you reckon Dad might buy one? Holidays would be great if we had a boat like this.'

'You can always ask,' had been Ingram's response.

Danny found the whole idea of sliding a long wriggling ragworm on to a barbed point until the steel was clothed in something resembling a wrinkled silk stocking deeply repugnant and insisted that Ingram did the business for him. 'It's alive,' he pointed out. 'Doesn't the hook hurt it?'

'Not as much as it would hurt you.'

'It's an invertebrate,' said his brother, who was leaning over the side of the boat and watching his various floats bob on the water, 'so it doesn't have a nervous system like us. Anyway, it's near the bottom of the food chain so it only exists to be eaten.'

'Dead things are the bottom of the food chain,' said Danny. 'Like the lady on the beach. She'd've been food if we hadn't found her.'

Ingram handed Danny his rod with the worm in place. 'No fancy casting,' he said, 'just dangle it over the side and see what happens.' He leaned back and tilted his baseball cap over his eyes, content to let the boys do the fishing. 'Tell me about the bloke who made the phone call,' he invited. 'Did you like him?'

'He was all right,' said Paul.

'He said he saw a lady with no clothes on and she looked like an elephant,' said Danny, joining his brother to lean over the side.

'It was a joke,' said Paul. 'He was trying to make us feel better.'

'What else did he talk about?'

'He was chatting up the lady with the horse,' said Danny, 'but she didn't like him as much as he liked her.'

Ingram smiled to himself. 'What makes you think that?'

'She frowned a lot.'

So what's new?

'Why do you want to know if we liked him?' asked Paul, his agile mind darting back to Ingram's original question. 'Didn't *you* like him?'

'He was all right,' said Ingram, echoing Paul's own answer. 'A bit of a berk for setting out on a hike on a hot day without any suntan lotion or water, but otherwise okay.'

'I expect they were in his rucksack,' said Paul loyally, who hadn't forgotten Harding's kindness even if his brother had. 'He put it down to make the telephone call then left it there because he said it was too heavy to lug down to the police car. He was going to pick it up again on his way back. It was probably water that was making it heavy.' He looked earnestly towards their host. 'Don't you think?'

Ingram closed his eyes under the brim of his cap. 'Yes,' he agreed, while wondering what had been in the rucksack that meant Harding hadn't wanted a policeman to see it. Binoculars? Had he seen the woman, after all? 'Did you describe the lady on the beach to him?' he asked Paul.

'Yes,' said the boy. 'He wanted to know if she was pretty.'

There were two hidden agendas behind the decision to send WPC Griffiths home with William and Hannah Sumner. The first derived entirely from the child's un-favourable psychiatric report and was intended to safeguard her welfare; the second was based on years of statistical evidence that showed a wife was always more likely to be murdered by her husband than by a stranger. However, because of the distances involved and the problems of jurisdiction – Poole being Dorsetshire Constabulary and Lymington being Hampshire Con-stabulary – Griffiths was advised that the hours would be long ones.

'Yes, but is he *really* a suspect?' Griffiths asked Galbraith.

'Husbands are always suspects.'

'Come on, guv, he was definitely in Liverpool because I phoned the hotel to check, and it's a hell of a long way from there to Dorset. If he's driven to and fro twice in five days, then he's done over a thousand miles. That's a hell of a lot of driving.'

'Which may explain why he fainted,' was Galbraith's dry response.

'Oh, great!' she said sarcastically. 'I've always wanted to spend quality time with a rapist.'

'There's no compulsion, Sandy. You don't have to do it if you don't want to, but the only other option is to leave Hannah in the care of foster parents until we're satisfied it's safe to return her to her father. How about you go back tonight and see how it goes? I've got a team searching the house at the moment, so I'll instruct one of the chaps to stay on and shadow you. Can you live with that?'

'What the hell!' she said cheerfully. 'With any luck, it'll give me a chance to work babies out of my system.'

As far as Sumner himself was concerned, Griffiths was the official 'friend' who was supplied by any police force to a family in distress. 'I can't possibly cope on my own,' he kept telling Galbraith as if it was the fault of the police that he found himself a widower.

'We don't expect you to.'

The man's colour had improved after being given something to eat when he admitted he'd had nothing since a cup of tea at breakfast that morning. Renewed energy had set him chasing explanations again. 'Were they kidnapped?' he asked suddenly.

'We don't think so. Lymington police checked the house inside and out and there's no indication of any sort of disturbance. The neighbour let them in with a spare key so the search was a thorough one. That doesn't mean we're ignoring the possibility of abduction, just that we're keeping an open mind. We're conducting a second search ourselves at the moment, but on the evidence so far it looks as if Kate and Hannah left of their own accord some time after the post was delivered on Saturday morning. The letters had been opened and stacked on the kitchen table.'

'What about her car? Could she have been taken from her car?'

Galbraith shook his head. 'It's parked in your garage.'

'Then I don't understand.' Sumner appeared genuinely confused. 'What happened?'

'Well, one explanation is that Kate met someone when she was out, a friend of the family perhaps, who persuaded her and Hannah to go for a sail in his boat.' He was careful to avoid any idea of a pre-arranged meeting. 'But whether she expected to be taken as far as Poole and the Isle of Purbeck we simply don't know.'

Sumner shook his head. 'She'd never have gone,' he said with absolute certainty. 'I keep telling you, she didn't like sailing. And, anyway, the only people we know with boats are couples.' He stared at the floor. 'You're not suggesting a couple could have done something like this, are you?' He sounded shocked.

'I'm not suggesting anything at the moment,' said Galbraith patiently. 'We need more information before we can do that.' He paused. 'Her wedding ring seems to be missing. We assume it was removed because it could identify her. Was it special in some way?'

Sumner held out a trembling hand and pointed to his own ring. 'It was identical to this one. We had them engraved inside with our initials. "K" entwined with "W".'

Interesting, thought Galbraith. 'When you're ready, I'd like a list of your friends, particularly the ones who sail. But there's no immediate hurry.' He watched Sumner crack his finger joints noisily, one after the other, and wondered what had attracted the pretty little woman in the mortuary to this gauche, hyperactive man.

Sumner clearly hadn't been listening. 'When was Hannah abandoned?' he demanded.

'We don't know.'

'My mother said she was found in Poole at lunchtime yesterday, but you said Kate died in the early hours of the morning. Doesn't that mean Hannah must have been on board when Kate was raped and was put ashore in Poole *after* Kate was dead? I mean, she couldn't possibly have been wandering around on her own for twenty-four hours before somebody saw her, could she?'

He was certainly no fool, thought Galbraith. 'We don't think so.'

'Then her mother was killed in front of her?' The man's voice rose. 'Oh my God, I'm not sure I can bear this! She's only a baby, for Christ's sake.'

Galbraith reached out a calming hand. 'It's far more likely she was asleep.'

'You can't know that.'

No, thought Galbraith, I can't. Like everything else in policework, I can only guess. 'The doctor who examined her after she was found thinks she was sedated,' he explained. 'But, yes, you're right. At the moment we can't be certain about anything.' He rested his palm briefly on the man's taut shoulder, then withdrew tactfully into his own space. 'But it really is better to stop tormenting yourself with what might have been. Nothing's ever as bleak as our imagination paints it.'

'Isn't it?' Sumner straightened abruptly and let his head flop on to the chair back so that he was looking at the ceiling. A long sigh whispered from his chest. 'My imagination tells me you're working on the theory that Kate was having an affair, and that the man she went with was her lover.'

Galbraith saw no point in pretending. The idea of an affair that had turned sour was the first they'd considered, particularly as Hannah had apparently accompanied her mother on whatever journey she had made. 'We can't ignore the possibility,' he said honestly. 'It would certainly explain why she agreed to go on board somebody's boat and take Hannah with her.' He studied the man's profile. 'Does the name Steven Harding mean anything to you?'

Sumner frowned. 'What's he got to do with it?'

'Probably nothing, but he was one of the people on the spot when Kate's body was found and we're questioning everyone connected with her death, however remotely.' He waited a moment. 'Do you know him?'

'The actor?'

'Yes.'

'I've met him a couple of times.' He steepled his hands in front of his mouth. 'He carried Hannah's buggy over the cobbles at the bottom of the High Street one day when Kate was struggling with some heavy shopping, and she asked me to thank him when we bumped into him about a week later. After that he started popping up all over the place. You know what it's like. You meet someone, and then you see them wherever you go. He's got a sloop on Lymington river and we used to talk sailing from time to time. I invited him back to the house once and he chewed my ear off for hours about some blasted play he was auditioning for. He didn't get the part, of course, but I wasn't surprised. He couldn't act his way out of a paper bag if his life depended on it.' His eyes narrowed. 'Do you think he did it?'

Galbraith gave a small shake of his head. 'At the moment, we're just trying to eliminate him from the inquiry. Were he and Kate friends?'

Sumner's lips twisted. 'Do you mean, were they having an affair?'

'If you like.'

'No,' he said adamantly. 'He's a galloping poof. He poses for pornographic gay magazines. In any case she can't . . . couldn't stand him. She was furious when I took him back to the house that time . . . said I should have asked her first.'

Galbraith watched him for a moment. The denial was overdone, he thought. 'How do you know about the gay magazines? Did Harding tell you?'

Sumner nodded. 'He even showed me one of them. He was proud of it. But then he loves all that. Loves being in the limelight.'

'Okay. Tell me about Kate. How long have you and she been married?'

He had to think about it. 'Getting on for four years. We met at work and married six months later.'

'Where's work?'

'Pharmatec UK in Portsmouth. I'm a research chemist there and Kate was one of the secretaries.'

Galbraith lowered his eyes to cloak his sudden interest. 'The drug company?'

'Yes.'

'What sort of drugs do you research?'

'Me personally?' He gave an indifferent shrug. 'Anything to do with the stomach.'

Galbraith made a note. 'Did Kate go on working after you married?'

'For a few months until she fell pregnant with Hannah.'

'Was she happy about the pregnancy?'

'Oh, yes. Her one ambition was to have a family of her own.'

'And she didn't mind giving up work?'

Sumner shook his head. 'She wouldn't have it any other way. She didn't want her children to be brought up the way she was. She didn't have a father, and her mother was out all day, so she was left to fend on her own.'

'Do you still work at Pharmatec?'

He nodded. 'I'm their top scientist.' He spoke the words matter-of-factly.

'So you live in Lymington and work in Portsmouth?'

'Yes.'

'Do you drive to work?'

'Yes.'

'That's a difficult journey,' said Galbraith sympathetically, doing a rough calculation in his head. 'It must take you – what? – an hour and a half of travelling each way. Have you ever thought of moving?'

'We didn't just think about it,' said Sumner with a hint of irony. 'We *did* it a year ago when we moved to Lymington. And, yes, you're right, it's an awful journey, particularly in the summer when the New Forest's packed with tourists.' He sounded unhappy about it.

'Where did you move from?'

'Chichester.'

Galbraith remembered the notes Griffiths had shown him after Sumner's telephone call. 'That's where your mother lives, isn't it?'

'Yes. She's been there all her life.'

'You too? A born and bred Chichester man?'

Sumner nodded.

'Moving must have been a bit of a wrench, particularly if it meant adding an hour to your journey each way?'

He ignored the question to stare despondently out of the window. 'You know what I keep thinking?' he said then. 'If I'd stuck to my guns and refused to budge, Kate wouldn't be dead. We never had any trouble when we lived in Chichester.' He seemed to realize immediately that his remarks could be interpreted in a number of ways and added what was presumably intended as an explanation: 'I mean, Lymington's full of strangers. Half the people you meet don't even live there.'

*

88

Galbraith had a quick word with Griffiths before she left to accompany William and Hannah Sumner home. She had been given time, while the SOCOs finished their search of Langton Cottage, to go home in order to change and pack a bag, and was dressed now in a baggy yellow jumper and black leggings. She looked very different from the severe young woman in the police uniform and Galbraith wondered wryly if the father and daughter would feel more or less comfortable with the Sloppy Joe. Less, he fancied. Police uniforms inspired confidence.

'I'll be with you early tomorrow morning,' he told her, 'and I need you to prod him a bit before I get there. I want lists of their friends in Lymington, a second list of friends in Chichester, and a third list of work friends in Portsmouth.' He ran a tired hand around his jaw, while he tried to organize his memory. 'It would be helpful if he splits those with boats, or with access to boats, from those without, and even more helpful if he separates Kate's personal friends from their joint friends.'

'Okey-doke,' she said.

He smiled. 'And try to get him to talk about Kate,' he went on. 'We need to know what her routine was, how she managed her day, which shops she used, that kind of thing.'

'No problem.'

'*And* his mother,' he said. 'I get the impression Kate forced him to move away from her, which may have caused some friction within the family.'

Griffiths looked amused. 'I don't blame her,' she said. 'He's ten years older than she was and he'd been living at home with Mummy for thirty-seven years before they got married.'

'How do you know?'

'I had a chat with him when I asked him for his previous address. His mother gave him the family home as a wedding present in return for him taking a small mortgage to help her buy a flat in some sheltered accommodation across the road.'

'A bit too close for comfort, eh?'

She chuckled. 'Bloody stifling, I should think.'

'What about his father?'

'Died ten years ago. Up until then it was a *ménage à trois*. Afterwards, a *ménage à deux*. William was the only child.'

Galbraith shook his head. 'How come you're so well informed? It can only have been a very little chat.'

She tapped the side of her nose. 'Sensible questions and a woman's intuition,' she said. 'He's been waited on all his life which is why he's so convinced he won't be able to cope.'

'Good luck then,' he said, meaning it. 'I can't say I envy you.'

'Someone has to look after Hannah.' She sighed. 'Poor little kid. Do you ever wonder what would have happened to you if you'd been abandoned the way most of the kids we arrest are abandoned?'

'Sometimes,' Galbraith admitted. 'Other times I thank God my parents pushed me out of the nest and told me to get on with it. You can be loved too much as well as too little, you know, and I'd be hard pushed to say which was the more dangerous.'

Chapter Eight

THE DECISION TO question Steven Harding was made at eight o'clock that Monday night when Dorset police received confirmation that he was on board his boat in the Lymington river; although the interview itself did not take place until after nine because the officer in charge, Detective Superintendent Carpenter, had to drive from Winfrith in order to lead it. DI John Galbraith, who was still in Poole, was instructed to make his own way to Lymington and meet his governor outside the harbour master's office.

Attempts had been made to raise Harding on his radio and his mobile telephone but, as both were switched off, the investigating officers had no way of finding out whether he would still be there on Tuesday morning. A call to his agent, Graham Barlow, had elicited only a furious tirade against arrogant young actors 'who are too big for their boots to attend auditions' and who could 'dream on about future representation'.

'Of course I don't know where he'll be tomorrow,' he had finished angrily. 'I haven't heard a cheep out of him since Friday morning so I've sacked the bugger. I wouldn't mind if he was making any money for me but he hasn't worked in months. From the way he talks, you'd think he was Tom Cruise. Ha! Pinocchio's nearer the mark . . . he's certainly wooden enough . . .'

Galbraith and Carpenter met up at nine o'clock. The Superintendent was a tall rangy man with a shock of dark hair and a ferocious frown that made him look permanently angry. His colleagues had ceased to notice it, but suspects were often intimidated by it. Galbraith had already rung through a brief report of his conversation with Sumner, but he went through it again for the Superintendent's benefit, particularly the reference to Harding being 'a galloping poof'.

'It doesn't square with what we've been told by his agent,' said Carpenter bluntly. 'He describes him as sex mad, says he's got girls falling over themselves to get into bed with him. He's a cannabis smoker, a heavy metal fanatic, collects adult movies and, when he's got nothing better to do, sits for hours in strip joints watching the girls shed their kit. He's got a thing about nudity so when he's on his own, either on the boat or in his flat, he prances around bollock-naked. Chances are we'll find him with his dick hanging out when we go aboard.'

'That's something to look forward to then,' said Galbraith gloomily.

Carpenter chuckled. 'He fancies himself – doesn't think he's doing the business unless he's got two birds on the go at one time. Currently there's a twenty-five-year-old in London called Marie, and another called Bibi or Didi, or something similar, down here. Barlow's given us the name of a friend of Harding's in Lymington, one Tony Bridges, who acts as his answering service when he's out at sea, so I've sent Campbell round to have a word with him. If he gets a line on anything he'll call through.' He tugged at his earlobe. 'On the plus side, the sailing lobby speak well of him. He's lived in Lymington all his life, grew up over a chip shop in the High Street, and he's been mucking around in boats since he was ten. He made it to the top of the waiting list for a river mooring just over three years ago – they're like gold dust apparently – whereupon he sank every last cent into buying *Crazy Daze*. He spends his free weekends on her, and the number of man-hours he's put into getting her shipshape would leave lesser men weeping. That's a quote from some fellow in the yacht club. The general consensus seems to be that he's a bit of a lad, but his heart's in the right place.'

'He sounds like a ruddy chameleon,' said Galbraith cynically. 'I mean that's three different versions of the same guy. Arse-bandit, rampant stud, and all-round good bloke. You pays your money and takes your choice, eh?'

'He's an actor, don't forget, so I doubt if any of them are accurate. He probably plays to the gallery whenever he's given a chance.'

'A liar, more like. According to Ingram, he said he grew up on a farm in Cornwall.' Galbraith raised his collar as a breeze blew down the river, reminding him that he had put on light clothes that morning when the air temperature had touched the low thirties. 'Do you fancy him for it?'

Carpenter shook his head. 'Not really. He's a bit too visible. I think our man's more likely to be textbook material. A loner . . . poor work record . . . history of failed relationships . . . probably lives at home with his mother . . . resents her interference in his life.' He raised his nose to sniff the air. 'At the moment, I'd say the husband sounds a more likely candidate.'

Tony Bridges lived in a small terraced house behind the High Street and gave a nod of agreement when the grey-haired detective sergeant at his door asked if he could talk to him for a few minutes about Steven Harding. He had no shirt or shoes on, just a pair of jeans, and he weaved unsteadily down the corridor as he led the way to an untidy sitting room. He was thin and sharp-featured, with a peroxide crew-cut that didn't suit his sallow complexion, but he smiled amiably enough as he gestured DS Campbell through the door. Campbell, who thought he smelt cannabis in the air, had the distinct impression that visits from the police were not unusual and suspected the neighbours had much to put up with.

The house gave the impression of multiple occupancy with a couple of bicycles leaning against the wall at the end of the corridor, and assorted clothes lying in heaps about the furniture and floor. Dozens of empty lager cans had been tossed into an old beer crate in a corner – left over, Campbell presumed, from a long-dead party – and overflowing ashtrays reeked into the atmosphere. Campbell wondered what the kitchen was like. If it was as rank as the sitting room, it probably had rats, he thought.

'If his car alarm's gone off again,' said Bridges, 'then it's the garage you want to talk to. *They* fitted the sodding thing and I'm sick to death of people phoning you lot about it when he's not here. I don't even know why he bothered to have it put in. The car's a pile of crap so I can't see anyone wanting to steal it.' He picked up an opened Enigma can from the floor and used it to point to a chair. 'Take a pew. Do you want a lager?'

'No thanks.' Campbell sat down. 'It's not about his alarm, sir. We're asking routine questions of everyone who knows him in order to eliminate him from an inquiry, and we were given your name by his agent.'

'What inquiry?'

'A woman drowned on Saturday night and Mr Harding reported finding the body.'

'Is that right? Shit! Who was it?'

'A local woman by the name of Kate Sumner. She lived in Rope Walk with her husband and daughter.'

'Fucking Nora! Are you serious?'

'Did you know her?'

Tony took a swill from the can. 'I knew *of* her but I never met her. She had this thing about Steve. He helped her out once with her kid and she wouldn't leave him alone. It used to drive him mad.'

'Who told you this?'

'Steve of course. Who else?' He shook his head. 'No wonder he drank himself stupid last night if he's the one who found her.'

'He wasn't. Some boys found her. He made the phone call on their behalf.'

Bridges pondered for several moments in silence, and it was clearly hard work. Whatever anaesthetic he'd taken – cannabis, alcohol or both – he was having trouble getting his mind into gear. 'This doesn't make sense,' he said with sudden belligerence, his eyes focusing on Campbell like two little spy cameras. 'I know for a fact Steve wasn't in Lymington on Saturday night. I saw him Friday night and he told me he was going to Poole for the weekend. His boat was out all Saturday and Sunday which means there's no way he could have reported a drowning in Lymington.'

'She didn't drown here, sir. She drowned off the coast about twenty miles from Poole.'

'Ah, shit!' He emptied the lager can with one swallow then crumpled it between his fist and threw it at the beer crate. 'Look, it's pointless asking me any more questions. I don't know anything about anyone drowning. Okay? I'm a mate of Steve's not his blasted keeper.'

Campbell nodded. 'Fair enough. So, as a mate, do you know if he has a girlfriend down here called Bibi or Didi, Mr Bridges?'

Tony levelled an accusing finger. 'What the hell *is* this?' he demanded. 'Over my dead body are these routine questions. What's going on?'

The DS looked thoughtful. 'Steve isn't answering his telephone so his agent's the only person we've been able to talk to. He told us Steve had a girlfriend in Lymington called Bibi or Didi and he suggested we contact you for her address. Is that a problem for you?'

'TO-ONY!' called a drunken female voice from upstairs. 'I'M WA-AITING!'

'Too right it's a problem,' said Bridges angrily. 'That's Bibi and she's *my* sodding girlfriend, not Steve's. I'll kill the bastard if he's been two-timing me.'

There was the sound of a body slumping on the floor upstairs. 'I'M GOING TO SLE-EP AGAIN, TONY!'

Carpenter and Galbraith travelled out to *Crazy Daze* in the harbour master's rib – a souped-up dinghy with a fibreglass keel and a steering column – captained by one of his young assistants. The night air had become noticeably cold after the heat of the day and both men wished they had had the sense to wear jumpers or fleeces under their jackets. A stiff breeze was funnelling down the Solent, making rigging lines rattle noisily against the forest of masts in the Berthon and Yacht Haven marinas. Ahead of them the Isle of Wight crouched like a slumbering beast against the shadowy sky and the lights from the approaching Yarmouth to Lymington ferry danced in reflection across the waves.

The harbour master had been amused by police suspicion over their fruitless attempts to raise Harding via radio or mobile telephone. 'Do the man a favour! Why should he waste his batteries on the odd chance that you lot want to talk to him? There's no shore power to boats on the buoys. He lights the saloon with a butane gas lamp – claims it's romantic – which is why he prefers a buoy in the river to a pontoon in a marina. That, and the fact that once on board the girls are dependent on him and his dinghy to get them off again.'

'Does he take many girls out there?' asked Galbraith.

'I wouldn't know. I've got better things to do than keep a tally of Steve's conquests. He prefers blondes, I know that. I've seen him with a right little stunner recently.'

'Small, curly blonde hair, blue eyes?'

'Far as I recall, she had straight hair, but don't quote me on it. I'm no good with faces.'

'Any idea what time Steve's boat left on Saturday morning?' asked Carpenter.

The harbour master shook his head. 'I can't even see it from here. Ask at the yacht club.'

'We already have. No luck.'

'Wait till the weekenders come down on Saturday then. They'll be your best bet.'

The rib slowed as it approached Harding's sloop. Yellow light glimmered in the midship portholes and a rubber dinghy bobbed astern in the wash from the ferry. From inside came the faint sound of music.

'Hey, Steve,' shouted the harbour master's lad, rapping smartly on the port planking. 'It's Gary. You've got visitors, mate.'

Harding's voice came faintly. 'Bog off, Gary! I'm sick.'

'No can do. It's the police. They want to talk to you. Come on, open up, and give us a hand.'

The music ceased abruptly and Harding hoisted himself through the open companionway into the cockpit. 'What's up?' he asked, surveying the two detectives with an ingenuous smile. 'I guess this has something to do with that woman yesterday? Were the boys lying about the binoculars?'

'We've a few follow-up questions,' said Detective Superintendent Carpenter with an equally ingenuous smile. 'Can we come on board?'

'Sure.' He hopped on to the deck and reached down to assist Carpenter before turning to help his companion.

'My shift ends at ten,' the lad called to the police officers. 'I'll be back in forty minutes to take you off. If you want to leave earlier call on your mobile. Steve knows the number. Otherwise get him to bring you back.'

They watched him turn away in a wide circle, carving a gleaming wake out of the water as he headed upriver towards the town.

'You'd better come below,' said Harding. 'It's cold out here.' He was dressed – much to Galbraith's relief – in the same sleeveless T-shirt and shorts he'd been wearing the day before, and he shivered as a wind blew across the salt flats at the entrance to the river. Barefoot himself, he looked critically at the policemen's shoes. 'You'll have to take those off,' he told them. 'It's taken me two years to get the planking looking like this and I don't want it marked.'

Obligingly, the two men unlaced their boots before padding across to the companionway in search of welcome warmth. The atmosphere inside the saloon was still redolent of the previous night's heavy drinking session and, even without the evidence of the empty whisky bottle which stood on the table, neither officer had any difficulty guessing why Harding had described himself as 'sick'. The muted light of the single gas-operated lamp served only to accentuate the hollows in his cheeks and the dark stubble around his unshaven jaw, and the brief glimpse they had of the tumbled sheets in the forward cabin before he closed the door left neither of them in any doubt that he'd spent most of the day sleeping off a ferocious hangover.

'What kind of follow-up questions?' he asked, sliding on to a bench seat at the side of the table and gesturing them to take the other.

'Routine ones, Mr Harding,' said the Superintendent.

'About what?'

'Yesterday's events.'

He pressed the heels of his palms against his lids and rotated them fiercely as if to drive out demons. 'I don't know any more than I told the other guy,' he said, eyes watering as he lowered his hands. 'And most of that was what the boys told me. They reckoned she drowned and got left on the beach. Were they right?'

'It certainly looks that way.'

He hunched forward over the table. 'I'm thinking about making a complaint against that copper. He was bloody rude, made out me and the kids had something to do with the body being there. I didn't mind for myself so much, but I was pretty pissed off for the boys. They were scared of him. I mean, let's face it, it can't be much fun finding a corpse – and then to have some idiot in hobnailed boots making the whole situation worse . . .' He broke off with a shake of his head. 'Matter of fact I think he was jealous. I was chatting up this bird when he came back, and he looked bloody furious about it. I reckon he fancies her himself, but he's such a dozy pillock he hasn't done anything about it.'

As neither Galbraith nor Carpenter rose in Ingram's defence, a silence fell during which the two policemen cast interested glances about the saloon. In other circumstances the light may well have been romantic, but to a couple of law officers intent on spotting anything that might connect its owner to a brutal rape and murder it was worse than useless. Too much of the interior was obscured by shadow and if there was evidence that Kate and Hannah Sumner had been on board the previous Saturday then it wasn't obvious.

'What do you want to know?' asked Harding then. He was watching John Galbraith as he spoke, and there was something in his eye – *triumph? amusement?* – that made Galbraith think the silence had been deliberate. He had given them an opportunity to look, and they had only themselves to blame if they were disappointed.

'We understand you berthed in Salterns Marina on Saturday night and stayed there most of Sunday?' said Carpenter.

'Yes.'

'What time did you tie up, Mr Harding?'

'I've no idea.' He frowned. 'Pretty late. What's that got to do with anything?'

'Do you keep a log?'

He glanced towards his chart table. 'When I remember.'

'May I look at it?'

'Why not?' He leaned over and retrieved a battered exercise book from the clutter of paper on the lid of the chart table. 'It's hardly great literature.' He handed it across.

Carpenter read the last six entries.

09.08.97.	10.09.	*Slipped mooring.*
" "	11.32.	*Rounded Hurst Castle.*
10.08.97.	02.17.	*Berthed, Salterns Marina.*
" "	18.50.	*Slipped mooring.*
" "	19.28.	*Exited Poole Harbour.*
11.08.97.	00.12.	*Berthed, Lymington.*

'You certainly don't waste your words much, do you?' he murmured, flicking back through the pages to look at other entries. 'Doesn't wind speed or course ever feature in your log?'

'Not often.'

'Is there a reason for that?'

The young man shrugged. 'I know the course to everywhere on the south coast so I don't need to keep reminding myself, and wind speed is wind speed. That's part of the beauty of it. Any journey takes as long as it takes. If you're the sort of impatient type who's only interested in arrivals then sailing will drive you nuts. On a bad day it can take hours to go a few miles.'

'It says here you tied up in Salterns Marina at 2.17 on Sunday morning,' said Carpenter.

'Then I did.'

'It also says you left Lymington at 10.09 on Saturday

102

morning.' He did a quick calculation. 'Which means it took you sixteen hours to sail approximately thirty miles. That's got to be a record, hasn't it? It works out at about two knots an hour. Is that as fast as this thing can go?'

'It depends on the wind and the tide. On a good day I can do six knots but the average is probably four. In fact I probably sailed sixty miles on Saturday because I was tacking most of the way.' He yawned. 'Like I said, it can take hours on a bad day, and Saturday was a bad day.'

'Why didn't you use your motor?'

'I didn't want to. I wasn't in a hurry.' His expression grew wary with suspicion. 'What's this got to do with the woman on the beach?'

'Probably nothing,' said Carpenter easily. 'We're just tying up some loose ends for the report.' He paused, assessing the young man thoughtfully. 'I've done a little sailing myself in the past,' he said then, 'and I'll be honest with you, I don't believe it took you sixteen hours to sail to Poole. If nothing else, the offshore winds as the land cooled in the late afternoon would have boosted your speed well over two knots. I think you sailed on past the Isle of Purbeck, perhaps with the intention of going to Weymouth, and only turned back to Poole when you realized how late it was getting. Am I right?'

'No. I hove to off Christchurch for a few hours to do some fishing and have a nap. That's why it took so long.'

Carpenter didn't believe him. 'Two minutes ago you gave tacking as the explanation. Now you're claiming a fishing break. Which was it?'

'Both. Tacking and fishing.'

'Why isn't it in your log?'

'It wasn't important.'

Carpenter nodded. 'Your approach to time seems a little' – he sought a suitable word – 'individualistic, Mr Harding. For example, you told the police officer yesterday that you were planning to walk to Lulworth Cove, but Lulworth's a good twenty-five miles from Salterns Marina, fifty in total if you intended to walk back again. That's an ambitious distance for a twelve-hour hike, isn't it, bearing in mind you told the harbour master at Salterns Marina you'd be back by late afternoon?'

Harding's eyes gleamed with sudden amusement. 'It doesn't look nearly as far by sea,' he said.

'Did you make it to Lulworth?'

'Like hell I did!' he said with a laugh. 'I was completely whacked by the time I reached Chapman's Pool.'

'Could that be because you travel light?'

'I don't understand.'

'You were carrying a mobile telephone, Mr Harding, but nothing else. In other words you set out on a fifty-mile hike on one of the hottest days of the year with no fluids, no money, no sunscreen protection, no additional clothes if you started to burn, no hat. Are you usually so careless about your health?'

He pulled a wry face. 'Look, all right it was stupid. I admit it. That's the reason I turned back after your

104

bloke drove the kids away. If you're interested, the return journey took twice as long as the journey out because I was so damn knackered.'

'About four hours then,' suggested DI Galbraith.

'More like six. I started after they left, which was 12.30 near enough, and got to the marina around 6.15. I drank about a gallon of water, had something to eat then set off for Lymington maybe half an hour later.'

'So the hike out to Chapman's Pool took three hours?' said Galbraith.

'Something like that.'

'Which means you must have left the marina shortly after 7.30 to be able to make the emergency call at 10.43.'

'If you say so.'

'I don't say so at all, Steve. Our information is that you were paying for your berth at eight o'clock which means you couldn't have left the marina until several minutes later.'

Harding linked his hands behind his head and stared across the table at the Inspector. 'Okay, I left at eight,' he said. 'What's the big deal?'

'The big deal is there's no way you could have hiked sixteen miles along a rough coastal path in two and a half hours' – he paused, holding Harding's gaze – 'and that includes the time you must have lost waiting for the ferry.'

There was no hesitation in his reply. 'I didn't go along the coastal path, or not to start off with anyway,' he said. 'I hitched a lift with a couple on the ferry who were heading for the country park near Durlston Head. They dropped me off by the gates leading up to the lighthouse and I got on to the path there.'

'What time was that?'

He shifted his gaze to the ceiling. 'Ten forty-three minus however long it takes to jog from Durlston Head to Chapman's Pool, I suppose. Look, the first time I remember checking my watch yesterday was just before I made the nine-nine-nine call. Up until then I couldn't have given a toss what time it was.' He looked at Galbraith again, and there was irritation in his dark eyes. 'I hate being ruled by the bloody clock. It's social terrorism to force people to conform to arbitrary evaluations of how long something should take. That's why I like sailing. Time's irrelevant and there's bugger all you can do about it.'

'What sort of car did the couple drive?' asked Carpenter, unmoved by the young man's flights of philosophical fancy.

'I don't know. A saloon of some sort. I don't notice cars.'

'What colour?'

'Blue, I think.'

'What were the couple like?'

'We didn't talk much. They had a Manic Street Preachers album on tape. We listened to that.'

'Can you describe them, Mr Harding?'

'Not really. They were ordinary. I spent most of the time looking at the backs of their heads. She had blonde hair and he had dark hair.' He reached for the whisky bottle and rolled it between his palms, beginning to lose his patience. 'Why the hell are you asking me these questions anyway? What the fuck does it matter how long it took me to get from A to B, or who I met along the way? Does everyone who dials nine-nine-nine get the third degree?'

'Just tying loose ends, sir.'

'So you said.'

'Wouldn't it be truer to say that Chapman's Pool was your destination, and not Lulworth Cove?'

'No.'

A silence developed. Carpenter stared fixedly at Harding while he continued to play with the whisky bottle. 'Were there any passengers on board your boat on Saturday?' he asked then.

'No.'

'Are you sure about that, sir?'

'Of course I'm bloody sure. Don't you think I'd have noticed them? It's hardly the *QE2*, is it?'

Carpenter leafed idly through the logbook. 'Do you *ever* carry passengers?'

'That's none of your business.'

'Maybe not, but we've been led to believe you're a bit of a lad.' He lifted an amused eyebrow. 'Legend has it that you regularly entertain ladies on board. I'm wondering if you ever take them sailing with you' – he jerked his head towards the cabin – 'or does all the action take place in there when you're moored up to your buoy?'

Harding took time to consider his answer. 'I take some of them out,' he admitted at last.

'How often?'

Another long pause. 'Once a month, maybe.'

Carpenter slapped the exercise book on to the table and drummed his fingers on it. 'Then why is there no mention of them in here? Surely you have a responsibility to record the names of everyone on board in case of an accident? Or perhaps you don't care that someone might drown because the coastguards assume you're the only person they're looking for?'

'That's ridiculous,' said Harding dismissively. 'The boat would have to turn turtle for a scenario like that and the log'd be lost anyway.'

'Have any of your passengers ever gone overboard?'

Harding shook his head but didn't say anything. His eyes flickered with open suspicion from one man to the other, tasting their mood in the way a snake flicks his tongue to taste scent on the air. There was something very studied about every movement he made, and Galbraith regarded him objectively, mindful that he was an actor. He had the impression that Harding was enjoying himself, but he couldn't think why this should be unless Harding had no idea the investigation involved rape and murder and was merely using the experience of an interrogation to practise 'method-acting' techniques.

'Do you know a woman by the name of Kate Sumner?' asked Carpenter next.

Harding pushed the bottle aside and leaned forward aggressively. 'What if I do?'

'That's not an answer to my question. Let me repeat it. Do you know a woman by the name of Kate Sumner?'

'Yes.'

'Do you know her well?'

'Well enough.'

'How well is well enough?'

'None of your bloody business.'

'Wrong answer, Steve. It's very much our business. It was her body you saw being winched into the helicopter.'

His reaction surprised them.

'I had a feeling it might be,' he said.

Chapter Nine

AHEAD ACROSS THE WATER, the lights of Swanage gleamed like brilliant jewels in the night. Behind, the dying sun dipped beneath the horizon. Danny Spender was yawning profusely, worn out by his long day and three hours' exposure to fresh sea air. He leaned against Ingram's comforting bulk while his older brother stood proudly at the wheel, steering *Miss Creant* home. 'He was a dirty person,' he confided suddenly.

'Who was?'

'That man yesterday.'

Ingram glanced down at him. 'What did he do?' he asked, careful to keep the curiosity out of his voice.

'He was rubbing his willy with his telephone,' said Danny, 'all the time the lady was being rescued.'

Ingram looked at Paul to see if he was listening but the other boy was too enthralled by the wheel to pay them any attention. 'Did Miss Jenner see him do it?'

Danny's eyelids drooped. 'No. He stopped when she came round the corner. Paul reckons he was polishing it – you know, like bowlers do with cricket balls to make them turn in the air – but he wasn't, he was being dirty.'

'Why does Paul like him so much?'

The child gave another huge yawn. 'Because he wasn't cross with him for spying on a nudie. Dad would be. He was *furious* when Paul got hold of some porno mags. I said they were boring but Paul said they were natural.'

Detective Superintendent Carpenter's telephone rang. 'Excuse me,' he said, retrieving it from his jacket pocket and flipping open the mouthpiece. 'Yes, Campbell,' he said. 'Right . . . go on . . .' He stared at a point above Steven Harding's head as he spoke, his inevitable frown lengthened and deepened by the shadows thrown by the gaslight as he listened to his DS's report on his interview with Tony Bridges. He clamped the receiver tight against his ear as the name 'Bibi' was mentioned, and lowered his eyes curiously to the young man opposite.

Galbraith watched Steven Harding while the one-sided conversation proceeded. The man was listening acutely, straining to pick up what was being said at the other end, all too aware that the topic under discussion was probably himself. Most of the time he stared at the table but once or twice he raised his eyes to look at Galbraith, and Galbraith felt a curious empathy with him as if he and Harding, by dint of their mutual ignorance of the conversation, were ranged against Carpenter. He had no sense that Harding was guilty, no intuition that he was sitting with a rapist; yet his training told him that that meant nothing. Sociopaths could be as charming and as unthreatening as the rest of humanity, and it was always a potential victim who thought otherwise.

111

Galbraith resumed his inspection of the interior, picking out shapes in the shadows beyond the gaslight. His eyes had become accustomed to the gloom and he was able to make out a great deal more now than he had ten minutes ago. With the exception of the clutter on the chart table, everything else was neatly stowed away in lockers or on shelves, and there was nothing to indicate the presence of a woman. It was a masculine environment of wooden planking, black leather seats and brass fittings, and no colour intruded anywhere to adorn its austere simplicity. Monastic, he thought, with approval. His own house, a noisy toy-filled establishment created by a wife who was a power in the National Childbirth Trust, was too cluttered and . . . God forbid, *child-centred!* . . . for an endlessly weary policeman.

The galley which was to starboard of the companion-way particularly interested him. It was built into an alcove beside the laddered steps and contained a small sink and Calor-gas hob set into a teak worktop with lockers below and shelves above. His attention had been caught by some articles pushed back into the shadows in the corner and, with the passage of time, he had been able to identify them as a half-eaten lump of cheese in a plastic wrapper with a Tesco's sticker and a bag of apples. He felt the shift of Harding's gaze as it followed his, and he wondered if the man had any idea that a forensic pathologist could detail what a victim had eaten before she died.

Carpenter disconnected and placed the telephone on the logbook. 'You said you had a feeling the body was Kate Sumner's,' he reminded Harding.

'That's right.'

'Could you elaborate? Explain when and why you got this feeling?'

'I didn't mean I had a feeling it was going to be *her*, only that it was bound to be somebody I knew otherwise you wouldn't have come out to my boat.' He shrugged. 'Put it this way, if you do this kind of follow up every time somebody makes an emergency call then it's not bloody surprising the country's awash with unconvicted criminals.'

Carpenter chuckled, although the frown didn't leave his face and remained fixed on the young man opposite. 'Never believe what you read in newspapers, Steve. Trust me, we always catch the criminals who matter.' He examined the actor closely for several seconds. 'Tell me about Kate Sumner,' he invited. 'How well did you know her?'

'Hardly at all,' said Harding with airy unconcern. 'I've met her maybe half a dozen times since she and her husband moved to Lymington. The first time was when she was having trouble pushing her little girl's buggy over the cobbles near the old Customs House. I gave her a hand with it, and we had a brief chat before she went on up the High Street to do her shopping. After that she always stopped to ask me how I was whenever she saw me.'

'Did you like her?'

Harding's gaze strayed towards the telephone while he considered his answer. 'She was all right. Nothing special.'

'What about William Sumner?' asked Galbraith. 'Do you like him?'

'I don't know him well enough to say. He seems okay.'

'According to him, he sees you quite often. He's even invited you back to his house.'

The young man shrugged. 'So? Loads of people invite me to their houses. It doesn't mean I'm close mates with them. Lymington's a sociable place.'

'He told me you showed him some photographs of yourself in a gay magazine. I'd have thought you'd need to be pretty friendly with a man to do that.'

Harding grinned. 'I don't see why. They're good photos. Admittedly he didn't think much of them, but that's his problem. He's pretty straight is old Will Sumner. Wouldn't show his tackle for anything, not even if he was starving, and certainly not in a gay mag.'

'I thought you said you didn't know him well.'

'I don't need to. You only have to look at him. He probably looked middle-aged when he was eighteen.'

Galbraith agreed with him, which made Kate's choice of a husband even odder, he thought. 'Still, it's an unusual thing to do, Steve, go round showing nude photos of yourself to other guys. Do you make a habit of it? Have you shown them round the yacht club, for example?'

'No.'

'Why not?'

Harding didn't answer.

'Maybe you just show them to husbands, eh?' Galbraith lifted an enquiring eyebrow. 'It's a great way to convince a man you've no designs on his wife. I mean if he thinks you're gay he'll think you're safe, won't he? Is that why you did it?'

'I can't remember now. I expect I was pissed and he was getting on my nerves.'

'Were you sleeping with his wife, Steve?'

'Don't be stupid,' said Harding crossly. 'I've already told you I hardly knew her.'

'Then the information we've been given that she wouldn't leave you alone and it was driving you mad is completely wrong?' said Carpenter.

Harding's eyes widened slightly, but he didn't answer.

'Did she ever come on board this boat?'

'No.'

'Are you sure?'

For the first time there was genuine nervousness in the man's manner. He hunched his shoulders over the table again and ran his tongue across dry lips. 'Look, I don't really get what all this is about. Okay, somebody drowned and I knew her – not very well, but I *did* know her. Okay – too – I can accept it looks like a bizarre coincidence that I was there when she was found – but, listen, I'm always meeting up with people I know. That's what sailing's about – bumping into guys that you had a drink with maybe two years before.'

'But that's the root of the problem,' said Galbraith reasonably. 'According to our information, Kate Sumner didn't sail. You've said yourself she was never on board *Crazy Daze*.'

'That doesn't mean she didn't accept a spur-of-the

moment invitation. There was a French Beneteau called *Mirage* anchored in Chapman's Pool yesterday. I saw her through the boys' binoculars. She was moored up in Berthon at the end of last week – I know that because they have this cute kid on board who wanted to know the code for the lavatories. Well – *Jesus!* – those French guys are just as likely to have met Kate as I was. Berthon's in Lymington, isn't it? Kate lives in Lymington. Maybe they took her for a spin?'

'It's a possibility,' agreed Carpenter. He watched Galbraith make a note. 'Did you catch the "cute kid's" name, by any chance?'

Harding shook his head.

'Do you know of any other friends who might have taken Kate out on Saturday?'

'No. Like I said, I hardly knew her. But she must have had some. Everyone round here knows people who sail.'

Galbraith jerked his head towards the galley. 'Did you go shopping on Saturday morning before you left for Poole?' he asked.

'What's that got to do with anything?' The truculence was back in his voice again.

'It's a simple question. Did you buy the cheese and apples that are in your galley on Saturday morning?'

'Yes.'

'Did you meet Kate Sumner while you were in town?'

Harding hesitated before he replied. 'Yes,' he admitted then. 'She was outside Tesco's with her little girl.'

'What time was that?'

'Nine-thirty, maybe.' He seized the whisky bottle

116

again and laid it on its side, placing his forefinger against the neck and turning it slowly. 'I didn't hang around because I wanted to get off, and she was looking for some sandals for her child. We said hi and went our separate ways, and that was it.'

'Did you invite her to go sailing with you?' asked Carpenter.

'No.' He lost interest in the bottle and abandoned it with its open neck pointing directly at the Superintendent's chest like the barrel of a rifle. 'Look, I don't know what you think I've done,' he said, ratcheting up his irritation, 'but I'm damn sure you're not allowed to ask me questions like this. Shouldn't there be a tape recorder?'

'Not when people are merely helping us with our inquiries, sir,' said Carpenter mildly. 'As a general rule, the taping of interviews follows the cautioning of a suspect for an indictable offence. Such interviews can only be conducted in a police station where the proper equipment allows an officer to insert a new blank tape into the recorder in front of the suspect.' He smiled without hostility. 'However, if you prefer, you can accompany us to Winfrith where we will question you as a voluntary witness under taped conditions.'

'No way. I'm not leaving the boat.' He stretched his arms along the back of the settee and gripped the teak edging as if to emphasize the point. The movement caused his right hand to brush against a piece of fabric that was tucked on to the narrow shelf behind the edging strip and he glanced at it idly for a moment before crushing it in his hand.

There was a short silence.

'Do you have a girlfriend in Lymington?' asked Carpenter.

'Maybe.'

'May I ask what her name is?'

'No.'

'Your agent suggested a name. He said she was called Bibi or Didi.'

'That's his problem.'

Galbraith was more interested in what was crushed inside Harding's fist because he had seen what it was. 'Do you have any children?' he asked him.

'No.'

'Does your girlfriend have children?'

No answer.

'You're holding a bib in your fist,' the DI pointed out, 'so presumably someone who's been on this boat has children.'

Harding uncurled his fingers and let the object drop on to the settee. 'It's been there for ages. I'm not much of a cleaner.'

Carpenter slammed his palm on to the table, making the phone and the whisky bottle jump. 'You're annoying me, Mr Harding,' he said severely. 'This isn't a piece of theatre put on for your benefit, it's a serious investigation into a young woman's drowning. Now you've admitted knowing Kate Sumner and you've admitted seeing her on the morning before she drowned, but if you've no knowledge of how she came to be lying on a shore in Dorset at a time when she and her daughter were assumed to be in Lymington then I advise you to answer our questions as straightforwardly and honestly as you can. Let me rephrase the question.' His eyes narrowed. 'Have you recently entertained a girlfriend on board this boat who has a child or children?'

'Maybe,' said Harding again.

'There's no maybe about it. Either you have or you haven't.'

He abandoned his 'crucifixion' pose to slump forward again. 'I've several girlfriends with children,' he said sulkily, 'and I've entertained them all off and on. I'm trying to remember who was the most recent.'

'I'd like the names of every one of them,' said Carpenter grimly.

'Well you're not going to get them,' said Harding with sudden decision, 'and I'm not answering any more questions. Not without a solicitor and not without the conversation being recorded. I don't know what the hell I'm supposed to have done but I'm buggered if you're going to stitch me up for it.'

'We're trying to establish how Kate Sumner came to drown in Egmont Bight.'

'No comment.'

Carpenter righted the whisky bottle and placed a finger on top of it. 'Why did you get drunk last night, Mr Harding?'

The man stared at the Superintendent but didn't say anything.

'You're a compulsive liar, lad. You said yesterday that you grew up on a farm in Cornwall when the truth is you grew up over a chip shop in Lymington. You told your agent your girlfriend's name was Bibi when in fact

119

Bibi's been your mate's steady girlfriend for the last four months. You told William Sumner you were a poof while everyone else round here seems to think you're Casanova. What's your problem, eh? Is your life so boring that you have to play-act some interest into it?'

A faint flush reddened Harding's neck. 'Jesus, you're a piece of shit!' he hissed furiously.

Carpenter steepled his hands over the telephone and stared him down. 'Have you any objections to us taking a look round your boat, Mr Harding?'

'Not if you've got a search warrant.'

'We haven't.'

Harding's eyes gleamed triumphantly. 'Don't even think about it then.'

The Superintendent studied him for a moment. 'Kate Sumner was brutally raped before being thrown into the sea to drown,' he said slowly, 'and all the evidence suggests that the rape took place on board a boat. Now let me explain the rules about searching premises, Mr Harding. In the absence of the owner's consent, the police have various courses open to them, one of which – assuming they have reasonable cause to suspect that the owner has been guilty of an arrestable offence – is to arrest him and then search any premises he controls in order to prevent the disposal of evidence. Do you understand the implications of what I've just said, bearing in mind that rape and murder are serious arrestable offences?'

Harding's face had gone very white.

'Answer me, please,' snapped Carpenter. 'Do you understand the implications of what I've just said?'

'You'll arrest me if I refuse.'

Carpenter nodded.

Shock was giving way to anger. 'I can't believe you're allowed to behave like this. You can't go round accusing people of rape just so you can search their boats without a warrant. That's abuse of police powers.'

'You're forgetting reasonable cause.' He enumerated points on his fingers. '*One*, you've admitted meeting Kate Sumner at 9.30 on Saturday morning shortly before you sailed; *two*, you've failed to give an adequate explanation of why it took you fourteen hours to sail between Lymington and Poole; *three*, you've offered conflicting stories about how you came to be on the coastal path above where Kate Sumner's body was found yesterday; *four*, your boat was berthed at a time and in the vicinity of where her daughter was discovered wandering alone and traumatized; *five*, you seem unwilling or unable to give satisfactory answers to straightforward questions . . .' He broke off. 'Do you want me to go on?'

Whatever composure Harding had was gone. He looked what he was, badly frightened. 'It's all just coincidence,' he protested.

'Including little Hannah being found near Salterns Marina yesterday? Was that a coincidence?'

'I guess so . . .' He stopped abruptly, his expression alarmed. 'I don't know what you're talking about,' he said, the pitch of his voice rising. 'Oh, shit! I need to think.'

'Well, think on this,' said Carpenter evenly, 'if, when we search the interior of this boat, we discover a single fingerprint belonging to Kate Sumner—'

121

'Look, okay,' he interrupted, breathing deeply through his nose and making damping gestures with his hands as if it was the detectives who needed calming and not himself. 'She and her kid have been on board, but it wasn't on Saturday.'

'When was it?'

'I can't remember.'

'That's not good enough, Steve. Recently? A long time ago? Under what circumstances? Did you bring them out in your dinghy? Was Kate one of your conquests? Did you make love to her?'

'No, dammit!' he said angrily. 'I hated the stupid bitch. She was always throwing herself at me, wanting me to fuck her and wanting me to be nice to that weird kid of hers. They used to hang around down by the fuelling pontoon in case I came in for diesel. It used to bug me, it really did.'

'So, let me get this straight,' murmured Carpenter sarcastically. 'To stop her pestering you, you invited her on board?'

'I thought if I was polite . . . Ah, what the hell! Go ahead, search the damn boat. You won't find anything.'

Carpenter nodded to Galbraith. 'I suggest you start in the cabin. Do you have another lamp, Steve?'

Harding shook his head.

Galbraith unhooked a torch from the aft bulkhead and flicked the switch to see if it was working. 'This'll do.' He propped open the cabin door and swung the beam around the interior, settling almost immediately on a small pile of clothes on the port shelf. He used the end of his biro to push a flimsy blouse, a bra and pair of panties to one side to reveal some tiny child's shoes nestling together on the shelf. He turned the beam of the torch full on them and stood back so they were visible to Carpenter and Harding.

'Who do the shoes belong to, Mr Harding?'

No answer.

'Who do the women's clothes belong to?'

No answer.

'If you have an explanation for why these articles are on board your boat, Steve, then I advise you to give it to us now.'

'They're my girlfriend's,' he said in a strangled voice. 'She has a son. The shoes belong to him.'

'Who is she, Steve?'

'I can't tell you. She's married, and she's got nothing to do with this.'

Galbraith emerged from the cabin with one of the shoes hooked on the end of his biro. 'There's a name written on the strap, guv, H. SUMNER. And there's staining on the floor in here.' He pointed the torch beam towards some dark marks beside the bunk bed. 'It looks fairly recent.'

'I need to know what caused the stains, Steve.'

In one lithe movement, the young man erupted out of his seat and grabbed the whisky bottle in both hands, swinging it violently to his left and forcing Galbraith to retreat into the cabin. 'Enough, okay!' he growled, moving towards the chart table. 'You're way off beam on this one. Now back off before I do something I'll regret. You've got to give me some space, for Christ's sake. I need to think.'

He was unprepared for the ease with which Galbraith plucked the bottle from his grasp and spun him round to face the teak clad wall while securing his wrists behind his back with handcuffs.

'You'll have plenty of time for thinking when we get you into a police cell,' said the DI unemotionally as he pushed the young man face-down on to the settee. 'I am arresting you on suspicion of murder. You do not have to say anything but it may harm your defence if you do not mention, when questioned, something you later rely on in court. Anything you do say may be given in evidence.'

Had William Sumner not had a key to his front door, Sandy Griffiths would have questioned whether he had ever lived in Langton Cottage because his knowledge of the house was minimal. Indeed, the police constable who had stayed behind to act as her shadow was better informed than he was, having watched the scene-of-crime officers meticulously examine every room. Sumner looked at her blankly each time she asked him a question. Which cupboard was the tea in? He didn't know. Where did Kate keep Hannah's nappies? He didn't know. Which towel or flannel was hers? He didn't know. Could he at least show her to Hannah's room so that she could put the child to bed? He looked towards the stairs. 'It's up there,' he said, 'you can't miss it.'

He seemed fascinated by the invasion of his home by the search team. 'What were they looking for?' he asked.

'Anything that will connect with Kate's disappearance,' said Griffiths.

'Does that mean they think I did it?'

Griffiths eased Hannah on her hip and turned the child's head into her shoulder in a somewhat futile attempt to block her ears. 'It's standard procedure, William, but I don't think it's something we should talk about in front of your daughter. I suggest you take it up with DI Galbraith tomorrow.'

But he was either too insensitive or too careless of his daughter's welfare to take the hint. He stared at a photograph of his wife on the mantelpiece. 'I couldn't have done it,' he said. 'I was in Liverpool.'

At the request of Dorsetshire Constabulary, Liverpool police had already begun preliminary inquiries at the Regal Hotel. It was early days, of course, but the account he'd settled that morning made interesting reading. Despite being a heavy user of the telephone, coffee lounge, restaurant and bar in the first two days, there was a period of twenty-four hours between lunchtime on Saturday and a noon drink in the bar on Sunday when he had failed to make use of a single hotel service.

Chapter Ten

DURING THE TWENTY minutes that he waited in the sitting room at Langton Cottage the following morning to speak to William Sumner, John Galbraith learnt two things about the man's dead wife. The first was that Kate Sumner was vain. Every photograph on display was either of herself, or of herself and Hannah, and he searched without success for a likeness of William, or even of an elderly woman who might have been William's mother. In frustration he ended up counting the pictures that were there – thirteen – each of which showed the same prettily smiling face within its framework of golden curls. Was this the cult of the personality taken to its extreme, he wondered, or an indication of a deep-seated inferiority which needed constant reminders that to be photogenic was a talent like any other?

The second thing he learnt was that he could never have lived with Kate. She delighted, it seemed, in applying frills to everything: lace curtains with frills, pelmets with frills, armchairs with frills – even the lampshades had tassels attached to them. Nothing, not even the walls, had escaped her taste for over-embellishment. Langton Cottage was of nineteenth-century origin with beamed ceilings and brick fireplaces, and instead of the plain white plaster that would have shown these features off to their best advantage, she had covered the walls of the sitting room – probably at considerable expense – with mock Regency wallpaper, adorned with gilt stripes, white bows and baskets of unnaturally coloured fruit. Galbraith shuddered at the desecration of what could have been a charming room and unconsciously contrasted it with the timbered simplicity of Steven Harding's sloop which was currently being put under a microscope by scene-of-crime officers while Harding, exercising his right to remain silent, cooled his heels in a police cell.

Rope Walk was a quiet tree-lined avenue to the west of the Royal Lymington and Town yacht clubs, and Langton Cottage had clearly not been cheap. As he knocked on the door at eight o'clock on Tuesday morning after two hours' sleep, Galbraith wondered how big a mortgage William had had to raise to buy it and how much he earned as a pharmaceutical chemist. He could see no logic behind the move from Chichester, particularly as neither Kate nor William appeared to have any links with Lymington.

He was let in by WPC Griffiths who pulled a face when he told her he needed to talk to Sumner. 'You'll be lucky,' she whispered. 'Hannah's been bawling her head off most of the night, so I doubt you'll get any sense out of him. He's had almost as little sleep as I've had.'

'Join the club.'

'You, too, eh?'

Galbraith smiled. 'How's he holding up?'

She shrugged. 'Not too well. Keeps bursting into tears and saying it's not supposed to be like this.' She lowered her voice even further. 'I'm really concerned about Hannah. She's obviously scared of him. She works herself into a tantrum the minute he enters the room then calms down rapidly as soon as he leaves. I ordered him to bed in the end to try and get her to sleep.'

Galbraith looked interested. 'How does he react?'

'That's the odd thing. He doesn't react at all. He just ignores it as if it's something he's grown used to.'

'Has he said why she does it?'

'Only that, being out at work so much, he's never had a chance to bond with her. It could be true, you know. I get the impression Kate swaddled her in cotton wool. There are so many safety features in this house that I can't see how Hannah was ever expected to learn anything. Every door has a child lock on it – even the wardrobe in her own bedroom – which means she can't explore, can't choose her own clothes or even make a mess if she wants to. She's almost three but she's still sleeping in a cot. That's pretty weird, you know. More like prison bars than a nursery. It's a damned odd way to bring up a child and, frankly, I'm not surprised she's a withdrawn little thing.'

'I suppose it's occurred to you that she might be scared of him because she watched him kill her mother,' murmured Galbraith.

Sandy Griffiths spread her hand and made a rocking motion. 'Except I don't see how he can have done it.

128

He's made a list of some colleagues who can alibi him for Saturday night in Liverpool, and if that holds good then there's no way he could have been shoving his wife in the water at 1.00 a.m. in Dorset.'

'No,' agreed Galbraith. 'Still . . .' He pursed his lips in thought. 'Do you realize the SOCOs found no drugs in this house at all, not even paracetamol? Which is odd considering William's a pharmaceutical chemist.'

'Maybe that's why there aren't any. He knows what goes into them.'

'Mmm. Or they were deliberately cleared out before we got here.' He glanced towards the stairs. 'Do you like him?' he asked her.

'Not much,' she admitted, 'but you don't want to go by what I say. I've always been a lousy judge of character where men are concerned. He could have done with a good smacking thirty years ago, in my opinion, just to teach him some manners but as things are, he seems to view women as serving wenches.'

He laughed. 'Are you going to be able to stick it out?'

She rubbed her tired eyes. 'God knows! Your chap left about half an hour ago, and there's supposed to be some relief coming when William's taken away to identify the body and talk to the doctor who examined Hannah. The trouble is, I can't see Hannah letting me go that easily. She clings to me like a limpet. I'm using the spare room to grab kip when I can, and I thought I'd try to organize some temporary cover while she's asleep so I can stay on the premises. But I'll need to get hold of my governor to organize someone locally.' She sighed. 'I suppose you want me to wake William for you.'

He patted her shoulder. 'No. Just point me towards his room. I'm happy to do the business.'

She was sorely tempted, but shook her head. 'You'll disturb Hannah,' she said, baring her teeth in a threatening grimace, 'and I swear to God I'll kill you if she starts howling again before I've had a fag and some black coffee. I'm bushed. I can't take any more of her screaming without mega-fixes of caffeine and nicotine.'

'Is it putting you off babies?'

'It's putting me off husbands,' she said. 'I'd have coped better if he hadn't kept hovering like a dark cloud over my shoulder.' She eased open the sitting-room door. 'You can wait in here till he comes. You'll love it. It has all the makings of a shrine.'

Galbraith heard footsteps on the stairs and turned to face the door as it opened. Sumner was in his early forties, but he looked a great deal older than that today and Galbraith suspected Harding would have been a lot harsher in his description if he could have seen Kate's husband like this. He was unshaven and dishevelled, and his face was inexpressibly weary, but whether from grief or lack of sleep, it was impossible to say. Nevertheless, his eyes shone brightly enough and Galbraith took note of the fact. Lack of sleep did not lead automatically to blunted intelligence.

'Good morning, sir,' he said. 'I'm sorry to bother you again so early but I've more questions to ask, and I'm afraid they won't wait.'

'That's all right. Sit down. I feel I was less than helpful last night but I was so whacked I couldn't think properly.' He took an armchair and left Galbraith to the sofa. 'I've made those lists you wanted. They're on the table in the kitchen.'

'Thanks.' He gave the man a searching look. 'Did you get any sleep?'

'Not really. I couldn't stop thinking about it. It's all so illogical. I could understand if they'd both drowned, but it doesn't make sense that Kate's dead and Hannah's alive.'

Galbraith agreed. He and Carpenter had been puzzling over that very fact most of the night. Why had Kate had to swim for her life while the toddler was allowed to live? The neat explanation – that the boat was *Crazy Daze*, that Hannah *had* been on board but had managed to release herself while Harding was walking to Chapman's Pool – failed to address the questions of why the child hadn't been pushed into the sea along with her mother, why Harding was so unconcerned about her wails being heard by other boat users in the marina that he'd left her on her own, and who had fed, watered and changed her nappy in the hours before she was found.

'Have you had time to go through your wife's wardrobe, Mr Sumner? Do you know if any of her clothes are missing?'

'Not that I can tell . . . but it doesn't mean much,' he added as an afterthought. 'I don't really notice what people wear, you see.'

'Suitcases?'

'I don't think so.'

'All right.' He opened his briefcase on the sofa beside him. 'I've some articles of clothing to show you, Mr Sumner. Please tell me if you recognize any of them.' He removed a polythene bag containing the flimsy blouse found on board *Crazy Daze* which he held out for the other man to look at.

Sumner shook his head, without taking it. 'It's not Kate's,' he said.

'Why so positive,' Galbraith asked curiously, 'if you didn't notice what she wore?'

'It's yellow. She hated yellow. She said it didn't suit people with fair hair.' He gestured vaguely towards the door. 'There's no yellow anywhere in the house.'

'Fair enough.' He took out the bags containing the bra and panties. 'Do you recognize either of these as belonging to your wife?'

Sumner reached out a reluctant hand and took both bags, examining the contents closely through the clear plastic. 'I'd be surprised if they were hers,' he said, handing them back. 'She liked lace and frills, and these are very plain. You can compare them with the other things in her drawers, if you like. You'll see what I mean.'

Galbraith nodded. 'I'll do that. Thank you.' He took out the bag with the child's shoes and laid them on his right palm. 'What about these?'

Sumner shook his head again. 'I'm sorry. All children's shoes look alike to me.'

'They have H. SUMNER printed inside the strap.'

He shrugged. 'Then they must be Hannah's.'

'Not necessarily,' said Galbraith. 'They're very small, more suited to a one-year-old than a three-year-old, and anyone can write a name into some shoes.'

'Why would they want to do that?'

'Pretence, perhaps.'

The other man frowned. 'Where did you find them?'

But Galbraith shook his head. 'I'm afraid I can't reveal that at this stage.' He held the shoes up again. 'Would Hannah recognize them, do you think? They may be a pair of cast-offs.'

'She might if the policewoman showed them to her,' said Sumner. 'There's no point in my trying. She screams her head off every time she sees me.' He swept imaginary dirt from the arm of the chair. 'The trouble is I spend so much time at work that she's never had the chance to get to know me properly.'

Galbraith gave him a sympathetic smile while wondering if there was any truth in the statement. Who could contradict him, after all? Kate was dead; Hannah was tongue-tied; and the various neighbours who'd already been interviewed claimed to know little about William. Or indeed, Kate herself.

'To be honest I've only met him a couple of times and he didn't exactly impress me. He works very hard, of course, but they were never ones for entertaining. She was quite sweet, but we were hardly what I'd call friends. You know how it is. You don't choose your neighbours; they get thrust upon you . . .'

'He's not what you'd call sociable. Kate told me once that he spends his evenings and weekends working out formulas on his computer while she watched soaps on the

telly. I feel awful about her dying like that. I wish I'd had more time to talk to her. I think she must have been quite lonely, you know. The rest of us all work, of course, so she was a bit of a rarity, staying at home and doing the housework . . .'

'He's a bully. He took my wife to task about one of the fencing panels between our gardens, said it needed replacing, and when she told him it was his ivy that was pulling it down, he threatened her with court proceedings. No, that's the only contact we've had with him. It was enough. I don't like the man . . .'

'I saw more of Kate than I saw of him. It was an odd marriage. They never did anything together. I sometimes wondered if they even liked each other very much. Kate was very sweet but she hardly ever talked about William. To be honest, I don't think they had much in common . . .'

'I understand Hannah cried most of the night. Does she usually do that?'

'No,' Sumner answered without hesitation, 'but then Kate always cuddled her when she was upset. She's crying for her mother, poor little thing.'

'So you haven't noticed any difference in her behaviour?'

'Not really.'

'The doctor who examined her after she was taken to Poole police station was very concerned about her, described her as unnaturally withdrawn, backward in her development and possibly suffering from some sort of psychological trauma.' Galbraith smiled slightly. 'Yet you're saying that's quite normal for Hannah?'

Sumner coloured slightly as if he'd been caught out in a lie. 'She's always been a little bit' – he hesitated – 'well, odd. I thought she was either autistic or deaf so we had her tested, but the GP said there was nothing wrong and just advised us to be patient. He said children were manipulative, and if Kate did less for her she'd be forced to ask for what she wanted and the problem would go away.'

'When was this?'

'About six months ago.'

'What's your GP's name?'

'Dr Attwater.'

'Did Kate take his advice?'

He shook his head. 'Her heart wasn't in it. Hannah could always make her understand what she wanted, and she couldn't see the point of forcing her to talk before she was ready.'

Galbraith made a note of the GP's name. 'You're a clever man, Mr Sumner,' he said next, 'so I'm sure you know why I'm asking you these questions.'

A ghost of a smile flickered across the man's tired face. 'I prefer William,' he said, 'and yes, of course I do. My daughter screams every time she sees me; my wife had ample opportunity to cheat on me because I'm hardly ever at home; I'm angry because I didn't want to move to Lymington; the mortgage on this place is way too high and I'd like to get shot of it; she was lonely because she hadn't made many friends; and wives are more usually murdered by their partners out of fury than by strangers out of lust.' He gave a hollow laugh. 'About the only thing in my favour is a cast-iron alibi and, believe me, I've spent most of the night thanking God for it.'

Under the rules governing police detention, there is a limit to how long a person may be held without charge, and the pressure to find evidence against Steven Harding mounted as the hours ticked by. It was notable more for its absence. The stains on the floor of the cabin, which had looked so promising the night before, turned out to be whisky-induced vomit – blood group A, matching Harding's – and a microscopic examination of his boat failed to produce any evidence that an act of violence had occurred on board.

If the pathologist's findings were right – *'bruising and abrasions to back (pronounced on shoulder blades and buttocks) and inside of thighs, indicative of forced inter-course on a hard surface such as a deck or an uncarpeted floor – some blood loss from abrasions in vagina'* – the wooden planking of the deck and/or saloon and/or cabin should have had traces of blood, skin tissue and even semen trapped between the grooved joints or under rogue splinters of wood. But no such traces were found. Dried salt was scraped in profusion from the deck planking, but while this might suggest he had scrubbed the topsides down with sea water to remove evidence, it was axiomatic that dried salt would be found on a sailing boat.

On the more likely probability that a blanket or rug had been spread on the hard surface before Kate Sumner had been forced on to it, every item of cloth on board was examined with similarly negative results, although it was all too obvious that any such item would have been thrown overboard along with Kate's clothes and anything else connecting her to the boat. Kate's body was re-examined inch by inch, in the hope that splinters of wood, linking her to *Crazy Daze*, had become embedded under her skin, but either the flaying action of the sea on open wounds had washed the evidence away or it had never been there in the first place. It was a similar story with her broken fingernails. If anything had ever been underneath them, it had long since vanished.

Only the sheets in the cabin showed evidence of semen staining but as the bedclothes hadn't been washed for a very long time it was impossible to say whether the stains were the product of recent intercourse. Indeed, as only two alien hairs were discovered on the pillows and bedclothes – neither of which was Kate's although both were blonde – the conclusion was that, far from being the promiscuous stallion portrayed by the harbour master, Steven Harding was in fact a lonely masturbator.

A small quantity of cannabis and a collection of unopened condoms were discovered in the bedside locker, together with three torn Mates wrappers minus their contents. No used condoms were found. Every container was examined for benzodiazepine, Rohypnol and/or *any* hypnotic. No indications were found. Despite a comprehensive search for pornographic photographs and magazines, none were found. Subsequent searches of Harding's car and flat in London were equally disappointing, although the flat contained thirty-five adult movies. All were on general release, however. A warrant was issued to search Tony Bridges' house in Lymington, but there was nothing to incriminate Steven Harding or to connect him or anyone else there with Kate Sumner. Despite extensive inquiries, police could come up with no other premises used or owned by Harding, and bar a single sighting of him talking to Kate outside Tesco's on Saturday morning, no one reported seeing them together.

There was fingerprint and palm evidence that Kate and Hannah Sumner had been on board *Crazy Daze* but too many of the prints were overlaid with other prints, few of which were Steven Harding's, for the SOCOs to be confident that the visit had been a recent one. Considerable interest was raised by the fact that twenty-five different sets of fingerprints, excluding Carpenter's, Galbraith's, Kate's, Hannah's and Steven's – at least five of the sets being small enough to be children's – were lifted from the saloon, some of which matched prints lifted from Bridges' house, but few of which were replicated in the cabin. Demonstrably, therefore, Harding had entertained people on board, although the nature of the entertainment remained a mystery. He explained it by saying he always invited fellow sailors into the saloon whenever he took a berth in a marina and, in the absence of proof to the contrary, the police accepted his explanation. Nevertheless, they remained curious about it.

In view of the cheese and apples in the galley, Kate Sumner's last meal looked like something the police could run with until the pathologist pointed out that it was impossible to link semi-digested food with a particular purchase. A *Tesco's* Golden Delicious, minced with gastric acids, showed the same chemical printout as a *Sainsbury's* Golden Delicious. Even the child's bib proved inconclusive when the fingerprint evidence on the plastic surface demonstrated that, while Steven Harding and two unidentified others had certainly touched it, Kate Sumner had not.

Briefed by Nick Ingram, attention was paid to the only rucksack found on the boat, a triangular black one with a handful of sweet wrappers in the bottom. Neither Paul nor Danny Spender had been able to give an accurate description of it – Danny: 'it was a big black one . . .'; Paul: 'it was quite big . . . I think it might have been green . . .' – but it told them nothing about what it might have contained on Sunday morning or indeed identified it as the one the boys had seen. Steven Harding, who seemed baffled by police interest in his rucksack, claimed it was certainly the one he had been using that day and explained he had left it on the hillside because it had a litre bottle of water in it, and he couldn't be bothered to lug it down to the boatsheds simply to lug it all the way up again. He further said that PC Ingram had never asked him about a rucksack which is why he hadn't mentioned it at the time.

The nail in the coffin of police suspicion was supplied by a cashier at Tesco's in Lymington High Street who had been on duty the previous Saturday.

''Course I know Steve,' she said, identifying his photograph. 'He comes in every Saturday for provisions.

Did I see him talking to a blonde woman and child last week? Sure I did. He spotted them as he was about to leave and he said, "Damn!" so I said, "What's the problem?" and he said, "I know that woman and she's going to talk to me because she always does," so I said, *jealous*-like, "She's very pretty," and he said, "Forget it, Dawn, she's married, and anyway I'm in a hurry." And he was right. She did talk to him, but he didn't hang around, just tapped his watch and scarpered. You want my opinion? He had something good lined up and he didn't want delaying. She looked mighty miffed when he left, but I didn't blame her for it. Steve's a bit of a hunk. I'd go for him myself if I wasn't a grandmother three times over.'

William Sumner claimed to know little about the management of Langton Cottage or his wife's regular movements. 'I'm away from the house for twelve hours a day, from seven in the morning till seven at night,' he told Galbraith as if it were something to be proud of. 'I was much more *au fait* with her routine in Chichester, probably because I knew the people and the shops she was talking about. Things register better when you recognize names. It's all so different here.'

'Did Steven Harding feature in her conversation?' asked Galbraith.

'Is he the bastard who had Hannah's shoes?' demanded Sumner angrily.

Galbraith shook his head. 'We'll get on a lot faster if you don't keep second-guessing me, William. Let me remind you that we still don't know if the shoes belonged to Hannah.' He held the other man's gaze. 'And, while I'm about it, let me *warn* you that if you start speculating on anything to do with this case, you could prejudice any prosecution we try to bring. And that could mean Kate's killer going free.'

'I'm sorry.' He raised his hands in apology. 'Go on.'

'Did Steven Harding feature in her conversation?' Galbraith asked again.

'No.'

Galbraith referred to the lists of names he had produced. 'Are any of the men on here ex-boyfriends? The ones in Portsmouth, for example. Did she go out with any of them before she went out with you?'

Another shake of the head. 'They're all married.'

Galbraith wondered about the naivety of that statement, but didn't pursue the issue. Instead, he went on to try and build a picture of Kate's early life. It was about as easy as building houses out of straw. The potted history that William gave him was notable more for its gaps than its inclusions. Her maiden name had been Hill, but whether that was her mother's or her father's surname, he didn't know.

'I don't think they were married,' he said.

'And Kate never knew him?'

'No. He left when she was a baby.'

She and her mother had lived in a council flat in Birmingham, although he had no idea where it was, which school Kate had gone to, where she had trained as a secretary or, even, where she had worked before joining Pharmatec UK. Galbraith asked him if she had any friends from that time with whom she had kept in contact, but William shook his head and said he didn't think so. He produced an address book from a drawer in a small bureau in the corner of the room and said Galbraith could check for himself. 'But you won't find anyone from Birmingham in there.'

'When did she move?'

'When her mother died. She told me once that she wanted to put as much distance between herself and where she grew up as she could, so she moved to Portsmouth and rented a flat over a shop in one of the back streets.'

'Did she say why distance was important?'

'I think she felt she'd have less of a chance to get on if she stayed put. She was quite ambitious.'

'For a career?' asked Galbraith in surprise, recalling Sumner's assertion the day before that Kate's one ambition had been to have a family of her own. 'I thought you said she was happy to give up working when she got pregnant.'

There was a short silence. 'I suppose you're planning to talk to my mother?'

Galbraith nodded.

He sighed. 'She didn't approve of Kate so she'll tell you she was a gold-digger. Not in so many words, perhaps, but the implication will be clear. She can be pretty vitriolic when she chooses.' He stared at the floor.

'Is it true?' prompted Galbraith after a moment.

'Not in my opinion. The only thing Kate wanted was something better for her children than she had herself. I admired her for it.'

'And your mother didn't?'

'It's not important,' said Sumner. 'She never approved of anyone I brought home, which probably explains why it took me so long to get married.'

Galbraith glanced at one of the vacuously smiling photographs on the mantelpiece. 'Was Kate a strong character?'

'Oh, yes. She was single-minded about what she wanted.' He gave a lopsided smile as he made a gesture that encompassed the room. 'This was it. The dream. A house of her own. Social acceptance. Respectability. It's why I know she'd never have had an affair. She wouldn't have risked this for anything.'

Yet another display of naivety? Galbraith wondered. 'Maybe she didn't realize there was a risk involved,' he said dispassionately. 'By your own admission, you're hardly ever here so she could easily have been conducting an affair that you knew nothing about.'

Sumner shook his head. 'You don't understand,' he said. 'It wasn't fear of *me* finding out that would have stopped her. She had me wound round her little finger from the first time I met her.' A wry smile thinned his lips. 'My wife was an old-fashioned puritan. It was fear of other people finding out that ruled her life. Respectability *mattered*.'

It was on the tip of the DI's tongue to ask this man if he had ever loved his wife, but he decided against it. Whatever answer Sumner gave, he wouldn't believe him. He felt the same instinctive dislike of William that Sandy Griffiths felt, but he couldn't decide if it was a chemical antipathy or a natural revulsion that was inspired by his own unshakeable hunch that William had killed his wife.

Galbraith's next port of call was The Old Convent, Osborne Crescent in Chichester where Mrs Sumner senior lived in sheltered accommodation at number two. It had obviously been a school once but was now converted into a dozen small flats with a resident warden. Before he went in, he stared across the road at the solidly rectangular 1930s semi-detached houses on the other side, wondering idly which had been the Sumners' before it was sold to buy Langton Cottage. They were all so similar that it was impossible to say, and he had a sneaking sympathy for Kate's desire to move. Being respectable, he thought, wasn't necessarily synonymous with being boring.

Angela Sumner surprised him because she wasn't what he was expecting. He had pictured an autocratic old snob with reactionary views, and found instead a tough, gutsy woman, wheelchair-bound by rheumatoid arthritis, but with eyes that brimmed with good humour. She told him to put his warrant card through her letter-flap before she'd allow him entrance, then made him follow her electrically operated chair down the corridor into the sitting room. 'I suppose you've given William the third degree,' she said, 'and now you're expecting me to confirm or deny what he's told you.'

'Have you spoken to him?' asked Galbraith with a smile.

She nodded, pointing to a chair. 'He phoned me yesterday evening to tell me that Kate was dead.'

He took the chair she indicated. 'Did he tell you how she died?'

She nodded. 'It shocked me, although to be honest I guessed something dreadful must have happened the minute I saw Hannah's picture on the television. Kate would never have abandoned the child. She doted on her.'

'Why didn't you phone the police yourself when you recognized Hannah's photograph?' he asked curiously. 'Why did you ask William to do it?'

She sighed. 'Because I kept telling myself it couldn't possibly be Hannah – I mean, she's such an unlikely child to be wandering around a strange town on her own – and I didn't want to appear to be causing trouble if it wasn't. I phoned Langton Cottage over and over again and it was only when it became clear yesterday morning that no one was going to answer that I phoned William's secretary and she told me where he was.'

'What kind of trouble would you have been causing?'

She didn't answer immediately. 'Let's just say Kate wouldn't have believed my motives were pure if I made a genuine error. You see, I haven't seen Hannah since they moved twelve months ago, so I wasn't 100 per cent sure I was right anyway. Children change so quickly at that age.'

It wasn't much of an answer, but Galbraith let it go for the moment. 'So you didn't know William had gone to Liverpool?'

'There's no reason why I should. I don't expect him

to tell me where he is all the time. He rings once a week and drops in occasionally on his way back to Lymington, but we don't live in each other's pockets.'

'That's quite a change, though, isn't it?' suggested Galbraith. 'Didn't you and he share a house before he was married?'

She gave a little laugh. 'And you think that means I knew what he was doing? You obviously don't have grown-up children, Inspector. It makes no difference whether they live with you or not, you still can't keep tabs on them.'

'I have a seven- and five-year-old who already have a more exciting social life than I've ever had. It gets worse, does it?'

'It depends on whether you approve of them spreading their wings. I think the more space you give them, the more likely they are to appreciate you as they get older. In any case, my husband converted the house into two self-contained flats about fifteen years ago. He and I lived downstairs, and William lived upstairs, and days could go by without our paths crossing. We lived quite separate lives, which didn't change much even after my husband died. I became more disabled, of course, but I hope I was never a burden to William.'

Galbraith smiled. 'I'm sure you weren't, but it must have been a bit of a worry, knowing he'd get married one day and all the arrangements would have to change.'

She shook her head. 'Quite the reverse. I was longing for him to settle down but he never showed any inclination to do it. He adored sailing, of course, and spent most of his free time out on his Contessa. He had girlfriends, but none that he took seriously.'

'Were you pleased when he married Kate?'

There was a short silence. 'Why wouldn't I be?'

Galbraith shrugged. 'No reason. I'm just interested.'

Her eyes twinkled suddenly. 'I suppose he's told you I thought his wife was a gold-digger?'

'Yes.'

'Good,' she said. 'I hate having to tell lies.' She raised the back of a gnarled hand to her cheek to wipe away a stray hair. 'In any case there's no point pretending I was happy about it when anyone round here will tell you I wasn't. She *was* a gold-digger, but that wasn't why I thought he was mad to marry her. It was because they had so little in common. She was ten years younger than he was, virtually uneducated and completely besotted by all the material things in life. She told me once that what she really enjoyed in life was *shopping*.' She shook her head in bewilderment that anything so mundane could produce a height of sensation. 'Frankly, I couldn't see what was going to keep them together. She wasn't remotely interested in sailing and refused point-blank to have anything to do with that side of William's life.'

'Did he go on sailing after they married?'

'Oh, yes. She didn't have a problem with him doing it, she just wouldn't go herself.'

'Did she get to know any of his sailing friends?'

'Not in the way you mean,' she said bluntly.

'What way's that, Mrs Sumner?'

'William said you think she was having an affair.'

'We can't ignore the possibility.'

'Oh, I think you can, you know.' She gave him an old-fashioned look. 'Kate knew the price of everything and the value of nothing, and she'd certainly have calculated the cost of adultery in terms of what she'd lose if William found out about it. In any case, she wouldn't have been having an affair with any of William's sailing friends in Chichester. They were all far more shocked by his choice of wife than I was. She made no effort to fit in, you see, plus there was a generation gap between her and most of them. Frankly, they were all completely bemused by her rather inane conversation. She had no opinions on anything except soap operas, pop music and film stars.'

'So what was her attraction for William? He's an intelligent man and certainly doesn't give the impression of someone who likes inane conversation.'

A resigned smile. 'Sex, of course. He'd had his fill of intelligent women. I remember him saying that the girlfriend before Kate' – she sighed – 'her name was Wendy Plater and she was such a nice girl . . . so suitable . . . that her idea of foreplay was to discuss the effects of sexual activity on the metabolism. I said, how interesting, and William laughed and said, given the choice, he preferred physical stimulation.'

Galbraith kept a straight face. 'I don't think he's alone, Mrs Sumner.'

'I'm not going to argue the point, Inspector. In any case, Kate was obviously far more experienced than he was even though she was ten years younger. She knew William wanted a family and she gave him a baby before you could say Jack Robinson.' He heard the reservation in her voice, and wondered about it. 'Her approach to marriage was to spoil her husband rotten, and William revelled in it. He didn't have to do a damn thing except take himself to work every day. It was the most old-fashioned arrangement you can imagine, with the wife as chief admirer and bottle-washer and the husband swanking around as bread-winner. I think it's what's known as a passive–aggressive relationship where the woman controls the man by making him dependent on her while giving the impression she's dependent on him.'

'And you didn't approve?'

'Only because it wasn't my idea of a marriage. Marriage should be a meeting of minds as well as bodies otherwise it becomes a waste ground where nothing grows. All she could talk about with any enthusiasm were her shopping expeditions and who she'd bumped into during the day, and it was quite clear William never listened to a word she said.'

He wondered if she realized William had yet to be eliminated as a suspect. 'So what are you saying? That he was bored with her?'

She gave his question long consideration. 'No, I don't think he was bored,' she said then, 'I think he just realized he could take her for granted. That's why his working day got progressively longer and why he didn't object to the move to Lymington. She approved of whatever he did, you see, so he didn't have to bother spending time with her. There was no challenge in the relationship.' She paused. 'I hoped children would be something they could share, but Kate appropriated Hannah at birth as something that was the preserve of women, and if I'm honest the poor little thing created even more distance between them. She used to roar her head off every time William tried to pick her up, and he soon got bored with her. I took Kate to task about it, as a matter of fact, told her she wasn't doing the child any good by swamping her in mother love, but it only made her angry with me.' She sighed. 'I shouldn't have interfered. It's what drove them away of course.'

'From Chichester?'

'Yes. It was a mistake. They made too many changes in their lives too quickly. William had to pay off the mortgage on my flat when he sold the house across the road, then take out a much larger one to buy Langton Cottage. He sold his boat, gave up sailing. Not to mention flogging himself to death driving to and from work every day. And all for what? A house he didn't even like very much.'

Galbraith was careful to keep the interest out of his voice. 'Then why did they move?'

'Kate wanted it.'

'But if they weren't getting on, why did William agree to it?'

'Regular sex,' she said crossly. 'In any case, I didn't say they weren't getting on.'

'You said he was taking her for granted. Isn't it the same thing?'

'Not at all. From William's point of view she was the perfect wife. She kept house for him, provided him with children and never pestered him once to put himself out.' Her mouth twisted into a bitter smile. 'They got on like a house on fire as long as he paid the mortgage and kept her in the manner to which she was rapidly becoming accustomed. I know you're not supposed to say these things any more but she was awfully common. The few friends she made were quite dreadful . . . loud . . . over made-up . . .' She shuddered. 'Dreadful!'

Galbraith pressed his fingertips together beneath his chin and studied her with open curiosity. 'You really didn't like her, did you?'

Again Mrs Sumner considered the question carefully. 'No, I didn't,' she said then. 'Not because she was overtly unpleasant or unkind, but because she was the most self-centred woman I've ever met. If everything – and I do *mean* everything – in life wasn't revolving around her she manoeuvred and manipulated until it did. Look at Hannah if you don't believe me. Why encourage the child to be so dependent on her unless she couldn't bear to compete for her affections?'

Galbraith thought of the photographs in Langton Cottage, and his own conclusion that Kate Sumner was vain. 'If it wasn't an affair that went wrong, then what do you think happened? What persuaded her to take Hannah on board someone's boat when she hated sailing so much?'

'What a strange question,' the woman said in surprise. '*Nothing* would have persuaded her. She was obviously forced on board. Why should you doubt that? Anyone who was prepared to rape and kill her then leave her child to wander the streets alone would obviously have no qualms about using threats to coerce her.'

'Except marinas and harbours are busy places and there have been no reports of anyone seeing a woman and child being put on board a boat against their will.' Indeed, as far as the police had been able to establish so far, there had been no sightings of Kate and Hannah Sumner at all at any of the access points to boats along the Lymington River. They hoped for better luck on Saturday when the weekenders returned but, meanwhile, they were working in the dark.

'I don't suppose there would have been,' said Angela Sumner stoutly, 'not if the man was carrying Hannah and threatening to hurt her if Kate didn't do what he said. She loved that child to distraction. She'd have done anything to prevent her being harmed.'

Galbraith was about to point out that such a scenario would have depended on Hannah's willingness to be carried by a man, which seemed unlikely in view of the psychiatric report and Angela Sumner's own admission that she screamed her head off every time her own father tried to pick her up, but he had second thoughts. The logic was sound even if the method had varied . . . Hannah had obviously been sedated . . .

Chapter Eleven

Memo

To: Detective Superintendent Carpenter
From: Detective Inspector Galbraith
Date: 12.8.97 – 9.15 p.m.
Re: **Kate & William Sumner**

Thought you'd be interested in the enclosed report/ statements. Of the various issues raised, the most telling seem to be:

1. Kate made few friends and those she had came from her own milieu.
2. She appears to have had little interest in her husband's friends/pursuits.
3. There are some unflattering descriptions of her – i.e.: manipulative, sly, deceitful, malicious.
4. William is under stress over money worries.
5. The 'dream house' was clearly Kate's idea but the consensus view is that William made a mistake buying it.

6. Finally, what on earth was the attraction? Did he marry her because she was pregnant?

Some interesting vibes, don't you think?

Witness statement: James Purdy,
Managing Director, Pharmatec UK

I've known William Sumner since he joined the company fifteen years ago at the age of twenty-five. I recruited him myself from Southampton University where he worked as an assistant to Professor Hugh Buglass after gaining his MSc. William led the research into two of our pharmaceutical drugs – Antiac and Counterac – which between them represent 12 per cent of the antacid market. He is a valued and valuable member of the team and is well respected in his profession. Until his marriage to Kate Hill in 1994 I would have described William as the eternal bachelor. He had an active social life but his real interests were work and sailing. I remember him telling me once that a wife would never allow him the sort of freedom his mother did. Various young women set their caps at him over the years but he was adroit at avoiding entanglement. I was surprised therefore when I heard that he and Kate Hill were planning to get married. She worked at Pharmatec for some twelve months in '93/'94. I was extremely sorry to hear about her death and have authorized extended leave for William while he comes to terms with his loss and sorts out the care of his daughter. As far as I am aware William was in Liverpool during the weekend of 9/10 August, although I had no contact with him after he left on the morning of Thursday, 7 August. I barely knew Kate Hill-Sumner while

she was here and have not seen or heard from her
since she left.

James Purdy

Witness statement: Michael Sprate, Services Manager, Pharmatec UK

Kate Hill-Sumner worked as part of my team from May
'93 to March '94 when she left the company. She had
no shorthand but her typing skills were above average.
I had one or two problems with her, principally in
relation to her behaviour. This could be very disruptive
at times. She had a sharp tongue and was not averse
to using it against the other secretaries. I would
describe her as a bully who had no qualms about
spreading malicious gossip in order to undermine
someone she had taken a dislike to. She became particularly difficult after her marriage to William Sumner
which she clearly felt gave her an elevated status and,
had she not decided to leave voluntarily, I would certainly have sought to have her transferred from my
department. I know William only slightly, so cannot
comment on their relationship as I have not seen or
heard from Kate since she left Pharmatec UK. I know
nothing about her death.

Michael Sprate

Witness statement: Simon Trew, Manager, R & D, Pharmatec UK

William Sumner is one of our leading scientists. His most successful research resulted in Antiac and Counterac. We are optimistic that something may come of the project he is working on at the moment, although he has hinted for some time now that he might be leaving us to work for one of our competitors. I believe the pressure to move has been coming from his wife. William took on an expensive mortgage some twelve months ago which he is having trouble honouring and the increase in salary we can offer him does not match the offer from elsewhere. All our employee contracts contain indemnity clauses relating to the unauthorized use of research ideas funded by Pharmatec UK, so if he decides to leave his research will remain with the company. I understand that he is reluctant to abandon the project at what he believes to be a crucial point, however his financial commitments may force his hand sooner than he would like. I have never met Kate Sumner. I joined the company two years after she left, and my relationship with William has always been strictly professional. I admire his experience and expertise but I find him difficult to get on with. He carries a permanent chip on his shoulder because he sees himself as undervalued, and this causes friction within the department. I can confirm that William left for Liverpool on the morning of Thursday, 7 August and that I spoke to him by telephone shortly before he delivered his paper on the afternoon of Friday, 8 August. He appeared to be in good spirits and confirmed a meeting with me for 10.00 a.m. on Tuesday, 12 August. In the event the meeting did not take place. I know nothing about Mrs Sumner's death.

Simon Trew

Witness statement: Wendy Plater, Research Scientist,
Pharmatec UK

I've known William Sumner for five years. We were very
close when I first joined the company, and I visited him
and his mother in Chichester and also went sailing
once or twice on his boat. He was a quiet man with a
dry sense of humour, and we spent some pleasant
times together. He always told me he wasn't the marrying kind, so I was very surprised when I heard that
Kate Hill had hooked him. If I'm honest, I thought he
had better taste, although I don't think he stood a
chance once she set her sights on him. There is
nothing nice I can say about her. She was uneducated,
vulgar, manipulative and deceitful, and she was out for
anything and everything she could get. I knew her
quite well before she married and I disliked her
intensely. She was a stirrer and a malicious gossiper,
and she was never happier than when she was pulling
people down to her own level or below. Lying was
second nature to her and she told some appalling lies
about me for which I have never forgiven her. The sad
part is William changed for the worse after his marriage. He's been a right bitch since he moved to
Lymington, constantly complaining about the people
he works with, disrupting team spirit and whingeing
on about how he's been cheated by the company. He
made a mistake selling his boat and taking on a huge
mortgage, and he's been venting his spleen on his
work colleagues. I believe Kate to have been a terrible

influence on him; however, I cannot conceive of a single circumstance that would have caused William to have anything to do with her death. The impression I have always had is that he was genuinely fond of her. I was at a disco on Saturday night, 9 August, with my partner, Michael Sprate. I haven't seen or heard from Kate Sumner since she left Pharmatec UK and I know nothing about her murder.

Wendy Plater

Witness statement: Polly Garrard, Secretary, Services,
Pharmatec UK

I knew Kate Hill very well. She and I shared an office
for ten months while she worked in Services. I felt sorry
for her. She had a hell of a life before she moved to
Portsmouth. She lived on a run-down council estate in
Birmingham, and she and her mother used to barricade
themselves behind their front door because they were
so terrified of the other tenants. I think her mother
worked in a shop and I think Kate learnt her typing
while she was still at school, but I can't swear to either.
I remember she told me once that she had been
working in a bank before her mother died and that
they'd sacked her because she took time off to care for
her ma. On another occasion she said she resigned
voluntarily in order to nurse her mother. I don't know
which story is true. She didn't talk much about her life
in Birmingham except to say it was pretty rough. She
was okay. I liked her. Everyone else thought she was a
bit sly – you know, out for what she could get – but I
just saw her as an incredibly vulnerable person who
was looking for security. It's true she took against
people and picked up bits of gossip about them and
spread them around, but I'm not convinced she did it
from malice. I think it made her feel better about herself
to know that other people weren't perfect. I visited her
a couple of times after she and William got married,
and on both occasions her mother-in-law was there.
Mrs Sumner Snr. was very rude. Kate married the son,

not the mother, so what business was it of hers if Kate talked with a Brummie accent and held her knife like a pencil? She was always lecturing Kate on how to bring up little Hannah and how to be a good wife, but as far as I could see she was making a success of both without any interference from anyone. The best thing she did was move to Lymington, and I'm really upset she's dead. I haven't seen her for over a year and I know nothing about her murder.

Polly Garrard

Addendum to report on Hannah Sumner ('Baby Smith') following conversation with William Sumner (father) and telephone conversation with Dr Attwater, GP

Physical: As before.

Psychological: Both father and doctor agree that Hannah's mother was overprotective and would not allow her to develop naturally by playing with other children or by being allowed to explore her own environment and make mistakes. She had some contact with a mothers' and toddlers' group but, as Hannah's play tends to be aggressive, her mother chose <u>less</u> exposure to other children rather than <u>more</u> as a means of dealing with it. Hannah's 'withdrawal' is manipulative rather than frightened, and her 'fear' of men has everything to do with the sympathetic reaction it inspires in women and nothing to do with any real terror. Both father and doctor describe Hannah as being of below-average intellect, and blame both this and her mother's overprotectiveness for her poor verbal skills. Dr Attwater has not seen Hannah since her mother's death; however, he is confident that my assessment of her does not differ materially from the assessment he made six months ago.

Conclusions: While I am prepared to accept that Hannah's backward development (which I believe to be serious) may not be due to any recent event, I can only reiterate that this child's welfare must be continuously monitored. Without supervision, I consider it probable that Hannah will suffer psychological, emotional and physical neglect as William Sumner (father) is immature, lacks parental skills and appears to have little affection for his daughter.

Dr Janet Murray

Chapter Twelve

STEVEN HARDING WAS released without charge shortly before 9.00 a.m. on Wednesday, 13 August 1997, when the review officer declined to authorize his continued detention due to lack of evidence. However, he was informed that both his car and his boat would be retained for 'as long as is necessary'. No further explanation was offered for their retention. With the co-operation of the Hampshire Constabulary, he was remanded on police bail to twenty-three Old Street, Lymington, the house of Anthony Bridges, and was ordered to present himself at Lymington police station daily so that a regular check could be kept on his movements.

On the advice of a solicitor, he had made a detailed statement about his relationship with Kate Sumner and his movements over the weekend of 9/10 August, although it added little to what he had already told the police. He explained the fingerprint evidence and the presence of Hannah's shoes on *Crazy Daze* in the following manner:

> They came on board in March when I had the boat
> lifted out of the water to clean and repaint the hull.

Crazy Daze was in Berthon's yard, sitting on a wooden cradle, and when Kate realized I couldn't get away from her because I had to finish the painting, she kept coming to the yard and hanging around, making a nuisance of herself and irritating me. In the end, just to get rid of her, I agreed to let her and Hannah climb the ladder and look at the inside while I stayed below. I told them to take their shoes off and leave them in the cockpit. When the time came for them to climb down again, Kate decided Hannah couldn't manage the ladder so lowered her down to me instead. I strapped Hannah into her buggy but I didn't notice whether or not she was wearing shoes. To be honest I never look at her much. She gives me the creeps. She never says anything, just stares at me as if I'm not there. Some time later I found some shoes in the cockpit with H. SUMNER written on the strap. Even if they were too small to be the ones Hannah was wearing that day, I have no other explanation for their presence there.

Although I knew where the Sumners lived, I did not return Hannah's shoes because I was sure that Kate had left them there deliberately. I did not like Kate Sumner and I did not want to be alone with her in her house because I knew she had a serious crush on me which I did not reciprocate. She was very peculiar and her constant pestering worried me. I can only describe her behaviour as harassment. She used to hang around by the yacht club waiting for me to come ashore in my dinghy. Most of the time she just stood and watched me, but sometimes she'd deliberately bump into me and rub her breasts against my arm. The mistake I made was to visit Langton Cottage with her husband shortly after she introduced me to him in the street at the end of last year. I believe that was the beginning of her infatuation. At no time was I inclined to respond to her advances.

Some time later, at the end of April, I think, I was moored up to the Berthon fuelling pontoon, waiting for the dockie to come and operate the pump, when Kate and Hannah walked down 'C' pontoon towards me. Kate said she hadn't seen me for a while but had spotted *Crazy Daze* and felt like a chat. She and Hannah came on board without invitation which annoyed me. I suggested Kate go into the aft cabin to retrieve Hannah's shoes from the port shelf. I knew there were some clothes belonging to other women in the cabin and I thought it would be a good thing if Kate saw them. I hoped it would make her realize that I wasn't interested in her. She left soon afterwards and when I went into the cabin, I found she'd taken off Hannah's nappy, which was dirty, and had ground the mess into the bedclothes. She had also left the shoes behind again. I believe both acts were done deliberately to show me that she was angry about the women's underclothes in the cabin.

I became seriously concerned about Kate Sumner's harassment of me when she found out where I parked my car and took to setting off the alarm to get Tony Bridges and his neighbours riled with me. I have no proof it was Kate who was doing it, although I am sure it must have been because I kept finding faeces smeared on the driver's handle. I did not tell the police about my suspicions because I was afraid of becoming even more involved with the Sumner family. Instead I sought out William Sumner some time in June and showed him photographs of myself in a gay magazine because I wanted him to tell his wife I was gay. I realize this must seem odd after I had shown Kate evidence that I entertain girlfriends on board *Crazy Daze* but I was becoming desperate. Some of the photographs were quite explicit and William was shocked by them. I don't know what he told his wife but, to my relief, she stopped harassing me almost immediately.

I have seen her in the street maybe five times since June but did not speak to her until the morning of Saturday, 9 August, when I realized I couldn't avoid her. She was outside Tesco's, and we said good morning to each other. She told me she was looking for some sandals for Hannah, and I said I was in a hurry to get off because I was sailing to Poole for the weekend. That was the extent of our conversation. I did not see her again. I admit that I was very aggrieved by her persecution of me, and developed a strong dislike for her, but I have no idea how she came to drown in the sea off the Dorset coast.

A long interview with Tony Bridges produced a corroborative statement. As DS Campbell had predicted, Bridges was known to the Lymington police as a cannabis user but they took a tolerant view of it. 'Once in a while his neighbours complain when he has a party in there, but it's alcohol that makes them raucous, not cannabis, and even the blue-rinse brigade are finally beginning to realize that.' Rather more surprisingly, he was also a respected chemistry teacher at one of the local schools. 'What Tony does in the privacy of his home is his own affair,' said his headmaster. 'As far as I'm concerned, the policing of my colleagues' morals outside school hours isn't part of my job description. If it were, I would probably lose some of my better staff. Tony's an inspirational teacher who enthuses children in a difficult subject. I have a lot of time for him.'

I've known Steven Harding for eighteen years. We attended the same primary and secondary schools and have been friends ever since. He sleeps in my house when his boat's out of commission or during the winter when it's too cold for him to stay on board. I used to know his parents quite well before they moved to Cornwall in 1991 but I have not seen them since. Steve sailed down to Falmouth two summers ago but I don't believe he's made any other visits to Cornwall. He divides his life between his flat in London and his boat in Lymington.

He told me on more than one occasion this year that he was having problems with a woman called Kate Sumner who was stalking him. He described her and her child as weird, and said they scared him. His car alarm kept going off and he told me he thought it was Kate Sumner who was activating it and asked me if he should report it to the police. It was a pretty odd story so I wasn't sure whether to believe him or not. Then he pointed out the faeces on the car door handle and told me how Kate Sumner had wiped her child's nappy on his sheets. I told him that if he brought the police into it it would get worse rather than better and suggested he find somewhere else to park his car. As far as I know, that sorted the problem.

I have never spoken to Kate or Hannah Sumner. Steve pointed them out to me once in the middle of Lymington then dragged me round a corner so we wouldn't have to speak to them. His reluctance was genuine. I believe he found her seriously intimidating. I met William Sumner once in a pub at the beginning of this year. He was drinking alone and invited Steve and me to join him. He knew Steve already because they'd been introduced to each other by Kate after Steve had helped her with her shopping. I left after about half an hour, but Steve told me later that he went back to William's house to continue a discussion they were having about sailing. He said William used to race a Contessa and was interesting to talk to.

Steve's a good-looking bloke and has an active sex life. He has at least two girls on the go at the same time because he's not interested in settling down. He's obsessed with sailing and told me once that he could never get serious about anyone who didn't sail. He's not the kiss-and-tell type and, as I never listen to names, I've no idea who he's got on the go at the moment. When he's not acting, he can always get regular work as a photographic model. Mostly he models clothes, but he's done a few sessions for pornographic magazines. He needs money to fund the flat in London and keep *Crazy Daze* afloat, and that kind of work pays well. He's not ashamed of the photographs but I've never known him show them around. I've no idea where he stores them.

I saw Steve on the evening of Friday, 8 August. He dropped in to tell me he was off to Poole the next day and wouldn't see me again until the following weekend. He mentioned that he had an audition in London on Monday, 11 August, and said he was planning to catch the last train back on Sunday night. Later, a mutual friend, Bob Winterslow, who lives near the station, told me that Steve had rung from his boat to ask if he could borrow a sofa Sunday night in order to catch the first train on Monday morning. In the event he stayed on board and missed his audition. This is standard for Steve. He tends to come and go as he pleases. I became aware that Steve had cocked up when his agent, Graham Barlow, phoned me on Monday morning to say there was no sign of Steve in London and he wasn't answering his mobile phone. I phoned friends to see if anyone knew where he was, then borrowed a dinghy to go out to *Crazy Daze*. I discovered that Steve was badly hungover, and that this was the reason for his non-appearance.

I spent the weekend, 9/10 August, with my girlfriend Beatrice 'Bibi' Gould whom I've known for four months. On Saturday night we went to a 'rave' at the Jamaica Club in Southampton, returning home at approximately 4.00 a.m. We slept through till some time Sunday p.m. I know nothing about Kate Sumner's death, although I am completely sure that Steven Harding had nothing to do with it. He is not an aggressive person.

(<u>Police note</u>: this rave certainly took place, but there is no way of checking whether A. Bridges & B. Gould were present. Rough estimate of numbers at the Jamaica Club on Saturday night: 1,000+.)

Beatrice Gould's statement supported Bridges' and Harding's in all relevant details.

I'm nineteen years old and I work as a hairdresser in Get Ahead in Lymington High Street. I met Tony Bridges at a pub disco about four months ago and he introduced me to Steve Harding a week later. They've been friends for a long time and Steve uses Tony's house as a base in Lymington when he can't stay on his boat for any reason. I've come to know Steve quite well over the time Tony and I have been together. Several of my friends would like to go out with him but he's not interested in settling down and tends to avoid heavy relationships. He's a good-looking bloke and, because he's an actor as well, girls throw themselves at him. He told me once that he thinks they see him as a stud, and that he really hates it. I know he's had a lot of problems in that way with Kate Sumner. He was nice to her once, and afterwards she wouldn't leave him alone. He said he thought she was lonely but that didn't give her the right to make his life a misery. It got to the point that he'd hide behind corners while Tony or I checked to see if she was on the other side. I think she must have been mentally disturbed. The worst thing she did was smear her daughter's dirty nappies on his car. I thought that was completely disgusting and told Steve that he should report her to the police.

I didn't see Steve the weekend of 9/10 August. I went to Tony's house at 4.30 p.m. on Saturday, 9 August, and at about 7.30 p.m. we left for the Jamaica Club in Southampton. We go there a lot because Daniel Agee is a brilliant DJ and we really like his style. I stayed at Tony's until 10.00 p.m. on Sunday night then went home. My permanent address is sixty-seven Shorn Street, Lymington, where I live with my parents but I spend most weekends and some weekday nights with Tony Bridges. I like Steve Harding a lot and I don't believe he had anything to do with Kate Sumner's death. He and I get on really well together.

Detective Superintendent Carpenter sat in silence while John Galbraith read through all three statements. 'What do you think?' he asked when the other had finished. 'Does Harding's story ring true? Is that a Kate Sumner you recognize?'

Galbraith shook his head. 'I don't know. I haven't got a feel for her yet. She was like Harding, a bit of a chameleon, play-acted different roles to suit different people.' He reflected for a moment. 'I suppose one thing in Harding's defence is that when she rubbed someone up the wrong way she did it in spades – really got under their skin in other words. Did you read those statements I sent you? Her mother-in-law didn't like her at all, and neither did Wendy Plater, William's ex-girlfriend, who was cut out of the running by Kate. You could argue it was straightforward jealousy on both counts, but I got the impression there was more to it than that. They used the same word to describe her. Manipulative. Angela Sumner referred to her as the most self-centred and calculating woman she had ever met, and the girlfriend said lying was second nature to her. William said she was single-minded about what she wanted and had him wound round her finger from the first time she met him.' He shrugged. 'Whether any of that means she was stalking a man she became infatuated with, I don't know. I wouldn't have expected her to be so blatant but' – he spread his hands in perplexity – 'she was pretty blatant in her pursuit of a comfortable lifestyle.'

'I hate these cases, John,' said Carpenter with genuine regret. 'The poor little woman's dead but her character's going to be blackened whichever way you look at it.' He pulled Harding's statement across the desk towards him and drummed his fingers on it in irritation. 'Shall I tell you what this smells of to me? The classic defence against rape. *She was panting for it, guv. Couldn't keep her hands off me. I just gave her what she wanted and it's not my fault if she cried foul afterwards. She was an aggressive woman and she liked aggressive sex.*' His frown deepened to a chasm. 'All Harding's doing is laying some neat groundwork in case we manage to bring charges against him. Then he'll tell us her death was an accident . . . she fell off the back of the boat and he couldn't save her.'

'What did you make of Anthony Bridges?'

'I didn't like him. He's a cocky little bastard, and a damn sight too knowledgeable about police interviews.

175

But his and his blousy girlfriend's stories tally so closely with Harding's that, unless they're operating some sort of sick conspiracy, I think we have to accept they're telling the truth.' A sudden smile banished his frown. 'For the moment anyway. It'll be interesting to see if anything changes after he and Harding have had a chance to talk together. You know we've bailed him to Bridges' address.'

'Harding's right about one thing,' said Galbraith thoughtfully. 'Hannah gives *me* the creeps, too.' He leaned forward, elbows on knees, a troubled expression on his face. 'It's codswallop about her screaming every time she sees a man. I was waiting for her father to bring me some lists he'd made, and she came into the room, sat down on the carpet in front of me and started to play with herself. She had no knickers on, just pulled up her dress and got going like there was no tomorrow. She was watching me the whole time she was doing it, and I swear to God she knew exactly what she was about.' He sighed. 'It was bloody unnerving, and I'll eat my hat if she hasn't been introduced to some sort of sexual activity, whatever that doctor said.'

'Meaning you've got your money on Sumner?'

Galbraith considered for a moment. 'Put it this way, I'd say he's a dead cert if, one: his alibi doesn't check out and, two: I can work out how he managed to have a boat waiting for him off the Isle of Purbeck.' His pleasant face broke into a smile. 'He gets under my skin something rotten, probably because he thinks he's so

176

damned clever. It's hardly scientific but, yes, I'd put my money on him any day before Steven Harding.'

For seventy-two hours, local and national newspapers had been carrying reports of a murder inquiry following the finding of a body on a beach on the Isle of Purbeck. On the theory that the dead woman and her daughter had been travelling by boat, sailors between South- ampton and Weymouth were being asked to come forward with any sightings of a small, blonde woman and/or a three-year-old child on the weekend of 9/10 August. During her lunch break that Wednesday, a shop assistant in one of the big department stores in Bourne- mouth went into her local police station and suggested diffidently that, while she didn't want to waste anyone's time, she thought that something she'd seen on Sunday evening might be connected to the woman's murder.

She gave her name as Jennifer Hale and said she'd been on a Fairline Squadron called *Gregory's Girl* belonging to a Poole businessman called Gregory Free- mantle.

'He's my boyfriend,' she explained.

The desk sergeant found the description amusing. She'd never see thirty again, and he wondered how old the boyfriend was. Approaching fifty, he guessed, if he could afford to own a Fairline Squadron.

'I wanted Gregory to come and tell you about it himself,' she confided, 'because he could have given you a better idea of where it was, but he said it wasn't worth the bother because I didn't have enough experience to know what I was looking at. He believes his daughters, you see. They said it was an oil drum and woe betide anyone who disagrees with them. He won't argue with them in case they complain to their mother when what he ought to be doing . . .' She heaved the kind of sigh that every potential stepmother has sighed down the ages. 'They're a couple of little madams, frankly. I thought we should have stopped at the time to investigate but' – she shook her head – 'it wasn't worth going into battle over. Frankly, I'd had enough for one day.'

The desk sergeant who had stepchildren of his own gave her a sympathetic smile. 'How old are they?'

'Fifteen and thirteen.'

'Difficult ages.'

'Yes, particularly when their parents . . .' She stopped abruptly, reconsidering how much she wanted to say.

'It'll get better in about five years when they've grown up a bit.'

A gleam of humour flashed in her eyes. 'Assuming I'm around to find out, which at the moment doesn't look likely. The younger one's not too bad, but I'd need a skin like a rhinoceros to put up with another five years of Marie. She thinks she's Elle McPherson and Claudia Schiffer rolled into one, and throws a tantrum if she isn't being constantly petted and spoilt. Still . . .' She returned to her reason for being there. 'I'm sure it wasn't an oil drum. I was sitting at the back of the flying bridge and had a better view than the others. Whatever it was, it wasn't metal . . . although it *was* black . . . it looked to me like an upturned dinghy . . . a rubber one.

I think it may have been partially deflated because it was pretty low in the water.'

The desk sergeant was taking notes. 'Why do you think it was connected with the murder?' he asked her.

She gave an embarrassed smile, afraid of making a fool of herself. 'Because it was a boat,' she said, 'and it wasn't far from where the body was found. We were in Chapman's Pool when the woman was lifted off by helicopter, and we passed the dinghy only about ten minutes after we rounded St Alban's Head on our way home. I've worked out that the time must have been about 6.15 and I know we were travelling at twenty-five knots because my boyfriend commented on the fact as we rounded the Head. He says you'll be looking for a yacht or a cruiser but I thought – well – you can drown off a dinghy just as easily as off a yacht, can't you? And this one had obviously capsized.'

Carpenter received the report from Bournemouth at three o'clock, mulled it over in conjunction with a map, then sent it through to Galbraith with a note attached.

Is this worth following up? If it hasn't beached between St Alban's Head and Anvil Point, then it'll have gone down in deep water somewhere off Swanage and is irretrievable. However, the timings seem very precise so, assuming it washed up before Anvil Point, your friend Ingram can probably work out where it is. You said he was wasted as a beat copper. Failing him, get on to the coastguards. In fact it might be worth going to them

*first. You know how they hate having their thunder
stolen by landlubbers. It's a long shot – can't see where
Hannah fits in or how anyone can rape a woman in a
dinghy without turning turtle – but you never know. It
could be that boat off the Isle of Purbeck you wanted.*

In the event the coastguards happily passed the buck to
Ingram, claiming they had better things to do at the
height of the summer season than look for 'imaginary'
dinghies in unlikely places. Equally sceptical himself,
Ingram parked at Durlston Head and set off along the
coastal path, following the route Harding claimed to
have taken the previous Sunday. He walked slowly,
searching the shoreline at the foot of the cliffs every fifty
yards through binoculars. He was as conscious as the
coastguards of the difficulties of isolating a black dinghy
against the glistening rocks that lined the base of the
headland, and constantly re-examined stretches he had
already decided were clear. He also had little faith in his
own estimate that a floating object seen at approximately
6.15 p.m. on Sunday evening, some three hundred yards
out from Seacombe Cliff – his guess at where a Fairline
Squadron might have been after ten minutes travelling
at twenty-five knots from St Alban's Head – could have
beached approximately six hours later halfway between
Blackers Hole and Anvil Point. He knew how unpredictable the sea was, and how very unlikely it was that a
partially deflated dinghy would even have come ashore.
The more probable scenario was that it was halfway to

180

France by now – always assuming it had ever existed – or twenty fathoms under.

He found it slightly to the east of where he had predicted, nearer to Anvil Point, and he smiled with justifiable satisfaction as the powerful lenses picked it out. It was upside down, held in shape by its wooden floor and seats, and neatly stranded on an inaccessible piece of shore. He dialled through to DI Galbraith on his mobile. 'How good a sailor are you?' he asked him. 'Because the only way you'll get close to this little mother is by boat. If you meet me in Swanage I can take you out this evening. You'll need waterproofs and waders,' he warned. 'It'll be a wet trip.'

Ingram invited along a couple of friends from the Swanage lifeboat crew to keep *Miss Creant* on station while he took Galbraith into the shore in his own inflatable. He killed the outboard motor and swung it up out of the water thirty yards from land, using his oars to manoeuvre them carefully through the crops of jagged granite that lay in wait for unwary sailors. He steadied the little craft against a good-sized rock, nodded to Galbraith to get out and start wading, then followed him into the water and used the painter to guide the lightened dinghy on to what passed for a beach in that desolate spot.

'There she is,' he said, jerking his head to the left while he lifted his inflatable clear of the waterline, 'but God only knows what she's doing out here. People don't abandon perfectly good dinghies for no reason.'

181

Galbraith shook his head in amazement. 'How the hell did you spot it?' he asked, gazing up at the sheer cliffs above them and thinking it must have been like looking for a needle in a haystack.

'It wasn't easy,' Ingram admitted, leading the way towards it. 'More to the point, how the hell did it survive the rocks?' He stooped over the upturned hull. 'It must have come in like this or its bottom would have been ripped out, and that means there won't be anything left inside. Still' – he raised an enquiring eyebrow – 'shall we turn it over?'

With a nod, Galbraith grasped the stern board while Ingram took a tuck in the rubber at the bow. They set it right way up with difficulty because the lack of air meant there was no rigidity in the structure and it collapsed in on itself like a deflated balloon. A tiny crab scuttled out from underneath and slipped into a nearby rock pool. As Ingram had predicted, there was nothing inside except the wooden floorboards and the remains of a wooden seat which had snapped in the middle, probably on its journey to and fro across the rocks. Nevertheless, it was a substantial dinghy, about ten feet long and four feet wide with its stern board intact.

Ingram pointed to the indentations where the screw clamps of an outboard motor had bitten into the wood, then squatted on his haunches to examine two metal rings screwed into the transom planking aft, and a single ring screwed into the floorboarding at the bow. 'It's been hung from davits off the back of a boat at some point. These rings are for attaching the wires before it's winched up tight against the davit arms. That way it

doesn't swing about while the host boat's in motion.'
He searched the outside of the hull for any sign of a
name, but there was none. He looked up at Galbraith,
squinting against the setting sun. 'There's no way this
dropped off the back of a cruiser without anyone noticing. Both winching wires would have to snap at the
same moment and the chances of that happening would
be minimal, I should think. If only one wire snapped –
the stern wire for example – you'd have a heavy object
swinging like a pendulum behind you and your steering
would go haywire. At which point you'd slow right
down and find out what the problem was.' He paused.
'In any case, if the wires had sheered they'd still be
attached to the rings.'

'Go on.'

'I'd say it's more likely it was launched off a trailer,
which means we need to ask questions at Swanage,
Kimmeridge Bay or Lulworth.' He stood up and glanced
towards the west. 'Unless it came out of Chapman's
Pool, of course, and then we need to ask how it got
there in the first place. There's no public access, so you
can't just pull a trailer down and launch a dinghy for the
fun of it.' He rubbed his jaw. 'It's curious, isn't it?'

'Couldn't you carry it down and pump it up *in
situ*?'

'It depends how strong you are. They weigh a ton
these things.' He stretched his arms like a fisherman
sizing a fish. 'They come in huge canvas holdalls but,
trust me, you need two people to carry them any distance, and it's a good mile from Hill Bottom to the
Chapman's Pool slip.'

'What about the boatsheds? The SOCOs took photographs of the whole bay and there are plenty of dinghies parked on the hard standing beside the sheds. Could it be one of those?'

'Only if it was nicked. The fishermen who use the boatsheds wouldn't abandon a perfectly good dinghy. I haven't had any reports of one being stolen but that might be because no one's noticed it's missing. I can run some checks tomorrow.'

'Joyriders?' suggested Galbraith.

'I doubt it.' Ingram touched his foot to the hull. 'Not unless they fancied the hardest paddle of their life to get it out into the open sea. It couldn't have floated out on its own. The entrance channel's too narrow and the thrust of the waves would have forced it back on to the rocks in the bay.' He smiled at Galbraith's lack of comprehension. 'You couldn't take it out without an engine,' he explained, 'and your average joyrider doesn't usually bring his own means of locomotion with him. People don't leave outboards lying around any more than they leave gold ingots. They're expensive items so you keep them under lock and key. That also rules out your pumping up *in situ* theory. I can't see anyone lugging a dinghy *and* an outboard down to Chapman's Pool.'

Galbraith eyed him curiously. 'So?'

'I'm thinking on the hoof here, sir.'

'Never mind. It sounds good. Keep going.'

'If it was stolen out of Chapman's Pool that makes it a premeditated theft. We're talking someone who was prepared to lug a heavy outboard along a mile-long path in order to nick a boat.' He lifted his eyebrows. 'Why

184

would anyone want to do that? And, having done it, why abandon ship? It's a bit bloody odd, don't you think? How did they get back to shore?'

'Swam?'

'Maybe.' Ingram's eyes narrowed to slits against the brilliant orange sun. He didn't speak for several seconds. 'Or maybe they didn't have to,' he said then. 'Maybe they weren't in it.' He lapsed into a thoughtful silence. 'There's nothing wrong with the stern board so the outboard should have pulled it under as soon as the sides started to deflate.'

'What does that mean?'

'The outboard wasn't on it when it capsized.'

Galbraith waited for him to go on and, when he didn't, he made impatient winding motions with his hand. 'Come on, Nick. What are you getting at? I know sweet FA about boats.'

The big man laughed. 'Sorry. I was just wondering what a dinghy like this was doing in the middle of nowhere without an outboard.'

'I thought you said it must have had one.'

'I've changed my mind.'

Galbraith gave a groan. 'Do you want to stop talking in riddles, you bastard? I'm wet, I'm freezing to death here and I could do with a drink.'

Ingram laughed again. 'I was only thinking that the most obvious way to take a stolen rib out of Chapman's Pool would be to tow it out, assuming you'd come in by boat in the first place.'

'In which case, why would you want to steal one?'

Ingram stared down at the collapsed hull. 'Because

you'd raped a woman and left her half-dead in it?' he suggested. 'And you wanted to get rid of the evidence? I think you should get your scene-of-crime people out here to find out why it deflated. If there's a blade puncture then I'd guess the intention was to have the boat and its contents founder in the open sea when the tow rope was released.'

'So we're back to Harding?'

The constable shrugged. 'He's your only suspect with a boat in the right place at the right time,' he pointed out.

Tony Bridges listened to Steven Harding's interminable tirade against the police with growing irritation. His friend paced the sitting room in a rage, kicking at anything that got in his way and biting Tony's head off every time he tried to offer advice. Meanwhile, Bibi, a silent and frightened observer to their mounting anger, sat cross-legged on the floor at Tony's feet, hiding her feelings behind a curtain of thick blonde hair and wondering whether it would make the situation better or worse if she announced her intention of going home.

Finally, Tony's patience snapped. 'Get a grip before I bloody *flatten* you,' he roared. 'You're acting like a two-year-old. Okay, so the police arrested you. Big deal! Just be grateful they didn't find anything.'

Steve slammed down into an armchair. 'Who says they haven't? They've refused to release *Crazy Daze* . . . my car's in a pound somewhere . . . What the hell am I supposed to do?'

'Get the solicitor on to it. That's what he's paid to do, for Christ's sake. Just don't keep bellyaching on to us. It's fucking *boring*, apart from anything else. It's not our fault you went to Poole for the sodding weekend. You should have come to Southampton with us.'

Bibi stirred uncomfortably on the floor at his feet. She opened her mouth to say something, then closed it again when caution prevailed. Anger was bubbling in the room like overheated yeast.

Harding slammed his feet on to the floor in a rage. 'The solicitor's worse than useless, told me the bastards were entitled to hold evidence for as long as is necessary or some legalized crap like that . . .' His voice tailed off on a sob.

There was a long silence.

This time fondness for Tony's friend got the better of caution and nervously Bibi raised her head. She scraped a gap in her hair to look at him. 'But if you didn't do it,' she said in her soft, rather childish way, 'then I don't see what you're worrying about.'

'Right,' agreed Tony. 'They can't prosecute you without evidence, and if they've released you then there isn't any evidence. QED.'

'I want my phone,' said Harding, surging to his feet again with crackling energy. 'What did you do with it?'

'Left it with Bob,' said Tony. 'Like you told me to do.'

'Has he put it on charge?'

'I wouldn't know. I haven't spoken to him since Monday. He was pretty stoned when I gave it to him, so the chances are he's forgotten all about it.'

'That's all I need.' The angry young man launched a kick at one of the walls.

Bridges took a pull at his lager can, eyeing his friend thoughtfully over the top of it. 'What's so important about the phone?'

'Nothing.'

'Then leave my fucking walls alone!' he bellowed, surging out of his own chair and thrusting his face into Harding's. 'Show some respect, you bastard! This is *my* house, not your crappy little boat.'

'Stop it!' screamed Bibi, cowering back behind the chair. 'What's wrong with you both? One of you's going to get hurt in a minute.'

Harding frowned down at her, then held up his hands. 'All right, all right. I'm expecting a call. That's why I'm twitched.'

'Then use the phone in the hall,' said Bridges curtly, flinging himself into the armchair again.

'No.' He backed towards the wall and leaned against it. 'What did the police ask you?'

'What you'd expect. How well you knew Kate . . . whether I thought the harassment was genuine . . . whether I saw you on Saturday . . . where *I* was . . . what kind of pornography you were into . . .' He shook his head. 'I knew that garbage would come back to haunt you.'

'Leave it out,' said Harding tiredly. 'I told you I'd had enough of your bloody lectures on Monday. What did you tell them?'

Tony frowned warningly at Bibi's bent head, then touched a hand to the back of her neck. 'Do you want to do me a favour, Beebs? Hop down to the off-licence and get an eight-pack. There's some money on the shelf in the hall.'

She rose to her feet with obvious relief. 'Sure. Why not? I'll leave them in the hall then go home. Okay?' She held out a reluctant hand. 'I'm really tired, Tony, and I could do with a decent night's kip. You don't mind, do you?'

'Of course not.' He gripped her fingers for a moment, squeezing them hard. 'Just so long as you love me, Beebs.'

She tore herself free, cradling her hand under her arm, and made for the hall. 'You know I do.'

He didn't speak again until he heard the front door close behind her. 'You want to be careful what you say around her,' he warned Harding. 'She had to give a statement, too, and it's not fair to get her any more involved than she is already.'

'Okay, okay . . . So what did you tell them?'

'Aren't you more interested in what I *didn't* tell them?'

'If you like.'

'Right. Well, I didn't tell them you shagged Kate's brains out.'

Harding breathed deeply through his nose. 'Why not?'

'I thought about it,' Bridges admitted, reaching for a packet of Rizla papers on the floor and setting about rolling himself a joint. 'But I know you too well, mate. You're an arrogant son of a bitch with an over-inflated opinion of yourself' – he squinted up at his friend with

a return of good humour in his eyes – 'but I can't see
you murdering anyone, particularly not a woman, and
never mind she was pissing you off something rotten. So
I kept shtoom.' He gave an eloquent shrug. 'But if I
live to regret it, I'll have your stinking hide . . . and
you'd better believe that.'

'Did they tell you she was raped before she was
murdered?'

Bridges gave a low whistle of understanding as if
pieces of a jigsaw were finally coming together. 'No
wonder they were so interested in your porno shoots.
Your average rapist's a sad bastard in a dirty mac who
jerks off over that kind of trash.' He pulled a plastic bag
out from the recesses of his chair and started to fill the
Rizla papers. 'They must have had a field day with those
photographs.'

Harding shook his head. 'I got rid of the lot over the
side before they came. I didn't want any' – he thought
about it – 'confusion.'

'Jesus, you're an arsehole! Why can't you be honest
for once? You got shit-scared that if they had evidence
of you performing sex acts with an under-age kid, they'd
have no trouble pinning a rape on you.'

'It wasn't for real.'

'Chucking the photos away was. You're an idiot,
mate.'

'Why?'

'Because you can bet your bottom dollar William will
have mentioned photos. *I* sure as hell did. Now the filth
will be wondering why they can't find any.'

'So?'

'They'll know you were expecting a visit.'

'So?' said Harding again.

Bridges cast him another thoughtful glance as he licked the edges of the spliff. 'Look at it from their point of view. Why would you be expecting a visit if you didn't know it was Kate's body they'd found?'

Chapter Thirteen

'WE CAN GO to the pub,' said Ingram, locking *Miss Creant* on to her trailer behind his Jeep, 'or I can give you some supper at home.' He glanced at his watch. 'It's 9.30, so the pub'll be pretty raucous by now and it'll be difficult to get anything to eat.' He started to peel off his waterproofs which still streamed water from his immersion in the sea at the bottom of the slip as he had guided *Miss Creant* on to the trailer while Galbraith operated the winch. 'Home, on the other hand,' he said with a grin, 'has drying facilities, a spectacular view and silence.'

'Do I get the impression you'd rather go home?' asked Galbraith with a yawn, levering off his inadequate waders and turning them upside down to empty them in a Niagara Falls over the slip. He was soaked from the waistband down.

'There's beer in the fridge and I can grill you a fresh sea bass if you're interested.'

'How fresh?'

'Still alive Monday night,' said Ingram, taking some spare trousers from the back of the Jeep and tossing them across. 'You can change in the lifeboat station.'

'Cheers,' said Galbraith setting off in stockinged feet

towards the grey stone building that guarded the ever-ready Swanage lifeboat, 'and I'm interested,' he called over his shoulder.

Ingram's cottage was a tiny two-up, two-down, backing on to the downs above Seacombe Cliff, although the two downstairs rooms had been knocked into one with an open-plan staircase rising out of the middle and a kitchen extension added to the back. It was clearly a bachelor establishment and Galbraith surveyed it with approval. Too often, these days, he felt he still had to be persuaded of the joys of fatherhood.

'I envy you,' he said, bending down to examine a meticulously detailed replica of the *Cutty Sark* in a bottle on the mantelpiece. 'Did you make this yourself?'

Ingram nodded.

'It wouldn't last half an hour in my house. I reckon anything I ever had of value was smashed within hours of my son getting his first football.' He chuckled. 'He keeps telling me he's going to make a fortune playing for Man United, but I can't see it myself.'

'How old is he?' asked Ingram, leading the way through to the kitchen.

'Seven. His sister's five.'

The tall constable took the sea bass from the fridge, then tossed Galbraith a beer and opened one for himself. 'I'd have liked children,' he said, splitting the fish down its belly, filleting out the backbone and splaying it spatchcock fashion on the grillpan. He was neat and quick in his movements, despite his size. 'Trouble is I never found a woman who was prepared to hang around long enough to give me any.'

Galbraith remembered what Steven Harding had said on Monday night about Ingram fancying the woman with the horse and wondered if it was more a case of the *right* woman not hanging around long enough. 'A guy like you'd do well anywhere,' he said, watching him take some chives and basil from an array of herbs on his window sill and chop them finely before sprinkling them over the sea bass. 'So what's keeping you here?'

'You mean apart from the great view and the clean air?'

'Yes.'

Ingram pushed the fish to one side and started washing the mud off some new potatoes before chucking them into a saucepan. 'That's it,' he said. 'Great view, clean air, a boat, fishing, contentment.'

'What about ambition? Don't you get frustrated? Feel you're standing still?'

'Sometimes. Then I remember how much I hated the rat race when I was in it and the frustrations pass.' He glanced at Galbraith with a self-deprecating smile. 'I did five years with an insurance company before I became a policeman, and I hated every minute of it. I didn't believe in the product, but the only way to get on was to sell more and it was driving me nuts. I had a long think over one weekend about what I wanted out of life, and gave in my notice on the Monday.' He filled the saucepan with water and put it on the gas.

The DI thought sourly of his various life, endowment and pension policies. 'What's wrong with insurance?'

'Nothing.' He tipped his can in the direction of the DI and took a swill. 'As long as you need it . . . as long as you understand the terms of the policy . . . as long as you can afford to keep paying the premiums . . . as long as you've read the small print. It's like any other product. Buyer beware.'

'Now you're worrying me.'

Ingram grinned. 'If it's any consolation, I'd have felt exactly the same about selling lottery tickets.'

WPC Griffiths had fallen asleep, fully clothed, in the spare room but woke with a start when Hannah started screaming in the next room. She leapt off the bed, heart thudding, and came face to face with William Sumner as he slunk through the child's doorway. 'What the hell do you think you're doing?' she demanded angrily, her nerves shot to pieces by her sudden awakening. 'You've been told not to go in there.'

'I thought she was asleep. I just wanted to look at her.'

'We agreed you wouldn't.'

'*You* may have done. *I* never did. You've no right to stop me. It's *my* house, and she's *my* daughter.'

'I wouldn't bank on that, if I were you,' she snapped. She was about to add: Your rights take second place to Hannah's at the moment, but he didn't give her the chance.

He clamped fingers like steel bands around her arms and stared at her with dislike, his face working uncontrollably. 'Who have you been talking to?' he muttered.

She didn't say anything, just broke his grip by raising her hands and striking him on both wrists, and with a choking sob he stumbled away down the corridor. But it was a while before she realized what his question had implied.

It would explain a lot, she thought, if Hannah wasn't his child.

Galbraith laid his knife and fork at the side of his plate with a sigh of satisfaction. They were sitting in shirt-sleeves on the small patio at the side of the cottage beside a gnarled old plum tree that flavoured the air with the scent of fermentation. A storm lantern hissed quietly on the table between them, throwing a circle of yellow light up the wall of the house and across the lawn. On the horizon, moon-silvered clouds floated across the surface of the sea like windblown veils.

'I'm going to have a problem with this,' he said. 'It's too damn perfect.'

Ingram pushed his own plate aside and propped his elbows on the table. 'You need to like your own company. If you don't, it's the loneliest place on earth.'

'Do you?'

The younger man's face creased into an amiable smile. 'I get by,' he said, 'as long as people like you don't drop in too often. Solitude's a state of mind with me, not an ambition.'

Galbraith nodded. 'That makes sense.' He studied the other's face for a moment. 'Tell me about Miss Jenner,' he said then. 'Harding gave us the impression he and she had quite a chat before you got back. Could he have said more to her than she's told you?'

'It's possible. She seemed pretty relaxed with him.'

'How well do you know her?'

But Ingram wasn't so easily drawn about his private life. 'As well as I know anyone else round here,' he said casually. 'What did you make of Harding, as a matter of interest?'

'Difficult to say. He gives a convincing performance of wanting nothing to do with Kate Sumner but, as my boss pointed out, dislike is as good a reason for rape and murder as any other. He claims she was harassing him by smearing crap all over his car because he'd rejected her. It might be true, but none of us really believes it.'

'Why not? There was a case down here three years ago when a wife smashed her husband's Jag through the front door of his lover's house. Women can get pretty riled when they're given the elbow.'

'Except he says he never slept with her.'

'Maybe that was her problem.'

'How come you're on his side all of a sudden?'

'I'm not. The rules say keep an open mind, and that's what I'm trying to do.'

Galbraith chuckled. 'He wants us to believe he's a bit of a stud, presumably on the basis that a man who has access to sex on tap doesn't need to rape anyone, but he can't or won't produce the names of women he's slept with. And neither can anyone else.' He shrugged. 'Yet no one questions his reputation for laddish behaviour. They're all quite confident he entertains ladies on his boat even though the SOCOs couldn't come up with any evidence to support it. His bedlinen's stiff with dried semen, but there were only two hairs on it that weren't his, and neither of them was Kate Sumner's. Conclusion, the guy's a compulsive masturbator.' He paused for reflection. 'The problem is his damn boat's positively monastic in every other respect.'

'I don't get you.'

'Not a whisper of anything pornographic,' said Galbraith. 'Compulsive masturbators, particularly the ones who go on to rape, wank their brains out over hard-core porn videos because sensation begins and ends with their dicks, and they need more and more explicit images to help them jerk off. So how does our friend Harding get himself aroused?'

'Memory?' suggested Ingram wryly.

Galbraith chuckled. 'He's done some pornographic photoshoots himself but claims the only copies he ever kept were the ones he showed William Sumner.' He gave a brief rundown of both Harding's and Sumner's versions of the story. 'He says he threw the magazine in the bin afterwards and, as far as he's concerned, porno shoots become history the minute he's paid.'

'More likely he got rid of everything over the side when it occurred to him I might put his name forward for further questioning.' Ingram thought for a moment. 'Did you ask him about what Danny Spender told me? Why he was rubbing himself with the phone?'

'He said it wasn't true, said the kid made it up.'

'No way. I'll stake my life on Danny getting that right.'

'Why then?'

'Reliving the rape? Getting himself excited because his victim had been found? Miss Jenner?'

'Which?'

'The rape,' said Ingram.

'Pure speculation, based on the word of a ten-year-old and a policeman. No jury will believe you, Nick.'

'Then talk to Miss Jenner tomorrow. Find out if she noticed anything before I got there.' He started to stack the dirty dishes. 'I suggest you use kid gloves, though. She's not too comfortable around policemen.'

'Do you mean policemen in general, or just you?'

'Probably just me,' said Ingram honestly. 'I tipped off her father that the man she'd married had bounced a couple of bad cheques, and when the old boy tackled him about it, the bastard did a runner with the small fortune he'd conned out of Miss Jenner and her mother. When his fingerprints were run through the computer, it turned out half the police forces in England were looking for him, not to mention the various wives he'd acquired along the way. Miss Jenner was number four, although as he never divorced number one, the marriage was a sham anyway.'

'What was his name?'

'Robert Healey. He was arrested a couple of years ago in Manchester. She knew him as Martin Grant but he admitted to twenty-two other aliases in court.'

'And she blames you because she married a creep?' asked Galbraith in disbelief.

'Not for that. Her father had had a bad heart for years and the shock of finding out they were on the verge of bankruptcy killed him. I think she feels that if I'd gone to her instead of him, she could somehow have persuaded Healey to give the money back and the old man would still be alive.'

'Could she?'

'I wouldn't think so.' He placed the dishes in front of him. 'Healey had the whole scam down to a fine art, and being open to persuasion wasn't part of his MO.'

'How did he work it?'

Ingram pulled a wry face. 'Charm. She was besotted with him.'

'So she's stupid?'

'No . . . just overly trusting . . .' Ingram marshalled his thoughts. 'He was a professional. Created a fictitious company with fictitious accounts and persuaded the two women to invest in it, or more accurately persuaded Miss Jenner to persuade her mother. It was a very sophisticated operation. I saw the paperwork afterwards, and I'm not surprised they fell for it. The house was littered with glossy brochures, audited accounts, salary cheques, lists of employees, Inland Revenue statements. You'd have to be very suspicious indeed to assume anyone would go to so much trouble to con you out of a hundred thousand quid. Anyway, on the basis that the company stock was going up by 20 per cent a year, Mrs Jenner cashed in all her bonds and securities and handed her son-in-law a cheque.'

'Which he converted back into cash?'

Ingram nodded. 'It passed through at least three bank accounts on the way, and then vanished. In all, he spent twelve months working the scam – nine months softening up Miss Jenner, and three months married to her – and it wasn't just the Jenners who got taken to the cleaners. He used his connection with them to draw in other people, and a lot of their friends got their fingers burnt as well. It's sad, but they've become virtual recluses as a result.'

'What do they live on?'

'Whatever she can make from the Broxton House livery stables. Which isn't much. The whole place is getting seedier by the day.'

'Why don't they sell it?'

Ingram pushed his chair back, preparatory to standing up. 'Because it doesn't belong to them. Old man Jenner changed his will before he died and left the house to his son, with the proviso that the two women can go on living there as long as Mrs Jenner remains alive.'

Galbraith frowned. 'And then what? The brother throws the sister on the streets?'

'Something like that,' said Ingram dryly. 'He's a lawyer in London, and he certainly doesn't plan to have a sitting tenant on the premises when he sells out to a developer.'

Before he left to interview Maggie Jenner on Thursday morning, Galbraith had a quick word with Carpenter to bring him up to speed on the beached dinghy. 'I've organized a couple of SOCOs to go out to it,' he told him. 'I'll be surprised if they find anything – Ingram and I had a poke around to see what had caused it to deflate and frankly it's all a bit of a mess – but I think it's worth a try. They're going to make an attempt to reflate it and float it off the rocks, but the advice is, don't hold your breath. Even if they get it back, it's doubtful we'll learn much from it.'

Carpenter handed him a sheaf of papers. 'These'll interest you,' he said.

'What are they?'

'Statements from the people Sumner said would support his alibi.'

Galbraith heard a note of excitement in his boss's voice. 'And do they?'

The other shook his head. 'Quite the opposite. There are twenty-four hours unaccounted for, between lunchtime on Saturday and lunchtime on Sunday. We're now blitzing everyone, hotel staff, other conference delegates, but those' – he levelled a finger at the documents in Galbraith's hand – 'are the names Sumner himself gave us.' His eyes gleamed. 'And if they're not prepared to alibi him, I can't see anyone else doing it. It looks as if you could be right, John.'

Galbraith nodded. 'How did he do it, though?'

'He used to sail, must know Chapman's Pool as well as Harding, must know there are dinghies lying around for the taking.'

'How did he get Kate there?'

'Phoned her Friday night, said he was bored out of his mind with the conference and was planning to come home early, suggested they do something exciting for a change, like spend the afternoon on Studland beach, and arranged to meet her and Hannah off the train in Bournemouth or Poole.'

Galbraith tugged at his earlobe. 'It's possible,' he agreed.

A child of three travels free by train, and the record of sales from Lymington station had shown that numerous single adult fares to Bournemouth and Poole had been sold on the Saturday, the trip being a quick and easy one through a change on to regular mainline trains at Brockenhurst. However, if Kate Sumner had purchased one of the tickets she had used cash rather than a cheque or credit card for the transaction. None of the railway staff remembered a small blonde woman with a child but, as they pointed out, the traffic through Lymington station on a Saturday in peak holiday season was so continuous and so heavy because of the ferry link to and from the Isle of Wight that it was unlikely they would.

'The only fly in the ointment is Hannah,' Carpenter went on. 'If he abandoned her in Lilliput before driving back to Liverpool, why did it take so long for anyone to notice her? He must have dumped her by 6 a.m., but Mr and Mrs Green didn't spot her until 10.30.'

Galbraith thought of the traces of benzodiazepine and paracetamol in her system. 'Maybe he fed, watered and cleaned her at six, then left her asleep in a cardboard box in a shop doorway,' he said thoughtfully. 'He's a pharmaceutical chemist, don't forget, so he must have a pretty good idea how to put a three-year-old under for several hours. My guess is he's been doing it for years.

By the way the child behaves around him she must have been a blight on his sex life from the day she was born.'

Meanwhile, Nick Ingram was chasing stolen dinghies. The fishermen who parked their boats at Chapman's Pool couldn't help. 'Matter of fact it's the first thing we checked when we heard the woman had drowned,' said one. 'I'd have let you know if there'd been a problem, but nothing's missing.'

It was the same story in Swanage and Kimmeridge Bay.

His last port of call, Lulworth Cove, looked more promising. 'Funny you should ask,' said the voice on the other end of the line, 'because we have had one go missing, black ten-footer.'

'Sounds about right. When did it go?'

'A good three months back.'

'Where from?'

'Would you believe it, off the beach. Some poor sod from Spain anchors his cruiser in the bay, ferries himself and his family in for a pub lunch, leaves the outboard in place with the starter cord dangling, and then tears strips off yours truly because it was hijacked from under his nose. According to him, *no one* in Spain would dream of stealing another chap's boat – never mind he makes it easy enough for the local moron to nick it – and then gives me a load of grief about the aggression of Cornish fishermen and how they were probably at the bottom of it. I pointed out that Cornwall's a good hundred miles away, and that Spanish fishermen are far more aggressive than the Cornish variety and *never* follow European Union rules, but he still said he was going to report me to the European Court of Human Rights for failing to protect Spanish tourists.'

Ingram laughed. 'So what happened?'

'Nothing. I took him and his family out to his sodding great bastard of a fifty-foot cruiser and we never heard another word. He probably put in for twice the dinghy's insurance value and blamed the vile English for its disappearance. We made inquiries, of course, but no one had seen anything. I mean, why would they? We get hundreds of people here during bank holiday week and anyone could have started it up with no trouble. I mean what kind of berk leaves a dinghy with an outboard in place? We reckoned it was taken by joyriders who sank it when they got bored with it.'

'Which bank holiday was it?'

'End of May. School half-term. The place was packed.'

'Did the Spaniard give you a description of the dinghy?'

'A whole bloody manifest more like. All ready for the insurance. Half of me suspected he wanted it to be nicked just so he could get something a bit more swanky.'

'Can you fax the details through?'

'Sure.'

'I'm particularly interested in the outboard.'

'Why?'

205

'Because I don't think it was on the dinghy when it went down. With any luck, it's still in the possession of the thief.'

'Is he your murderer?'

'Very likely.'

'Then you're in luck, mate. I've got all sorts of serial numbers here, courtesy of our Spanish friend, and one of them's the outboard.'

Chapter Fourteen

Subject: Steven Harding

Mr and Mrs Harding live at 18 Hall Road, a modest
bungalow to the west of Falmouth. They retired to
Cornwall in 1991 after running a fish and chip shop in
Lymington for 20+ years. They used a considerable
proportion of their capital to put their only child, Steven,
through a private drama college following his failure to
gain any A level passes at school, and feel aggrieved
that they now live in somewhat straitened circumstances as a result. This may in part explain why their
attitude towards their son is critical and unfriendly.

They describe Steven as a 'disappointment' and
evince considerable hostility towards him because of
his 'immoral lifestyle'. They blame his wayward behaviour – 'he is only interested in sex, drugs and rock and
roll' – and lack of achievement – 'he has never done a
day's serious work in his life' – on laziness and a belief
that 'the world owes him a living'. Mr Harding, who is

207

proud of his working-class roots, says Steven looks down on his parents which explains why Steven has been to see them only once in six years. The visit – during the summer of 1995 – was not a success and Mr Harding's views on his son's arrogance and lack of gratitude were explosive and earthy. He uses words like 'poser', 'junky', 'parasite', 'oversexed', 'liar', 'irresponsible' to describe his son, although it is clear that his hostility has more to do with his inability to accept Steven's rejection of working-class values than any real knowledge of his son's current lifestyle as they have had no contact with him since July 1995.

Mrs Harding cites a schoolfriend of Steven's, Anthony Bridges, as a malign influence on his life. According to her, Anthony introduced Steven to shoplifting, drugs and pornography at the age of twelve and Steven's lack of achievement stems from a couple of police cautions he and Anthony received during their teenage years for drunk and disorderly behaviour, vandalism, and theft of pornographic materials from a newsagent. Steven became rebellious and impossible to control after these episodes. She describes Steven as 'too handsome for his own good', and says that girls were throwing themselves at him from an early age. She says Anthony, by contrast, was always overshadowed by his friend and that she believes this is why it amused Anthony to 'get Steven into trouble'. She feels very bitter that Anthony, despite his previous history, was bright enough to go to university and find himself a job in teaching while Steven had to rely on the funding his parents provided for which they have received no thanks.

When Mr Harding asked Steven how he was able to afford to buy his boat *Crazy Daze*, Steven admitted he had received payment for several hard-core pornography sessions. This caused such distress to his parents that they ordered him from their house in July 1995 and have neither seen nor heard from him since. They know nothing about his recent activities, friends or acquaintances and can shed no light on the events of 9/10 August 1997. However, they insist that, despite all his faults, they do not believe Steven to be a violent or aggressive young man.

Chapter Fifteen

MAGGIE JENNER WAS raking straw in one of the stables when Nick Ingram and John Galbraith drove into Broxton House yard on Thursday morning. Her immediate reaction, as it was with all visitors, was to retreat into the shadows, unwilling to be seen, unwilling to have her privacy invaded, for it required an effort of will to overcome her natural disinclination to participate in anything that involved people. Broxton House, a square Queen Anne building with pitched roof, red-brick walls and shuttered upper windows, was visible through a gap in the trees to the right of the stableyard and she watched the two men admire it as they got out of the car, before turning to walk in her direction.

With a resigned smile, she drew attention to herself by hefting soiled straw through the stable doorway on the end of a pitchfork. The weather hadn't broken for three weeks, and sweat was running freely down her face as she emerged into the fierce sunlight. She was irritated by her own discomfort, and wished she'd put on something else that morning or that PC Ingram had had the courtesy to warn her he was coming. Her checkered cheesecloth shirt gripped her damp torso like a stocking and her jeans chafed against the inside of her thighs. Ingram spotted her almost immediately and was amused to see that, for once, the tables were turned and it was she who was hot and bothered and not he, but his expression as always was unreadable.

She propped the pitchfork against the stable wall and wiped her palms down her already filthy jeans before smoothing her hair off her sweaty face with the back of one hand. 'Good morning, Nick,' she said. 'What can I do for you?'

'Miss Jenner,' he said, with his usual polite nod. 'This is Detective Inspector Galbraith from Dorset HQ. If it's convenient, he'd like to ask you a few questions about the events of last Sunday.'

She inspected her palms before tucking them into her jeans pockets. 'I won't offer to shake hands, Inspector. You wouldn't like where mine have been.'

Galbraith smiled, recognizing the excuse for what it was, a dislike of physical contact, and cast an interested glance around the cobbled courtyard. There was a row of stables on each of three sides, beautiful old red-brick buildings with solid oak doors, only half a dozen of which appeared to have occupants. The rest stood empty, doors hooked back, brick floors bare of straw, hay baskets unfilled, and it was a long time, he guessed, since the business had been a thriving one. They had passed a faded sign at the entrance gate, boasting: BROXTON HOUSE RIDING & LIVERY STABLES, but, like the sign, evidence of dilapidation was everywhere, in the crumbling brickwork that had been thrashed by the elements for a couple of hundred years, in the cracked and peeling paintwork and the broken windows in the tack room and office which no one had bothered – *or could afford?* – to replace.

Maggie watched his appraisal. 'You're right,' she said, reading his mind. 'It has enormous potential as a row of holiday chalets.'

'A pity when it happens, though.'

'Yes.'

He looked towards a distant paddock where a couple of horses grazed half-heartedly on drought-starved grass. 'Are they yours as well?'

'No. We just rent out the paddock. The owners are supposed to keep an eye on them, but they're irresponsible, frankly, and I usually find myself doing things for their wretched animals that was never part of the contract.' She pulled a rueful smile. 'I can't get it into their owners' heads that water evaporates and that the trough needs filling every day. It makes me mad sometimes.'

'Quite a chore then?'

'Yes.' She gestured towards a door at the end of the row of stables behind her. 'Let's go up to my flat. I can make you both a cup of coffee.'

'Thank you.' She was an attractive woman, he thought, despite the muck and the brusque manner, but he was intrigued by Ingram's stiff formality towards her which wasn't readily explained by the story of the bigamous husband. The formality, he thought, should be on her side. As he followed them up the wooden stairs, he decided the constable must have tried it on at some point and been comprehensively slapped down for playing outside his own league. Miss Jenner was top-drawer material, even if she did live in something resembling a pigsty.

The flat was the antithesis of Nick's tidy establishment. There was disorder everywhere, bean bags piled in front of the television on the floor, newspapers with finished and half-finished crosswords abandoned on chairs and tables, a filthy rug on the sofa which smelt unmistakably of Bertie, and a pile of dirty washing-up in the kitchen sink. 'Sorry about the mess,' she said. 'I've been up since five, and I haven't had time to clean.' To Galbraith's ears, this sounded like a well-worn apology that was trotted out to anyone who might be inclined to criticize her lifestyle. She swivelled the tap to squeeze the kettle between it and the washing-up. 'How do you like your coffee?'

'White, two sugars, please,' said Galbraith.

'I'll have mine black please, Miss Jenner. No sugar,' said Ingram.

'Do you mind Coffeemate?' Maggie asked the Inspector, sniffing at a cardboard carton on the side. 'The milk's off.' Cursorily she rinsed some dirty mugs under the tap. 'Why don't you grab a seat? If you chuck Bertie's blanket on the floor one of you can have the sofa.'

'I think she means you, sir,' murmured Ingram as they retreated into the sitting room. 'Inspector's perks. It's the best seat in the place.'

'Who's Bertie?' whispered Galbraith.

'The Hound of the Baskervilles. His favourite occupation is to shove his nose up men's crotches and give them a good slobbering. The stains tend to hang around through at least three washes, I find, so it pays to keep your legs crossed when you're sitting down.'

'I hope you're joking!' said Galbraith with a groan. He had already lost one pair of good trousers to the previous night's soaking in the sea. 'Where is he?'

'Out on the razzle, I should think. His second favourite occupation is to service the local bitches.'

The DI lowered himself gingerly into the only armchair. 'Does he have fleas?'

With a grin, Ingram jerked his head towards the kitchen door. 'Do mice leave their droppings in sugar?' he murmured.

'Shit!'

Ingram removed himself to a window sill and perched precariously on the edge of it. 'Just be grateful it wasn't her mother who was out riding on Sunday,' he said in an undertone. 'This kitchen's sterile by comparison with hers.' He had sampled Mrs Jenner's hospitality once four years ago, the day after Healey had fled, and he'd vowed never to repeat the experience. She had given him coffee in a cracked Spode cup that was black with tannin, and he had gagged continuously while drinking it. He had never understood the peculiar mores of the impoverished landed gentry who seemed to believe the value of bone china outweighed the value of hygiene.

They waited in silence while Maggie busied herself in the kitchen. The atmosphere was ripe with the stench of horse manure, wafted in from a pile of soiled straw in the yard outside, and the heat baking the interior of the flat through the uninsulated roof was almost unbearable. In no time at all both men were red in the face and mopping at their brows with handkerchieves, and whatever brief advantage Ingram thought he had gained over Maggie was quickly dispelled. A few minutes later she emerged with a tray of coffee mugs which she handed around before sinking on to Bertie's blanket on the sofa.

'So what can I tell you that I haven't already told Nick?' she asked Galbraith. 'I know it's a murder inquiry because I've been reading the newspapers, but as I didn't see the body I can't imagine how I can help you.'

Galbraith pulled some notes from his jacket pocket. 'In fact it's rather more than a murder inquiry, Miss Jenner. Kate Sumner was raped before she was thrown into the sea, so the man who killed her is extremely dangerous and we need to catch him before he does it again.' He paused to let the information sink in. 'Believe me, any help you can give us will be greatly appreciated.'

'But I don't know anything,' she said.

'You spoke to a man called Steven Harding,' he reminded her.

'Oh, good God,' she said, 'you're not suggesting he did it?' She frowned at Ingram. 'You've really got it in for that man, haven't you, Nick? He was only trying to help in all conscience. You might as well say any of the men who were in Chapman's Pool that day could have killed her.'

Ingram remained blandly indifferent to both her frown and her accusations. 'It's a possibility.'

'So why pick on Steve?'

'We're not, Miss Jenner. We're trying to eliminate him from the inquiry. Neither I nor the Inspector wants to waste time investigating innocent bystanders.'

'You wasted an awful lot of time on Sunday doing it,' she said acidly, stung by his dreary insistence on treating her with forelock-tugging formality.

He smiled, but didn't say anything.

She turned back to Galbraith. 'I'll do my best,' she said, 'although I doubt I can tell you much. What do you want to know?'

'It would be helpful if you can start by describing your meeting with him. I understand you rode down the track towards the boatsheds and came across him and the boys beside PC Ingram's car. Is that the first time you saw him?'

'Yes, but I wasn't riding Jasper then. I was leading him because he was frightened by the helicopter.'

'Okay. What were Steven Harding and the two boys doing at that point?'

She shrugged. 'They were looking at a girl on a boat through the binoculars, at least Steve and the older brother were. I think the younger one was bored by it all. Then Bertie got overexcited—'

Galbraith interrupted. 'You said *they* were looking through binoculars. How did that work exactly? Were they taking it in turns?'

'No, well, that's wrong. It was Paul who was looking, Steve was just holding them steady for him.' She saw his eyebrows lift in enquiry and anticipated his next question. 'Like this.' She made an embracing gesture with her arms. 'He was standing behind Paul, with his arms round him, and holding the binoculars so Paul could look through the eyepieces. The child thought it was funny and kept giggling. It was rather sweet really. I think he was trying to take his mind off the dead woman.' She paused to collect her thoughts. 'Actually, I thought he was their father, till I realized he was too young.'

'One of the boys said he was playing around with his telephone before you arrived. Did you see him do that?'

She shook her head. 'It was clipped to his waistband.'

'What happened next?'

'Bertie got overexcited, so Steve grabbed him and then suggested we put the boys at ease by encouraging them to pat Bertie and Sir Jasper. He said he was used to animals because he'd grown up on a farm in Cornwall.' She frowned. 'Why is any of this important? He was just being friendly.'

'In what way, Miss Jenner?'

Her frown deepened and she stared at him for a moment, clearly wondering where his questions were leading. 'He wasn't making a nuisance of himself if that's what you're getting at.'

'Why would I think he was making a nuisance of himself?'

She gave an irritated toss of her head. 'Because it would make things easier for you if he was,' she suggested.

'How?'

'You want him to be the rapist, don't you? Nick certainly does.'

Galbraith's grey eyes appraised her coolly. 'There's a little more to rape than making a nuisance of yourself. Kate Sumner had been dosed with a sleeping drug, she had abrasions to her back, strangle marks at her neck, rope burns to her wrists, broken fingers and a ruptured vagina. She was then thrown ... *alive* ... into the sea by someone who undoubtedly knew she was a poor swimmer and wouldn't be able to save herself, even assuming she came round from the effects of the drug. She was also pregnant when she died which means her baby was murdered with her.' He smiled slightly. 'I realize that you're a very busy person and that the death of an unknown woman is hardly a priority in your life, but PC Ingram and I take it more seriously, probably because we both saw Kate's body and were distressed by it.'

She looked at her hands. 'I apologize,' she said.

'We don't ask questions for the fun of it,' said Galbraith without hostility. 'Matter of fact, most of us find this sort of case very stressful, although the public rarely recognizes it.'

She raised her head and there was the glimmer of a smile in her dark eyes. 'Point taken,' she said. 'The problem is, I get the impression you're homing in on Steve Harding just because he was there, and that seems unreasonable.'

Galbraith exchanged a glance with Ingram. 'There are other reasons why we're interested in him,' he said, 'but the only one I'm prepared to tell you at the moment is that he'd known the dead woman for quite some time. For that reason alone we'd be investigating him, whether he was at Chapman's Pool on Sunday or not.'

She was thoroughly startled. 'He didn't say he knew her.'

'Would you have expected him to? He told us he never saw the body.'

She turned to Ingram. 'He can't have done, can he? He said he was walking from St Alban's Head.'

'There's a very good view of Egmont Bight from the coastal path up there,' Ingram reminded her. 'If he had a pair of binoculars, he could have picked her out quite easily.'

'But he didn't,' she protested. 'All he had was a telephone. You made that point yourself.'

Galbraith debated with himself how to put the next question and opted for a straightforward approach. The woman must have a stallion or two in her stables, so she was hardly likely to faint at the mention of a penis. 'Nick says Harding had an erection when he first saw him on Sunday. Would you agree?'

'Either that or he's incredibly well endowed.'

'Were you the cause of it, do you think?'

She didn't answer.

'Well?'

'I've no idea,' she said. 'My feeling at the time was that it was probably the girl on the boat who had got him excited. Walk along Studland beach any sunny day and you'll find a hundred randy eighteen- to twenty-four-year-olds cowering in the water because their dicks react independently of their brains. It's hardly a crime.'

Galbraith shook his head. 'You're a good-looking woman, Miss Jenner, and he was standing close to you. Did you encourage him in any way?'

'No.'

'It *is* important.'

219

'Why? All I know is the poor bloke wasn't in absolute control of himself.' She sighed. 'Look, I'm really sorry about the woman. But if Steve was involved, then he never gave me any indication of it. As far as I was concerned, he was a young man out for a walk who made a phone call on behalf of a couple of children.'

Galbraith laid a forefinger on a page of his notes. 'This is a quote from Danny Spender,' he said. 'Tell me how true it is. "He was chatting up the lady with the horse but I don't think she liked him as much as he liked her." Is that what was happening?'

'No, of course it wasn't,' she said with annoyance, as if the idea of being chatted-up was pure anathema to her, 'though I suppose it might have looked like that to the children. I said he was brave for grabbing Bertie by the collar, so he seemed to think that laughing a lot and slapping Jasper on the rump would impress the boys. In the end I had to move the animals into the shade to get them away from him. Jasper's amenable to most things, but not to having his bottom smacked every two minutes, and I didn't want to be prosecuted if he lashed out suddenly.'

'So was Danny right about you not liking him?'

'I don't see that it matters,' she said uncomfortably. 'It's a subjective thing. I'm not a very sociable person so liking people isn't my strong point.'

'What was wrong with him?' he went on imperturbably.

'Oh, God, this is ridiculous!' she snapped. 'Nothing. He was perfectly pleasant from beginning to end of our conversation.' She cast an angry sideways glance towards Ingram. 'Almost ridiculously polite, in fact.'

'So why didn't you like him?'

She breathed deeply through her nose, clearly at war with herself about whether to answer or not. 'He was a toucher,' she said with a spurt of anger. 'All right? Is that what you wanted? I have a thing against men who can't keep their hands to themselves, Inspector, but it doesn't make them rapists or murderers. It's just the way they are.' She took another deep breath. 'And while we're on the subject – just to show you how little faith you can put in my judgement of men – I wouldn't trust any of you further than I could throw you. If you want to know why, ask Nick.' She gave a hollow laugh as Galbraith lowered his eyes. 'I see he's already told you. Still . . . if you want the juicier details of my relationship with my bigamous husband, apply in writing and I'll see what I can do for you.'

The DI, reminded of Sandy Griffiths's similar *caveat* regarding her judgement of Sumner, ignored the tantrum. 'Are you saying Harding touched *you*, Miss Jenner?'

She gave him a withering glance. 'Of course not. I never gave him the opportunity.'

'But he touched your animals, and that's what put you against him?'

'No,' she said crossly. 'It was the boys he couldn't keep his hands off. It was all very macho . . . hail-fellow-well-met stuff . . . you know, a lot of punching of shoulders and high fives . . . to be honest it's why I

221

thought he was their father. The little one didn't like it much – he kept pushing him away – but the older one revelled in it.' She smiled rather cynically. 'It's the kind of shallow emotion you only ever see in Hollywood movies so I wasn't in the least bit surprised when he told Nick he was an actor.'

Galbraith exchanged a questioning glance with Ingram.

'I'd say that's an accurate description,' admitted the constable honestly. 'He was very friendly towards Paul.'

'How friendly?'

'*Very*,' said Ingram. 'And Miss Jenner's right. Danny kept pushing him away.'

'*Child seducer?*' wrote Galbraith in his notebook. 'Did you see Steve abandon a rucksack on the hillside before he took the boys down to Nick's car?' he asked Maggie then.

She was looking at him rather oddly. 'The first time I saw him was at the boatsheds,' she said.

'Did you see him retrieve it after Nick drove the boys away?'

'I wasn't watching him.' Her forehead creased into lines of concern. 'Look . . . aren't you jumping to conclusions again? When I said he was touching the boys I didn't mean . . . that is . . . it wasn't inappropriate . . . just, well, *overdone*, if you like.'

'Okay.'

'What I'm trying to say is I don't think he's a paedophile.'

'Have you ever met one, Miss Jenner?'

'No.'

'Well, they don't have two heads, you know. Nevertheless, point taken,' he assured her in a conscious echo of what she'd said herself. Gallantly he lifted his untouched mug from the floor and drank it down before taking a card from his wallet and passing it across. 'That's my number,' he said, getting up. 'If anything occurs to you that you think's important, you can always reach me there. Thank you for your help.'

She nodded, watching as Ingram moved away from the window. 'You haven't drunk *your* coffee,' she said with a malicious gleam in her eyes. 'Perhaps you'd have preferred it with sugar after all. I always find the mouse droppings sink to the bottom.'

He smiled down at her. 'But dog hairs don't, Miss Jenner.' He put on his cap and straightened the peak. 'My regards to your mother.'

Kate Sumner's papers and private possessions had filled several boxes, which the investigators had been working their way through methodically for three days, trying to build a picture of the woman's life. There was nothing to link her with Steven Harding, or with any other man.

Everyone in her address book was contacted without results. They proved, without exception, to be people she had met since moving to the south coast and matched a neat Christmas card list in the bottom drawer of the bureau in the sitting room. An exercise book was found in one of the kitchen cupboards, inscribed: '*Weekly Diary*', but turned out, disappointingly, to be a precise record of what she spent on food and household bills, and tallied, give or take a pound or two, with the allowance William paid her.

Her correspondence was composed almost entirely of business letters, usually referring to work on the house, although there were a few private letters from friends and acquaintances in Lymington, her mother-in-law, and one, with a date in July, from Polly Garrard at Pharmatec UK.

Dear Kate,

It's ages since we had a chat and every time I ring the phone's off the hook or you're not there. Give me a buzz when you can. I'm dying to hear how you and Hannah are getting on in Lymington. It's a waste of time asking William. He just nods and says: 'Fine.'

I'd really love to see the house since you've had all the decorating done. Maybe I could take a day off and visit you when William's at work? That way he can't complain if all we do is sit and gossip. Do you remember Wendy Plater? She got drunk a couple of weeks ago at lunchtime and called Purdy 'a tight-arsed prick' because he was in the hall when she came staggering back late and he told her he was going to dock her wages. God, it was funny! He would have sacked her on the spot if good old Trew hadn't spoken up for her. She had to apologize, but she doesn't regret any of it. She says she's never seen Purdy go purple before!

I thought of you immediately, of course, which
is why I've been ringing. It really is <u>ages</u>. <u>Do</u> call.
Thinking of you,
    Love,
        Polly Garrard

Attached to it by paper clip was the draft of an answer
from Kate.

Dear Polly,
    Hannah and I are doing well, and of course
you must come and visit us. I'm a bit busy at the
moment, but will ring as soon as I can. The house
looks great. You'll love it.
    ~~You promised on your honour~~ The story about
Wendy Plater was really funny!
    Hope all's well with you.
    Speak soon,
        Love,
            Kate

The Spender brothers' parents looked worried when
Ingram asked if he and DI Galbraith could talk to Paul
in private. 'What's he done?' asked the father.

Ingram removed his cap and smoothed his dark hair
with the flat of his hand. 'Nothing as far as I know,' he
said with a smile. 'It's just a few routine questions, that's
all.'

'Then why do you want to talk to him in private?'

Ingram's frank gaze held his. 'Because the dead woman was naked, Mr Spender, and Paul's embarrassed to talk about it in front of you and your wife.'

The man gave a snort of amusement. 'He must think we're the most frightful prudes.'

Ingram's smile broadened. 'Just parents,' he said. He gestured towards the lane in front of their rented cottage. 'He'll probably feel more comfortable if he talks to us outside.'

In the event Paul was surprisingly open about Steven Harding's 'friendliness'. 'I reckon he fancied Maggie and was trying to impress her by how good he was with kids,' he told the policemen. 'My uncle's always doing it. If he comes to our house on his own he doesn't bother to talk to us, but if he brings one of his girlfriends he puts his arms round our shoulders and tells us jokes. It's only to make them think he'd be a good father.'

Galbraith chuckled. 'And that's what Steve was doing?'

'Must have been. He got much more friendly after she turned up.'

'Did you notice him playing with his phone at all?'

'You mean the way Danny says?'

Galbraith nodded.

'I didn't watch him because I didn't want to be rude, but Danny's pretty sure about it, and he should know because he was staring at him all the time.'

'So why was Steve doing that, do you think?'

'Because he forgot we were there,' said the boy.

'In what way exactly?'

Paul showed the first signs of embarrassment. 'Well,

you know,' he said earnestly, 'he sort of did it without thinking . . . my dad often does things without thinking, like licking his knife in restaurants. Mum gets really angry about it.'

Galbraith gave a nod of agreement. 'You're a bright lad. I should have thought of that myself.' He stroked the side of his freckled face, considering the problem. 'Still, rubbing yourself with a telephone's a bit different from licking your knife. You don't think it's more likely he was showing off?'

'He looked at a girl through the binoculars,' Paul offered. 'Maybe he was showing off to her?'

'Maybe.' Galbraith pretended to ponder some more. 'You don't think it's more likely he was showing off to you and Danny?'

'Well . . . he talked a lot about ladies he'd seen in the nude, but I sort of got the feeling most of it wasn't true . . . I think he was trying to make us feel better.'

'Does Danny agree with you?'

The boy shook his head. 'No, but that doesn't mean anything. He reckons Steve stole his T-shirt so he doesn't like him.'

'Is it true?'

'I don't think so. It's just an excuse because he's lost it and Mum gave him an earbashing. It's got DERBY FC on the front and it cost a fortune.'

'Did Danny have it with him on Sunday?'

'He says it was in the bundle round the binoculars but I don't remember it.'

'Okay.' Galbraith nodded again. 'So what does Danny think Steve was up to?'

'He reckons he's a paedophile,' said Paul matter-of-factly.

WPC Sandra Griffiths whistled tunelessly to herself as she made a cup of tea in the kitchen at Langton Cottage. Hannah was sitting mesmerized in front of the television in the sitting room, while Sandy was blessing the memory of whatever genius had invented the electronic nanny. She turned towards the fridge in search of milk and found William Sumner standing directly behind her. 'Did I frighten you?' he asked as she gave a little start of surprise.

You know you did, you stupid bastard . . . ! She forced a smile to her face to disguise the fact that he was beginning to give her the creeps. 'Yes,' she admitted. 'I didn't hear you come in.'

'That's what Kate used to say. She'd get quite angry about it sometimes.'

Who can blame her . . . ? She was beginning to think of him as a voyeur, a man who got his rocks off by secretly watching a woman go about her business. She had stopped counting the number of times she'd glimpsed him peering round a door jamb like an unwelcome intruder in his own house. She put distance between herself and him by removing the teapot to the kitchen table and pulling out a chair. There was a lengthy silence during which he sulkily kicked the toe of his shoe against the table leg, shoving the top in little jerks against her belly.

'You're afraid of me, aren't you?' he said suddenly.

'What makes you think that?' she asked as she held the table firm against his kicks.

'You were afraid last night.' He looked pleased, as if the idea excited him, and she wondered how important it was to him to feel superior.

'Don't flatter yourself,' she declared bluntly, lighting a cigarette and blowing the smoke deliberately in his direction. 'Trust me, if I'd been remotely afraid, I'd have taken your fucking balls off. Cripple first and ask questions later, that's my motto.'

'I don't like you smoking or swearing in this house,' he said with another petulant kick at the table leg.

'Then put in a complaint,' she answered. 'It just means I'll be reassigned.' She held his gaze for a moment. 'And that wouldn't suit you one little bit, would it? You're too damn used to having an unpaid skivvy about the place.'

Ready tears sprang to his eyes. 'You don't understand what it's like. Everything worked so well before. And now . . . well, I don't even know what I'm supposed to be doing.'

His performance was amateur at best, diabolical at worst, and it brought out the bully in Griffiths. *Did he think she found male helplessness attractive?* 'Then you should be ashamed of yourself,' she snapped. 'According to the health visitor you didn't even know where the vacuum cleaner was, let alone how to work it. She came here to teach you elementary parenting and housekeeping skills because no one – and I repeat *no one* – is going to allow a three-year-old child to remain in the care of a man who is so patently indifferent to her welfare.'

He moved around the kitchen, opening and shutting cupboard doors as if to demonstrate familiarity with their contents. 'It's not my fault,' he said. 'That's how Kate wanted it. I wasn't allowed to interfere in the running of the house.'

'Are you sure it wasn't the other way round?' She tapped the ash off her cigarette into her saucer. 'I mean you didn't marry a wife, did you? You married a housekeeper who was expected to run this house like clockwork and account for every last penny she spent.'

'It wasn't like that.'

'What was it like then?'

'Living in a cheap boarding house,' he said bitterly. 'I didn't marry a wife *or* a housekeeper, I married a landlady who allowed me to live here as long as I paid my rent on time.'

The French yacht, *Mirage,* motored up the Dart river early on Thursday afternoon and took a berth in the Dart Haven Marina on the Kingswear side of the estuary, opposite the lovely town of Dartmouth and alongside the steam railway line to Paignton. Shortly after they made fast, there was a blast on a whistle and the three o'clock train set off in a rush of steam, raising in the Beneteau's owner a romantic longing for days he himself couldn't remember.

By contrast his daughter sat sunk in gloom, unable to comprehend why they had moored on the side of the river that boasted nothing except the station when everything that was attractive – shops, restaurants, pubs, people, life, *men!* – was on the other side in Dartmouth. Scornfully, she watched her father take out the video camera and search through the case for a new tape in order to film steam engines. He was like a small boy, she thought, in his silly enthusiasms for the treasures of rural England when what really mattered was London. She was the only one of her friends who had never been there, and it mortified her. God, but her parents were *sad*!

Her father turned to her in mild frustration, asking where the unused tapes were, and she had to admit there were none. She'd used them all to film irrelevancies in order to pass the time, and with irritating tolerance (he was one of those understanding fathers who refused to indulge in rows) he played the videos back, squinting into the eyepiece, in order to select the least interesting for reuse.

When he came to a tape of a young man scrambling down the slope above Chapman's Pool towards two boys, followed by shots of him sitting alone on the foreshore beyond the boatsheds, he lowered the camera and looked at his daughter with a worried frown. She was fourteen years old, and he realized he had no idea if she was still innocent or whether she knew exactly what she'd been filming. He described the young man and asked her why she had taken so much footage of him. Her cheeks flushed a rosy red under her tan. No particular reason. He was there and he was – she spoke with defiance – handsome. In any case, she knew him. They'd introduced themselves when they'd chatted together in Lymington. *And* he fancied her. She could tell these things.

Her father was appalled.

His daughter flounced her shoulders. What was the big deal? So he was English? He was just a good-looking guy who liked French girls, she said.

Bibi Gould's face fell as she swung light-heartedly out of the hairdressing salon in Lymington where she worked and saw Tony Bridges standing on the pavement, half-turned away from her, watching a young mother hoist a toddler on to her hip. Her relationship, such as it was, with Tony had become more of a trial than a pleasure and for a brief second she thought about retreating through the door again until she realized he had seen her out of the corner of his eye. She forced a sickly smile to her lips. 'Hi,' she said with unconvincing jauntiness.

He stared at her with his peculiarly brooding expression, taking note of the skimpy shorts and cropped top that barely covered her tanned arms, legs and midriff. A blood vessel started to throb in his head, and he had trouble keeping the temper out of his voice. 'Who are you meeting?'

'No one,' she said.

'Then what's the problem? Why did you look so pissed to see me?'

'I didn't.' She lowered her head to swing her curtain

of hair across her eyes in a way he hated. 'I'm just tired, that's all . . . I was going home to watch telly.'

He reached out a hand to grip her wrist. 'Steve's done a vanishing act. Is he the one you're planning to meet?'

'Don't be stupid.'

'Where is he?'

'How would I know?' she said, twisting her arm to try to release herself. 'He's your friend.'

'Has he gone to the caravan? Did you say you'd meet him there?'

Angrily, she succeeded in tugging herself free. 'You've got a real problem with him, you know . . . you should talk to someone about it instead of taking it out on me all the time. And for your information, not everyone runs away to hide in Mummy and Daddy's sodding caravan every time things go wrong. It's a dump, for Christ's sake . . . like your house . . . and who wants to fuck in a dump?' She rubbed her wrist where his fingers had left a Chinese burn on her skin, her immature nineteen-year-old features creasing into a vicious scowl. 'It's not Steve's fault you're so spaced out most nights you can't get it up, so don't keep pretending it is. The trouble with you is you've lost it, but you can't bloody well see it.'

He eyed her with dislike. 'What about Saturday? It wasn't me who passed out on Saturday. I'm sick to death of being fucked about, Beebs.'

She was on the point of giving a petulant toss of her head and saying sex with him had become so boring that she might as well be comatose as not when caution persuaded her against it. He had a way of getting his own back that she didn't much like. 'Yeah, well, you can't blame me for that,' she muttered lamely. 'You shouldn't buy dodgy E off your dodgy mates, should you? A girl could die that way.'

Chapter Sixteen

FAX:

From: PC Nicholas Ingram Date: 14 August – 7.05 p.m.
To: DI John Galbraith Re: **Kate Sumner murder inquiry**

....

Sir,

I've had some follow-up thoughts on the above, particularly in relation to the pathologist's report and the stranded dinghy, and as it's my day off tomorrow I'm faxing them through to you. Admittedly they are based entirely on the presumption that the stranded dinghy was involved in Kate's murder, but they suggest a new angle which may be worth considering.

I mentioned this a.m. that: 1) there's a possibility the dinghy was stolen from Lulworth Cove at the end of May, in which case the thief and Kate's murderer could be one and the same person; 2) that if my 'towing' theory was correct, there was a good chance the out-board engine (Make: Fastrigger; Serial No: 240B

5006678) was removed and remains in the thief's possession; 3) you take another look at Steven Harding's log to see if he was in Lulworth Cove on Thursday, 29 May; 4) if he had a second dinghy stowed on board *Crazy Daze* – which only required a foot pump to reflate it – it would solve some of your forensic problems; 5) he probably has a lock-up somewhere which you haven't yet discovered and which may contain the stolen outboard.

***I have since had time to consider the logistics of how the dinghy was actually removed from Lulworth Cove in broad daylight and I've realized that Harding or indeed any boat owner would have had some difficulty.

It's important to recognize that *Crazy Daze* must have anchored in the middle of Lulworth Bay and Harding could only have come ashore in his own dinghy. Joyriders going for a spin would have attracted little attention (the assumption would be that the boat belonged to them) but a man on his own, coping with two dinghies, would have stood out like a sore thumb, particularly as the only way he could have removed them from the Cove (unless he was prepared to waste time deflating them) was to tow them in tandem or parallel behind *Crazy Daze*. It is highly unusual for a yacht to have two dinghies and, once the theft had been reported, that fact is bound to have registered with the coastguards in the lookout point above Lulworth.

I think now that a more likely scenario for the theft was removal by foot. Let's say an opportunist thief spotted that the outboard wasn't padlocked, released

its clamps and carried it away quite openly to his car/
house/garage/caravan. Let's say he wandered back half
an hour later to see if the owners had returned and,
finding they hadn't, he simply hoisted the dinghy above
his head and carried that away too. I'm not suggesting
that Kate Sumner's murder was premeditated at this
early stage, but what I am suggesting is that the
opportunist theft of the Spanish dinghy in May gave
rise to an ideal method in August for the disposal of her
body. (NB: thefts of or from boats represent some of the
highest crime statistics along the south coast.) I
strongly advise, therefore, that you try to find out if
anyone connected with Kate was staying in or near
Lulworth between 24–31 May. I suspect the sad irony
will be that she, her husband and her daughter were –
there are several caravan parks and campsites round
Lulworth – but I think this will please you. It strength-
ens the case against the husband.

For reasons that follow, I am no longer confident that
you'll find the outboard. Assuming the intention was for
the stolen dinghy, plus contents (i.e. Kate) to sink, then
the outboard must have been on board.

You may remember my querying the 'hypothermia'
issue in the pathologist's report when you showed it to
me on Monday. The pathologist's view is that Kate was
swimming in the water for some considerable time,
prior to drowning, which caused her stress and cold. At
the time I wondered why it took her so long to swim a
comparatively short distance and I suggested that she
was more likely to suffer hypothermia from being
exposed to air temperature at night rather than sea

temperature – the latter being generally warmer. It would depend of course on how good a swimmer she was, particularly as the pathologist refers to her entering the sea a <u>minimum</u> of half a mile WSW of Egmont Bight, and I assumed she must have swum a great deal further than his estimate. However, you told Miss Jenner this morning that Kate was a poor swimmer, and I have been wondering since how a poor swimmer could have remained afloat long enough in difficult seas to show evidence of hypothermia before death. I have also been wondering why her killer was confident of making it safely back to shore, since there are no lights on that part of the coast and the currents are unpredictable.

One explanation which covers the above is that Kate was raped ashore, her killer presumed her dead after the strangulation attempt and the whole 'drowning' exercise was designed to dispose of her body off an isolated stretch of coast.

Can you buy this reasoning? 1) He bundled her naked and unconscious body into the stolen dinghy, then took her a considerable distance – Lulworth Cove to Chapman's Pool = 8 nautical miles approx. – before he tied her to the outboard and left the dinghy to sink with its contents (wind-chill factor would already have caused hypothermia in a naked woman); 2) once set adrift, Kate came round from the strangulation attempt/ Rohypnol and realized she had to save herself; 3) her broken fingers and nails could have resulted from her struggle to break free of her bonds then release the clamps holding the outboard in place in order to eject its weight, probably capsizing the dinghy in the pro-

238

cess; 4) she used the dinghy as a float and only became separated from it when she lapsed into unconsciousness or became too tired to hold on; 5) in all events, I am guessing the dinghy travelled <u>much closer to shore than the pathologist's estimate</u> otherwise the boat would have become swamped and the killer himself would have been in trouble; 6) killer climbed the cliffs and returned to Lulworth/Kimmeridge via the coastal path during the dark hours of the night.

This is as far as my thoughts have taken me, but if the dinghy <u>was</u> involved in the murder then it must have come from the west – Kimmeridge Bay or Lulworth Cove – because the craft was too fragile to negotiate the race around St Alban's Head. I realize none of this explains Hannah, although I can't help feeling that if you can discover where the stolen dinghy was hidden for two months, you may also discover where Kate was raped and where Hannah was left while her mother was being drowned.

(NB: None of the above rules out Harding – the rape <u>may</u> have taken place on his deck with the evidence subsequently washed away, and the dinghy <u>may</u> have been towed behind *Crazy Daze* – but does it make him a less likely suspect?)

Nick Ingram

Chapter Seventeen

THE SUN HAD been up less than an hour on Friday morning when Maggie Jenner set off along the bridle-way behind Broxton House, accompanied by Bertie. She was on a skittish bay gelding called Stinger, whose owner came down from London every weekend to her cottage in Langton Matravers to ride hard around the headlands as an antidote to her high-pressured job as a money broker in the City. Maggie loved the horse but loathed the woman whose hands were about as sensitive as steam hammers and who viewed Stinger in the same way as she probably viewed a snort of cocaine – as a quick adrenaline fix. If she hadn't agreed to pay well over the odds for the livery service Maggie provided, Maggie would have refused her business without a second's hesitation but, as with most things in the Jenners' lives, compromise had become the better part of staving off bankruptcy.

She turned right at St Alban's Head Quarry, negoti-ating her way through the gate and into the deep, wide valley that cleaved a grassy downland passage towards the sea between St Alban's Head to the south and the high ground above Chapman's Pool to the north. She nudged her mount into a canter and sent him springing across the turf in glorious release. It was still cool but there was barely a breath of wind in the air, and as always on mornings like this her spirits soared. However bad existence was, and it could be very bad at times, she ceased to worry about it here. If there was any point to anything, then she came closest to finding it, alone and free, in the renewed optimism that a fresh sun generated with each daybreak.

She reined in after half a mile, and walked the gelding towards the fenced coastal path which hugged the slopes of the valley on either side in a series of steep steps cut into the cliffs. It was a hardy rambler who suffered the agony of the downward trek only to be faced with the worse agony of the upward climb, and Maggie, who had never done either, thought how much more sensible it was to ride the gully in order to enjoy the scenery. Ahead, the sea, a sparkling blue, was flat calm without a sail in sight and she slipped lightly from the saddle while Bertie, panting from the exertion of keeping up, rolled leisurely in the warming grass beside the gelding's hooves. Looping Stinger's reins casually round the top rail of the fence, she climbed the stile and walked the few yards to the cliff edge to stand and glory in the vast expanse of blueness where the line of demarcation between sky and sea was all but invisible. The only sounds were the gentle swish of breakers on the shore, the sigh of the animals' breaths and a lark singing in the sky above . . .

It was difficult to say who was the more startled, therefore, Maggie or Steven Harding, when he rose out of the ground in front of her after hoisting himself over the cliff edge where the downland valley dropped towards the sea. He crouched on all fours for several seconds, his face pale and unshaven, breathing heavily and looking a great deal less pretty than he had five days before. More like a rapist; less like a Hollywood lead. There was a quality of disturbing violence about him, something calculating in the dark eyes that Maggie hadn't noticed before, but it was his abrupt rearing to full height that caused her to shriek. Her alarm transmitted itself immediately to Stinger who pranced backwards, tearing his reins free of the fence, and thence to Bertie who leapt to his feet, hackles up.

'YOU STUPID BASTARD!' Maggie shouted at him, giving vent to her fear in furious remonstration as she heard Stinger's snort of alarm and stamping hooves. She turned away from Harding in a vain attempt to catch the excited gelding's reins before he bolted.

Pray God, he didn't . . . he was worth a fortune to Broxton House Livery Stables . . . she couldn't afford it if he damaged himself . . . pray God, pray God . . .

But Harding, for reasons best known to himself, darted across her path in Stinger's direction and the gelding, eyes rolling, took off like lightning up the hill.

'OH, SHIT!' Maggie stormed, stamping her foot and raging at the young man, her face red and ugly with ungovernable fury. 'How could you be so bloody infantile, you – you CREEP! What the *hell* did you think you were doing! I swear to Christ if Nick Ingram knew you were here he'd *crucify* you! He already thinks you're a fucking PERVERT!'

242

She was completely unprepared for his backhand slap that caught her a glancing blow across the side of her face and as she hit the ground with a resounding thud, the only thought in her head was: What on earth does this idiot think he's doing . . . ?

Ingram squinted painfully at his alarm clock when his phone rang at 6.30 a.m. He lifted the receiver and listened to a series of high-pitched, unintelligible squeaks at the other end of the line which he recognized as coming from Maggie Jenner.

'You'll have to calm down,' he said when she finally took a breath. 'I can't understand a word you're saying.'

More squeaks.

'Pull yourself together, Maggie,' he said firmly. 'You're not a wimp so don't behave like one.'

'I'm sorry,' she said with a commendable attempt to compose herself. 'Steven Harding hit me so Bertie went for him . . . there's blood everywhere . . . I've rigged up a tourniquet on his arm but it's not working properly . . . I don't know what else to do . . . I think he's going to die if he doesn't get to hospital.'

He sat up and rubbed his face furiously to eradicate sleep. He could hear the white noise of empty space and the sound of birdsong in the background. 'Where are you?'

'At the end of the quarry gully . . . near the steps on the coastal path . . . halfway between Chapman's Pool and St Alban's Head . . . Stinger's bolted and I'm afraid he's going to break a leg if he trips on his reins . . . we'll lose everything . . . I think Steve's dying . . .' Her voice faded as she turned away from the signal. 'Manslaughter . . . Bertie was out of control . . .'

'I'm losing you, Maggie,' he shouted.

'Sorry.' Her voice came back in a rush. 'He's not responding to anything. I'm worried Bertie's severed an artery but I can't get the tourniquet tight enough to stop the bleeding. I'm using Bertie's lead but it's too loose and the sticks here are all so rotten they just keep breaking.'

'Then forget the lead and use something else – something you can get a grip on – a T-shirt maybe. Wind it round his arm as tight as you can above the elbow then keep twisting the ends to exert some pressure. Failing that, try and locate the artery on the underside of his upper arm with your fingers and press hard against the bone to stop the flow. But you've got to keep the pressure on, Maggie, otherwise he'll start bleeding again, and that means your hands are going to hurt.'

'Okay.'

'Good girl. I'll get help to you as fast as I can.' He cut her off and dialled Broxton House. 'Mrs Jenner?' he said, flicking over to the loudspeaker when the receiver was lifted at the other end. 'It's Nick Ingram.' He flung himself out of bed and started to drag on some clothes. 'Maggie needs help and you're the closest. She's trying to stop a man bleeding to death in the quarry gully. They're at the coastal path end. If you take Sir Jasper and get up there PDQ, then the man stands a chance, otherwise—'

'But I'm not dressed,' she interrupted indignantly.

'I couldn't give a shit,' he said bluntly. 'Get your arse up there and give your daughter some support because, by God, it'll be a first if you do.'

'How dare—'

He cut her off, and set in motion the series of calls that would result in the Portland Search and Rescue helicopter being scrambled in the direction of St Alban's Head for the second time in less than a week when the ambulance service expressed doubt about their ability to reach a man in a remote grassy valley before he bled to death.

By the time Nick Ingram reached the scene, having driven his Jeep at breakneck speed along narrow lanes and up the bridleway, the drama was effectively over. The helicopter was on the ground some fifty yards from the scene of the accident, engine idling, Harding was conscious and sitting up being attended by an SAR paramedic, and another hundred yards to the south of the helicopter and halfway up the hillside, Maggie was busy trying to catch Stinger who rolled his eyes and backed away from her every time she came too close. She was clearly trying to head him off from the cliff edge but he was too frightened of the helicopter to move in its direction, and all she was succeeding in doing was driving him towards the three-foot-high fence and the perilously steep steps that edged the cliff. Celia, clad in a pair of pyjama trousers and a tannin-stained bedjacket, stood arrogantly to one side with one hand grasping Sir

Jasper's reins tightly beneath his chin and the other wound into the looped end in case he, too, decided to bolt. She favoured Ingram with a frosty glare, designed to freeze him in his tracks, but he ignored her and turned his attention to Harding.

'Are you all right, sir?'

The young man nodded. He was dressed in Levi's and a pale green sweatshirt, both of which were copiously splattered with blood, and his lower right arm was tightly bandaged.

Ingram turned to the paramedic. 'What's the damage?'

'He'll live,' said the man. 'The two ladies managed to stop the bleeding. He'll need stitching so we'll take him to Poole and get him sorted there.' He drew Nick aside. 'The young lady could do with some attention. She's shaking like a leaf, but she says it's more important to catch the horse. The trouble is he's torn his reins off and she can't get close enough to get a grip on his throat strap.' He jerked his head towards Celia. 'And the older one's not much better. She's got arthritis, and she wrecked her hip riding up here. By rights, we ought to take them with us, but they're adamant they won't leave the animals. There's also a time problem. We need to get moving, but the loose horse is going to bolt in real earnest the minute we take off. It's terrified out of its wits already and damn nearly skidded over the cliff when we landed.'

'Where's the dog?'

'Vanished. I gather the young lady had to thrash him

with his lead to get him off the lad, and he's fled with his tail between his legs.'

Nick rumpled his sleep-tousled hair. 'Okay, can you give us another five minutes? If I help Miss Jenner round up the horse, we may be able to persuade her mother to go in for some treatment. How about it?'

The paramedic turned to look at Steven Harding. 'Why not? He says he's strong enough to walk but it'll take me a good five minutes to get him in and settled. I don't fancy your chances much, but good luck.'

With a wry smile, Nick put his fingers to his lips and gave a piercing whistle before scanning both hillsides with narrowed eyes. To his relief, he saw Bertie rise out of the grass on the breast of Emmetts Hill about two hundred and fifty yards away. He gave another whistle and the dog came like a torpedo towards him. He raised his arm and dropped him to the ground when he was still fifty yards away, then went back to Celia. 'I need a quick decision,' he told her. 'We've got five minutes to catch Stinger before the helicopter leaves, and it strikes me Maggie'll have more chance if she's riding Sir Jasper. You're the expert. Do I take him up to her or do I leave him with you, bearing in mind I know nothing about horses and Jasper's likely to be just as frightened of the noise as Stinger is?'

She was a sensible woman and didn't waste time on recriminations. She handed the loop of the reins into his left hand and guided his right into position under Jasper's chin. 'Keep clicking your tongue,' she said, 'and he'll follow. Don't try and run, and don't let go. We can't afford to lose both of them. Remind Maggie they'll both go mad the minute the helicopter takes off so tell her to ride like the devil for the middle of the headland and give herself some space.'

He set off up the slope, whistling Bertie to follow and gathering him into his left leg so that the dog walked like a shadow beside him.

'I didn't realize it was his dog,' said the paramedic to Celia.

'It's not,' she said thoughtfully, shading her eyes against the sun to watch what happened.

She saw her daughter come stumbling down towards the tall policeman, who had a quick word with her then hefted her lightly into Jasper's saddle before, with a gesture of his arm, he sent Bertie out in a sweeping movement towards the cliff edge to circle round behind the excited gelding. He followed in Bertie's wake, placing himself as an immovable obstacle between the horse and the brink, while directing the dog to hamper Stinger's further retreat up the hillside by dashing to and fro above him. Meanwhile, Maggie had turned Sir Jasper towards the quarry site and had kicked him into a canter. Faced with the unpalatable alternatives of a dog on one side, a helicopter on the other and a man behind, Stinger chose the sensible option of pursuing the other horse towards safety.

'Impressive,' said the paramedic.

'Yes,' said Celia even more thoughtfully. 'It was, wasn't it?'

*

Polly Garrard was about to leave for work when DI John Galbraith rang her front doorbell and asked if she was willing to answer a few more questions about her relationship with Kate Sumner. 'I can't,' she told him. 'I'll be late. You can come to the office if you like.'

'Fine, if that's the way you want it,' he assured her. 'It might make things difficult for you, though. You probably won't want eavesdroppers to some of the things I'm going to ask you.'

'Oh, shit!' she said immediately. 'I knew this was going to happen.' She opened the door wide. 'You'd better come in,' she said, leading the way into a tiny sitting room, 'but you can't keep me long. Half an hour max, okay? I've already been late twice this month and I'm running out of excuses.'

She dropped on to one end of a sofa, hooking an arm over its back, and inviting him to sit at the other end. She twisted round to face him, one leg curled beneath her so that her skirt rose up to her crotch and her breasts stood out in response to her pulled-back shoulder. The pose was deliberate, thought Galbraith with some amusement, as he lowered himself on to the seat beside her. She was a well-built young woman with a taste for tight T-shirts, heavy make-up and blue nail varnish, and he wondered how Angela Sumner would have coped with Polly as a daughter-in-law in place of Kate. For all her real or imagined sins, Kate seemed to have looked the part of William's wife even if she did lack the necessary social and educational skills that would have satisfied her mother-in-law.

'I want to ask you about a letter you wrote to Kate in

July which concerns some of the people you work with,' he told Polly, taking a photocopy of it out of his breast pocket. He spread it on his knee and handed it to her. 'Do you remember sending that?'

She read it through quickly, then nodded. 'Yup. I'd been phoning on and off for about a week, and I thought, what the hell, she's obviously busy, so I'll drop her a note instead and get her to phone me.' She screwed her face into cartoon pique. 'Not that she ever did. She just sent a scrotty little note, saying she'd call when she was ready.'

'This one?' He handed her a copy of Kate's draft reply.

She glanced at it. 'I guess so. That's what it said, more or less. It was on some fancy headed notepaper, I remember that, but I was pissed that she couldn't be bothered to write a decent letter back. The truth is, I don't think she wanted me to go. I expect she was afraid I'd embarrass her in front of her Lymington friends. Which I probably would have done,' she added in fairness.

Galbraith smiled. 'Did you visit the house when they first moved?'

'Nope. Never got invited. She kept saying I could go as soon as the decorating was finished, but' – she pulled another face – 'it was just an excuse to put me off. I didn't mind. Fact is, I'd probably have done the same in her shoes. She'd moved on – new house, new life, new friends – and you grow out of people when that happens, don't you?'

'She hadn't moved on completely,' he pointed out. 'You still work with William.'

Polly giggled. 'I work in the same building as William,' she corrected him, 'and it gets up his nose something rotten that I tell everyone he married my best friend. I know it's not true – it never was, really – I mean I liked her and all that, but she wasn't the best-friend type, if you know what I mean. Too self-contained by half. No, I just do it to annoy William. He thinks I'm common as muck, and he nearly died when I told him I'd visited Kate in Chichester and met his mother. I'm not surprised. God, she was an old battleaxe! Lecture, lecture, lecture. Do this. Don't do that. Frankly, I'd've wheeled her in front of a bus if she'd been *my* mother-in-law.'

'Was there ever a chance of that?'

'Do me a favour! I'd need to be permanently comatose to marry William Sumner. The guy has about as much sex appeal as a turnip!'

'So what did Kate see in him?'

Polly rubbed her thumb and forefinger together. 'Money.'

'What else?'

'Nothing. A bit of class, maybe, but an unmarried bloke with no children and money was what she was looking for, and an unmarried bloke with no children and money is what she got.' She cocked her head on one side, amused by his expression of disbelief. 'She told me once that William's tackle, even when he had a stiffy, was so limp it was more like an uncooked sausage than

251

a truncheon. So I said, how does he do the business? And she said, with a pint of baby oil and my finger up his fucking arse.' She giggled again at Galbraith's wince of sympathy for another man's problems. 'He loved it, for Christ's sake! Why else would he marry her with his mother spitting poison all over the place? Okay, Kate may have wanted money, but poor old Willy just wanted a tart who'd tell him he was bloody brilliant whether he was or not. It worked like a dream. They both got what they wanted.'

He studied her for a moment, wondering if she was quite as naive as her words made her sound. 'Did they?' he asked her. 'Kate's dead, don't forget.'

She sobered immediately. 'I know. It's a bugger. But there's nothing I can tell you about that. I haven't seen her since she moved.'

'All right. Tell me what you do know. Why did your story about Wendy Plater insulting James Purdy remind you of Kate?' he asked her.

'What makes you think it did?'

He quoted from her letter. ' "*She*" – meaning Wendy – "*had to apologize, but she doesn't regret any of it. She says she's never seen Purdy go purple before! I thought of you immediately, of course . . .*" ' He laid the page on the bench between them. 'Why that last bit, Polly? Why should Purdy going purple make you think of Kate Sumner?'

She thought for a moment. 'Because she used to work at Pharmatec?' she tried unconvincingly. 'Because she thought Purdy was a prick? It's just a figure of speech.'

He tapped the copy of Kate's draft reply. 'She crossed out, "*You promised on your honour*", in this before going on to write, "*The story about Wendy Plater was really funny!*"' he said. 'What did you promise her, Polly?'

She looked uncomfortable. 'Hundreds of things, I should think.'

'I'm only interested in the one that had something to do with either James Purdy or Wendy Plater.'

She removed her arm from the back of the seat and hunched forward despondently. 'It's got nothing to do with her being killed. It's just something that happened.'

'What?'

She didn't answer.

'If it really does have nothing to do with her murder, then I give you my word it'll go no further than me,' he said reassuringly. 'I'm not interested in exposing her secrets, only in finding her killer.' Even as he spoke, he knew the statement was untrue. All too often, justice for a rape victim meant that she had to endure the humiliation of her secrets being exposed. He looked at Polly with unexpected sympathy. 'But I'm afraid *I'm* the one who has to decide whether it's important.'

She sighed. 'I could lose my job if Purdy ever finds out I told you.'

'There's no reason why he should.'

'You reckon?'

Galbraith didn't say anything, having learnt from experience that silence often exerted more pressure than words.

'Oh, what the hell!' she said then. 'You've probably guessed anyway. Kate had an affair with him. He was

253

crazy about her, wanted to leave his wife and everything, then she blew him away and said she was going to marry William instead. Poor old Purdy couldn't believe it. He's no spring chicken, and he'd been rogering himself stupid to keep her interested. I think he may even have told his wife he wanted a divorce. Anyway, Kate said he went purple and then collapsed on his desk. He was off work for three months afterwards, so I reckoned he must have had a heart attack, but Kate said he couldn't face coming back while she was still there.' She shrugged. 'He started work again the week after she left so maybe she was right.'

'Why did she choose William?' he asked. 'She wasn't any more in love with him than she was with Purdy, was she?'

Polly repeated the gesture of rubbing her thumb and fingers together. 'Dosh,' she said. 'Purdy's got a wife and three grown-up children, all of whom would have demanded their cut before Kate got a look in.' She pulled a wry face. 'Like I said, what she really wanted was an unmarried guy without children. She reckoned if she was going to have to bust a gut to make some plonker happy, she wanted access to everything he owned.'

Galbraith shook his head in perplexity. 'Then why bother with Purdy at all?'

She hooked her arm over the sofa again and thrust her tits into his face. 'She didn't have a father, did she? Any more than I do.'

'So?'

'She had a thing about older men.' She opened her

eyes wide in flirtatious invitation. 'Me, too, if you're interested.'

Galbraith chuckled. 'Do you eat them alive?'

She looked pointedly at his fly. 'I swallow them whole,' she said with a laugh.

He shook his head in amusement. 'You were telling me why Kate bothered with Purdy,' he reminded her.

'He was the boss,' she said, 'the guy with the loot. She thought she'd take him for a few bob, get him to pay for improvements on her flat, while she looked around for something better. The trouble was, she didn't reckon on him getting as smitten as he did so the only way to get rid of him was to be cruel. She wanted security, not love, you see, and she didn't think she'd get it from Purdy, not after his wife and children had taken their slice. He was thirty years older than she was, remember. Also, he didn't want any more kids, and that was all she really wanted, kids of her own. She was pretty screwed up in some ways, I guess because she'd had a tough time growing up.'

'Did William know about her affair with Purdy?'

Polly shook her head. 'No one knew except me. That's why she swore me to secrecy. She said William would call the wedding off if he ever found out.'

'Would he have done?'

'Oh, for sure. Look, he was thirty-seven years old, and he wasn't the marrying kind. Wendy Plater nearly got him up to scratch once till Kate put a spanner in the works by telling him she was a lush. He dumped her so quick, you wouldn't believe.' She smiled reminiscently. 'Kate practically had to put a ring through his nose to get him to the registry office. It might have been different if his mother had approved but old Ma Sumner and Will were like Derby and Joan, and Kate had to work her socks off every night to make sex more attractive to the silly sod than having his laundry done on a regular basis.'

'Was it true about Wendy Plater?'

Polly looked uncomfortable again. 'She gets drunk sometimes but not on a regular basis. Still, as Kate said, if Will had wanted to marry her, he wouldn't have believed it, would he? He just seized on the first good excuse to get out.'

Galbraith looked down at Kate Sumner's childish writing in the draft letter she'd written to Polly and wondered about the nature of ruthlessness. 'Did the affair with Purdy continue after she married William?'

'No,' said Polly with conviction. 'Once Kate made up her mind to something, that was it.'

'Would that stop her having an affair with someone else? Let's say she was bored with William and met someone younger – would she have been unfaithful in those circumstances?'

Polly shrugged. 'I don't know. I sort of thought she might have something going because she hasn't bothered to phone me for ages, but that doesn't mean she did. It wouldn't have been serious, anyway. She was pleased as punch about moving to Lymington and getting a decent house and I can't see her giving all that up very easily.'

Galbraith nodded. 'Have you ever known her use faeces as a means of revenge?'

'What the hell's fee-sees?'

'Crap,' Galbraith explained obligingly, 'turds, dung, number twos.'

'Shit!'

'Exactly. Have you ever known her smear crap over anyone's belongings?'

Polly giggled. 'No. She was much too prissy to do anything like that. A bit of a hygiene freak, actually. When Hannah was a baby she used to swab the kitchen down every day with Dettol in case there were any germs. I told her she was crazy – I mean germs are everywhere, aren't they – but she still went on doing it. I can't see her touching a turd in a million years. She used to hold Hannah's nappies at arm's length after she'd changed her.'

Curiouser and curiouser, thought Galbraith. 'Okay. Give me a rough idea of the timetable. How soon after she told Purdy she was going to marry William did the wedding actually take place?'

'I can't remember. A month maybe.'

He did a quick calculation in his head. 'So if Purdy was off for three months, then it was two months after the wedding that she left work because she was pregnant?'

'Something like that.'

'And how pregnant was she, Polly? Two months? Three months? Four months?'

A resigned expression crossed the young woman's face. 'She said as long as it looked like her it wouldn't matter, because William was so besotted he'd believe anything she told him.' She read Galbraith's expression correctly as one of contempt. 'She didn't do it out of malice. Just desperation. She knew what it was like to grow up in poverty.'

Celia's adamant refusal to go with Harding in the helicopter and her inability to bend at the hip meant that she was either going to have to walk home in extreme pain or travel flat on her back on the floor of Ingram's Jeep which was full of oilskins, waders and fishing tackle. With a wry smile he cleared a space and bent to pick her up. However, she was even more adamant in her refusal to be carried. 'I'm not a child,' she snapped.

'I don't see how else we can do it, Mrs Jenner,' he pointed out, 'not unless you slide in on your front and lie face down where I usually put my fish.'

'I suppose you think that's funny.'

'Merely accurate. I'm afraid it's going to be painful whatever we do.'

She looked at the uncomfortable, ridged floor and gave in with bad grace. 'Just don't make a meal of it,' she said crossly. 'I hate fuss.'

'I know.' He scooped her into his arms and leaned into the Jeep to deposit her carefully on the floor. 'It's going to be a bumpy ride,' he warned, packing the oilskins around her as wadding. 'You'd better shout if it gets too much for you and I'll stop.'

It was already too much but she had no intention of telling him so. 'I'm worried about Maggie,' she said through gritted teeth. 'She ought to be back by now.'

'She'll have led Stinger towards the stables not away from them,' he told her.

'Are you ever wrong about anything?' she asked acidly.

'Not where your daughter's knowledge of horses is concerned,' he answered. 'I have faith in her, and so should you.' He shut the door on her and climbed in behind the wheel. 'I'll apologize in advance,' he called as he started the engine.

'What for?'

'The lousy suspension,' he murmured, letting out the clutch and setting off at a snail's pace across the chewed-up turf of the valley. She didn't make a sound the entire way back and he smiled to himself as he drew into the Broxton House drive. Whatever else she was, Celia Jenner was a gutsy lady, and he admired her for it.

He opened the back door. 'Still alive?' he asked, reaching in for her.

She was grey with pain and fatigue but it took more than a bumpy ride to kill the spark. 'You're a very irritating young man,' she muttered, as she clamped her arm round his neck again and grunted with pain as he shifted her along the floor. 'But you were right about Martin Grant,' she admitted grudgingly, 'and I've always regretted that I didn't listen to you. Does that please you?'

'No.'

'Why not? Maggie would tell you it's the closest I'll ever come to an apology.'

He smiled slightly, hefting her against his chest and stepping away from the Jeep. 'Is being stubborn something to be proud of?'

'I'm not stubborn, I'm principled.'

'Well, if you weren't so' – he grinned at her – 'principled, you'd be in Poole hospital by now getting proper treatment.'

'You should always call a spade a spade,' she said crossly. 'And, frankly, if I was half as stubborn as you seem to think I am, I wouldn't even be in this condition. I object to having my arse mentioned over the telephone.'

'Do you want *another* apology?'

She looked up and caught his eye, then looked away again. 'For goodness sake put me down,' she said. 'This is so undignified in a woman of my age. What would my daughter say if she saw me like this?'

He took no notice of her and strode across the weed-strewn gravel towards her front door, only lowering her to the ground when he heard the sound of running feet. Maggie, flustered and breathless, appeared round the corner of the house, a walking stick in each hand. She handed them to her mother. 'She's not allowed to ride,' she told Nick, bending over to catch her breath. 'Doctor's orders. But thank God she never takes anyone's advice. I couldn't have managed on my own, and I certainly couldn't have got Stinger back without Sir Jasper.'

Nick held supporting hands under Celia's elbows while she balanced herself on the sticks. 'You should have told me to get stuffed,' he said.

She inched forward on her sticks like a large crab. 'Don't be ridiculous,' she muttered irritably. 'That's the mistake I made last time.'

Chapter Eighteen

Statement

Witness:	James Purdy, Managing Director, Pharmatec UK
Interviewer:	DI Galbraith

Some time during the summer of 1993, I was working late in the office. As far as I was aware, everyone else had left the premises. On my way out at approximately 9.00 p.m., I noticed a light shining in an office at the end of the corridor. The office belonged to Kate Hill, secretary to the Services Manager, Michael Sprate, and, because I was impressed by the fact that she was working late, I went in to commend her on her commitment. She had been drawn to my attention when she first joined the company because of her size. She was slim and small with blonde hair and remarkable blue eyes. I found her very attractive, but that was not my reason for going into her office that night. She had never given any indication that she was interested in me. I was surprised and flattered, therefore, when she got up from her desk and said she had stayed late in the hope that I would come in.

I am not proud of what happened next. I'm fifty-eight years old and I've been married thirty-three years, and no one has ever done to me what Kate did that night. I know it sounds absurd, but it's the sort of thing most men dream of: that they'll walk into a room one day and a beautiful woman, for no reason at all, will offer them sex. I was extremely worried afterwards because I assumed she must have had an ulterior motive for doing it. I spent the next few days in fear. At the very least I expected her to take liberties in her dealings with me; at the worst I expected some sort of blackmail attempt. However, she was extremely discreet, asked nothing in return, and was always polite whenever I saw her. When I realized there was nothing to fear, I became obsessed with her and dreamt about her night after night.

Some two weeks later, she was again in her office when I passed, and the experience was repeated. I asked her why and she said: 'Because I want to.' From that moment on, there was nothing I could do to control myself. In some ways, she is the most beautiful thing that has ever happened in my life, and I do not regret one moment of our affair. In other ways, I look back on it as a nightmare. I did not believe hearts could be broken, but mine was broken several times by Kate, never more so than when I heard she was dead.

Our affair continued for several months until January 1994. For the most part it was conducted in Kate's flat, although once or twice, under the guise of business trips, I took her to hotels in London. I was prepared to divorce my wife in order to marry Kate, even though I have always loved my wife and would never do anything willingly to hurt her. I can only describe Kate as a fever in the blood that temporarily upset my equilibrium because, once exorcized, I was able to return to normal.

On a Friday at the end of January 1994, Kate came into my office at about 3.30 p.m., and told me she was going to marry William Sumner. I was terribly distressed and remember little of what happened next. I know I passed out and when I came round again I was in hospital. I was told I had had a minor heart attack. I have since confessed to my wife everything that happened.

As far as I am aware, William Sumner knows nothing about my relations with Kate before their marriage. I have certainly not told him, nor have I led him to believe that we were even remotely friendly. It did occur to me that his daughter might be mine, but I have never mentioned it to anyone as I would not lay claim to the child.

I can confirm that I have had no contact with Kate Hill-Sumner since the day in January 1994 when she told me of her decision to marry William Sumner.

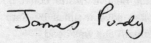

Statement

Witness: Vivienne Purdy, The Gables, Drew Street,
             Fareham
Interviewer: DI Galbraith

....

I first learnt of my husband's affair with Kate Hill some
four weeks after his heart attack in January 1994. I
cannot remember the precise date, but it was either the
day she married William Sumner or the day after. I
found James in tears and I was worried because he had
been making such good progress. He told me he was
crying because his heart was breaking, and he went on
to explain why.

I was neither hurt nor surprised by his confession.
James and I have been married a long time, and I knew
perfectly well that he was having a relationship with
someone else. He has never been a good liar. My only
emotion was relief that he had finally decided to clear
the air. I felt no animosity towards Kate Hill-Sumner for
the following reasons.

It may sound insensitive but I would not have
regarded it as the worst misfortune that could have
happened to me to lose the man I had lived with for
thirty years. Indeed, in some ways I would have welcomed it as an opportunity to start a new life, free of
duty and responsibility. Prior to the events of 1993/94
James was a conscientious father and husband, but his

family had always taken second place to his personal ambitions and desires. When I realized that he was having an affair, I made discreet enquiries about the financial position should divorce become inevitable, and satisfied myself that a division of our property would allow me considerable freedom. I renewed my career as a teacher some ten years ago, and my salary is an adequate one. I have also made sensible pension provisions for myself. As a result, I would certainly have agreed to a divorce had James asked for one. My children are grown up and, while they would be unhappy at the thought of their parents separating, I knew that James would continue to be interested in them.

I explained all this to James in the spring of 1994, and showed him the correspondence I had had with my solicitor and my accountant. I believe it concentrated his mind on the choices open to him and I am confident that he put aside any thought of attempting to rekindle the affair with Kate Hill-Sumner. I hope I don't flatter myself when I say it came as a shock to him to realize that he could no longer take my automatic presence in his life for granted, and that he took this possibility rather more seriously than he took his relationship with Kate Hill-Sumner. I can say honestly that I have no lingering resentment towards James or Kate because it was I who was empowered by the experience. I have a great deal more confidence in myself and my future as a result.

I was aware that William and Kate Hill-Sumner had a child some time in autumn 1994. By simple calculation, I recognized that the child could have been my husband's. However, I did not discuss the issue with him. Nor indeed with anyone else. I could see no point in causing further unhappiness to the parties involved, particularly the child.

I have never met Kate Hill-Sumner nor her husband.

Vivienne Pendy

Chapter Nineteen

INSIDE BROXTON HOUSE, Nick Ingram abandoned both women in the kitchen to put through a call to the incident room at Winfrith. He spoke to Detective Superintendent Carpenter, and gave him details of Harding's activities that morning. 'He's been taken to Poole hospital, sir. I shall be questioning him later about the assault but meanwhile you might want to keep an eye on him. He's not likely to go anywhere in the short term because his arm needs stitching, but I'd say he's out of control now or he wouldn't have attacked Miss Jenner.'

'What was he trying to do? Rape her?'

'She doesn't know. She says she shouted at him when her horse bolted so he slapped her and knocked her to the ground.'

'Mmm.' Carpenter thought for a moment. 'I thought you and John Galbraith decided he was interested in little boys.'

'I'm ready to be proved wrong, sir.'

There was a dry chuckle at the other end. 'What's the first rule of policing, son?'

'Always keep an open mind, sir.'

'Legwork first, lad. Conclusions second.' There was another brief silence. 'The DI's gone off in hot pursuit of William Sumner after reading your fax. He won't be at all pleased if Harding's our man after all.'

'Sorry, sir. If you can give me a couple of hours to go back to the headland, I'll see if I can find out what he was up to. It'll be quicker than sending any of your chaps down.'

In the event, he was delayed by the wretched state of the two Jenner women. Celia was in such pain she was unable to sit down and so she stood in the middle of the kitchen, legs splayed and leaning forward on her two sticks, looking more like an angry praying mantis than a crab. Meanwhile, Maggie's teeth chattered non-stop from delayed shock. 'S-s-sorry,' she kept saying, as she took a filthy, evil-smelling horse blanket from the scullery and draped it round her shoulders, 'I'm j-just s-s-so c-cold.'

Unceremoniously, Ingram shoved her on to a chair beside the Aga and told her to stay put while he dealt with her mother. 'Right,' he said to Celia, 'are you going to be more comfortable lying down in bed or sitting up in a chair?'

'Lying down,' she said.

'Then I'll set up a bed on the ground floor. Which room do you want it in?'

'I don't,' she said mutinously. 'It'll make me look like an invalid.'

He crossed his arms and frowned at her. 'I haven't got time to argue about this, Mrs Jenner. There's no way you can get upstairs, so the bed has to come to you.' She didn't answer. 'All right,' he said, heading for the hall. 'I'll make the decision myself.'

'The drawing room,' she called after him. 'And take the bed out of the room at the end of the corridor.'

Her reluctance, he realized, had more to do with her unwillingness to let him go upstairs than fear of being seen as an invalid. He had had no idea how desperate their plight was until he saw the wasteland of the first floor. The doors stood open to every room, eight in all, and there wasn't a single piece of furniture in any but Celia's. The smell of long-lying dust and damp permeating through an unsound roof stung his nostrils and he wasn't surprised that Celia's health had begun to suffer. He was reminded of Jane Fielding's complaints about selling the family heirlooms to look after her parents-in-law, but their situation was princely compared with this.

The room at the end of the corridor was obviously Celia's own, and her bed probably the only one left in the house. It took him less than ten minutes to dismantle and reassemble it in the drawing room, where he set it up close to the french windows, overlooking the garden. The view was hardly inspiring, just another wasteland, untended and uncared for, but the drawing room at least retained some of its former glory, with all its paintings and most of its furniture still intact. He had time to reflect that few, if any, of Celia's acquaintances could have any idea that the hall and the drawing room represented the extent of her remaining worth. But what sort of madness made people live like this, he wondered? Pride? Fear of their failures being known? Embarrassment?

He returned to the kitchen. 'How are we going to do this?' he asked her. 'The hard way or the easy way?'

Tears of pain squeezed between her lids. 'You really are the most provoking creature,' she said. 'You're determined to take away my dignity, aren't you?'

He grinned as he put one arm under her knees and the other behind her back, and lifted her gently. 'Why not?' he murmured. 'It may be my only chance to get even.'

'I don't want to talk to you,' said William Sumner angrily, barring the front door to DI Galbraith. Hectic spots of colour burned in his cheeks, and he kept tugging at the fingers of his left hand as he spoke, cracking the joints noisily. 'I'm sick of the police treating my house like a damn thoroughfare, and I'm sick of answering questions. Why can't you just leave me alone?'

'Because your wife's been murdered, sir,' said Galbraith evenly, 'and we're trying to find out who killed her. I'm sorry if you're finding that difficult to cope with but I really do have no option.'

'Then talk to me here. What do you want to know?'

The DI glanced towards the road where an interested group of spectators was gathering. 'We'll have the Press here before you know it, William,' he said dispassionately. 'Do you want to discuss your alleged alibi in front of an audience of journalists?'

Sumner's jittery gaze jumped towards the crowd at

his gate. 'This isn't fair. Everything's so bloody public. Why can't you make them go away?'

'They'll go of their own accord if you let me in. They'll stay if you insist on keeping me on the doorstep. That's human nature, I'm afraid.'

With a haunted expression, Sumner seized the policeman's arm and pulled him inside. Pressure was beginning to take its toll, thought Galbraith, and gone was the self-assured, if tired, man of Monday. It meant nothing in itself. Shock took time to absorb, and nerves invariably began to fray when successful closure to a case remained elusive. He followed Sumner into the sitting room and, as before, took a seat on the sofa.

'What do you mean, *alleged* alibi?' the man demanded, preferring to stand. 'I was in Liverpool, for God's sake. How could I be in two places at once?'

The DI opened his briefcase and extracted some papers. 'We've taken statements from your colleagues, hotel employees at the Regal and librarians at the university library. None of them supports your claim that you were in Liverpool on Saturday night.' He held them out. 'I think you should read them.'

Witness statement: Harold Marshall, MD Campbell Ltd, Lee Industrial Estate, Lichfield, Staffordshire

I remember seeing William at lunch on Saturday, 9 August 1997. We discussed a paper in last week's *Lancet* about stomach ulcers. William says he's working on a new drug that will beat the current frontrunner into a cocked hat. I was sceptical, and we had quite a debate. No, I didn't see him at the dinner that evening but then I wouldn't expect to. He and I have been attending these conferences for years, and it'll be a red-letter day when William decides to let his hair down and join the rest of us for some light-hearted entertainment. He was certainly at lunch on Sunday because we had another argument on the ulcer issue.

Witness statement: Paul Dimmock, Research Chemist, Wryton's, Holborne Way, Colchester, Essex

I saw William at about 2.00 p.m. Saturday afternoon. He said he was going to the university library to do some research, which is par for the course for him. He never goes to conference dinners. He's only interested in the intellectual side, hates the social side. My room was two doors down from his. I remember seeing the DO NOT DISTURB notice on the door when I went up to bed about half-past midnight, but I've no idea when he got back. I had a drink with him before lunch on Sunday. No, he didn't seem at all tired. Matter of fact he was in better form than usual. Positively cheerful in fact.

Witness statement: Anne Smith, Research Chemist, Bristol University, Bristol

I didn't see him at all on Saturday but I had a drink with him and Paul Dimmock on Sunday morning. He gave a paper on Friday afternoon and I was interested in some of the things he said. He's researching the drug treatment of stomach ulcers and it sounds like good stuff.

Witness statement: Carrie Wilson, Chambermaid, Regal Hotel, Liverpool

I remember the gentleman in number two-two-three-five. He was very tidy, unpacked his suitcase and put everything away in the drawers. Some of them don't bother. I finished about midday on Saturday, but I made up his room when he went down to breakfast and I didn't see him afterwards. Sunday morning, there was a DO NOT DISTURB notice on his door so I left him to sleep. As I recall he went down at about 11.30 and I made up his room then. Yes, his bed had certainly been slept in. There were science books scattered all over it, and I think he must have been doing some studying. I remember thinking he wasn't so tidy after all.

Witness statement: David Forward, Concierge, Regal Hotel, Liverpool

We have limited parking facilities, and Mr Sumner reserved a parking space at the same time as he reserved his room. He was allocated number thirty-four which is at the back of the hotel. As far as I'm aware the car remained there from Thursday 7 to Monday 11. We ask guests to leave a set of keys with us, and Mr Sumner didn't retrieve his until the Monday. Yes, he could certainly have driven his car out if he had a spare set. There are no barriers across the exit.

Witness statement: Jane Riley, Librarian, University Library, Liverpool
(Shown a photograph of William Sumner)

273

Quite a few of the conference members came into the library on Saturday, but I don't remember seeing this man. That doesn't mean he wasn't here. As long as they have a conference badge, and know what they're looking for, they have free access.

Witness statement: Les Allen, Librarian, University Library, Liverpool
(Shown a photograph of William Sumner)
He came in on Friday morning. I spent about half an hour with him. He wanted papers on peptic and duo-denal ulcers, and I showed him where to find them. He said he'd be back on Saturday, but I didn't notice him. It's a big place. I only ever notice the people who need help.

'You see our problem?' asked Galbraith when Sumner had read them. 'There's a period of twenty-one hours, from two o'clock on Saturday till 11.30 on Sunday, when no one remembers seeing you. Yet the first three statements were made by people whom you told us would give you a cast-iron alibi.'

Sumner looked at him in bewilderment. 'But I was there,' he insisted. 'One of them must have seen me.' He stabbed a finger at Paul Dimmock's statement. 'I met up with Paul in the foyer. I told him I was going to the library and he walked part of the way with me. That had to be well after two o'clock. Dammit, at two o'clock I was still arguing the toss with that bloody fool Harold Marshall.'

Galbraith shook his head. 'Even if it was four o'clock,

it makes no difference. You proved on Monday that you can do the drive to Dorset in five hours.'

'This is absurd!' snapped Sumner nervously. 'You'll just have to talk to more people. Someone must have seen me. There was a man at the same table as me in the library. Ginger-haired fellow with glasses. He can prove I was there.'

'What was his name?'

'I don't know.'

Galbraith took another sheaf of papers out of his briefcase. 'We've questioned thirty people in all, William. These are the rest of the statements. There's no one who's prepared to admit they saw you at any time during the ten hours prior to your wife's murder or the ten hours after. We've also checked your hotel account. You didn't use any hotel service, and that includes your telephone, between lunch on Saturday and pre-lunch drinks on Sunday.' He dropped the papers on to the sofa. 'How do you explain that? For example, where did you eat on Saturday night? You weren't at the conference dinner and you didn't have room service.'

Sumner set to cracking his finger joints again. 'I didn't have anything to eat, not a proper meal anyway. I hate those blasted conference dinners, so I wasn't going to leave my room in case anyone saw me. They all get drunk and behave stupidly. I used the mini-bar,' he said, 'drank the beer and ate peanuts and chocolate. Isn't that on the account?'

Galbraith nodded. 'Except it doesn't specify a time. You could have had them at ten o'clock on Sunday morning. It may explain why you were in such good spirits when you met your friends in the bar. Why didn't you order room service if you didn't want to go down?'

'Because I wasn't that hungry.' Sumner lurched towards the armchair and slumped into it. 'I knew this was going to happen,' he said bitterly. 'I knew you'd go for me if you couldn't find anyone else. I was in the library all afternoon, then I went back to the hotel and read books and journals till I fell asleep.' He lapsed into silence, massaging his temples. 'How could I have drowned her anyway?' he demanded suddenly. 'I don't have a boat.'

'No,' Galbraith agreed. 'Drowning does seem to be the one method that exonerates you.'

A complex mixture of emotions – *relief? triumph? pleasure?* – showed briefly in the man's eyes. 'There you are then,' he said childishly.

'Why do you want to get even with my mother?' asked Maggie when Ingram returned to the kitchen after settling Celia and phoning the local GP. Some colour had returned to her cheeks and she had finally stopped shaking.

'Private joke,' he said, filling the kettle and putting it on the Aga. 'Where does she keep her mugs?'

'Cupboard by the door.'

He took out two and transferred them to the sink, then opened the cupboard underneath and found some washing-up liquid, bleach and pan scourers. 'How long has her hip been bad?' he asked, rolling up his sleeves and setting to with the scourers and the bleach to render the sink hygienic before he even began to deal with the stains in the mugs. From the strong whiffs of dirty dog and damp horse blankets that seemed to haunt the kitchen like old ghosts, he had a strong suspicion that the sink was not entirely dedicated to the purpose of washing crockery.

'Six months. She's on the waiting list for a replacement operation but I can't see it happening before the end of the year.' She watched him sluice down the draining board and sink. 'You think we're a couple of sluts, don't you?'

''Fraid so,' he agreed bluntly. 'I'd say it's a miracle neither of you has gone down with food poisoning, particularly your mother when her health's not too brilliant in the first place.'

'There are so many other things to do,' she said dispiritedly, 'and Ma's in too much pain most of the time to clean properly . . . or says she is. Sometimes I think she's just making excuses to get out of it because she thinks it's beneath her to get her hands dirty. Other times . . .' She sighed heavily. 'I keep the horses immaculate but cleaning up after myself and Ma is always at the bottom of the list. I hate coming up here anyway. It's so' – she sought a suitable word – 'depressing.'

He wondered she had the nerve to stand in judgement on her mother's lifestyle, but didn't comment on it. Stress, depression and waspishness went together in his experience. Instead, he scrubbed the mugs, then filled them with diluted bleach and left them to stand. 'Is that why you moved down to the stables?' he asked her, turning round.

'Not really. If Ma and I live in each other's pockets we argue. If we live apart we don't. Simple as that. Things are easier this way.'

She looked thin and harassed, and her hair hung in limp strands about her face as if she hadn't been near a shower for weeks. It wasn't surprising in view of what she'd been through that morning, particularly as the beginnings of a bruise were ripening on the side of her face, but Ingram remembered her as she used to be, pre-Robert Healey, a gloriously vibrant woman with a mischievous sense of humour and sparkling eyes. He regretted the passing of that personality – it had been a dazzling one – but she was still the most desirable woman he knew.

He glanced idly around the kitchen. 'If you think this is depressing, you should try living in a hostel for the homeless for a week.'

'Is that supposed to make me feel better?'

'This one room could house an entire family.'

'You sound like Ava, my bloody sister-in-law,' she said testily. 'According to her, we live in the lap of luxury despite the fact that the damn place is falling down about our ears.'

'Then why don't you stop whingeing about it and do something constructive to change it?' he suggested. 'If you gave this room a lick of paint it would brighten it up and you'd have less to feel depressed about and more to be thankful for.'

'Oh, my God,' she said icily, 'you'll be telling me to take up knitting next. I don't need DIY therapy, Nick.'

'Then explain to me how sitting around moaning about your environment helps you? You're not helpless, are you? Or maybe it's you, and not your mother, who thinks that getting her hands dirty is demeaning?'

'Paint costs money.'

'Your flat over the stables costs a damn sight more,' he pointed out. 'You baulk at forking out for some cheap emulsion, yet you'll pay two sets of gas, electricity and telephone bills just in order to avoid having to get on with your mother. How does that make things easier, Maggie? It's hardly sound economics, is it? And what are you going to do when she falls over and breaks her hip so badly she's confined to a wheelchair? Pop in once in a while to see she hasn't died of hypothermia in the night because she hasn't been able to get into bed on her own? Or will that be so depressing you'll avoid her entirely?'

'I don't need this,' she said tiredly. 'It's none of your business anyway. We manage fine on our own.'

He watched her for a moment, then turned back to the sink, emptying the mugs of bleach and rinsing them under the tap. He jerked his head towards the kettle. 'Your mother would like a cup of tea, and I suggest you put several spoonfuls of sugar in it to bring up her energy levels. I also suggest you make one for yourself. The GP said he'd be here by eleven.' He dried his hands on a tea towel and rolled down his sleeves.

'Where are you going?' she asked him.

'Up to the headland. I want to try and find out why

Harding came back. Does your mother have any freezer bags?'

'No. We can't afford a freezer.'

'Cling film?'

'In the drawer by the sink.'

'Can I take it?'

'I suppose so.' She watched him remove the roll and tuck it under his arm. 'What do you want it for?'

'Evidence,' he said unhelpfully, making for the door.

She watched him in a kind of despair. 'What about me and Ma?'

He turned with a frown. 'What about you?'

'God, I don't know,' she said crossly. 'We're both pretty shaken, you know. That bloody man hit me, in case you've forgotten. Aren't the police supposed to stay around when women get attacked? Take statements or something?'

'Probably,' he agreed, 'but this is my day off. I turfed out to help you as a friend, not as a policeman, and I'm only following up on Harding because I'm involved in the Kate Sumner case. Don't worry,' he said with a comforting smile, 'you're in no danger from him, not while he's in Poole, but dial nine-nine-nine if you need someone to hold your hand.'

She glared at him. 'I want him prosecuted which means I want you to take a statement now.'

'Mmm, well, don't forget I'll be taking one from him, too,' Ingram pointed out, 'and you may not be so eager to go for his jugular if he opts to counter prosecute on the grounds that he's the one who suffered the injuries because you didn't have your dog under proper control. It's going to be your word against his,' he said, making for the door, 'which is one of the reasons why I'm going back up there now.'

She sighed. 'I suppose you're hurt because I told you to mind your own business?'

'Not in the least,' he said, disappearing into the scullery. 'Try angry or bored.'

'Do you want me to say sorry?' she called after him. 'Well, okay . . . I'm tired . . . I'm stressed out and I'm not in the best of moods but' – she gritted her teeth – 'I'll say sorry if that's what you want.'

But her words fell on stony ground because all she heard was the sound of the back door closing behind him.

The Detective Inspector had been silent so long that William Sumner grew visibly nervous. 'There you are then,' he said again. 'I couldn't possibly have drowned her, could I?' Anxiety had set his eyelid fluttering and he looked absurdly comical every time his lid winked. 'I don't understand why you keep hounding me. You said you were looking for someone with a boat, but you know I haven't got one. And I don't understand why you released Steven Harding when WPC Griffiths said he was seen talking to Kate outside Tesco's on Saturday morning.'

WPC Griffiths should learn to keep her mouth shut, thought Galbraith in annoyance. Not that he blamed her. Sumner was bright enough to read between the lines of newspaper reports about 'a young Lymington actor being taken in for questioning', and then press for answers. 'Briefly,' he said, 'then they went their separate ways. She talked to a couple of market stallholders afterwards, but Harding wasn't with her.'

'Well, it wasn't me who did it.' He winked. 'So there must be someone else you haven't found yet.'

'That's certainly one way of looking at it.' Galbraith lifted a photograph of Kate off the table beside him. 'The trouble is looks are so often deceptive. I mean, take Kate here. You see this?' He turned the picture towards the husband. 'The first impression she gives is that butter wouldn't melt in her mouth, but the more you learn about her the more you realize that isn't true. Let me tell you what I know of her.' He held up his fingers and ticked the points off as he spoke. 'She wanted money and she didn't really mind how she got it. She manipulated people in order to achieve her ambitions. She could be cruel. She told lies if necessary. Her goal was to climb the social ladder and become accepted within a milieu she admired and, as long as it brought the goalposts closer, she was prepared to play-act whatever role was required of her, sex being the major weapon in her armoury. The one person she couldn't manipulate successfully was your mother, so she dealt with her in the only way possible by moving away from her influence.' He dropped his hand to his lap and looked at the other man with genuine sympathy. 'How long was it before you realized you'd been suckered, William?'

'I suppose you've been talking to that bloody police-woman?'

'Among other people.'

'She made me angry. I said things I didn't mean.'

Galbraith shook his head. 'Your mother's view of your marriage wasn't so different,' he pointed out. 'She may not have used the terms "landlady" or "cheap boarding house", but she certainly gave the impression of an unfulfilled and unfulfilling relationship. Other people have described it as unhappy, based on sex, cool, boring. Are any of those descriptions accurate? Are they all accurate?'

Sumner pressed his finger and thumb to the bridge of his nose. 'You don't kill your wife because you're bored with her,' he muttered.

Galbraith wondered again at the man's naivety. Boredom was precisely why most men killed their wives. They might disguise it by claiming provocation or jealousy but, in the end, a desire for something different was usually the reason – even if the difference was simply escape. 'Except I'm told it wasn't so much a question of boredom, but more a question of you taking her for granted. And that interests me. You see, I wonder what a man like you would do if the woman you'd been taking for granted suddenly decided she wasn't going to play the game any more.'

Sumner stared back at him with disdain. 'I don't know what you're talking about.'

'Or if', Galbraith went on relentlessly, 'you discovered that what you'd been taking for granted wasn't true. Such as being a father, for example.'

*

Ingram's assumption was that Harding had come back for his rucksack because, despite the man's claim that the rucksack found on board *Crazy Daze* was the one he'd been carrying, Ingram remained convinced that it wasn't. Paul and Danny Spender had been too insistent that it was big for Ingram to accept that a triangular one fitted the description. Also, he remained suspicious about why Harding had left it behind when he took the boys down to the boatsheds. Nevertheless, the logic of why he had descended to the beach that morning, only to climb up again empty-handed, was far from obvious. Had someone else found the rucksack and removed it? Had Harding weighted it with a rock and thrown it into the sea? Had he even left it there in the first place?

In frustration, he slithered down a gully in the shale precipice to where the grassy slope at the end of the quarry valley undulated softly towards the sea. It was a western-facing cliff out of sight of the sun, and he shivered as the cold and damp penetrated his flimsy T-shirt and sweater. He turned to look back towards the cleft in the cliff, giving himself a rough idea of where Harding must have emerged in front of Maggie. Shale still pattered down the gully Ingram himself had used, and he noticed what was obviously a recent slide further to the left. He walked over to it, wondering if Harding had dislodged it in his ascent, but the surface was damp with dew and he decided it must have happened a few days previously.

He turned his attention to the shore below, striding down the grass to take a closer look. Pieces of driftwood and old plastic containers had wedged themselves into cracks in the rocks, but there was no sign of a black or green rucksack. He felt exhausted suddenly, and wondered what the hell he was doing there. He'd planned to spend his day in total idleness aboard *Miss Creant*, and he really didn't appreciate giving it up for a wild-goose chase. He raised his eyes to the clouds skudding in on a south-westerly breeze and sighed his frustration to the winds . . .

Maggie put a cup of tea on the table beside her mother's bed. 'I've made it very sweet,' she said. 'Nick said you needed your energy levels raising.' She looked at the dreadful state of the top blanket, worn and covered in stains, then noticed the tannin dribbles on Celia's bed-jacket. She wondered what the sheets looked like – it was ages since Broxton House had boasted a washing machine – and wished angrily that she had never introduced the word 'slut' into her conversation with Nick.

'I'd rather have a brandy,' said Celia with a sigh.

'So would I,' said Maggie shortly, 'but we haven't got any.' She stood by the window, looking at the garden, her own cup cradled between her hands. 'Why does he want to get even with you, Ma?'

'Did you ask him?'

'Yes. He said it was a private joke.'

Celia chuckled. 'Where is he?'

'Gone.'

'I hope you thanked him for me.'

'I didn't. He started ordering me about so I sent him away with a flea in his ear.'

Her mother eyed her curiously for a moment. 'How odd of him,' she said, reaching for her tea. 'What sort of orders was he giving you?'

'Snide ones.'

'Oh, I see.'

Maggie shook her head. 'I doubt you do,' she said, addressing the garden. 'He's like Matt and Ava, thinks society would have better value out of this house if we were evicted and it was given to a homeless family.'

Celia took a sip of her tea and leaned back against her pillows. 'Then I understand why you're so angry,' she said evenly. 'It's always irritating when someone's right.'

'He called you a slut and said it was a miracle you hadn't come down with food poisoning.'

Celia pondered for a moment. 'I find that hard to believe if he wasn't prepared to tell you why he wanted to get even with me. Also, he's a polite young man, and doesn't use words like "slut". That's more your style, isn't it, darling?' She watched her daughter's rigid back for a moment but, in the absence of any response, went on: 'If he'd *really* wanted to get even with me, he'd have spiked my guns a long time ago. I was extremely rude to him, and I've regretted it ever since.'

'What did you do?'

'He came to me two months before your wedding with a warning about your fiancé, and I sent him away' – Celia paused to recall the words Maggie had used – 'with a flea in his ear.' Neither she nor Maggie could ever think of the man who had wheedled his way into their lives by his real name, Robert Healey, but only by the name they had come to associate with him, Martin Grant. It was harder for Maggie who had spent three months as Mrs Martin Grant before being faced with the unenviable task of informing banks and corporations that neither the name nor the title belonged to her. 'Admittedly the evidence against Martin was very thin,' Celia went on. 'Nick accused him of trying to con Jane Fielding's parents-in-law out of several thousand pounds by posing as an antiques dealer – with everything resting on old Mrs Fielding's insistence that Martin was the man who came to their door – but if I'd listened to Nick instead of castigating him . . .' She broke off. 'The trouble was he made me angry. He kept asking me what I knew of Martin's background, and when I told him Martin's father was a coffee-grower in Kenya, Nick laughed and said, how convenient.'

'Did you show him the letters they wrote to us?'

'*Supposedly* wrote,' Celia corrected her. 'And, yes, of course I did. It was the only proof we had that Martin came from a respectable background. But, as Nick so rightly pointed out, the address was a PO box number in Nairobi which proved nothing. He said anyone could conduct a fake correspondence through an anonymous box number. What he wanted was Martin's previous address in Britain and all I could give him was the address of the flat Martin was renting in Bournemouth.' She sighed. 'But as Nick said, you don't have to be the son of a coffee-planter to rent a flat, and he told me I'd be wise to make a few enquiries before I allowed my daughter to marry someone I knew nothing about.'

Maggie turned to look at her. 'Then why didn't you?'

'Oh, I don't know.' Her mother sighed. 'Perhaps because Nick was so appallingly pompous . . . Perhaps because on the one occasion that I dared to question Martin's suitability as a husband' – she lifted her eyebrows – 'you called me a meddling bitch and refused to speak to me for several weeks. I think I asked you if you could really marry a man who was afraid of horses, didn't I?'

'Ye-es,' said her daughter slowly, 'and I should have listened to you. I'm sorry now that I didn't.' She crossed her arms. 'What did you say to Nick?'

'More or less what you just said about him,' said Celia. 'I called him a jumped-up little oik with a Hitler complex and tore strips off him for having the brass nerve to slander my future son-in-law. Then I asked him which day Mrs Fielding claimed to have seen Martin and, when he told me, I lied and said she couldn't possibly have done because Martin was out riding with you and me.'

'Oh my God!' said Maggie. 'How could you do that?'

'Because it never occurred to me for one moment that Nick was right,' said Celia with an ironic smile. 'After all, he was just a common or garden policeman and Martin was such a gent. Oxford graduate. Old Etonian. Heir to a coffee plantation. So who wins the prize for stupidity now, darling? You or me?'

Maggie shook her head. 'Couldn't you at least have told me about it? Forewarned might have been forearmed.'

'Oh, I don't think so. You were always so cruel about

Nick after Martin pointed out that the poor lad blushed like a beetroot every time he saw you. I remember you laughing and saying that even beetroots have more sex appeal than overweight Neanderthals in policemen's uniforms.'

Maggie squirmed at the memory. 'You could have told me about it afterwards.'

'Of course I could,' said Celia bluntly, 'but I didn't see why I should give you an excuse to shuffle the guilt off on to me. You were just as much to blame as I was. You were living with the wretched creature in Bournemouth, and if anyone should have seen the flaws in his story it was you. You weren't a child in all conscience, Maggie. If you'd asked to visit his office just once, the whole edifice of his fraud would have collapsed.'

Maggie sighed in exasperation – with herself – with her mother – with Nick Ingram. 'Don't you think I know that? Why do you think I don't trust anyone any more?'

Celia held her gaze for a moment, then looked away. 'I've often wondered,' she murmured. 'Sometimes I think it's bloody-mindedness, other times I think it's immaturity. Usually I put it down to the fact that I spoilt you as a child and made you vain.' Her eyes fastened on Maggie's again. 'You see it's the height of arrogance to question other people's motives when you consistently refuse to question your own. Yes, Martin was a conman but why did he pick on us as his victims? Have you ever wondered about that?'

'We had money.'

'Lots of people have money, darling. Few of them

get defrauded in the way that we did. No,' she said with sudden firmness, 'I was conned because I was greedy, and you were conned because you took it for granted that men found you attractive. If you hadn't, you'd have questioned Martin's ridiculous habit of telling everyone he met how much he loved you. It was *so* American and *so* insincere, and I can't understand why any of us believed it.'

Maggie turned back to the window so that her mother wouldn't see her eyes. 'No,' she said unevenly. 'Neither can I – now.'

A gull swooped towards the shore and pecked at something white tumbling at the water's edge. Amused, Ingram watched it for a while, expecting it to take off again with a dead fish in its beak, but when it abandoned the sport and flapped away in disgust, screaming raucously, he walked down the waterline, curious about what the intermittent flash of white was that showed briefly between each wave. *A carrier bag caught in the rocks? A piece of cloth?* It ballooned unpleasantly as each swell invaded it, before rearing abruptly in a welter of spume as a larger wave flooded in.

Chapter Twenty

GALBRAITH LEANED FORWARD, folding his freckled hands under his chin. He looked completely unalarming, almost mild in fact, like a round-faced schoolboy seeking to make friends. He was quite an actor, like most policemen, and could change his mood as occasion demanded. He tempted Sumner to confide in him. 'Do you know Lulworth Cove, William?' he murmured in a conversational tone of voice.

The other man looked startled but whether from guilt or from the DI's abrupt switch of tack it was impossible to say. 'Yes.'

'Have you been there recently?'

'Not that I recall.'

'It's hardly the sort of thing you'd forget, is it?'

Sumner shrugged. 'It depends what you mean by recently. I sailed there several times in my boat, but that was years ago.'

'What about renting a caravan or a cottage? Maybe you've taken the family there on holiday?'

He shook his head. 'Kate and I only ever had one holiday and that was in a hotel in the Lake District. It was a disaster,' he said in weary recollection. 'Hannah wouldn't go to sleep so we had to sit in our room, night after night, watching the television to stop her screaming the place down and upsetting the other guests. We thought we'd wait until she was older before we tried again.'

It sounded convincing, and Galbraith nodded. 'Hannah's a bit of a handful, isn't she?'

'Kate managed all right.'

'Perhaps because she dosed her with sleeping drugs?'

Sumner looked wary. 'I don't know anything about that. You'd have to ask her doctor.'

'We already have. He says he's never prescribed any sedatives or hypnotics for either Kate or Hannah.'

'Well then.'

'You work in the business, William. You can probably get free samples of every drug on the market. And, let's face it, with all these conferences you go to, there can't be much about pharmaceutical drugs you don't know.'

'You're talking rubbish,' said Sumner, winking uncontrollably. 'I need a prescription like anyone else.'

Galbraith nodded again as if to persuade William that he believed him. 'Still . . . a difficult, demanding child wasn't what you signed up for when you got married, was it? At the very least it will have put a blight on your sex life.'

Sumner didn't answer.

'You must have thought you'd got yourself a good bargain at the beginning. A pretty wife who worshipped the ground you trod on. All right, you didn't have much in common with her, and fatherhood left a lot to be desired, but all in all life was rosy. The sex was good, you had a mortgage you could afford, the journey to work was a doddle, your mother was keeping tabs on your wife during the day, your supper was on the table when you came home of an evening, and you were free to go sailing whenever you wanted.' He paused. 'Then you moved to Lymington and things started to turn sour. I'm guessing Kate grew less and less interested in keeping you happy because she didn't need to pretend any more. She'd got what she wanted – no more supervision from her mother-in-law . . . a house of her own . . . respectability – all of which gave her the confidence to make a life for herself and Hannah which didn't include you.' He eyed the other man curiously. 'And suddenly it was your turn to be taken for granted. Is that when you began to suspect Hannah wasn't yours?'

Sumner surprised him by laughing. 'I've known since she was a few weeks old that she couldn't possibly be mine. Kate and I are blood group O, and Hannah's blood group A. That means her father has to be either blood group A or AB. I'm not a fool. I married a pregnant woman and I had no illusions about her, whatever you or my mother may think.'

'Did you challenge Kate with it?'

Sumner pressed a finger to his fluttering lid. 'It was hardly a challenge. I just showed her an Exclusions of Paternity table on the ABO system and explained how two blood group O parents can only produce a group O child. She was shocked to have been found out so easily but, as my only purpose in doing it was to show her I wasn't as gullible as she seemed to think I was, it never became an issue between us. I had no problem acknowledging Hannah as mine which is all Kate wanted.'

'Did she tell you who the father was?'

He shook his head. 'I didn't want to know. I assume it's someone I work with – or have worked with – but as she broke all contact with Pharmatec after she left, except for the odd visit from Polly Garrard, I knew the father didn't figure in her life any more.' He stroked the arm of his chair. 'You probably won't believe me, but I couldn't see the point of getting hot under the collar about someone who had become an irrelevance.'

He was right. Galbraith didn't believe him. 'Presumably the fact that Hannah isn't your child explains your lack of interest in her?'

Once again the man didn't answer and a silence lengthened between them.

'Tell me what went wrong when you moved to Lymington,' Galbraith said then.

'Nothing went wrong.'

'So you're saying that from day *one*' – he emphasized the word – 'marriage was like living with a landlady? That's a pretty unattractive proposition, isn't it?'

'It depends what you want,' said Sumner. 'Anyway, how would *you* describe a woman whose idea of an intellectual challenge was to watch a soap opera, who had no taste in anything, was so houseproud that she believed cleanliness was next to godliness, preferred overcooked sausages and baked beans to rare steak, and accounted voluntarily for every damn penny that either of us ever spent?'

There was a rough edge to his voice which to Galbraith's ears sounded more like guilt at exposing his wife's shortcomings than bitterness that she'd had them, and he had the impression that William couldn't make up his mind if he'd loved his wife or loathed her. But whether that made him guilty of her murder, Galbraith didn't know.

'If you despised her to that extent, why did you marry her?'

Sumner rested his head against the back of his chair and stared at the ceiling. 'Because the *quid pro quo* for helping her out of the hole she'd dug for herself was sex whenever I wanted it.' He turned to look at Galbraith, and his eyes were bright with unshed tears. 'That's all *I* was interested in. That's all any man's interested in. Isn't it? Sex on tap. Kate would have sucked me off twenty times a day if I'd told her to, just so long as I kept acknowledging Hannah as my daughter.'

The memory brought him little pleasure, apparently, because tears streamed in murky rivers down his cheeks while his uncontrollable lid winked . . . and winked . . .

It was an hour and a half before Ingram returned to Broxton House, carrying something wrapped in layers of cling film. Maggie saw him pass the kitchen window and went through the scullery to let him in. He was soaked to the skin and supported himself against the door jamb, head hanging in exhaustion.

'Did you find anything?' she asked him.

He nodded, lifting the bundle. 'I need to make a

phone call but I don't want to drip all over your mother's floor. I presume you were carrying your mobile this morning, so can I borrow it?'

'Sorry, I wasn't. So no. I got it free two years ago in return for a year's rental, but it was so bloody expensive I declined to renew my subscription and I haven't used it in twelve months. It's in the flat somewhere.' She held the door wide. 'You'd better come in. There's an extension in the kitchen, and the quarry tiles won't hurt for getting water on them.' Her lips gave a brief twitch. 'They might even benefit. I dread to think when they last saw a mop.'

He padded after her, his shoes squelching as he walked. 'How did you phone me this morning if you didn't have a mobile?'

'I used Steve's,' she said, pointing to a Philips GSM on the kitchen table.

He pushed it to one side with the back of his finger and placed the cling film bundle beside it. 'What's it doing here?'

'I put it in my pocket and forgot about it,' she said. 'I only remembered it when it started ringing. It's rung five times since you left.'

'Have you answered it?'

'No. I thought you could deal with it when you came back.'

He moved across to the wall telephone and lifted it off its bracket. 'You're very trusting,' he murmured, punching in the number of the Kate Sumner incident room. 'Supposing I'd decided to let you and your mother stew in your own juice for a bit?'

'You wouldn't,' she said frankly. 'You're not the type.'

He was still wondering how to take that when he was put through to Detective Superintendent Carpenter. 'I've fished a boy's T-shirt out of the sea, sir . . . almost certainly belonging to one of the Spender boys. It's got a Derby County FC logo on the front, and Danny claimed Harding stole it from him.' He listened for a moment. 'Yes, Danny could have dropped it by accident . . . I agree, it doesn't make Harding a paedophile.' He held the phone away from his ear as Carpenter's barking beat against his eardrums. 'No, I haven't found the rucksack yet, but as a matter of fact . . . only that I've a pretty good idea where it is.' More barking. 'Yes, I'm betting it's what he came back for . . .' He grimaced into the receiver. 'Oh, yes, sir, I'd say it's definitely in Chapman's Pool.' He glanced at his watch. 'The boat-sheds in an hour. I'll meet you there.' He replaced the receiver, saw amusement at his discomfort in Maggie's eyes, and gestured abruptly towards the hall. 'Has the doctor been to see your mother?'

She nodded.

'Well?'

'He told her she was a fool not to take the paramedic's offer to have her admitted as an emergency this morning, then patted her on the head and gave her some painkillers.' Her lips twitched into another small smile. 'He also said she needs a Zimmer frame and wheelchair, and suggested I drive to the nearest Red Cross depot this afternoon and see what they can do for her.'

'Sounds sensible.'

'Of course it does, but since when did sense feature in my mother's life? She says if I introduce any such contraptions into her house, she won't use them and she'll never speak to me again. And she means it, too. She says she'd rather crawl on her hands and knees than give anyone the impression she's passed her sell-by date.' She gave a tired sigh. 'Ideas on a postcard, please, care of Broxton House Lunatic Asylum. What the hell am I supposed to do?'

'Wait,' he suggested.

'What for?'

'A miraculous cure or a request for a Zimmer frame. She's not stupid, Maggie. Logic will prevail once she gets over her irritation with you, me and the doctor. Meanwhile, be kind to her. She crippled herself for you this morning, and a little gratitude and TLC will probably have her on her feet quicker than anything.'

'I've already told her I couldn't have done it without her.'

He looked amused. 'Like mother like daughter, eh?'

'I don't understand.'

'*She* can't say sorry. *You* can't say thank you.'

Sudden light dawned. 'Oh, I see. So that's why you went off in a huff two hours ago. It was gratitude you wanted. How silly of me. I thought you were angry because I told you to mind your own business.' She wrapped her arms about her thin body and gave him a tentative smile. 'Well, thank you, Nick, I'm extremely grateful for your assistance.'

He tugged at his forelock. 'Much obliged I'm sure,

Miss Jenner,' he said in a rolling burr. 'But a lady like you don't need to thank a man for doing his job.'

Her puzzled eyes searched his for a moment before it occurred to her he was taking the piss and her over-wrought nerves snapped with a vengeance. 'Fuck off!' she said, landing a furious fist on the side of his jaw before marching into the hall and slamming the door behind her.

Two Dartmouth policemen listened with interest to what the Frenchman told them while his daughter stood in embarrassed silence beside him, fidgeting constantly with her hair. The man's English was good, if heavily accented, as he explained carefully and precisely where he and his boat had been the previous Sunday. He had come, he said, because he had read in the English newspapers that the woman who had been lifted off the shore had been murdered. He placed a copy of Wednes-day's *Telegraph* on the counter in case they didn't know which inquiry he was referring to. 'Mrs Kate Sumner,' he said. 'You are acquainted with this matter?' They agreed they were, so he produced a video cassette from a carrier bag and put it beside the newspaper. 'My daughter made a film of a man that day. You understand – I know nothing about this man. He may – how you say – be innocent. But I am anxious.' He pushed the video across the desk. 'It is not good what he is doing, so you play it. Yes? It is important, perhaps.'

*

Harding's mobile telephone was a sophisticated little item with the capacity to call abroad or be called from abroad. It required an SIM card (Subscriber Identification Module) and a PIN number to use it, but as both had been logged in, presumably by Harding himself, the phone was operational. If it hadn't been, Maggie wouldn't have been able to use it. The card had an extensive memory and, depending on how much the user programmed into it, could store phone numbers and messages, plus the last ten numbers dialled out and the last ten dialled in.

The screen was displaying '5 missed calls' and a 'messages waiting' sign. With a wary look towards the door into the hall, Ingram went into the Menu, located 'Voice mail' followed by 'Mail box', pressed the 'Call' button and held the receiver to his ear. He massaged his cheek tenderly while he listened, wondering if Maggie had any idea how powerful her punch was.

'*You have three new messages,*' said a disembodied female voice at the other end.

'*Steve?*' A lisping, lightweight – *foreign?* – voice, although Ingram couldn't tell if it was male or female. '*Where are you? I'm frightened. Please phone me. I've tried twenty times since Sunday.*'

'*Mr Harding?*' A man's voice, definitely foreign. '*This is the Hotel Angelique, Concarneau. If you wish us to keep your room, you must confirm your reservation by noon today, using a credit card. I regret that without such confirmation the reservation cannot be honoured.*'

'*Hi,*' said an Englishman's voice next. '*Where the fuck are you, you stupid bastard? You're supposed to be kipping*' *here, for Christ's sake. Dammit, this is the address you've been bailed to and I swear to God I'll take you to the cleaners if you get me into any more trouble. Just don't expect me to keep my mouth shut next time. I warned you I'd have your stinking hide if you were playing me for a patsy. Oh, and in case you're interested, there's a sodding journalist nosing round who wants to know if it's true you've been questioned about Kate's murder. He's really bugging me, so get your arse back PDQ before I drop you in it up to your neck.'*

Ingram touched 'End' to disconnect, then went through the whole process again, jotting down bullet points on the back of a piece of paper which he took from a notepad under the wall telephone. Next he pressed the arrow button twice to scroll up the numbers of the last ten people who had dialled in. He discounted 'Voice mail' and made a note of the rest, together with the last ten calls Harding had made, the first of which was Maggie's call to him. For further good measure – *To hell with it! In for a penny in for a pound!* – he scrolled through the entries under 'Names' and took them down together with their numbers.

'Are you doing something illegal?' asked Maggie from the doorway.

He had been so engrossed he hadn't heard the door open, and he looked up with a guilty start. 'Not if DI Galbraith already has this information.' He flattened his palm and made a rocking motion. 'Probable infringement of Harding's rights under the Data Protection Act, if he hasn't. It depends whether the phone was on *Crazy Daze* when they searched it.'

301

'Won't Steven Harding know you've been playing his messages when you give it back to him? Our answer-phone never replays the ones you've already listened to unless you rewind the tape.'

'Voice mail's different. You have to delete the messages if you don't want to keep hearing them.' He grinned. 'But if he's suspicious, let's just hope he thinks you buggered it up when you made your phone call.'

'Why drag me into it?'

'Because he'll know you phoned me. My number's in the memory.'

'Oh God,' she said in resignation. 'Are you expecting me to lie for you?'

'No.' He stood up, lacing his hands above his head and stretching his shoulder muscles under his damp clothes. He was so tall he could almost touch the ceiling and he stood like a Colossus in the middle of the kitchen, easily dominating a room that was big enough to house an entire family.

Watching him, Maggie wondered how she could ever have called him an overweight Neanderthal. It had been Martin's description, she remembered, and it galled her unbearably to think how tamely she had adopted it herself because it had raised a laugh among people she had once regarded as friends but whom she now avoided like the plague. 'Well, I will,' she said with sudden decision.

He shook his head as he lowered his arms. 'It wouldn't do me any good. You couldn't lie to save your life. And that's a compliment, by the way,' he said as she started to scowl, 'so there's no need to hit me again. I don't admire people who lie.'

'I'm sorry,' she said abruptly.

'No need to be. It was my fault. I shouldn't have teased you.' He started to gather the bits and pieces from the table.

'Where are you going now?'

'Back to my house to change, then down to the boatsheds at Chapman's Pool. But I'll look in again this afternoon before I go to see Harding. As you so rightly pointed out, I need to take a statement from you.' He paused. 'We'll talk about this in detail later, but did you hear anything before he appeared?'

'Like what?'

'Shale falling?'

She shook her head. 'All I remember is how quiet it was. That's why he gave me such a fright. One minute I was on my own, the next he was crouching on the ground in front of me like a rabid dog. It was really peculiar. I don't know what he thought he was doing but there's a lot of scrub vegetation and bushes round there so I think he must have heard me coming and ducked down to hide.'

He nodded. 'What about his clothes? Were they wet?'

'No.'

'Dirty?'

'You mean before he bled all over them?'

'Yes.'

She shook her head again. 'I remember thinking that

he hadn't shaved, but I don't remember thinking he was dirty.'

He stacked the cling film bundle, notes and phone into a pile and lifted them off the table. 'Okay. That's great. I'll take a statement this afternoon.' He held her gaze for a moment. 'You'll be all right,' he told her. 'Harding's not going to come back.'

'He wouldn't dare,' she said, clenching her fists.

'Not if he has any sense,' murmured Ingram, moving out of her range.

'Do you have any brandy in your house?'

The switch was so abrupt that he needed time to consider. 'Ye-es,' he murmured cautiously, fearing another assault if he dared to question why she was asking. He suspected four years of angry frustration had gone into her punch, and he wished she'd chosen Harding for target practice instead of himself.

'Can you lend me some?'

'Sure. I'll drop it in on my way back to Chapman's Pool.'

'If you give me a moment to tell Ma where I'm going, I'll come with you. I can walk back.'

'Won't she miss you?'

'Not for an hour or so. The painkillers have made her sleepy.'

Bertie was lying on the doorstep in the sunshine as Ingram drew the Jeep to a halt beside his gate. Maggie had never been inside Nick's little house but she had always resented the neatness of his garden. It was like a reproach to all his less organized neighbours with its beautifully clipped privet hedges and regimented hydrangeas and roses in serried ranks before the yellow-stone walls of the house. She often wondered where he found the time to weed and hoe when he spent most of his free hours on his boat, and in her more critical moments put it down to the fact that he was boring and compartmentalized his life according to some sensible duty roster.

The dog raised his shaggy head and thumped his tail on the mat before rising leisurely to his feet and yawning. 'So this is where he comes,' she said. 'I've often wondered. How long did it take you to train him, as a matter of interest?'

'Not long. He's a bright dog.'

'Why did you bother?'

'Because he's a compulsive digger, and I got fed up with having my garden destroyed,' he said prosaically.

'Oh God,' she said guiltily. 'Sorry. The trouble is he never takes any notice of me.'

'Does he need to?'

'He's *my* dog,' she said.

Ingram opened the Jeep door. 'Have you made that clear to him?'

'Of course I have. He comes home every night, doesn't he?'

He reached into the back for the stack of evidence. 'I wasn't questioning ownership,' he told her. 'I was questioning whether or not Bertie knows he's a dog. As far as he's concerned, he's the boss in your establishment. He gets fed first, sleeps on your sofa, licks out your dishes. I'll bet you even move over in bed in order to make sure he's more comfortable, don't you?'

She coloured slightly. 'What if I do? I'd rather have him in my bed than the weasel that used to be in it. In any case, he's the closest thing I've got to a hot-water bottle.'

Ingram laughed. 'Are you coming in or do you want me to bring the brandy out? I guarantee Bertie won't disgrace you. He has beautiful manners since I took him to task for wiping his bottom on my carpet.'

Maggie sat in indecision. She had never wanted to go inside because it would tell her things about him that she didn't want to know. At the very least it would be insufferably clean, she thought, and her bloody dog would shame her by doing exactly what he was told.

'I'm coming in,' she said defiantly.

Carpenter took a phone call from a Dartmouth police sergeant just as he was about to leave for Chapman's Pool. He listened to a description of what was on the Frenchman's video then asked: 'What does he look like?'

'Five eight, medium build, bit of a paunch, thinning dark hair.'

'I thought you said he was a young chap.'

'No. Mid-forties, at least. His daughter's fourteen.'

Carpenter's frown dug trenches out of his forehead. 'Not the bloody Frenchman,' he shouted, 'the toe-rag on the video!'

'Oh, sorry. Yes, he's young all right. Early twenties, I'd say. Longish dark hair, sleeveless T-shirt and cycling shorts. Muscles. Tanned. A handsome bugger, in fact. The kid who filmed him said she thought he looked like Jean-Claude Van Damme. Mind you, she's mortified about it now, can't believe she didn't realize what he was up to, considering he's got a rod like a fucking salami. This guy could make a fortune in porno movies.'

'All right, all right,' said Carpenter testily. 'I get the picture. And you say he's wanking into a handkerchief?'

'Looks like it.'

'Could it be a child's T-shirt?'

'Maybe. It's difficult to tell. Matter of fact, I'm amazed the French geezer spotted what the bastard was up to. It's pretty discreet. It's only because his knob's so damn big that you can see anything at all. The first time I watched it I thought he was peeling an orange in his lap.' There was a belly laugh at the other end of the line. 'Still, you know what they say about the French. They're all wankers. So I guess our little geezer's done a spot of it himself and knew what to look for. Am I right or am I right?'

Carpenter, who spent all his holidays in France, cocked a finger and thumb at the telephone and pulled the trigger – bloody racist, he was thinking – but there was no trace of irritation in his voice when he spoke. 'You said the young man had a rucksack. Can you describe it for me?'

'Standard camping type. Green. Doesn't look as if it's got much in it.'

'Big?'

'Oh, yes. It's a full-size job.'

'What did he do with it?'

'Sat on it while he jerked himself off.'

'Where? Which part of Chapman's Pool? Eastern side? Western side? Describe the scenery for me.'

'Eastern side. The Frenchman showed me on the map. Your wanker was down on the beach below Emmetts Hill, facing out towards the Channel. Green slope behind him.'

'What did he do with the rucksack after he sat on it?'

'Can't say. The film ends.'

With a request to send the tape on by courier, together with the Frenchman's name, proposed itinerary for the rest of his holiday and address in France, Carpenter thanked the sergeant and rang off.

'Did you make this yourself?' asked Maggie, peering at the *Cutty Sark* in the bottle on the mantelpiece as Ingram came downstairs in uniform, buttoning the sleeves of his shirt.

'Yes.'

'I thought you must have done. It's like everything else in this house. So' – she waved her glass in the air – '*well behaved.*' She might have said masculine, minimal or monastic, in an echo of Galbraith's description of Harding's boat, but she didn't want to be rude. It was as she had predicted, insufferably clean, and insufferably boring as well. There was nothing to say this house belonged to an interesting personality, just yards of pallid wall, pallid carpet, pallid curtains and pallid uphol- stery, broken occasionally by an ornament on a shelf. It never occurred to her that he was tied to the house through his job but, even if it had, she would still have expected splashes of towering individualism among the uniformity.

He laughed. 'Do I get the impression you don't like it?'

'No, I do. It's – er—'

'Twee?' he suggested.

'Yes.'

'I made it when I was twelve.' He flexed his huge fingers under her nose. 'I couldn't do it now.' He straightened his tie. 'How's the brandy?'

'Very good.' She dropped into a chair. 'Does exactly what it's supposed to do. Hits the spot.'

He took her empty glass. 'When did you last drink alcohol?'

'Four years ago.'

'Shall I give you a lift home?'

'No.' She closed her eyes. 'I'm going to sleep.'

'I'll look in on your mother on my way back from Chapman's Pool,' he promised her, shrugging on his jacket. 'Meanwhile, don't encourage your dog to sit on my sofa. It's bad for both your characters.'

'What will happen if I do?'

'The same thing that happened to Bertie when he wiped his bottom on my carpet.'

Despite another day of brilliant sunshine, Chapman's Pool was empty. The south-westerly breeze had created an unpleasant swell, and nothing was more guaranteed to discourage visitors than the likelihood of being sick over their lunch. Carpenter and two detective constables followed Ingram away from the boatsheds towards an area marked out on the rocky shore with pieces of driftwood.

'We won't know until we see the video, of course,' said Carpenter, taking his bearings from the description the Dartmouth sergeant had given of where Harding had been sitting, 'but it looks about right. He was certainly on this side of the bay.' They were standing on a slab of rock at the shoreline and he touched a small pebble cairn with the toe of his shoe. 'And this is where you found the T-shirt?'

Ingram nodded as he squatted down and put his hand in the water that lapped against the base of the rock. 'But it was well and truly wedged. A gull had a go at getting it out, and failed, and I was saturated doing my retrieval act.'

'Is that important?'

'Harding was dry as a bone when I saw him so it can't have been the T-shirt he came back for. I think that's been here for days.'

'Mmm.' Carpenter pondered for a moment. 'Does fabric easily get wedged between rocks?'

Ingram shrugged. 'Anything can get wedged if a crab takes a fancy to it.'

'Mmm,' said Carpenter again. 'All right. Where's this rucksack?'

'It's only a guess, sir, and a bit of a flaky one at that,' said Ingram standing up.

'I'm listening.'

'Okay, well, I've been puzzling about the ruddy thing

310

for days. He obviously didn't want it anywhere near a policeman or he'd have brought it down to the boat-sheds on Sunday. By the same token it wasn't on his boat when you searched it – or not in my opinion anyway – and that suggests to me that it's incriminating in some way and he needed to get rid of it.'

'I think you're right,' said Carpenter. 'Harding wants us to believe he was carrying the black one we found on his boat, but the Dartmouth sergeant described the one on the video as green. So what's he done with it, eh? And what's he trying to hide?'

'It depends on whether the contents were valuable to him. If they *weren't*, then he'll have dropped it in the ocean on his way back to Lymington. If they *were*, he'll have left it somewhere accessible but not too obvious.' Ingram shielded his eyes from the sun and pointed towards the slope behind them. 'There's been a mini-avalanche up there,' he said. 'I noticed it because it's just to the left of where Miss Jenner said Harding appeared in front of her. Shale's notoriously unstable – which is why these cliffs are covered in warnings – and it looks to me as though that fall's fairly recent.'

Carpenter followed his gaze. 'You think the ruck-sack's under it?'

'Put it this way, sir, I can't think of a quicker or more convenient way of burying something than to send an avalanche of shale over the top of it. It wouldn't be hard to do. Kick out a loose rock, and hey presto, you've got a convenient slide of loose cliff pouring over whatever it is you want to hide. No one's going to notice it. Slides like that happen every day. The Spender brothers set one off when they dropped their father's binoculars, and I can't help feeling that might have given Harding the idea.'

'Meaning he did it on Sunday?'

Ingram nodded.

'And came back this morning to make sure it hadn't been disturbed?'

'I suspect it's more likely he intended to retrieve it, sir.'

Carpenter brought his ferocious scowl to bear on the constable. 'Then why wasn't he carrying it when you saw him?'

'Because the shale's dried in the sunshine and become impacted. I think he was about to go looking for a spade when he ran into Miss Jenner by accident.'

'Is that your best suggestion?'

'Yes, sir.'

'You're a bit of a suggestion-junky, aren't you, lad?' said Carpenter, his frown deepening. 'I've got DI Galbraith chasing over half of Hampshire on the back of the suggestions you faxed through last night.'

'It doesn't make them wrong, sir.'

'It doesn't make them right either. We had a team scouring this area on Monday, and they didn't find a damn thing.'

Ingram jerked his head towards the next bay. 'They were searching Egmont Bight, sir, and with respect no one was interested in Steven Harding's movements at that point.'

'Mmm. These search teams cost money, lad, and I like a little more certainty before I commit taxpayers' money to guesses.' Carpenter stared out across the sea. 'I could understand him revisiting the scene of the crime to relive his excitement – it's the sort of thing a man like him might do – but you're saying he wasn't interested in that.'

Ingram had said no such thing, but he wasn't going to argue the point. For all he knew, the Superintendent was right anyway. Maybe that's exactly what Harding had come back for. His own avalanche theory looked horribly insignificant beside the magnitude of a psychopath gloating over the scene of murder.

'Well?' demanded Carpenter.

The constable smiled self-consciously. 'I brought my own spade, sir,' he said. 'It's in the back of my Jeep.'

Chapter Twenty-one

GALBRAITH STOOD UP and walked across to one of the windows which overlooked the road. The crowd of earlier had dispersed, although a couple of elderly women still chatted on the pavement, glancing occasionally towards Langton Cottage. He watched them for several minutes in silence, envying the normality of their lives. How often did they have to listen to the dirty little secrets of murder suspects? Sometimes, when he heard the confessions of men like Sumner, he thought of himself in the role of a priest offering a kind of benediction merely by listening, but he had neither the authority nor the desire to forgive sins and invariably felt diminished by being the recipient of their furtive confidences.

He turned to face the man. 'So a more accurate description of your marriage would be to say it was a form of sexual slavery? Kate was so desperate to make sure her daughter grew up in the sort of security she herself never enjoyed that you were able to blackmail her?'

'I said she *would* have done it, not that she did or that I ever asked her to.' Triumph crept stealthily into Sumner's eyes as if he had won an important point.

'There's no median way with you, is there? Half an hour ago you were treating me like a cretin because you thought Kate had suckered me into marrying her. Now you're accusing me of sexual slavery because I got so tired of her lies about Hannah that I pointed out – very mildly, as a matter of fact – that I knew the truth. Why would I buy her this house if she had no say in the relationship? You said yourself I was better off in Chichester.'

'I don't know. Tell me.'

'Because I loved her.'

Impatiently, Galbraith shook his head. 'You describe your marriage as a war zone, then expect me to swallow garbage like that. What was the real reason?'

'That *was* the real reason. I loved my wife, and I'd have given her whatever she wanted.'

'At the same time as blackmailing her into giving you blow jobs whenever you fancied it?' The atmosphere in the room was stifling, and he felt himself grow cruel in response to the cruelty of Kate and William's marriage. He couldn't rid himself of memories of the tiny, pregnant woman on the pathologist's slab and Dr Warner's casual raising of her hand in order to shake it to and fro in convincing demonstration that the fingers were broken. The noise of grating bone had lodged in Galbraith's head like a maggot, and his dreams were of charnel houses. 'You see, I can't make up my mind whether you loved or hated her. Or maybe it was a bit of both? A love/hate relationship that turned sour?'

Sumner shook his head. He looked defeated suddenly, as if whatever game he was playing was no longer worth the candle. Galbraith wished he understood what William was trying to achieve through his answers, and studied the man in perplexity. William was either extremely frank, or extremely skilful at clouding an issue. On the whole he gave the impression of honesty, and it occurred to Galbraith that, in a ham-fisted way, he was trying to demonstrate that his wife was the sort of woman who could easily have driven a man to rape her. He remembered what James Purdy had said about Kate. *'No one has ever done to me what Kate did that night . . . It's the sort of thing most men dream of . . . I can only describe Kate as a fever in the blood . . .'*

'Did she love you, William?'

'I don't know. I never asked her.'

'Because you were afraid she'd say no?'

'The opposite. I knew she'd say yes.'

'And you didn't want her to lie to you?'

The man nodded.

'I don't like being lied to,' murmured Galbraith, his eyes fixing on Sumner's. 'It means the other person assumes you're so stupid you'll believe anything they say. Did she lie to you about having an affair?'

'She wasn't having an affair.'

'She certainly visited Steven Harding on board his boat,' Galbraith pointed out. 'Her fingerprints are all over it. Did you find out about that? Maybe you suspected that the baby she was carrying wasn't yours? Maybe you were afraid she was going to foist another bastard on to you?'

Sumner stared at his hands.

'Did you rape her?' Galbraith went on remorselessly. 'Was that part of the *quid pro quo* for acknowledging Hannah as your daughter? The right to take Kate whenever you wanted her?'

'Why would I want to rape her when I didn't need to?' he asked.

'I'm only interested in a yes or a no, William.'

His eyes flashed angrily. 'Then no, dammit. I never raped my wife.'

'Maybe you dosed her with Rohypnol to make her more compliant?'

'No.'

'Then tell me why Hannah's so sexually aware?' Galbraith said next. 'Did you and Kate perform in front of her?'

More anger. 'That's revolting.'

'Yes or no, William.'

'No.' The word came out in a strangled sob.

'You're lying, William. Half an hour ago, you described how you had to sit with her in a hotel bedroom because she wouldn't stop crying. I think that happened at home as well. I think sex with Kate involved Hannah as an audience because you got so fed up with Hannah being given as the excuse for the endless brushes off that you insisted on doing it in front of her. Am I right?'

He buried his face in his hands and rocked himself to and fro. 'You don't know what it's like . . . she wouldn't leave us alone . . . she never sleeps . . . pester, pester all the time . . . Kate used her as a shield . . .'

'Is that a yes?'

317

The answer was a whisper of sound. 'Yes.'

'WPC Griffiths said you went into Hannah's room last night. Do you want to tell me why?'

Another whisper. 'You won't believe me if I do.'

'I might.'

Sumner raised a tear-stained face. 'I wanted to look at her,' he said in despair. 'She's all I've got left to remind me of Kate.'

Carpenter lit a cigarette as Ingram's careful spadework disclosed the first strap of a rucksack. 'Good work, lad,' he said approvingly. He dispatched one of the DCs to his car to collect some disposable gloves and polythene sheeting, then watched as Ingram continued to remove the shale from around the crumpled canvas.

It took Ingram another ten minutes to release the object completely and transfer it to the polythene sheet. It was a heavy-duty green camper's rucksack, with a waist strap for extra support and loops underneath for taking a tent. It was old and worn, and the integral backframe had been cut out for some reason, leaving frayed canvas edges between the stitched grooves that had contained it. The frays were old ones, however, and whatever had persuaded the owner to remove the frame was clearly ancient history. It sat on the sheeting, collapsed in on itself under the weight of its straps, and whatever it contained took up less than a third of its bulk.

Carpenter instructed one detective constable to seal

each item in a forensic bag as he took it out and the other to note what it was, then he squatted beside the rucksack and carefully undid the buckles with gloved fingertips, flipping back the flap. 'Item,' he dictated. 'One pair of 20×60 binoculars, name worn away, possibly Optikon . . . one bottle of mineral water, Volvic . . . three empty crisp packets, Smith's . . . one baseball cap, New York Yankees . . . one blue and white checked shirt – men's – made by River Island . . . one pair of cream cotton trousers – men's – also made by River Island . . . one pair of brown safari-style boots, size seven.'

He felt inside the pockets and took out some rancid orange peel, more empty crisp packets, an opened packet of Camel cigarettes with a lighter tucked in among them, and a small quantity of what appeared to be cannabis, wrapped in cling film. He squinted up at the three policemen.

'Well? What do you make of this little lot? What's so incriminating about it all that Nick mustn't know he had it?'

'The C,' said one. 'He didn't want to be caught in possession.'

'Maybe.'

'God knows,' said the other.

The Superintendent stood up. 'What about you, Nick? What do you think?'

'I'd say the shoes are the most interesting item, sir.'

Carpenter nodded. 'Too small for Harding, who's a good six foot, and too big for Kate Sumner. So what's he doing carrying a pair of size-seven shoes round with him?'

No one volunteered an answer.

DI Galbraith was on his way out of Lymington when Carpenter phoned through instructions to locate Tony Bridges and put the 'little bastard' through the wringer. 'He's been holding out on us, John,' he declared, detailing the contents of Harding's rucksack, what was on the Frenchman's video and repeating verbatim the messages that Ingram had taken from the voice mail. 'Bridges *must* know more than he's been telling us so arrest him on conspiracy if necessary. Find out why and when Harding was planning to leave for France, and get a fix on the wanker's sexual orientation if you can. It's all bloody odd, frankly.'

'What happens if I can't find Bridges?'

'He was in his house two or three hours ago because the last message came from his number. He's a teacher, don't forget, so he won't have gone to work, not unless he has a holiday job. Campbell's advice is: check the pubs.'

'Will do.'

'How did you get on with Sumner?'

Galbraith thought about it. 'He's cracking up,' he said. 'I felt sorry for him.'

'Less of a dead cert then?'

'Or more,' said Galbraith dryly. 'It depends on your viewpoint. She was obviously having an affair which he knew about. I think he *wanted* to kill her . . . which is probably why he's cracking up.'

Fortunately for Galbraith, Tony Bridges was not only at home but stoned out of his head into the bargain. So much so that he was completely naked when he came to the front door. Galbraith had momentary qualms about putting anyone in his condition through Carpenter's 'wringer', but they were only momentary. In the end the only thing that matters to a policeman is that witnesses tell the truth.

'I told the stupid sod you'd check up on him,' Bridges said garrulously, leading the way down the corridor into the chaotic sitting room. 'I mean you don't play silly buggers with the filth, not unless you're a complete moron. His problem is he won't take advice – never listens to a word I say. He reckons I sold out and says my opinions don't count for shit any more.'

'Sold out to what?' asked Galbraith, picking his way towards a vacant chair and remembering that Harding was said to favour nudity on board *Crazy Daze*. He wondered gloomily if nakedness had suddenly become an essential part of youth culture, and hoped not. He didn't much fancy the idea of police cells full of smack-heads with hairless chests and acne on their bottoms.

'The establishment,' said Bridges, sinking cross-leg-ged on to the floor and retrieving a half-smoked spliff from an ashtray in front of him. 'Regular employment. A salary.' He proffered the joint. 'Want some?'

Galbraith shook his head. 'What sort of employment?' He had read all the reports on Harding and his
friends, knew everything there was to know about
Bridges, but it didn't suit him at the moment to reveal
it.

'Teaching,' the young man declared with a shrug. He
was too stoned – or *appeared* to be too stoned, as
Galbraith was cynical enough to remind himself – to
remember that he had already given the police this
information before. 'Okay the pay's not brilliant, but,
hell, the holidays are good. And it's got to be better
than flaunting your arse in front of some two-bit photographer. The trouble with Steve is he doesn't like kids
much. He's had to work with some right little bastards
and it's put him off.' He lapsed into contented silence
with his joint.

Galbraith assumed a surprised expression. 'You're a
teacher?'

'That's right.' Bridges squinted through the smoke.
'And don't go getting hot under the collar. I'm a
recreational cannabis user and I've no more desire to
share my habit with children than my headmaster has to
share his whisky.'

The excuse was so simplistic and so well tutored by
the cannabis lobby that it brought a smile to the DI's
face. There were better arguments for legalization, he
always thought, but your average user was either too
thick or too high to produce them. 'Okay, okay,' he
said, raising his hands in surrender. 'This isn't my patch
so I don't need the lecture.'

'Sure you do. You lot are all the same.'

'I'm more interested in Steve's pornography. I gather you don't approve of it?'

A closed expression tightened the young man's features. 'It's cheap filth. I'm a teacher. I don't like that kind of crap.'

'What kind of crap is it? Describe it to me.'

'What's to describe? He's got a todger the size of the Eiffel Tower and he likes to display it.' He shrugged. 'But that's his problem, not mine.'

'Are you sure about that?'

Bridges squinted painfully through the smoke from his spliff. 'What's that supposed to mean?'

'We've been told you live in his shadow.'

'Who by?'

'Steve's parents.'

'You don't want to believe anything they say,' he said dismissively. 'They stood in judgement on me ten years ago, and have never changed their opinion since. They think I'm a bad influence.'

Galbraith chuckled. 'And are you?'

'Let's put it this way, *my* parents think Steve's a bad influence. We got into a bit of trouble when we were younger, but it's water under the bridge now.'

'So what do you teach?' Galbraith asked, looking around the room and wondering how anyone could live in such squalor. More interestingly, how could anyone so rank boast a girlfriend? Was Bibi as squalid?

Campbell's description of the set-up after his interview with Bridges on Monday had been pithy. 'It's a pit,' he said. 'The bloke's spaced out, the house stinks, he's shacked up with a slapper who looks as if she's slept with half the men in Lymington, and he's a teacher for Christ's sake.'

'Chemistry.' He sneered at Galbraith's expression, misinterpreting it. 'And, yes, I do know how to synthesize lysergic acid diethylamide. I also know how to blow up Buckingham Palace. It's a useful subject, chemistry. The trouble is' – he broke off to draw pensively on his spliff – 'the people who teach it are so bloody boring they turn the kids off long before they ever get to the interesting bits.'

'But not you?'

'No. I'm good.'

Galbraith could believe it. Rebels, however flawed, were always charismatic to youth. 'Your friend is in Poole hospital,' he told the young man. 'He was attacked by a dog on the Isle of Purbeck this morning and had to be shipped out by helicopter to have his arm stitched.' He looked at Bridges enquiringly. 'Any idea what he was doing there? In view of the fact he was bailed to this address and presumably you have some knowledge of what he gets up to.'

'Sorry, mate, that's where you're wrong. Steve's a closed book to me.'

'You said you warned him I'd come checking.'

'Not you personally. I don't know you from Adam. I told him the filth would come. That's different.'

'Still, if you had to warn him, Tony, then you must have known he was about to leg it. So where was he planning to go and what did he plan to do?'

'I told you. The guy's a closed book to me.'

'I thought you were at school together.'

'We've grown apart.'

'Doesn't he doss here when he's not on his boat?'

'Not often.'

'What about his relationship with Kate?'

Bridges shook his head. 'Everything I know about her is in my statement,' he said virtuously. 'If I knew anything else I'd tell you.'

Galbraith looked at his watch. 'We've got a bit of a problem here, son,' he said affably. 'I'm on a tight schedule so I can only give you another thirty seconds.'

'To do what, mate?'

'Tell the truth.' He unclipped his handcuffs from his belt.

'Pull the other one,' scoffed Bridges. 'You're not going to arrest me.'

'Too right I am. And I'm a hard bastard, Tony. When I arrest a lying little toe-rag like you, I take him out just as he is, never mind he's got a bum like a pizza and his prick's shrunk in the fucking wash.'

Bridges gave a throaty chuckle. 'The Press would crucify you. You can't drag a naked guy through the streets for illegal possession. It's hardly even a crime any more.'

'Try me.'

'Go on then.'

Galbraith snapped one bracelet on to his own wrist, then leaned forward and snapped the other on to Tony's. 'Anthony Bridges, I am arresting you on suspicion of conspiracy in the rape and murder last Saturday night of Mrs Kate Sumner of Langton Cottage and the grievous bodily assault this morning of Miss Margaret

Jenner of Broxton House.' He stood up and started walking towards the door, dragging Bridges behind him. 'You do not have to say anything but it may harm your defence—'

'Shit!' said the young man stumbling to his feet. 'This is a joke, right?'

'No joke.' The DI twitched the spliff out of the young man's fingers and flicked it, still alight, into the corridor. 'The reason Steven Harding was attacked by a dog this morning is because he attempted to assault another woman in the same place that Kate Sumner died. Now you can either tell me what you know, or you can accompany me to Winfrith where you will be formally charged and interviewed on tape.' He looked the man up and down, and laughed. 'Frankly, I couldn't give a toss either way. It'll save me time if you talk to me now, but' – he shook his head regretfully – 'I'd hate your neighbours to miss the fun. It must be hell living next door to you.'

'That spliff's going to set my house on fire!'

Galbraith watched the joint smoulder gently on the wooden floorboards. 'It's too green. You're not curing it properly.'

'You'd know, of course.'

'Trust me.' He yanked Bridges down the corridor. 'Where were we? Oh, yes. It may harm your defence if you do not mention, when questioned, something you later rely on in court.' He pulled open the door and ushered the man outside. 'Anything you do say may be given in evidence.' He prodded Bridges on to the pavement in front of a startled old lady with fluffy white hair and eyes as big as golf balls behind pebble spectacles. 'Morning, ma'am,' he said politely.

Her mouth gaped.

'I've parked behind Tesco's,' he told Bridges, 'so it'll probably be quicker if we go up the High Street.'

'You can't take me up the High Street like this. Tell him, Mrs Crane.'

The elderly woman leaned forward, putting a hand behind her ear. 'Tell him what, dear?'

'Oh, Jesus! Never mind! Forget it!'

'I'm not sure I can,' she murmured in a confidential tone. 'Did you know you were naked?'

'Of course I know!' he shouted into her deaf ear. 'The police are denying me my rights and you're a witness to it.'

'That's nice. I've always wanted to be a witness to something.' Her eyes brimmed with sudden amusement. 'I'll tell my husband about it. He'll be pleased as punch. He's been saying for years that the only thing that happens when you burn the candle at both ends is the wick gets smaller.' She gave a joyful laugh as she moved on. 'And, you know, I always thought it was a joke.'

Galbraith grinned after her. 'What do you want me to do with your front door?' he asked, grabbing the handle. 'Slam it shut?'

'Jesus no!' Bridges lurched backwards to stop the door closing. 'I haven't got a key for Christ's sake.'

'Losing your nerve already?'

'I could sue you for this.'

'No chance. This was your choice, remember. I explained that if I had to arrest you I would take you out as you were and your response was: Go on then.'

Bridges looked wildly up the road as a man rounded the corner, and Galbraith was rewarded with a scrambling stampede for the safety of the corridor. He shut the door and stood with his back to it, halting further flight by a jerk on the handcuffs. 'Right. Shall we start again? Why did Steve go back to Chapman's Pool this morning?'

'I don't know. I didn't even know he was there.' His eyes widened as Galbraith reached for the door handle again. 'Listen, dickhead, that guy coming up the street's a journalist, and he's been pestering me all morning about Steve. If I'd known where the bastard was I'd have sent the bloke after him but I can't even get him to answer his mobile.' He jerked his head towards the sitting room. 'At least let's get out of earshot,' he muttered. 'He's probably listening at the door and you don't want the Press on your back any more than I do.'

Galbraith released the handcuffs on his own wrist and followed Bridges into the sitting room again, treading on the spliff as he went. 'Tell me about the relationship between Steve and Kate,' he said, resuming his seat. 'And make it convincing, Tony,' he added, taking his notebook from his pocket with a sigh, 'because A: I'm knackered; B: you're getting up my nose; and C: it's completely immaterial to me if your name is plastered across the newspapers tomorrow morning as a probable suspect on a rape and murder charge.'

*

'I never did understand the attraction. I only met her once and, as far as I'm concerned, she's the most boring woman I've ever come across. It was in a pub one Friday lunchtime, and all she could do was sit and look at Steve as if he were Leonardo DiCaprio. Mind you, when she started talking, it was even worse. God, she was stupid! Having a conversation with her was like listening to paint dry. I think she must have lived on a diet of soap operas because whatever I said reminded her of something that had happened in *Neighbours* or *EastEnders*, and it got on my tits after a while. I asked Steve later what the hell he thought he was doing, and he laughed and said he wasn't interested in her for her conversation. He reckoned she had a dream of an arse, and that was all that mattered. To be honest, I don't think he ever intended it to get as serious as it did. She met him in the street one day after the incident with Hannah's buggy, and invited him back to her house. He said it was all pretty mind-blowing. One minute he was struggling to find something to talk about over a coffee in the kitchen, and the next she was climbing all over him. He said the only bad part was that the kid sat in a highchair watching them do it because Kate said Hannah would scream her head off if she tried to take her out.

'As far as Steve was concerned, that was it. That's what he told me anyway. Wham, bam, thank you, ma'am, and bye-bye. So I was a bit surprised when he asked if he could bring her here on a couple of occasions in the autumn term. It was during the day while her husband was at work so I never saw her. Other times, they did it on his boat or in her house, but mostly they did it in his Volvo estate. He'd drive her out into the New Forest and they'd dose the kid with paracetamol so she'd sleep on the front seat while they set to in the back. All in all it went on for about two months until he started to get bored. The trouble was Kate had nothing going for her except her arse. She didn't drink, she didn't smoke, she didn't sail, she had no sense of humour and all she wanted was for Steve to get a part in *EastEnders*. It was pathetic really. I think it was the ultimate dream for her, to get hitched to a soap star and swan around being photographed on his arm.

'In all honesty, I don't think it ever occurred to her that he was only balling her because she was available and didn't cost him a penny. He said she was completely gobsmacked when he told her he'd had enough and didn't want to see her again. That's when she turned nasty. I guess she'd been conning idiots like her husband for so long it really pissed her off to find she'd been taken for a ride by a younger guy. She rubbed crap all over the sheets in his cabin, then she started setting off his car alarm and smearing shit all over his car. Steve got incredibly uptight about it. Everything he touched had crap on it. What really bugged him was his dinghy. He came down one Friday and found the bottom ankle-deep in water and slushy turds. He said she must have been saving them up for weeks. Anyway, that's when he started talking about going to the police.

'I told him it was a crazy idea. If you get the filth involved, I said, you'll never hear the end of it. And it won't be just Kate who's after you, it'll be William, too. You can't go round sleeping with other guys' wives and expect them to turn a blind eye. I told him to cool down and move his car to another parking place. So he said, what about his dinghy? And I said I'd lend him one that she wouldn't recognize. And that was it. Simple. Problem sorted. As far as I know he didn't have any more aggro from her.'

It was a while before Galbraith responded. He had been listening attentively, and making notes, and he finished writing before he said anything. 'Did you lend him a dinghy?' he asked.

'Sure.'

'What did it look like?'

Bridges frowned. 'The same as any dinghy. Why do you want to know that?'

'Just interested. What colour was it?'

'Black.'

'Where did you get it from?'

He started to pluck Rizla papers from their packet and make a patchwork quilt of them on the floor. 'A mail order catalogue, I think. It's the one I had before I bought my new rib.'

'Has Steve still got it?'

He hesitated before shaking his head. 'I wouldn't know, mate. Wasn't it on *Crazy Daze* when you searched it?'

Thoughtfully, the DI tapped his pencil against his teeth. He recalled Carpenter's words of Wednesday: '*I didn't like him. He's a cocky little bastard, and a damn sight too knowledgeable about police interviews.*' 'Okay,' he said next. 'Let's go back to Kate. You say the problem was sorted. What happened then?'

'Nothing. That's it. End of story. Unless you count the fact that she ends up dead on a beach in Dorset the weekend Steve just happens to be there.'

'I do. I also count the fact that her daughter was found wandering along a main road approximately two hundred yards from where Steve's boat was moored.'

'It was a set up,' said Bridges. 'You should be giving William the third degree. He had far more reason to murder Kate than Steve did. She was two-timing him, wasn't she?'

Galbraith shrugged. 'Except that William didn't hate his wife, Tony. He knew what she was like when he married her and it made no difference to him. Steve, on the other hand, had got himself into a mess and didn't know how to get out of it.'

'That doesn't make him a murderer.'

'Perhaps he thought he needed an ultimate solution.'

Bridges shook his head. 'Steve's not like that.'

'And William Sumner is?'

'I wouldn't know. I've never met the bloke.'

'According to your statement you and Steve had a drink with him one evening.'

'Okay. Correction. I don't *know* the bloke. I stayed fifteen minutes tops and exchanged maybe half a dozen words with him.'

Galbraith steepled his fingers in front of his mouth and studied the young man. 'But you seem to know a lot about him,' he said. 'Kate, too, despite only meeting each of them once.'

Bridges returned his attention to his patchwork quilt, sliding the papers into different positions with the balls of his fingers. 'Steve talks a lot.'

Galbraith seemed to accept this explanation because he gave a nod. 'Why was Steve planning to go to France this week?'

'I didn't know he was.'

'He had a reservation at a hotel in Concarneau which was cancelled this morning when he failed to confirm it.'

Bridges' expression became suddenly wary. 'He's never mentioned it.'

'Would you expect him to?'

'Sure.'

'You said you and he had grown apart,' Galbraith reminded him.

'Figure of speech, mate.'

A look of derision darkened the Inspector's eyes. 'Okay, last question. Where's Steve's lock-up, Tony?'

'What lock-up?' asked the other guilelessly.

'All right. Let me put it another way. Where does he store the equipment off his boat when he's not using it? His dinghy and his outboard, for example.'

'All over the place. Here. The flat in London. The back of his car.'

Galbraith shook his head. 'No oil spills,' he said. 'We've searched them all.' He smiled amiably. 'And don't try and tell me an outboard doesn't leak when it's laid on its side because I won't believe you.'

Bridges scratched the side of his jaw but didn't say anything.

'You're not his keeper, son,' murmured Galbraith kindly, 'and there's no law that says when your friend digs a hole for himself you have to get into it with him.'

The man pulled a wry face. 'I did warn him, you know. I said he'd do better to volunteer information rather than have it dragged out of him piecemeal. He wouldn't listen, though. He has this crazy idea he can control everything when the truth is he's never been able to control a damn thing from the first day I met him. Talk about a loose cannon. Sometimes, I wish I'd never met the stupid bugger because I'm sick to death of telling lies for him.' He shrugged. 'But, hey! He *is* my friend.'

Galbraith's boyish face creased into a smile. The young man's sincerity was about as credible as a Ku Klux Klan assertion that it wasn't an association of racists, and he was reminded of the expression: with friends like this who needs enemies? He glanced idly about the room. There were too many discrepancies, he thought, particularly in relation to fingerprint evidence, and he felt he was being steered in a direction he didn't want to go. He wondered why Bridges thought that was necessary.

Because he knew Harding was guilty? Or because he knew he wasn't?

Chapter Twenty-two

A CALL FROM Dorsetshire Constabulary to the manager of the Hotel Angelique in Concarneau, a pretty seaside town in southern Brittany, revealed that Mr Steven Harding had telephoned on 8 August, requesting a double room for three nights from Saturday, 16 August for himself and Mrs Harding. He had given his mobile telephone as the contact number, saying he would be travelling the coast of France by boat during the week 11–17 August and could not be sure of his exact arrival date. He had agreed to confirm the reservation not less than twenty-four hours prior to his arrival. In the absence of any such confirmation, and with rooms in demand, the manager had left a message with Mr Harding's telephone answering service and had cancelled the reservation when Mr Harding failed to return his call. He was not acquainted with Mr Harding and was unable to say if Mr or Mrs Harding had stayed in the hotel before. Where exactly was his hotel in Concarneau? Two streets back from the waterfront, but within easy walking distance of the shops, the sea, and the lovely beaches.

And the marinas, too, of course.

*

A complete check of the numbers listed in Harding's mobile telephone, which had been unavailable to the police at the time of his arrest because it had been under a pile of newspapers in Bob Winterslow's house, produced a series of names already known and contacted by the investigators. Only one call remained a mystery, either because the subscriber had deliberately withheld the number or because it had been routed through an exchange – possibly a foreign one – which meant the SIM card had been unable to record it.

'Steve? Where are you? I'm frightened. Please phone me. I've tried twenty times since Sunday.'

Before he returned to Winfrith, Detective Superintendent Carpenter took Ingram aside for a briefing. He had spent much of the last hour with his telephone clamped to his ear, while the PC and the two DCs continued to dig into the shale slide and scour the shoreline in a fruitless search for further evidence. He had watched their efforts through thoughtful eyes while jotting the various pieces of information that came through to him into his notebook. He was unsurprised by their failure to find anything else. The sea, as he had learnt from the coastguards' descriptions of how bodies vanished without trace and were never seen again, was a friend to murderers.

'Harding's being discharged from Poole hospital at five,' he told the constable, 'but I'm not ready to talk to him yet. I need to see the Frenchman's video and question Tony Bridges before I go anywhere near him.'

He clapped the tall man on the back. 'You were right about the lock-up, by the way. He's been using a garage near the Lymington yacht club. John Galbraith's on his way there now to have a look at it. What I need you to do, lad, is nail our friend Steve for the assault on Miss Jenner and hold him on ice till tomorrow morning. Keep it simple – make sure he thinks he's only being arrested for the assault. Can you do that?'

'Not until I've taken a statement from Miss Jenner, sir.'

Carpenter looked at his watch. 'You've got two and a half hours. Pin her to her story. I don't want her weaseling out because she doesn't want to get involved.'

'I can't force her, sir.'

'No one's asking you to,' said Carpenter irritably.

'And if she isn't as amenable as you hope?'

'Then use some charm,' said the Superintendent, thrusting his frown under Ingram's nose. 'I find it works wonders.'

'The house belongs to my grandfather,' said Bridges, directing Galbraith to pass the yacht club and take the road to the right which was lined with pleasant detached houses set back behind low hedges. It was at the wealthier end of town, not far from where the Sumners lived in Rope Walk, and Galbraith realized that Kate must have passed Tony's grandfather's house whenever she walked into town. He realized, too, that Tony must come from a 'good' family, and he wondered how they viewed their rebellious offspring and if they ever visited his shambolic establishment. 'Grandpa lives on his own,' Tony went on. 'He can't see to drive any more so he lends me the garage to store my rib.' He indicated an entrance a hundred yards farther on. 'In here. Steve's stuff is at the back.' He glanced at the DI as they drew to a halt in the small driveway. 'Steve and I have the only keys.'

'Is that important?'

Bridges nodded. 'Grandpa hasn't a clue what's in there.'

'It won't help him if it's drugs,' said Galbraith unemotionally, opening his door. 'You'll all be for the high jump, never mind how blind, deaf or dumb any of you are.'

'No drugs,' said Bridges firmly. 'We never deal.'

Galbraith shook his head in cynical disbelief. 'You couldn't afford to smoke the amount you do without dealing,' he said in a tone that brooked no disagreement. 'It's a fact of life. A teacher's salary couldn't fund a habit like yours.' The garage was detached from the house and set back twenty yards from it. Galbraith stood looking at it for a moment before glancing up the road towards the turning into Rope Walk. 'Who comes here the most?' he asked idly. 'You or Steve?'

'Me,' said the young man readily enough. 'I take my rib out two or three times a week. Steve just uses it for storage.'

Galbraith gestured towards the garage. 'Lead the way.' As they walked towards it, he caught the twitch of a curtain in one of the downstairs windows, and he wondered if Grandpa Bridges was quite as ignorant about what went into his garage as Tony claimed. The old, he thought, were a great deal more curious than the young. He stood back while the young man unlocked the double doors and pulled them wide. The entire front was taken up with a twelve-foot orange rib on a trailer but, when Tony pulled it out, an array of imported but clearly illicit goods was revealed at the back – neat stacks of cardboard boxes with VIN DE TABLE stencilled prominently on them, trays of Stella Artois lager, wrapped in polythene, and shelves covered in multi-pack cartons of cigarettes. Well, well, thought Galbraith with mild amusement, did Tony really expect him to believe that good old-fashioned smuggling of 'legal' contraband was the worst crime either he or his friend had ever been engaged in? The screed floor interested him more. It was still showing signs of damp where someone had hosed it down, and he wondered what had been washed away in the process.

'What's he trying to do?' he asked. 'Stock an entire off-licence? He's going to have a job persuading Customs and Excise this is for his own use.'

'It's not that bad,' protested Bridges. 'Listen, the guys in Dover bring in more than this every day via the ferries. They're coining it in. It's a stupid law. I mean, if the Government can't get its act together to bring down the duty on liquor and fags to the same level as the rest of Europe, then of course guys like Steve are going to do a bit of smuggling. Stands to reason. Everyone does it. You sail to France and you're tempted, simple as that.'

'And you end up in jail when you get busted. Simple as that,' said the DI sardonically. 'Who's funding him? You?'

Bridges shook his head. 'He's got a contact in London who buys it off him.'

'Is that where he takes it from here?'

'He borrows a mate's van and ships it up about once every two months.'

Galbraith traced a line in the dust on top of an opened box lid, then idly flipped it back. The bottoms of all the boxes in contact with the floor showed a tidemark where water had saturated them. 'How does he get it ashore from his boat?' he asked, lifting out a bottle of red table wine and reading the label. 'Presumably he doesn't bring it in by dinghy or someone would have noticed?'

'As long as it doesn't look like a case of wine there isn't a problem.'

'What *does* it look like?'

The young man shrugged. 'Something ordinary. Rubbish bags, dirty laundry, duvets. If he sticks a dozen bottles into socks to stop them rattling then packs them in his rucksack no one gives him a second glance. They're used to him transporting stuff to and from his boat – he's been working on it long enough. Other times he moors up to a pontoon and uses a marina trolley. People pile all sorts into them at the end of a weekend. I mean if you shove a few trays of Stella Artois down a sleeping bag, who's going to notice? More to the point, who's going to care? Everyone stocks up at the hypermarkets in France before they come home.'

Galbraith made a rough count of the wine boxes. 'There's six-hundred-odd bottles of wine here. It'd take him hours to move these a dozen at a time, not to mention the lager and the fags. Are you seriously saying no one's ever questioned why he's plying to and fro in a dinghy with a rucksack?'

'That's not how he shifts the bulk of it. I was only pointing out that it's not as difficult to bring stuff off boats as you seem to think it is. He moves most of it at night. There are hundreds of places along the coast you can make a drop as long as there's someone to meet you.'

'You, for example?'

'Once in a while,' Bridges admitted.

Galbraith turned to look at the rib on its trailer. 'Do you go out in the rib?'

'Sometimes.'

'So he calls you on his mobile and says I'll be in such-and-such a place at midnight. Bring your rib and the mate's van and help me unload.'

'More or less, except he usually comes in about three o'clock in the morning and two or three of us will be in different places. It makes it easier if he can choose the nearest to where he is.'

'Like where?' asked Galbraith dismissively. 'I don't swallow that garbage about there being hundreds of drop-off points. This whole coast is built over.'

Bridges grinned. 'You'd be amazed. I know of at least ten private landing stages on rivers between Chichester and Christchurch where you can bet on the owners being absent twenty-six weekends out of fifty-two, not to mention slips along Southampton Water. Steve's a good sailor, knows this area like the back of his hand and, providing he comes in on a rising tide in order to avoid being stranded, he can tuck himself pretty close into shore. Okay, we may get a bit wet, wading to and fro, and we may have a trek to the van, but two strong guys can usually clear a load in an hour. It's a doddle.'

Galbraith shook his head, remembering his own soaking off the Isle of Purbeck and the difficulties involved in winching boats up and down slips. 'It sounds like bloody hard work to me. What does he make on a shipment like this?'

'Anything between five hundred and a thousand quid a trip.'

'What do you make out of it?'

'I take payment in kind. Fags, lager, whatever.'

'For a drop?'

Bridges nodded.

'What about rent on this garage?'

'Use of *Crazy Daze* whenever I want it. It's a straight swap.'

Galbraith eyed him thoughtfully. 'Does he let you sail it or just borrow it to shag your girlfriends?'

Bridges grinned. 'He doesn't let *anyone* sail it. It's his pride and joy. He'd kill anyone who left a mark on it.'

'Mmm.' Galbraith lifted a white wine bottle out of another box. 'So when was the last time you used it for a shag?'

'A couple of weeks ago.'

'Who with?'

'Bibi.'

'Just Bibi? Or do you shag other girls behind her back?'

'Jesus, you don't give up, do you? Just Bibi, and if you tell her any different I'll make a formal complaint.'

Galbraith tucked the bottle back into its box with a smile and moved on to another one. 'How does it work? Do you call Steve in London and tell him you want the boat for the weekend? Or does he offer it to you when he doesn't want it?'

'I get to use it during the week. He gets to use it at weekends. It's a good deal, suits everyone.'

'So it's like your house? Anyone and everyone can pile in for a quick shag whenever the mood takes them?' He flicked the young man a look of disgust. 'It sounds pretty sordid to me. Do you all use the same sheets?'

'Sure.' Bridges grinned. 'Different times, different customs, mate. It's all about enjoying life these days, not being tied to conventional views of how to conduct yourself.'

Galbraith seemed suddenly bored with the subject. 'How often does Steve go to France?'

'It probably works out at an average of once every two months. It's no big deal, just booze and fags. If he clears five thousand quid in a year he reckons he's done well. But it's peanuts, for Christ's sake. That's why I told him he should come clean. The worst that can happen is a few months in jail. It would be different if he was doing drugs but' – he shook his head vigorously – 'he wouldn't touch them with a bargepole.'

'We found cannabis in one of his lockers.'

'Oh, come on,' said Bridges with a sigh. 'So he

smokes the odd joint. That doesn't make him a Colombian drugs baron. On that basis, anyone who enjoys a drink is smuggling alcohol by the lorry load. Look, trust me, he doesn't bring in anything more dangerous than red wine.'

Galbraith moved a couple of boxes. 'What about dogs?' he asked, lifting a plastic kennel out from behind them and holding it up for Bridges to look at.

The young man shrugged. 'A few times maybe. Where's the harm? He always makes sure they've got their anti-rabies certificates.' He watched a frown gather on Galbraith's forehead. 'It's a stupid law,' he repeated like a mantra. 'Six months of quarantine costs the owner a fortune, the dogs are miserable while it's happening, and not a single one has ever been diagnosed with rabies in all the time this country's been enforcing the rabies regulations.'

'Cut the crap, Tony,' said the DI impatiently. 'Personally, I think it's a crazy law that allows a smackhead like you within a hundred miles of impressionable children, but I'm not going to break your legs to keep you away from them. How much does he charge?'

'Five hundred, and I'm no fucking smackhead,' he said with genuine irritation. 'Smack's for idiots. You should bone up on your drug terminology.'

Galbraith ignored him. 'Five hundred, eh? That's a nice little earner. What does he make per person? Five *thousand*?'

There was a distinct hesitation. 'What are you talking about?'

'Twenty-five different sets of fingerprints inside *Crazy*

Daze, not counting Steve's or Kate and Hannah Sumner's. You've just accounted for two – yours and Bibi's – that still leaves twenty-three unaccounted for. That's a lot of fingerprints, Tony.'

Bridges shrugged. 'You said it yourself, he runs a sordid establishment.'

'Mmm,' murmured Galbraith, 'I did say that, didn't I?' His gaze shifted towards the trailer again. 'Nice rib. Is it new?'

Bridges followed his gaze. 'Not particularly, I've had it nine months.'

Galbraith walked over to look at the two Evinrude outboards at the stern. 'It looks new,' he remarked, running a finger along the rubber. 'Immaculate in fact. When did you last clean it?'

'Monday.'

'And you hosed the garage floor for good measure, did you?'

'It got wet in the process.'

Galbraith slapped the inflated sides of the rib. 'When did you last take it out?'

'I don't know. A week ago maybe.'

'So why did it need cleaning on Monday?'

'It didn't,' said Bridges, his expression growing wary again. 'I just like to look after it.'

'Then let's hope Customs and Excise don't rip it apart looking for drugs, my son,' said the policeman with poorly feigned sympathy, 'because they're not going to buy your story about red wine being Steve's most dangerous import any more than I do.' He jerked his head towards the back of the garage. 'That's just a blind in case you're sussed for anything more serious. Like illegal immigration. Those boxes have been in there for months. The dust's so thick I can write my name in it.'

Ingram stopped at Broxton House on his way home to check on Celia Jenner and was greeted enthusiastically by Bertie who bounded out of the front door, tail wagging. 'How's your mother?' he asked Maggie as he met her in the hall.

'Much better. Brandy and painkillers have put her on cloud nine and she's talking about getting up.' She headed for the kitchen. 'We're starving so I'm making some sandwiches. Do you want some?'

He followed with Bertie in tow, wondering how to tell her politely that he'd rather go home and make his own, but kept his counsel when he saw the state of the kitchen. It was hardly up to hospital standards, but the smell of cleaning rising from the floor, worktops, table and units was a huge advance on the ancient, indescribable aroma of dirty dog and damp horse blankets that had shocked his scent and taste buds earlier. 'I wouldn't say no,' he said. 'I haven't had anything to eat since last night.'

'What do you think?' she asked, setting to with a loaf of sliced bread, cheese and tomatoes.

He didn't pretend he didn't know what she was talking about. 'All in all a vast improvement. I prefer the floor this colour.' He touched the toe of one large boot to a quarry tile. 'I hadn't realized it was orange or that my feet weren't supposed to stick to it every time I moved.'

She gave a low laugh. 'It was damned hard work. I don't think it's had a mop on it for four years, not since Ma told Mrs Cottrill she couldn't afford her any more.' She glanced critically around the room. 'But you're right. A coat of paint would make a hell of a difference. I thought I'd buy some this afternoon and slap it on over the weekend. It won't take long.'

He should have brought the brandy up a long time ago, he realized, marvelling at her optimism. He would have done if he'd known she and her mother had been on the wagon for four years. Alcohol, for all its sins, wasn't called a restorative for nothing. He cast an interested eye towards the ceiling which was festooned with cobwebs. 'It'll slap right off again unless you shift that little lot as well. Do you have a stepladder?'

'I don't know.'

'I've got one at home,' he said. 'I'll bring it up this evening when I've finished for the day. In return will you put off your paint-buying trip long enough to give me a statement about Harding's assault on you this morning? I'll be questioning him at five o'clock and I want your version of the story before I do.'

She looked anxiously towards Bertie who, at Ingram's fingered command, had taken up station beside the Aga. 'I don't know. I've been thinking about what you said and now I'm worried he's going to accuse Bertie of being out of control and attacking *him*, in which case

I'll be faced with a prosecution under the Dangerous Dogs Act and Bertie will be put down. Don't you think it would be better to let it drop?'

Nick pulled out a chair and sat on it, watching her. 'He'll probably try to bring a counter prosecution, anyway, Maggie. It's his best defence against anything you might say.' He paused. 'But if you let him get in first then you'll be handing him the advantage. Is that what you want?'

'No, of course it isn't, but Bertie *was* out of control. He sank his teeth into the stupid idiot's arm and I couldn't get him off for love or money.' Angrily, she turned a ferocious glare on her dog, then stabbed her knife into a tomato and splattered seeds all over the chopping board. 'I had to thrash him in the end to make him release his hold and I won't be able to deny it if Steve takes me to court.'

'Who attacked first, Bertie or Steve?'

'Me probably. I was screaming abuse at Steve so he lashed out at me, then the next thing I knew Bertie was hanging off his arm like a great hairy leech.' Unexpectedly, she laughed. 'Actually, in retrospect, it's quite funny. I thought they were dancing until red saliva came out of Bertie's mouth. I just couldn't understand what Harding thought he was playing at. First he appears out of nowhere, then he runs at Stinger, then he slaps me and starts dancing with my dog. I felt as if I was in a madhouse.'

'Why do you think he slapped you?'

She smiled uncomfortably. 'Presumably because I made him angry. I called him a pervert.'

'That's no excuse for slapping you. Verbal abuse does not constitute an assault, Maggie.'

'Then maybe it should.'

'The man hit you,' he remarked curiously. 'Why are you making excuses for him?'

'Because, thinking back, I was incredibly rude. I certainly called him a creep and a bastard and I said you'd crucify him if you knew he was there. It's your fault really. I wouldn't have been so frightened if you hadn't come and questioned me about him yesterday. You planted the idea that he was dangerous.'

'*Mea culpa*,' he said mildly.

'You know what I mean.'

He acknowledged the point gravely. 'What else did you say?'

'Nothing. I just screamed at him like a fishwife because he gave me such a shock. The trouble is, he was shocked, too, so we both sort of lashed out without thinking . . . he in his way . . . me in mine.'

'There's no excuse for physical violence.'

'Isn't there?' she asked dryly. 'You excused mine earlier.'

'True,' he admitted, rubbing his cheek reminiscently. 'But if I'd retaliated, Maggie, you'd still be unconscious.'

'Meaning what? That men are expected to show more responsibility than women?' She glanced at him with a half-smile. 'I don't know whether to accuse you of being patronizing or ignorant.'

'Ignorant every time,' he said. 'I know nothing about women except that very few of them could land me a knock-out blow.' His eyes smiled at her. 'But I know damn well that I could flatten any of them. Which is why – unlike Steve Harding – I wouldn't dream of raising my hand against one.'

'Yes, but you're so wise and so middle-aged, Nick,' she said crossly, 'and he isn't. In any case, I don't even remember the way it happened. It was all over so quickly. I expect that sounds pathetic, but I've realized I'm not much good as a witness.'

'It just makes you normal,' he said. 'Very few people have accurate recall.'

'Well, the truth is I think he wanted to try and catch Stinger before he bolted and only hit out when I called him a pervert.' Her shoulders sagged despondently as if the brandy-courage in her blood had suddenly evaporated. 'I'm sorry to disappoint you. I used to see everything so straightforwardly before I got taken to the cleaners by Martin, but now I can't make up my mind about anything. I'd have insisted on a prosecution like a shot this morning but now I realize I'd *die* if anything happened to Bertie. I love the stupid animal to distraction, and I absolutely refuse to sacrifice him on a point of principle. He's worth a slap from a toe-rag any day. Goddammit he's *faithful*. All right, he visits you from time to time but he always comes home to love me at night.'

'Okay.'

There was a short silence.

'Is that all you're going to say?'

'Yes.'

She eyed him with suspicion. 'You're a policeman. Why aren't you arguing with me?'

'Because you're intelligent enough to make your own decisions, and nothing I can say will change your mind.'

'That's absolutely right.' She slapped some butter on a piece of sliced bread and waited for him to say something else. When he didn't, she grew nervous. 'Are you still going to question Steve?' she demanded.

'Of course. That's my job. Helicopter rescues don't come cheap, and someone has to account for why this morning's was necessary. Harding was admitted to hospital with dog bites, so I have a responsibility to establish whether the attack on him was provoked or unprovoked. One of you was assaulted this morning and I have to try and find out which. If you're lucky, he'll be feeling as guilty as you are and there'll be a stalemate. If you're unlucky, I'll be back this evening requesting a statement from you in answer to his assertion that you had no control over your dog.'

'That's blackmail.'

He shook his head. 'As far as I'm concerned you and Steven Harding have equal rights under the law. If he says Bertie made an unprovoked attack on him I will investigate the allegation, and if I think he's right I'll submit my findings to the Crown Prosecution Service and suggest they prosecute you. I may not like him, Maggie, but if I think he's telling the truth I will support him. That's what society pays me for, irrespective of personal feeling and irrespective of how it may affect the people involved.'

She turned round, back against the worktop. 'I had no idea you were such a cold fucking bastard.'

He was unrepentant. 'And I had no idea you thought you ranked above anyone else. You'll get no favours from me, not where the law's concerned.'

'Will you favour me if I give you a statement?'

'No, I'll be as fair to you as I am to Harding but my advice is that you'll gain an advantage by getting your statement in first.'

She whipped the knife off the chopping board and waved it under his nose. 'Then you'd bloody well better be right,' she said fiercely, 'or I'll take your testicles off – *personally* – and laugh while I'm doing it. I *love* my dog.'

'So do I,' Ingram assured her, putting a finger on the hilt of the knife and moving it gently to one side. 'The difference is I don't encourage him to slobber all over me in order to prove it.'

'I've sealed the garage for the moment,' Galbraith told Carpenter over the phone, 'but you'll have to sort out priorities with Customs and Excise. We need a scene-of-crime team down here pronto, but if you want a hard charge on which to hold Steven Harding, then C and E can probably deliver for you. My guess is he's been ferrying illegal immigrants in wholesale and dropping them off along the south coast . . . Yes, it would certainly explain the fingerprint evidence in the saloon area. No, no sign of the stolen Fastrigger outboard . . .' He felt the young man beside him stir, and he glanced at him with a distracted smile. 'Yes, I'm bringing Tony Bridges in now. He's agreed to make a new statement . . . Yes, very co-operative. William? . . . No, it doesn't eliminate him any more than it eliminates Steve . . . Mmm, back to square one, I'm afraid.' He tucked the telephone into his breast pocket and wondered why he'd never thought of taking up acting himself.

At the other end, Superintendent Carpenter looked at his receiver in surprise for a moment before cutting the line. He hadn't a clue what John Galbraith had been talking about.

Although he hadn't been aware of it, Steven Harding had been under observation by a woman detective constable from the moment he was admitted to the hospital. She sat out of sight in the Sister's office, making sure he stayed put, but in the event he appeared in no hurry to leave. He flirted constantly with the nurses and, much to the WDC's irritation, the nurses reciprocated. She spent the waiting hours pondering the naivety of women, and wondered how many of these selfsame nurses would argue vehemently that they hadn't given him any encouragement if and when he decided to rape them. In other words, what constituted encouragement? Something a woman would describe as innocent flirting? Or something a man would call a definite come-on?

It was with some relief that she handed over responsibility to PC Ingram in the corridor outside. 'The Sister's discharging him at five but the way things are going, I'm not sure he'll be leaving at all,' she said ruefully.

'He's got every nurse wound round his little finger and he looks set for the duration. Frankly, if they turf him out of this bed, it wouldn't surprise me if he ends up in a nice warm one somewhere else. I can't see the attraction myself but then I've never been too keen on wankers.'

Ingram gave a muted laugh. 'Hang around. Watch the fun. If he doesn't walk out of his own accord on the dot of five, I'll clap the irons on him in there.'

'I'm game,' she agreed cheerfully. 'You never know, you might need a hand.'

The video film was difficult to watch, not because of its content, which was as discreet as the Dartmouth sergeant had promised, but because the picture rose and fell with the movement of the Frenchman's boat. Nevertheless, his daughter had succeeded in capturing considerable footage of Harding in close detail. Carpenter, sitting behind his desk, played it through once, then used the remote to rewind to where Harding had first sat down on his rucksack. He held the image on pause and addressed the team of detectives crammed into his office. 'What do you think he's doing there?'

'Releasing Godzilla?' said one of the men with a snigger.

'Signalling to someone,' said a woman.

Carpenter played back a few frames to follow, in reverse, the panning of the camera lens across the shadowy, out-of-focus glare of the white motor cruiser and the blurry bikini-clad figure lying face down across the bows. 'I agree,' he said. 'The only question is, who?'

'Nick Ingram listed the boats that were there that day,' said another man. 'They shouldn't be too difficult to track down.'

'There was a Fairline Squadron with two teenage girls on board,' said Carpenter, passing across the report from Bournemouth about the abandoned dinghy. '*Gregory's Girl* out of Poole. Start with that one. It's owned by a Poole businessman called Gregory Freemantle.'

Ingram detached himself from the wall and blocked the corridor as Steven Harding, arm in sling, came through the door of the ward at 4.45. 'Good afternoon, sir,' he said politely. 'I hope you're feeling better.'

'Why would you care?'

Ingram smiled. 'I'm always interested in anyone I help to rescue.'

'Well, I'm not going to talk to you. You're the bastard who got them interested in my boat.'

Ingram showed his warrant card. 'I questioned you on Sunday. PC Ingram, Dorsetshire Constabulary.'

Harding's eyes narrowed. 'They say they can keep *Crazy Daze* for as long as is necessary but won't explain what gives them the right. I haven't done anything so they can't charge me, but they can sure as hell steal my boat for no reason.' His angry gaze raked Ingram. 'What does "as long as is necessary" mean, anyway?'

'There can be any number of reasons why it's deemed

necessary to retain seized articles,' explained the constable helpfully, if somewhat misleadingly. The rules surrounding retention were woolly in the extreme and policemen had few qualms about smothering so-called evidence in mountains of paperwork to avoid having to return it. 'In the case of *Crazy Daze*, it probably means they haven't finished the forensic examination, but once that's done you should be able to effect its release almost immediately.'

'Bollocks to that! They're holding it in case I abscond to France.'

Ingram shook his head. 'You'd have to go a little further than France, Steve,' he murmured in mild correction. 'Everyone's mighty co-operative in Europe these days.' He stood aside and gestured down the corridor behind him. 'Shall we go?'

Harding backed away from him. 'Dream on. I'm not going anywhere with you.'

'I'm afraid you must,' said Ingram with apparent regret. 'Miss Jenner's accused you of assault which means I have to insist that you answer some questions. I would prefer it if you came voluntarily but I will arrest you if necessary.' He jerked his chin towards the corridor behind Harding. 'That doesn't lead anywhere – I've already checked it out.' He pointed towards a door at the end where a woman was consulting a noticeboard. 'This is the only exit.'

Harding began to ease his arm out of its sling, clearly fancying his chances in a sprint dash against this simple, forelock-tugging, sixteen-stone yokel in a uniform, but something changed his mind. Perhaps it was the fact that Ingram stood four inches taller than he did. Perhaps the woman by the door signalled that she was a detective. Perhaps he saw something in Ingram's lazy smile that persuaded him he might be making a mistake . . .

He gave an indifferent shrug. 'What the hell! I've nothing else to do. But it's your precious Maggie you should be arresting. She stole my phone.'

Chapter Twenty-three

SECURED IN the passenger seat of the police Range Rover where Ingram could keep an eye on him, Harding sat huddled in moody silence for most of the trip back to Swanage. Ingram made no attempt to talk to him. Once in a while their eyes met when the policeman was checking traffic to his left, but he felt none of the empathy for Harding that Galbraith had experienced on *Crazy Daze*. He saw only immaturity in the young man's face and despised him because of it. He was reminded of every juvenile delinquent he'd arrested down the years, not one of whom had had the experience or the wisdom to understand the inevitability of consequence. They saw it in terms of retribution and justice and whether they would do 'time', never in terms of the slow destruction of their lives.

It was as they drove through the little town of Corfe Castle, with its ruined medieval ramparts commanding a gap in the Purbeck chalk ridge, that Harding broke the silence. 'If you hadn't jumped to conclusions on Sunday,' he said in a reasonable tone of voice, 'none of this would have happened.'

'None of what?'

'Everything. My arrest. This.' He touched a hand to his sling. 'I shouldn't be here. I had a part lined up in London. It could have been my breakthrough.'

'The only reason you're here is because you attacked Miss Jenner this morning,' Ingram pointed out. 'What have the events of Sunday got to do with that?'

'She wouldn't know me from Adam but for Kate's murder.'

'That's true.'

'And you won't believe I didn't have anything to do with that – none of you will – but it's not fair,' Harding complained with a sudden surge of bitterness. 'It's just a bloody awful coincidence, like the coincidence of bumping into Maggie this morning. Do you think I'd have shown myself to her if I'd known she was there?'

'Why not?' The car sped up as they exited the thirty-mile speed limit.

He turned a morose stare on Ingram's profile. 'Have you any idea what it's like to have your movements monitored by the police? You've got my car, my boat. I'm supposed to stay at an address you've chosen for me. It's like being in prison without the walls. I'm being treated like a criminal when I haven't done anything, but if I lose my temper because some stupid woman treats me like Jack the Ripper I get accused of assault.'

Ingram kept his eyes on the road ahead. 'You hit her. Don't you think she had a right to treat you like Jack the Ripper?'

'Only because she wouldn't stop screaming.' He gnawed at his fingernails. 'I guess you told her I was a rapist, so of course she believed you. That's what got me riled. She was fine with me on Sunday, then today . . .' He fell silent.

'Did you know she might be there?'

'Of course not. How could I?'

'She rides that gully most mornings. It's one of the few places she can give her horses a good gallop. Anyone who knows her could have told you that. It's also one of the few places with easy access to the beach from the coastal path.'

'I didn't know.'

'Then why are you so surprised she was scared of you? She'd have been scared of any man who appeared out of nowhere on a deserted headland when she wasn't expecting it.'

'She wouldn't have been scared of you.'

'I'm a policeman. She trusts me.'

'She trusted *me*,' said Harding, 'until you told her I was a rapist.'

It was the same point Maggie had made and Ingram conceded it was a fair one – to himself if not to Harding. It was the grossest injustice to destroy an innocent person's reputation, however it was done, and while neither he nor Galbraith had said that the young man was a rapist, the implication had been clear enough. They continued for a while in silence. The road to Swanage led south-east along the spine of Purbeck and the distant sea showed intermittently between folds of pastureland. The sun was warm on Ingram's arm and neck but Harding, sitting in shade on the left-hand side of the car, hunched tighter into himself as if he was cold and stared sightlessly out of the window. He seemed lost in lethargy, and Ingram wondered if he was still trying to concoct some sort of defence or whether the events of the morning had finally taken their toll.

'That dog of hers should be shot,' he said suddenly.

Still concocting a defence then, thought Ingram, while wondering why it had taken him so long to get round to it. 'Miss Jenner claims he was only trying to protect her,' he said mildly.

'It bloody savaged me.'

'You shouldn't have hit her.'

Harding gave a long sigh. 'I didn't mean to,' he admitted as if realizing that continued argument would be a waste of time. 'I probably wouldn't have done it if she hadn't called me a pervert. The last person who did that was my father and I flattened him for it.'

'Why did he call you a pervert?'

'Because he's old-fashioned and I told him I'd done a porno shoot to make money.' The young man balled his hands into fists. 'I wish people would just keep their noses out of my business. It gets on my tits the way everyone keeps lecturing me about the way I live my life.'

Ingram shook his head in irritation. 'There's no such thing as a free lunch, Steve.'

'What's that got to do with anything?'

'Live now, pay later. What goes around, comes around. No one promised you a rose garden.'

Harding turned to stare out of the passenger window, offering a cold shoulder to what he clearly felt was a patronizing police attitude. 'I don't know what the fuck you're talking about.'

Ingram smiled slightly. 'I know you don't.' He glanced sideways. 'What were you doing on Emmetts Hill this morning?'

'Just walking.'

There was a moment's silence before Ingram gave a snort of laughter. 'Is that the best you can do?'

'It's the truth,' he said.

'Like hell it is. You've had all day to work this one out but by God, if that's the only explanation you've been able to come up with, you must have a very low opinion of policemen.'

The young man turned back to him with an engaging smile. 'I do.'

'Then we'll have to see if we can change your mind.' Ingram's smile was almost as engaging. 'Won't we?'

Gregory Freemantle was pouring himself a drink in the front room of his flat in Poole when his girlfriend showed in two detectives. The atmosphere was thick enough to cut with a knife and it was obvious to both policemen that they had walked in on a humdinger of a row. 'DS Campbell and DC Langham,' she said curtly. 'They want to talk to you.'

Freemantle was a Peter Stringfellow lookalike, an ageing playboy with straggling blond hair and the beginnings of desperation in the sagging lines around his eyes and chin. 'Oh God,' he groaned, 'you're not taking her seriously about that bloody oil drum, are you? She doesn't know the first thing about sailing' – he paused to consider – 'or children for that matter, but it doesn't stop her being lippy.' He raised one hand and worked his thumb and forefingers to mimic a mouth working.

He was the kind of man other men take against instinctively, and DS Campbell glanced sympathetically at the girlfriend. 'It wasn't an oil drum, sir, it was an upturned dinghy. And, yes, we took Miss Hale's information very seriously.'

Freemantle raised his glass in the woman's direction. 'Good one, Jenny.' His eyes were already showing alcohol levels well above average, but he still downed two fingers of neat whisky without blinking. 'What do you want?' he asked Campbell. He didn't invite them to sit down, merely turned back to the whisky bottle and poured himself another drink.

'We're trying to eliminate people from the Kate Sumner murder inquiry,' Campbell explained, 'and we're interested in everyone who was in Chapman's Pool on Sunday. We understand you were there on a Fairline Squadron.'

'You know I was. She's already told you.'

'Who was with you?'

'Jenny and my two daughters, Marie and Fliss. And it was a bloody nightmare if you're interested. You buy a boat to keep everyone happy, and all they can do is snipe at each other. I'm going to sell the damn thing.' His drink-sodden eyes filled with self-pity. 'It's no fun going out on your own, and it's even less fun taking a menagerie of cats with you.'

'Was either of your daughters wearing a bikini and lying face-down on the bow between 12.30 and one o'clock on Sunday, sir?'

'I don't know.'

'Does either of them have a boyfriend called Steven Harding?'

He shrugged indifferently.

'I'd be grateful for an answer, Mr Freemantle.'

'Well, you're not going to get one because I don't know and I don't care,' he said aggressively. 'I've had a bucketful of women today, and as far as I'm concerned the sooner they're all genetically engineered to behave like Stepford wives the better.' He raised his glass again. 'My wife serves me with notice that she intends to bankrupt my company in order to take three-quarters of what I'm worth. My fifteen-year-old daughter tells me she's pregnant and wants to run away to France with some long-haired git who fancies himself as an actor, and my girlfriend' – he lurched his glass in Jenny Hale's direction – 'that one over there – tells me it's all my fault because I've waived my responsibilities as a husband and a father. So cheers! To men, eh!'

Campbell turned to the woman. 'Can you help us, Miss Hale?'

She looked questioningly towards Gregory, clearly seeking his support, but when he refused to meet her eyes, she gave a small shrug. 'Ah, well,' she said, 'I wasn't planning on hanging around after this evening anyway. Marie, the fifteen-year-old, was wearing a bikini and was sunbathing on the bow before lunch,' she told the two policemen. 'She lay on her tummy so that her father wouldn't see her bump and she was signalling to her boyfriend who was jerking off on the shore for her benefit. The rest of the time she wore a sarong to disguise the fact that she's pregnant. She has since told us that her boyfriend's name is Steve Harding and that he's an actor in London. I knew she was plotting something because she was hyped up from the moment we left Poole, and I realized it must be to do with the boy on the shore because she became completely poisonous after he left and has been a nightmare ever since.' She sighed. 'That's what the row has been about. When she turned up today in one of her tantrums I told her father he should take some interest in what's really going on because it's been obvious to me for a while that she's not just pregnant but has been taking drugs as well. Now open war has broken out.'

'Is Marie still here?'

Jenny nodded. 'In the spare bedroom.'

'Where does she normally live?'

'In Lymington with her mother and sister.'

'Do you know what she and her boyfriend were planning to do on Sunday?'

She glanced at Gregory. 'They were going to run away together to France, but when that woman's body was found they had to abandon the plan because there were too many people watching. Steve has a boat apparently which he'd left at Salterns Marina, and the idea was for Marie to vanish into thin air out of Chapman's Pool after saying she was going for a walk to Worth Matravers. They thought if she changed into some men's clothes that Steve had brought with him, and slogged it back across land to the ferry, they could be on their way to France by the evening and no one would ever know where she'd gone or who she was with.' She shook her head. 'Now she's threatening to kill herself if her father doesn't let her leave school and go and live with Steve in London.'

While the garage in Lymington, and its contents, were being taken apart systematically by scene-of-crime officers in search of evidence, Tony Bridges was being formally interviewed as a witness and under taped conditions by Detective Superintendent Carpenter and DI Galbraith. He refused to repeat anything he had said to Galbraith about his or Harding's alleged smuggling activities, however, and, as that particular matter was being passed to Customs and Excise, Carpenter was less exercised by the refusal than he might otherwise have been. Instead, he chose to shock Bridges by showing him the videotape of Harding masturbating, then asked him if his friend made a habit of performing indecent acts in public.

Surprisingly, Bridges *was* shocked.

'Jesus!' he exclaimed, wiping his forehead with his sleeve. 'How would I know? We lead separate lives. He's never done anything like that around me.'

'It's not that bad,' murmured Galbraith who was sitting beside Carpenter. 'Just a discreet wank. Why are you sweating over it, Tony?'

The young man eyed him nervously. 'I get the impression it's worse than that. You wouldn't be showing it to me otherwise.'

'You're a bright lad,' said Carpenter, freeze-framing the video at the point where Harding was cleaning himself up. 'That's a T-shirt he's using. You can just make out the Derby FC logo on the front. It belongs to a ten-year-old kid called Danny Spender. He thinks Steve stole it off him around midday on Sunday and half an hour later we see him ejaculating all over it. You know the guy better than anyone. Would you say he has a yen for little boys?'

Bridges looked even more startled. 'No,' he muttered.

'We have a witness who says Steve couldn't keep his hands off the two lads who found Kate Sumner's body. One of the boys describes him using his mobile telephone to bring on an erection in front of them. We have a policeman who says he maintained the erection while the boys were around him.'

'Ah, shit!' Bridges ran his tongue round dry lips. 'Listen, I always thought he hated kids. He can't stand working with them, can't stand it when I talk about teaching.' He looked towards the frozen image on the television screen. 'This has to be wrong. Okay, he's got a thing about sex – talks about it too much – likes blue movies – boasts about three-in-a-bed romps, that kind of thing – but it's always with women. I'd have bet my last cent he was straight.'

Carpenter leaned forward to examine the other man closely, then shifted his gaze to look at the television screen. 'That really offends you, doesn't it? Why is that, Tony? Did you recognize anyone else in the sequence?'

'No. I just think it's obscene, that's all.'

'It can't be worse than the pornography shoots he does.'

'I wouldn't know. I've never seen them.'

'You must have seen some of his photographs. Describe them for us.'

Bridges shook his head.

'Do they include kids? We know he's done some gay poses. Does he pose with children as well?'

'I don't know anything about it. You'll have to talk to his agent.'

Carpenter made a note. 'Paedophile rings pay double what anyone else pays.'

'It's got nothing to do with me.'

'You're a teacher, Tony. You have more responsibility than most people towards children. Does your friend pose with children?'

He shook his head.

'For the purposes of the tape,' said Carpenter into the microphone, 'Anthony Bridges declined to answer.' He consulted a piece of paper in front of him. 'On Tuesday you told us Steve wasn't the kiss-and-tell type, now you're saying he boasts about three-in-a-bed sex. Which is true?'

'The boasting,' he said with more confidence, glancing at Galbraith. 'That's how I know about Kate. He was always telling me what they did together.'

Galbraith wiped a freckled hand around the back of his neck to massage muscles made sore by too much driving that day. 'Except it sounds like all talk and no action, Tony. Your friend goes in for solitary pursuits. On beaches. On his boat. In his flat. Did you ever wonder if he was lying about his relationships with women?'

'No. Why should I? He's a good-looking bloke. Women like him.'

'All right, let me put it another way. How many of these women have you actually met? How often does he bring them to your house?'

'He doesn't need to. He takes them to his boat.'

'Then why is there no evidence of that? There were a couple of articles of women's clothing and a pair of Hannah's shoes on board but nothing to suggest that a woman was ever in the bed with him.'

'You can't know that.'

'Oh, come on,' said Galbraith in exasperation, 'you're a chemist. His sheets have semen stains all over them but nothing that remotely suggests there was anyone else in the bed with him when he ejaculated.'

Bridges looked rather wildly towards the Superintendent. 'All I can tell you is what Steve told me. It's hardly my fault if the stupid sod was lying.'

'True,' agreed Carpenter, 'but you do keep shoving his prowess down our throats.' He produced Bridges' statement from a folder on the table and spread it flat in front of him, holding it down with his palms stretched on either side. 'You seem to have a bit of a thing about him being good-looking. This is what you said at the beginning of the week. "*Steve's a good-looking bloke*",' he read, ' "*and has an active sex life. He has at least two girls on the go at the same time . . .*" ' He lifted enquiring eyebrows. 'Do you want to comment on that?'

It was clear that Tony had no idea where this line of questioning was leading and needed time to think. A fact which interested both policemen. It was as if he were trying to predict moves in a chess game, and had begun to panic because checkmate looked inevitable. Every so often his eyes flicked towards the television screen, then dropped away rapidly as if the frozen image was more than he could bear. 'I don't know what you want me to say.'

'In simple terms, Tony, we're trying to square your portrayal of Steve with the forensic evidence. You want us to believe your friend had a prolonged affair with an older married woman but we're having difficulty substantiating that any such affair happened. For example, you told my colleague that Steve took Kate to your house on occasion, yet, despite the fact that your house clearly hasn't been cleaned in months, we couldn't find a single fingerprint belonging to Kate Sumner anywhere inside it. There is also nothing to suggest that Kate was ever in Steve's car, although you claim that he drove her to the New Forest on numerous occasions for sex in the back of it.'

'He said they needed out-of-the-way places in case they were spotted together. They were scared of William finding out because, according to Steve, he was so jealous he'd go berserk if he knew he was being two-timed.' He wilted before Carpenter's unconvinced expression. 'It's not my fault if he was lying to me,' he protested.

'He described William to us as middle-aged and straight,' said Carpenter thoughtfully. 'I don't recall him suggesting he was aggressive.'

'That's what he told me.'

Galbraith stirred on his chair. 'So your entire knowledge of Steve's *alleged'* – he put careful stress on the word – 'affair with Kate came from a single meeting with her in a pub and whatever Steve chose to tell you about her?'

Bridges nodded but didn't answer.

'For the purposes of the tape, Anthony Bridges gave a nod of agreement. So was he ashamed of the relationship, Tony? Is that why you only got to meet her once? You said yourself, you couldn't understand what the attraction was.'

'She was married,' he said. 'He was hardly going to parade a married woman around the town, was he?'

'Has he *ever* paraded a woman around town, Tony?'

There was a long silence. 'Most of his girlfriends are married,' he said then.

'Or mythical?' suggested Carpenter. 'Like claiming Bibi as a girlfriend?'

Bridges looked baffled, as if he was struggling with half-heard, dimly understood truths that were suddenly making sense. He didn't answer.

Galbraith levelled a finger at the television screen. 'What we're beginning to suspect is that the talk was a smokescreen for no action. Maybe he was pretending to like women because he didn't want anyone to know that his tastes lay in an entirely different direction? Maybe the poor bastard doesn't want to recognize it himself and lets off steam quietly in order to keep himself under control?' He turned the finger accusingly on Bridges. 'But if that's true, then where does it leave you and Kate Sumner?'

The young man shook his head. 'I don't understand.'

371

The DI took his notebook from his pocket and flipped it open. 'Let me quote some of the things you said about her: "*I think she must have lived on a diet of soap operas . . .*" "*Kate said Hannah would scream her head off . . .*" "*I guess she'd been conning idiots like her husband for so long . . .*" I could go on. You talked about her for fifteen minutes, fluently and with no prompting from me.' He laid his notebook on the table. 'Do you want to tell us how you know so much about a woman you only met once?'

'Everything I know is what Steve told me.'

Carpenter nodded towards the recording machine. 'This is a formal interview under taped conditions, Tony. Let me rephrase the question for you so there can be no misunderstandings. Bearing in mind that the Sumners are recent newcomers to Lymington, that both Steven Harding and William Sumner have denied there was any relationship between Steven and Kate Sumner, and that you, Anthony Bridges, claim to have met her only once, how do you explain your extensive and accurate knowledge of her?'

Marie Freemantle was a tall, willowy blonde with waist-length wavy hair and huge doe-like eyes which were awash with tears. Once assured that Steve was alive and well and currently answering questions about why he had been at Chapman's Pool on Sunday, she dried her eyes and favoured the policemen with a heavily practised triangular smile. If they were honest, both men were moved by her prettiness when they first saw her, although their sympathies were soon frayed by the self-centred, petulant nature beneath. They realized she wasn't very bright when it became clear that it hadn't occurred to her they were questioning her because Steven Harding was a suspect in Kate Sumner's murder. She chose to talk to them away from her father and his girlfriend, and her spite was colossal, particularly towards the woman whom she described as an interfering bitch. 'I hate her,' she finished. 'Everything was fine till she stuck her nose in.'

'Meaning you've always been allowed to do what you liked?' suggested Campbell.

'I'm old enough.'

'How old were you when you first had sex with Steven Harding?'

'Fifteen.' She wriggled her shoulders. 'But that's nothing these days. Most girls I know had sex at thirteen.'

'How long have you known him?'

'Six months.'

'How often have you had sex with him?'

'Lots of times.'

'Where do you do it?'

'Mostly on his boat.'

Campbell frowned. 'In the cabin?'

'Not often. The cabin stinks,' she said. 'He takes a blanket up on deck and we do it in the sunshine or under the stars. It's great.'

'Moored up to the buoy?' asked Campbell, with a rather shocked expression. Like Galbraith earlier, he was wondering about the generation gap that seemed to have opened, unobserved, between himself and today's youth. 'In full view of the Isle of Wight ferry?'

'Of course not,' she said indignantly, wriggling her shoulders again. 'He picks me up somewhere and we go for a sail.'

'Where does he pick you up?'

'All sorts of places. Like he says, he'd get strung up if anyone knew he was going with a fifteen-year-old, and he reckons if you don't use the same place too often, no one notices.' She shrugged, recognizing that further explanation was necessary. 'If you use a marina once in two weeks, who's going to remember? Then there's the salt flats. I walk round the path from the Yacht Haven and he just shoots in with his dinghy and lifts me off. Sometimes I go to Poole by train and meet him there. Mum thinks I'm with Dad, Dad thinks I'm with Mum. It's simple. I just phone him on his mobile and he tells me where to go.'

'Did you leave a message on his phone this morning?'

She nodded. 'He can't phone me in case Mum gets suspicious.'

'How did you meet him in the first place?'

'At the Lymington yacht club. There was a dance there on St Valentine's Day and Dad got tickets for it because he's still a member even though he lives in Poole now. Mum said Fliss and me could go if Dad watched out for us, but he got shit-faced as usual and left us to get on with it. That's when he was going out with his bitch of a secretary. I really *hated* her. She was always trying to put him against me.'

Campbell was tempted to say it wouldn't have been

difficult. 'Did your father introduce you to Steve? Did he know him?'

'No. One of my teachers did. He and Steve have been friends for years.'

'Which teacher?'

'Tony Bridges.' Her full lips curved into a malicious smile. 'He's fancied me for ages and he was trying to make this pathetic move on me when Steve cut him out. God, he was pissed about it. He's been needling away at me all term, trying to find out what's going on, but Steve told me not to tell him in case he got us into trouble for under-age sex. He reckons Tony's so fucking jealous he'd make life hell for us if he could.'

Campbell thought back to his interview with Bridges on Monday night. 'Perhaps he feels responsible for you.'

'That's not the reason,' she said scornfully. 'He's a sad little bastard – *that's* the reason. None of his girl-friends stay with him because he's stoned most of the time and can't do the business properly. He's been going out with this hairdresser for about four months now, and Steve says he's been feeding her drugs so she won't complain about his lousy performance. If you want my opinion there's something wrong with him – he's always trying to touch up girls in class – but our stupid headmaster's too thick to do anything about it.'

Campbell exchanged a glance with his colleague. 'How does Steve know he's been feeding her drugs?' he asked.

'He's seen him do it. It's like a Mickey Finn. You dissolve a tablet in lager and the girl passes out.'

'Do you know what drug he's using?'

Another shrug. 'Some sort of sleeping pill.'

'I'm not going to explain anything without a solicitor here,' said Bridges adamantly. 'Look, this was one sick woman. You think that kid of hers is weird? Well, trust me, she's as sane as you and me compared with her mother.'

WPC Griffiths heard the sound of smashing glass from the kitchen, and lifted her head in immediate concern. She had left Hannah watching television in the sitting room and, as far as she knew, William was still in his study upstairs where he had retreated, angry and resentful, after his interview with DI Galbraith. With a perplexed frown, she tiptoed along the corridor and pushed open the sitting-room door to find Sumner standing just inside. He turned an ashen face towards her then gestured helplessly towards the little girl who stalked purposefully about the room, picking up pictures of her mother and throwing them with high-pitched guttural cries into the unlit fireplace.

Ingram put a cup of tea in front of Steven Harding and took a chair on the other side of the table. He was puzzled by the man's attitude. He had expected a long interview session, punctuated by denials and counter accusations. Instead Harding had admitted culpability and agreed with everything Maggie had written in her statement. All that awaited him now was to be formally charged and held over till the next morning. His only real concern had been his telephone. When Ingram had handed it to the custody sergeant and formally entered it into the inventory of Harding's possessions, Harding had looked relieved. But whether because it had been returned or because it was switched off, Ingram couldn't tell.

'How about talking to me off the record?' he invited. 'Just to satisfy my own curiosity. There's no tape. No witnesses to the conversation. Just you and me.'

Harding shrugged. 'What do you want to talk about?'

'You. What's going on. Why you were on the coastal path on Sunday. What brought you back to Chapman's Pool this morning.'

'I already told you. I fancied a walk' – he made a good attempt at a cocky grin – 'both times.'

'All right.' He splayed his palms on the edge of the table, preparatory to standing up. 'It's your funeral. Just don't complain afterwards that no one tried to help you. You've always been the obvious suspect. You knew the victim, you own a boat, you were on the spot, you told lies about what you were doing there. Have you any idea how all that is going to look to a jury if the CPS decides to prosecute you for Kate Sumner's rape and murder?'

'They can't. They haven't got any evidence.'

'Oh, for Christ's sake grow up, Steve!' he said in irritation, subsiding on to his chair again. 'Don't you read the newspapers? People have spent years in prison on less evidence than Winfrith have against you. All right, it's only circumstantial but juries don't like co-incidence any more than the rest of us and, frankly, your antics of this morning haven't helped any. All they prove is that women make you angry enough to attack them.' He paused, inviting a reply that never came. 'If you're interested, in the report I wrote on Monday, I mentioned that both Miss Jenner and I thought you were having difficulty coping with an erection. Afterwards one of the Spender boys described how you were using your telephone as a masturbation aid before Miss Jenner arrived.' He shrugged. 'It may have had nothing to do with Kate Sumner, but it won't sound good in court.'

A dull flush spread up Harding's throat and into his face. 'That sucks!'

'True nevertheless.'

'I wish to God I'd never helped those kids,' he said with a burst of anger. 'I wouldn't be in this mess but for them. I should have walked away and left them to cope on their own.' He pushed his hair off his face with both hands and rested his forehead in his palms. 'Jesus Christ! Why do you have to put something like that in a report?'

'Because it happened.'

'Not like that it didn't,' he said sullenly, the flush of humiliation lingering in his cheeks.

'Then how?' Ingram watched him for a moment. 'Headquarters think you came back to gloat over the rape and that's what caused your erection.'

'That's bullshit!' said the young man angrily.

'What other explanation is there? If it wasn't the

thought of Kate Sumner's body that excited you then it had to be Miss Jenner or the boys.'

Harding raised his head and stared at the policeman, his eyes widening in shocked revulsion. 'The boys?' he echoed.

It crossed Ingram's mind that the facial expression was a little too theatrical, and he reminded himself, as Galbraith had done, that he was dealing with an actor. He wondered what Harding's reaction would be when he was told about the videotape. 'You couldn't keep your hands off them,' he pointed out. 'According to Miss Jenner, you were hugging Paul from behind when she rounded the boatsheds.'

'I don't believe this,' said Harding in desperation. 'I was only showing him how to use the binoculars properly.'

'Prove it.'

'How can I?'

Ingram tilted his chair back and stretched his long legs out in front of him, lacing his hands behind his head. 'Tell me why you were at Chapman's Pool. Let's face it, whatever you were doing can't be any worse than the constructions that are being put on your actions at the moment.'

'I'm not saying another word.'

Ingram stared at a mark on the ceiling. 'Then let me tell you what I think you were doing. You went there to meet someone,' he murmured. 'I think it was a girl and I think she was on one of the boats, but whatever plans you'd made with her were scuppered when the place started jumping with policemen and sightseers.' He shifted his attention back to Harding. 'But why the secrecy, Steve? What on earth were you intending to do with her that meant you'd rather be arrested on suspicion of rape and murder than give an explanation?'

It was two hours before a solicitor arrived, courtesy of Tony's grandfather, and after a brief discussion with his client, and following police assurances that, because of his alibi, Tony was not under suspicion of involvement in Kate Sumner's death, he advised him to answer their questions.

'Okay, yes, I got to know Kate pretty well. She lives – lived – about two hundred yards from my grandfather's garage. She used to come in and talk to me whenever I was in there because she knew I was a friend of Steve's. She was a right little tart, always flirting, always opening those baby blue eyes of hers and telling stories about how this and that man fancied her. I thought it was a come-on, particularly when she said William had a problem getting it up. She told me she went through pints of baby oil to help the poor sod out, and it made her laugh like a drain. Her descriptions were about as graphic as you can get, but she didn't seem to care that Hannah was listening or that I might get to be friendly with William.' He looked troubled, as if the memory haunted him. 'I told you she was sick. Matter of fact, I think she enjoyed being cruel to people. I reckon she made that poor bastard's life hell. It certainly gave her a kick slapping me down when I tried to kiss her. She spat in my face, and said she wasn't that desperate.' He fell silent.

'When was this?'

'End of February.'

'What happened then?'

'Nothing. I told her to fuck off. Then Steve started dropping hints that he was balling her. I think she must have told him I'd made a pass, so he thought he'd swagger a bit just to rub it in. He said everyone had had her except me.'

Carpenter pulled forward a piece of paper and flicked the plunger on his pen. 'Give me a list,' he said. 'Everyone you know who had anything to do with her.'

'Steve Harding.'

'Go on.'

'I don't know of anyone else.'

Carpenter laid his pen on the table again and stared at the young man. 'That's not good enough, Tony. You describe her as a tart, then offer me one name. That gives me very little confidence in your assessment of Kate's character. Assuming you're telling the truth, we know of only three men who had a relationship with her – her husband, Steven Harding and one other from her past.' His eyes bored into Bridges'. 'By any standards that's a modest number for a thirty-year-old woman. Or would you call any woman who's had three lovers a tart? Your girlfriend, for example? How many partners has Bibi had?'

'Leave Bibi out of this,' said Bridges angrily. 'She's got nothing to do with it.'

Galbraith leaned forward. 'She gave you your alibi for Saturday night,' he reminded him. 'That means she has a great deal to do with it.' He folded his hands in front of his mouth and studied Bridges intently. 'Did she know you fancied Kate Sumner?'

The solicitor laid a hand on the young man's arm. 'You don't need to answer that.'

'Well, I'm going to,' he said, shaking himself free. 'I'm fed up with them trying to drag Bibi into it.' He addressed Galbraith. 'I didn't fucking well fancy Kate. I loathed the stupid bitch. I just thought she was easy, that's all, so I tried it on once. Listen, she was a cock-teaser. It gave her a buzz to get blokes excited.'

'That's not what I asked you, Tony. I asked you if Bibi knew you fancied Kate.'

'No,' he muttered.

Galbraith nodded. 'But she knew about *Steve* and Kate?'

'Yes.'

'Who told her? You or Steve?'

Bridges slumped angrily in his chair. 'Steve mostly. She got really worked up when Kate started smearing Hannah's crap all over his car so he told her what had been going on.'

Galbraith leaned back, letting his hands drop to the table top. 'Women don't give a toss about a car unless the guy who drives it matters to her. Are you sure your girlfriend isn't playing away from home?'

Bridges erupted out of his seat in a fury of movement. 'You are *so* fucking patronizing. You think you know it all, don't you? She got mad because there was shit all over the handle when she tried to open the door. That's what got her worked up. Not because she cares about Steve or the car, but because her hand was covered in crap. Are you so stupid you can't work that out for yourselves?'

'But doesn't that prove my point?' said Galbraith unemotionally. 'If she was driving Steve's car, she must have had more than a nodding acquaintance with him.'

'*I* was driving it,' said Bridges, ignoring the solicitor's restraining hand to lean across the table and thrust his face into the Inspector's. 'I checked the driver's handle and it was clean, so I released the locks. What never occurred to me was that the bloody bitch might have changed tactics. This time the crap was on the passenger's side. Now, get this, dickhead. It was still soft when Bibi touched it so that meant Kate must have put it there minutes before. It also meant that Bibi's hand stank to high bloody heaven. Can you follow all that or do you want me to repeat it?'

'No,' said Galbraith mildly. 'The tape recorder's pretty reliable. I think we got it.' He nodded towards the chair on the other side of the table. 'Sit down, Tony.' He waited while Bridges resumed his seat. 'Did you see Kate walk away?'

'No.'

'You should have done. You said the faeces was still soft.'

Tony pulled both hands across his peroxided hair and bent forward over the table. 'There were plenty of places she could have been hiding. She was probably watching us.'

'Did you ever wonder if you were the target and not Steve? You describe her as sick and say she spat at you.'

'No.'

'She must have known Steve allows you to drive his car.'

'Once in a while. Not often.'

Galbraith flipped another page of his notebook. 'You told me this afternoon that you and Steve had an arrangement regarding your grandfather's garage and *Crazy Daze*. A straight swap, you called it.'

'Yes.'

'You said you took Bibi there two weeks ago.'

'What of it?'

'Bibi doesn't agree with you. I phoned her at her parents' house two hours ago, and she said she's never been on *Crazy Daze*.'

'She's forgotten,' he said dismissively. 'She was drunk as a skunk that night. What does it matter anyway?'

'Let's just say we're interested in discrepancies.'

The young man shrugged. 'I don't see what difference it makes. It's got nothing to do with anything.'

'We like to be accurate.' Galbraith consulted his notebook. 'According to her, the reason she's never been on *Crazy Daze* is because Steve banned you from using it the week before you met her. "*Tony trashed the boat when he was drunk,*"' he read, '"*and Steve blew his stack. He said Tony could go on using the car but* Crazy Daze *was off limits.*"' He looked up. 'Why did you lie about taking Bibi on board?'

'To wipe the stupid smirk off your face, I expect. It pisses me off the way you bastards behave. You're all

384

fascists.' He hunched forward, eyes burning angrily. 'I haven't forgotten you were planning to drag me through the streets in the buff even if you have.'

'What's that got to do with Bibi?'

'You wanted an answer so I gave you one.'

'How about this for an answer instead? You knew Bibi had been on board with Steve, so you decided to offer an explanation for why her fingerprints were there. You knew we'd find yours because you went out to *Crazy Daze* on Monday, and you thought you'd be safe pretending you and Bibi had been there together. But the only place we lifted your prints in the cabin, Tony, was on the forward hatch, while Bibi's were all over the headboard behind the bed. She likes being on top, presumably?'

He dropped his head in misery. 'Fuck off.'

'It must drive you up the wall the way Steve keeps stealing your girlfriends.'

Chapter Twenty-four

MAGGIE LOWERED HER aching arms and tapped pointedly on her watch when Nick shouldered his way through the scullery door, carrying an aluminium stepladder. She was perched precariously on a garden chair on top of the kitchen table, her hair sticky with cobwebs, her rolled-up sleeves saturated with water. 'What sort of time do you call this?' she demanded. 'It's a quarter to ten and I have to be up at five o'clock tomorrow morning to see to the horses.'

'Good God, woman!' he declared plaintively. 'A night without sleep won't kill you. Live dangerously and see how you enjoy it.'

'I expected you hours ago.'

'Then don't marry a policeman,' he said, setting up his ladder under the uncleaned part of the ceiling.

'Chance'd be a fine thing.'

He grinned up at her. 'You mean you'd contemplate it?'

'Absolutely not,' she said, as if offering him a challenge to even try and chat her up. 'All I meant was that no policeman has ever asked me.'

'He wouldn't dare.' He opened the cupboard under

the sink and hunkered down to inspect it for cleaning implements and buckets. She was above him – like the rare occasions when she met him on horseback – and she felt an awful temptation to take advantage of the fact by dripping water on to the back of his neck. 'Don't even think about it,' he said, without looking up, 'or I'll leave you to do the whole bloody lot on your own.'

She chose to ignore him, preferring dignity to humiliation. 'How did you get on?' she asked, stepping down from the chair to dunk her sponge in the bucket on the table.

'Rather well.'

'I thought you must have done. Your tail's wagging.' She climbed back on to the chair. 'What did Steve say?'

'You mean apart from agreeing with everything in your statement?'

'Yes.'

'He told me what he was doing at Chapman's Pool on Sunday.' He looked up at her. 'He's a complete idiot, but I don't think he's a rapist or a murderer.'

'So you were wrong about him?'

'Probably.'

'Good. It's bad for your character to have everything your own way. What about paedophile?'

'It depends on your definition of paedophilia.' He swung forward a chair and straddled it, resting his elbows along the back, content to watch her work. 'He's besotted with a fifteen-year-old girl who's so unhappy at home she keeps threatening to kill herself. She's an absolute stunner apparently, nearly six feet tall, looks twenty-five, ought to be a supermodel and turns heads wherever she goes. Her parents are separated and fight like cat and dog – her mother's jealous of her – her father has a string of bimbos – she's four months pregnant by Steve – refuses to have an abortion – weeps all over his manly bosom every time she sees him' – he lifted a sardonic eyebrow – 'which is probably why he finds her attractive – and is so desperate to have the baby and so desperate to be loved that she's twice tried to slit her wrists. Steve's solution to all this was to whisk her off to France in *Crazy Daze* where they could live' – another sardonic lift of an eyebrow – 'love's young dream without her parents having any idea where she'd gone or who she'd gone with.'

Maggie chuckled. 'I told you he was a good Samaritan.'

'Bluebeard, more like. She's fifteen.'

'And looks twenty-five.'

'If you believe Steve.'

'Don't you?'

'Put it this way,' he said dispassionately, 'I wouldn't let him within half a mile of a daughter of mine. He's oversexed, deeply enamoured with himself and has the morals of an alleycat.'

'A bit like the weasel I married in other words?' she asked dryly.

'No question about it.' He grinned up at her. 'But then I'm prejudiced of course.'

There was a glint of amusement in her eyes. 'So what happened? He got sidetracked by Paul and Danny and the whole thing went pear-shaped?'

He nodded. 'He realized, when he had to identify himself, that there was no point going on with it and signalled to his girlfriend to abandon it. Since when, he's had one tearful conversation with her over his mobile on his way back to Lymington on Sunday night, and hasn't been able to talk to her since because he's either been under arrest or separated from his phone. The rule is, she always calls him, and as he hasn't heard from her he's terrified she's killed herself.'

'Is it true?'

'No. One of the messages on his mobile was from her.'

'Still . . . poor boy. You've locked him up again, haven't you? He must be worried sick. Couldn't you have let him talk to her?'

He wondered at the vagaries of human nature. He would have bet on her sympathies being with the girl. 'Not allowed.'

'Oh, come on,' she said crossly. 'That's just cruel.'

'No. Common sense. Personally, I wouldn't trust him further than I could throw him. He's committed several crimes, don't forget. Assault on you, sex with an under-age girl, conspiracy to abduct, not to mention gross indecency and committing lewd acts in public . . .'

'Oh my God! You haven't charged him with having an erection, have you?'

'Not yet.'

'You *are* cruel,' she said in disgust. 'It was obviously his girlfriend he was looking at through the binoculars. On that basis you should have arrested Martin every time he put his hand on my arse.'

'I couldn't,' he said seriously. 'You never objected, so it didn't constitute an assault.'

There was a twinkle in her eye. 'What happened to indecency?'

'I never caught him with his trousers down,' he said with regret. 'I did try, but he was too bloody quick every time.'

'Are you winding me up?'

'No,' he said. 'I'm courting you.'

Half-asleep, Sandy Griffiths squinted at the luminous hands on her clock through gritty eyes, saw that it was three o'clock, and tried to remember if William had gone out earlier. Yet again, something had disturbed her intermittent dozing. She thought it was the front door closing, although she couldn't be sure if the sound had been real or if she'd dreamt it. She listened for footfalls on the stairs but, hearing only silence, stumbled out of bed and dragged on her dressing gown. Babies she thought she could probably cope with – a husband, *NEVER* . . .

She switched on the landing lamp and pushed open Hannah's bedroom door. A wedge of light cut across the cot, and her alarm subsided immediately. The child sat in the concentrated immobility that seemed to be her nature, thumb in mouth, staring wide-eyed with her curiously intense gaze. If she recognized Griffiths, she didn't show it. Instead she looked through her as if her mind saw images behind and beyond the woman that had no basis in reality, and Griffiths realized she was fast asleep. It explained the cot and the locks on all the doors. They were there to protect a sleepwalker, she understood belatedly, not to deprive a conscious child of adventure.

From outside, muffled by closed doors, she heard the sound of a car starting, followed by gears engaging and the scrunch of tyres on the drive. What the hell did the bloody man think he was doing now, she wondered? Did he seriously believe that abandoning his daughter in the early hours of the morning would endear him to social services? *Or was that the whole point?* Had he decided to ditch the responsibility once and for all?

Wearily she leaned against the door jamb and studied Kate's blank-eyed, blonde-haired replica with compassion and thought about what the doctor had said when he saw the smashed photographs in the fireplace. '*She's angry with her mother for deserting her . . . it's a perfectly normal expression of grief . . . get her father to cuddle her . . . that's the best way to fill the gap . . .*'

William Sumner's disappearance raised a few eyebrows in the incident room at Winfrith when Griffiths notified them of it, but little real interest. As so often in his life, he had ceased to matter. Instead, the spotlight turned on Beatrice 'Bibi' Gould who, when police knocked on her parents' door at 7.00 a.m. on Saturday morning, inviting her back to Winfrith for further questioning, burst into tears and locked herself in the bathroom, refusing to come out. When threatened with immediate arrest for obstruction, and on the promise that her parents could accompany her, she finally agreed to come out. Her fear seemed out of proportion to the police request and when asked to explain it she said, 'Everyone is going to be angry with me.'

Following a brief appearance before magistrates on his assault charge, Steven Harding, too, was invited for further questioning. He was chauffeured by a yawning Nick Ingram who took the opportunity to impart a few facts of life to the immature young man at his side. 'Just for the record, Steve, I'd break your legs if it was my fifteen-year-old daughter you'd got pregnant. As a matter of fact, I'd break your legs if you even laid a finger on her.'

Harding was unrepentant. 'Life's not like that any more. You can't order girls to behave the way you want them to behave. They decide for themselves.'

'Watch my lips, Steve. I said it's *your* legs I'd be breaking, not my daughter's. Trust me, the day I find a twenty-four-year-old man besmirching a beautiful child of mine is the day that bastard will wish he'd kept his zip done up.' Out of the corner of his eye he watched words begin to form on Harding's lips. 'And don't tell me she wanted it just as much as you did,' he snarled, 'or I'd be tempted to break your arms as well. Any little jerk can persuade a vulnerable adolescent into bed with him as long as he promises to love her. It takes a man to give her time to learn if the promise is worth anything.'

Bibi Gould refused to have her father in the interview room with her, but begged for her mother to sit with her and hold her hand. On the other side of the table, Detective Superintendent Carpenter and DI Galbraith took her through her previous statement. She quailed visibly in front of Carpenter's frown, and he only had to say: 'We believe you've been lying to us, young lady,' for the floodgates of truth to open.

'Dad doesn't like me spending weekends at Tony's . . . says I'm making myself cheap . . . He'd have gone spare if he'd known I'd passed out. Tony said it was alcohol poisoning because I was vomiting blood, but I think it was the bad E that his friend sold him . . . I was sick for hours after I came round . . . Dad would have killed me if he'd known . . . He hates Tony . . . He thinks he's a bad influence.' She laid her head on her mother's shoulder and sobbed heartily.

'When was this?' asked Carpenter.

'Last weekend. We were going to this rave in Southampton so Tony got some E from this bloke he knows . . .' She faltered to a stop.

'Go on.'

'Everyone's going to be angry,' she wailed. 'Tony said why should we get his friend into trouble just because Steve's boat was in the wrong place.'

With considerable effort Carpenter managed to smooth his frown into something approaching fatherly kindness. 'We're not interested in Tony's friend, Bibi, we're only interested in getting an accurate picture of where everyone was last weekend. You've told us you're fond of Steven Harding,' he said disingenuously, 'and it will help Steve considerably if we can clear up some of the discrepancies around his story. You and Tony claimed you didn't see him on Saturday because you went to a rave in Southampton. Is that true?'

'It's true we didn't see him.' She sniffed. 'At least I didn't . . . I suppose Tony might have done . . . but it's not true about the rave. It didn't start till ten, so Tony said we might as well get in the mood earlier. The trouble is I can't remember much about it . . . We'd been drinking since five and then I took the E . . .' She wept into her mother's shoulder again.

'For the record, Bibi, you're telling us you took an Ecstasy tablet supplied to you by your boyfriend, Tony Bridges?'

She was alarmed by his tone. 'Yes,' she whispered.

'Have you ever passed out before in Tony's company?'

'Sometimes . . . if I drink too much.'

Pensively, Carpenter stroked his jaw. 'Do you know what time you took the tablet on Saturday?'

'Seven, maybe. I can't really remember.' She blew her nose into a Kleenex. 'Tony said he hadn't realized how much I'd been drinking, and that if he had he wouldn't have given it to me. It was awful . . . I'm never going to drink or take Ecstasy ever again . . . I've been feeling ill all week.' She raised a wan smile. 'I reckon it's true what they say about it. Tony thinks I was lucky not to die.'

Galbraith was less inclined to be fatherly. His private opinion of her was that she was a blousy slag with too much puppy fat and too little self-control, and he seriously pondered the mysteries of nature and chemistry that meant a girl like this could cause a previously sane man to behave with insanity. 'You were drunk again on

Monday,' he reminded her, 'when DS Campbell visited Tony's house in the evening.'

She flicked him a sly up-from-under look that curdled any remnants of sympathy he might have had. 'I only had two lagers,' she said. 'I thought they'd make me feel better – but they didn't.'

Carpenter tapped his pen on the table to bring her attention back to him. 'What time did you come round on Sunday morning, Bibi?'

She shrugged self-pityingly. 'I don't know. Tony said I was sick for about ten hours, and I didn't stop till seven o'clock on Sunday evening. That's why I was late back to my parents'.'

'So about nine o'clock on Sunday morning then?'

She nodded. 'About that.' She turned her wet face to her mother. 'I'm ever so sorry, Mum. I'm never going to do it again.'

Mrs Gould squeezed the girl's shoulder and looked pleadingly at the two policemen. 'Does this mean she'll be prosecuted?'

'What for, Mrs Gould?'

'Taking Ecstasy?'

The Superintendent shook his head. 'I doubt it. As things stand, there isn't any evidence that she took any.' *Rohypnol, maybe* . . . 'But you're a very stupid young woman, Bibi, and I trust you won't come whining to the police with your troubles the next time you accept unknown and unidentified tablets from a man. Like it or not, you bear responsibility for your own behaviour, and the best advice I can offer you is to listen to your father once in a while.'

Good one, guv, thought Galbraith.

Carpenter tented his fingers over Bibi's previous statement. 'I don't like liars, young woman. None of us does. I think you told another lie last night to my colleague DI Galbraith, didn't you?'

Her eyes stretched in a kind of panic but she didn't answer.

'You said you've never been on *Crazy Daze* when we think you have.'

'I haven't.'

'You volunteered a set of your fingerprints at the beginning of the week. They match several sets found in the cabin of Steve's boat. Would you care to explain their presence in light of your denial that you've never been there?' He scowled at her.

'It's . . . Tony doesn't know, you see . . . oh God!' She shook with nerves. 'It was just . . . Steve and I got drunk one night when Tony was away. He'd be so *hurt* if he found out . . . he's got this thing about Steve being good-looking, and it'd *kill* him if he found out that we . . . well, you know . . .'

'That you had intercourse with Steven Harding on board *Crazy Daze*?'

'We were drunk. I don't even remember much about it. It didn't *mean* anything,' she said desperately, as if disloyalty could be excused when alcohol loosened inhibitions. But perhaps the concept of *in vino veritas* was too obscure for an immature nineteen-year-old to understand.

'Why are you so frightened of Tony finding out?' asked Carpenter curiously.

'I'm not.' Her eyes stretched wider in a visible demonstration that she was lying.

'What does he do to you, Bibi?'

'Nothing. It's just . . . he gets really jealous sometimes.'

'Of Steve?'

She nodded.

'How does he show it?'

She licked her lips. 'He's only done it once. He jammed my fingers in the car door after he found me in the pub with Steve. He said it was an accident, but . . . well . . . I don't think it was.'

'Was that before or after you slept with Steve?'

'After.'

'So he knew what you and Steve had done?'

She pressed her hands to her face. 'I don't see how he could have done . . . he wasn't around for the whole week but he's been – well, *odd* – ever since . . .'

'When did this happen?'

'Last half-term.'

Carpenter consulted his diary. 'Between 24 and 31 May?'

'It was a bank holiday, I know that.'

'Fine.' He smiled encouragingly. 'Only one or two more questions, Bibi, and then we're done. Do you remember an occasion when Tony was driving you somewhere in Steve's car and Kate Sumner had smeared the passenger door handle with her daughter's faeces?'

She pulled an expression of disgust. 'It was horrible. I got it all over my hand.'

'Can you remember when that was?'

She thought about it. 'I think it was the beginning of June. Tony said he'd take me to the flicks in Southampton but I had to wash my hands so much to get all the filth off that in the end we never went.'

'After you'd slept with Steve then?'

'Yes.'

'Thank you. Last question. Where did Tony stay while he was away?'

'*Miles* away,' she said with emphasis. 'His parents have a caravan at Lulworth Cove and Tony always goes there on his own when he needs to recharge his batteries. I keep telling him he should give up teaching because he really *hates* children. He says if he has a nervous breakdown it'll be *their* fault, even though everyone else will say it was because he smoked too much cannabis.'

Steven Harding's interview was tougher. He was informed that Marie Freemantle had given the police a statement about her relationship with him and that, because of her age, he could well face charges. Nevertheless, he declined the services of a solicitor, saying he had nothing to hide. He seemed to assume that Marie had been questioned as a result of his off-the-record conversation with Nick Ingram the previous evening, and neither Carpenter nor Galbraith disabused him of the fact.

'You are currently in a relationship with a fifteen-year-old by the name of Marie Freemantle?' said Carpenter.

'Yes.'

'Whom you knew to be under-age when you first had sexual intercourse with her?'

'Yes.'

'Where does Marie live?'

'Fifty-four Dancer Road, Lymington.'

'Why did your agent tell us you have a girlfriend called Marie living in London?'

'Because that's where he thinks she lives. He got her some work and, as she didn't want her parents to know about it, we gave the address of a shop in London that acts as a postal drop.'

'What sort of work?'

'Nude work.'

'Pornography?'

Harding looked uncomfortable. 'Only soft porn.'

'Video or stills?'

'Stills.'

'Were you in the shots with her?'

'Some,' he admitted.

'Where are those photographs now?'

'I dropped them over the side of my boat.'

'Because they showed you performing indecent acts with an under-age girl?'

'She doesn't look under-age.'

'Answer the question, Steve. Did you put them over the side because they showed you performing indecent acts with an under-age girl?'

Harding nodded.

'For the purposes of the tape, Steven Harding nodded agreement. Did Tony Bridges know you were sleeping with Marie Freemantle?'

'What's Tony got to do with it?'

'Answer the question, Steve.'

'I don't think so. I never told him.'

'Did he see the photographs of her?'

'Yes. He came out to my boat on Monday and they were on the table.'

'Did he see them before Monday?'

'I don't know. He trashed my boat four months ago.' He ran his tongue round his dry mouth. 'He might have found them then.'

Carpenter leaned back, his fingers toying with his pen. 'Which would have made him angry,' he said, more as a statement than a question. 'She's a pupil of his and he had a fondness for her himself, albeit a hands-off one because of his position, which you knew about.'

'I – er – guess so.'

'We understand you met Marie Freemantle on 14 February. Was that while you were having a relationship with Kate Sumner?'

'I didn't have a relationship with Kate.' He blinked nervously, trying like Tony the night before to pre-guess the direction the questions were going. 'I went back to her house one time and she kind of . . . well . . . threw herself at me. It was okay, but I've never been that keen on older women. I made it clear I wasn't interested in anything long term and I thought she understood. It was just a quick shag in her kitchen – nothing to get excited about.'

'So when Tony tells us the relationship went on for three or four months, he's lying?'

'Oh, Jesus!' Harding's nervousness increased. 'Listen,

I may have given him that impression. I mean I knew Kate . . . you know, as an acquaintance . . . for quite a while before we actually got it together, and I may have . . . well, given Tony the idea there was a bit more to it than there actually was. It was a joke, really. He's a bit of a prude.'

Carpenter watched him for a moment, before lowering his eyes to a piece of paper on the table in front of him. 'Three months after meeting Marie, some time during the week 24–31 May, you had a one-night stand with Bibi Gould, Tony Bridges' girlfriend. Is that right?'

Harding gave a small groan. 'Oh, come on! That really *was* nothing. We got drunk in the pub and I took her back to *Crazy Daze* to sleep it off because Tony was away and his house was locked up. She came on to me a bit strong and . . . well, to be honest, I don't remember much about it. I was rat-arsed and couldn't swear that anything happened worth recording.'

'Does Tony know?'

He didn't answer immediately. 'I don't – look, why do you keep going on about Tony?'

'Answer the question, please. Does Tony know that you slept with his girlfriend?'

'I don't know. He's been a bit off recently, so I've been wondering if he saw me ferrying her back to the slip the next morning.' With a worried gesture, he pulled at the hair that flopped across his forehead. 'He was supposed to be staying the whole week in his folks' caravan, but Bob Winterslow said he saw him that day at his grandad's place, getting ready to tow his rib out.'

'Can you remember which day it was?'

'Bank holiday Monday. Bibi's hairdressing salon doesn't open on bank holidays which is why she was able to stay over on Sunday night.' He waited for Carpenter to speak, and when he didn't, he gave a small shrug. 'Listen, it was no big deal. I planned to square it with Tony if he ever said anything' – another shrug – 'but he never did.'

'Does he normally say something when you sleep with his girlfriends?'

'I don't make a habit of it, for Christ's sake. The trouble is . . . well, Bibi was like Kate. You try and be nice to a woman, and the next minute they're climbing all over you.'

Carpenter frowned. 'Are you saying they forced you to have intercourse with them?'

'No, but—'

'Then spare me the excuses.' He consulted his notes again. 'How did your agent get the idea Bibi was your girlfriend?'

Harding tugged at his hair again and had the grace to look embarrassed. 'Because I told him she was a bit of a goer.'

'Meaning she'd be amenable to pornographic stills?'

'Yes.'

'Would your agent have mentioned that to Tony?'

Harding shook his head. 'If he had, Tony would have taken me apart.'

'Except he didn't take you apart over Kate Sumner, did he?'

The young man was clearly baffled by the question. 'Tony didn't know Kate.'

'How well did *you* know her, Steve?'

'That's the crazy thing,' he said. 'Hardly at all . . . okay, we did it once but . . . well, it doesn't mean you get to know someone, does it? I avoided her afterwards because it was embarrassing. Then she started treating me as if I'd wronged her in some way.'

Carpenter pulled out Harding's statement. 'You claimed she was obsessed with you, Steve. "*I knew she had a serious crush on me . . .*"' he read. '"*She used to hang around by the yacht club waiting for me to come ashore . . . Most of the time she just stood and watched me, but sometimes she'd deliberately bump into me and rub her breasts against my arm . . .*" Is any of that true?'

'I may have exaggerated a bit. She did hang around for about a week till she realized I wasn't interested. Then she sort of . . . well, abandoned the idea, I suppose. I didn't see her again till she did the thing with the nappy.'

Carpenter sorted Tony Bridges' statement from the pile. 'This is what Tony said: "*He told me on more than one occasion this year that he was having problems with a woman called Kate Sumner who was stalking him . . .*" Did you decide to exaggerate a bit when you told Tony?'

'Yes.'

'Did you refer to Kate as a "tart"?'

He hunched his shoulders. 'It was just an expression.'

'Did you tell Tony Kate was easy?'

'Listen, it was a joke. He used to have a real hang-up

about sex. Everyone used to tease him, not just me . . . then Bibi came along and he . . . well, lightened up.'

Carpenter studied him closely for a moment. 'So did you sleep with Bibi for a joke?'

Harding stared at his hands. 'I didn't do it for any particular reason. It just happened. I mean she really *was* easy. The only reason she hangs around with Tony is because she's got a thing about me. Look' – he hunched further into his seat – 'you don't want to get the wrong idea about all of this.'

'What wrong idea's that, Steve?'

'I don't know, but you seem to have it in for Tony.'

'With reason,' said Carpenter, easing another piece of paper from the pile in front of him and hiding the contents with cupped fingers. 'We've been told you watched him feed Bibi a drug called' – he lowered his eyes to the paper, as if the word were written there – '*Rohypnol* so she wouldn't complain about his perform-ance. Is that true?'

'Oh, shit!' He rested his head in his hands. 'I suppose Marie's been spouting her mouth off?' His fingers caressed his temples in soft, circular movements, and Galbraith was fascinated by the gracefulness of his actions. He was an extraordinarily beautiful young man and it didn't surprise him that Kate had found him more attractive than William.

'Is it true, Steve?'

'Sort of. He told me he slipped it to her once when she was giving him a load of grief but I didn't see him do it, and for all I know he was lying through his teeth.'

'How did he know about Rohypnol?'

'Everyone knows.'

'Did you tell him?'

Harding lifted his head to look at the paper in front of the Superintendent, clearly wondering how much information was written there. 'His grandad hasn't been sleeping too well since his wife died so the GP prescribed him Rohypnol. Tony was telling me about it, so I laughed and said it could sort all his problems if he could get hold of some of it. It's not my fault if the stupid fucker used it.'

'Have you used it, Steve?'

'Do me a favour! Why would I need to?'

A faint smile crossed Carpenter's face as he changed tack. 'How soon after the incident with the nappy did Kate start smearing Hannah's faeces on your car and setting the alarm off?'

'I don't know. A few days, maybe.'

'How did you know it was her?'

'Because she'd left Hannah's crap on the sheets in my boat.'

'Which was some time towards the end of April?' Harding nodded. 'But she didn't start this' – Carpenter sought a suitable phrase – ' "dirty campaign" until after she realized you weren't interested in pursuing a relationship with her?'

'It's not my *fault*,' he said despairingly. 'She was . . . *so . . . fucking . . . boring.*'

'The question I asked you, Steve,' repeated Carpenter patiently, 'was did she start her "dirty" campaign after she realized you weren't interested in her?'

'Yes.' He jabbed the heels of his palms against his

eyelids in an effort to recall detail. 'She just made my life hell until I couldn't stand it any longer. That's when I thought of persuading William to tell her I was an arse-bandit.'

The Superintendent ran a finger down Harding's statement. 'Which was in June?'

'Yes.'

'Any particular reason why you waited a month and a half to put a stop to it?'

'Because it was getting worse not better,' the young man said with a sudden rush of anger as if the memory still rankled deeply. 'I thought she'd run out of steam if I was patient, but when she started targeting my dinghy, I decided enough was enough. I reckoned she'd start on *Crazy Daze* next, and there was no way I was going to let her do that.'

Carpenter nodded as if he thought the explanation a reasonable one. He pulled out Harding's statement again and ran his finger down it. 'So you sought out William and showed him photographs of yourself in a gay magazine because you wanted him to tell his wife you were gay?'

'Yes.'

'Mmm.' Carpenter reached for Tony Bridges' statement. 'Tony, on the other hand, says that when you told him you were going to report Kate to the police for harassing you, he advised you to move your car instead. According to him *that's* what sorted the problem. In fact, he thought it was pretty funny when we told him last night that your solution to Kate's harassment was to show William gay pictures of yourself. He said: "*Steve always was as thick as two short planks.*"'

Harding shrugged. 'So? It worked. That's all I was interested in.'

Slowly, Carpenter squared the papers on the table in front of him. 'Why do you think that was?' he asked. 'I mean, you're not seriously suggesting that a woman who was so angry at being rejected that she was prepared to harass and intimidate you for weeks would meekly give up when she found out you were gay? Or are you? Admittedly I'm no expert in mental disorders but I'd guess the intimidation would become markedly worse. No one likes to be made a fool of, Steve.'

Harding stared at him in perplexity. 'Except she *did* stop.'

The Superintendent shook his head. 'You can't stop something you never started, son. Oh, she certainly wiped Hannah's nappy on your sheets in a moment of irritation, which probably gave Tony the idea, but it wasn't Kate who was getting her own back on you, it was your friend. It was a peculiarly apt revenge after all. You've been crapping on his doorstep for years. It must have given him a hell of a buzz to pay you back in your own coin. The only reason he stopped was because you were threatening to go to the police.'

A sickly smile washed across Harding's face like wet water colour. He looked ill, thought Carpenter with satisfaction.

*

William Sumner's mother had long since given up trying to induce her son to talk. Her initial surprise at his unheralded appearance in her flat had given way to fear and, like a hostage, she sought to appease and not to confront. Whatever had brought him back to Chichester was not something he wanted to share with her. He seemed to alternate between anger and anguish, rocking himself to and fro in bouts of frenetic movement only to collapse in tear-sodden lethargy when the fit passed. She was unable to help him. He guarded the telephone with the singlemindedness of a madman and, handicapped by immobility and dread, she withdrew into silent observation.

He had become a stranger to her in the last twelve months and a kind of subdued dislike drove her towards cruelty. She found herself despising him. He had always been spineless, she thought, which was why Kate had gained such an easy ascendancy over him. Her mouth pinched into lines of contempt as she listened to the dry sobs that racked his thin frame and, when he finally broke his silence, she realized with a sense of inevitability that she could have predicted what he was going to say. '. . . I didn't know what to do . . .'

She guessed he had killed his wife. She feared now he had also killed his child.

Tony Bridges rose to his feet as the cell door opened and viewed Galbraith with an uneasy smile. He was diminished by incarceration, a small insignificant man who had discovered what it meant to have his life controlled by others. Gone was the cocksure attitude of yesterday, in its place a nervous recognition that his ability to persuade had been blunted by the stone wall of police distrust. 'How long are you going to keep me here?'

'As long as it takes, Tony.'

'I don't know what you want from me.'

'The truth.'

'All I did was steal a boat.'

Galbraith shook his head. He fancied he saw a momentary regret in the frightened gaze that briefly met his before he stood back to let the young man pass. It was remorse of a kind, he supposed.

'. . . I didn't mean to do it. I didn't do it – not really. Kate would still be alive if she hadn't tried to push me over the side. It's her fault she's dead. We were getting on fine until she made a lunge at me, then the next thing I knew she was in the water. You can't blame me for that. Don't you think I'd have drowned Hannah too if I'd intended to kill her mother . . . ?'

Chapter Twenty-five

BROXTON HOUSE SLUMBERED peacefully in the afternoon sunshine as Nick Ingram pulled up in front of the porticoed entrance. As always he paused to admire its clean, square lines and, as always, regretted its slow deterioration. To him, perhaps more than to the Jenners, it represented something valuable, a living reminder that beauty existed in everything; but then he, despite his job, was enduringly sentimental, and they were not. The double doors stood wide open, an invitation to any passing thief, and he picked up Celia's handbag from the hall table as he passed on his way to the drawing room. Silence lay across the house like a blanket of dust, and he worried suddenly that he had come too late. Even his own footfalls on the marble floor were just a whisper in the great emptiness that surrounded him.

He eased open the drawing-room door and stepped inside. Celia was propped up in bed, bifocals slipping off the end of her nose, mouth open, snoring quietly, with Bertie's head on the pillow beside her. They looked like a tableau out of *The Godfather*, and Nick was hard-pushed not to laugh out loud. The sentimentalist in him viewed them fondly. Maybe Maggie was right, he thought. Maybe happiness was more to do with bodily contact than with hygiene. Who cared about tannin in teacups when you had a hairy hot-water bottle who was prepared to lie with you and love you when no one else would? He tapped lightly on one of the door panels and watched with amusement as Bertie opened a cautious eye then closed it again in obvious relief when he realized Nick wasn't going to make any demands on his loyalty.

'I'm not asleep, you know,' said Celia, raising a hand to adjust her spectacles. 'I heard you come in.'

'Am I disturbing you?'

'No.' She hoisted herself into a more upright position, tugging her bedjacket across her chest in a belated attempt to safeguard her dignity.

'You shouldn't leave your bag on the hall table,' he told her, walking across to put it on the bed. 'Anyone could steal it.'

'They're welcome to it, my dear. There's nothing in it worth taking.' She examined him closely. 'I prefer you in uniform. Dressed like that, you look like a gardener.'

'I said I'd help Maggie with the painting and I can't paint in my uniform.' He pulled forward a chair. 'Where is she?'

'Where you told her to be. In the kitchen.' She sighed. 'I worry about her, Nick. I didn't bring her up to be a manual labourer. She'll have navvy's hands before she's finished.'

'She already has. You can't muck out stables and scrub horse buckets day after day and keep your hands pretty. The two are mutually exclusive.'

She tut-tutted disapprovingly. 'A gentleman doesn't notice that kind of thing.'

He'd always been fond of her. He didn't know why except that her forthright approach appealed to him. Perhaps she reminded him of his own mother, a down-to-earth Cockney who had been dead for ten years. Certainly he found people who spoke their minds easier to get on with than those who cloaked their feelings in hypocritical smiles. 'He probably does, you know. He just doesn't mention it.'

'But that's the whole point, you silly fellow,' she said crossly. 'A gentleman is known by his manners.'

He grinned. 'So you prefer a man who lies to a man who is honest? That's not the impression you gave me four years ago when Robert Healey did his bunk.'

'Robert Healey was a criminal.'

'But an attractive one.'

She frowned at him. 'Have you come here to annoy me?'

'No, I came to see if you were all right.'

She waved a hand in dismissal. 'Well, I am. Go and find Maggie. I'm sure she'll be pleased to see you.'

He made no move to go. 'Were either of you ever called as a witness in Healey's trial?' he asked her.

'You know we weren't. He was only tried for his last fraud. All the rest of us had to take a back seat in case we confused the issue, and that made me more angry than anything. I wanted my day in court so that I could tell the little beast what I thought of him. I was never going to get my money back, but at least I could have taken my pound of flesh.' She folded her arms across her chest like armour plating. 'However, it's not a subject I wish to dwell on. It's unhealthy to rake over the past.'

'Did you read the reports of the trial?' he went on, ignoring her.

'One or two,' she said curtly, 'until I gave up in fury.'

'What made you furious?'

A small tic started above her lip. 'They described his victims as lonely women, desperate for love and attention. I've never been so incensed about anything. It made us look such fools.'

'But your case wasn't tried,' he pointed out, 'and that description applied to his last victims – two elderly unmarried sisters who lived alone in an isolated farmhouse in Cheshire. A perfect target for Healey, in other words. It was only because he tried to speed up the fraud by forging their names on cheques that he was discovered. The sisters' bank manager was worried enough to go to the police.'

The tic fluttered on. 'Except I sometimes think it was true,' she said with difficulty. 'I never thought of us as lonely, but we did rather blossom when he came into our lives and I'm humiliated every time I remember it.'

Ingram reached into the back pocket of his jeans and pulled out a newspaper clipping. 'I brought something I want to read to you. It's what the judge told Healey before he passed sentence.' He smoothed the paper on his lap. ' "*You're an educated man with a high IQ and an engaging manner*",' he read, ' "*and these qualities make you extremely dangerous. You display a ruthless disregard for your victims' feelings while at the same time exercising considerable charm and intelligence to convince them of your sincerity. Too many women have been taken in by you for anyone to believe that THEIR"'* – he stressed the word – '"*gullibility was the only reason for your success, and I am persuaded that you represent a real menace to society."'* He laid the clipping on the bed. 'What the judge recognized is that Healey *was* a charming and intelligent man.'

'It was pretence,' she said, reaching for the comfort of Bertie's ears and tugging at them. 'He was an actor.'

Ingram thought of Steven Harding's very moderate acting skills, and shook his head. 'I don't think so,' he said gently. 'No one could keep up a pretence like that for a year. The charm was genuine which is what you and Maggie were attracted by, and it seems to me that the problem you both have is coming to terms with that. It makes his betrayal so much worse if you liked him.'

'No.' She pulled a tissue from under her pillow and blew her nose. 'What upsets me more is that I thought he liked *us*. We're not so difficult to love, are we?'

'Not at all. I'm sure he adored you both. Everyone else does.'

'Oh, don't be absurd!' Celia snapped. 'He wouldn't have stolen from us if he had.'

'Of course he would.' Ingram propped his chin in his hands and stared at her. 'The trouble with you, Mrs J, is that you're a conformist. You assume everyone does and should behave the same way. But Healey was a professional conman. Theft was his business. He'd made a ten-year career out of it, don't forget. That doesn't mean he wasn't fond of you, any more than it would mean I wasn't fond of you if I had to arrest you.' His mouth twitched into a crooked smile. 'We do what we're good at in this life if we don't want to starve, and we cry all the way to the bank if it upsets us.'

'That's nonsense.'

'Is it? Do you think I take pleasure arresting a ten-year-old kid for vandalism when I know he comes from a lousy home, truants because he can't read, and is likely to get a belting from his drunken mother because she's too stupid to deal with him in any other way? I caution the boy because that's what I'm paid to do, but I'm always a damn sight fonder of him than I am of his mother. Criminals are human like everyone else, and there's no law that says they aren't likable.'

She peered at him over her bifocals. 'Yes, but *you* didn't like Martin, Nick, so don't pretend you did.'

'No, I didn't,' he admitted, 'but it was a personal thing. I thought the guy was a grade A prat. If I'm honest, though, I never believed for one moment that Mrs Fielding was telling the truth when she accused him of trying to steal her antiques. As far as I was concerned he was whiter than white . . . bloody perfect, in fact . . . every young woman's dream.' The smile became even more crooked. 'I assumed – and still do because it didn't fit Healey's MO – that it was Mrs Fielding's senility talking, and the only reason I came to you about it was because I couldn't resist the opportunity to take him down a peg or two.' He raised his eyes to hers. 'It certainly didn't give me any insights into what he was really up to. Even when Simon Farley told me he'd passed a couple of dud cheques in the pub and asked me to get it sorted quietly because he didn't want any fuss, it never occurred to me that Martin was a professional. If it had, I'd have approached it differently, and maybe you wouldn't have lost your money and maybe your husband would still be alive.'

'Oh, for God's sake!' she said gruffly, pulling so hard on Bertie's ears that the poor animal furrowed his brow in pain. 'Don't you start feeling guilty, too.'

'Why not? If I'd been older and wiser I might have done my job better.'

With an uncharacteristic display of tenderness, she laid a hand on his shoulder. 'I have enough trouble coping with my own guilt without carrying yours and Maggie's as well. According to Maggie, her father dropped dead because she was shouting at him. *My* recollection is that he threw a two-week tantrum then dropped dead after a drinking bout in his study. If my son is to be believed, he died of a broken heart because Maggie and I treated him like a cipher in his own house.' She sighed. 'The truth is Keith was a chronic alcoholic with a history of heart disease who could have died at any moment, although clearly Martin's shenanigans didn't help. And it wasn't as though it was Keith's money that was stolen. It was mine. My father left me ten thousand in his will twenty years ago, and I managed to work it up to over a hundred thousand by playing the stock market.' She frowned in irritation at the memory, before giving Ingram's shoulder a sudden sharp rap. 'This is ridiculous. When all's said and done, the only person to blame is Robert Healey and I refuse to let anyone else take responsibility.'

'Does that include you and Maggie or are you going to go on wearing sackcloth and ashes so that the rest of us feel guilty by association?'

She regarded him thoughtfully for a moment. 'I was right about you yesterday,' she said. 'You are a *very* provoking young man.' She flapped a hand towards the hall. 'Go away and make yourself useful. Help my daughter.'

'She's doing a fine job on her own. I'll probably just stand back and watch.'

'I wasn't talking about painting the kitchen,' Celia retorted.

'Neither was I, but the answer's still the same.'

She peered at him blankly for a moment, then gave a throaty chuckle. 'On the principle that everything comes to him who waits?'

'It's worked up till now,' he said, reaching for one of her hands and holding it lightly. 'You're a gutsy lady, Mrs J. I always wanted to know you better.'

'Oh, for goodness sake, get on with you!' she said, smacking him away. 'I'm beginning to think Robert Healey was a novice compared with you.' She wagged a finger at him. 'And don't call me Mrs J. It's appallingly *infra dig* and makes me sound like a cleaner.' She closed her eyes and took a deep breath as if she were about to bestow the crown jewels on him. 'You may call me Celia.'

*

'... I couldn't think properly, that was the trouble ... if she'd just listened to me instead of shouting all the time ... I suppose what surprised me was how strong she was ... I wouldn't have broken her fingers otherwise ... it was easy ... they were tiny, like little wishbones, but it's not the kind of thing a man wants to do ... put it this way, I'm not proud of it ...'

Nick found Maggie in the kitchen, arms crossed, staring out of the window at the horses in the drought-starved paddock. The ceiling had received a coat of brilliant white emulsion but none of the walls had yet been touched, and the paint-roller had been abandoned to harden in the tray. 'Look at those poor brutes,' she said. 'I think I'm going to phone the RSPCA and have their beastly owners prosecuted.'

He knew her too well. 'What's really bugging you?'

She swung round defiantly. 'I heard it all,' she said. 'I was listening outside the door. I suppose you thought you were being clever?'

'In what way?'

'Martin took the trouble to seduce Mother before he seduced me,' she said. 'At the time I was impressed by his tactics. Afterwards, I decided it was the one thing that should have warned me he was a cheat and a liar.'

'Perhaps he found her easier to get on with,' Nick suggested mildly. 'She's good news, your ma. And, for the record, I have no intention of seducing you. It'd be like fighting my way through half a mile of razor wire – painful, unrewarding, and bloody hard work.'

She favoured him with a twisted smile. 'Well, don't expect *me* to seduce *you*,' she said tartly, 'because you'll be waiting for ever if you do.'

He prized the paint-roller out of the tray and held it under a running tap in the sink. 'Trust me. Nothing is further from my mind. I'm far too frightened of having my jaw broken.'

'Martin didn't have a problem.'

'No,' he said dryly. 'But then Martin wouldn't have had a problem with the Elephant Man as long as there was money in it. Does your mother have a scrubbing brush? We need to remove the hardened paint from this tray.'

'You'll have to look in the scullery.' She watched in an infuriated silence while he scrabbled around among four years' detritus in search of cleaning implements. 'You're such a hypocrite,' she said then. 'You've just spent half an hour boosting Ma's self-esteem by telling her how lovable she is, but I get compared with the Elephant Man.'

There was a muffled laugh. 'Martin didn't sleep with your mother.'

'What difference does that make?'

He emerged with a bucket full of impacted rags. 'I'm having trouble with the fact that you sleep with a dog,' he said severely. 'I'm buggered if I'll turn a blind eye to a weasel as well.'

There was a brief silence before Maggie gave a splutter of laughter. 'Bertie's in bed with Ma at the moment.'

'I know. He's about the worst guard dog I've ever encountered.' He took the bundle of cloth out of the bucket and held it up for inspection. 'What the hell is this?'

More laughter. 'They're my father's Y-fronts, you idiot. Ma uses them instead of J-cloths because they don't cost anything.'

'Oh, right.' He put the bucket in the sink to fill it with water. 'I can see the logic. He was a big fellow, your dad. There's enough material here to cover a three-piece suite.' He separated out a pair of striped boxer shorts. 'Or a deckchair,' he finished thoughtfully.

Her eyes narrowed suspiciously. 'Don't even think about using my father's underpants to seduce me, you bastard, or I'll empty that entire bucket over your head.'

He grinned at her. 'This isn't seduction, Maggie, this is courtship. If I wanted to seduce you I'd have brought several bottles of brandy with me.' He wrung out the boxer shorts and held them up for inspection. 'However . . . if you think these would be effective . . . ?'

'. . . *most of the time it's just me, the boat and the sea . . . I like that . . . I feel comfortable with space around me . . . people can get on your nerves after a while . . . they always want something from you . . . usually love . . . but it's all pretty shallow . . . Marie? She's okay . . . nothing great . . . sure I feel responsible for her, but not for ever . . . nothing's for ever . . . except the sea . . . and death . . .*'

Chapter Twenty-six

JOHN GALBRAITH PAUSED beside William Sumner's car in the Chichester street and stooped to look in through the window. The weather was still set fair and the heat from the sun-baked roof warmed his face. He walked up the path towards Angela Sumner's flat and rang the doorbell. He waited for the chain to rattle into place. 'Good afternoon, Mrs Sumner,' he said when her bright eyes peered anxiously through the gap. 'I think you must have William in there.' He gestured towards the parked car. 'May I talk to him?'

With a sigh, she released the chain and pulled the door wide. 'I wanted to phone you but he pulled the wire out of the wall when I suggested it.'

Galbraith nodded. 'We've tried your number several times but there was never any answer. If the phone wasn't plugged in, that explains it. I thought I'd come anyway.'

She turned her chair to lead him down the corridor. 'He keeps saying he didn't know what to do. Does that mean he killed her?'

Galbraith laid a comforting hand on her shoulder. 'No,' he said. 'Your son isn't a murderer, Mrs Sumner.

He loved Kate. I think he'd have given her the earth if she'd asked him for it.'

They paused in the sitting-room doorway. William sat huddled in an armchair, arms wrapped protectively about himself and the telephone in his lap, his jaw dark with stubble and his eyes red-rimmed and puffy from too much weeping and too little sleep. Galbraith studied him with concern, recognizing that he bore some of the responsibility for pushing him towards the brink. He could excuse his prying into William's and Kate's secrets on the grounds of justice, but it was a cold logic. He could have been kinder, he thought – one could always be kinder – but, sadly, kindness rarely elicited truth.

He squeezed Angela Sumner's shoulder. 'Perhaps you could make us a cup of tea,' he suggested, moving aside for her wheelchair to reverse. 'I'd like to have a few words with William alone, if that's possible.'

She nodded gratefully. 'I'll wait till you call me.'

He closed the door behind her and listened to the whine of the battery fading into the kitchen. 'We've caught Kate's killer, William,' he said, taking the seat opposite the man. 'Steven Harding has been formally charged with her abduction, rape and murder and will be remanded to prison shortly to await trial. I want to stress that Kate was not a party to what happened to her, but on the contrary fought hard to save herself and Hannah.' He paused briefly to search William's face, but went on when there was no reaction. 'I'm not going to pretend she didn't have sex with Steven Harding prior to the events of last week because she did. However, it was a brief affair some months ago, and followed a prolonged campaign by Harding to break her down. Nevertheless – and this is important' – he glossed the truth deliberately in Kate's favour – 'it's clear she made up her mind very quickly to put an end to the relationship when she recognized that her marriage was more important to her than a mild infatuation with a younger man. Her misfortune was her failure to recognize that Steven Harding is self-fixated and dangerously immature and that she needed to be afraid of him.' Another pause. 'She was lonely, William.'

A strangled sob issued from the other man's mouth. 'I've been hating her so much . . . I knew he was more than a casual acquaintance when she said she didn't want him in the house any more. She used to flirt with him at the beginning, then she turned vicious and started calling him names . . . I guessed he'd got bored with her . . .'

'Is that when he showed you the photographs?'

'Yes.'

'Why did he do that, William?'

'He said he wanted me to show them to Kate but . . .' He lifted a trembling hand to his mouth.

Galbraith recalled something Tony had said the previous evening. '*The only reason Steve does pornography is because he knows it's inadequate guys who're going to look at it. He doesn't have any hang-ups about sex so it gives him a buzz to think of them squirming over pictures of him . . .*'

'But he really wanted to show them to you?'

Sumner nodded. 'He wanted to prove that Kate would sleep with anyone – even a man who preferred other men – rather than sleep with me.' Tears streamed down his face. 'I think she must have told him I wasn't very good. I said I didn't want to see the pictures, so he put the magazine on the table in front of me and told me to' – he struggled with the words, closing his eyes in pain, as if to blot out the memory – ' "suck on it".'

'Did he say he'd slept with Kate?'

'He didn't need to. I knew when Hannah let him pick her up in the street that something was going on . . . she's never let me do that.' More tears squeezed from his tired eyes.

'What *did* he say, William?'

He plucked at his mouth. 'That Kate was making his life hell by smearing Hannah's nappies on his possessions, and that if I didn't make her stop he'd go to the police.'

'And you believed him?'

'Kate was – like that,' he said with a break in his voice. 'She could be spiteful when she didn't get her own way.'

'Did you show her the magazine?'

'No.'

'What did you do with it?'

'Kept it in my car.'

'Why?'

'To look at . . . remember . . .' He rested his head against the back of the chair and stared at the ceiling. 'Have something to hate, I suppose.'

'Did you tackle Kate about it?'

'There was no point. She'd have lied.'

424

'So what did you do?'

'Nothing,' he said simply. 'Went on as if nothing had happened. Stayed late at work . . . sat in my study . . . avoided her . . . I couldn't *think*, you see. I kept wondering if the baby was mine.' He turned to look at the policeman. 'Was it?'

Galbraith leaned forward and clamped his hands between his knees. 'The pathologist estimated the foetus at fourteen weeks, making conception early May, but Kate's affair with Harding finished at the end of March. I can ask the pathologist to run a DNA test if you want absolute proof, but I don't think there's any doubt Kate was carrying your son. She didn't sleep around, William.' He paused to let the information sink in. 'But there's no doubt Steven Harding accused her wrongly of harassment. Yes, she lashed out once in a moment of pique, but probably only because she was annoyed with herself for having given in to him. The real culprit was a friend of Harding's. Kate rejected him, so he used her as a shield for his own revenge without ever considering the sort of danger he might be putting her into.'

'I never thought he'd do anything to her . . . Jesus! Do you think I wanted her killed? She was a sad person . . . lonely . . . boring . . . God, if she had anything going for her she kept it well hidden . . . Look, I know this sounds bad – I'm not proud of it now – but I found it funny the way Steve reacted. He was shit-scared of her. That stuff about dodging round corners was all true. He thought she was going to attack him in the middle of the street if she managed to catch him unawares. He kept talking about

the movie Fatal Attraction, *and saying Michael Douglas's mistake was not to let the Glenn Close character die when she tried to kill herself.'*

'Why didn't you tell us this before?' Carpenter had asked.

'Because you have to believe someone's guilty before you get yourself into trouble. In a million years I wouldn't have thought Steve had anything to do with it. He doesn't go in for violence.'

'Try violation instead,' Carpenter had said. *'Off-hand, can you think of anything or anyone your friend has not violated? Hospitality ... friendship ... marriage ... women ... young girls ... every bloody law you can think of ... Did it never occur to you, Tony, that someone so intensely sociopathic as Steven Harding, so careless of other people's sensibilities, might represent a danger to a woman he thought had been terrorizing him?'*

Sumner continued to stare at the ceiling, as if answers lay somewhere within its white surface. 'How did he get her on to his boat if she wasn't interested any more?' he asked flatly. 'You said no one had seen her with him after he spoke to her outside Tesco's.'

'She smiled at me as if nothing had happened,' Harding had told them, *'asked me how I was and how the acting was going. I said she had a bloody nerve even talking to me after what she'd done, and she just laughed and told me to grow up. "You did me a favour," she said. "You taught me to appreciate William, and if I don't hold any grudges why should you?" I told her she knew fucking well why I held a grudge, so she started to look cross. "It was payment in kind," she said. "You were*

crap." Then she walked away. I think that's what made me angry – I hate it when people walk away from me – but I knew the woman in Tesco's was watching so I crossed the High Street and went down behind the market stalls on the other side of the road, watching her. All I planned to do was have it out with her, tell her she was lucky I hadn't gone to the police . . .'

'Saturday's market day in Lymington High Street,' said Galbraith, 'so the place was packed with visitors from outside. People don't notice things in a crowd. He followed her at a distance, waiting for her to turn towards home again.'

'She looked pretty angry so I think I must have upset her. She turned down Captain's Row, so I knew she was probably going home. I gave her a chance, you know. I thought if she took the top road I'd let her go, but if she took the bottom road past the yacht club and Tony's garage I'd teach her a lesson . . .'

'He has the use of a garage about two hundred yards from your house,' Galbraith went on. 'He caught up with her as she was passing it and persuaded her and Hannah to go inside. She'd been in several times before with Harding's friend, Tony Bridges, so it obviously didn't occur to her there was anything to worry about.'

'Women are such stupid bitches. They'll fall for anything as long as a bloke sounds sincere. All I had to do was tell her I was sorry, and squeeze a couple of tears out – I'm an actor so I'm good at that – and she was all smiles again and said, no, she was sorry, she hadn't meant to be cruel and couldn't we let bygones be bygones and stay friends? So I said, sure, and why didn't I give her some

*champagne out of Tony's garage to show there were no
hard feelings? You can drink it with William, I said, as
long as you don't tell him it came from me. If there'd been
anyone in the street or if old Mr Bridges had been at his
curtains, I wouldn't have done it. But it was so bloody
easy. Once I'd closed the garage doors, I knew I could do
anything I wanted . . .'*

'You need to remember how little she knew about
him, William. According to Harding himself, her entire
knowledge of him came from two months of constant
flattery and attention while he wanted to get her into
bed, a brief period of unsatisfactory love-making on
both sides which resulted in *him* giving her the cold
shoulder and *her* taking petty revenge with Hannah's
nappy on his cabin sheets, then four months of mutual
avoidance. As far as she was concerned, it was old
history. She didn't know his car was being daubed with
faeces, didn't know he'd approached you and told you
to warn her off, so when she accepted a glass of champagne in the garage, she genuinely thought it was the
peace-offering he said it was.'

'*If she hadn't told me William was away for the
weekend I wouldn't have gone through with it, but you
kind of get the feeling that some things are meant to
happen. It was her fault really. She kept on about how she
had nothing to go home for, so I offered her a drink. If
I'm honest, I'd say she was up for it. You could tell she was
pleased as bloody punch to find herself alone with me.
Hannah wasn't a problem. She's always liked me. I'm
about the only person, other than her mother, who could
pick her up without her screaming . . .'*

'He put her to sleep, using a benzodiazepine hypnotic drug called Rohypnol which he dissolved in the champagne. It's been called the date-rape drug because it's easy to give to a woman without her knowing. It's powerful enough to keep her out for six to ten hours, and in the cases reported so far, women claim intermittent periods of consciousness when they know what's happening to them but an inability to do anything about it. We understand there are moves to change it to a schedule 3 controlled drug in 1998, add a blue dye to it and make it harder to dissolve, but at the moment it's open to abuse.'

'*Tony keeps his drug supplies in the garage, or did until he heard you'd arrested me, then he went in and cleared the whole lot out. He'd taken the Rohypnol off his grandad when the poor old bugger kept falling asleep during the daytime. He found him in the kitchen once with the gas going full blast because he'd nodded off before he had time to put a match to it. Tony was going to chuck the Rohypnol out but I told him it could do him some good with Bibi so he kept it. It worked like a treat on Kate. She went out like a light. The only problem was, she let Hannah drink some of the champagne as well, and when Hannah went out she fell over backwards with her eyes wide open. I thought she was dead . . .*'

'He's very unclear what he was intending to do to Kate. He talks about teaching her a lesson but whether the intention was always to rape her then kill her, he can't or won't say.'

'*I wasn't going to hurt Kate, just give her something to think about. She'd been pissing me off with the crap thing, and it had been really bugging me. Still, I had to have a rethink when Hannah keeled over. That was pretty frightening, you know. I mean, killing a kid, even if it was an accident, is heavy stuff. I thought about leaving them both there while I scarpered to France with Marie but I was afraid Tony might find them before I met up with her, and I'd already told him I was going to Poole for the weekend. I guess it was the fact that Kate was so small that made me think about taking them both with me . . .'*

'He took them on board under everyone's noses,' said Galbraith. 'Just motored *Crazy Daze* into one of the visitors' pontoons near the yacht club and carried Kate on in the canvas holdall that takes his dinghy when it's not in use. They're substantial items, apparently, big enough to take eight feet of collapsed rubber, plus the seat and the floor boarding, and he says he had no trouble folding Kate into it. He took Hannah on board in his rucksack and carried the buggy quite openly under his arm.'

'People never question anything if you're up front about what you're doing. I guess it has something to do with the British psyche, and the fact we never interfere unless we absolutely have to. But you kind of want them to sometimes. It's almost as if you're being forced to do things you don't really want to do. I kept saying to myself, ask me what's in the bag, you bastards, ask me why I'm carrying a baby's buggy under my arm. But no one did, of course . . .'

'Then he left for Poole,' said Galbraith. 'The time was getting on for midday by then and he says he hadn't thought what he was going to do beyond smuggling

Kate and Hannah aboard. He talks about being stressed out, and being unable to think properly' – he raised his eyes to Sumner – 'rather like your description of yourself earlier, and it does seem as if he opted to do nothing, left them imprisoned and unconscious inside the bags on the principle of out of sight out of mind.'

'*I guess I'd realized all along I was going to have to dump them over the side but I kept putting it off. I'd sailed out into the Channel to get some space around me, and it was around seven o'clock when I hauled them up on deck to get it over with. I couldn't do it, though. I could hear whimpering coming out of the rucksack so I knew Hannah was still alive. I felt good about that. I never wanted to kill either of them . . .*'

'He claims Kate started to come round at about 7.30 which is when he released her, and let her sit beside him in the cockpit. He also claims it was her idea to take her clothes off. However, in view of the fact that her wedding ring is also missing, we think the truth is he decided to strip her body of anything that could identify her before he threw her overboard.'

'*I know she was frightened, and I know she probably did it to try to get into my good books, but I never asked her to strip and I never forced her to have sex with me. I'd already made up my mind to take them back. I wouldn't have altered course otherwise, and she'd never have ended up in Egmont Bight. I gave her something to eat because she said she was hungry. Why would I do that if I was going to kill her . . .?*'

'I know this is distressing for you, William, but we believe he spent hours fantasizing about what he was going to do with her before he killed her, and when he'd stripped her he went ahead and played out those fantasies. However, we don't know how conscious Kate was or how much she knew about what was going on. One of the difficulties we have is that *Crazy Daze* shows no recent signs of Kate and Hannah being on board. What we think happened is that he kept Kate naked on the deck for about five hours between 7.30 and half-past midnight which would explain the evidence of hypothermia and the lack of forensic evidence connecting her with the interior. We're still looking for evidence on the topsides but I'm afraid he had hours during the trip back to Lymington on Sunday to scrub the deck clean with buckets of salt water.'

'Okay, I was way out of line at the beginning, I'll admit that. Things got out of control for a while – I mean I panicked like hell when I thought Hannah was dead – but by the time it was dark I'd got it all worked out. I told Kate that if she promised to keep her mouth shut I'd take her to Poole and let her and Hannah off there. Otherwise, I'd say she came on board willingly, and as Tony Bridges knew she had the hots for me, no one would believe her word against mine, particularly not William . . .'

'He says he promised to take Kate to Poole, and she may have believed him, but we don't think he had any intention of doing it. He's a good sailor, yet he steered a course that brought him back to land to the west of St Alban's Head when he should have been well to the east. He's arguing that he lost track of his position because Kate kept distracting him, but it's too much of a coincidence that he put her into the sea where he did, bearing in mind he was planning to walk there the next morning.'

'*She should have trusted me. I told her I wasn't going to hurt her. I didn't hurt Hannah, did I . . . ?*'

'He says she lunged at him and tried to push him overboard, and in the process went over herself.'

'*I could hear her shouting and thrashing about in the water, so I brought the helm round to try and locate her. But it was so dark I couldn't see a damn thing. I kept calling to her but it all went silent very quickly and in the end I had to give up. I don't think she could swim very well . . .*'

'He's claiming he made every attempt to find her but thinks she must have drowned within a few minutes. He refers to it as a terrible accident.'

'*Of course it was a coincidence we were off Chapman's Pool. It was pitch black, for Christ's sake, and there's no lighthouse at St Alban's Head. Have you any idea what it's like sailing at night when there's nothing to tell you where you are? I hadn't been concentrating, hadn't taken the tidal drift and wind changes into account. I was pretty sure I'd sailed too far west which is why I altered course to sail due east, but it wasn't until I came within sight of the Anvil Point lighthouse that I had any idea I was within striking distance of Poole. Look, don't you think I'd have killed Hannah as well if I'd meant to kill Kate . . .?*'

When Galbraith fell silent, Sumner finally dragged his gaze away from the ceiling. 'Is that what he'll say in court? That she died by accident?'

'Probably.'

'Will he win?'

'Not if you stand up for her.'

'Maybe he's telling the truth,' said the other man listlessly.

Galbraith smiled slightly. Kindness *was* a mug's game. 'Don't ever say that in my presence again, William,' he said with a rasp in his throat. 'Because, so help me God, I'll beat the fucking daylights out of you if you do. I saw your wife, remember. I wept for her before you even knew she was dead.'

Sumner blinked in alarm.

Galbraith straightened. 'The bastard drugged her, raped her – several times we think – broke her fingers because she attempted to release her daughter from the rucksack, then put his hands round her neck and throttled her. But she wouldn't die. So he tied her to a spare outboard his friend had given him and set her adrift in a partially inflated dinghy.' He thumped his fist into his palm. 'Not to give her a chance of life, William, but to make sure she died slowly and in fear, tormenting herself about what he was going to do to Hannah and regretting that she'd ever dared to take revenge on him.'

'The kid never cried once after I took her out of the rucksack. She wasn't frightened of me. As a matter of fact I think she felt sorry for me because she could see I was upset. I wrapped her in a blanket and laid her on the floor in the cabin and she went to sleep. I might have panicked if she'd started crying in the marina, but she didn't. She's a funny kid. I mean she's obviously not very bright, but you get the feeling she knows things . . .'

'I don't know why he didn't kill Hannah, except that he seems to be afraid of her. He says now that the fact she's alive is proof he didn't want Kate to die either, and he may have decided that as she was never going to be a threat to him he could afford to let her live. He says he changed her, fed her and gave her something to drink from the bag that was on the back of the buggy, then took her off the boat in his rucksack. He left her asleep in the front garden of a block of flats on the Bournemouth to Poole road, a good mile from Lilliput, and seems to be more shocked than anyone that she was allowed to walk all the way back to the marina before anyone questioned why she was on her own.'

There was some paracetamol in the buggy bag so I dosed her up with it to make sure she was asleep when I took her off the boat. Not that I really needed to. I reckon the Rohypnol was still working because I sat and watched her in the cabin for hours and she only woke up once. There's no way she could have known where Salterns Marina was, so how the hell did she find her way back to it? I kept telling you she was weird. But you wouldn't believe me . . .'

'On the trip back to Lymington he put everything overboard that could connect him in any way at all with Kate and Hannah – the dinghy holdall, Kate's clothes, her ring, the buggy, Hannah's dirty nappy, the rug he wrapped her in – but he forgot the sandals that Kate left behind in April.' Galbraith smiled slightly. 'Although the odd thing is he says he did remember them. He took them out of a locker after he left Hannah asleep on the cabin floor and put them in the buggy bag, and he says now that the only person who could have hidden them under the pile of clothes was Hannah.'

'I got sidetracked worrying about fingerprints. I couldn't make up my mind whether to clean the inside of Crazy Daze or not. You see I knew you'd find Kate and Hannah's fingerprints from when they were on board in April and I wondered if it would be better to pretend that visit had never happened. In the end I decided to leave it exactly the way it's been for the last three months because I didn't want you lot imagining I'd done something worse than I had. And I was right, wasn't I? You wouldn't have released me on Wednesday if you'd found any evidence that I set out to hurt Kate the way you're saying I did . . .'

Sumner's eyes welled again but he didn't say anything.

'Why didn't you tell me Kate and Harding had had an affair?' Galbraith asked him.

It was a moment before William answered and, when he did, he lifted a trembling hand in supplication, like a beggar after charity. 'I was ashamed.'

'For Kate?'

'No,' he whispered, 'for myself. I didn't want anyone to know.'

To know what? Galbraith wondered. That he couldn't keep his wife interested? That he'd made a mistake marrying her? He reached over and took the telephone from Sumner's lap. 'If you're interested, Sandy Griffiths says Hannah's been walking round the house all day, looking for you. I asked Sandy to tell her I'd be bringing you home, and Hannah clapped her hands. Don't make a liar out of me, my friend.'

He shook with grief. 'I thought she'd be better off without me.'

'No chance.' He raised the man to his feet with a hand under his arm. 'You're her father. How could she possibly be better off without you?'

Chapter Twenty-seven

MAGGIE LAY ON the floor stretching her aching back while Nick meticulously poked a loaded paint brush into all the nooks and crannies that she'd missed. 'Do you think Steve would have done it if Tony Bridges hadn't wound him up by smearing crap all over the place?'

'I don't know,' said Nick. 'The Superintendent's convinced he's an out-and-out psychopath, says it was only a matter of time before his obsession with sex spilled over into rape, so maybe he'd have done it anyway, with or without Tony Bridges. I suppose the truth is Kate was in the wrong place at the wrong time.' He paused, remembering the tiny hand waving in the spume. 'Poor woman.'

'Still . . . does Tony walk away scot-free? That's hardly fair, is it? I mean he must have known Steve was guilty.'

Nick shrugged. 'Claims he didn't, claims he thought it was the husband.' He dabbed gently at a spider and watched it scurry away into the shadows. 'Galbraith told me he and Carpenter hung Tony up to dry last night for keeping quiet the first time they interviewed him, and

Tony's excuse was that Kate was such a bitch he didn't see why he should help the police screw her husband. He reckoned Kate got what she deserved for spouting off about the poor bastard's performance. He has trouble on that front himself, apparently, so his sympathies were with William.'

'And this man's a *teacher*?' she said in disgust.

'Not for much longer,' Nick reassured her, 'unless his fellow inmates have a yen for chemisty. Carpenter's thrown the book at him – perverting the course of justice, supplying drugs, false imprisonment of his girlfriend, rape of said girlfriend under the influence of Rohypnol, incitement to murder . . . even' – he chuckled – 'criminal damage to Harding's car . . . and that's not to mention whatever Customs and Excise choose to throw at him.'

'Serves him right,' said Maggie unsympathetically.

'Mmm.'

'You don't sound convinced.'

'Only because I can't see what prison will do for someone like Tony. He's not a bad guy, just a misguided one. Six months' community service in a home for the disabled would do him more good.' He watched the spider sink into a pool of wet emulsion. 'On a scale of one to ten, spasmodic impotence doesn't even register compared with severe physical or mental handicap.'

Maggie sat up and clasped her arms about her knees. 'I thought policemen were supposed to be hard bastards. Are you going soft on me, Ingram?'

He looked down at her with a gleam of amusement in his dark eyes. 'Courtship's like that, I'm afraid. The hardness comes and goes whether you like it or not. It's nature.'

She lowered her face to her knees, refusing to be diverted. 'I don't understand why Steve drowned Kate off Chapman's Pool,' she said next. 'He knew he was going there the next morning and he must have realized there was a chance she'd wash up on the beach. Why would he want to put his meeting with Marie in jeopardy?'

'I'm not sure you can apply logic to the actions of someone like Harding,' he said. 'Carpenter's view is that, once he had Kate on board, there would only ever be one place he'd kill her. He says you can tell from the Frenchman's video how hyped-up he was by all the excitement.' He watched the spider lift his legs from the wet paint and wave them in useless protest. 'But I don't think Steve expected her body to be there. He'd broken her fingers and tied her to an outboard so it must have been a hell of a shock to find she'd managed to free herself. Presumably the intention was to gloat over her grave before absconding with Marie. Carpenter thinks Harding's an embryo serial killer so in his view Marie's lucky to be alive.'

'Do you agree with him?'

'God knows.' He mourned the spider's inevitable death as the exhausted creature dipped its abdomen into the paint. 'Steve says it was a terrible accident, but I've no idea if he's telling the truth. Carpenter doesn't believe him and neither does DI Galbraith, but I have a real problem accepting that anyone so young can be so evil. Let's just say I'm glad you had Bertie with you yesterday.'

'Does Carpenter think he wanted to kill me, too?'

Nick shook his head. 'I don't know. He asked Steve what was so important about the rucksack that he'd risked going back for it, and do you know what Steve said? "My binoculars." So then Carpenter asked him why he'd left it there at all, and he said: "Because I'd forgotten the binoculars were in it."'

'What does that mean?'

Nick gave a low laugh. 'That there was nothing in it he wanted, so he decided to dump it. He hadn't had any sleep, he was knackered and Marie's desert boots kept banging against his back and giving him blisters. All he wanted to do was get rid of it as fast as possible.'

'Why is that funny?'

'It's the exact opposite of why I thought he'd left it there.'

'No, it's not,' she contradicted him. 'You told me it would incriminate him because he used it to carry Hannah off his boat.'

'But he didn't kill Hannah, Maggie, he killed Kate.'

'So?'

'All I did by finding it was help the defence. Harding will argue it proves he never intended to murder anyone.'

He sounded depressed, she thought. 'Still,' she said brightly, I suppose they'll be offering you a job at headquarters. They must be awfully impressed with you. You homed in on Steve as soon as you saw him.'

'And homed straight out again the minute he spun me a plausible yarn.' Another low laugh, this time self-deprecating. 'The only reason I took against him was because he got up my nose, and the Superintendent knows that. I think Carpenter thinks I'm a bit of a joke. He called me a suggestion-junky.' He sighed. 'I'm not sure I'm cut out for CID work. You can't take a wild guess then invent arguments to support the theory. That's how miscarriages of justice happen.'

She cast him a speculative glance. 'Is that something else Carpenter said?'

'More or less. He said the days are long past when policemen could play hunches. It's all about putting data into computers now.'

She felt angry on his behalf. 'Then I'll phone the bastard and give him a piece of my mind,' she said indignantly. 'If it hadn't been for you, it would have taken them months to make the connection between Kate and Harding – if ever, frankly – and they'd never have found that stranded dinghy or worked out where it was stolen from. He ought to be congratulating you, not finding fault. *I'm* the one who got it all wrong. There's obviously a flaw in my genes that makes me gravitate towards scumbags. Even Ma thought Harding was the most frightful creep. She said: "Fancy making such a performance over a dog bite. I've had far worse, and all anyone offered me was TCP."'

'She'll have my guts for garters when she finds out I made her wreck her hip for a murderer.'

'No, she won't. She says you remind her of James Stewart in *Destry Rides Again*.'

'Is that good?'

'Oh, yes,' said Maggie with a sardonic edge to her voice. 'She goes weak at the knees every time she sees it. James Stewart plays a peace-loving sheriff who brings law and order to a violent city by never raising his voice or drawing his gun. It's fantastically sentimental. He falls in love with Marlene Dietrich who throws herself in front of a bullet to protect him.'

'Mmm. Personally, I've always fancied myself as Bruce Willis in *Die Hard*. The heroic, bloodstained cop with his trusty arsenal who saves the world and the woman he loves by blasting hell out of Alan Rickman and his gang of psychopaths.'

She giggled. 'Is this another attempt at seduction?'

'No. I'm still courting you.'

'I was afraid you might be.' She shook her head. 'You're too nice, that's your trouble. You're certainly too nice to blast hell out of anyone.'

'I know,' he said despondently. 'I don't have the stomach for it.' He climbed down the stepladder and squatted on the floor in front of her, rubbing his tired eyes with the back of his hand. 'I was beginning to like Harding. I still do in a funny kind of way. I keep thinking what a waste it all is and what a difference it would have made if someone, somewhere, had warned him that everything has a price.' He reached up to put the paint brush in the tray on the table. 'To be fair to Carpenter, he *did* congratulate me. He even said he'd support me if I decided to apply for the CID. According to him, I have potential' – he mimicked the Superintendent's growl – 'and he should know because he hasn't been a Super for five years for nothing.' He smiled his crooked smile. 'But I'm not convinced that's where my talents lie.'

'Oh, for God's sake!' she declared, revealing more of her genes than she knew. 'You'd make a brilliant detective. I can't think what you're worried about. Don't be so bloody cautious, Nick. You should seize your chances.'

'I do . . . when they make sense to me.'

'And this one doesn't?'

He smiled and stood up, removing the tray to the sink and running water into it. 'I'm not sure I want to move away.' He glanced about the transformed room. 'I rather like living in a backwater where the odd suggestion makes a difference.'

Her eyes fell. 'Oh, I see.'

He rinsed the emulsion out of the brush in silence, wondering if she did, and if 'I see' was going to be her only response. He propped the brush to dry on the draining board, and seriously considered whether fighting his way through half a mile of razor wire wouldn't be the more sensible option after all. 'Shall I come back tomorrow? It's Sunday. We could make a start on the hall.'

'I'll be here,' she said.

'Okay.' He walked across to the scullery door.

'Nick?'

'Yes?' He turned.

'How long do these courtships of yours usually take?'

An amiable smile creased his eyes. 'Before what?'

'Before . . .' She looked suddenly uncomfortable. 'Never mind. It was a silly question. I'll see you tomorrow.'

'I'll try not to be late.'

'It doesn't matter if you are,' she said through gritted teeth. 'You're doing this out of kindness, not because you have to. I haven't asked you to paint the whole house, you know.'

'True,' he agreed, 'but it's a courtship thing. I thought I'd explained all that.'

She clambered to her feet with flashing eyes. 'Go *away*,' she said, pushing him through the door and bolting it behind him. 'And for God's sake bring some brandy with you tomorrow,' she yelled. 'Courtship stinks. I've decided I'd rather be seduced.'

The television was on and Celia, remote control in hand, was chuckling to herself when Maggie tiptoed into the drawing room to see if she was all right. Bertie had abandoned the stifling heat of the bed and was stretched out on his back on the sofa, legs akimbo. 'It's late, Ma. You ought to be asleep.'

'I know, but this is so funny, darling.'

'You said it was wall-to-wall horror movies.'

'It is. That's why I'm laughing.'

Maggie fixed her mother with a perplexed frown, then seized the remote control and killed the picture. 'You were listening,' she accused her.

'Well . . .'

'How *could* you?'

'I needed a pee,' said Celia apologetically, 'and you weren't exactly whispering.'

'The doctor said you weren't to walk around on your own.'

'I had no option. I called out a couple of times but you didn't hear me. In any case' – her eyes brimmed with humour – 'you were getting on so well that I decided it would be tactless to interrupt you.' She appraised her daughter in silence for a moment, then abruptly patted the bed. 'Are you too old to take some advice?'

'It depends what it is,' said Maggie, sitting down.

'Any man who invites the woman to make the running is worth having.'

'Is that what my father did?'

'No. He swept me off my feet, rushed me to the altar, and then gave me thirty-five years to repent at leisure.' Celia smiled ruefully. 'Which is why the advice is good. I fell for your father's over-inflated opinion of himself, mistook obstinacy for masterfulness, alcoholism for wit, and laziness for charisma . . .' She broke off apologetically, realizing that it was her daughter's father she was criticizing. 'It wasn't all bad,' she said robustly. 'Everyone was more stoical in those days – we were taught to put up with things – and look what I got out of it. You . . . Matt . . . the house . . .'

Maggie leaned forward to kiss her mother's cheek. 'Ava . . . Martin . . . theft . . . debts . . . heartache . . . a wonky hip . . .'

'Life,' countered Celia. 'A still-viable livery stable . . . Bertie . . . a new kitchen . . . a future . . .'

'Nick Ingram?'

'Well, why not?' said Celia with renewed chuckles. 'If I was forty years younger and he showed the remotest interest in me, I certainly wouldn't need a bottle of brandy to get things moving.'